Wild Jasmine

❀ ❀

Bertrice Small

BALLANTINE BOOKS
NEW YORK

To Susan Jane Petersen,
President of Ballantine Books,
a peace offering.

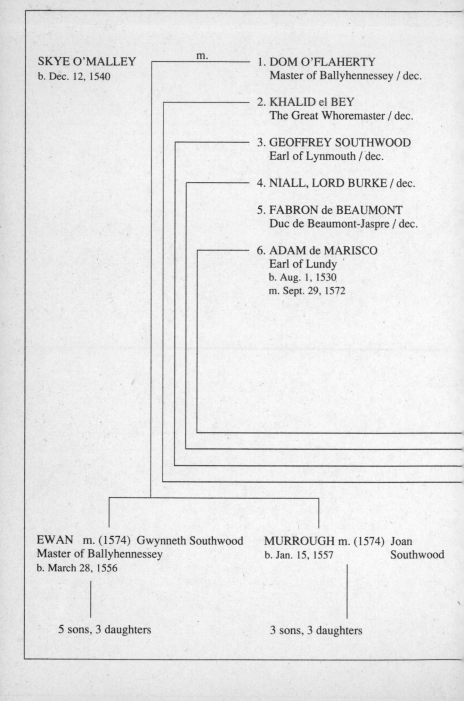

SKYE O'MALLEY
b. Dec. 12, 1540

m.

1. DOM O'FLAHERTY
   Master of Ballyhennessey / dec.

2. KHALID el BEY
   The Great Whoremaster / dec.

3. GEOFFREY SOUTHWOOD
   Earl of Lynmouth / dec.

4. NIALL, LORD BURKE / dec.

5. FABRON de BEAUMONT
   Duc de Beaumont-Jaspre / dec.

6. ADAM de MARISCO
   Earl of Lundy
   b. Aug. 1, 1530
   m. Sept. 29, 1572

EWAN m. (1574) Gwynneth Southwood
Master of Ballyhennessey
b. March 28, 1556

5 sons, 3 daughters

MURROUGH m. (1574) Joan
b. Jan. 15, 1557   Southwood

3 sons, 3 daughters

The Genealogy of SKYE O'MÁLLEY
and her husbands
and their children

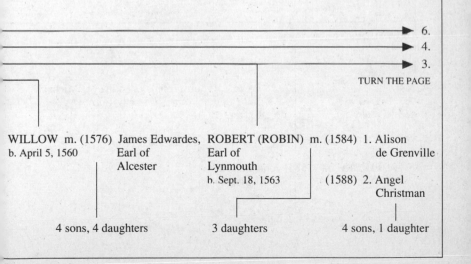

6.

4.

3.

TURN THE PAGE

WILLOW m. (1576) James Edwardes,   ROBERT (ROBIN) m. (1584) 1. Alison
b. April 5, 1560   Earl of   Earl of   de Grenville
                               Alcester   Lynmouth
                                                        b. Sept. 18, 1563   (1588) 2. Angel
                                                                                              Christman

            4 sons, 4 daughters   3 daughters   4 sons, 1 daughter

(Genealogy Continued)

3. GEOFFREY SOUTHWOOD
   Earl of Lynmouth/dec.

4. NIALL, LORD BURKE/dec.

5. FABRON de BEAUMONT
   Duc de Beaumont-Jaspre/dec.

6. ADAM de MARISCO
   Earl of Lundy
   b. Aug. 1, 1530
   m. Sept. 29, 1572

JOHN
b. Dec. 1, 1564
d. Apr. 9, 1566

PADRAIC m. (1603) Valentina St. Michael,
Lord Burke   Lady Burrows
b. Jan. 30, 1569

1 son, 1 daughter

DEIRDRE m. (1584) John Blakeley
b. Dec. 12, 1567   Lord Blackthorn

3 sons, 4 daughters

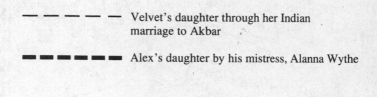

— — — — — Velvet's daughter through her Indian
marriage to Akbar

▬▬▬▬▬▬▬ Alex's daughter by his mistress, Alanna Wythe

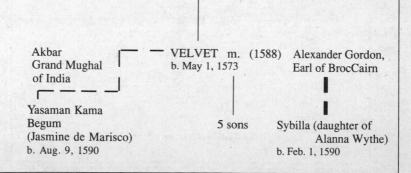

Akbar
Grand Mughal
of India

VELVET m. (1588) Alexander Gordon,
b. May 1, 1573   Earl of BrocCairn

Yasaman Kama
Begum
(Jasmine de Marisco)
b. Aug. 9, 1590

5 sons

Sybilla (daughter of
Alanna Wythe)
b. Feb. 1, 1590

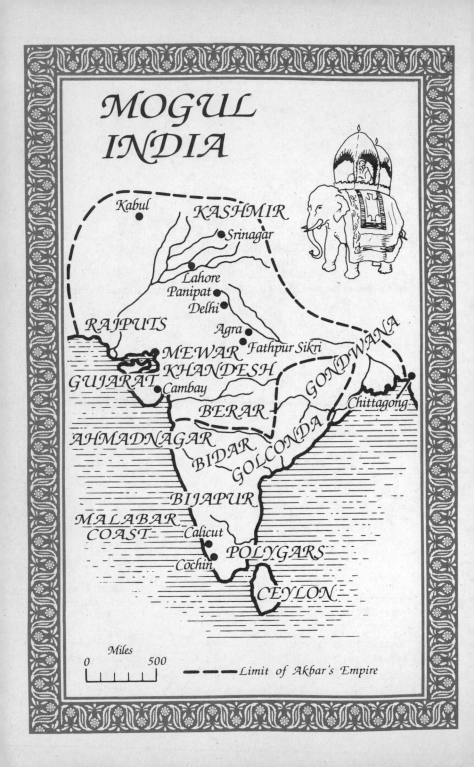

MOGUL
INDIA

Kabul

KASHMIR

Srinagar

Lahore
Panipat
Delhi

RAJPUTS

Agra
Fathpur Sikri

MEWAR
KHANDESH
GUJARAT Cambay

GONDWANA

Chittagong

BERAR

AHMADNAGAR

BIDAR

GOLCONDA

BIJAPUR

MALABAR
COAST Calicut

Cochin

POLYGARS

CEYLON

Miles
0   500

— — — Limit of Akbar's Empire

THE PLAYERS

IN INDIA

Yasaman Kama Begum—The daughter of India's ruler and his English wife, called Candra

Jalal-ud-Din Muhammad Akbar—The Grand Mughal of India, 1556–1605

Hamida Banu Begum, called Mariam Makani—Akbar's mother

Rugaiya Begum—His first wife, Yasaman's foster mother

Jodh Bai—A favorite wife, mother of his heir

Salim—Akbar's oldest son and heir

Man Bai, Nur Jahan—Salim's favorite wives

Murad, Daniyal, Shahzad-Kanim Begum, Shukuran Nisa Begum, Aram Banu Begum—Akbar's other children

Yusef Ali Khan—The defeated former ruler of Kashmir, now Akbar's loyal general

Jamal Darya Khan—Yusef Khan's youngest and most loyal son

Yaqub Khan, Haider Khan—His other surviving sons

Father Cullen Butler—Yasaman's tutor, a priest

Alain O'Flaherty—Factor of the O'Malley-Small trading house in India

Captain Michael Small—Captain of the *Cardiff Rose*

Lady Juliana Bourbon—A physician

Adali—Yasaman's high steward

Rohana, Toramalli—Yasaman's twin serving women

Ali—The fisherman of Wular Lake

Balna—The parrot Hiraman's keeper

IN ENGLAND

Skye O'Malley de Marisco, Countess of Lundy—Jasmine de Marisco's grandmother, and the family matriarch

Adam de Marisco, Earl of Lundy—Her husband, Jasmine's grandfather

Velvet de Marisco Gordon, Countess of BrocCairn—Their daughter, Jasmine's natural mother

Alexander Gordon, Earl of BrocCairn—Her husband

Sybilla Gordon—Alex Gordon's legitimized bastard daughter

James, Adam Charles, Robert, Henry, and Edward Gordon—Velvet and Alex's sons

Ewan and Gwenneth O'Flaherty—Skye's eldest son, and his wife

Murrough and Joan O'Flaherty—Skye's second son, and his wife

Willow and James Edwardes, Earl and Countess of Alcester—Skye's eldest daughter and her husband

Robin and Angel Southwood, Earl and Countess of Lynmouth—Skye's third son, and his wife

Deirdre and John Blakeley, Lord and Lady Blackthorne—Skye's second daughter and her husband

Padraic and Valentina Burke, Lord and Lady Burke—Skye's youngest son, and his wife

Conn and Aidan St. Michael, Lord and Lady Bliss—Skye's brother and his wife

Thomas Ashburne, Earl of Kempe—A friend of the family

Rowan Lindley, Marquess of Westleigh—His cousin

James Leslie, Earl of Glenkirk—The king's confidant

King James Stuart—King of England 1603–1625

Anne of Denmark—His queen

Henry Stuart—Their eldest son and heir

Elizabeth Stuart, Charles Stuart—Their daughter and their youngest son

Robert Carr, Viscount Rochester—The king's favorite

Frances Howard, Lady Essex—A lady of the court

Daisy Kelly—Lady de Marisco's tiring woman

IN IRELAND

Rory Maguire—Of Maguire's Ford

Fergus Duffy—A village leader

Bride Duffy—His wife

Eamon Feeny—A royal land agent

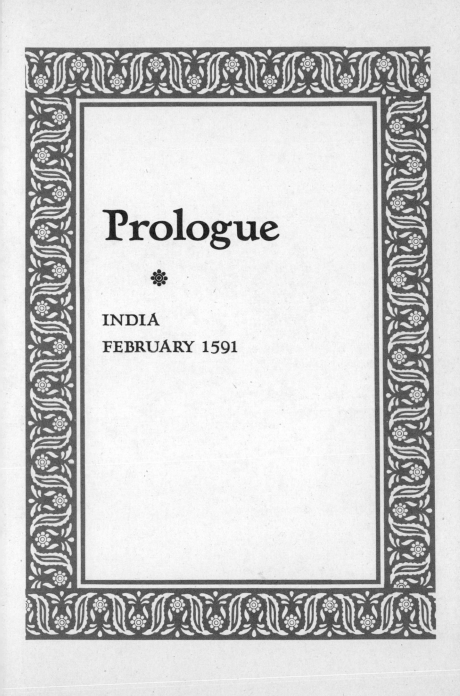

Prologue

❋

INDIA
FEBRUARY 1591

He could not tear himself away from the window of the tower, but there was nothing now to see. The coastal road stretched into infinity, the caravan long gone. There was not even the faintest puff of taupe dust on the horizon any longer to indicate its passing. He had no idea how long he had stood there before the window. The gray light of dawn had long since given way to the hot, bright yellow light of day. The insects in the trees about the palace had begun to hum and sing, a certain sign of hot weather, and yet he was cold.

His face felt wet. Reaching up, he realized that he was silently crying. He had not wept since he was a very small boy, he thought, surprised. Tears were not an integral part of his personality, although he was a kind and gentle man. He stared for a long moment at the evidence of his sorrow shining damply on his fingertips. Then he rubbed his chest, for it ached almost unbearably. His eyes scanned the road again, straining in the vivid light, seeing nothing. *She was gone.*

With this reality hammering in his brain, Akbar, the

Grand Mughal of India, turned from the window and sat heavily upon the only piece of furniture in the small room— a long couch with an open end, which was covered in a red- and deep blue–striped brocade. He was numb with the pain of his great loss. *Candra*. His beautiful and most favorite young wife. Torn from his side by a cruel twist of fate. The ache in his chest grew and deepened, and Akbar did not know if he would survive it. *Candra. Candra. Candra.* Her name pounded in his head, and his senses swam dizzily.

When he came to himself again, he was amazed to find that it was night once more. Moonlight silvered the room where he sat in his painful desolation. His mouth was in- credibly dry and, despite the heat of the season, he was still cold. The Grand Mughal attempted to marshal himself. Can- dra, his English rose, was gone. But for their daughter, Yas- aman, it was as if she had never even existed. He shivered with the eerie thought. Candra had indeed existed. She had been warm and vibrant, and so alive with the joy of living. Perhaps it was just her youth—but no, it was not simply that.

The English girl, brought to him as a captive by the Por- tuguese, had been brave and intelligent. Although it had not been easy for her, she had come to accept the fact that she was thousands of miles from her homeland and would never see it again. She had made peace with that fact and, having done so, had been content to make her life with him. He had loved her. He still did, and he believed that she had come to love him. She had said she did, and Candra was not a woman to dissemble.

The warm night wind brought the scent of jasmine to his tower room, and Akbar sighed deeply as if in pain. Jasmine, called Yasaman in the Indian tongue, had been Candra's favorite. She had even named their child for the flower. *Their child!* What was to become of her?

When Candra's priestly uncle had arrived to take her home, Akbar had been forced to relinquish the woman he loved to her family, to another husband thought dead, but now, by some miracle, alive and desirous of regaining his wife. He had had no choice but to send Candra back, but he would not allow her to take their child, for he was older and wiser than she was. Yasaman would have been considered ill-born by Candra's family. God only knew what would have happened to the child. Here with her father, however, she would be raised the royal Mughal princess that she was. She would be happy, and she would be loved. Akbar knew that Candra's world could not guarantee that future for his youngest child.

Candra had not left her daughter willingly. Akbar had had to drug her, and when she realized it, she had crawled from her bed where they had lain together to Yasaman's cradle. She had stared down at the sleeping baby for a long, deep moment, and then Candra had raised her beautiful emerald-green eyes to him and said, *I shall never forgive you for this.* Her words could have destroyed him, had he not realized they were only a means of venting her frustration.

Remember that I love you, he told her. *That has not stopped, nor will it ever.*

And I, God help me, love you, my lord Akbar, she had replied. *Do not forget me.*

Never! He had said the word then, and now, alone in his tower, he repeated it fiercely. "No, my beloved and beautiful English rose, I will never forget you!"

Once the Wheel of Love has been set in motion, there is no absolute rule. He could even now hear her voice as she had whispered that last farewell to him before falling into her drugged slumber. He had held her sleeping form in his arms for some minutes before surrendering her. Now, as the memory of the moment returned so vividly to him, Akbar felt the tightening in his chest once more, and a sudden, sharp pain in his head sent him sliding into unconsciousness.

"Akbar! Akbar! Open the door!" A furious pounding finally aroused him, and stumbling to his feet, he saw that it was once again day. *But what day?* He remembered his pain, but he had absolutely no idea for how long he had lain stricken. Was someone calling him, or were his befuddled wits playing a jest upon him? With strangely clumsy fingers he unbolted the door and opened it.

"My son!"

Shocked, he recognized his mother standing before him. What was she doing here? She did not live in his palace.

"My son!" Hamida Banu Begum, known to her intimates as Mariam Makani, was a slender, elegant woman to whom age had been quite kind despite the harsh life she had lived in her youth. The black hair of her girlhood had turned silver with the years, but for one ebony lock that ran directly down the center of her head as if dividing it. Her face was little lined, and her black eyes intelligent. Now those eyes brimmed over with sympathy. Akbar might be the most powerful ruler in the east, but he was first and foremost her son. His sorrow was her sorrow.

"Mother. How came you here?" he asked her softly.

"Your wives Rugaiya Begum and Jodh Bai sent for me to come, my son. They have told me of Candra's fate. I weep with you." Mariam Makani reached up with a gentle hand and stroked her son's face. Then she gasped. Akbar's turban was not upon his head. His long hair hung down his back. When she had last seen him, that hair had been shining black. Now it was snow white, as was his facial hair.

"It was not necessary for you to come, Mother," he said. "I know how you dislike travel."

"Akbar, my son," his mother said gently, "have you no idea how long you have been in this room? Candra's caravan left here four mornings ago." He looked at her, astounded, as she continued. "Although they respect your grief, Rugaiya Begum and Jodh Bai grew frightened when you would not respond to their calls. They did not dare to have the door broken down, and so they decided to send for me. You have been known to grieve hard in the past, but always in sight of those who love you best. This time you locked yourself away. They did not know what to think. Then, too, we would not want my dear grandson, Salim, to gain the wrong notion regarding your sorrow. He is a charming boy, but given to jumping to conclusions." Her eyes twinkled gently up at him.

Akbar, however, was not amused. "Salim is a rash man, and you are correct, Mother. He would use any excuse to usurp my place in this land; but he shall not. He will not be ruler here until I am dead."

"I did not mean—" Mariam Makani began, shocked, but Akbar interrupted her.

"My heir is what he is, Mother. Rash. Impatient, and eager to step into my boots. It is the truth, and we both know it. You see it even if you will not admit directly to it. Salim wheedles 'round you, and has always been able to do so. You dote upon him, even as you dote upon me. Since your youth you have a weakness for Mughal men, my mother."

Mariam Makani chuckled, but then she grew serious again. "What is to happen to the tiniest of my grandchildren? What of Yasaman?"

"I have given her to Rugaiya Begum to raise," he answered. "She has longed for a child of mine for all the years of our marriage. She is the first of my wives, but until now I could not fulfill her only desire of me because she is barren. She was Candra's friend, and she has loved Yasaman since the day my daughter was born. She will be a good mother to the princess."

Mariam Makani nodded, satisfied with his decision. "Will my granddaughter grow up believing Rugaiya Begum is her natural mother?" she asked him.

Akbar shook his head. "No," he said simply, and then he continued, "It is important that Yasaman know her heritage. The English will soon be trading with India."

"Aiiieee!" his mother cried, beating briefly upon her breast. "Are the Portuguese and their arrogance not enough of a plague upon this land, my son? You would admit more barbarians?"

"The Portuguese have grown arrogant with my kindness," Akbar told his mother. "Some behave as if they are conquerors instead of here on my sufferance. I will introduce the English into India, and instead of giving us difficulty, they will give each other difficulty as they strive for supremacy over one another. From what Candra told me, the English are a fair-minded and honest people." He patted his mother's hand. "You simply do not like foreigners and their ways, Mother. Admit to this failing, you who have virtually no faults."

"I do not count it a blemish upon my character that I do not like foreigners and their foreign ways," she told him sharply. Then she tapped his cheek with a long finger. "Do not presume to criticize me, Akbar. In your lifelong search for the truth, you have forgotten that according to the Holy Koran: Paradise lies at a mother's feet. Now you must cease to grieve for your English wife and come out of here so that you may go about the business of ruling your realm. You are Akbar, the Grand Mughal, not some lovelorn boy, broken-hearted over his first romance. Go and get your turban. It has fallen from your head. Your hair has gone white in your sorrow, my son. You do not want to startle anyone."

"I will shave it all off," he said, "as proof of my grief over Candra's loss."

Mariam Makani nodded. "Your moustache too," she told him. "I will go myself and get the razor and the basin. No one must see you like this, my son." She turned to go, her plum-colored silk robes swinging gracefully about.

"Bring me a change of clothes as well, Mother," he called after her, and then he moved back into the tower room to gaze a final time out of the window. The day was bright and hot, as it had been four mornings ago when his beloved had been taken from him. The coastal road was empty. The insects hummed in the trees about the palace. Akbar sighed. Candra was gone. He would never see her beautiful face again. He would never love her exquisite body again. He had nothing but his memories. His memories and their daughter, Yasaman. In a perverse way, he had failed Candra; he had been unable to change her fate. He would not fail Yasaman. The child was all he had left of their brief but extraordinary love. No, he would not fail Yasaman.

PART I

Yasaman

❀

INDIA
1597–1605

❦

1

❦

A giggle, with a distinctly mischievous ring to it, came from somewhere near the tall orchid trees that soared gracefully into the late spring afternoon.

"My *princess!* Where are you?" The head eunuch of Yasaman Kama Begum's household staff moved anxiously through the Grand Mughal's gardens. "Where has that imp of Azrael gotten to?" he muttered crankily to himself. He stopped to listen, but only the noisy chatter of birds met his sharp ears.

"Adali! Have you found Yasaman yet?" Rugaiya Begum called to him impatiently from an open balcony in the princess's palace.

"Nay, my lady, but I will," the eunuch answered. Then he heard the giggle of the child again. His brown eyes grew crafty, and he said in a wheedling tone, "I hear you, my princess. Come to Adali and he will give you your favorite sweetmeats." The air about him was silent again but for the birds.

"Mariam Makani will soon be here, Adali." Rugaiya Begum was beginning to sound anxious. She now stood upon

13

a colonnaded porch that opened directly into the gardens. Yasaman's grandmother was the highest-ranking lady in the kingdom. One did not keep her waiting when she chose to visit. Rugaiya Begum sighed deeply. Yasaman was such a mischievous child, but why oh why had she chosen today to tease them all?

"You look troubled, Aunt."

Rugaiya Begum jumped, startled by the sound of Prince Salim's voice. "Salim! Oh, Allah! Is your grandmother here already?" Her face grew distressed.

"Grandmother is coming here? Today? I did not know," the prince replied. "No, she is not with me, but what is it that troubles you so?"

"Mariam Makani is due at any moment," Rugaiya Begum said, "and your little sister has taken this moment to play one of her games. Adali cannot find her. She is hiding in the gardens from us and she will not come out!"

Prince Salim chuckled indulgently. "I will ferret her out," he said, and moved down the steps from the colonnaded porch into the garden. "Yasaman, my little sweetmeat, where are you?" he called in dulcet tones.

"Salim? Is it you?" his sister's voice called back.

"It is I, my adorable one. Come out! Our grandmother is coming to visit at any time now. You know how she dislikes being kept waiting." His dark eyes scanned the greenery before him, seeking for some movement that would betray the child.

"You must find me!" she teased him wickedly.

He laughed. He had never imagined when this youngest child of his father's had been born six years ago that he, a grown man even then, could be overwhelmingly enchanted by so small a human being. His own children had never appealed to him so; but he adored this baby half sister of his. "Very well, you naughty monkey, I shall find you, and when I do, I shall spank your little bottom for this lack of respect," the prince threatened.

Yasaman giggled in reply.

Salim glanced back at his aunt and saw that she was looking even more frantic. The time for subtlety was obviously over. Carefully, he looked about the garden, seeking some small thing out of place, and then he saw it—a small scrap of red gauze amid the Crown Imperials. Softly he crept toward the spot, and then, with a noisy cry, he swooped down to capture his crouching prey. With a shriek of surprise she squirmed from his grasp, black hair flying, and dashed past him, but Salim was quicker. Catching his little sister once again, he lifted her up and carried her kicking and raging to where Rugaiya Begum awaited. A firm but loving smack upon her small posterior silenced her temporarily.

"Here is your daughter, Aunt," Salim said. He set the child upon her bare feet, but kept a firm hand upon her head.

"Thank you, Salim," Rugaiya Begum said. "Will you stay and have refreshments with us when your grandmother arrives? She will count it a great bonus to see you too."

"I thank you for your invitation, Aunt. Yes, I will stay," he replied.

"How did you find me when Adali could not?" Yasaman demanded, looking up at her adored eldest brother, her startling turquoise-blue eyes curious.

"I looked carefully about the garden, my little monkey, and saw the edge of your skirt," he told her with a superior smile. "There it was fluttering bright and scarlet amongst the yellow Crown Imperials."

"Adali's eyes are not as sharp as yours, my brother," Yasaman noted as the eunuch came noisily puffing up to them.

"I will deliver her to Toramalli and Rohana to be prepared," Adali said to Rugaiya Begum, taking Yasaman's little hand in his. "You have been most naughty, my princess," he scolded his little mistress as he led her into the palace.

"It is not fun always being good, Adali," she answered him.

Her honesty brought a smile to the faces of both Rugaiya Begum and Prince Salim.

"She has brought you much joy, hasn't she, Aunt?" the young man said.

"She is the child of my heart, even if I did not bear her," Rugaiya Begum said quietly. "I wonder if Candra thinks often of her."

"Perhaps she does," the prince said. He had not known his father's young English wife particularly well. She had been with them so short a time. "Then again," Salim said, "perhaps she does not think of Yasaman at all. She was, after all, returned to another husband. Surely she has had other children. Those children and their care would possibly take her mind from Yasaman."

"How could a woman forget her first child?" Rugaiya said indignantly. "I do not believe that Candra has ever forgotten her daughter! She was not that kind of woman."

The prince shrugged. "In the almost six years since she has been gone, has she ever once written a letter to inquire of the child's well-being, Aunt?"

"It was agreed that she would not," Rugaiya said quietly. "It would be far too painful for her."

Again Salim shrugged. "My father was right to retain custody of Yasaman. Here she is safe and beloved of all who know her. It would not have been so in that foreign land."

"You cannot know that for certain," Rugaiya Begum said, some instinct deep within her wanting to defend the other half of her daughter's heritage. Though separated by many years, Candra had been her friend.

Before the prince might reply, a servant arrived to tell Rugaiya Begum, "The queen mother's procession approaches, gracious lady."

"Send for the princess Yasaman," she told the servant. "She must be here to greet Mariam Makani."

"It has already been done, gracious lady," the servant replied a trifle smugly.

"Your diligence and foresight are to be commended, Ali," Rugaiya Begum said dryly, dismissing the servant.

"Mama Begum! Mama Begum!" Yasaman danced out onto the portico. Her scarlet skirt had been changed for one of turquoise-blue silk gauze with large gold coin-shaped dots. The hem of the skirt was edged in a two-inch band of gold. Her short-sleeved half blouse was made of cloth-of-gold and had a modest little round neckline that seemed to be at war with the wide area of bare skin between the bottom of the blouse and the waistband of her skirt. On the child's narrow and elegant little feet were slippers that matched her skirt. Her ebony hair was pulled back from her face and fashioned into a single long braid that had been woven with pearls and hung down her back. Yasaman wore a small necklace of pink diamonds, and there were pink diamond studs in her tiny earlobes. Her unique blue eyes had been outlined in kohl, rendering them even more brilliant.

"Mama Begum!" Yasaman said insistently a third time, and having gained Rugaiya Begum's attention, she smiled winningly. Placing the palms of her hands together, she bowed her head prettily, then looking up, asked, "Do you think the old queen, my grandmother, will be pleased with me?"

"Yes, I do," Rugaiya Begum assured the child, "but you must not call Mariam Makani the 'old queen,' my little one. Your grandmother is a great lady in this land."

"Should her eyes be outlined so with kohl, Aunt?" Salim suddenly demanded. The effect, he thought, seemed to make Yasaman appear older than her six years. For the first time he saw a small glimpse of a woman within his youngest sister. It was a startling revelation.

"It is a special occasion, Salim," Rugaiya Begum said with a smile.

"I do not know if I like it," he replied. "It makes her look like a Nautch girl."

"Salim!" Rugaiya Begum was shocked.

"What is a Nautch girl?" demanded Yasaman.

"A pretty dancing girl," her mother quickly replied, "but

you are a princess, not a dancing girl. Salim! Apologize to your sister at once!" Rugaiya Begum's dark eyes flashed angrily at her husband's eldest son and heir. A Nautch girl was indeed a dancing girl, but she was also more often than not a prostitute as well. That Salim would use such language around his sister distressed Rugaiya Begum.

"I do apologize, Aunt, for I did not mean to offend. I sought for a word to describe my displeasure with Yasaman's appearance. I should have said I thought the kohl about her eyes too sophisticated for a little girl of six." The prince took Rugaiya Begum's hands in his and touched his head to them in a gesture of obeisance.

"I am six and a half!" Yasaman said sharply to her brother, and the look on her face was so like Akbar's that both Salim and Rugaiya Begum could not restrain their laughter.

"It is good to enter a happy house so filled with laughter," came a strong, sweet voice, and the queen mother swept into the garden smiling.

"Grandmother!" Yasaman launched herself at the old lady and, wrapping her little arms about Mariam Makani's neck, kissed her cheek.

"Let me look at you! Let me look at you!" her grandmother said, unwrapping the arms that embraced her. Yasaman pirouetted gracefully. "Ahh, yes," Mariam Makani noted. "You have grown taller since my last visit, my child. Are you studying hard? Your father is a great believer in education. He has educated not only your brothers, but your older sisters as well."

"Yes, Grandmother, I am studying very hard," Yasaman assured her. "I can do my numbers. I am learning the history of our people. I am also learning French and Portuguese, as well as English, which I am told was Candra Begum's language."

"Who has your sire chosen for your tutor, my child?" Mariam Makani demanded, her black eyes curious.

"He is a priest, Grandmother. His name is Father Cullen

Butler, and he is a great deal of fun; not at all like that sour
old Father Xavier and the other priests. Father Cullen laughs
at Baba, my monkey, and the naughty things he does. He
even brings Baba treats and does not call him the devil's
own spawn, as does Father Xavier," Yasaman told her ear-
nestly. "Baba ate Father Xavier's rosary. It made him sick
for a day."

"I do not like these Christians that my son has allowed
into our land," Mariam Makani said.

"They hold no more power over my lord Akbar than do
the mullahs or the priests of the Buddhists, the Hindus, or
the Jains," Rugaiya Begum reassured her mother-in-law,
and taking her by the arm, she led her into the palace.
"Come and let us have some refreshment, my gracious lady."

"Salim!" the old woman called, and he hurried to her side.
"Are you well, my boy? And your wives and children?"

"All well, Grandmother. I thank you for asking. May I
say how happy I am to see you so blooming with health and
vigor. You have yet the beauty of a young woman." He
kissed her cheek.

"Flatterer!" She chuckled, but she was pleased by the flattery. "Are you to take refreshment with us then?"

"When the lady Rugaiya Begum told me of your visit, I
would not go until I had seen you. Yes, I will be pleased to
take refreshment with you," Salim told her.

They sat by a long reflecting pool that ran almost the
entire length of the entry hall. Above them soft light filtered
through the latticed jasper set into the bottom of the dome
that capped the palace. Great porcelain tubs decorated with
blue designs lined the walls of the lovely little hall. Long-
leafed cardamom with its sprays of blue and white-lipped
yellow-green flowers, as well as yellow, cream, and white gin-
ger lilies, their long-tubed flowers sweetly scenting the air,
filled the tubs. A golden chandelier hung down and, in the
evenings, lit the entry. So the room had been in the time
of Candra, and so it had remained, but for the couches

Rugaiya Begum had placed near the water, along with several small, low, brass and ebony tables.

The servants, soft-footed and discreet in their white robes, brought out platters upon which were set slices of fresh melon, pomelos, and small bananas, as well as little pastries made from chopped nuts, shredded coconut, and honey. Blue and white porcelain cups of Assam tea, made even more fragrant by the addition of cloves, were passed around. There were tiny bowls of pistachio and pine nuts. Yasaman sat curled up within her eldest brother's embrace. She giggled as he fed her bits of sweetmeats and as he nibbled at her fingers when she, in turn, pressed bits of fruit and pastry upon him.

"It is good to see the love between the eldest and the youngest," their grandmother noted with a smile.

"He spoils her too much," Rugaiya Begum said, "as does her father when he comes to see her."

"When my son is no longer here, Yasaman will have a powerful ally and protector in her brother Salim," Mariam Makani answered her daughter-in-law wisely.

"Yasaman will be long married by that day," Rugaiya Begum replied. "Her husband will protect her."

"Her husband will not be the Grand Mughal. Salim will," Mariam Makani said tartly.

"Why do not brothers and sisters marry, Grandmother?" Yasaman asked, overhearing them. "I can think of no better husband to have than my brother Salim."

"It is unhealthy to mix blood that is so close, my child," the old woman answered. "It is considered an abomination by all faiths for a brother and sister to know each other as a man and a woman know each other. Ask your priest. That is one thing upon which we will agree, although there is little else."

"Yet in the ancient culture of Egypt," Salim told them, "it was mandatory for the ruler to wed with his sister, that their royal blood not be tainted by foreigners. Only their children could inherit the throne of Egypt."

Yasaman giggled innocently. "Then when I grow up, my brother, I shall wed with you. Our children shall rule India for a thousand generations to come." She wound her arms about his neck and kissed him upon the lips. Then she looked archly at her audience.

"When you grow up," Rugaiya Begum said, "you will marry a most handsome young prince, my Yasaman. He will come for you one day riding upon a fine elephant. The beast will be bedecked in silken cloths and jewels, and there will be a gold howdah upon its back. Your prince will have dark eyes and a sweet voice to sing you love songs. He will carry you away to his kingdom, where you will have many sons and live happily ever after. Look! It is all here in the teacup." Rugaiya Begum turned the little blue and white cup so that her daughter could see the black leaves in it.

"But I want to marry Salim!" Yasaman's mouth pouted and her eyes grew mutinous.

"Well, you cannot," her grandmother said briskly. "What of Salim's dear wives—Man Bai, the mother of your nephew Khusrau, and your niece, Sultan un-Nisa Begum; and Nur Jahan, his new passion and wife of less than a year? You would hurt their feelings if you stole Salim away from them."

"They are old," Yasaman said, making a face. "Why, Man Bai is at least three years past twenty. She will be even older when I am ready to marry, and so will Nur Jahan."

Salim laughed. "What a wicked little creature you are, baby sister," he said indulgently, and plucking a bright jewel from his jacket, he gave it to her.

She gazed up at him adoringly.

"I have brought you a present, Yasaman," Mariam Makani said, in an attempt to change the subject.

The child was immediately diverted by her natural youthful greed and, slipping off her eldest brother's lap, turned to stand before the old queen. "What have you brought me, Grandmother?" she demanded. "Can I wear it? Can I play with it?"

The elderly woman cackled at her granddaughter's eagerness. "You are a true Mughal, child," she said. "Your hands are ever outstretched, grasping all you desire, or think you desire." She nodded to her personal servant, who had been standing behind her couch. The eunuch hurried off, to return but a moment later carrying an absolutely beautiful bird upon his arm. There was a small gold band about the creature's left ankle, to which was attached a thick gold chain that the eunuch grasped.

It was a large bird with glorious plumage—a bright gold breast, and turquoise-blue wings and tail. There was a patch of blue-black about his large hooked beak and his lively dark eyes. Upon his head was a small half cap of green feathers. The creature, made a trifle nervous by his new surroundings, flapped his wings strongly, revealing them to be bright gold underneath.

"A parrot!" Yasaman was wide-eyed with delight. She had a pony and an elephant, but she loved animals.

"His name is Hiraman," began Mariam Makani.

"Like the Raja Parrot in the story of Princess Labam!" Yasaman said excitedly.

"Perhaps it is the same bird," the old lady said slyly, and then she looked at the parrot. "Hiraman, this is your new mistress. Make your salaam."

To everyone's surprise, the parrot lifted its right foot, ducked its head slightly, and said in a gravelly voice, "Live a hundred years, lady!"

"Ohhhhhh!" Yasaman breathed, quite awed. "It talks, Grandmother! Hiraman talks!"

"Indeed he does, child," she agreed, smiling.

"It is a wonderful gift you have brought Yasaman, Mariam Makani," Rugaiya Begum said, and before she might admonish her daughter for a lack of manners, Yasaman was speaking.

"Oh, thank you, Grandmother! It is the best present I have ever received!" the little girl said enthusiastically.

"Hiraman has his own keeper, Yasaman," her grandmother told the child. "You may come forward and meet your new mistress," Mariam Makani called, and a tiny woman stepped into their vision. "This is Balna," the old queen said. "She is full-grown, though she stands but three feet high. She knows how to feed and care for Hiraman."

Balna fell to her knees and, touching her head to Yasaman's slipper, said, "I but live to serve you, my princess."

"You may rise, Balna," the little girl replied. "Why are you so small?"

"It is the will of Allah, my princess," Balna answered as she scrambled to her feet.

"How old are you?" Yasaman demanded.

"I am sixteen, my princess," Balna said. She was a pretty girl with pale brown skin and large, expressive amber-colored eyes. Her dark hair was neatly braided into two long plaits.

"Can Hiraman say and do other things?" Yasaman wanted to know.

"Indeed, my princess, he most certainly can," Balna told Yasaman, "but he is quite tired from his journey now and would probably like nothing better than a piece of banana and his perch."

"I'll give it to him!" Yasaman said eagerly, and before anyone could stop her, she had broken off a piece of peeled banana and was thrusting it toward the parrot.

Hiraman cocked his head and looked directly at Yasaman. Then reaching out, he gently took the fruit from her little fingers, saying most distinctly, "Thank you, lady."

"*He thanked me, Grandmother!* Hiraman Parrot thanked me for the banana!" Yasaman said excitedly.

The bird, his banana now clutched in one of his claws, said, "Thank you, lady! Thank you!" and began to eat.

Salim burst out laughing. "This is indeed an excellent present you have brought my baby sister, Grandmother. I do not ever remember you bringing me anything quite so fine."

"You did not deserve it," the old lady told him bluntly. "You have been in a rebellion of one kind or another against my son, your father, since your birth. Yasaman, however, respects her father."

"But you love me, Grandmother," he gently teased her, putting his arm about her.

"I love you," she answered, "but your father will always come first in my heart, Salim."

"Yet you have defended me to him on many an occasion," he rejoined.

"Would that I did not have to, my grandson. You are Akbar's eldest son and heir. You must understand that loyalty and respect go with that position and privilege. You are too eager to inherit all that is your father's, Salim."

His arm dropped from about her. "I am a man, Grandmother. I do not seek to supplant my father, but I need to have him rely upon me and not upon others, like Abul Fazl."

"Foolish boy!" his grandmother said irritably. "Abul Fazl is your father's historian. No more! He does naught but keep a record of your father's reign."

"He is my father's friend. My father asks his advice. He does not ask my advice!" Salim said angrily.

Mariam Makani snorted. "They are together constantly, Salim. You are little with your father, and yet he adores you above all his children, even Yasaman. If he occasionally asks Abul Fazl's advice, it is because Abul Fazl is there and you are not. You have your own life and duties. You have a family and your children. You must learn to rule through your father's example, but you will not rule here in this land until Akbar is gone." She pierced her grandson with a sharp look. "And may that be many years hence and I long gone myself."

"Salim would never harm Papa," Yasaman said, intuitive and clever for her years.

"Of course I would not harm our father," the prince replied smoothly, and, bending, he picked the little girl up in his arms. "I must go now, little monkey. Come with me to the gate." He smoothed her dark hair. "Your hair is as black as night and as soft as silk," he said almost to himself.

"He needs but a light rein," his grandmother said as she watched them moving away.

"He is ambitious to rule and, at times, cannot hide it," Rugaiya Begum replied. As deeply fond of Salim as she was, she could not ignore his faults, as all the other ladies of the zenana could. How many times had Salim gotten into his father's bad books only to have the other women of the household beg and plead for his restoration to his father's good graces? Akbar, Allah help him, loved Salim. He always forgave him. One day, Rugaiya Begum feared, he would not. One day Salim would step over that invisible line in the sands of life.

"He is a good boy," Mariam Makani continued.

"He is a grown man with wives and children," Rugaiya answered the old lady.

"He is the best of Akbar's sons," Mariam Makani continued.

"Aye, he is," Rugaiya agreed. "I pity Murad and Daniyal. They have spent their lives in Salim's shadow. How hard it has been for them knowing that no matter how good they were at anything, Salim would rule over them one day. It is what has driven them to liquor and opiates which may someday kill them. They have not their father's strength of will. So often the sons of a man like Akbar are lacking."

"It is all those Hindu women he marries," Mariam Makani grumbled. "Their blood is weak, and they breed weak sons."

"Salim's mother is a Rajput, the highest caste," Rugaiya Begum reminded her mother-in-law, "and he is not weak."

"True. True, my dear. Perhaps it is just that no one can compare to my son. Even his sons."

"You do not fool me, Mariam Makani." Rugaiya Begum laughed. "You dote on Salim as does every other female of his acquaintance."

The old woman chuckled. "I admit to it." She smiled. "But how can I not? Salim has such great charm."

Rugaiya Begum argued no further with her mother-in-law on the subject of Prince Salim. Instead she signaled her servants to pour them fresh tea. Salim did indeed have charm, but it was a dangerous charm. He used it to gain everything he wanted, but underneath he was ambitious and ruthless. Nothing stood in the way of Salim's desires. Nothing and no one except Akbar, who turned a blind eye to his son's faults, although he knew them, and continued to call him by the pet name he had given him in babyhood: *Shaikho Baba*.

Salim did have his good points. He was good to his women and his children. He loved animals, though he could be a vigorous and overly zealous hunter. He loved beautiful things and was already famed for his collection of fine art, particularly European prints which he liked to have set in gold frames decorated with Mughal floral borders. His collection of Chinese porcelain grew with each passing year. Recently he had begun to accumulate beautifully made wine cups of all kinds, and jeweled daggers.

His energy and curiosity were his strong points; but he had an eccentric side to his personality that sometimes could be whimsical, and other times just plain capricious. His large sexual appetite was considered by many a strength, by others a weakness, as was his fondness for good wine and his occasional foray into opium. He was wise enough to know his responsibilities, however, Rugaiya Begum thought, and did not as often indulge himself in these vices as did his two younger brothers. More than anything else, Salim Muhammad desired to rule India. He would do nothing to jeopardize that.

Yasaman came running back to them, chattering even as she came. "Salim says he will take me on a tiger hunt soon! Several of the beasts have been sighted near Agra. Can I go, Mama Begum? Can I go? Please! *Please!*" She danced around the two women.

"We are leaving for Kashmir shortly, my daughter," her foster mother told her. "It is your father's wish that you spend most of the year there rather than here in Lahore. The climate is better for you."

"I don't want to go to Kashmir," Yasaman pouted. "I want to go on a tiger hunt with Salim. I never have any fun!"

"No fun! No fun!" Hiraman Parrot said, and the beautiful bird shook his head from side to side sadly.

They looked, astounded, at him for a brief moment and then began to laugh. Even Yasaman was unable to keep from giggling, and her bad mood instantly dissipated.

"Hiraman Parrot is so funny," she bubbled, and then she turned to her grandmother. "He really is the best present I have ever had!"

Mariam Makani smiled at her youngest grandchild, showing betel-stained teeth. "I am glad to have made you so happy, child," she said. "Hiraman Parrot will remind you of me while I am away from you."

"Why do you not come to Kashmir, Grandmother?" Yasaman asked.

"Because I am an old lady, my child, and I love my home best of all. I have traveled much in my life, but I do not have to travel now if I do not want to, and I do not. I am happiest amongst my own things."

"I love Kashmir," Yasaman said. "I love the palace there that Papa built for Candra that is now mine. I love the lakes and the mountains. It is so peaceful."

"Do you not like Lahore?" her grandmother asked.

"Not as much as Kashmir," Yasaman replied. "Lahore is such a large and noisy city, Grandmother. I do not like its walls, and I cannot see the mountains unless I go outside the city. The land is so dry, except near the canals which draw water from the river that runs by the city. How can a land be so brown and arid with a river in its midst, Grandmother?"

Mariam Makani shook her head. "I do not know, my child. Perhaps you should ask your tutor. The Christian priests claim to know everything." She frowned slightly and then continued, "But this palace is a fine place to live, is it not? You are not crowded within the zenana like the other women of this family. You have your own little palace within the palace gardens. Did you know that your Mama Begum and Papa played here as children?"

Yasaman nodded her head, smiling. "Mama Begum says that Papa used to catch beetles and chase her with them. Big, black, ugly beetles!" she said, making an ugly face. Hunching her shoulders and raising her hands up, she wiggled her fingers pretending to be a beetle.

Rugaiya Begum recoiled in mock horror, which sent her daughter into a fresh fit of giggles, particularly as her mother cried out, "Oh, Yasaman, do not do that! It terrifies me so!" Then, reaching out, she pulled the little girl into her warm embrace and hugged her. "Do not contort your beautiful face so, my darling. What if a wicked jinn saw you thus and liked it enough to cast a spell upon you so it would always remain that way?"

"Ohhh, no Mama Begum!" Yasaman gasped, quickly looking about, her turquoise eyes wide, and she snuggled into her mother's arms.

Rugaiya Begum chuckled. "I think it is time for you to bid your grandmother farewell, my daughter. Both Balna and Hiraman Parrot look tired and need to be shown to their quarters. Take them to Adali."

"Yes, Mama Begum," the child answered, slipping from Rugaiya's arms, kissing her on the cheek as she drew away. "Good-bye, Grandmother. I am so happy you came to visit with me today." Yasaman kissed the old lady on both of her cheeks. "I hope you will come to see me again very soon."

"And bring you another wonderful present, my child?" Mariam Makani asked slyly, her dark eyes bright and amused.

"Ohhh, Grandmother, you could never give me another present as wonderful as Hiraman Parrot!" Yasaman exclaimed, and then taking the parrot's keeper by the hand, she led her off.

"Has my son chosen a husband for her yet?" Mariam Makani asked.

"She is too young," Rugaiya replied. "You know how Akbar feels about marrying too young. Yasaman is not quite seven yet. There is plenty of time."

"She grows so quickly," Mariam Makani noted. "She will be taller than most girls, but already she is a beauty. Akbar is wise to wait with her. She will only grow more beautiful with each passing year. Her bride price will be great, and her husband a man of much influence and power. That is as it should be for a daughter of Akbar the Great." She paused in her conversation to drink deeply from her cup. "Do you speak to her of Candra Begum?"

Rugaiya nodded. "Yes," she said. "It is not fair that she not know of the mother who gave birth to her and who left her so very reluctantly. Their separation was not of Candra's making. Given the choice—and she was not—Candra would never have left her child."

"I am sorry I did not know her," Mariam Makani said. "Akbar grieved greatly for her; and you and Jodh Bai speak so fondly of her. What was she like?"

Rugaiya Begum was somewhat surprised by her mother-in-law's query. Mariam Makani had never before inquired about Candra. In the brief time that Candra had been with them, Mariam Makani had been traveling on a religious pilgrimage. She had been home but a few days when her son's two favorite wives had sent for her out of desperation. Candra was gone and Akbar had locked himself in a high tower of the Lahore palace. Candra's weeping servants, Rohana and Toramalli, had brought the infant Princess Yasaman to Rugaiya Begum. They were virtually incoherent with their grief.

"Candra was a beautiful woman," Rugaiya said slowly, striving to remember the face of her long-ago friend. "She was quite different from anyone we have ever seen. Even the Portuguese women are similar to us in coloring, as you know. Candra had skin like polished silk. It was as white as the mountain snows. Her eyes were as green as the emeralds you wear, Mariam Makani; and her hair! Ahh, what hair she had! It was a deep, rich brown, and it was filled with fiery red lights. She called the color," and here Rugaiya Begum cudgeled her memory for a long moment, *"Auburn!"* she finished triumphantly.

"I have always known it was from Candra that Yasaman gained her light-colored eyes," the elderly woman replied, "but I thought their eyes would be the same color. Emerald-green you say. How interesting. I have seen blue-eyed Englishmen at my son's court; but none have had eyes like a turquoise, as does Yasaman. I wonder if there is one with such eyes in Candra's family? But tell me, Rugaiya Begum, of Candra herself. Her beauty I suspected, for my grand-daughter is beautiful. The fairest of Akbar's children, in fact. Tell me of the woman my son loved so deeply." Mariam Makani reached for a honeyed pastry and popped it into her mouth.

"Candra was intelligent," Rugaiya said quietly. "She had exquisite manners. The first time Jodh Bai saw her in the baths, Candra recognized in Jodh Bai a woman of royalty and bowed as they passed. She was kind, and there was no meanness in her at all. Almira and some of Akbar's other wives were fiercely jealous of her. They set themselves against Candra and took every opportunity they could find to insult her. She met their insolence with spirited courtesy, accepting none of their slights, and defending her position with gallantry. Her demeanor infuriated them." Rugaiya chuckled.

"Did she truly love my son?"

"Oh, yes! And when Yasaman was born to Candra, she was radiant with her happiness. Then when Yasaman was but six months of age, tragedy struck. Candra's uncle, a Christian priest, arrived at court. Candra's first husband had not been killed as she had thought. Both he and her family wanted Candra back. I am told she refused to go, telling Akbar that she would sooner be the lowest of the low within his household than to be parted from him."

"But my son's sense of honor would not permit such a thing," Mariam Makani said knowingly. "Foolish man! He sacrificed his own happiness and Candra's for his honor. Had it been me, I should have killed the priest and put an end to it then and there!" She snorted with impatience at her son's past behavior. "Still, some good came of it. You are a good mother to my granddaughter, Yasaman. Her kismet is a fortunate one, I believe."

"So the astrologers predicted at her birth," Rugaiya replied.

Mariam Makani rose to her feet. "I have tarried with you a long time this day," she noted. "It is past time I went to my own home."

"Your presence has honored our house," Rugaiya murmured, standing politely. "I hope, Mariam Makani, that you will come again soon."

"Perhaps before you leave for Kashmir at the end of the month," her mother-in-law promised.

Rugaiya Begum escorted her guest to her elephant, waiting politely as Mariam Makani was helped into her gold and scarlet howdah, waving as the old queen mother's small procession wended its way from her courtyard. Only then did she turn back into the little palace, hurrying up the staircase to the second level and down the hallway to her daughter's bedchamber. Yasaman had already been bathed and fed. She was tucked into her small bed, her beautiful blue and gold parrot in his brass cage within her sight.

Rugaiya Begum smiled and said, "I have come to bid you good-night, my child. Have you had a happy day?"

Yasaman smiled sleepily. "Oh, yes, Mama Begum!"

Rugaiya Begum bent down and kissed the little girl's cheek. "May God give you sweet dreams, my daughter," she said.

"Tell me of Candra again," Yasaman begged. Her eyes were heavy, but her tone determined.

Rugaiya positioned herself on the edge of the child's bed. To argue would be useless. Yasaman was very stubborn when she wanted something. She would fall asleep within five minutes if not thwarted. "Once upon a time," Rugaiya Begum began, "there was a beautiful princess who came from many months' distance away, over the vast seas to the land of the great emperor Akbar. She was the most beautiful maiden that the emperor had ever seen, and he immediately fell in love with her and made her his fortieth wife. He called her Candra in honor of the moon, for she was, he said, as fair as the moon. After several months a child was born from the love shared by Akbar and Candra. Candra loved her child with all her heart, and the infant princess was named Yasaman Kama. Yasaman for the jasmine flowers whose scent was Candra's favorite, and Kama, which means *love*, for the little girl had been conceived and born of love."

Yasaman's eyes suddenly widened. "Papa!" she cried joyfully, holding out her arms to her father even as Rugaiya Begum arose, bowing to her husband, her hands folded in a gesture of respect.

"My little love," the emperor said with a warm smile for this youngest of his children. He bent to kiss her, then sat down upon the edge of her bed. "What story does your Mama Begum tell you?" he asked.

"The story of Candra!" the little girl replied excitedly. "It is my favorite story of all, Papa, except for its sad ending. How I wish it had a happier ending."

Akbar's expressive dark eyes clouded for a moment with the painful memory and he sighed sadly, deeply.

"My dearest lord," Rugaiya Begum said, "I beg your forgiveness, but I have never thought it right that Yasaman not know the truth."

He looked up at her, and she almost cried out at the hurt she saw in his face. Then he took her hand in his and answered, "I gave you our daughter to raise, my dear wife. You can do no wrong with her in my eyes. Continue with your tale now, for Yasaman will not rest until it is finished, will you, my little love?"

Yasaman shook her head most vigorously.

"Now, where was I?" Rugaiya wondered aloud, remembering quite clearly where she had stopped, but enjoying her daughter's excitement.

"The little girl had been conceived and born of love," Yasaman prompted her.

"Ahh, yes," she said, and then continued, "When the child was but a half a year old, a wise man came from Candra's native land. He brought terrible news, and Candra was forced to leave her beloved daughter and the emperor, Akbar. She did not want to go, but more important, she did not want to leave her child. Akbar, however, would not allow his little daughter to be taken from him; and so Candra placed her baby into the keeping of her friend, Rugaiya Begum. 'Be the Mama Begum to my child as I cannot now be,' she said, and Rugaiya Begum, whom Allah had not blessed with a child of her own womb, happily agreed because she loved her friend, and she loved the baby. Candra left the emperor's lands, never to be seen again by him or the others who loved her.

"It is known that she reached her own land safely, and each year upon the birthday of Yasaman Kama Begum, the emperor, Akbar, sends a perfect pearl to Candra's mother, who is Yasaman's other grandmama, that Candra's family may be reassured that the child thrives."

Yasaman's eyes were now shut tightly. Her breathing had slowed and her left thumb crept slowly into her mouth. The two adults rose from their places at the side of her bed and departed the room. Rugaiya Begum led her husband to the small dining room within the palace, for he had come to take supper with her.

"I must apologize for the simplicity of the meal, my lord, but you did not give me a great deal of notice," she said.

"I enjoy your simple meals, my dear wife," he told her. "Each day in the main palace I must eat in state. There are a minimum of five hundred dishes served to me. No one eating with me can touch a morsel until each of these dishes is presented to me. It is exhausting."

Rugaiya lowered her head to hide her smile. Akbar was the ruler of this vast land. He might complain of all the pomp surrounding his daily life, but if he really desired to make that life more simple, he had but to command it. The truth was, he generally enjoyed all the fuss, although occasionally, like this evening, he sought a more simple life. Raising her eyes, she signaled her servants to begin serving them.

The meal began with a watermelon sherbet to cleanse the palate for the delights to come. A honey loaf sprinkled with poppy seeds was put upon the table, followed by a leg of delicately cooked baby lamb, chicken in a mustard leaf curry, a river fish with red chili, bowls of carrots, tiny, sharp herbed pickles, and saffron rice. Akbar tore the loaf in half and helped himself generously to each of the dishes offered him. When he had finished, a lemon sherbet was brought to him, and then lychees, peeled, in a dish of light wine were set before him along with a tray of fresh fruits, a bowl of shelled pistachios, and a plate of rose petals encased in crystallized honey.

He ate with gusto, and when he was finished he said, "I sleep better for your simple meals, my dear Rugaiya."

"So do we all, my lord," she answered him with a smile. "We are no longer as young as we once were."

"I am not *that* old," he protested.

"Do not forget, my lord," Rugaiya teased him mischievously, "that I am well aware of your exact age. We are cousins, after all, as well as husband and wife."

He chuckled. "It is true," he agreed, "but I am still young enough to enjoy a comely maiden in my bed."

"Is any man *ever* too old for a comely maiden?" she replied wickedly. It pleased her that after all these years she could still make him laugh. Now, more than ever, he needed to laugh.

"Have you always been this wise," he teased back, "or is it *your* age? Remember, I know how old you are too!"

"But you are far too noble to disclose that information publicly, my lord, I am certain," she said.

Again he laughed, but then he grew a trifle sober and asked her, "Why do you not tell Yasaman exactly why Candra was taken from us? Does she not ever ask just what the 'terrible news' brought by the wise man was? She is normally as curious as a monkey."

"But she is still just a child, my lord, barely out of her babyhood. For now it is enough that Candra loved her and did not want to leave her. She would not understand even if I attempted to explain the truth to her. Later on when she is older and capable of more intricate thought, I will tell her precisely what happened if she wants to know. It may not be important to her then."

"Why did you tell her at all then, my dear one?"

"Because if I had not, one day you may be certain someone would have. There is no way anyone would believe Yasaman was a child of your seed and my womb. It is obvious I am not her natural mother. I am plump and big-boned. My eyes are black. My skin is a wheaten-gold in color. Yasaman, on the other hand, is slender and delicately made. Her turquoise eyes give her away as the daughter of another woman. Her skin is the color of heavy cream, and her black hair, though it is as straight as yours, my lord, shines with hidden fire, even as Candra's did.

"There would come a day when someone, out of mischief,

or jealousy, or just plain meanness, would have told Yasaman of Candra. They would not know the truth as I know the truth. Did you not order Abul Fazl, your personal historian, to erase all mention of Candra from his writings of your reign? I know that you did it because of your great pain over the matter, but others would not know that. They would try and make something unkind of it. They would hurt my child, and I will never allow anyone to hurt her! As long as there is breath in my body and strength in my arms, no one shall harm our daughter!"

Akbar nodded, and taking her hand in his, he pressed it lovingly. "I chose wisely when I gave Yasaman to you, Rugaiya. I can remember back to when Candra came to me about how jealous Shaikho Baba was of me, for he wanted her for himself. When Yasaman was born he even suggested she might not be my daughter but the get of some Portuguese who had first taken Candra for his own pleasure. He was very angry in his deep disappointment, yet today he adores his little sister."

"No one looking at Yasaman could doubt she was your child, my dear lord," Rugaiya Begum said. "The tiny mole between her upper lip and her left nostril is the twin to yours, but for its size, which is smaller; and although she does not resemble you exactly, her imperious look when she is thwarted is your look." She laughed. "She quite cows the servants with that look."

"Yes," he agreed. "I have seen it. Her fierce Tatar ancestry shows in that look." Then he looked deep into his first wife's eyes and told her, "You are a good mother, Rugaiya Begum. Yasaman is fortunate to have your love, to be in your care."

"She is the child of my heart, my dear lord. I thank God each day that you have entrusted me with her care."

"I am of a mind to rest comfortably this night," Akbar answered her. "May I stay in your bed, my dearest Rugaiya?"

"No comely maiden, my lord?" she gently mocked him.

"Sometimes old friends are the best," he replied, smiling at her and touching her soft cheek with gentle fingers.

"Do you not mean old wives?" she teased him back.

"No," he said quietly. "You are my friend, Rugaiya Begum. I have thirty-nine wives, of which you are the first; but I have few true friends upon whom I can count. You are amongst those few."

"We are fortunate to have each other, are we not?" she said.

"Yes," he agreed, and rising, he led her from the dining room, back up the staircase to her chamber.

✹

2

✹

The fisherman, casting his nets in the still, dark waters of the lake, peered curiously at the palace of the Grand Mughal's daughter. He was quite near to it, perhaps closer than he should have been, but the fish were running into the shore tonight. Besides, Yasaman Kama Begum did not mind. Had she not personally given him permission to fish these waters by her home? He was the envy of all the men in the village, he thought, pushing his chest out with his pride; but had he not saved the princess's cat from a watery death? A young creature of obviously little sense, it had unwisely leapt from the marble terrace in pursuit of a noisy, arrogant duck. He chuckled with the memory.

He had seen the cat, an elegant beastie with long silvery-white fur, stalking the duck from the terrace top. The fisherman had assumed it was merely a feline exercise until the cat, perhaps taunted to rashness by the squawking duck, had leapt out high over the water, landing with a resounding splash and a howl of surprise which was half muffled by the water in its mouth. The duck, protesting this invasion of its territory, lifted itself off the lake with an indignant flap and flew away.

Almost immediately a chattering monkey had appeared upon the terrace wall, to be followed by a young girl who shrieked her distress. The fisherman, who had daughters of his own, realized that this was a beloved pet. Diving into the calm waters of the lake, he hauled the cat out and dumped it in his boat, which was little more than a hollowed-out log. The cat, in its terror, scratched him badly. Without thinking, the fisherman cursed loudly, likening the cat's mother to the bottom of a cesspit.

"Mama Begum says that no one should use such language," the girl said, but then she giggled.

The fisherman was astounded to be addressed by the cat's mistress. He did not need to be told who she was. She was the Grand Mughal's youngest and, so it was said, most beloved daughter. He dared not speak again, and climbing back into his boat, he cast his eyes down.

"If you will row but a bit closer," Yasaman Kama Begum said, "you can, I believe, hand Fou-Fou up to me."

The fisherman looked up and gaped at her foolishly.

"The cat, good sir," the princess gently explained.

"The cat," he repeated, and then looked down into the bottom of his vessel where the stupid creature crouched, eyeing him balefully and growling low. *Yes, the cat!* The fisherman realized that in being where he should not be, the sooner he departed, the less likely it was that questions would be asked of him. Stooping quickly, he reached for the beast which, with an angry hiss, struck out at him with a claw. Startled, the fisherman drew back.

"Bad Fou-Fou!" the young girl scolded. "This man saved your foolish life and but wishes to return you to me."

The cat's ears perked at the sound of its mistress's voice, and looking up, it meowed piteously. The fisherman quickly lifted the diverted animal from the boat's bottom and handed it to the princess.

"Oh, thank you, good sir," she said to him with a winning smile. "You must be rewarded for your bravery. My father would not have it otherwise. What is your name?"

Allah help me! the fisherman thought. I will surely be punished now for fishing so close to the royal palace, but there was no help for it. "My name is Ali, great lady," he said, bowing awkwardly, painfully conscious of his bare feet and dirty loincloth.

"You should not have been fishing so near to my palace, should you, Ali?" the princess said wisely. "Had you not, however, I should have lost my dear Fou-Fou. He was given to me by my brother Salim, who will one day be Grand Mughal. Fou-Fou is a most important cat, and you are responsible for saving her life." She smiled at him, showing perfect little white teeth. "Do you come so close because the fishing is good here, Ali?"

He nodded, afraid. She knew he should not have been there. He would certainly be punished.

"Then tomorrow, Adali, who is the high steward of my household, shall go to the village and present your headman with my written permission for you to fish in the waters near my palace. Do you have sons, Ali?"

"Two, great lady," he answered her, his heart hammering with excitement.

"And sons-in-law?" she further queried.

"Three," he said, suddenly realizing that what was said about this royal princess was absolutely true. She was the most beautiful female ever begat.

Yasaman Kama Begum nodded thoughtfully, and then said, "You may bring two of these men with you if you choose, Ali the fisherman. More would be an intrusion, *and* none may come without you. This privilege will span your lifetime only. This is my reward to you for saving my pet."

"Thank you, great lady! Thank you!" His head was swimming with delight. Fishing rights by the princess's palace, among the richest fishing grounds on the lake! He was going to be a wealthy man! "Thank you! Thank you!" he babbled. He wanted to row quickly home to tell his wife and family of his good fortune, but he would not. He had fishing to attend to.

"It is I who should thank you, Ali the fisherman." She smiled again. "Fou-Fou thanks you too," she assured him.

He would always remember her smile, Ali thought as he recalled that afternoon three years before, when his kismet had placed him in the wrong place at the right time. He had indeed grown wealthy by her kindness; but his family had many needs that seemed to grow with his fortune. Only he could fish this spot, with two of his offspring or his sons-in-law. So it was necessary to continue laboring. Now his youngest daughter was getting married, and there was a great deal his wife insisted she must have. The fisherman was just as glad to have an excuse to get away from his house and all the chattering women. His happiness had always been here on the lake.

He gazed at the nearby palace, which in the twilight seemed to float upon the waters of the lake. There were lanterns decorating the terrace tonight, and he could hear the sounds of flutes and drums. Candles fixed into little rounds of wood had been lit and set afloat in the lake. It was most magical and a perfect way to celebrate the princess's birthday. He knew it was her birthday because she had spoken to him when she saw him just a few days ago.

"I will be thirteen," she had said. "My father and brother are coming to see me. I shall be given my weight in precious jewels, Ali. I have been every year since my birth."

"You must be very rich, great lady," he had observed.

"I suppose I am," she replied modestly.

The fisherman smiled to himself. She was a most charming young girl, and he would always bless her for his good fortune. He hoped her kismet would be a happy one, but then why wouldn't it be? She was a princess. Ali cast his nets gracefully and gazed toward the terrace where two figures now stood intertwined. One of them was Yasaman Kama Begum, the other a man. The fisherman discreetly turned his back upon them. He was curious, but then it was not his business.

"Why does that fisherman come so close to your palace?" Salim demanded of his sister.

She peered through the fast-darkening evening and then answered him, "It is Ali; the man who saved Fou-Fou three years ago. You know I gave him fishing rights."

"What I know is that you have grown more fair, if that is possible," the prince replied. He drew her tightly against him and was excited to feel the soft flesh of her young breasts give against his chest.

"Mama Begum is going to speak to Father while he is here about the candidates for my hand in marriage," she told him, looking up into his face, her dark lashes fluttering just slightly.

"You are too young for marriage!" he growled in an angry voice.

"I am not," she replied calmly. "I bleed each month like all women of childbearing age. I am ready. You were not much older than I am now when you first wed."

"You know nothing of men, sweet sister," he murmured, and his hand caressed her silky head. "Besides, I will not let you go, Yasaman. I want you by me when I come into my inheritance. Remember how we spoke on it when you were little?"

"So you admit I am no longer a child," she teased him.

"I admit nothing! Sweet sister, do you not remember the kings and queens of ancient Egypt?" He bent his head and gently kissed her brow.

"The ones who wed each other in order to keep their bloodline pure? Aye, brother, I remember, but do you not recall our grandmother says that such a thing is unclean?" His arms about her were both exciting and frightening, she decided. Salim, twenty-one years her senior, seemed so sophisticated and worldly.

"She is a querulous old woman! What does she know of

life, my lotus blossom?" He pressed his lips to her temple once again. *Allah! How he wanted her!* It was madness, he knew, but for several years now he had lusted after his half sister with a passion that frightened even him. He seemed to have no control over it, and it had only grown worse as Yasaman had matured and grown more beautiful.

He had three wives. Man Bai, Amara, and the elegant Nur Jahan. He loved them. Yet still he wanted Yasaman. The thought of another man's lingham piercing her sweet yoni was more than he could bear. He felt his own member hardening at the thought. *Yasaman!* The mere thought of her consumed him with a raging, burning passion.

"Am I to be a spinster then, like our poor sister, Aram-Banu?" Yasaman demanded, shifting nervously at the unfamiliar pressure against her leg.

"Aram-Banu is a child," he told her.

"Aram-Banu is older than I am, Salim!" she retorted spiritedly.

"In years, aye, sweet sister, but Aram-Banu has the mind of a child. She is too simpleminded to be given to any man for a wife, else Father would have married her off to his advantage long ago." Reaching out, he cupped her face in his hand. "I cannot bear the thought of losing you, little monkey. Tell Father you will accept no husband now, and stay with me." He smiled down at her. "You know that I adore you, Yasaman." He ran his thumb along her full lips. She opened those lips and took his thumb in her mouth, sucking teasingly upon it for a moment. He believed he would lose control entirely as thoughts of her mouth upon a more intimate part of him filled his head. Yet practical instinct told him she was still half a child and had no real knowledge of her effect upon him.

"There you two are!" Rugaiya Begum had come upon them, although they had not heard her approach. "Yasaman, run along and change your garments. Your father's messenger has just arrived to say that Akbar is only an hour away."

The girl pulled easily from her brother's grasp and, without so much as a backward glance, hurried off. The prince and the older woman stared at each other a long, hard moment.

Then Rugaiya Begum said, "Your father and I are going to choose suitors for Yasaman while he is here. It is time we began to consider an advantageous marriage for her."

"Under the law, she cannot marry until she is fourteen," Salim replied. "I think it is much too soon to betroth her."

"Your father made the laws, and he can amend them, Salim. I cannot protect Yasaman the way a husband can." Rugaiya Begum answered him.

"Does she need protection, lady? Who would harm the Grand Mughal's daughter?"

She knew! The bitch had a sharp eye and a keener judgment of his character than any other. Whenever he had gotten in his father's bad graces over the years, he could always rely upon the ladies of his father's zenana to aid him. All but Rugaiya Begum. She loved him for his mother's sake, but unlike the others, even his grandmother, she was not fooled by him.

"You will want to change your clothes, Salim, or perhaps you would prefer to leave," she said, ignoring his question. Then she turned away, hurrying back into the house.

Rugaiya Begum went to her daughter's apartments, where Yasaman was bathing in a marble pool of perfumed water with the aid of her two body servants, Rohana and Toramalli. Looking about her, Rugaiya Begum sighed. The child was still such an innocent. Fou-Fou, the long-haired white cat Yasaman so doted upon, lay sprawled indolently upon a silken couch. Baba, the monkey, had perched himself upon the rolled arm of the couch and was eating a piece of fruit which was dripping juice all over the silk fabric. The parrot, Hiraman, strutted fretfully about the pool muttering, "Water! Water!" beneath its breath and watching Yasaman nervously.

Rugaiya Begum shook her head. Yasaman had been too

cosseted and too sheltered! It was all her fault that Yasaman was too immature to marry, and yet . . . Rugaiya Begum bit her lip in vexation. Was she mistaken? Surely Salim did not lust after his little sister! It had to be the imagination of an old woman seeing shadows where there were none. Still, Akbar was not well, although he hid it from everyone but his physician and her. A marriage had to be arranged for Yasaman eventually. Now was as good a time as any to settle the matter. Her instincts had never failed her before, but she was still loath to believe that the prince desired Yasaman as a woman. If Yasaman were married, however, the matter would be settled for good and all. If she was right, this would be but one of Salim's temporary passions. A royal marriage for his sister would cool his ardor and bring him to his senses.

"What have you decided to wear, my child?" she asked her daughter.

"The peacock-blue- and gold-striped pajama, and a cloth-of-gold kurti with my new shabnam peshwaz, Mama Begum," Yasaman answered as she stepped from the marble bathing pool.

Rugaiya Begum looked closely at her daughter for the first time in a long while and realized, to her surprise, that Yasaman had the body of a woman. Her breasts were high cones of smooth pale skin that would grow quite lush with age. Her legs were long and shapely. With a young body like that, her desires would only increase as each day went by. No wonder she was so susceptible to Salim. Yasaman's body was maturing faster than her emotions, which, of course, were confusing the girl, who did not know yet what to do with those emotions.

"A perfect choice, dearest one, but then you always had an instinct for style," Rugaiya Begum complimented her daughter. Then she said in a more serious tone, "We must speak, my daughter, for you have done something you knew would displease me, and yet you did it."

"What is that, Mama Begum?" Yasaman replied sweetly,

raising her arms to allow her servants to dry her off before massaging her with almond oil.

"You were wrong to ask your brother to come to your birthday celebration, Yasaman," Rugaiya Begum said.

"Next to Papa and you, he is my favorite person," the girl answered.

"Your father has not, nor will he ever forgive Salim for his part in the murder of Abul Fazl."

"Salim did not murder Abul Fazl!" Yasaman defended her brother.

"No," agreed Rugaiya Begum. "Your brother did not wield the weapon that pierced the heart of Abul Fazl; but he most certainly directed Bir Singh of Orchha to do so. It is no secret, Yasaman. You know it to be so. Bir Singh has publicly said your brother promised him his patronage and a rich reward for the deed."

"The cowardly bandit lies!" Yasaman exclaimed angrily, but at the same time she felt uncomfortable. She had heard the gossip, and Salim had always been jealous of her father's friend, the historian. Abul Fazl had been a gentle, wise man with a wonderful sense of humor. He had always been especially kind to her, and Yasaman's conscience nagged her. Still, she loved her brother. She could not believe he would do such a thing!

"A man on the run such as Bir Singh exposes his compatriots in order to divert the whole punishment from himself, my child."

"Father forgave Salim," Yasaman muttered with a total lack of logic.

"Your father had no choice but to publicly forgive Salim," Rugaiya Begum explained gently. "Your two other brothers, Murad and Daniyal, are not fit to rule. *Salim is the only heir.* Only the intercession of your grandmother and Gulbadan Begum, your father's elderly aunt, saved Salim. Your father was ready to disinherit him and declare Salim's son, Prince Khusrau, the next Mughal.

"Publicly your father has reconciled himself with your brother. Privately he does not want to see him. You have been incredibly thoughtless, Yasaman. You should have asked me before you sent to Salim. Abul Fazl was murdered one year ago this very day."

Yasaman turned, her young face shocked. "Ohh, Mama Begum! I did not know!"

"There was no need for you to know, my child, until now. Had you not asked Prince Salim to come, it would never have been necessary to tell you that your father's dearest friend and advisor was murdered on your twelfth birthday. It is tragic that a day your father has always held in esteem and joy became one of sadness for him."

"Oh, Mama Begum, I would not hurt my father! You know how much I love him!" Yasaman cried.

"Then send Adali to your brother with the message that he must leave here before your father arrives," Rugaiya Begum advised.

"Yes! Yes!" Yasaman agreed. Calling the eunuch who was her high steward, she instructed him nervously, her eyes flicking back and forth from the eunuch's face to her mother's for approval.

Adali nodded solemnly, his brown eyes meeting Rugaiya Begum's for a brief moment of total understanding. Then, with a bow to his young mistress, he hurried off.

"There, there, my child," Rugaiya Begum said, gathering her daughter into her arms to soothe her. "Everything will be all right now, I promise you." She patted Yasaman, all the while thinking, Salim will rush off in a temper if I know him, and I do. We'll not be bothered with him for a long while now.

She was incorrect, however. She had returned to her own quarters to dress when Adali came to her.

"The prince says he will leave the palace so that his sister's birthday celebration will not be spoilt. He will remain in the vicinity, however, so he may visit with her, as they have been separated these many months and he has missed her company. He asks that you tender his respects to his father. One of his servants will remain to present the prince's birthday gift to the princess."

Rugaiya Begum frowned. "I had hoped he would leave us entirely," she said, disappointed.

"I understand, gracious lady," Adali replied, nodding.

"Do you, I wonder?" Rugaiya Begum said almost to herself.

"The prince lusts after his sister, which is wrong," Adali answered her softly.

Rugaiya Begum gasped, shocked to hear her own fears voiced aloud by another. "Is it so obvious then, Adali?" she questioned him.

"Only to you and to me, gracious lady. We both know how the prince behaves when he desires something he cannot or should not have. We have both watched over our little princess since she was born, and we would keep her safe from all wickedness. What will you do, gracious lady?" Though Adali was a servant, he was a trusted one, and Rugaiya Begum thought, he was also a friend.

"My lord Akbar will be here in Kashmir for several days, Adali. In that time I hope to broach the matter of Yasaman's marriage. I believe if we can settle her with a husband, Prince Salim's unnatural desires will dissolve."

The high steward nodded in agreement. "As always, gracious lady, I stand in awe of your wisdom," he said.

Rugaiya Begum smiled. "We have had many adventures together over our dear child, haven't we, Adali? Do you remember the time she felt sorry for her father's fighting elephants and let them loose?"

"And they wandered through the city of Lahore trumpeting piteously and frightening the general population, who thought they were under attack?" Adali wheezed with laughter.

"Even Akbar found it funny," Rugaiya Begum chuckled,

"although afterwards he scolded her most severely. He had to pay for all the damages too, particularly in the open market where the fruits and vegetables were sold. Those elephants ate everything in sight!"

"But our good and gracious master also explained to our little princess that the fighting elephants were trained to go into battle and, indeed, enjoyed it. When Yasaman understood that by loosing the beasts she had frightened them, for they felt lost and afraid, she repented of her naughtiness. I remember our lord Akbar telling her that if ever again she thought that a cruelty was being perpetrated upon an animal, she was to come to him first. How he loves the creatures, and he has taught his daughter to love and cherish them too."

Before they might continue with their reminiscences, however, they heard the sound of the drums that accompanied the emperor in his travels. Akbar was approaching the palace.

"Find Yasaman!" Rugaiya Begum instructed Adali, and he ran off to do so.

Rugaiya Begum turned to look at herself in the full-length mirror that she possessed, and was pleased with the reflection that looked back at her. She wore a jaguli: a high-waisted dress long favored by her Mughal ancestors. It had an open neck and long, tight-fitting sleeves. The skirt flowed regally about her. The midnight-blue color was particularly flattering, and the silken skirt was dotted with silver stars that seemed to match her hair. She wore a long necklace of fat Indian Ocean pearls and Ceylon sapphires that echoed the sapphires in her ears.

"Well," she said to herself in a low voice, "I am becoming an old woman, but by Allah, I am a handsome old woman!" She chuckled and patted her beautiful silvery hair, which she wore parted in the center and wound into an elegant knot at the nape of her neck. Her plain but kindly face was lined around her lively black eyes, but barely touched elsewhere. She took great pride in her soft, fine skin which quite belied the fact that she would be sixty on her next birthday in the spring.

"Mama Begum! Mama Begum! Papa is almost in the courtyard!" Yasaman danced into her view. "Ohhh, how beautiful you are!"

Rugaiya Begum smiled happily and replied, "You far outshine me, my daughter. I am astounded by the evidence of my eyes. You are really quite grown up."

"*Am I?*" Yasaman's voice was somewhat breathless with her excitement.

Rugaiya Begum turned from her mirror and gently patted her daughter's cheek. "Yes you are."

"Do you think Papa will be pleased with my costume? My aunt, the lady Jodh Bai, sent me this shabnam peshwaz. It is the muslin of the morning dew. Only a Mughal's daughter may have peshwaz of shabnam."

"Yes, I know that," said Rugaiya Begum, a small smile tugging at the corners of her mouth. "There are other fine muslins, like White of the Clouds when the Rain is Spent; the Jasmine Flower White; White of the August Moon; but, of course, only plain princesses can wear those. Only a royal Mughal princess can wear the shabnam muslin. It goes quite well with your peacock-blue and cloth-of-gold pajama and kurti. I like what Toramalli has done with your hair too."

Yasaman's long black tresses were loose, but her maidservant had fashioned a single braid amid the thick cloud of hair, weaving it with small pearls and diamonds, which hung down her back and glittered with her every movement. Then she had powdered Yasaman's hair with gold dust. In the princess's small ears, diamonds sparkled also.

"You look perfect," her mother assured her. "Let us go now and greet your father."

Hand in hand they entered the courtyard just as the emperor arrived. Akbar would be sixty-one in the autumn. He was still a handsome man, and if his concealed ill health had taken a toll on him, it was not visible. He was dressed all in white, from the silk dastar turban on his head to the jama, a long coat-tunic with a full skirt that covered his long pants, which were called cuddidara pajamas. Only his patka, a sash of cloth-of-gold studded with sparkling diamonds, broke the pristine purity of his snow-white costume.

Climbing off his horse, he turned and opened his arms to his wife and daughter. "At last!" he said with a deep sigh, and then he pretended to look about. "Rugaiya, my dear, where is Yasaman? Why is she not here to greet her old father?"

"Papa!" Yasaman giggled and ran into his embrace. "It is me!"

The emperor set her back down and declared, "No! You cannot be my little daughter! You are far too seductive a maiden. My Yasaman is but a child." His dark eyes were twinkling.

"Papa! This is my thirteenth birthday! I am a grown woman now," Yasaman declared.

"Are you certain that you are Yasaman Kama Begum?" he teased her. "You are not some fairy maid come to steal her presents, are you?"

"*Presents?*" Yasaman pretended she was offended, but then she began to giggle.

"You are not entirely grown-up yet, I am relieved to see," Akbar told her dryly.

"Do you not want me to grow up?" Yasaman asked her father, taking him by the hand to lead him into her palace.

"The older you grow, my little rosebud, the older I grow," he told her. "It is the natural order of things, but not necessarily how I would want it."

"If you could change anything, Papa, what would it be?" she asked him curiously.

"There is not a great deal I would change, my child," he answered slowly. "I think I would have wanted my twin sons, Hussein and Hassan, to live instead of dying at birth. And, of course, I would have wanted Candra to remain with us. And perhaps if the great God would give me the opportunity to change things, Abul Fazl would be here with us today." He sighed and a sad look came into his eyes. "So many people I have loved. *Gone*."

"Do not be sad, Papa," Yasaman said, looking up at her father. Mama Begum and I love you. We are here, and for all those gone, there are others yet with you."

The emperor looked into his daughter's young face for a long moment. "You are growing up," he said quietly. "You have said a very wise thing, my daughter."

They had moved from the courtyard through the palace and were now coming out onto the lakeside terrace where the celebration was to be held.

"Good evening, my gracious lord," Adali said, coming up to Akbar and bowing low. "The boats are even now approaching with the royal ladies."

Akbar nodded and, with his daughter and senior wife, watched as the barges, festively decorated with twinkling lanterns, made their way over the placid waters to bump against the small marble quay at Yasaman's palace, at the foot of a short flight of steps. As each boat disgorged its passengers, it moved back into the lake to bob at anchor. Yasaman greeted her guests individually.

Watching them come, Rugaiya Begum considered that time had not been kind to most of Akbar's other wives. Zada Begum, the second wife Akbar had taken, never changed. She had been a gray-brown mouse of a woman her entire life. Older than her husband by several years, she was now wizened and stooped. Still, she managed a smile for Yasaman, who sweetly kissed her wrinkled cheek and personally led her to a comfortable cushioned seat. Zada Begum had always been a haughty woman and had never acknowledged Candra; but for some unknown reason she had always had a soft spot for Yasaman.

The third wife, Salima Begum, was the mother of Yasaman's eldest sister, Shahzad-Kanim Begum. She, too, had never accepted Candra, but Yasaman was a different matter. Yasaman was blood kin to her own child; a royal Mughal princess, not some foreigner whom she held in contempt. Tall and thin, her hair was now iron-gray, and her Mughal nose had grown more hawklike with age.

"How old are you now, child?" she demanded of Yasaman.

"Thirteen this day, my honored aunt," was the polite reply. Yasaman had learned early that the prickly Salima Begum was not to be trifled with.

"You have the breasts of an older woman," remarked Salima Begum bluntly. "It is time you were married."

"So my mother says," Yasaman agreed pleasantly.

"Does she indeed?" Salima Begum noted. "Well, she is right for once!" Then she passed on to sit with Zada Begum, who was her best friend.

The other consorts arrived. Almira, the mother of Prince Murad, had once been a beautiful, passionate creature over whom Akbar had caused a minor scandal. Now she was a hollow-eyed and embittered woman. Strangely for one so young, Yasaman understood this *aunt*. She greeted her in a kindly fashion, but received barely a nod from Almira in return.

Leila, the princess of Khandesh, the mother of Akbar's second daughter, Shukuran Nisa Begum, kissed Yasaman politely and passed on. After her came Roopmati, the princess of Bikaner, the mother of the charming but weak-willed Prince Daniyal, Yasaman's youngest brother. There was Kamlavati, the princess of Jaisalmer, and her cousin Sadera, the princess of Puragadh. They were pleasant ladies, but none of them really knew Yasaman, for she lived apart from them in her own palaces in Lahore and Kashmir. The lady Waqi and her daughter, Yasaman's sister, Aram-Banu Begum, arrived and were warmly welcomed. Waqi had been a mere concubine who had somehow managed, in a very brief encounter with Akbar, to conceive his child. She was a good-hearted woman whose life revolved about her impaired daughter, now aged twenty-two, and the many works of charity she performed, for she was a devout Muslim.

"I knew that shabnam peshwaz would look perfect on you!" said Akbar's favorite wife, Jodh Bai, who arrived last.

Yasaman hugged her happily and kissed her cheek. "I love it, dearest aunt! I have never had such a fine peshwaz." Then she leaned over and whispered softly in Jodh Bai's ear, "Salim was here! He is coming back to see me when Father is gone."

"*I know,*" Jodh Bai whispered back. "That is why I am late. My son came to see me too!" Time had changed the mother of Akbar's heir little. She was petite in stature, her famed long, dark hair still as black as a raven's wing. Golden-brown eyes twinkled conspiratorially in a remarkably smooth-skinned face. She adored her only child and was delighted by the close bond between him and his half sister.

"Why are you the only one amongst us who does not grow old?" grumbled Rugaiya Begum as she joined them.

Jodh Bai laughed her tinkling laughter. "Perhaps my face remains young as did my mother's and my grandmother's before me; but my bones are old now, Rugaiya, I swear it! On damp summer mornings my knees ache most fiercely."

The guests having all assembled, it was time for Yasaman's traditional birthday weighing. The double scales were brought forth and set up in the middle of the terrace. The young princess was helped into her seat on one side of the scales. Then two servants, carrying an open chest of loose gemstones, came forth. They set the chest upon the ground and slowly, using small gold scoops, began to carefully fill the other scale pan with brightly colored jewels and vari-colored pearls. After a while the scales began to tilt, until finally they were balanced so finely that a feather would have created an imbalance.

"You do not look as if you weigh more than last year, my daughter," Akbar said, "but you do. It is, I think, the height you have attained." He helped her from her seat. "My birthday gift to you will be a nice addition to your personal wealth."

"It is her breasts." Salima Begum nodded wisely to Zada Begum. "She has fine breasts for a young girl. I will wager they would weigh heavily in a man's hands." She chuckled.

The other women now came forward with their gifts for the princess. There was the usual assortment of silk scarves and saris; perfumes, gold bracelets, and earrings. Aram-Banu Begum brought her youngest sister a little cage with two lovebirds.

"They are for you," she said slowly, struggling to remember the words exactly as her mother had taught her. "I raised them myself. My mama says you like birds."

"I shall love them dearly, my revered elder sister, especially knowing that you raised them for me yourself," Yasaman told Aram-Banu Begum, and she hugged her.

"She has a good heart," the lady Waqi observed wisely. "Not like others here I might name. You have raised her well, my lady Rugaiya Begum."

"I thank you, Lady Waqi," Rugaiya Begum said with a kindly smile. Poor Waqi. She had been but a passing fancy with Akbar, and only the fact she had borne his child saved her from total obscurity. If Aram-Banu had been normal, she would have married well, and Waqi would have spent a comfortable old age in a rich son-in-law's house spoiling her grandchildren. Her daughter's feeble mind denied her all these things. She would grow old in the zenana.

"I have a most special gift for our Yasaman," Jodh Bai announced, and all eyes turned to her.

"What is it, Aunt?" Yasaman asked, surprised. She had believed her shabnam peshwaz Jodh Bai's gift.

Jodh Bai signaled to her servant. The eunuch hurried forth to present Yasaman with a sandalwood box with gold filigreed corners and a matching filigreed lock. The lock, however, was only decorative. As he held the box, Yasaman lifted the lid to reveal its contents. The interior was lined in beaten gold, and upon a scarlet satin pillow rested a book.

"It is a Pillow Book, my dearest," Jodh Bai told Yasaman. "It is the very same Pillow Book I gave Candra those many years ago. Now it is yours."

Yasaman's eyes filled with tears. She looked away, embarrassed for a brief moment. Then, regaining control over her emotions, she said, "You could have given me nothing that would have pleased me more. To have something that Candra cherished is almost too much to bear, dear aunt. It makes me feel closer to her." Yasaman lifted the book from its box. It was exquisitely bound in peacock-blue silk, its edges of pure gold studded with tiny pearls and diamonds. Opening the first ivory-vellum page she read aloud the words that were written in gold upon it.

" 'Once the Wheel of Love has been set in motion, there is no absolute rule.' " Her heart seemed to beat a little faster as the words echoed in the night. "Ohh, how perfectly romantic! It's from the *Kama Sutra*, isn't it?"

"Yes," said Jodh Bai, a little surprised. "You have read the *Kama Sutra*?"

"Only some of it, Aunt. It disturbs poor Father Cullen when I do, and so I only read it occasionally."

"If the *Kama Sutra* upsets the priest, I can only imagine what a Pillow Book is going to do," Jodh Bai said mischievously.

"There is nothing wrong with a Pillow Book," Rugaiya Begum said indignantly. "These priests! Why they deny their manhood is a mystery I shall never solve. They have linghams like other men, and yet all they use them for is to pee. It is a terrible waste, I tell you! If Allah had wanted a race of men who didn't use their linghams for joy, then he would have so created them! Pay no attention to Father Cullen, my daughter. A Pillow Book but prepares a young girl for the marriage bed by allowing her to see what will go on there. Ignorance has no virtue, and fear should play no part in lovemaking."

"Is she not perhaps a little too young for a Pillow Book?" Akbar asked.

Before Rugaiya Begum might reply, Jodh Bai said, "No, my good lord, she is not. Look closely at Yasaman. Salima is correct. The girl has the breasts of a mature woman. She is ripe for marriage."

"It is time we spoke of finding a husband for Yasaman, my lord," Rugaiya Begum said now that this perfect opportunity had presented itself to her. "In another year Yasaman will be of marriageable age. It would be good to settle the matter soon," she finished, casting her friend, Jodh Bai, a grateful look.

"Yes, I suppose you are correct, my dear Rugaiya," Akbar said, "but let us speak on it later."

"As my lord wishes," Rugaiya Begum agreed, surmising that his reluctance to discuss the matter stemmed from the presence of the other consorts, all of whom had grown suddenly still as they strained to hear the conversation between their shared husband and his first wife.

Since it was past time for the evening meal, Rugaiya Begum signaled her servants discreetly. Under Adali's firm direction, they moved about the terrace offering the guests fruit and sweetmeats. Because she knew the older of the wives particularly enjoyed them, Yasaman had asked that Turkish paste candies be served. There was tea to drink, both smoky black Assam and a delicate green tea from China that had a faint flavor and aroma of apricots. Food was an important part of the zenana life, and the wives of Akbar enjoyed it as much as anyone.

Behind a screen the musicians played softly. Some young dancing girls entertained the ladies, and they were followed by a wizened old man who charmed a snake from its woven basket. A large bright moon gave the feeling of daylight,

and when a light breeze sprang up, Rugaiya Begum called to
Adali to bring kites. Akbar enjoyed kite flying, and the wind
was just right this evening for the delicate paper toys.

"I want the tiger," Yasaman said.

"But I want it too," teased her father.

"It is my birthday," the girl reasoned with him. "Therefore, I should have whatever I so desire, Papa, and I desire
the tiger kite!"

"I am forced to agree with you, my daughter," the
emperor told her gracefully. "I shall take the elephant kite
instead."

"Aram-Banu! Come and join us!" Yasaman called to her
sister. "There is a peacock for you."

Delighted to be included, Aram-Banu arose and took hold
of the silken string attached to her kite, which Adali had
already begun flying for her. Yasaman came to stand next
to her sister and gently instructed her in the art so that the
childlike woman's kite would not crash to earth. Aram-Banu
might be slower than most women her age, but she had a
full-blown Mughal temper when frustrated or thwarted.

"Yasaman will be a good mother one day," Rugaiya Begum
said, pleased by her daughter's kind behavior.

"Why should she not be?" Jodh Bai demanded. "She has
had the best example possible in you, my dear friend."

"If I had not been here for her, you would have been,"
Rugaiya Begum replied practically.

"I could not have raised her the way you raised her," Jodh
Bai insisted. "Behold my son Salim, dear friend."

"He will be a fine emperor one day," Rugaiya insisted.
"He is simply impatient."

"And stubborn and full of pride," Jodh Bai said. "He is
my child, and I love him. I want to believe him perfect even
if I know better."

"Like his father," Rugaiya Begum chuckled, "and like my
darling daughter, Yasaman."

"You defend Salim. Yet of all the women in his father's house, you have never interceded for him or been won over by his charm," Jodh Bai noted.

"No, I have not," her friend agreed. "Salim must learn that not all women will succumb to his magnetism. He must be able to accept when he is wrong. I have always been the voice of Salim's conscience. I will continue to be as long as I walk this earth. If he learns from his errors, he will one day be a good and just emperor. I believe he can accomplish this."

The celebration ended shortly afterward. The servants brought bowls of rose water and soft towels to the ladies that they might remove the sticky sweet residue of the dessert from their fingers. Yasaman politely saw her guests to their boats and, kissing each aunt and her elder sister, waved them all off. Only Akbar and her mother remained. Hugging her parents, the princess bid them a good-night and sought her own bed. It had been a most exciting day, but she knew that her mother and father wanted to discuss possible plans for her marriage. As for herself, she wanted to examine in detail the Pillow Book Jodh Bai had brought her, the book that had once belonged to Candra—the woman who had given her life and then disappeared back into her own world.

Akbar called to Adali, "Come and help me out of these clothes, old friend, and then bring me a cup of light wine."

The steward quickly divested the emperor of his jama coat and his patka. "Bring his majesty a lungi," he instructed a slave woman. Then, kneeling, he removed Akbar's slippers and cuddidara pajamas. He handed each garment to a young eunuch who stood attentively by his side. When he had removed all of his master's clothing, he swathed him in the lungi which the slave woman had brought him. The garment was a simple length of cloth that wrapped about his hips several times and was tucked in at the waist. It was the traditional at-home garb of the Mughals. "There, my gracious lord," Adali said, finishing his task and impatiently waving the young eunuch away.

"Ahhhh," Akbar replied, comfortable at last.

Adali permitted himself a small grin as, hurrying over to a little table, he poured his master the required beverage, handing it to him and bowing himself off the terrace. He knew the importance of the conversation about to take place. He wanted that conversation to begin. Carefully, he stationed himself in the shadows where he could hear all, but not be seen.

The emperor lowered himself onto a large couch and, stretching out, sipped his wine. Rugaiya Begum sat on a low stool by his side and waited for her lord to broach the subject she had already attempted with him. Finally he said, "She is still too young to marry under our law, Rugaiya."

"Nonetheless, we must choose a husband for her, my lord, for that day, a year from now, when she will not be too young to marry," his wife replied.

"You love her so dearly," he observed, "that I did not believe you would ever want to discuss her marriage. Well, now that you have brought it up, there are several eligible princes available for Yasaman. The raja of Orissa, or perhaps the heir to Khandesh or Mewar."

"Orissa would be too hot for Yasaman," Rugaiya Begum said. "You know she absolutely wilts in the heat, and the dampness off the Bay of Bengal would kill her before her time. I see a similar problem with Khandesh, and besides, I'm not certain how the lady Leila would like it if you married Yasaman to the son of the man who overthrew her father. As for Mewar, you cannot make peace with them or bribe them with our daughter. I am astounded you would even suggest it. They are very troublesome people, the folk of Mewar," Rugaiya Begum concluded.

Akbar hid a small smile. Rugaiya Begum had obviously already decided upon Yasaman's future husband. It was a mere formality that she consult with him. "Perhaps," he said slowly, "you are right about Orissa, Khandesh, and Mewar, my dear. Do you have another suggestion you want to make to me? You, of course, are Yasaman's mother and want only what is best for her."

Rugaiya Begum chuckled. How well he knew her. "Yasaman," she began, "loves Kashmir above all places. Each year she manages to spend more and more time here and less in Lahore and Agra. She has actually spent most of this year here. I think that nothing would make her happier than if she could remain here for the rest of her life. Yusef Khan, the former ruler of Kashmir, who is now your most loyal general, has several surviving sons. The eldest, Yaqub Ali Khan, is, for all his recent submission to you, a rebel, and the middle son, Haider, follows him. Jamal Darya Khan does not."

"How old is Jamal Khan?" the emperor asked.

"He is twenty-three, my lord," she replied.

"Does he have any wives?"

"No. He has a zenana, not a large one—perhaps a half a dozen women of whom he is fond, but not overly attached.

"Yaqub Khan is some years Prince Jamal's senior and has a different mother. This youngest son is the offspring of a lady from a respectable but not very important Kashmiri family. The story, I am told, is that Yusef Khan married her when her father, a loyal government official, begged him to take the girl into his zenana. The man was on his deathbed. There was no other family, and he feared for his child. She was quite lovely—Prince Jamal is a particularly handsome young man.

"Upon seeing the maiden, Yusef Khan agreed to marry her and to provide for her, which was, of course, far more than the official had hoped. The wedding was celebrated almost immediately, before the dying father. Yusef Khan took the maiden to his bed that very night, and proof of the consummation was brought to her father the next morning.

He died that same day. Then several weeks later the new bride announced that she was expecting a child. It is said that Yusef Khan was most pleased, although Yaqub Khan's mother was not, particularly when the new baby turned out to be another son.

"This prince was raised by his mother from his earliest years to be totally loyal to his father and his father's wishes. It is how the grateful lady repaid her debt to her lord. That is why, when Yusef Khan so gracefully accepted defeat at your hands in the battle for Kashmir and then became one of your most loyal generals, Prince Jamal did not rebel against you as did his brother, Yaqub Khan.

"I knew Prince Jamal's mother. She died two years ago, but she was a good and gracious woman. I believe this young prince would be a perfect husband for Yasaman. When you learn to trust him yourself as you trust his father, you might even make him governor here in your name. You cannot help but bind the Kashmiri people closer to you, my dear Akbar, by making a son of their former ruling family your voice and marrying your own beloved daughter to him as well.

"Forgive me for speaking the unspeakable, but you will not always be here for Yasaman, and neither will I. One day Salim will rule, and with his favorite sister married to Kashmir's governor, his northern flank will be safe. You must think on the future when you think of Yasaman's marriage and Salim's kingship," she finished.

"You have thought this out most carefully, haven't you, my dear Rugaiya? I will, of course, want to meet this young paragon of princely virtue before rendering a decision in the matter." Akbar smiled at his wife. "Does Yasaman know Prince Jamal?"

Rugaiya Begum shook her head in the negative. "Yasaman knows nothing but the simple life she has always lived within the safety of her family. It has not been necessary that she know anything else."

He nodded slowly. "No. You are wise, my dear, in the ways of your motherhood. Salima was correct, however, when she said the girl had matured physically. She is suddenly quite beautiful. Indeed, the most beautiful of all my children. I wish Candra could see her now. Perhaps it is best we marry her young. Her mother was young when I took her as my wife." For a moment his eyes were misty with his memories. "Young and very passionate," he said softly, "and so beautiful."

"So you still think of her," Rugaiya Begum answered him. "I certainly have never forgotten her. Sometimes Yasaman will gesture in a certain manner, or glance in a particular way, and I see Candra."

Akbar looked at her and said candidly, "A day has not gone by since Candra was taken from me that I have not thought of her, my dear. I did not stop loving her because she was no longer here. The proof of my great love for my English rose is Yasaman. I want only what is best for her. If you say that Prince Jamal Darya Khan is the best husband our daughter can have, then I trust your judgment."

"I thank you, my dearest lord," Rugaiya Begum said. "I have indeed thought long and hard on this matter. Although she is half of our blood, and has been raised in India, Yasaman has Candra's blood in her as well. There is an independence and determination about her that is totally alien. The Kashmiri peoples are independent-minded too. Here she will be freer to be herself."

"And," the emperor continued with a smile, "once Yasaman delves into that Pillow Book Jodh Bai gave her tonight, her youthful curiosity will quickly assert itself. Who better to be the recipient of that curiosity than an eager and equally passionate young bridegroom?"

"Do you remember," Rugaiya Begum reminded him, "how you could not breach Candra's defenses at first, and you came to Jodh Bai and me for aid? The book was originally intended as a gift for Jodh Bai's niece who was to be married, but instead she offered to send it to Candra."

The memory was a bittersweet one for Akbar, but still he smiled and said, "She was so curious, and yet shy of it. I remember sitting with her and turning the pages for her, watching her slow arousal until at last she yielded herself to me. I have relived that night a thousand times and again a thousand in my mind over the years." He sighed deeply.

"And now the book belongs to the child she bore you," Rugaiya Begum said. "I wonder if perhaps I should not have let her have it until after her marriage is arranged."

Akbar shook his head. "She is innocent, but curious, Rugaiya. I think it better to allow her curiosity an innocent release."

While her parents spoke on the things that would decide her future, Yasaman had stood patiently as her two women servants removed her clothing and sponged her with rose water. Twin sisters, Rohana and Toramalli were twenty-four years of age and identical in features but for one thing. They each carried a small flower-shaped birthmark set at the edge of an eye. Toramalli's, however, was situated by the corner of her right eye, and Rohana's was by the corner of her left eye. They had expressive dark brown eyes, golden skin, and long, straight black hair. They had been barely ten years of age when the Mughal had presented them to Candra, and when she had departed India, they had remained to serve her child.

Rohana undid her mistress's long black hair and brushed it free of gold dust. Then she perfumed it with jasmine oil. Toramalli brought her lady a large, light shawl to wrap about her, for the evening had turned cool. Then the two servants escorted Yasaman to her bed.

"Leave me," the princess told them. "Go to your own beds."

The twin sisters bowed themselves from the bedchamber.

Alone, Yasaman leapt from her bed to fetch a small oil lamp and the Pillow Book. Setting the lamp on the little round table next to her bed, Yasaman settled herself down and opened the book. The small shawl slid about her shoulders, but she didn't notice. She leafed past the title page with its cryptic words from the *Kama Sutra* to the page with the first painting. The colors were clear and bright. The picture depicted a prince, fully clothed, wearing a lotus crown, seated with his equally clothed consort.

Yasaman found herself slightly disappointed. There was nothing at all titillating about it. Yasaman knew enough about the Hindu faith to know that the lotus crown indicated that the wearer had attained a high level of spiritual awareness. Did a man have to reach such a spiritual plateau in order to make love to a woman? And what about the woman? Or did she misunderstand entirely? Perhaps men also wore lotus crowns when they made love to a woman. Yes! That had to be it! She turned the page to find she was totally mistaken.

The second painting showed the prince unclothed and crownless, his consort also unclothed. The young woman, looking coyly from beneath her eyelashes, cuddled against her lord, who had quite a firm grasp on one of her breasts, while his other hand roamed freely over the lady's bare belly. *This* was definitely more interesting, Yasaman thought, encouraged. She closed her eyes and tried to imagine what it would feel like to have a man fondling her so intimately. She couldn't even begin to conceive such a thing because she had never known a man romantically, nor had she even known a man about whom she might fantasize romantically. The only men she had ever known were her father, Abul Fazl, her brothers, Adali—who was a eunuch—and Father Cullen, who might as well be one. Salim was so handsome, though, it would be easy to think of him as a lover if he wasn't her brother.

She turned the page of the book to find that the prince

and his consort were now quite intimately entwined, gazing lovingly into one another's eyes. The prince's lingham was thrust boldly forward in anticipation of the pleasure to come. Closing her eyes, Yasaman tried her hardest to imagine how such a moment would feel. Her shawl fell completely away from her shoulders. With a deep sigh she cupped her own breast in her hand and then shivered at the tiny thrill of excitement she felt race through her.

And at that moment the faintest of footfalls caught her attention. Her eyes flew open just as a man slipped into her chamber from the terrace. Yasaman blushed guiltily in the half darkness as she recognized the silhouette of her brother, Salim, in the moonlight. He stepped into the room saying, "Still awake, little monkey?" His eyes slid with surprise over her lush nudity.

"Salim!" she squealed softly. "It is late! What on earth are you doing here?" Her erotic thoughts at first made her forget her nudity, but then she drew her shawl up.

"I promised you I would be back," he told her, walking across the chamber and seating himself by her side. *Allah!* he thought. What a magnificent body she has, my sweet baby sister. *She must be mine! I can let no other man have her!*

"I did not think you meant tonight," Yasaman replied, suddenly uncomfortable, and a little annoyed that he had interrupted her fantasy just as it was becoming interesting.

He heard the irritation in her voice. Though it was slight, and no one else would have heard it, he knew every nuance of her emotions. She fascinated him and always had. There was something different about Yasaman he could not quite pinpoint, but she was unlike any other female he knew. Then his eye caught the book in her lap. "What is this, little monkey?" he asked her, seeing quite clearly what it was.

"It is a Pillow Book. Your mother gave it to me tonight. It once belonged to the Rose Princess," Yasaman said.

"A Pillow Book? Of course! Both Man Bai and Nur Jahan had Pillow Books among their bridal chests. Of course I did not need them," he told her boastfully. "So Rugaiya Begum is really considering a betrothal for you, Yasaman?"

"Papa and Mama Begum could hardly wait for me to leave them tonight so they might discuss it," Yasaman admitted. "I wonder who they will choose to be my husband."

"And you could barely wait to leave so you might learn all the knowledge the Pillow Book contains," he teased her gently, ignoring her last remark.

"Salim!" she said, pretending outrage, but then she sighed. "All the Pillow Book can do is show me *how* a man and a woman make love, my brother."

"And that is not enough?" he probed gently. *Allah!* Was he to be provided an opportunity he had not even dared to imagine? His heart hammered in his ears and he felt his blood racing excitedly in his veins.

"I cannot help but be curious as to how I would *feel,*" Yasaman replied, "if I were the consort in that picture. Is that wrong of me, Salim? What if they choose a husband for me, but I do not like it when he makes love to me? How do I even know I will like to make love at all? Oh, it is so difficult to be a maiden!"

Salim put his arm about his young sister, his fingers gently caressing her flesh. How soft it was! "Of course you are not wrong to wonder these things, Yasaman," he said soothingly. "All girls do. There is really quite a simple solution to your problem, you know. Girls with older brothers have solved this same problem the same way since the beginning of time, little monkey." How delicious her hair smelled.

"How?" she asked, looking curiously into his handsome face. Why had she never noticed before how sensual Salim's mouth was?

"Together we can emulate what is on the pages of the Pillow Book. *Not,* mind you," he continued quickly, seeing her look of surprise and seeking to reassure her, "the full consummation of a man and a woman's love. No, no! Your precious maidenhead belongs to your husband, my sister;

but there is nothing to prevent me from teaching you what will please that husband as outlined here on the pages of the Pillow Book. I know how very much you dislike appearing at a disadvantage." And as if to emphasize his point, Salim reached out, his hand finding one of her breasts, and cupped it within his palm. Very gently the ball of his thumb rubbed against her nipple. He heard her sharp intake of breath. "You will not," he murmured hotly in her ear, "look foolish, my sister, if you will but trust me." Lowering his head for a moment, he kissed her rounded shoulder.

Yasaman felt a sharp spur to her pride, but nonetheless her conscience pricked her. "You know it is wrong to imitate the ancient lords of Egypt," she said low. "They all say it is wrong, Salim."

"But we will not do that, my sister," he promised her. "There is far more to learn of passion than a man's lingham slipping into a woman's yoni. Trust me, little monkey. I will make you the most accomplished of brides."

"Will my husband want an accomplished bride?" she questioned him sharply. "Should not my knowledge of passion come from him?" Should she like Salim's hand upon her breast? Yet surely something so nice was not wrong.

"As long as your maidenhead is intact, my sister," Salim told Yasaman with assurance, "he will care naught but for the pleasure you give him." He dropped another kiss upon her naked shoulder.

"I am still not sure this is right," Yasaman told him slowly, but her pride and her natural inquisitiveness were overcoming her scruples.

"I must remove my lungi, little monkey," he told her, sliding off the bed and standing up. Let her see him nude. He was proud of his body. It was hard and firm. There was no fat on him, despite a fondness for wine.

Yasaman pondered a long moment. Then she nodded. His hand on her breast had given her a lovely, tingly feeling once she had gotten over the shock of the intimacy. She wanted that feeling back. He was only touching her. There couldn't be anything wrong with just his touching her.

With a supreme burst of self-discipline, Salim masked his feeling of triumph as he unwrapped his lungi and laid it aside. For tonight he would keep a tight rein on his own desires. If Yasaman proved as passionate as he believed she was, there would come a night soon when she would not care what transpired between them. Indeed, she would beg him to plunge himself into her. He knew she was the female side of him. Once she overcame her childish fears, she would want him every bit as much as he wanted her!

Standing proudly, he watched from beneath hooded lids as she carefully looked him over. Then he returned to her side. "Turn the page, Yasaman," he commanded her, and she obeyed.

"What in Allah's name is this prince doing to his consort?" Yasaman demanded of her brother. She stared curiously at the picture which showed the beautiful maiden now upon her back, the prince between her open legs, his pointed tongue licking at her most intimate spot. The woman looked blissful, her sloe eyes half closed, as if she knew some special secret.

"It is the first great pleasure a man can offer his consort while preserving her maidenhead intact," Salim told her.

"Show me!"

"Not quite yet, Yasaman," he told her. Allah! How eager she was, but he must go slowly if he was to have her completely. "You have such lovely breasts, my sister," he murmured. "I would like to caress them. That, too, gives pleasure." He was now seated cross-legged, facing her. He leaned forward, reaching out with both his hands, and began to stroke her breasts fervently. "Give me your sweet lips," he told her. "I would kiss you, but not like a brother kisses a sister; rather as a man kisses a woman."

"You can do both things at once? That is quite marvelous!" she exclaimed. She leaned forward, pursing her lips as she did so.

Allah! Her innocence was so provocative, and it aroused him mightily. He kissed her firmly, then commanded, "Open your mouth, Yasaman, and give me your tongue."

"Why?" She drew back from him for a moment, looking curious.

"Because that, too, gives pleasure," he replied. *"Sweet, hot, melting pleasure."*

Closing her eyes, Yasaman obeyed him. She was both surprised and delighted to feel delicious little shivers racing up and down her spine as his tongue caressed her tongue with long, slow strokes, while his hands continued to gently crush and caress her breasts. "Mmmmmmmm," she murmured, quite pleased by this new and dawning knowledge.

He drew away from her mouth just enough to speak once again. "We will add a third element, my sister. So far it is you who are receiving all the pleasure. When I kiss you again, reach down and take my lingham within your delicate little hands. It is at rest, but perhaps your untutored touch can arouse it and give me pleasure too."

"Oh Salim," she cried, "it is really impossible to do all these wonderful things at one time, isn't it? Besides, I have never touched a man's lingham before. I do not know if I dare!" She glanced down shyly at his male organ; the love weapon, she had heard it called. His seemed most impressive, although she had never seen another.

"We can do everything, Yasaman, and much more, I promise you," he assured her. "Take my lingham within your soft, pale hands, for you are the Mughal's daughter and should fear nothing!"

Their lips met once more and, reaching out, she found his manhood. Gently she caressed it, her hand enclosing it, squeezing it, releasing it and stroking it lightly. To her amazement, Salim's lingham both grew in length and breadth. It hardened until it was like a pillar of iron in her hands. When he groaned suddenly, Yasaman pulled away, saying frantically, "I have not hurt you, Salim, have I? Oh, I did not mean to harm your love weapon!"

"No," he reassured her through gritted teeth. *Allah!* He had not expected that she would arouse him so thoroughly, so completely, so quickly. She was only a maiden! He wanted to press forward until he filled her yoni to overflowing with his passion; but he also instinctively knew that now was not the time. If she grew frightened and cried out, it could be the end for him. His father was in the palace tonight.

Salim knew that should the old man discover what he was about with Yasaman, Akbar would not hesitate to replace him as his heir with Salim's own son, Khusrau. This time there would be no pleas for amnesty from the ladies of the household. Mariam Makani, his mother, and all the important consorts, adored Yasaman. As for Rugaiya Begum, she was not his friend. They would never forgive him for this incestuous seduction. Indeed, they would encourage his father to destroy him. Akbar would probably administer the death blow himself if he discovered his son in a clandestine and prohibited relationship with his naive young sister.

Yasaman trusted him so completely.

"Why then did you cry out?" she questioned him, piercing his thoughts.

"Because you gave me great pleasure, my sister," he told her, struggling to regain control of his body, on fire with her touch. *He had to distract himself.* "Let me give you a similar delight now, Yasaman. We will imitate the page you have open in the Pillow Book." He stroked her cheek, kissing her lips lightly. "Lie back, little monkey, and spread your legs for me. Be careful you do not tumble off the bed. It is very small, I can see." He learned forward and placed a satin bolster beneath her neck and shoulders.

"It is not meant for two people, Salim," she told him, and carefully positioned herself. "What are you going to do?"

He knelt between her limbs and leaned forward to caress the soft folds of flesh offered up so innocently to him, saying softly, "What the prince in the picture is doing, my precious one. Hidden within your nether lips, my sweet, is a tiny jewel of great sensitivity. Only the most delicate of touches can arouse it, allowing you pleasure as you have never before experienced." With two elegant fingers he lightly stroked the soft, plump mound beneath his hot eyes. Yasaman squirmed nervously, a half giggle escaping her at the tickly feeling his touch gave her as his two thumbs gently pulled the folds apart.

Fascinated, Yasaman watched as Salim bent farther forward, his dark head pushing between her open thighs. She glanced over at the page of the Pillow Book. Yes. It was quite correct. *Then suddenly she felt it.* Tiny, feathery touches to her most intimate self. A momentary panic raced through her. *What was Salim doing?* Her head rolled to one side and then the other. His hands were pressed flat on either side of her. *What was he doing?* The shock of realization raced through her. *His tongue!* He was putting his tongue on her! Her heart beat wildly. Briefly she considered whether he should be doing this to her, and yet . . . yet.

She shivered, and then quite suddenly relaxed. Salim would not hurt her. *He would not!* Indeed, his tongue on her hot flesh was quite pleasurable. She made a soft sound, and, as if by some sort of signal, her body felt surprisingly languid and violently tense all at the same time. She sighed and her eyes closed of their own volition, allowing her to float free. It was so lovely. So deliciously lovely. She was melting into nothingness.

He groaned low and then growled softly to her, "Do you feel the pleasure, Yasaman? Do you feel it?" Allah! She was like no other. He would never be able to get enough of her honeyed cream.

"*More,*" she begged him shamelessly.

For a moment longer he complied, but then Salim realized

that Yasaman would soon no longer be satisfied with just this charming foreplay he offered. He wanted her, but there was so much more for her to learn and know before they consummated their mutual passion. He would not spoil that time with unseemly haste now. When the time came she would beg him for everything he could offer, and he would give it to her gladly. He flicked his tongue back and forth against her little jewel, drawing her first taste of hot, sweet passion to an end. She shuddered a final time and cried out softly.

Raising himself from between her quivering thighs, he silenced her with a deep kiss, plunging his tongue, still wet with her juices, into her mouth to subdue her. His hard body covering her soft one, he reveled for a long moment in the firmness of her full breasts.

Then, not daring to remain atop her lest he lose complete control, Salim rolled to one side and sat up. "There, my sister," he told her in a deceptively calm voice, "you have tasted passion. Did you like it?"

Yasaman opened her turquoise-blue eyes and looked directly at him. "Yes," she said softly. "I liked it very much, Salim. Will my husband give me pleasure like that?"

"Yes," he told her, "if he is a good lover."

"I do not want to marry any man who is not," was her ingenuous answer. "How can we tell beforehand, Salim?"

"His reputation should precede him," the prince answered, amused. Yes, Yasaman was his equal in matters of passion. He would teach her everything, and she would be for him alone. A fourth wife could be nothing but good fortune. Four had always been his lucky number. Man Bai, his cousin, the mother of his children; loyal and sweet. Amara, adoring and politically correct. Nur Jahan, quick, intelligent, ambitious for him and herself, too, if the truth be known. Yasaman, his half sister. Passionate and hot-blooded. His equal and his refuge. Together they would be perfect!

"Look!" Yasaman had recovered and had turned to the next page of the Pillow Book. "The consort has taken her lord's lingham into her own mouth. That gives him pleasure, doesn't it, Salim?"

"Yes," he said, struggling to restrain the shudder welling within him. *Not yet*, his more cautious self warned him. If you allow her that, there will be no going back.

"May I give you pleasure in that manner, then?" she asked.

"Not tonight, my sister," he told her, pleased with the look of disappointment that sprang into her eyes. "It is late. You have learned much already and are an apt pupil. Let us save some pleasures for another time."

"*When?*" she demanded eagerly.

"I will come to you tomorrow night, my sweet sister; when all have again gone to their beds. Will you like that?" He arose from her bed, and picking up his lungi, wrapped it around his burning loins.

"Yes," she told him slowly, "but it will seem like a hundred years, Salim."

"Passion anticipated is usually best, Yasaman," he told her wisely. "Now come and bid me a proper good-night, little monkey."

She sprang from the bed and, to his delighted amusement, wrapped her arms about his neck, her body pressing hotly against his. Their lips met in a torrid kiss that left him frankly breathless. *Patience!* the inner voice warned him. He drew back and, with a cool smile, calmly departed her chamber, although he did not want to go.

Yasaman watched him leave. With a sigh she picked up the Pillow Book, then glancing regretfully at it, closed it and put it away. Smoothing the wrinkles from her bed, she lay down again, but sleep seemed elusive now. Slowly her hand crept to that magical spot between her legs and she pushed between the folds of flesh.

How moist she was. *Moist and hot.* Her fingers began to

play lightly within the wetness. A tiny tingle of delight raced through her. It was nowhere near the pleasure his facile tongue had given, but it offered relief from the anxious irritation that seemed to have suffused her entire body. Her fingers played fiercely and more fiercely until at last, with a sigh of relief, she felt herself relaxing. Her breathing became slow and even as she slipped from a waking state into a deep sleep.

From the shadows of the room a shapeless form emerged and silently padded across the floor. Taking the Pillow Book from where Yasaman had placed it, Adali picked it up and hurried from the chamber. He had observed everything that had happened between his little princess and her brother. The child had been entrusted to his care since she was six months old, and never before had he allowed evil to come so close to her. He had been aware of Prince Salim's wicked intentions toward Yasaman for several years now, watching carefully each time brother and sister were together. Ever vigilant for the safety of his princess, he often saw danger long before others saw it, even the good Rugaiya Begum. Many times he had quietly prevented harm coming to his little lady without anyone else knowing. But this was different. Tonight he had been forced to watch the prince weave his sensuous spell about Yasaman while he remained helplessly silent, for his knowledge could be his death warrant. Prince Salim was totally ruthless, as Abul Fazl's murder had proven. Adali knew he could not aid his young mistress from beyond the grave. He realized he was facing a problem that required someone of greater stature and power than he had. He knocked softly upon the door of Rugaiya Begum's chamber, hoping against hope as he did that the emperor would not be there with her.

The door was opened by Rugaiya Begum's chief serving woman, Laili. "She has already retired, Adali," Laili said irritably. She, herself, had been sleeping.

"Nonetheless, I must see her," he replied. This was Princess Yasaman's house, and he was the princess's high steward. Laili could not refuse him.

"Come in, then," she said, and grumbling beneath her breath, went into her mistress's bedchamber, returning a few moments later to wave him into the room.

"You may go to your bed," Adali instructed her. "My lady Rugaiya Begum will not need you again this night." He closed the door firmly behind the serving woman, pressing his ear against it until he was certain she had gone off.

Rugaiya Begum was seated in her bed, her silver hair braided into one thick plait. "Sit here," she told him, patting the side of the bed. "If she comes back to listen, she will hear nothing if we are close." Rugaiya Begum knew that if Adali would seek her presence at so late an hour, the matter was indeed urgent. "Now tell me what it is," she finished as he sat beside her.

"Tonight," he said without further ado, "I secreted myself in Princess Yasaman's room. Do not ask why, my lady, for I am not even certain myself. Some deep instinct, perhaps, warned me to be there."

Rugaiya Begum nodded, but said nothing, listening with growing horror as he described what he had seen in Yasaman's bedchamber. "Princess Yasaman responded with innocent ardor to the prince's overtures," Adali concluded. "She is a most passionate young girl who shows promise of becoming a very passionate woman. It is to be expected. Her father is a passionate man, and Candra a passionate woman."

"But that passion must not be directed toward Salim!" Rugaiya Begum exclaimed. "Ohh, he is wicked, Adali! He knows that he is wrong, but he attempts to seduce Yasaman, who really knows no better. *What can I do?* If anything happens to my lord, how can I protect Yasaman from her brother? *I cannot!*"

"You cannot wait to marry her off, my lady Begum," Adali said bluntly. As an old and valued servant, he was permitted to freely speak his mind. "The princess must be married before the onset of winter. She must not return south again to Lahore."

"You know the law, Adali, as well as I do," Rugaiya Begum said desperately. "No girl below the age of fourteen, or boy below the age of sixteen, may be married. Yasaman is only thirteen."

"You are allowing your maternal fears to overcome your own good sense, my lady Begum," Adali scolded her. "You have said yourself that the emperor made the laws and that he can amend them if he so chooses."

"But what possible reason can I give Akbar for wanting to press ahead so quickly with Yasaman's betrothal and marriage?" Rugaiya Begum was beginning to look haggard with her worry.

"There is only one reason that will sway him, my lady Begum," Adali told her. *"The truth."*

Rugaiya Begum grew pale. "I cannot tell him such a thing," she protested.

"You must!" he insisted. "The Mughal is no fool, lady, and he is, Allah forgive me my words, dying. Who knows when the black camel of death will arrive to take him away. It will be sooner rather than later, as we both know. When he has left this world, who will protect our princess? Neither you nor I have the power."

"Will a husband?" Rugaiya Begum responded. "Once Salim is the Grand Mughal, who is there more powerful than he?"

"Prince Salim is capricious in many of his actions, I will admit, my lady Begum," the eunuch replied, "but he knows his lust is wrong, no matter how he may rationalize it. If the princess is married and happy, I do not believe he will attempt to spoil her happiness, for he loves her. If she is a mother, so much the better."

"But does he love himself more, I wonder?" Rugaiya Begum mused. "Even I have never been certain of just how far he would go. This murder of Abul Fazl truly surprised me. Salim always used to pride himself on his self-discipline where wine and opium are concerned. He saw what they have done to his brothers, Murad and Daniyal. Yet I have heard disturbing stories of late about Salim's excesses and drunkenness. When under the influence of wine and opium together, he does things he would not otherwise dare. I am told he recently had a young page who offended him castrated; and a servant beaten to death. This instability of character frightens me, Adali."

"Then you must certainly tell our lord Akbar the truth, my lady Begum. The prince will obviously stop at nothing. The princess must be protected at all costs. When you spoke with our lord tonight, did he have any suggestions for a husband for our little lady?"

"Of course," Rugaiya Begum said, "but none were suitable. There is but one prince for Yasaman. Jamal Darya Khan."

Adali raised his eyebrows slightly in approval of Rugaiya Begum. "An admirable choice, my lady Begum," he said. "If our princess weds a Kashmiri prince, she will be well out of her brother's sphere of influence. Excellent! When will you discuss this with the Mughal?"

"Let him sleep the night, Adali, although Allah knows I will not! My lord and I will settle this matter in the morning before he returns to his own palace. There can be no delay in Yasaman's wedding. Ahh, my poor daughter. She is so young!"

"She is also strong like Candra, my lady Begum," Adali said. "Whatever fate life has in store for her, she will meet the challenge and triumph. *This I know in my heart.*"

❀

3

❀

The emperor awakened early, as was his custom, and bathed. He spent several minutes in spiritual meditation, but when he arose from his knees expecting to find his breakfast being served, he instead saw his first wife, Rugaiya Begum, enter the room. He thought that she was showing her age for the first time. There were purple patches beneath her fine eyes.

"A word, my lord, before your meal, I pray you. It is most important, or I should not disturb you. Will you walk by the lake with me?" She slipped her arm through his, looking into his face with a silent plea.

He nodded but said nothing, realizing that her unspoken request meant they should go somewhere they could not be overheard. The morning air was sweet and cool. The sun was just rising over the mountains, and mist hung above the placid, mirrorlike waters of Wular Lake.

"My words will shock and certainly anger you, my lord," Rugaiya Begum told him as they strolled along the shore. A mewling gull swooped low over the water looking for a meal.

"You must swear to me on the soul of your father, Humayun, that you will not retaliate against the guilty."

"What is so terrible that you must seek to extract such a promise from me, my wife?" he asked her. *Salim.* It had to be Salim. The source of most of his pain was Salim; but never before had Rugaiya taken his part. Interesting.

"I will say nothing more unless you will swear to me, my lord," Rugaiya Begum insisted stubbornly.

"Then I must so swear," Akbar replied. "I cannot remember ever having you ask such a thing of me, my dear. It must be very serious. It is Salim, of course, but it is not like you to defend him. Why?" It disturbed him to see her looking so distraught, as if she had not slept the entire night.

"Yes, it is about Salim, my lord. But it is about Yasaman too," and then she told him in careful and minute detail exactly what Adali had told her.

Akbar listened, his wheaten complexion growing darker with his rising anger. By some supreme strength of will he managed to remain silent until she had finished her horrific tale; and then he said, "I should have killed him last year when he murdered Abul Fazl. Prince Khusrau is sixteen, old enough and certainly more than competent to be my heir. Was I not myself younger when I became the Mughal, Rugaiya? Everyone has constantly excused Salim his rash ways throughout his life because of his charm; and I have forgiven him time after time because he was my firstborn surviving son and so dear to my heart.

"One year ago he murdered my best friend, for he was jealous of him, always jealous of him. He constantly complained I favored Abul Fazl over him, which was not true. Abul Fazl was my friend, Salim my son and heir. It was our friendship Salim was jealous of, Rugaiya. Now he attempts to involve his innocent sister in an incestuous relationship. He lusts after her as if she were not of his own blood! He must die, Rugaiya. There is nothing else for it but that he must die!" Akbar's face was anguished as he pronounced the words.

"No, my lord," Rugaiya Begum calmly told him, putting a comforting hand upon his hand. "Salim has good qualities as well as evil ones. He has trained his whole life for the future that will one day be his. In time he will be a good ruler. Abul Fazl's murder was a terrible act. I cannot excuse it, but I understand why the prince acted as he did. You must not have your son's death upon your hands, my dearest lord! Not now.

"The solution to our problem is really most simple. Let Yasaman be married now to the son of Yusef Khan. Let her remain here in Kashmir. Send Salim south and keep him there. Mewar has never been fully subdued. Let Salim work his abundance of energy off there. With a young, ardent husband, it is likely that Yasaman will quickly have children. She will be content and happy. Her brother will be happy for her and forget his evil intentions."

"That he has touched her in so intimate a manner enrages me, Rugaiya!" the emperor said angrily. "He had not the right! Allah! Yasaman is barely past childhood!"

"Yes, and it angers me as well, my lord, but there is nothing that we can do to change what has already happened," she told him sensibly. "Imagine our good Adali, forced to remain in the shadows watching as Salim worked his seduction of Yasaman. He remained silent despite his outrage so that he might save Yasaman from any further assault. If Salim had known he was there, he would have killed Adali himself. Adali kept his head in order to fight Salim another day. We must be as brave and as clever, my husband. Salim must not know that we are aware of this dark passion he harbors for his sister. Right now he believes he *must* have Yasaman. If he learns we suspect him, he will do what he has to do to fulfill that desire."

"But he will have to know of Yasaman's marriage," Akbar

said. "He will ask why I am permitting her to wed at thirteen
when the law most clearly says a maid may not marry until
she is fourteen. What am I to say to him, my good wife? To
say I simply desire it will not be enough for Salim."

Rugaiya Begum smiled. "It is quite simple, my lord. You will
tell Prince Salim that you fear for Yaqub Khan's loyalty despite
his father's faithful service to you. Tell Salim that you wish to
ensure Yusef Khan's family's future trustworthiness by an immediate marriage between Yasaman and his younger son. Tell
him that you may eventually make Prince Jamal Darya Khan
governor of Kashmir, binding him, his family, and the Kashmiri people even closer to our family. It is a logical and states-
manlike act, and worthy of you, my dearest lord."

Akbar smiled slowly. "I had forgotten how wise and clever
you are, Rugaiya. You have spent too many years away from
me raising our daughter to womanhood." He leaned over
and kissed her cheek. "I will speak with Yusef Khan this
very day and arrange matters. *And* I will send the lady Juliana to examine Yasaman to be certain that Salim has not
violated her innocence."

"Adali shares our secret, my lord, but there must be one
other to bear this burden. The priest. Yasaman has been
raised within the Christian faith, as her mother would have
wanted, but like you, she is eclectic in her religious tastes.
Still, we will need the priest's cooperation in preparing her
for this very great change in her life."

They swung about to return to the palace.

"Very well, Rugaiya, I will leave it to your good judgment.
Let me eat now and then get about my business. Yusef Khan
is here visiting his family, so the matter of Yasaman's marriage may be concluded swiftly."

Making obeisance to her husband, Rugaiya Begum sought
out Father Cullen Butler, the priest attached to Yasaman's
household. He had just finished his morning prayers and, as
she had with Akbar, she invited him to walk with her along
the lakeshore.

"I need your help, Father Cullen," she said.

"You know you have but to ask, my lady," he assured her in a voice soft with the lilt of his native Ireland.

He was a tall, slender man approaching his middle years. He kept his dark brown hair cropped close and simple in style. His fine blue eyes, however, were always lively and inquiring. He had come to them when Yasaman was in her second year, for Akbar had requested a priest for his daughter's household from the head of the Jesuits in India. Although it had caused a mild stir at the time, the fuss quickly died down. Akbar was known to be interested in all religions, and each of the princes had had priests for tutors at one time or another. Cullen Butler had fit easily into the household. He was fascinated with Indian life and, unlike other priests, did not condemn or criticize. It was quickly discovered that he had a ribald sense of humor, which quite endeared him to the servants.

"For some time now," Rugaiya Begum began, "I have noticed that Prince Salim's interests in Yasaman appeared to be more that of a man attracted to a woman, and less of a brother for his sister. I attempted to thrust these wicked thoughts from my mind. I did not want to believe what my own instinct was telling me. It was totally unthinkable!"

"You have changed your mind, however," the priest said to her, "haven't you, my lady? Why?" His blue eyes were now serious.

"Last night," she told him, "Salim began a campaign of seduction. He entered Yasaman's bedchamber, and . . . and . . . Oh! I cannot tell you the wickedness! Had it not been for Adali . . ." She stopped, unable to continue for the moment.

"Adali caught them?" the priest inquired, striving to get the whole story before the poor woman dissolved into tears.

"Adali had become suspicious of Prince Salim," Rugaiya Begum said, regaining a strong hold on her distress. "He secreted himself in Yasaman's chamber last night and observed all that went on between them.

"The lady Jodh Bai brought Yasaman a Pillow Book yesterday. It had belonged to Candra. She was naturally curious. She was looking through the book when her brother arrived. He suggested that together they might emulate some of the paintings in order that she not be totally ignorant of lovemaking when she marry. He told her that there were ways in which a virgin could obtain great pleasure without losing her virginity."

"Christ's bloody bones!" the priest exploded, much to Rugaiya Begum's shock. She had never before heard him swear so volubly. Cullen Butler looked so fiercely at the older woman that she almost drew back in fright. "Did he breach her maidenhead?" he asked bluntly.

"No! No!" Rugaiya Begum assured him. "Adali swore he did not. Speak with him yourself, Father. He believes the prince waits for a more propitious moment to ravish her completely."

"Something must be done to stop the devil from his wickedness," Cullen Butler said. "What is it you propose, my lady, and how may I help you?"

"I have suggested to my lord Akbar that Yasaman be married immediately. Certainly Salim will desist in his evil if she is happy with a husband."

"And who is the prince you have chosen?" the priest asked.

"Jamal Darya Khan, the younger son of Yusef Khan," Rugaiya Begum said.

Cullen Butler nodded, thoughtful. "A lusty young man, I hear, but loyal to our lord Akbar, like his father. She would stay here in Kashmir," he said almost to himself. "Aye! It is a good choice, my lady. You will want me, of course, to prepare Yasaman for a quick marriage."

"Yes," Rugaiya Begum told him. "She will not be pleased by the news, I fear. We have let her be a little girl for so long, and now suddenly, before she has the chance to be a young girl, we are telling her she must become a woman. You know how Yasaman prizes her freedom. It will be difficult for her to curb that part of her nature, but she will have to once she is married.

"She is still really too young, but we cannot find another way to protect her from Salim. I tell you this in confidence— the emperor is not very well. The events of the last year have taken a great toll upon his health, although he strives not to show any weakness. When he is no longer here, I will not be able to protect my daughter from Salim. None of us will except a husband."

"Aye," the priest agreed, but he was not certain that she was right. Salim was a determined young man who let little stand in the way of his carnal desires. Several years ago he had fallen violently in love with Nur Jahan. Akbar had opposed such a match, not believing that Zain Khan Koka's daughter was a good consort for a future Mughal, despite her beauty. The girl was far too clever to suit Akbar, and outspoken as well. She openly reciprocated Salim's passion. Indeed, she encouraged it, as did her mother.

Zain Khan Koka was one of Akbar's cleverest and most successful generals. Their families had been close for generations. The girl had been half raised in Akbar's house. He had always thought her like a sister to Salim. The emperor felt there was an impropriety in such a marriage, but finally he was prevailed upon to give Salim his way.

"After all," as Zain Khan Koka himself explained to his master, "there is no blood tie between our children, my gracious lord."

Even Salim's beloved first wife, Man Bai, and his second wife, Amara, the Princess of Bikaner, had petitioned the Mughal to give Salim his way in the matter. The marriage had taken place. Now Salim's lusts were directed toward his youngest sister, and Akbar was a dying man. It is not good, the priest thought worriedly.

"How should we approach the princess, my lady?" he inquired of Rugaiya Begum.

"We must wait until my lord Akbar has concluded the

match with Yusef Khan," she told him. "He will send for
him this very day, as the general is here in Kashmir to visit
with his family. I think that if the marriage is a happy one,
and the young Jamal proves himself, that the emperor might
give him charge over Kashmir in his name."

"Is Prince Jamal not Yusef Khan's youngest son, my lady?
What will the others think of such a thing?"

"Surely they must understand that they have not been
faithful," Rugaiya Begum answered him. "Besides, only three
of Yusef Khan's four sons are still living. Yaqub, the eldest,
who cannot be trusted; Haider, the middle son, whom my
lord does not trust, believing him to be like Prince Yaqub;
and Jamal, the youngest, who has proved his loyalty. Ahmed,
the second son, died fighting in a civil war against his uncle
several years ago. If my lord puts Kashmir into the keeping
of any man, it will be Prince Jamal, providing he continues
to be loyal."

Even as Rugaiya Begum and the priest spoke together,
Akbar had returned to his apartments. He ate a quick meal
consisting of wheat bread and a custard apple, washed down
with a cup of hot, sweet black tea. Finished, he rose from
his table and, without even seeing his daughter, he called
for his horse. Escorted by his bodyguards, he rode back to
his own palace nearby on the lake.

Wular Lake. He remembered the first time he had seen it,
how he had known instantly that Candra would love this
land of cool waters and high mountains. He chuckled to
himself remembering how she disliked the heat of the plains
and the dust of Lahore; but she had tried so hard not to
complain. For Candra, he had built the palace in which his
daughter now lived; hiring twice the number of workers ordinarily needed on such a site, paying them twice what they
were used to receiving, all in order that the palace be ready
for his beloved young wife when she gave birth to their child.
It had been here that Yasaman had been born, and she grew

up loving Kashmir every bit as much as her mother had. Now he was going to give her in marriage to a prince of this land. She would remain here always, and that was good. Rugaiya was correct. Jamal Darya Khan was the perfect match for their daughter.

Akbar rode up to the royal palace, giving orders to one of his aides as he arrived. "Find Yusef Khan. Bring him to me at once. I will be in my private reception room."

It was early in the day still, and yet the moment it was known that the emperor had returned, officials immediately started besieging him with problems of one kind or another.

"Not yet! Not yet!" he told them, and his dark eyes twinkled. "You are like ants in an anthill, scurrying about filled with your own importance. Are we being invaded in any part of the realm?"

"No, my lord," the officials chorused.

"Is anyone of import ill or dying?"

"No, my lord."

"Then leave me be until after I have spoken with my friend, Yusef Khan," he told them. "And someone bring tea and honey cakes. Is the Grand Mughal to appear niggardly and inhospitable?" He waved them away, and they went. Akbar chuckled. *Bureaucrats!* It seemed to be impossible to run a government without them; or perhaps bureaucrats were like a parasitic growth developing upon a government instead of on a tree or rotting wood, sapping its strength and vitality until it could no longer function properly. It was an interesting thought.

His private reception room was a cool and pleasant place, its walls decorated with wonderful paintings of court life done in bright, fresh colors. Furnished simply and sparingly, it looked out upon the lake. It was quite remote from the rest of the palace. The only entry to the room was from the terrace, and the other three walls were solid. It was a difficult place upon which to eavesdrop. A servant soon arrived with boiling tea and a plate of freshly made poppy-seed cakes.

"I will serve my guest when he arrives," the emperor said, and the bowing servant departed.

Yusef Khan came without an escort as he knew his way about the palace and its grounds quite well. He had once lived here. "My lord." He knelt and placed the emperor's foot upon his head.

Akbar accepted the obeisance and then told his general, "Rise and sit with me."

Together the two men sat down upon the pillows strewn about a low table. The emperor poured them cups of tea and shoved the plate with the poppy-seed cakes into the center of the table. The amenities observed, he stared directly at Kashmir's former ruler and spoke.

"You have proved your loyalty to me many times over these last few years despite our difficult beginnings. Now I will reward you in a manner you will not have expected. I want your youngest son, Jamal Darya Khan, for my youngest daughter, Yasaman Kama Begum. What say you to that, my good Yusef Khan?"

Kashmir's previous ruler was truly stunned by the Mughal's words. When his own father had died, his uncle had attempted to usurp the Kashmiri throne, but the Mughal had helped him to regain his rightful inheritance. Akbar had asked in return only that Yusef Khan swear his fealty to the Mughal Empire. Yusef Khan had quickly agreed; but then he had reneged on his promise, until finally Akbar had come into Kashmir and taken it away from him.

Nonetheless, he had been forgiven. He had eventually proved his worth as one of Akbar's most reliable generals, but his place in the emperor's court was constantly being endangered by his eldest son, Yaqub. His son Haider was equally rebellious, but he was also a coward.

His youngest son, Jamal, however, had become the joy of his father's life by virtue of his noble behavior. Now both he and the boy would profit by it. Akbar's words, in effect, told him that Kashmir would eventually be ruled by his family again, although as a vassal state. It was enough!

"My lord! There are no words that can possibly express the joy your words have given me! I am astounded that you would honor my family so. I swear to you on my son's behalf that the princess Yasaman will be treated like the young queen she deserves to be!"

"I am told your son has a small zenana, but no consort, Yusef. Is this true?" Akbar asked, coming directly to the point. "Yasaman must be her husband's first consort; the mother of his heir. No Imperial Mughal princess can accept a lesser portion in life."

"Jamal has no wife, and only five women in his zenana, sire. None has been with him for very long. There are no children yet," Yusef Khan told his lord.

"Is there any one woman who holds his heart?" Akbar demanded. "Tell the truth, for I will learn it eventually. I do not want Yasaman unhappy. She can adjust as long as she understands what is involved. I would like it if your son could love her, but I realize that such a thing may not be possible."

"Jamal is a charming young man, very much like his late mother," Yusef Khan said. "To my knowledge, no one woman enthralls him. The reason his zenana is so small, and the women in it of recent purchase, is that he becomes easily bored with his maidens."

"Is he not virile, then?" the emperor inquired. Frequently a man had difficulties and blamed his women for the problem.

"He is, I have heard, quite virile," Yusef Khan replied. "I believe his restlessness stems from boredom. I do not think that any woman has ever intrigued him enough to win his heart. I cannot guarantee that he will love your daughter, my lord. You know as well as I do that arranged marriages are usually nothing more than alliances for land, or gold, or power. Your daughter is young. Why not just allow her the opportunity to fall in love? She is the last of your children and not important dynastically."

Akbar sighed deeply. "If such a choice were available to me, Yusef Khan, I should gladly take it; but alas, it is not. I must take you into my confidence, my friend. I have not been well for several years now. Indeed, I believe I may be dying. I want to see my daughter wed, and perhaps I may even see one of her children before the thread of my life is snapped. I dare not leave her fate to her brother. Salim adores Yasaman and, indeed, has often stated that no man is worthy of her. Such an attitude, while charming, is, I am sure you realize, very impractical. Yasaman could easily end up an ancient maiden. No, Yusef Khan. My daughter is meant to marry and have children, and if God so wills it, a husband who loves her. She has been raised away from my court. While she realizes her place, her life has been a simple one, and she is happiest here in Kashmir.

"A union between our children could cement relations between our families for generations. It would make Kashmir truly an important part of my empire. What greater gift can I offer your people than my own dear daughter? Tell me, Yusef Khan, do you believe your son Jamal is capable of ruling Kashmir in my name?"

"He is intelligent, my lord," Yusef Khan answered, the blood singing in his ears, "and he knows how to be loyal."

"Then perhaps if the marriage between our children is a happy one, and if it prospers, Jamal Khan could find himself governing here for me," Akbar told his general calmly. "Shall we begin the marriage negotiations then, Yusef Khan?"

The general nodded. "I will this very day obtain my son's consent to this marriage, my lord."

When Yusef Khan had departed, Akbar considered his own position. During the years of his rule he had been responsible for a number of civil reforms. Unwilling participants could no longer be simply bartered off in marriage by greedy families. The consent of both the bride and the bridegroom, as well as that of the parents, had to be obtained before a settlement could even be discussed. There was a tax for the license, the cost of which depended upon the financial status of the parties involved. He would charge himself twenty muhrs for Yasaman's marriage tax; double that of a rich man. But first he had to convince his youngest daughter that this marriage was in her best interests, and that she could be happy with Prince Jamal.

He suspected it would not be an easy task. Yasaman, overly protected by them all, was not really ready for marriage. And Salim would have to be sent away, lest he make some attempt to thwart his father's plans for his sister. Akbar had no fear that Prince Jamal would not consent to the match. At twenty-three the young man would fully understand the great opportunity being offered to him. He was intelligent, if his father was to be believed.

The prince would have surprised his overlord greatly if Akbar had been privy to the conversation between Yusef Khan and his son later that morning. Kashmir's former ruler had been rowed across Wular Lake to his son's palace. There he found Jamal Khan having a late morning meal upon the terrace. Yusef Khan forced himself to move slowly, with the dignity expected of his station.

"Dismiss your servants," he ordered Jamal Khan, and when they were finally alone, he said, "The Mughal wants you as husband for his youngest daughter!" His voice was pitched higher with his excitement than it normally would have been.

"No," said the prince, and helped himself to a bowl of pomelos that had been peeled and sectioned.

"No?" His father looked astounded.

"No," Jamal Khan repeated, and popped a piece of the juicy fruit into his mouth.

"Why?" demanded Yusef Khan. "Have you fallen in love with another woman?"

"There is no woman who claims my heart," Jamal Khan told his father, "but I am not of a mind to marry the daughter of the man who stripped my family of its inheritance—the man for whom you go to war, not in your own interest, my father, or in that of Kashmir's, but in the interest of the Mughal Empire."

"Listen to me, Jamal, my son. I have never admitted this aloud to a living soul, although it has eaten at my heart these many years. I dishonored the name of this family, may Allah forgive me. In the year in which you were born, my father, Ali Khan Chak, died. My uncle, Abdal Khan, sought to usurp me. I fled to the Mughal court to seek the emperor's help; and he gave it to me because I swore that once I regained Kashmir, I would be his most loyal vassal.

"So I was restored to my throne, my uncle driven away, but I did not do Akbar the homage I had promised him. He sent for me several times, and although I promised I would come, I did not; nor did I have any intention of coming. I believed Kashmir too far from the Mughal court for Akbar to be further bothered with us; but he persisted.

"Finally I sent your brother Haider to the Mughal court, but the emperor, who was now in Panjab and practically at our back door, summoned me once again. This time I sent your eldest brother, Yaqub, but it was still not enough. Yaqub fled the emperor's court without his permission. Akbar had frightened him by venting his outrage at my behavior before him. The emperor then sent an army to Kashmir, and we lost our lands. Perhaps my eventual obeisance would have restored our family's fortunes, but your brother Yaqub spent several years rebelling and fighting with the Mughals, to atone, he believed, for his former cowardice. They sent a harsh governor to rule over us in retaliation. You surely remember how hard a time that was.

"All of this came about because of my dishonorable actions. I had given my word to Akbar that I would accept him as my overlord. I broke that word. Now, however, our family has the opportunity to regain what was once ours. Akbar has said plainly that if this marriage is a successful one, he will appoint you to govern Kashmir in his name."

"But what if this match you two old men propose is not happy, my father? What then? Must I spend the rest of my life dancing attendance upon some spoilt Mughal princess so that Kashmir be ours once more? Let my brother Yaqub, who was once your rightful heir, or my middle brother Haider, marry the girl and regain Kashmir for us."

"The emperor wants you, Jamal. He did not ask for one of my other sons. He named you specifically. Besides, both Yaqub and Haider are too old for her and have grown children. Yasaman Kama Begum must be her husband's first consort, and the mother of his heir," his father told him firmly.

"I am unhappy to disappoint you, my father, for I honor you above all men," Jamal Khan replied.

"You will not disappoint me, my son," Yusef Khan replied calmly. "You will remember how well I did my duty twenty-four years ago when I married the daughter of one of my minor officials who was dying, as the poor girl had no family to care for her."

The prince flushed at this mention of his mother's marriage.

"I did not need another wife, my son, but my duty bid me to honor a dying man's wish. To my surprise, your mother proved a delightful companion, and then she bore me you. I did not really need another son, Jamal, nor would you be here this day had I not honored my obligations. Not honoring another obligation cost me Kashmir. Be reasonable, my son. You must have a wife. It is past time for you to settle down and give me grandchildren. *An Imperial Mughal princess!* Think on it, Jamal! You will have an Imperial Mughal princess for your wife."

"I am thinking on it, Father. It fills me with dread. What if this girl is ugly? Or bad-tempered? Or worst of all, stupid? I cannot be a stud for the emperor's favorite little mare, even for Kashmir! What am I to do if we do not like each other?"

"You will do what all men in that position do, my son," Yusef Khan told him wisely. "You will make a compromise with yourself. You will be mannerly and gallant to your wife, and once you have produced a son or two, you will take another wife; always remembering to honor the good woman who is the mother of your heirs. It is not necessary to like a woman to couple with her. I have never particularly liked Yaqub's mother, but I have always honored her with my respect."

"I want to love my wife," Jamal Khan stubbornly told his father.

"You are a true Kashmiri romantic, my son," was his father's smiling reply. "Do not despair over this marriage, Jamal. I have never heard anyone say a bad word about the princess. Indeed, I am told she rewarded a local fisherman with exclusive rights to fish the waters by her palace because he saved her cat from drowning. A selfish or spoiled girl would not have done such a thing. It shows thoughtfulness on her part. It is very possible that you will learn to love your bride.

"While you are thinking of what all of this will mean for you, Jamal, think of Yasaman Kama Begum. She is not, from what I have heard, a stupid girl who will blindly accept a marriage to just anyone. Do you not believe her doubts and fears over this marriage are similar to yours? A marriage is between two people, and can only be successful if they both want it to be. Nor is one person alone responsible for the happiness or the tragedy that befalls a marriage. I think your women have spoiled you into believing you are a special fellow," Yusef Khan concluded.

"I really have no choice, have I, Father? I must give my consent to this match," the prince said gloomily.

Yusef Khan nodded. "You must, but it is not, I suspect, a fate worse than death, Jamal. I will send to my lord Akbar immediately. Together you and I will visit the palace. Shall we decide now what presents will be part of the sachaq? I realize this is my responsibility as the father of the bridegroom, but I thought perhaps you would like to have a hand in selecting the articles we will send to Yasaman Kama Begum."

"The princess follows Islam?" Jamal Khan was surprised. "So many of the Mughal's wives are Rajput that I assumed this princess would be also."

"There is some mystery about Yasaman Kama Begum's mother. She has been raised by the lady Rugaiya Begum, the Mughal's first wife, who is of Islam, so I assume the girl follows the Prophet's way. I do not think my lord Akbar would object if you asked him about the princess's true mother, my son. He will understand you seek to learn about your bride's heritage so you may understand her."

Yusef Khan dispatched a messenger to the palace with the news that the prince Jamal Darya Khan had given his consent to a marriage between himself and Yasaman Kama Begum. The messenger returned with an answer. The emperor would see Yusef Khan and his son late that afternoon. Together father and son began the process of selecting betrothal gifts for the royal bride.

Akbar was elated to receive the consent of the Kashmiri prince—not that he thought for a moment that the young man would not give his consent. No man in his right mind would dare to refuse the Grand Mughal's daughter as a wife. Akbar called for his horse and, with his bodyguard beside him, rode back to his daughter's palace, which was but two miles distant.

Rugaiya Begum greeted him, looking distressed. "Salim is here, and he is with Yasaman," she told her husband.

"They are not alone?" Akbar replied anxiously.

"No. Rohana and Toramalli have been given strict instructions," she said.

Akbar put a comforting arm about Rugaiya Begum. "Jamal Khan has given his consent to a marriage between himself and Yasaman. We must now gain Yasaman's consent, and quickly! Take me to her, my dear."

"What will you do, my lord?"

"Wait and see, Rugaiya, and do not be surprised by anything I do. Salim thinks he is ready to step into my boots, but I am a far better tactician than he will ever be, though I am old and ill." The emperor followed his wife through the little marble palace and out onto the wide terrace that faced the lake. There he saw his son and daughter seated upon a couch, their dark heads together as if they were plotting some mischief. "My children," his voice boomed out genially, as always.

"Papa!" Yasaman pulled away from her brother and, rising, ran to kiss her father.

"Good day, my rosebud!" Akbar said gaily. "I bring you the most wonderful news!"

"Father." Salim arose, quickly wiping the surprise from his features, but not before Akbar had seen it. Coming to his father, he knelt, putting the emperor's foot on his head as a sign of homage.

"Shaikho Baba, my beloved son!" Akbar said, and, bending, lifted his son up and kissed him upon both cheeks. "It is good to see you. Your mother told me that you were here. Why did you not join us last night for your sister's birthday celebration?"

"Forgive me, Father, but I was not certain how I would be received by you. I did not wish to spoil Yasaman's birthday," Salim answered honestly.

"I have pardoned you, Shaikho Baba, and what is past is past," Akbar replied, sounding, to Rugaiya's surprise, as if he actually meant it. "I am glad you are here because I have wonderful news for Yasaman. You are to be married, my daughter! I have found you a lusty young prince to be your bridegroom. What think you of that, my rosebud?"

I am to be married! They have found me a prince! For a moment her heart soared with delight, and then Yasaman grew afraid. "What if the prince doesn't like me, Papa?" she said.

"How can he not love you, my darling?" her father reassured her. "Even now his heart is beating faster with the knowledge that you will soon be his; and I know that he, too, is wondering if you will love him. He is a young man, Yasaman, and you will be his first consort. The mother of his sons. Will you give your consent to this match, my daughter? You will be so happy, I promise you!"

"Who is this prince?" Salim demanded, unable to keep the jealousy from his voice. Yasaman could not marry. *She was his!*

"He is Yusef Khan's youngest son, Jamal Darya Khan, Shaikho Baba. When he weds with Yasaman, I shall give them Kashmir to rule in my name and yours. What think you of that, my son? I have secured our northern flank most effectively for generations to come. I can attain security and happiness for both my beloved children with one stroke. Tell your sister she must give her consent, for I know how she values your opinion, Shaikho Baba. This handsome man will make her very happy."

Salim felt the rage welling up within him, and for a moment he actually saw a red haze before his eyes, so great was his anger. Yasaman! *His Yasaman!* She was being taken away from him! He wanted to shriek with frustration, but he could not. The marriage would make no difference between them. When his father died, Yasaman would be his, and no one, not even a Kashmiri prince, would prevent it.

With a supreme effort he forced his fury back deep within his soul, and smiling at his sister, said, "This is a fine thing our father has done for you, little monkey! By all means accept this prince for a husband. When I think on it myself,

I can think of no prince better suited to you. You love Kashmir, and now it will be yours. You will remain here forever, which I know will please you, with your dislike of our dusty plains and hot summer weather."

Her nerves made her hesitate. She begged her brother once more, "Are you certain I should accept this marriage, Salim?" Her heart-shaped face looked up at him anxiously.

"Of course he thinks you should," Akbar said jovially, "don't you, Shaikho Baba?"

"Yes, of course you should accept," Salim said heartily through gritted teeth. His lips were turned up in a smile, but his eyes hid his angry thoughts. Somehow, he realized, his father had maneuvered him like a puppet to cooperate in this business. He had had no other choice. Helplessly he swallowed his fury.

"I am so happy for you, my daughter," Rugaiya Begum said, adding her voice to the discussion. Yasaman turned, and Rugaiya's heart cried out to her child.

"Mama Begum, oh please tell me what I should do."

Rugaiya Begum shook her head. "My daughter, this decision must be yours alone. Remember, however, that it is a woman's fate to marry. Your father has chosen a mate for you whom he believes will make you happy. I knew Prince Jamal's mother briefly in the years before her death. This young man loved and honored that lady. He is good-hearted. I believe him to be a perfect husband for you."

"I know you would not lie to me, and so I will accept this prince for a husband; but I need to have you near me. Will you stay here in Kashmir with me, Mama Begum?" Yasaman begged.

Rugaiya Begum cast Akbar a look that plainly told him she would acquiesce to her daughter's request; and then she said, "Do you think I intend being in Lahore and Agra when my grandchildren are in Kashmir? Of course I will remain here, Yasaman!"

The joy in the girl's young face almost broke her parents'

hearts. How they loved her! Salim's face was not quite as happy, although he continued to smile. Yasaman turned to her father. "I will accept Prince Jamal Darya Khan for my husband, my lord father," she said formally.

Akbar kissed his daughter on both of her cheeks, relief pouring through him. Although he had pretended confidence to assure Rugaiya, he had not really been certain that he could pull off this coup. Salim was so unpredictable—but then he caught his son by surprise, allowing him no time to think up excuses for Yasaman not to marry Prince Jamal. Now he must get Salim out of Kashmir so that he could engineer a quick wedding ceremony between his daughter and her intended husband. Seeing the dark, lustful looks his son was casting in his sister's direction, Akbar thought the quicker the marriage was celebrated and consummated, the better. Yasaman was really in jeopardy.

The Grand Mughal returned to his own palace to meet with Yusef Khan and his son. He wanted to talk seriously with this young man who was to be his son-in-law. Jamal Khan must understand how very precious Yasaman was to him and to the future emperor. He must not think he could mistreat her. Suddenly the Mughal found himself worried at the haste with which this marriage must be accomplished.

Akbar was encouraged, however, by his first glimpse of Yusef Khan's son. Jamal Khan was tall; indeed he was at least two inches taller than the emperor himself. His skin was pale gold and fresh-looking, and he had the body of a man accustomed to regular exercise. *Good!* Akbar thought. He is obviously not one of these effete princes, like so many in the south. The young man's hair was black as night, and his doe eyes a meltingly romantic deep brown, typical of the Kashmiri men. His features, Akbar noted with pleasure, were excellent. He was, in fact, extremely handsome; his forehead and cheekbones high, his nose slim and classic, his lips full, his chin oval in shape. The children of this union should be gorgeous, the emperor considered, and he was pleased.

"My gracious lord!" Yusef Khan knelt, touching his head to the floor before Akbar's feet.

Jamal Khan, however, looked Akbar directly in the eyes before emulating his father's behavior. He said nothing.

Proud, Akbar thought to himself. He is proud. I can see that although he has given his consent, he is not happy with this situation. That was interesting. Any other young prince would be falling all over himself to become the Mughal's son-in-law. I will have to know why he is so reticent, Akbar decided.

"Arise," the Mughal told his guests. "Let us sit and talk."

The three men settled themselves around a table upon which servants placed a large bowl of fruit and cups of steaming green tea from China. The tea had the fragrance of peaches. The servants withdrew.

"Introduce me properly to your son, Yusef Khan," Akbar said, and the general complied.

Jamal Khan greeted his overlord politely, but cautiously.

Never one to beat about the bush, the Mughal said, "You have, your father tells me, given your consent to this marriage; yet I sense you have reservations. Tell me what disturbs you. I will answer all your questions truthfully and try to soothe your fears. This is a good match for you and my daughter, Yasaman, as well as for Kashmir."

"So it would appear, my lord," Jamal Khan said quietly. His voice was musical and in the medium range tonally. "But you are correct. I am hesitant."

"Would it be the natural hesitancy of a lusty young man about to take a wife, Jamal Khan?" the emperor said, and his dark eyes twinkled.

Jamal Khan laughed. "Perhaps, my lord, it is. To be frank with you, I am not sure I am ready to be a husband."

"No man ever is," the emperor replied with a chuckle. "What else troubles you?"

"Nothing really troubles me, my lord, but I should like to

know a little more about the princess. I know the lady Rugaiya Begum has raised her, but it is said that she is not the lady who gave life to Yasaman Kama Begum. Is this so? Who did give birth to your daughter, and why did she not raise her own child?"

"Yasaman's mother was an English lady of a wealthy and noble family." Akbar sighed deeply, and then continued with his tale. He spoke quietly, but the sorrow was visible in his fine dark eyes as he did so.

"A day has not gone by since Candra was taken from me that I have not thought about her. I loved her. My love for her has never changed, though fate parted us," he sadly concluded. Then Akbar paused, and looking at the prince, asked, "What else do you wish to know, Jamal Khan?"

Yusef Khan sent his son a beseeching look. He was frankly embarrassed to have been allowed this very private glimpse into his lord's secret soul. *Cease!* the look begged, but Jamal Khan ignored his father and instead said, "What faith does the princess follow?"

"Like her father," Akbar replied, "she has been taught the tenets of every known religion. She takes what she deems good from each, but such a faith has no name unless you would call it tolerance. She has also been taught scholarly subjects by a priest, Father Cullen Butler. He will remain with her household as long as it pleases her."

Jamal Khan nodded and said, "You say she has been taught scholarly subjects. What are they?"

"Languages, for one," Akbar answered. "She speaks Arabic; Hindi; the dialect of Kashmir; her mother's tongue, English; Portuguese and French—the Western tongues having been taught her by the priest who also instructed her in a language called Latin, which is not generally spoken today in Europe except in the Church. It amused him, however, to teach her. She can read and write in all those tongues. She knows mathematics and astronomy. She plays several instruments and dances beautifully." He smiled. "Although she is young, she is an amusing conversationalist. You will never be bored with her."

"My son." Yusef Khan had finally regained his voice. "I think you have asked our lord Akbar more than enough questions."

"He has not asked me the most important question of all, Yusef," the Mughal teased, seeing his general's distress, but impressed by Prince Jamal's determination to learn what he felt he needed to learn. Akbar looked at the prince and asked, "Do you not wish to know if she is beautiful, Jamal Khan?"

"It would not, I think, make any difference, my lord," the prince replied honestly. "This is a political match, is it not?"

"Most matches among our class are, Jamal Khan," was Akbar's equally honest answer. "I have forty wives and most of them were foisted upon me. One of my brides I lusted after in my youth, and forced her husband to divorce her so I might have her. Unfortunately, the passion faded quickly. Too often passion does, and if there is nothing else there, it is sad for both parties involved. But there was always something to like, I found, in each woman. I sought it out and concentrated upon it. Rugaiya Begum, Yasaman's foster mother, is very dear to me. She is my cousin and we grew up together. Prince Salim's mother, Jodh Bai, the Amber Princess, was a delightful surprise. I fell in love with her, and I have never stopped loving her. So, too, with Candra."

"Does the princess look like her mother?" Jamal Khan inquired.

Akbar thought for a long moment, and then he said, "Yes and no. Candra had beautiful hair that was rich, red-brown in color. I had never seen anything like it before, nor have I since. Her eyes were green, and her skin fairer than any I have encountered in a lifetime. The English are not sallow folk like the Portuguese women. My daughter, however, has night-black hair, and her eyes are the color of fine turquoise.

Her skin is fair, like heavy cream, but not quite as fair as her mother's. Her face is shaped like a heart, unlike Candra's and mine, but she does have her mother's full mouth and long, slim nose. She has my look in her eyes, which are almond-shaped; and the mole I bear between my upper lip and left nostril, although the mark upon her is, of course, smaller, more feminine."

"Is she beautiful?" Jamal Khan asked, now frankly curious.

"You will judge for yourself, my young prince," the emperor told him and arose from his seat. "We will go secretly to Yasaman's palace, where you may observe her without her knowing you are there." Akbar walked swiftly from the room, giving orders as he went.

Both Yusef Khan and his son, surprised, scrambled to their feet and followed their overlord. Horses were brought, and the distance between the two palaces was quickly traveled. The emperor sent a mounted messenger ahead to warn Rugaiya Begum of his coming. She met them at the entrance to Yasaman's palace.

A most handsome women, Yusef Khan thought, as Rugaiya Begum salaamed to her guests, her large hands together in a gesture of obeisance. "My dear lord, you come at a most inopportune time. Yasaman has just gone to her bath," she told her husband and his companions.

Akbar smiled, obviously not in the least disturbed by her announcement. "Excellent!" he said. "The prince has come to see for himself if Yasaman is beautiful. What better place than her bath to discover this?"

"My lord!" Rugaiya Begum was frankly shocked.

"Once," the emperor said, boldly ignoring her and addressing his companions, "I observed Candra in her bath. It was before we came together as man and woman. I must admit that despite my great experience with women at that time, it still whetted my appetite for her fair flesh." He turned back to his wife. "You will lead the way, my dear, and then see that one of Yasaman's serving girls encourages her mistress from the bath, that Prince Jamal may observe our daughter in all her natural beauty. She will ravish his heart, I am certain, for all her youth."

Adali came to greet the emperor, and Rugaiya Begum instructed him of Akbar's wishes. The eunuch's eyebrows twitched just slightly, to the Mughal's amusement. Adali was a very proper fellow, and the overeagerness to serve he had possessed in his youth had, in his middle years, given way to just a touch of pomposity.

The high steward of Yasaman's household was a half-caste, the product of a liasion between an Indian mother and a French seaman father. He had been gelded in his youth when a famine made it necessary to sell him into slavery. His bilingual abilities had made his fortune when Candra had been introduced into the zenana of the Grand Mughal. Candra spoke neither Arabic nor Portuguese, but she did speak French. Adali's French, although a cruder version of his mistress's, allowed Candra to assimilate into the zenana with the eunuch acting as her translator. When Candra had been returned to her native land, Adali had been appointed high steward of Yasaman's household. He watched over the princess scrupulously, and, Akbar thought, if a eunuch could feel paternal, Adali's feelings toward Yasaman Kama Begum were certainly that of a father for a beloved child. The Mughal could not be jealous, though. It pleased him to have his youngest child surrounded by such caring people.

"There is a wall of jasper carved like a screen that faces the steps leading down to the princess's bathing pool, my lord," Adali said. "It is possible for you and your guests to secrete yourselves behind it without being observed, yet you will be able to see the princess. My lady knows the way. I will go ahead and instruct Rohana in your wishes." He bowed politely and, turning, glided smoothly off.

"Adali is the high steward of my daughter's house. He and all her servants will stay with Yasaman," Akbar said. "I think you will be quite pleased with Yasaman's dowry."

"My household could use someone with discipline," Jamal Khan noted, looking about him at the cleanliness and order of this place. The housekeeping in his own palace left a great deal to be desired, but that was because since his mother had died there was no one to instruct the servants. That was a wife's duty, but the prince had no wife. He was beginning to see advantages to this marriage that he had not seen before.

"We must speak softly lest Yasaman hear us and be embarrassed," Akbar instructed them.

"It is not really necessary that I go with you," Yusef Khan said. He was very uncomfortable with the situation, although he realized that the emperor was cleverly overcoming his son's reluctance by showing him the princess as only a husband should see her. Still, he would never be able to look his daughter-in-law in the eye if he saw her so. "Princess Yasaman's beauty and goodness are well-known," he finished lamely.

"Apparently not to your son," Akbar replied, amused. He fully recognized his general's discomfort and respected his sensibilities. Still, he could not resist teasing him a bit further. "Do you not want to see that the girl is perfect, Yusef?"

"No, my lord," came the agonized reply. "I accept your word in this matter, as I do in all things."

Akbar chuckled. "Go through there," he said, pointing to a wide arched opening. "You will find a cool breeze upon the terrace, and we will join you shortly, my friend."

Yusef Khan gratefully complied.

"Well now, my son," the Mughal said, his voice heavy with unspoken meaning, "shall we go observe your bride in all her glory? You will not be disappointed, Jamal Khan."

"Her beauty will be appreciated, my lord, but I am not so young or so unfamiliar with women that I am not aware there must be more between a man and wife for the marriage to be happy. My father took my mother as a favor to a dying friend. He thought her beautiful and sweet, but she was, in fact, quite clever. She caught his interest immediately, and she held that interest her entire lifetime as his wife."

"You loved your mother," Akbar said, as a statement of fact, not a question. "It is good for a man to love and respect his mother. It is the woman who gives a man life; who nourishes the man in his early years; from whom he learns his first, and perhaps most important lessons. Love and respect my daughter who will be the mother of your sons, Jamal Khan, and you will be a contented man. My own mother has often been a thorn in my thumb, but she is wise. She loves me above all others, and I love and honor her above all others."

Rugaiya Begum now led them through a door, her fingers going to her lips as she warned them to silence. The room into which they entered smelled heavily of jasmine flowers. They stood motionless behind the carved jasper screen, allowing their eyes to become used to the filtered sunlight and the rich perfumed steam rising from the bathing pool.

"Look," the emperor said softly, and then he discreetly turned away.

Jamal Khan stared intently at the girl who rose up from the water, walking halfway up the flight of stairs that led out of the pool, pausing a moment to grasp her long black hair and wring it free of moisture.

"Let me, my princess," a pretty young serving woman said, coming forward to help her mistress. She quickly pinned the girl's hair atop her head with several ivory pins.

Yasaman stood facing the carved screen, totally unaware she was being observed. She gracefully raised her arms above her head, as was her habit, when Rohana came to sponge her off. Her breasts, quite breathtaking for one so young, thrust forward, their nipples pert and rosy.

She was tall, Jamal observed, with wonderful long legs and slender, high-arched feet. None of his women were tall. If he held her in his arms, where would her head reach? Her waist was so tiny, he thought, he could probably span it with his hands, but her hips were wonderfully voluptuous. Her smooth thighs were firm-fleshed, and the mound between them plump, the groove separating her nether lips a deep slash of mauve shadow. To his surprise he felt his own body responding to her, and he flushed. She was only a virgin, he told himself. *But what a virgin!* his inner self replied.

She smiled at something her servant said, and he was treated to a glimpse of even, white teeth, not yet stained with betel, as were the teeth of so many women. He had thought her beautiful as she stood there, but when she smiled she was extraordinary. If there had been any doubts in his mind about the match, they were now swept away by his sight of the exquisite girl standing so artlessly before him in her innocent nudity.

Akbar watched the series of emotions as they were exposed so unconsciously upon the handsome face of Jamal Khan. His eyes met those of Rugaiya Begum, and she nodded so slightly that had it been anyone else, he would not have noted her approval. Akbar put a firm hand beneath the prince's elbow and guided him from the room.

"You are satisfied, Jamal Khan? As you can see, my daughter is flawless and without blemish."

The prince nodded, struggling to find his voice. *"When?"* he finally managed to ask.

"As soon as it can be arranged," the emperor told him.

Jamal Khan's senses now cleared. He was once again filled with questions. "Why the haste? The girl is only thirteen, and the law says she cannot be wed until she is fourteen."

"The haste," Akbar said smoothly, "is because my daughter has a suitor—she is not aware of him, of course—among the Afghan tribes. There are some who think I should marry her off there for the sake of peace. But the northern tribes are a contentious lot. It would not be of any use to give them my precious daughter. Once she had gone through the Khyber Pass, she would be lost to me. She is gently bred and would not survive in such barbaric surroundings.

"My son, Salim, has only recently brought me word of a plot to kidnap Yasaman for this tribal prince. The conspirators are men of Islam, however. If Yasaman is married elsewhere, they will give up their pursuit of her.

"Your father and I will give it out that this was a match made between us several years ago, with the wedding scheduled now because you cannot wait to claim my child, so great is your love for her. I can waive the law. As you saw, Yasaman already has the body of a woman, even if she has yet to know a man."

Jamal Khan nodded. *"She is beautiful,"* he said, almost to himself. "It would not be far from the truth to say I cannot wait to possess myself of her loveliness, my lord."

"Then we may proceed with the formalities, Jamal Khan?"

"Yes, my lord! The sooner the better!"

"Then let us go and tell your good father, for he is a man who worries constantly. I would not want to be the cause of sending him to an early grave. He will be as eager as I to enjoy the grandchildren this match will bring for both of us." They exited out onto the terrace, and Akbar said enthusiastically, "Yusef, my friend! We are to have a wedding!"

4

The sachaq was brought to Yasaman Kama Begum. Although she had been expecting it, she was not quite prepared for the generosity of Prince Jamal's family. The sachaq, prenuptial gifts to the bride, was presented to her on a variety of black lacquered trays decorated in bright, cheerful colors with flowers, fruits, animals, and other designs. One tray contained a selection of gold and silver bracelets and anklets. Another contained earrings in the same metals. A tray of pearl jewelry—necklaces, earrings, and hair ornaments—was followed by trays of diamonds, rubies, sapphires, emeralds, and one of prettily colored semiprecious stones. Even Rugaiya Begum was moved to amazement by this lavishness.

Tray after tray followed. One contained a stack of shabnam peshwazes, almost brilliant in their whiteness. Another was piled high with saris of the finest materials and in beautiful colors, some plain, some striped with gold or silver, some decorated with designs. A tray of rare oils and perfumes was presented to the princess, and a tiny tray with an alabaster pot of mehdi, festive red dye, was brought.

"I will not smear that awful stuff upon my person, tradition or no tradition," Yasaman declared firmly, and her mother laughed.

A tray of beautiful fruits was next: pomelos, custard apples, mangosteens, bananas, and coconuts, as well as rare oranges and an odd, prickly, oval fruit sprouting green leaves, which sat in the very center of the tray.

"What is *that*?" Yasaman demanded of the servant holding the tray before her. "I have never seen anything like it before."

"It is called a pineapple, gracious lady."

"Is it edible? Where does it come from?"

"When it is peeled, gracious lady, the yellow fruit within is juicy and both sweet and tart. I know not from where it comes, but it is a rare delicacy, I am told."

"My father brought one home from one of his voyages once," Adali, who had been overseeing the presentation of the sachaq, told them. "The fruit is grown on certain South Sea islands."

"Was it good?" Yasaman wanted to know.

"Delicious," he assured her.

Finally the last tray was brought. Unlike its black lacquered predecessors, this one was solid gold, and upon it, sitting most regally, was a small coal-black kitten wearing a dainty diamond collar. Even its whiskers were black, but its eyes were the color of clear, golden amber.

"Ohhh!" Yasaman breathed with delight, and reaching out, lifted the small beast off his tray. Gently she cuddled the little creature and was rewarded with a faint, barely formed purr. "Is he not beautiful, Mama Begum? What a wonderful gift!"

"I think Fou-Fou will be very jealous," Rugaiya Begum said. "She has never had to share you with another cat before."

"Jiinn will make a fine mate for her," Yasaman told her mother.

"Jiinn, is it?" Rugaiya Begum laughed. "And you are certain it is a male?"

"It is indeed a gentleman cat, gracious lady," the servant who had carried the tray spoke up in a singsong voice.

The kitten meowed, and Fou-Fou, in her usual indolent position upon a silken couch, was stirred to curiosity. Leaping from her perch she came forward. Yasaman set the kitten upon the cool tiles of the chamber floor. As if she were unable to believe her eyes, Fou-Fou stopped in her tracks, staring hard. The kitten meowed again, and the white female crouched and hissed. Undaunted, the black kitten launched himself forward and pounced on her. Flabbergasted by this sudden turn of events, the fat white cat tumbled over onto her back even as tiny Jiinn landed upon her fat belly and scampered forward up her furry length to press his dark nose against Fou-Fou's dainty pink one.

"Allah help us!" Rugaiya Begum cried, expecting to see the spoiled white cat turn angrily upon the bold kitten and kill it. But before their astonished eyes, an utterly besotted look came into Fou-Fou's lime-green ones. Lifting her head up, she began to vigorously lick the kitten, who started to purr quite loudly. Jiinn tolerated her adoration for a brief minute and then, squirming forward, he began to chew upon Fou-Fou's ear.

"They love each other!" Yasaman squealed, delighted. "I think it is a very good omen for my marriage, don't you, Mama Begum?" Then she looked up at the servant who had brought the kitten. "Is the prince handsome?" she asked him shyly.

"*Very* handsome, my lady princess," the servant told her with a grin.

Yasaman turned to her mother. "Why can I not see Prince Jamal before we are married, Mama Begum? You saw Papa before you were married. You even talked with him. Why can I not see the prince?"

"Your father and I were first cousins, Yasaman. We grew up together," Rugaiya Begum explained to her daughter for the hundredth time as Adali shooed the visiting servants from the princess's apartments. The steward didn't intend to allow them to remain and take back any juicy gossip to their own palace. "It isn't necessary or even proper that you and Prince Jamal meet until after the wedding ceremony is performed."

"When will that be?" Yasaman's heart was beating quickly with her excitement, and her color was high.

"First the Mehr must be agreed upon, and then the Nikah can be performed by the qazi," Rugaiya Begum said.

"Why do we need a Mehr? Surely Jamal Khan cannot divorce me. I am Yasaman Kama Begum, the daughter of the Grand Mughal. Wouldn't it be treason if he divorced me?"

"What if you and he cannot get on, my child? It is unlikely, but it could happen. Your father would not want you to spend the rest of your life in misery. The Mehr is a sum of money the bridegroom must pay you if your marriage is dissolved. His status and your status will determine the amount. I think Jamal Khan will strive very hard to make you happy, my daughter, for it would, I think, impoverish his family for several generations to come were he to divorce you. The Mehr is Islam's way of protecting a woman from an unscrupulous husband."

"I do not follow Islam," Yasaman said quietly. "I follow my conscience. There is much good in Islam, and much good in Christianity, Candra's religion, and Judaism as well. I have studied the teachings of Zoroaster, and the Buddha, and the Jain. I like the Hindu custom of not harming any living thing; but no one religion seems to satisfy me. Who's to know what is really right except, perhaps, God Himself?"

"Your bridegroom is of Islam," Rugaiya Begum reminded her daughter, "and he will raise his sons in its faith."

"But I will teach them what I have learned as well," Yasaman said. "They will make their own choice in the end, even as I will."

"Even Salim chooses Islam, despite Akbar and despite the fact that Jodh Bai is a Hindu," Rugaiya Begum said, and then wished she had remained silent, for she had not meant to mention Salim.

"Speaking of my brother, where is he?" Yasaman asked. "I have not seen him in the two days since he and you and Papa advised me to accept this marriage."

The older woman drew a deep breath. "Your brother has gone south to Mewar for your father on matters concerning the empire," she said calmly.

"He will not be here for my wedding?" The young girl's face was a mixture of outrage and disappointment.

Rugaiya Begum decided she would not argue this matter, and so she said, "Either your father had to go to Mewar, or Salim had to go, my daughter. I know how greatly you and your brother care for one another, but your father loves you too. Would you deny an old man the pleasure of seeing the last of his daughters married? Salim understood."

But Salim had not understood, and Rugaiya Begum knew it.

"I do not comprehend it," he said, close to open anger and defiance. "Suddenly Yasaman must be married, and it must be now," he complained to his aunt and his father. "You even waive your own laws to suit this matter. Why can I not be here to see my sister married? A day or two at the most. What can it possibly matter?"

"It does matter," Akbar said implacably. "There is trouble in Mewar. I need you to go, Shaikho Baba, and prevent the difficulties from spreading. You know the trial Mewar is to me. Is this how you will behave when you sit alone on my throne? Putting your own pleasures ahead of your duty to India and to the empire?"

"If it is so important, then you go," Salim replied rudely. Why, he asked himself, were they so anxious to see him ride away?

Akbar, however, pretended he was not offended by the insult and he laughed. "That is what old men have heirs for, Shaikho Baba! One day you will have the same advantage over Khusrau as I have over you."

"Why not let Khusrau go to Mewar," Salim said cleverly. "He is sixteen. It is certainly past time he learned his responsibilities. As the heir after me, he certainly can represent the Mughal every bit as much as I can, and then I may remain for my sister's wedding."

"As the next Mughal, you will have more authority than my grandson, Shaikho Baba, but your idea has merit. Take Khusrau with you," Akbar replied, "and teach him as I have taught you."

Rugaiya Begum watched the emotions playing swiftly over the prince's face. "We will miss you, my nephew," she told him. "May Allah protect you and Khusrau."

"I will see Yasaman before I go," Salim said, realizing that there was no escape from his father's will, save rebellion. It was not worth it. Not this time. Yasaman would be here in Kashmir for him whenever he wanted her. Besides, he would have this afternoon and this evening with her, and he would ensure it was a pleasurable time for them both.

"Please do not see my daughter, Salim," Rugaiya Begum said. "It will upset her to know you are going and that you will not be here for her wedding day. You know how very much she dotes upon you, but if you truly love her, you will leave her in peace."

"Your aunt is correct, my son," Akbar agreed. "It is better you go now while your sister is distracted with the preparations for her wedding."

He knew! His father knew! Salim was suddenly certain. *But how?* How could he possibly know? He couldn't! I'm imagining it, Salim decided. Akbar may be all-powerful, but there is no way under heaven that he could be privy to my secret thoughts. I have been very careful. No one saw me entering or leaving Yasaman's chamber the night of her birthday. *No! He does not know. He cannot!*

"If you would prefer that I not see Yasaman, then so be it, dear aunt, my father. I would not want to be the cause of my sister's unhappiness at a time when she should be happiest. Give her my love and tell her I wish I might be with her, but my duty rules otherwise." Salim bowed politely to his elders and then took his leave of them.

But Salim had certainly not understood, Rugaiya Begum knew, even as she lied to Yasaman. However, it did not matter any longer. He was gone! Yasaman was safe from his incestuous lust and would shortly be the wife of Jamal Khan. Salim would eventually lose interest if his sister was happily married and he rarely saw her. Their lives would proceed smoothly forward. Perhaps she would never even have to see her nephew again, Rugaiya considered. She saw no necessity to ever travel south now that her daughter was to be settled here in Kashmir. Yasaman's deep sigh drew her attention again. "Salim knew his duty, my daughter," she said.

"I know, Mama Begum," Yasaman agreed, "but I am still sad that my brother cannot be with me on so important a day."

"As is he," Rugaiya said with a degree of truth, "but fate has decreed it otherwise. You must always accept what fate offers you and make the best of it that you can."

"And fate," Akbar said, entering the chamber, "has decreed that tomorrow be our Yasaman's wedding day!" He put an arm around them both and chuckled benevolently. There was no mistaking the fact that the Mughal was vastly pleased.

"*Tomorrow?*" Yasaman cried. "It is so soon! Why tomorrow?"

"Because the Mehr has been agreed upon, and a most expensive young lady you are, my daughter." He chucked again and then said, "My astrologer has carefully compared your natal chart with that of Prince Jamal. He declares tomorrow is the only day for the next several months that the signs are propitious enough for this wedding to take place. So tomorrow we will have a wedding."

Rugaiya Begum heard the qualifying note in her husband's voice, but she waited until Yasaman had gone to bed that evening to discuss it with him. *"Propitious enough?* What did your astrologer mean by that, my dear lord? What is wrong? Are they still ill-suited? I do not want Yasaman in a bad marriage even in order to allow her to escape Salim's advances."

Akbar sighed and, lying upon his back, his arms beneath his head, said quietly, "Ali says they are well-matched in every aspect. There will be no trouble in the mating, and there will even be love between them. There is, however, in Jamal's chart a hidden danger, but Ali could not say what it was. It is, he says, blurred, as if fate had not yet decided Jamal's kismet or did not wish to reveal itself."

"And Yasaman's chart? What does it say?" Rugaiya Begum asked nervously.

"Ali says there is great happiness in store for Yasaman, but tragedy as well. He says there are several children ahead for Yasaman. Rugaiya, my love, let us not think on the future tonight. Let us think on the present. Happiness. Tragedy. Children. Is that not all our fates?"

"Yes," she agreed.

"When will the prince arrive?" Akbar asked her, taking a lock of her silvery hair in his hand and kissing it.

"In late afternoon, my lord. We will have the Henna-bandi ceremony first, and then the qazi will perform the ceremony. Then the prince will be introduced to his bride. There will be feasting, and dancing and other entertainments. Then Yasaman and her husband will leave for his palace across the lake," Rugaiya Begum concluded.

"Hmmmm, that is good," he said absently, and she could hear the weariness in his voice.

"Go to sleep, my dear lord," she said softly. Rugaiya Begum knew that within a day or two of their daughter's marriage, Akbar would gather up his household and begin the trek south for Lahore and Agra. It was rare he remained in any one place for very long. She wondered if once she remained in Kashmir, she would ever see Akbar again in this life. Then she chided herself for being a foolish old woman. Nothing would keep Akbar from Kashmir and the grand-children Yasaman would have. Yes, everything was going to be all right now, Rugaiya Begum thought. The Salim matter was settled, to her deep relief. She slept the sleep of a woman at peace.

Outside the small palace, the moon played upon the still, dark waters of the lake. The night air seemed perfumed with the thousands of flowers in the gardens. Yasaman had slipped from her sleeping chamber to walk upon the terrace. She knew that she should be sleeping, but she could not. Her mind hummed along like a hive of bees. Tomorrow she was to be married. It had happened so quickly. She was not really prepared for it, but her father was not well. Mama Begum had told her that quite frankly. Her father wanted her settled with a good husband. He wanted to see her chil-dren before he died. It was only natural, she supposed. Her father was known to be a very doting grandfather to the children of his sons and daughters.

Children. Yasaman knew how children were conceived and born. Every young girl did. There was no mystery about it. Was she expected to copulate with a stranger, she wondered, even if he was her husband? Would she be allowed time to get to know this stranger? Her father had not forced Candra to his bed, she knew. He wooed her and won her with pas-sion and with deep love, Rugaiya Begum had told her.

Love. Another variable. Would she and Jamal Khan learn to love one another? Would they even like one another? Dear lord! She prayed they would. Her mind was filled with so many questions to which she had no answers.

She walked to the edge of the terrace and saw that Ali, the fisherman, was almost directly below. "Good evening, Ali," she greeted him. "Are the fish running well tonight?"

Looking up, he flashed her a smile. "Always in a bright, full moon, gracious lady," he told her.

"I am to be married tomorrow, Ali," Yasaman told her friend.

"*Married?*" The fisherman was surprised. He had heard no word of a royal marriage. The marriage of the Mughal's daughter should be a great time of rejoicing, not some secret ceremony as this obviously was to be.

"Yes, Ali," Yasaman continued. "I am to be married to Prince Jamal Khan. What think you of that?" Perhaps the fisherman would tell her something of her husband-to-be, who had also, like Ali, lived his whole life in Kashmir. Peasants lived for gossip.

"The son of Yusef Khan?" the fisherman asked.

"Yes," Yasaman answered him. "Is he handsome? Do people speak well of him? You must tell me what you know."

"Yes, my princess, I have seen the prince. He is taller than your father and very handsome, all the ladies think. I have heard nought of evil about him. He is an obedient son to his father."

"Oh," she said. That was not particularly promising. In fact, it was dull. She had hoped Ali knew some interesting fact that would help her to understand this stranger she was to marry tomorrow.

"Good night, Princess. May Allah bless you with many sons, gracious lady," the fisherman said, and he began to row away from her, eager to return to his village and spread the news.

"Thank you, Ali," Yasaman said forlornly, and moved back from the edge of the parapet. Stretching out upon a silken couch on the terrace, she gazed up at the full August moon, thinking a thought she had often had. Candra sees this same moon. *Candra.* The woman who had given her life. *Her mother.* No, Candra was not her mother, Yasaman decided. A mother was someone who stayed with her child no matter what. Rugaiya Begum, the gentle and loving woman who had raised her, who had always been there for her, was her mother.

But she had always been curious about the English woman, Yasaman admitted to herself. To the best of her knowledge they had told her everything that they knew, but it was so little. Yet there was still a tie of sorts between them. Candra's family had never lost interest in her.

Each year, her father sent the most beautiful, flawless pearl he could find to Candra's mother through the factor of her trading company in Cambay. Her English grandmother, Yasaman knew, also had yearly correspondence with her father. What would they think of this marriage? she wondered.

"My child, what are you doing up so late?" Father Cullen Butler was suddenly by her side, his dark robes making a slight breeze. "Are you troubled in some measure?"

"I was thinking of Candra, Father," Yasaman answered. She motioned him to a comfortable padded stool by her side. "Sit down, Father."

The priest seated himself, asking as he did so, "Do you think often of Candra, my dear lady?"

"Only sometimes," Yasaman revealed candidly. "I know that I have been told everything about her that my father knows; but sometimes I wish I knew more. About her family. Mama Begum says that Papa corresponds with my other grandmother. Yet never have I been shown one of those letters. What do they write about? Does my grandmother write about Candra? Does Candra ever ask about me?" She sighed deeply. "Now that I am to be married and will eventually, God willing, become a mother myself, this other part of me somehow seems more important than it ever has before." Then she laughed ruefully. "Alas, that you cannot tell me what I need to know, Father, but you were not here when my . . . when Candra was here."

For a moment it seemed as if the priest was debating something with himself. Then he said to Yasaman, "It is true that I was not here when Candra was, my lady, but I can shed some light on that which you desire to know."

"*You can?*" Yasaman sat up and, leaning forward,

demanded, "Tell me what you know, Father! Oh, please tell me!"

"I have been privy to your maternal grandmother's correspondence with your father. As you know, the Mughal can neither read nor speak Candra's tongue. They communicated in French. Your grandmother de Marisco also writes to your father in French. But though your father speaks French, he cannot read it, and he does not wish his Jesuit friends to be cognizant of the letters. As you know, I am just a simple priest and not a member of that revered order of the religious. I read your grandmother's letters to him.

"Your grandmother, Lady de Marisco, is not English born. She comes from an island nation to the west of England called Ireland, but she has not lived there since her girlhood. Although of the noble class, she has a great natural instinct for the business of trading. Many years ago she went into partnership with a friend of her second husband. That gentleman is now deceased, but the company name remains the same. It is the O'Malley-Small Trading Company. Your grandmother has become very wealthy through it.

"Each year, as you know, she writes your father to tell him she has received the pearl he sends her. Sometimes she writes of Candra, who as you now know was reunited with her first husband. They have several sons now, which means you have other brothers. Lady de Marisco always asks after you. Are you pretty? How do your studies go? Do you look like your mother? Do you ever ask after them? Each year it is the same, and she ends the missive by sending her love to you."

"What does my father reply?" Yasaman asked, curious.

"Nothing, my lady," the priest said. "He will only send the pearl to your grandmother so that Candra will not worry about you; so that they know you are alive and that you flourish. Candra did not, as you know, wish to leave you. Because he loved her, the Mughal cannot bear the thought of her suffering needless anguish over your fate, which is why he maintains this tenuous contact at all.

"Why does Papa send the pearl to my grandmother and not to Candra?" Yasaman wondered aloud.

"If the Mughal sent it to Candra, it would but open old wounds between them. Then, too, you must remember that Candra is married. It is certain that her husband does not want to be reminded of that period in Candra's life when, thinking him dead, she wed another man and bore that other man a child. I have taught you the tenets of the Holy Mother Church, my dear lady. You know that a woman may only have one husband, as a husband must cleave only unto one wife."

Yasaman nodded and then she said wistfully, "I wonder if Candra ever thinks of me, Father Cullen. Do you think she would like me? I wish I could tell her of my marriage. If I wrote her a letter, would you see that it was sent off?"

"I do not think that would be wise, my dear lady," the priest replied gently, feeling absolutely wretched at the look of disappointment that came to the young girl's face. "I will personally see that your grandmother de Marisco knows of your happiness. Both she and Candra would be very proud of you, Princess, if they could know you, but, alas, they cannot. Better to leave things the way they are. You have never really been unhappy over the loss of the lady who bore you, for you did not know her. Rugaiya Begum has been a good and loving mother to you. You owe her respect, loyalty, and your love."

"She has it," Yasaman said. "Do you really think I will be happy, Father Cullen?" she queried him anxiously. "I wish this marriage were not so hurried an event."

"Dear child," the priest said, "you know that your father is not well."

"Is he dying?" she asked half fearfully. She could not really imagine Akbar dying. He was the Mughal. He was her father. He had always been there for her, and she assumed he always would be.

"We must all die eventually. The lord Akbar is of an age where life is shorter than it is longer. You are the last of his children. He wants very much to have you settled. That vanity in him that we all possess desires to see grandchildren of your union. Therefore, the sooner you wed, the sooner he will see those grandchildren." Cullen Butler chuckled. "All these many thoughts, my dear little lady! You are, I suspect, being attacked by a disease known the world over to maidens about to embark upon the road to marriage. They call this malady 'bridal nerves.' Most young girls facing their wedding day are beset by them."

"I just wish I knew more about Prince Jamal, Father. Why, I have never even seen him!"

"Many brides, both here in India and in Europe, never see their bridegrooms before the wedding day. There is nothing unusual in it. It is the way of the nobility and the wealthier classes throughout the world. Marriage is a sacrament between two people, as I have taught you, my dear lady."

"Not in Islam," Yasaman said. "Marriage in Islam is a contract between two people. That is why the Iman cannot bless it until the Mehr is fixed. Papa says I am a most expensive bride. It is unlikely the prince will ever divorce me, for I would cost his family too much gold. Besides, I am the Mughal's daughter, and my brother, Salim, will follow our father as Mughal one day. Jamal Khan would not dare ever insult my family."

"That is true," the priest agreed, "and because it is so, my dear lady, I would beg you to allow me to marry you and Prince Jamal in the faith of Candra into which you were baptized. It would please her family very much, I know. Remember, I was sent here to India by Holy Mother Church to keep you on the path of the true faith. In this I have failed, I fear, for you are not truly devout; but if I can give you the sacrament of marriage, then perhaps I will not have failed entirely."

"I do not know, Father." Yasaman considered carefully. "I do not think it would be allowed."

"Why not?" the priest said with unaccustomed belliger- ence. "Has not your father married many of his wives in both the faiths of Islam and the Hindu? Did not your brother, Salim, celebrate his marriage to Princess Man Bai in both her faith and his? Why should it be any different for you? Man Bai was but the daughter of the Raja of Amber. *You are the Mughal's daughter!* Should your wishes be consid- ered less than a daughter of Amber?"

Her pride pricked, it did not take Yasaman long to decide the matter. "You are right," she said, "and I know it would please Candra's family, Father Cullen."

"Indeed it would, my lady," the priest agreed, smiling to himself, pleased.

"Then so be it! I will speak with my father in the morning. The wedding will not be celebrated until the late afternoon. I suspect, however, that a Christian marriage will have to be performed in secret. Islam and the Hindu faith are natural to India. Christianity is not. Still, it matters not, does it? I will be wed in the faiths of those who gave me life. I think that most fitting, Father."

He nodded, content. She had studied the faith of her mother's family quite assiduously, but then, to his disap- pointment, she had also studied other faiths just as carefully. He was not really certain what she believed, and he dared not press her, lest he be sent away. It was important that he remain with her.

Yasaman suddenly yawned quite broadly.

"Good," Cullen Butler said with a small smile. "You are finally sleepy, my dear lady. Let me escort you into your chamber."

"Ummm," she agreed. Standing up, she allowed him to

lead her into her sleeping chamber, but before she could lay aside her large, beautiful, soft shawl, her only covering, he bowed himself quickly from her presence.

Yasaman smiled to herself. Father Cullen, like all the priests she knew, was embarrassed by nudity. It was so silly. Tossing aside the Kashmir shawl, Yasaman fell gratefully into her bed, asleep almost before her head could touch the pillow. It was a dreamless sleep, and when she was finally awakened in the morning by her two body servants, Rohana and Toramalli, Yasaman felt wonderfully refreshed.

"Tell my father I want to see him," she instructed Adali as he entered her chamber to greet her.

"At once, dearest princess," the eunuch said.

"It is a perfect day for a wedding, my lady," Toramalli said with a broad smile. "The kitchens have been busy since before dawn with all the baking. There is to be wheat bread, honey loaves, and Rumali roti bread!"

"And both purple and green rice, as well as rice covered with sheets of beaten gold and silver!" Rohana chimed in excitedly.

"Do not forget the sacrificial lamb," Yasaman said mischievously.

The two sisters look puzzled for a moment, and then suddenly understanding the jest, they burst out laughing, rolling their fine dark eyes about most comically. When they were finally able to contain themselves, Toramalli asked, "Shall we prepare your bath, my lady?"

"No," she told them. "I will bathe before the wedding; but I should like to be sponged with jasmine water now."

Rohana hurried to fetch a silver basin into which she had ladled cool water scented with jasmine oil. Together she and her sister washed their mistress and then helped her to dress in a hyacinth-colored jaguli. The traditional high-waisted dress of the Mughal's had long, tight-fitting sleeves and a long flowing skirt. The hem of the skirt was decorated in a gold design, as were the cuffs of the sleeves. The embroidered opening at the neck of the gown revealed a modest glimpse of Yasaman's young breasts.

Toramalli began to brush the princess's long, black hair with a brush dipped in jasmine oil, freeing it of the tangles it had gained during the night. Watching from the entry to the room, Akbar thought how very much her lovely hair reminded him of his own when he had been younger. He remembered how surprised Candra had been to find his hair long, and dark, and soft. Their daughter had inherited that small bit of him along with the mole he had between his upper lip and his left nostril. On Yasaman, though the mole was very much smaller, it was without a doubt the mark of the Mughal. His father, Humayun, had possessed that mark, although none of his other children did.

Shaking himself free of his thoughts, he stepped into his daughter's chamber. "Good morning, my rosebud!" he said jovially.

"Papa!" Yasaman arose and, running to him, kissed him. Then turning to her serving women, she said, "Go! We are not to be disturbed by anyone."

Adali, who had returned with his master, bowed, surprised, but dutifully shepherded Toramalli and Rohana from the room.

"Ahhh," the emperor said, intrigued. "What is this, Yasaman? Secrets? What secrets can my innocent young rosebud have?"

"Yes, my father," she answered, looking directly into his dark eyes. "A secret of sorts."

"What is it, my daughter?" he asked her. "It must be important for you to dismiss your body servants. You know I will refuse you nothing within reason, especially on this, your wedding day."

"Jamal Khan practices the faith of Islam, does he not?" she asked.

Akbar nodded. "He does."

"And are we to be married officially in that faith?" she continued.

"Yes. I did not think you would object, Yasaman. Your mind is an open one, I know," her father said.

"Yet both you and my brothers have married in not only the faith of Islam, but in the faith of your brides as well when it proved different. I would have that same privilege, my father. I wish to be married first, privately, in my mother's faith. Candra's. The mother who bore me."

He was at first stunned, and then said, "I do not know if Jamal Khan will accept such a thing."

"You are the Mughal," she told him implacably, in a tone he recognized as his own. "It is your will, my father, not the will of Jamal Khan, which shall prevail in this matter."

"You do not practice Candra's faith," he reasoned cleverly with her.

"No, I do not," she agreed honestly, "but I was baptized in it, *and* I respect the Christian faith. I have never renounced Candra's faith. So under both the laws of Islam and the laws of Christians, I am considered a Christian. I wish to be married in that faith before I am married under Islam. It will please me, my father, because it will allow me to continue that small tie that binds me to the English half of me. I know it would please both Candra as well as my other grandmother when you write to them of my marriage, as I know you will. It will certainly make Father Cullen happy, and he will feel less of a failure with regard to my lack of piety."

Yesterday she had been a child, he thought. Now she was speaking to him as if she were a grown woman; and even if he still wasn't certain that she really was mature, he respected her for it. "How do you know I will write to your grandmother in England, Yasaman? I do not correspond with her. To do so would be futile."

"No," Yasaman answered him with a little smile, "you do not write to her, but I know that each year she writes to you inquiring after me. This time you will write to her when you send the pearl, won't you? If you do not, I will. I think Candra will want to know that I am married."

"Have you ever been unhappy, my child?" he asked her, curious, for she had never before shown such interest in the other half of her heritage.

"Never!" she responded honestly. "I would be no one but who I am. Yasaman Kama Begum, the daughter of the Grand Mughal and Rugaiya Begum, his first consort."

"And the wife of Jamal Khan?" he said.

"And the wife of Jamal Khan," she replied, *"but only if I may be married first by Father Cullen."*

"Candra was stubborn too," he told her.

"Was she?" Yasaman's eyes twinkled mischievously.

"Yes," he nodded, and then he said, "I will grant your request, my daughter. Jamal Khan will somehow manage to live with our decision."

Jamal Khan, however, was not in the least distressed by the revelation that he would first be married by a Christian priest. When he arrived for the wedding to learn this new fact from the Mughal, he said practically, "My sons will be raised in the faith of the Prophet, my lord. That is all I care about. If it pleases the princess to be married in both faiths, then it pleases me too."

He and his father were with the emperor in a small receiving room of Yasaman's palace. None were aware that the princess watched and listened from the window outside. Although reassured by his words, her eyes were riveted upon the young man who would shortly become her husband. They had not lied. He was very handsome, but more important, he seemed to be a reasonable man. She had seen enough. Quietly she slipped through the thick foliage and worked her way around the building to the terrace facing the lake.

"Mistress, where have you been?" Adali hurried forward and, taking her arm, escorted her to her bath.

"I wanted to get a look at the prince, Adali. Is it not natural that I be curious? We are to be married in an hour. Have my aunts and my sister, Aram-Banu, arrived yet? They must perform the Henna-bandi ceremony before the marriage can take place. Tradition must be observed, but ohh, I hate that disgusting dye! Do not even consider attempting to redden my hands and feet with it today, Adali, or I vow I will snatch you bald!"

The eunuch chuckled. "No, mistress, your views on the henna are well-known. There is none in the palace, save the pot the prince sent you, and it will be used to dye his hands. Come now and bathe. The guests will soon be arriving."

"There are no guests but family and a few of my father's honored generals who are with the court," she told him. "This is a most hurried affair, Adali."

Before he might reply, the door to Yasaman's chambers opened and Rugaiya Begum entered, accompanied by another lady.

"I have brought the lady Juliana, my daughter. She must examine you before you bathe that she may attest to your health to your bridegroom's family."

The lady Juliana bowed politely and smiled at Yasaman. She was a plump woman of medium height with wonderful white skin and black hair and eyes. She was an Armenian Christian, married to Philip Bourbon, a member of the royal house of Navarre. Her husband was an architect who had built India's first Christian church only last year in the city of Agra. The lady Juliana was a physician and responsible for the health and well-being of Akbar's zenana.

"I am perfectly healthy," Yasaman protested, annoyed. No one had mentioned this before.

"Indeed, Princess, I would be most inclined to agree," the

lady Juliana replied, noting the girl's bright eyes and the fresh color of her skin. "Nonetheless, I have promised your father that I would examine you, and so I must. Show me your hands, child." She took Yasaman's hands and looked carefully at them. "As soon as you can, Princess, remove the ceremonial Mehdi. It seeps into the skin and I believe it a poison."

"I will not stain my skin with henna," Yasaman told her. "I never have. I dislike it intensely."

"Good!" the physician replied. "Now please open your mouth."

Yasaman complied.

"Her teeth are very sound," the lady Juliana said. "There is no rot nor betel stains, and her breath is fresh. She appears to be in good health, but we must check what we cannot see, eh? Come and lie upon your bed, child. Yusef Khan and his son will want me to swear to your virginity, and so I must. Sit first, however, and I will check to be certain that there are no cankers in your breasts." She began to gently palpate the girl's flesh.

Yasaman blushed deeply but said nothing. She was mortally embarrassed by the examination, but she knew she must submit as gracefully as possible.

A basin of water was brought. The physician washed her hands and then said, "Lie back now, child, and open your legs for me. You must not be frightened, but in order to attest to your purity, I must insert my finger into your yoni to be certain your innocence is honest."

"H-How can you tell?" Yasaman asked nervously, extremely uncomfortable at this unexpected turn of events.

"Before a girl becomes a woman, she has a small shield of thin skin blocking full admittance into her yoni. She becomes a woman when her husband's lingham pierces that shield, rending it asunder and removing her virginity forever. Then and only then can his seed find its way to her hidden garden and take root." The physician leaned forward, sniffing delicately, and then gently inserted a single finger into Yasaman. Her hand pressed carefully down upon the girl's belly. Finally she looked up at Rugaiya Begum and nodded, saying, "She is intact, my lady Begum, and very tight. She will give her husband much pleasure."

Juliana Bourbon arose and washed her hands again in the basin that Rohana presented her, drying them off on a towel Toramalli handed her. "Go to your bath now, Princess. You are, I am pleased to report, in excellent health, as I shall tell your father and the bridegroom."

Yasaman struggled shakily to her feet and said politely, "You will remain, my lady Juliana, as my guest at the wedding."

"I am honored, Princess," was the physician's equally polite reply, and she bowed low to Yasaman. Then, escorted by Rugaiya Begum, she departed.

Yasaman bathed in her bathing pool which was scented with jasmine oil, her namesake fragrance. In her father's household there was a perfumery, called the Khushbu Khana, that produced all kinds of oils, scents, and fragrances for the ladies of the royal house.

Exiting the pool, she was anointed with oil and her dark hair was braided with fine gold threads strung with tiny, glittering diamonds. Her wedding garments were then brought. They consisted of a red silk sari wrought with gold threads, over which was placed a cloth-of-gold angya-kurti, which was a jacketlike garment extending to the waist. The angya-kurti was heavily embroidered with gold and silver threads and diamonds. A necklace of diamonds and rubies was put about her neck, and earrings of the same gemstones hung from her ears. Thin bracelets of gold and silver were pushed up on her slender arms, and gold anklets with bells affixed about her ankles. Her gold slippers were embroidered in glittering little diamonds. The orhni, which was a mantle used as a head covering, was also wrought with gold throughout and had a wide band of gold along its hem.

Adali fastened a small veil across Yasaman's face. It was pale gold in color and quite diaphanous. "Come, my princess," he said, taking her by the hand. "Father Cullen will perform the Christian ceremony in your receiving room. He has set up a small altar there, but we must be quick, for we have received word that the Iman is on his way."

The priest awaited them and began the ceremony immediately. Yasaman did not dare to look at her bridegroom, but kept her eyes lowered modestly. There would be no mass, only the exchanging of vows and the blessing of the union. It was quickly over, and the prince, without even a backward glance at his bride, hurried from the room.

Yasaman was outraged. "How dare he not greet me!" she said furiously, her color high beneath her veil.

"He does not yet consider you his wife, my rosebud," Akbar said. "He accepted your wishes in this matter most gracefully, but in his mind you will not be his wife until the Iman has spoken."

"Then let us get on with it, my father!" she told him. "I have some things I wish to say to this prince! As I cannot say them until I am his wife in his eyes, we had best do the deed." She swept from the room, Rugaiya Begum running to catch up with her daughter, Akbar and Father Cullen following at a slower pace. The two men were highly amused. Yasaman's hot Mughal temper was not unfamiliar to either of them.

Yasaman's official wedding was to take place upon the wide terrace overlooking Wular Lake. It was the sunset hour, and the lake was still, the air windless. The Iman from the local mosque had arrived. He was astounded to have been asked to officiate at such an important event, and had been instructed by his two wives to remember everything. He jovially greeted Prince Jamal, whom he had known since childhood, and congratulated him on his good fortune.

"The princess is, I am told, a most beautiful and gentle lady, my lord. You are indeed fortunate." He lowered his voice. "It will be good to have our own royal family in Kash-mir once again."

Jamal Khan nodded, saying, "But you must always re-member, my good Abd Hassan, that Kashmir is now a loyal province of the Imperial Mughal Empire."

"Of course, my lord," the Iman replied smoothly.

Standing in the shadows of a terrace door, Yasaman ob-served her bridegroom. He wore white silk cuddidara paja-mas and a full-skirted white silk tunic embroidered in diamonds and pearls. His patka sash was made of cloth-of-gold. He was bare-headed, but upon his feet he wore Persian-style high-heeled sandals called kafsh. They made him seem tall, although she suspected in his bare feet he would not be much taller than she was. She, however, was taller than the other women in her family.

"Have you seen enough now to satisfy your curiosity?" Rugaiya Begum whispered. "He has extremely fine eyes, I think."

"He is impressive in his fine feathers, but I wonder how impressive he will be without them," Yasaman said boldly. Still, for all her sharp words, she could see his limbs were straight and well-muscled.

"Men, my daughter, are more at a disadvantage with-out their clothes than women," Rugaiya Begum chortled, "but if his lingham is strong, you will not care, I promise you."

"It is time," Akbar said, coming up to them. He was garbed in white and gold and covered with diamonds. To-gether he and Rugaiya Begum, equally magnificent in cloth-of-gold and diamonds, led Yasaman out onto the terrace.

The Iman stood with his back to the lake. Jodh Bai, Salima Begum, Zada Begum, and the lady Waqi stood before him holding up a golden canopy beneath which Jamal Khan and his father, Yusef Khan, waited. The bride joined them, with her parents by her side.

The Iman intoned. "A contract of marriage has been

agreed to between these two young people before us now. Prince Jamal, speak your vows."

"I, Jamal Darya Khan, take you, Yasaman Kama Begum, daughter of Mohammad Akbar, as my lawfully married wife before God and in front of this company in accordance with the teachings of the Koran. I promise to do everything to make this marriage an act of obedience to God, to make it a relationship of love, mercy, peace, faithfulness, and cooperation. Let God be my witness, because God is the best of all witnesses. Amen." He had not looked at her even once.

"Princess Yasaman, speak your vows," the Iman said.

Yasaman stared straight ahead, furious with this man who was almost her husband. Her voice was strong, however, when she spoke. She was the Mughal's daughter and would not be intimidated.

"I, Yasaman Kama Begum, take you, Jamal Darya Khan, son of Yusef Ali Khan, as my lawfully married husband before God and in front of this company in accordance with the teachings of the Koran. I promise to do everything to make this marriage an act of obedience to God, to make it a relationship of love, mercy, peace, faithfulness, and cooperation. Let God be my witness, because God is the best of all witnesses. Amen."

"They are married," the Iman pronounced, and he gazed out over the assembled guests. "Let us pay homage to Jamal Darya Khan and his bride. Huzzah! Huzzah! Huzzah!"

The family on both sides echoed the religious leader loudly. Then, in the company of her mother and the other women, the bride was led to her table for the feast while Akbar escorted the groom and his other male guests to their table.

"My child, I am so happy for you!" Jodh Bai, dainty and as charming as ever in a rose-pink sari, hugged Yasaman.

"You look young enough to be the bride yourself, dear aunt," Yasaman told her. "I thank you for your good wishes."

Jodh Bai beamed with pleasure at the compliment.

"A fine young man," said Salima Begum, resplendent in orange and gold. "He looks like he can give a woman much pleasure. You've read your Pillow Book, Yasaman, but until you've had a lusty young man love you, the pictures mean nothing. I can remember when your father was young and full of fiery juices. Aiiyeee! What a man he was in his youth! I wish you the same joy!"

"You have done well by Candra's daughter," Zada Begum said to Rugaiya Begum. The usually mousy little lady was quite elegant today in purple and gold garb. "Very well, indeed. She will be Kashmir's queen."

"I have done well by *my daughter*," Rugaiya Begum said stiffly.

"Oh!" Nervously, Zada Begum flushed bright red. "Yes, of course! How rude of me, Rugaiya Begum! I do beg your pardon."

Rugaiya Begum nodded coolly, and Zada Begum scurried quickly away to the opposite end of the table.

"She has always been such a fool," Salima Begum said to Rugaiya Begum, "but she means no harm, I know."

"She is your friend, Salima. You would understand her better than the rest of us," was the tart reply.

Salima Begum chuckled. "You are as prickly as a rosebush where that child is concerned, Rugaiya, but you need not be. You are her mother, the only mother she can remember, and nothing can change that fact. Yasaman loves you better than any, do you not, my child?"

"Yes, Aunt, I do!" Yasaman answered. She put her arms about her mother's neck and lovingly kissed her cheek.

A great feast was served to the wedding guests, beginning with cool lemon-flavored sherbets to cleanse the palate. Loaves of wheat bread, their tops glazed with egg yoke, were placed on the tables as well as round, sweet honey loaves, their tops black with poppy seeds; and silk handkerchief bread, called Rumali roti, made from wafer-thin sheets of

wheat flour. This last was only served on very special occasions. There were bowls of herbal pickles, carrots, and pulses
which were peas, beans, and edible seeds.

Rohana had been correct, there were several kinds of rice:
saffroned, dyed a rich royal purple, as well as green and
bridal red. Several bowls of rice were covered with thin sheets
of beaten gold or silver. No expense had been spared, for
this was the Mughal's daughter.

Roasted game birds cooked in clay tandoor pots were
brought, as well as roasted chickens, sea tortoise, several va-
rieties of fish, an especially hot curry of chicken, lambs' brains
and testicles in a mustard leaf curry, roasted kids, and a lamb
dish that had been cooked in red chili. The women ate as
heartily as the men, but the noise from the men's tables was
far greater.

When the main course was cleared away, fresh fruits,
tiny pastry horns filled with honey and chopped nuts, pistachios, pine nuts, lychees, and candied rose petals were
served, along with both green and black teas. The guests
had the choice of flavoring their tea with cardamons or
cloves for added zest.

The sun had set in a marvelous blaze of rich colors as
they ate. Torches were lit and they cast a warm light over
the terrace as the dancing girls arrived to entertain the guests.
First, however, a famous Kashmiri singer named Tahira, accompanying herself on a sitar, sang several ghazals, the clas-
sical Persian love songs so adored by the Mughals.

The air was still and warm for mid-August. Yasaman had
picked at her food, her mind roiling with all that had happened over the last few days. *Married.* She was a married
woman now, and she hadn't even said a single word to her
husband, nor had he said a word to her. It was an interesting
situation in which she found herself.

"My daughter," Rugaiya Begum said softly in her ear. "It
is time for you to leave me now and go with your husband."

"*Go? Go where?*" Yasaman was startled. "Are we not to

live here, Mama Begum?" This was something that had never been discussed with her.

Rugaiya Begum looked distressed as she realized Yasaman's dilemma. "My child," she said gently, "I assumed that you knew you would live in Jamal Khan's palace. It is just across the lake."

"Will you live with us, Mama Begum?"

"No, my daughter. I will remain here."

"I will not go! I will not live in some strange place with some strange man who has not even had the courtesy to speak a single kind word to me!" Her voice was beginning to border on the hysterical.

"*Yasaman!*" Rugaiya Begum's voice was suddenly stern. This was not the time, she knew, for softness. "It was indeed foolish of us to believe you understood everything this marriage entailed. I will not, however, allow you to embarrass your father, or Yusef Khan, or your husband, with a silly fit. Go with Jamal Khan tonight. His palace, I am sure, is lovely. If you wish to make changes, I am certain he will not object. If, my darling, you are truly unhappy there, then I am certain we can persuade your prince to come and live here. Now, go into your chambers. Do what you need to do before you leave. Toramalli and Rohana will join you in the morning. If you can do without Adali, I should like to keep him here with me, but you will know better about that tomorrow after you have inspected your new home. Remember, the next time you consider indulging yourself in a fit of hysterics, that you are the Mughal's daughter. Whatever a Mughal may feel, Yasaman, we mask it from the world lest they use our feelings against us."

Yasaman arose slowly, almost heavily, from her place. Then she drew a deep breath as if clearing away her emotions. "I did not understand, Mama Begum. I shall only be a moment."

Rugaiya Begum patted her daughter gently and watched

her go, her heart aching at having had to speak so sharply to her. She could never remember having done so before.

"Why this great hurry to marry the child off?" Jodh Bai said softly to her old friend, "and do not tell me the official story about a betrothal having been made years ago as part of a peace between Kashmir and the empire. I know it to be a lie."

"Akbar is growing old, Jodh Bai," Rugaiya Begum began, but the tiny brown-eyed woman cut her off, raising her hand up in a signal to stop the older woman's speech.

"*The truth*, Rugaiya Begum. Not some tale that you and Akbar have concocted. Have we been so long apart that you cannot tell me the truth? This is the child that our sweet friend, Candra, bore our husband. The daughter that you have loved and raised with tenderness. *Tell me the truth!*"

"The truth would be a knife to your heart, Jodh Bai," Rugaiya Begum said. "I love you too much to be the instrument of any hurt that would strike you. Do not press me, I beg you!"

"*The truth!*" Jodh Bai insisted.

Rugaiya Begum sighed. She could indeed refuse to tell her friend, but Jodh Bai would not be satisfied. She would continue to press her, and she would certainly press Akbar. "It is Salim," Rugaiya Begum said finally, and she quickly explained before Yasaman returned and overheard them.

Jodh Bai's soft eyes filled with tears. "Ahhh," she said, "what are we to do with my son? That he would do such a thing fills me with pain."

"The matter is settled, my old friend," Rugaiya Begum told her. "Salim will now lose interest. Think no more on it, I beg you."

Jodh Bai nodded. "But Yasaman is so young to be married," she replied. "She does not even know this young man who is now her husband."

"His reputation is spotless, I assure you, dear friend,"

Rugaiya Begum said. "Even with such a threat hanging over my child, I would not let her go to someone unsuitable, but hush! She is returning." Rugaiya Begum rose to her feet and held out her hands to her daughter. "You are ready?"

"I am ready, Mama Begum," was the reply.

Discreetly, Rugaiya Begum and Jodh Bai, who had also gotten to her feet, escorted Yasaman across the terrace. They moved down a narrow flight of marble steps to the gaily decorated little boat, which was called a shikara, that awaited her. The boat was painted in red lacquer with beautiful designs in gold swirling across its surface. A brightly striped red and gold awning shaded the deep blue satin bench which was decorated with plump multicolored pillows. The boatman, who stood at attention in the stern of the little vessel, bowed low to the princess as the two older women helped her into the boat, each hugging her before they let her go.

"Your husband will join you in but a moment, my daughter," Rugaiya Begum told Yasaman. "May Allah bless your union and make you fruitful."

"Indeed, may you be the mother of many sons," Jodh Bai echoed Rugaiya Begum's good wishes. "I will come and see you before we return south."

"Thank you, Mama Begum. Thank you, my aunt." Yasaman looked straight ahead, not daring to make eye contact with them lest her fears suddenly overcome her again and she begin to sob. This marriage was becoming quite terrifying. She almost cried out when she heard their footsteps retreating up the staircase. Instead she concentrated upon Ali, the fisherman, who, with his sons and most of their adult family, were crammed into their fishing boats nearby. Shyly she waved to them, and was rewarded with a small cheer, their good wishes for her happiness floating across the quiet waters of the lake.

"They will capsize themselves in their enthusiasm," a masculine voice said. The boat tipped with his weight as he entered it and sat next to her. He knew the story of Ali's luck. Everyone on the lake did. It would appear the tale had not been an exaggeration.

"Would you have me be rude and ignore them?" Yasaman said sharply. She would not look at him. How easily he could converse with her, she thought. Yet he had still not formally greeted her. Oh, why did I agree to this marriage? she wailed silently.

"And is the Mughal's daughter never rude?" he gently mocked her. "Indeed, if it is so, then I have gained a true paragon for a wife."

"Ohhh!" Her head snapped about and she glared up at him. "You, my lord, are absolutely insufferable! Not once since our marriage vows were spoken have you had the courtesy to speak to me! Now you would give me a lesson in good manners? And mock me unfairly in the bargain? If the law allowed it, I should divorce you this minute!"

Jamal Darya Khan was overcome with a deep urge to laugh, but he manfully contained himself. The incredible turquoise-blue eyes blazing up at him were the most beautiful eyes he had ever seen. What was more, his sense of fairness forced him to admit that she was absolutely correct. It was he who had been rude to her by ignoring her totally.

He had been not just a little annoyed at the way his father and the Mughal had maneuvered him into this marriage; but that was certainly not the girl's fault. Allah only knew, the match was extremely advantageous to his family. His bride, too, had undoubtedly been coerced in some benign manner. She was very young, and so beautiful that even sitting here next to her, he could not quite believe that this incredible loveliness was now his.

"Princess," he said gently, "custom, as you know, keeps a bride and bridegroom separated on their wedding day." Reaching up, he undid her pale gold gauze veil to revel in her features fully. "Ahhhh," he sighed deeply, one hand covering his heart in an expressive gesture as the other hand delicately traced the outline of her jaw, "you are so extravagantly fair, my bride!"

A blush suffused her cheeks. She was unable to continue looking at him. Her black lashes lowered, brushing against her creamy skin, even as her anger melted easily away. She felt momentarily tongue-tied. She felt shy; suddenly gauche. None of it was comfortable for Yasaman, who was used to being in full control of her emotions.

He tipped her face up. "Look at me, my bride. I have never seen eyes as magnificent as yours are. I am totally overcome with your innocent beauty. Tell me that you forgive me. I would not have you angry with the man whose heart you have so quickly captured."

She caught his gaze in hers, thinking how meltingly beautiful his own velvet-brown eyes were. Then her mind began to function once again and she said, "You have me at a disadvantage, my lord. I am unused to such compliments and know not how to answer. Should I tell you that you are even more handsome than my brother, Salim?"

He smiled into her face, and she thought that his smile was a lovely one, his teeth so pearly and white against the pale gold of his skin. "I am happy that mine are the first lover's praises to be heard by your dainty, shell-like ears," he told her.

Yasaman giggled. She could not help it. *"Shell-like ears?"* She giggled again. "My lord, such an outrageous term for a less than beautiful feature of the body. I may be young, but I am not a fool."

Jamal Khan laughed aloud. "I swear," he told her, "I am so carried away by your beauty, Princess, that I begin to babble." Then he took her hand in his. "Can we be friends now?"

"I am not certain," she said quietly. "I do not know you yet, my lord. Indeed, I know little about you except that you are an obedient son."

"And I know as little of you, my princess, except that you were born to the Mughal and his English wife, but raised by Rugaiya Begum."

They sat silently for the next several minutes as the shikara was swiftly rowed across the lake. Then Jamal Khan spoke once again.

"Look, my princess! The moon is rising."

She looked in the direction that he was pointing and said, "It was full on my birthday, a few days ago. Alas, it has begun to wane."

"Even as my love for you begins to grow," he promised her.

Yasaman blushed again. His words were so wonderfully thrilling. She had never imagined that a man could say such lovely things, and what was more, he sounded so sincere. Perhaps, just perhaps, this marriage was not a bad thing and would work out. Still, she knew not what to answer him back. So she remained quiet.

He took her hand in his and squeezed it gently. Then, raising it up, he turned it over and placed a warm kiss upon her palm. "Such a dainty hand, my princess," he murmured low. "I am overcome with the thought that soon that hand will caress me."

The touch of his mouth upon her skin set her heart to leaping in her chest. *"Ohhh,"* she gasped as the sensation suffused her body, leaving her weak with the simple pleasure his first kiss had created.

Now it was his turn to be silent. How old was she? he wondered, trying to remember. *Thirteen!* She had just turned thirteen, but she already had her woman's flow, he had been told. Allah in his heavenly garden! She was, it was quite obvious, so innocent; not that the knowledge wasn't pleasurable. He found himself suddenly overcome with delight that no other man had touched her, or complimented her, or kissed her lips as he soon intended kissing them.

She was a pure virgin, although she would certainly know what was expected of her; what was to come. She would have her Pillow Book, as all brides did. He had never possessed a virgin before. The few women he kept in his zenana were experienced in the arts of pleasing a man's sensual nature. There was nothing that he could teach them. Yasaman, however, was totally untutored, and it would be he who would instruct her.

The little boat lightly bumped the marble quay of his palace. The boatman sprang out and made the vessel fast. He then discreetly disappeared from view, leaving them alone. Jamal Khan stood up and stepped from the boat onto the quay, turning to draw Yasaman behind him.

"At present you will not find my . . . our home as fine a palace as your own. You have my permission to do whatever you so choose to make it a pleasant and happy place for us to live in, my princess. Buy what you will. The servants have been perhaps lax in their duties since my mother's death. They are now in your charge, as are all matters pertaining to this household."

"It will take me a few days to explore everything, to learn which of the servants is lazy, or simply negligent because of lack of guidance," Yasaman said. "My own body servants, Toramalli and Rohana, will be here tomorrow. Mama Begum would like Adali, my high steward, to remain with her, but I may need his services."

"Your chambers will have been prepared for you," Jamal Khan told her. "I left orders with the women in my zenana to do so. They should best know what pleases another woman. Come now, Princess."

"A moment, my lord," Yasaman said. "I must speak with you, but do not wish to be overheard by any."

"What is it, my bride? You have but to ask me and I will grant you your dearest desire," he vowed romantically.

"Perhaps not when you have heard me out, my lord," she said softly.

He looked curiously at her, but nonetheless said, "Speak."

"I am your lawfully married wife, my lord, but we do not yet know each other. I know that men will couple for pure pleasure with women unknown to them. I, however, as you know, have been gently raised. I find it repugnant that you would expect me to yield my body to you tonight, or any night for that matter, until some affection has grown between us. I do not know if you will understand this, but I must, nonetheless, appeal to you. I have been enjoined by my mother to accept my lord's decision in all matters, and so I will." She lowered her eyes modestly.

"And if I say I want you in my bed tonight, Princess, you will accept my decision in the matter?" he asked her.

"I have no real choice, my lord, do I? As an obedient wife I must, though it would grieve me greatly to find your lust far greater than your desire for relations between us to be pleasing and harmonious," Yasaman told him sweetly.

Jamal Khan laughed. "No girl your age should be so skilled with words, my princess. You are, I think, much too clever for a simple man of Kashmir as myself. Better you turn your talents to giving your husband a thousand and one nights of supreme delights. Still, I am of a mind to grant your request. Several days ago we knew naught of each other, yet now we find ourselves bound together for a lifetime. Should my lusts threaten to overwhelm me, the women in my zenana know well how to please me, as you will also in time. For now let us just be friends."

"Mama Begum says that the best marriages begin with the making of friends, my lord. She has never lied to me," Yasaman said.

"Come," he said, taking her hand once more. "Let me show you your new home. I am astounded that the servants are nowhere in evidence to welcome their new mistress, and the torches are not lit upon the terraces, or the lamps within the house."

He led her up the steps from the quay onto a lovely marble terrace similar to the one bordering her own palace. Here, however, she could see even in the waning moonlight that the plantings were obviously neglected, overgrown, or simply dying. Yasaman frowned. Here was something that would need her immediate attention. Gardens were most important to the Mughals. This year's growing season was almost done, but there was next year's to consider.

They passed beneath an arched entry into the building, and Jamal Khan said, "These are your quarters, Princess, but again I ask, why are there no lamps lit? I left orders your chambers were to be cleaned and made welcoming for you."

"The servants are obviously lax, my lord," Yasaman observed. "I must, I can see, take them in hand at once."

"Since my mother's death there has been little order here. I am a man and do not know what to do," he replied helplessly.

Yasaman laughed softly. "As long as you are well-fed and have clean clothes," she teased him, "you are content, eh, my lord? As long as you can hunt and there are pretty women to sing to you and tend to your more passionate nature, eh? But what of the ladies in your zenana? Is there not one amongst them who might have directed the servants?"

"It is not their function to direct servants," he said somewhat sheepishly. "Their duties lie elsewhere, as you surely know."

Yasaman's mother had always said that men, no matter their ages, were like little boys. Yasaman had had virtually no contact with men of any sort in her short lifetime, other than those comfortable gentlemen who belonged to her immediate family. She was certainly beginning to understand now exactly what Mama Begum had meant. As long as his personal needs were fulfilled and his life was not uncomfortable, Jamal Khan had been content to let his palace fall into disrepair, his servants run wild, and his women lie lazily about like fungus on a tree. These things were going to change, she thought grimly to herself, but right now she needed sleep. It had been an exhausting day.

"We must find someone to light us lamps," she told him in her most practical tone.

"The zenana is through that door," he said, pointing into the half gloom of the room. "This is the women's part of the palace."

Together they crossed the chamber. Jamal Khan opened the door, ushering his new wife into his zenana. Warm, golden light greeted them. The room was well-furnished with brightly upholstered couches, large floor pillows, low tables of ebony and brass, and fine rugs covering the marble floors. There were five women in the zenana. They looked up at the entry of the prince and his bride with fluttering cries of greeting. They arose to surround Jamal, totally ignoring Yasaman as they nudged her aside quite rudely.

"My lord, you have returned!" The speaker was a small, golden-skinned woman with long, straight, blue-black hair and slanted black eyes. She wound herself sinuously about Jamal Khan, looking adoringly up at him.

"Samira, why is the princess's apartment not prepared? Did I not tell you to direct the servants to do so?" He disentangled the clinging woman from his person.

"My lord! I am not some steward, or wife, to order servants to the cleaning of a house. I have been trained only to give my lord pleasure." She pouted up at him for a brief moment and then smiled winningly. "Would you like me to give you pleasure now, my lord? Is that why you have joined us? We are ready to do your bidding, are we not, ladies?" She glanced at her companions, her eyes narrowing dangerously.

"Oh, yes, my lord! Let us offer you pleasure!" the others chorused obediently, clustering about him again, touching him intimately.

Jamal Khan was at a loss for words, embarrassed at the open rudeness his women were displaying, but before he might gather himself to act, Yasaman said coldly, "Who are these creatures, *husband*? If they are indeed the ladies of your zenana, they are obviously as ill-trained and as bad-mannered as your servants. I can see that I have my work cut out for me."

Four of the women wilted visibly beneath her scorn, but the one called Samira put her hands upon Jamal Khan's shoulders, pressing herself boldly at him. She looked into his face and said, "My lord! Will you allow this girl to speak to me thusly? Am I not your favorite woman? Chastise this stranger at once!" Samira stamped her little foot for emphasis, her long hair swinging about her.

Her outrageous words spurred him to action. The prince put Samira aside more firmly, now saying angrily, "It is you whom I will chastise, woman! On your knees, all of you! This is Yasaman Kama Begum, the daughter of the Grand Mughal. *My bride.* She is mistress here, not any of you. You knew I was to bring her back tonight. Yet you have deliberately disobeyed me when I requested that you prepare a welcome for her. You will be beaten, every one of you!"

The four quiet women threw themselves at Jamal Khan's feet, crying, "Mercy, my lord! We would have prepared the welcome as you bid us, but Samira would not let us!"

Now Samira wrapped herself about his feet, sobbing piteously. "*They lie!* How could I, one small woman, prevent them from doing their duty?" And then she said slyly, "Besides, my lord, if this is your wedding night, will not the princess be spending it with you?"

"Of course I will," Yasaman said quickly. "Let us end this, my lord, and tomorrow I will see that all is made aright. Show mercy, my prince. There shall be no beatings. I am tired now and would seek my bed."

"You will not get much sleep, Princess, if our master loves you as well as he loves us," Samira said boldly, smirking as Yasaman paled visibly.

Jamal Khan slapped Samira for her less than subtle innuendo, but she did not flinch, pleased to have gained his special attention once more. Turning from her, he gently led Yasaman from the zenana.

They were only halfway to the door when Yasaman pulled away from him and, whirling about, said, "You would do well to seek your beds, ladies. Your master will not need your *services* this night; and tomorrow a new regime will begin, altering life as you have known it here. I have little use for idleness."

"So," he said, as he led her through the little palace to his own quarters, "the little kitten I have married is, when aroused, a fierce tigress." He chuckled, amused. She had not only surprised him, but he found he had been rather pleased by her swift retaliation toward Samira's viciousness. Many a wife's life had been made difficult by a clever concubine. He could already see Samira would not have that advantage over Yasaman.

"You would do well to remember that I am the tiger's daughter," Yasaman said fiercely. "The woman, Samira, is rude beyond my bearing. There can be but one mistress in this house. I will not tolerate any further disrespect."

"You are indeed the mistress here, Princess," he assured her. "This house and all in it are yours to command. Know that I will not allow any irreverence to be shown toward you. You are not just the Mughal's daughter, Yasaman Kama Begum, *you are my wife*."

They entered his quarters, and again all was dark and there were no servants to be found. Still, the room was placed in such a manner that the moon lit it well enough for them to find their way.

"Where am I to sleep?" she asked him.

"The bed is there," he said, pointing to a large bed set upon a raised dais.

She walked to it and wearily sat down. "Where will you sleep, my lord?"

"There is but one bed here, Princess. We will share it," was his answer.

Yasaman quickly stood up. "You promised me that we . . ." She flushed and struggled for the right words.

Jamal Khan walked over to his young bride and tipped her face up that he might see it. "It is a promise I will keep, Princess," he told her seriously, "however, there is but one bed in this room. I do not intend to sleep on the floor."

"Then I will," she declared stubbornly.

"No," he said, "you will not. Lady, do I appear to be some lust-crazed monster, unable to survive the night without a taste of your sweet flesh? If you prefer," he told her wickedly, "I can return to the zenana and leave you in full possession of this chamber."

"*No!*" Yasaman squeaked. She would sooner die than allow those wretched zenana women to know what transpired, or did not transpire, between her husband and herself. *And he knew it!* "Do not be smug," she told him tartly. "Even here in the dark I can tell you are smirking."

Jamal Khan chuckled and began to remove his wedding finery.

"*What are you doing now?*" she demanded nervously.

"It is not my habit to sleep in my clothes," he said mildly, and he turned from her as he continued to slowly disrobe.

She stood silent and still for a long moment, and then began to undress herself. She hadn't realized how warm she had been until she removed her heavily embroidered angyakurti. She laid it, along with her orhni, carefully upon a chair. To the pile she added her slippers, and her jewelry, and finally her sari. "I have nothing with which to brush my hair," she grumbled as she undid the bejeweled braid and ran her fingers through her dark hair. "Nor can we wash." She shook her head. "Never again, my lord, will you be subjected to such a poor welcome in your own house, I promise you." She lay down upon the bed and turned her back to him.

Jamal Khan watched her undress from beneath his thick, lowered lashes. To stare would have been rude and would have embarrassed or frightened her. He hadn't forgotten his glimpse of her in her bath. But that had been so brief. Just enough of a look, he thought, to whet his appetite, but not enough to allow him complete knowledge of her magnificent form. He was astounded by the lush curves and full breasts of the young girl who was now his wife. How easily, he thought uncomfortably, he had promised to honor her virtue; but of course that had been before he had seen her full beauty in his bed.

He lay down upon the other side of the bed, turning his back to her back. "Are you asleep?" he asked her softly.

"No," she answered.

"Before we sleep," he said, "will you do one thing for me?"

"What is that, my lord?" She moved just slightly.

"Will you say my name? We have been married for several hours now, and I have yet to hear my name upon your lips, Yasaman."

"Good night, Jamal," she replied. "God grant you a good rest."

"Good night, Yasaman," he murmured low. *I do not think I will be unhappy being your husband, my proud princess.*

They slept.

5

When Yasaman awoke she was confused for a moment as to where she was. Then, as memory reasserted itself, she rolled over to find she was alone. Had he gone to one of his women? she wondered, surprised to find that she was jealous. Why should she be jealous of a man she hardly knew? She arose and wrapped her sari about her body, annoyed that there was again no water for washing. The servants were worse than lax. Walking out onto the terrace that bordered the chamber, she was pleased to find that it was early morning. Jamal was seated at a table eating, quite alone.

Joining him, she said, "Good morning, my lord. I am pleased to see that at least you have been fed. Would that someone show me the same courtesy." She helped herself to a banana.

"Indeed, Princess, you do have your work cut out for you," he agreed, watching her neatly peel the fruit.

"This is all mine to oversee?" She waved her hand airily. "You will not interfere with my management or authority?

Last night you said so," Yasaman reminded him, wanting to be certain she understood.

"You are the mistress here, Princess," he said. Then he smiled at her. "You are very beautiful, Yasaman, when you sleep."

"Only when I sleep?" What had made her say such a thing? Was this flirting? She blushed.

He laughed. "You are beautiful at all times," he replied diplomatically, and then he amended his words teasingly, "at least as far as I can see, my princess, based upon our short acquaintance."

He was flirting with her! Her heart accelerated and her cheeks grew even pinker. She distinctly felt at a disadvantage. She wished she were safely back in her own palace across Wular Lake playing with her cats, but she was not. She was a married woman; no, not yet a woman. She was a bride, and she had a formidable task ahead of her if she was to put her husband's house in order. She could see he thought her an amusing child. She would gain his respect and hopefully, in time, his love.

"I have much to do, my lord," she told him formally. "Please excuse me," and she turned away from him, hurrying back into the little palace.

Her sense of direction being good, Yasaman left her husband's apartment, making her way through the building and back into the women's quarters. In the daylight her own rooms appeared in even worse repair than they had last night. They were dingy, old-fashioned, and appallingly dirty. She could see that once they had been elegant, for the tiles were beautiful and the walls inlaid with lapis, carnelian, malachite, mother-of-pearl, coral, and obsidian. Obviously, they had belonged to his mother, and even more obviously, they had not been cleaned in the years since her death. She mentally noted that the rugs were missing.

"My lady!" The dual voices belonged to her twin servants. Toramalli's glance swept the room. "Surely this is not your chamber," she said, shocked, as a puffball of dust wafted by her foot.

"I'm afraid it is," Yasaman said, "but we cannot blame the prince. His servants and his women are out of control for lack of a guiding hand. We have our work cut out for us, I fear, if we are to make our new home livable."

"My lady! Come out onto the terrace and see," Rohana said indignantly. "The trunks sent two days ago remain where our people delivered them! We are only fortunate it did not rain. Although the dew has not been good for them, there is no damage, I am relieved to report. It is untenable that you should be treated in so shameful a fashion!"

"Run quickly, Rohana, and tell our boatman I must see him before he returns across the lake," Yasaman instructed her servant.

The girl called down to the boatman. He leapt from his vessel and hurried up the steps to the terrace, bowing low before the princess.

"Take a message to my mother," Yasaman told him. "Say I must have Adali and at least half a dozen of our best house servants this very morning without delay."

"Yes, Princess!" the man replied.

They watched as he departed, rowing the boat, it seemed, with more speed than he usually did.

"*Now*," said Yasaman, "we must regain control of my lord's zenana. There are five women in it, of whom one is particularly bold. The others seem afraid of her. We must either pull the stinger from this queen bee's tail or destroy her. She will eventually decide her own fate."

Rohana and Toramalli followed their mistress as she made her way back into the building and into the zenana. Though silent, their eyes widened at the luxury of these quarters compared with Yasaman's apartment. Neither twin was stupid. They quickly realized the deliberate insult leveled at Yasaman by the zenana women. A look of understanding passed between them. They knew what these foolish creatures did not know. Their mistress might be young, but she was very determined and she would have her way. If Yasaman had made up her mind that she would take total control of this palace and of the prince, then she would.

"Good morning, ladies," Yasaman said coolly, and not even waiting for an answer, continued, "Samira—that is your name, isn't it? Present these others to me immediately."

Caught totally by surprise, Samira complied with the authoritative tone of Yasaman's voice before she even realized what she was doing. By then, of course, it was too late. She had already lost face before her companions. "Layla, Nilak, Lalita, and Thyra," she finished curtly, wanting to claw the little smile from Yasaman's face.

"Lalita, you are of India, are you not? You will always stand when I speak with any of you. It is only mannerly," Yasaman chided them firmly.

The woman called Lalita arose quickly and politely bowed to the princess. "Yes," she said. "I come from the south, Golconda."

" 'Yes, my lady,' " Yasaman gently instructed her. "You must each remember that I am the mistress of this house now. I must be treated with dignity."

"Yes, my lady," Lalita replied. She was a tiny, dark-skinned woman with a sweet expression on her round face.

"Layla. Nilak. You are Persian, I believe," Yasaman said. "Layla means Dark as Night in the Persian tongue. Nilak, a bluish lilac flower. Your names are as lovely as you both are."

The two young women, pale-skinned with blue-black hair and black eyes, arose and bowed. "Yes, my lady. Thank you, my lady," they chorused brightly. Samira scowled.

Yasaman's head turned to look at the young woman with the golden hair. She had never before seen such hair. "Thyra? What sort of a name is that?" she asked.

Thyra stood now and bowed almost arrogantly. "I am Greek," she said, and her cool eyes looked directly at Yasaman, but the princess did not flinch. Finally, with a small smile and a shrug of defeat, Thyra lowered her gaze.

"Do you not wish to know where I come from?" demanded Samira, irritated to be so ignored.

"Wherever you come from," Yasaman told her, "they did not teach you any manners!"

"I come from Samarkand," Samira said proudly. "My father was a great general!"

"Your father was a common soldier who bred you on a street whore," Thyra said mockingly. She had had all she wanted of Samira. "Why else would you be a slave in a zenana?"

Samira grabbed up a small fruit knife and snarled, "I will cut your heart out for that insult, foreign bitch!"

With lightning speed Toramalli slapped the knife from Samira's hand, much to the woman's surprise. "Do not ever arm yourself in my mistress's presence again," she said fiercely, "else I will have the pleasure of killing you."

Samira's rage turned from Thyra to Yasaman's servant. *"Who,"* she demanded angrily, *"are you?"*

"I am Toramalli. I guard the princess now, as I have ever since her birth. You are not fit to breathe the same air she does, woman of the streets. You had best beware me."

"Enough!" Yasaman said quietly. "Samira, please go through the palace and seek out the servants. Tell them that I would see them immediately on the main lakeside terrace.

"I am not your messenger," Samira said rudely. "Find the servants yourself, *my lady!*" She stood boldly before Yasaman, feet apart, chin thrust forward. "I am the prince's favorite. You cannot make me do anything I do not want to do."

"I do not repeat a command twice," Yasaman said softly. "Go now as I bid you, or you will find yourself for sale in the marketplace before the noon hour, Samira. Believe me when I tell you it is within my power to do so." Then Yasaman turned on her heel and left the zenana, followed by her two faithful women.

When she had gone, Thyra laughed. "You had best do as

she says, Samira. She is young, our master's bride, but she will, I can see, have her way. Or if you wish, do us the favor of being more disobedient. None of us would be sorry to see you go."

"Go yourself," Samira replied. "I am not that little girl's slave. I belong to Prince Jamal. Her threat is meaningless, Thyra. Do you think he would let his wife sell any of his women? She is daring with a boldness that comes of having had a man's lingham up your yoni for the first time.

"She thinks he loves her and will let her do whatever she wants to do. She will quickly learn differently. I will speak with our master when he comes to us tonight, and he will come. A woman can lose her virginity only once. After that she becomes like other women, distinguishable only by her degree of erotic skills. I doubt a carefully nurtured little royal blossom has such skills as we possess."

"Do not be a fool, Samira! This girl is not just a wife. She is the Mughal's daughter," Thyra said. "She was married to Prince Jamal for a reason. Already there are rumors that the Mughal means to give our master Kashmir to rule in his name. That will only happen, however, if the Mughal's daughter is a happy bride. Now go and do her bidding, lest her wrath fall on all of us!"

"You are the fool, Thyra!" Samira snapped. "This princess is an inexperienced girl! He will use her vigorously until she is with child. Then he will have done his duty and not bother with her again. Do you think he will find her fascinating when she is fat and swelling like an overripe melon? A Mughal's daughter is for breeding sons and nothing more. We are the important women in his life, not that whey-faced bitch!"

"I will go and fetch the servants," Lalita said to Thyra. "As long as they appear, the princess will not know which one of us did her bidding. She will be satisfied, and we will avoid a confrontation." She hurried out.

Samira smiled smugly. Then, taking up an ivory comb, she began to dress her long hair.

"Samira is right, of course," Layla assured Nilak and Thyra. "She is very knowledgeable regarding men."

"Perhaps, and perhaps not," Thyra replied. "She cannot predict with certainty if the prince will lose his heart to his new wife or not. Zenana women are for young, unmarried men, *and* old married men. There is a period between the two when we are simply not needed. Now that our master has taken a wife, he may take three more. What use are we to him then?

"We might escape this princess's wrath if we are pleasant company and do not anger her. I know that is too much to ask of you, Samira, isn't it? Our days here, ladies, are numbered, I fear. Prepare yourself. This woman of Samarkand will seal our doom sooner rather than later. Then we will find ourselves on the block once more."

Layla and Nilak looked unhappily at each other, but Samira just laughed at Thyra's words and continued to dress her hair, dipping her comb into heavily scented musk oil. Thyra shook her head. She wouldn't be sorry to find herself away from Samira, who, she thought, would sow discord even in paradise.

The servants were surprised to find themselves summoned by a woman from the zenana. The zenana women were rarely seen but by those few female slaves who brought them their daily food and occasionally cleaned their chambers. The servants' life was a good one because the prince, their master, required little of them. They had more than enough to eat, and comfortable sleeping quarters as well. Most spent their days at leisure, fishing or sunning themselves, or working in the little gardens they cultivated for themselves. They sold this produce of Jamal Khan's land for extra rupees, with which they purchased little luxuries and forbidden wine.

Yasaman awaited them on the lakeside terrace, her foot tapping impatiently. She was flanked by Adali, Rohana, and Toramalli. The servants fell to their knees, their heads touching the terrace floor; then they sat back upon their heels, looking up expectantly at their new mistress.

"Who is high steward here?" were the first words she spoke to them.

"The steward died a year ago, gracious princess," came the reply.

"Who are you?" Yasaman demanded.

"I am Hassan, the head cook, gracious princess."

Yasaman saw the gauze mask hanging about Hassan's neck. Of course he was the cook. She should have noted it sooner, and would have were she not so angry. "Since there is no high steward here, the high steward from my own palace will take immediate charge. This is Adali, and he speaks with my voice. You will obey him in all things, unquestioningly and with dispatch. There is much work to do here. You have badly neglected your duties; but I will not blame you entirely, for there was no one to oversee you. This is my lord's home, and all will be harmonious for him from this day forth." She smiled briefly at them, then, turning, departed, Rohana and Toramalli walking in her wake.

Adali looked out over the nervous faces. "I was with the princess's mother," he began, "and I have looked after Yasaman Kama Begum's household since her birth. *I cannot be bribed.* The past is past. Today you each begin anew. That is how my mistress wishes it to be, though frankly, I think her too lenient in this case. Beware of my wrath. I do not possess her kindness. Now, we have much work ahead of us. The princess's apartments must be ready by sunset for her habitation. Hassan the cook!"

"My lord steward?" the cook spoke up quickly.

"For supper the princess wishes a fresh lake fish, broiled. A roasted chicken, and perhaps a small curry. She will speak with you later as to the prince's likes and dislikes. She, however, prefers simple meals and enjoys a variety of fruits and vegetables."

"Yes, my lord steward!"

"You and your kitchen help are dismissed. I will question the rest of you, each in his turn," Adali said, and proceeded to do just that. As each department of the household staff was identified, the eunuch set them about their tasks until he was finally alone on the terrace. With a satisfied smile, he hurried off to his mistress's apartments.

"All the cleaning in the world will not make these rooms a pleasant place to be," Yasaman wailed as the servants worked about her.

"Let me send for your own things from your own palace," Adali suggested. "The furnishings here are outdated and old-fashioned. It will not take long to have them brought across the lake."

"The walls are impossible," Yasaman said. "The designs are caked with filth, and there are stones pried from them that will take months to repair."

"We will hang carpets and tapestries, my lady," Adali soothed her, "and once your own furniture is in place, it will seem quite friendly. Where are your trunks?"

"Upon the terrace where our people left them two days ago," Rohana told him, frowning. "There is also no private bath for our mistress, Adali!"

"Where are the women's baths, then?" he asked her.

"In the zenana," Rohana said. "What are we to do, Adali? Our mistress cannot share a bath with those *creatures* of the prince's."

He nodded in agreement. The whole situation was absolutely untenable. This is what came of having to arrange a hasty union for Yasaman Kama Begum. This palace was absolutely not ready to receive her, let alone any decent woman. She could not remain, Adali decided. "My lady," he said to his young mistress. "I would suggest that you return to your own palace until we can set this one in order. Let me speak to the prince. I know he will agree with me. It will take time to make these rooms fit for your habitation."

Yasaman looked about her. To return home to Rugaiya

Begum would be such an anticlimax, but she was a realist. There simply wasn't any choice. The furniture in her apartments was worn or rotting. Their efforts to clean the place were resulting in clouds of dust. She sneezed several times, and then she burst out laughing.

"I will sleep in my own house," she told them, "but I must remain during the day to oversee the renovations. The salon of the zenana is quite large, Adali, and there is a fountain in the room. Let us call the builders and take a portion of that room to make a private bath for me. The plumbers can run piping beneath the floor into the new bath for a water supply." She sneezed twice more. "Go to my lord, Adali, and tell him of what we would do. He will not gainsay us."

And, indeed, Jamal Khan did not. He returned to Yasaman's apartments in Adali's company and, looking about, grimaced. "You are correct, Princess, in your assessment of these rooms," he agreed. "It will take time to make them habitable. Do whatever you must. I will not deny you."

"Will you join me at night, my lord, at my own palace?" she asked. "There is more than enough room for you."

"I think it best, Princess, that I remain here to be certain our servants do not slip back into their slothful ways," he told her.

"Nonsense, my lord," Adali told the prince. "Go with your bride! I will oversee all. You will forgive my saying it, but you are not used to such things as the running of a household, my lord. I am."

"You are correct, Adali," Jamal Khan answered the eunuch gratefully. This Adali was a clever fellow who was obviously going to make life quite pleasant. "Time alone with my bride will give me time to get to know her better," the prince said. He smiled warmly at Yasaman, and she smiled shyly back.

"Go now," Adali encouraged them. "It is a fine late summer's day. The lake is perfect for a relaxing cruise. Rohana and Toramalli will return to you later."

"I will teach you to fish," Jamal Khan told his bride.

"Will I have to bait my own hook?" she asked him nervously, and he chuckled indulgently, thinking her charming even as he took her hand to lead her from the palace.

Behind them, Adali looked askance, while Rohana and Toramalli found themselves unable to restrain their giggles. Yasaman Kama Begum was a most experienced fisherwoman and had been since the age of five. She could also ride a horse astride like a warrior, and had been hunting for tiger and gazelle with her father many times. Like Akbar, she loved the chase and was fearless to the point of being reckless, much to the worry of Rugaiya Begum. Still, she was an expert at handling her own weapons, both bow and gun. Akbar and Salim were united in their admiration of her abilities, which had eased Rugaiya Begum's fears somewhat.

Adali chuckled. "I can see who will truly be in charge of this marriage," he said to his two companions.

"It is as it should be," Toramalli answered him pertly. "Men should confine themselves to making love and seeing their families can pay the merchant's bills."

"Bold baggage," the eunuch sniffed. "What makes you so wise in the ways of men?" Then he threw up his hands and sighed dramatically. "No! I do not want to know how you obtained your wisdom. It is better I think of you and your sister as sweet, biddable girls."

"We are indeed sweet, but perhaps not as biddable as you would have us, dear Adali," Rohana told him. "Still, together we all serve our mistress well, do we not?"

He chuckled once again. "Aye, we do serve her well. We have not failed Candra in that."

"Do you think she ever thinks of us, Adali?" Toramalli asked.

"I wonder what she is like today," Rohana replied. "Do you think she is still as beautiful as she was those many years ago? Do you think she found happiness again with her other lord? Does she think of our little mistress?"

"Questions! Questions!" the eunuch fussed at them, although if the truth were known, he had had the same thoughts of Candra. He recalled his last glimpse of her; pale, wan, half drugged; but with what part of her awareness remained, her concern was only for the infant daughter she had been forced to leave behind. Yes. He had thought of her many times. "These are questions we cannot possibly know the answers to," he grumbled at them as reality returned, "and while we stand idly chattering, our work awaits us.

Yasaman sat demurely in a small boat just off her own palace across the lake.

"It is really quite simple," Jamal Khan was explaining to his bride, thinking how sweet she looked in pale green trousers and matching bodice. He stood within the small vessel, balancing himself carefully, a bamboo fishing pole in his hands. "Just bait the hook like this and then you are ready." Demonstrating, he neatly dropped the fishing line into the water.

She sat, eyes wide, and asked, "Like this?" as she quickly baited her own hook and, with a quick flick of her wrist, sent her line into the lake.

Surprised, he asked, "Is it possible that you have done this before, Princess?"

"Perhaps," she teased coyly, struggling to keep the laughter out of her voice.

"Either you have or you haven't," he said, and the fact of how little he knew his wife was suddenly brought home to him.

"Ohhh!" Yasaman replied in answer, jumping to her feet. "I think I have a bite, my lord!"

"Stand still!" he ordered her sharply. Their boat was rocking quite dangerously.

"Ohhhhh!" she wailed again, eyes twinkling, her amusement bubbling over into gales of laughter as she moved backward and forward.

He realized too late that she was doing it deliberately. Jamal Khan lost his precarious footing, but as he tumbled into the water he shouted at her, *"Vixen!"* The water closed over him for a brief moment before he struggled to the surface. He splashed about, glowering fiercely toward the boat. To his shock, he realized that she was no longer in the little vessel. His heart began to pound furiously. What could have possibly happened to her? *"Yasaman!"* he cried frantically. *"Yasaman!"*

"You called, my lord?"

He turned about in the water to discover her bobbing quite calmly next to him. *"You can swim!"* His tone had an accusatory ring to it.

She laughed. "Of course I can swim. How could I grow up on this lake and not learn to swim? You swim. Did you have no sisters? Girls can swim as well as boys, my lord."

"And you fish too," he said, "don't you?"

Yasaman laughed again. "Of course, but you were so sweet to teach me that I could not resist teasing you just a bit. So now, my lord, you know three things about me. I swim, I fish, and I have a wicked sense of humor like my father. I had best warn you that I hunt and ride as well. I am quite proficient with bow, spear, and musket, it is said."

"There is something else I know about you," he told her as he treaded water next to her. His brown eyes twinkled mischievously.

"What is it?"

"You have an extravagantly beautiful body, Yasaman," and he laughed as she blushed.

"Villain!" she cried and, reaching out, yanked his dark hair before she dunked him beneath the waters of the lake.

"I was right!" he declared after he came up sputtering and laughing. It had never occurred to him that a wife could be fun. "You are a vixen!"

"Something else you have learned about me today!" she

mocked him, swimming away from him toward the marble steps that led down from the boat quay of her palace.

Chuckling, Jamal Khan gathered up his fishing pole, which was floating nearby. Putting it into the bottom of the boat, he pulled himself in behind it and paddled back to the shore.

Yasaman, having hauled herself from the water, was now wringing out her long black hair. Her sheer green trousers and her green and gold silk choli, a short-sleeved bodice, left little to the imagination when wet. Looking down at him, she once more felt her cheeks grow warm at the admiring look he gave her. He was wearing only a dhoti. She thought his muscled legs and smooth chest quite impressive. He tied their boat fast and climbed the steps to join her.

"It is fortunate we did not have to fish for our supper, my princess," he said mischievously.

Yasaman nodded. "I prefer curry anyway. I will ask Mama Begum to have the cook prepare lamb curry for supper."

"Where will we sleep afterward? There is nothing left in your chambers, Yasaman. It has all been taken across the lake to our palace."

"There are guest chambers, my lord."

"We will need only one," he replied. "As you did not want my zenana women to know of our little arrangement, I would prefer your servants not know. Servants gossip. It would quickly be all over Kashmir that Jamal Khan's bride was still a virgin. It is a state I do not think I will allow you to long retain. We are, I see, becoming fast friends."

"Why should anyone care if we are intimate or not, my lord? Is it not our business and no one else's?" His words disturbed her, but she instinctively knew he would keep his promise to her.

"That is true, Yasaman, it is our business alone, but it would still not prevent gossip. There would be those who thought me foolish to allow a maiden's fears to overrule my own desires. They would assume that I was weak and could be manipulated. If I am to govern Kashmir in your father's name, I must appear strong, even if my secret heart is soft. For the love and respect I feel for my own father, for the respect your father deserves of me, I will govern this province well."

Yasaman Kama Begum looked into her bridegroom's eyes with new regard. Loyalty to family and duty were things she well understood. She hardly knew this man, and yet she knew him quite well by his words. "I believe," she said thoughtfully, "that I can love you one day, my lord Jamal."

He smiled down at her; a smile of great sweetness, and then he gently caressed her face. "I believe I will learn to love you as well, my princess. A woman who can fish is indeed a pearl beyond price."

Yasaman burst out laughing. "You have a sense of humor too," she said. "You are the perfect man, my lord. Loyalty, duty, and humor! I can ask for no more."

"But there is more, Yasaman," he told her seriously. "There is my heart, and I offer it to you gladly."

"I cannot refuse so gracious a gift, Jamal," she returned softly, her heart beating a little faster. He was really the most romantic man she had ever met. When she had dreamed of a lover that short while ago, Jamal, faceless then, had been exactly what she had longed for. She could not wait to share her happiness with her brother, Salim. She would write him tomorrow. Salim, who loved his favorite wives deeply, would surely understand and be happy for her.

Watching them from a window in the palace, now hand in hand, Rugaiya Begum said a small prayer of thanks to Allah. Her instincts had been right in this matter. The handsome young Kashmiri prince was the perfect husband for her daughter, especially as neither of them had ever been in love before. Rugaiya Begum knew that her child was still untouched, for Yasaman had shared that knowledge with her, but even if she hadn't, Rohana and Toramalli had also told her. They had whisked the sheets from the prince's bed themselves this morning that they might protect their mistress's privacy. Without pressure the two young people would eventually fall in love and nature would take its sweet course. The older woman smiled, contented.

Several days later, Yasaman and her husband, assured by Adali that the prince's palace was now habitable, returned across the lake. Adali had told his mistress of his discovery that the zenana rooms were actually a part of her apartments. In Jamal Khan's mother's day there had been no zenana, he had concluded. All its rooms, including the lovely little marble bath, had certainly belonged to the prince's mother. The zenana women were usurping Yasaman's quarters.

"Share the bath for now, my lady," he counseled her. "I will see you have it to yourself whenever you want it. Perhaps the prince will not need a zenana in future."

Yasaman agreed with his wisdom, for she trusted the eunuch.

Akbar and his court departed Kashmir for Lahore and then Agra. For the first time in her life Yasaman remained behind. As the autumn deepened, she felt her energy rising along with a pure joy of living. She had never been so happy in her life. She loved her mountain kingdom, and she was, she realized, beginning to care for Jamal Khan. The more they were together, the more she got to know him and the better she liked him. He was not indolent like so many of the southerners she knew. He had no taste for intrigue or politics. He was a young man with an honest, straightforward outlook on life. As Akbar's unofficial governor, he worked hard at the rather dull business of the administration of the Mughal government in Kashmir. Jamal Khan was not a man to toil constantly, however. He liked to hunt, and he had taken Yasaman with him on several occasions. He was quite astounded by her facility with weapons, even proud of her talent.

As the days passed, he became more enchanted by the girl herself. He had not once visited his zenana since his marriage. It had become quite a sore point with Samira, who, unaware of the true relationship between Jamal and Yasaman, was convinced their neglect was Yasaman's fault. This was something she could not fathom. The princess was an untutored child. She, Samira, was a skilled courtesan. So were her companions.

Adali watched the situation until it had almost come to the boiling point. The zenana women were unhappy in their enforced virtue. The prince was growing restless with his noble chastity. As for Yasaman, she was irritable, beset by a longing she didn't understand, and euphoric and despondent by turns. She flung herself into seeing that her household ran perfectly. Adali decided that the time was ripe for the plan of action he had formulated in his wily mind the morning after the marriage had taken place, when he had learned from Rohana and Toramalli of their mistress's desire to know her husband better before they were intimate.

The prince hunted alone one chilly autumn day. He came home ill-humored, for he had found no game at all and had been caught several miles from home in a cold rainstorm.

"My lord," Adali petitioned him in dulcet tones, "you need the company of your zenana women tonight. I know you have kept from them since your marriage, but sometimes a variety of delights is just what a man needs after a disappointing day."

Jamal Khan thought on Adali's words. His pent-up energy was almost burning him from the inside out. There he was with a zenana of luscious treats, *and he had not had a woman in two months!* He had been patient. He was willing to remain patient, but where was it written that a man must be faithful to but a single woman? He didn't know any who were. His own father had a houseful of women. His father-in-law had forty wives, not to mention a zenana large enough to populate a small city.

The words were from his mouth before he could think another thought. "Tell the zenana women that I will join them this evening, Adali," he told his new high steward.

"Very good, my lord prince," Adali murmured deferentially. "Shall I tell the princess you will have your evening meal alone?"

Logic did no good. Jamal Khan felt guilty. The last thing he wanted to do was have a meal with his trusting young wife while contemplating an evening of lustful pleasures with his zenana. "Yes," he said. "Tell the princess my mood is foul and I would not inflict myself upon her. Tell her I will see her in the morning."

"Yes, my lord," Adali said, hiding his own delight. Bowing, he hurried off.

Disappointed, Yasaman nonetheless accepted the message. Men were as prone to moodiness as women, Mama Begum had often said. Rohana and Toramalli, alert to their mistress's state of dejection, tried to cheer her with her favorite chicken curry and lychee nuts in a honey syrup. Yasaman picked at her food and decided she was not interested in playing a game of chess with Rohana. She would retire early for lack of anything better to do.

She was awakened by the sound of soft music and laughter coming from the zenana. At first she was not even certain of what she heard. In her two months as Jamal Khan's wife, there had never been any unseemly noise from the other side of the wall. Curious, Yasaman arose and slipped out onto the terrace that she shared with the zenana. Standing behind a carved marble screen, she peered into the room, for the draperies were not drawn. Layla and Nilak were seated upon a divan lightly strumming upon stringed instruments. Yasaman cast her eyes about for the other women and gasped softly in shock, for Jamal Khan was with them.

They were all naked, she realized, and her husband stood quite still as Samira knelt before him, her hand firmly grasping his lingham as she suckled upon it. The golden-skinned woman's thighs were parted, allowing the Greek woman, Thyra, to lie with her head between them. Lalita lay atop Thyra, her head between the fair woman's legs, her hands outstretched to balance herself. For a moment the significance of the erotic tableau did not register on Yasaman, and then she gasped again.

Jamal Khan's fingers kneaded Samira's head strongly. His eyes were half closed, and deep pleasure was very evident upon his face. Yasaman stood very quietly, not even feeling the icy marble beneath her bare feet or the light chilly wind that had begun to blow off the lake. She was fascinated by what she was seeing. *It was a living Pillow Book.*

Thyra had begun to moan softly when the prince said to Samira, "Cease, woman! I will not be unmanned yet."

Samira looked up at him, her black eyes heavy with her own passion. Then swinging herself about, she bent forward in a kneeling position, her small round bottom facing her master. Thyra and Lalita rolled away from her, entwining their arms about each other as they frantically kissed. Jamal Khan knelt directly behind Samira.

"Enter me through the portal of Sodom, my lord," she begged him. "You know the pleasure it gives us both."

He pulled the twin halves of her bottom apart, and Thyra, seeing his need through the haze of her own lust, broke away from Lalita. Scrambling across the floor to her master, she grasped his great shaft and led it to the target. Jamal Khan grasped Samira firmly about the hips and began to press against the dainty, puckered orifice. For a moment it was unyielding, but then, like a bud, it began to open, giving way to the rigid rod of flesh that demanded entry.

She whimpered, but she also made an obviously conscious effort to relax for him, her back dipping lower. Suddenly the inflexible became flexible. He pushed through into her body.

Slowly, slowly, he screwed his way forward into her dense-
ness, even as her back arched more to facilitate him and she
wiggled her body with her rising pleasure. Finally he could
go no farther, and Samira purred with satisfaction as she felt
the pouch containing his seed slap against her flesh.

"Ohhhh, my lord!" she said huskily. "How I love being
the mare to your stallion! Use me! Use me, I beg you! Do
not be gentle!"

Watching her husband piston Samira with growing vigor,
Yasaman felt a stab of jealousy. Jamal had refused to join
her this evening for supper and chess because his mood was
foul? He certainly did not look as if his mood were foul now.
His look was one of smug satisfaction as Samira began to
howl and gasp beneath him. Then, with a great shudder and
a roar, the prince withdrew from Samira's body as she
sprawled forward sobbing with pleasure.

Immediately Layla and Nilak rushed forward, a basin of
scented water and love cloths in their hands. Tenderly they
bathed their lord's lingham as Lalita offered him a cup of
wine that had been laced with aphrodisiacs. He gulped it
down, grinning as his vigor was restored by both the wine
and the sensual ministrations of their hands. His arms about
Layla and Nilak, he escorted them a few feet to a large silken
feather mattress that had been placed upon the floor.

"Layla, my little flower," he said to her, and she giggled
as he pulled her down atop him. "Ride the stallion, little
flower," Jamal Khan commanded his zenana woman, but
poor Layla was so aroused by all that had already taken
place that she was scarcely atop her master when her own
pleasure quickly came and quickly departed.

"Ohhhhh!" she complained bitterly as shudders of delight
raced through her.

Jamal Khan laughed and lifted her off him. "Who will be
next, my beauties?" he teased his women. "I have a randy
lingham tonight that needs much attention."

Nilak and Lalita both attempted to mount their master,

and their frantic efforts dissolved into a quarrel between the two women that allowed Thyra to take advantage of the situation. Deliberately and with great care the Greek girl bathed his member once again. Then mounting him, she slowly sheathed his length within her own eager body.

Yasaman watched, fascinated as Thyra arched her back, her arms behind her that she might balance upon her hands. Thyra writhed sensually atop her master, making small, deep noises of satisfaction as she moved. Jamal Khan reached up and began to fondle his concubine's large white breasts, his fingers leaving faint reddish marks upon the girl's skin. The Greek's movements changed suddenly. Her hips began a frantic motion, and she was quite audibly panting and crying out by turns.

Yasaman did not even start when a soft wool shawl was wrapped about her. "He has betrayed me," she said softly.

"No, he has not," Adali told her. "He is a man, and men have needs that can only be satisfied by the flesh of a woman. You do not need to be told this, my princess. For two months you have held your husband at bay and he has been patient."

"I wanted to know him," she protested.

"I understand, but you would have gone on like this unless convinced otherwise, wouldn't you, my princess?"

"Sometimes," Yasaman told him as she turned to move away from the zenana scene, "I think I should be very afraid of you, my dear old Adali. I am not certain that you should know me better than I know myself; but then I remember that you love me, and so I cannot be afraid of you."

"Come inside," he said to her. "The night is cold, and you will catch a chill, my lady."

"Tomorrow my husband goes to hunt again," Yasaman reminded the eunuch. "He is meeting his elder brother, Yaqub Ali Khan, in the hills, and he will be gone for several days. Take the zenana women into the city and dispose of them. Thyra, Nilak, Layla, and Lalita leave with a good slave merchant. As for Samira, sell her yourself in the public marketplace. Surely some tribesman or brothel keeper will find her to his taste. Her greedy yoni will no longer entertain my husband's eager lingham. Just knowing she is in my house this night enrages me! I would kill her if I could!" Yasaman declared angrily.

"And the monies from the sale, my lady?" Adali inquired. "What shall I do with the proceeds of these sales?"

"They will go into my household treasury, Adali," Yasaman replied. "And gather together the workmen. Now that I am to reclaim my entire apartment, I want to redecorate it so that my husband will enjoy coming here. Do you think there is room for a nursery here?"

Adali grinned broadly. "Possibly, my lady, but when we must address that issue, perhaps it would be better to add an additional wing to the palace for the children. It would guarantee you and the prince your privacy. Lovers, I am told, prefer privacy, my lady." He helped his mistress back into her bed and drew the coverlet over her. "You will be lovers, Princess. I already see the dawn of love within both the prince's eyes and yours. It is time."

"Yes," she agreed with him. "It is time."

Adali left her, and Yasaman quickly slept. When she awoke she quickly learned that Jamal Khan had already departed, but he had left her a gift. Smiling, Yasaman undid the bejeweled silk handkerchief to find a fine blue and white porcelain bowl. She admired it, and then Rohana put it away even as Toramalli appeared with a tray laden with fresh, late melon, a boiled egg, yogurt, and bread with which to break her fast.

"Where is Adali?" she asked them.

"He has gone to the city, as you instructed, my lady," Toramalli answered softly.

"*They are gone?*"

"They are gone," her servant reassured Yasaman, and she could not help but smile at her mistress.

"Good!" Yasaman declared, and then for a brief moment she looked stricken. "I have never done anything so terrible," she admitted.

"They should not have been here when you first came two months ago as the prince's bride," Toramalli said indignantly.

"A man with a beautiful young wife does not need a zenana full of inferior women," Rohana added. "You are the Mughal's daughter, my lady, not the child of some provincial nobleman. It was insulting that the prince did not rid your house of those creatures!"

"Perhaps he was too kindhearted," Yasaman answered, "but now the deed is done. I hope he will not be angry with me."

Jamal Darya Khan returned home five days later. Although the sport had been good, he had been forced to bear the company of not just his elder brother, Yaqub, but his next elder brother, Haider. He did not like either of the men, both of whom had been grown when he was born. Throughout his childhood they had alternated between ignoring him and reminding him of his mother's inferiority in comparison with their two mothers. He bore them for the sake of his father. He would not have accepted Yaqub's invitation had he but known Haider would be with them. Yaqub was a braggart and a whiner. Haider, however, reminded Jamal of a poisonous snake. He was too wily by far.

His brothers were embittered with the loss of Kashmir to the Mughals, never mind the unsavory part that they had played in that loss. They were jealous that the youngest of their siblings had been honored with the Mughal's favorite daughter as a wife. They had heard rumors that Jamal Darya Khan would eventually be named official Mughal governor of Kashmir. They were martial, dense men of little vision. He had spent the entire time he was hunting with them explaining Akbar's reasons for giving him Yasaman.

When he left them, he was certain that they still believed the Grand Mughal's actions were a plot to hurt them. After all, it was Yaqub Ali Khan who was Yusef Khan's eldest son, and after him came Haider, not Jamal, as they had told him over and over again in the time he was in their sour company.

Consequently, Jamal Khan arrived home tired, irritable, and eager for some entertaining company. His zenana women had been most diverting the night before his departure. He had ignored them for far too long. It was a mistake he did not intend making again. He wanted a bath first, a good supper second, and then an evening of sport with his ladies. He grinned in anticipation, thinking about their silken flesh, their fine breasts, and their variety of sensual talents.

His naughty thoughts made his lingham bob up and down in the bath with a randy motion, to the amusement of his attendants. The male slaves teased him wickedly, praising his reputed prowess, suggesting he would wear himself out before it was time. Jamal Khan did not notice the looks that passed between his servants when he bragged that he would wear out every yoni in his zenana this evening, so eager was he for their erotic company. Instead, his servants suddenly grew quiet, bathing him and massaging their master with sandalwood oil. They wrapped him in a clean white dhoti when they were through, and Jamal Khan retired to his quarters for a light meal.

When he had eaten and was rested, he arose, walking leisurely through his palace to the women's quarters. He had not yet greeted his wife, but it would wait until morning. For now all he could think of was being entrapped between a pair of soft but firm thighs. He passed the door to Yasaman's chamber and moved on, but where the door to the zenana had been, there was now a solid wall. Confused, Jamal Khan stopped, thinking that he had been so engrossed in his own thoughts that he had gone too far; but when he turned and faced the wall, he could plainly see that there was but one door to the women's quarters—through Yasaman's chamber.

"Fetch the high steward," he told one of the guards at the door to his wife's chamber.

The soldier ran off, and Jamal Khan paced silently during the minutes it took for Adali to make his appearance.

"My lord?" Adali's robes were dancing about him. He had obviously run all the way, a fact the prince noted and was pleased by.

"Where is the entry to the zenana, Adali?" Jamal Khan demanded.

"That is a matter you had best discuss with the princess, my lord," Adali answered politely.

"I am asking *you*," Jamal Khan said through gritted teeth.

"My lord, I cannot answer you," Adali told him, and it was obvious that he was uncomfortable. "Please take this up with my mistress."

"I do not wish to see your mistress tonight, Adali," Jamal Khan told him, his anger barely in check. "I want to sport with my women in the zenana, but the door to the zenana no longer exists."

"Because the zenana no longer exists," he heard Yasaman say.

Jamal Khan whirled about, her words barely penetrating his mind, so great was his shock.

"Come in, my lord," she said, drawing him into her chamber. She shut the door behind him. He quickly saw that they were alone, and he realized she looked particularly beautiful tonight. Her silk skirt was black, flecked with small gold stars, and the fabric was so sheer he could see her slender legs through it. Her choli molded her breasts, her nipples visible through the black silk with its embroidered gold neckline and sleeves.

Jamal Khan looked about him. Something had changed. This was no bedchamber. It was suddenly a salon with comfortable divans, large pillows, tables of ebony inlaid with mother-of-pearl, brass tray tables and beautiful ruby glass and brass lamps, both hanging and standing upon brass pedestals. The gorgeous blue and gold parrot that Yasaman possessed was showcased in a corner. His tiny keeper Balna sat nearby, embroidering on a silken cloth which was to be a new cage cover. Fou-Fou was sprawled upon a divan in her usual reclining position, and the black kitten he had given Yasaman as a betrothal gift now lay by her side. Even the monkey, Baba, was there, eyeing the prince suspiciously as he silently peeled a small piece of fruit. The room had a comfortable, warm feeling to it, Jamal Khan thought as he looked about it. He couldn't ever remember it looking so fine.

He saw through the door that connected this room with the zenana, a bedchamber. "Where are my women?" he demanded, remembering why he was here.

"I have sold them," she said calmly. "Do sit down, my lord, and tell me of your trip. Was there much game? I do hope you brought back a deer. I love its meat!"

"You sold my zenana women? How did you dare do such a thing?" Jamal Khan was absolutely outraged by his wife's actions. He glowered at her fiercely. Then he was quite taken aback when she spoke to defend herself. It wasn't a defense. It was an attack!

"How did you dare to bring me to this place, my lord, without properly preparing it?" she countered, stamping her foot angrily. "In your mother's time, may Allah bless her worthy soul, there was no zenana here. These were your mother's rooms, and you gave most of them over to those low *creatures* while cramming your wife into a single chamber. Your women did not respect me, and no wonder! I was even forced to share a bath with them! There was no room for my servants or my things, and you obviously were quite oblivious to it all. Your only interest was in yourself.

"Well, I am the Mughal's daughter! I will not be abused

by you or by those females who found such dubious favor in your eyes. This is my home. You, yourself, gave me charge over it to do as I pleased. This apartment is simply not large enough for me and for any others. If you wish a zenana, my lord, then you must build another wing to this palace to house it. In the meantime, I have sold your women and taken the monies from their sale to decorate my rooms properly." She glared at him fiercely, daring him to dispute her.

Jamal Khan could only stare in amazement at Yasaman as he digested her words. *She had sold his zenana for monies to finance her decoration scheme?* Suddenly the humor in the situation hit him. What a woman she was! He began to laugh, and he continued laughing for several long minutes while she stood there before him refusing to be stared down. Tears of mirth ran down his cheeks. His sides ached. She was indeed the Mughal's daughter. He would get fine, strong sons and beautiful, willful daughters on her.

His laughter died as swiftly as it had begun. The getting of sons and daughters required a degree of intimacy that they had yet to attain, *and* he no longer had his zenana women upon which to slack his lusts. Yasaman Kama Begum was the most beautiful woman he had ever seen. The prince felt his desire rising. *He wanted her. Now. Tonight.*

"Having sold my zenana women," he said thoughtfully, "you must surely be prepared to serve me as they served me, Yasaman. You cannot dispose of them, yet continue to deny me."

She said nothing, but those incredibly fascinating turquoise-blue eyes of hers widened just imperceptibly. She was very still, like some wild creature about to be flushed from its cover. He reached out with an arm, his hand sliding about her waist to draw her near to him.

"You have not answered me, Yasaman," he said softly. "Are you ready to minister to *all* of my needs as a good wife should?" His other hand reached up to caress her face, which felt warm to his touch.

Her senses were swimming. She could hear the beat of her own heart in her ears. For a moment she couldn't even draw a breath. She felt as if she were being smothered. She cast her eyes about, instinctively seeking for help, but her servants, in the room but a moment ago, had suddenly all disappeared. *They were alone.*

He bent and kissed her forehead softly. "Yasaman, my proud princess, answer me."

It was as if the kiss had released her from some spell. "I am ready to be your wife, my lord," she murmured low. "You will have no need for any others now."

"Give me your lips," he replied, "and let us seal the bargain between us, my jasmine blossom." He brushed her mouth lightly with his and said, "You are so young, Yasaman. So fair. You cannot possibly have any knowledge of how great my desire for you is at this moment."

Reaching behind her, he unfastened her choli and removed it. Her full breasts enchanted him with their smooth roundness. He cupped them in his two hands, his thumbs lightly brushing the nipples. Her soft hiss told him of her arousal.

Next he undid her ghagra skirt and let it puddle about her ankles, rendering her totally nude. Standing away from her a moment, he enjoyed the sight of his wife as God had made her. He could feel his lingham straining the fabric of his dhoti. He, too, was aroused.

She stood silent and still, mesmerized by his warm brown eyes, shivering just slightly as the cool night air touched her skin. Or was it perhaps the touch of his hands upon her shoulders? He drew her near again. His fingers made small circles of sensation, smoothing around and down her back, over her buttocks and up again to touch her face once more. He held her head between his strong, gentle hands for a minute. Then his lips met hers once again.

Yasaman eagerly gave herself up to his kisses, her arms slipping about his neck in a welcoming embrace. She had been waiting for this all her life. The mouth on hers was warm and tender. It spoke to her without words, the firm but delicate pressure conveying the loving passion he felt for her. His breath was just faintly perfumed with mint, she noted, when in response to his silent signal she parted her lips and their tongues touched, circling each other in an erotic ballet of sweetly moist sensation. Yasaman sighed deeply, her own emotions stirring with innocent enthusiasm.

Content in his embrace, with eager little hands she undid his dhoti, bringing him to a natural state. Shyly but with growing boldness, she caressed him in return; stroking his smooth back, cupping his taut buttocks with her palms. Her breath caught in her throat as she felt his lingham, already firm, against her thigh. Her startled eyes flew to his face.

"I did not know that a virgin could arouse a husband so, my lord," she told him wonderingly.

"Perhaps not every virgin," he responded, "but certainly this virgin, my jasmine blossom." With a sweet smile he lifted her into his arms and walked toward her bedchamber.

"My Pillow Book!" she exclaimed to him. "I must have my Pillow Book else I cannot be certain what to do, Jamal!"

"Tonight," he told her, smiling again into her eyes, "I will guide you, my love, in all that you must know. Tonight I will teach you to enjoy passion. In the nights that follow, Yasaman, I will show you other ways of giving me pleasure, but tonight I will give you that special joy that only a man who loves a woman can give to her, and in doing so, I will gain equal joy. There is a saying from the *Ananga Ranga* which goes, 'How delicious an instrument is woman, when artfully played upon; how capable is she of producing the most exquisite harmonies, or executing the most complicated variations of love, and giving the most Divine of erotic pleasures.' " He lay her down upon the bed, joining her and tenderly caressing her breasts.

Yasaman watched him as he touched her; watched as her nipples responded to his touch, again filled with a dawning wonder as she felt her heart seemingly expand within her chest, radiating a warmth she had never before experienced. She did not know if it was love or desire that she was feeling, but whatever it was, it was most pleasant.

"In Lahore," she told him softly, "in the bedchamber of the woman who gave me life, there is a large shamsa upon the wall. In the center of the sunburst is a rosette of gold, red, and blue; and in the very center of the rosette is a circle inscribed with several verses. The first is from the *Kama Sutra*. It reads: 'Once the Wheel of Love has been set in motion, there is no absolute rule.' I think I am beginning to understand what that means, Jamal."

He drew slowly and sensuously upon the nipple of her breasts, sending a sensation of pleasure through her being. Then he said, "Do you love me, Yasaman?"

"I am not certain what love between a man and a woman is, Jamal," was her ingenuous reply. "You are most experienced in such matters, so I would ask you, do you love me?"

He pondered a moment and then he said, "I must, my Yasaman, else I should have beaten you for selling my zenana women off." His brown eyes twinkled down at her.

"Perhaps," she told him, "I care for you a little, my lord, else the thought of that bitch, Samira, in your arms would not drive me so wild with rage!" She pulled his head down and kissed him fiercely.

Jamal Khan's heart leapt within his chest. Marriage to a pleasant woman was the best he had dared to hope for, but somehow he had been blessed. He did love her. Her artless confession of angry jealousy told him that she did indeed love him, even if she was not quite certain of the emotion yet.

He kissed her back, nibbling upon her lips, tempering her fury with deep, slow kisses that set her to sighing with delight. He let his lips wander across her sensitive body, finding the hollow of her throat; the perfumed curve of a round shoulder; the deep, scented valley between her wonderful breasts; the flesh of her flat belly, which seemed to vibrate beneath his warm lips.

Yasaman sighed again. His mouth on her skin was like nothing she had ever experienced. Within, she felt a longing ache she thought would surely kill her if it was not satisfied. There was a sweetness between them that she had not felt when she and Salim had practiced those pages from her Pillow Book. Suddenly she knew that what they had done was wrong. Whatever Salim may have told her of the passion between ancient royals, it was wrong. *This was right!* She reached out and caressed the back of Jamal's neck with her fingers. His skin was so soft to her touch. She hadn't realized before that men had soft skin. His dark hair was silky as she twined her hands through it.

He brushed the soft flesh of her thighs, pressing gently between them, touching her more intimately. Her heart began to beat fiercely. She realized she very much wanted the sweet intimacy that existed between lovers. She wanted it desperately.

"Rid me now of my virginity, my lord Jamal," she begged him. "I find I am suddenly afraid of the unknown. I do not want to fear you. Take me quickly that my fears may ease and we may begin to enjoy one another!"

He understood her plea, but he also knew that the first experience with physical passion should bring not just pain, but pleasure as well. "Trust me, my blossom, not to harm you," he begged her.

Twisting his body about, he found her secret jewel with his mouth. His tongue touched the tender pink flesh with quick, sure strokes. When he had almost brought her into bloom, he swung his body over hers, preparing to enter her yoni.

Yasaman grasped his lingham between her two hands and guided him, her turquoise eyes never once leaving his warm, dark eyes. Slowly he penetrated, struggling with himself to go gently, hesitating just a fraction when he saw the shock of pain in her eyes.

"No!" she gasped, and thrust her young body up to absorb him completely, the pain slowly leaving her expression, to be replaced with a look of surprise.

It was then he began to move upon her, riding her as he would a finely bred mare, pacing himself to give her her first taste of adult pleasure before he took his own, watching the joy creep into her eyes; her cry of newborn ecstasy filling him with pure delight as he finally released his passion.

When, after their first bout with Eros, they lay content in each other's embrace, Yasaman said, "There is another saying inscribed upon that same shamsa I told you of, my lord. The second verse reads: 'Your being contains mine; now I am truly part of you. Together as one, we form an unbroken circle of love.' I did not fully understand that saying until now. Is it not right that such sweetness create another being?"

"Oh, Yasaman," he answered her, astounded by her youthful wisdom, "I think you understand far more than you even realize. The Mahabharata says: 'The wife is half the man, his priceless friend; Of pleasure, virtue, wealth, his constant source; A help throughout his earthly years; Through life unchanging, even beyond its end.' So, I believe, will be true of you. I am all the more fortunate for it, my jasmine blossom."

Yasaman pulled away from her husband and, raising herself up to balance upon her elbow, looked into his handsome face. Her own visage was pale with what was most certainly shock. "How did you know that verse from the Mahabharata, Jamal? Someone told you, of course!"

"Told me what?" he replied. "I have studied the Mahabharata, Yasaman. That verse was a particular favorite of mine. I always felt it described exactly how a man should feel about his wife. Perhaps it was my reason for not taking a spouse before now." He touched her face gently. "You are ashen, my love. What is it? Has our first shared passion been too much for you?"

"The verse you have quoted me from the Mahabharata, Jamal, is the third and final verse inscribed upon the shamsa in Candra's bedchamber. It is almost as if she has blessed our union, is it not?"

He was astounded by her words, but then he smiled. "Yes," he agreed. "Perhaps in a way she has, my love. Such a blessing is, I believe, very lucky for us. He kissed her tenderly. "Very fortunate indeed!"

❀

6

❀

Man Bai, the first wife of Prince Salim, was hysterical. She had always been a delicate creature with a highstrung personality, subject to fits of depression. Her servants sent for her beloved aunt, Jodh Bai, the Mughal's wife, who was also Man Bai's mother-in-law.

"My child! My child!" Jodh Bai gathered her niece into her embrace, stroking Man Bai's silky, perfumed dark hair soothingly. "What has distressed you so?" she asked.

For a time Man Bai could not answer. She simply wept on in a tragic, heartbroken fashion. The older woman comforted the younger as best she could.

"You must make the emperor s-stop!" Man Bai said finally.

"Stop what, my child?" Jodh Bai asked patiently.

By a supreme effort of will, Man Bai pulled herself together and said, "The emperor is angry with my lord Salim again. He is threatening once more to set my husband aside in favor of our son, Khusrau."

Jodh Bai felt a stab of irritation. She was disgusted with this game her husband and son played between them. Still, for her niece's sake she had to remain calm. "My lord Akbar is always saying he will disinherit Salim for one offense or another, Man Bai. He has never done it, nor will he ever really do it," she reassured the distraught woman.

"But this time," Man Bai told her, "my son, Khusrau, and my brother, Madho Singh, have joined forces. They speak openly about ridding the Mughal lion of the thorn in his paw. Oh, Aunt! I have raised my son to be loyal to his grandfather and his father. My wicked brother leads him astray. I am so ashamed!"

"The shame is not yours, Man Bai, but rather my grandson's and my nephew's. Do not fear, my child. There will be no rebellion against Salim, and my lord Akbar will never disinherit him. I will speak with my brother, your father, the raja of Amber. He will speak most forcefully, I assure you, with Madho Singh.

Man Bai, however, did not long remain reassured. That very evening, the evening of the first full moon of spring, the women of Salim's zenana gathered together to celebrate in the open courtyard. All were garbed in pink, and other than the moon itself, there was no light.

Nur Jahan, Salim's favorite wife, found herself next to Man Bai. "That traitor you have spawned deserves to die for his disloyalty, not to be rewarded with a rich and nubile princess!" she hissed in sweetly venomous tones.

"Do not dare to speak of my son so," Man Bai responded spiritedly. "He is a good boy and loves his father."

"An unnatural son who would rebel against his father," Nur Jahan retorted angrily. "Khusrau is no fit heir for my lord Salim.

"My lord looks among his other sons for a worthier heir. He is quite pleased, I am told, with Prince Khurram in particular. The emperor loves the lad too." Laughing at the stunned look on Man Bai's face, Nur Jahan danced gaily off.

Man Bai broke away from the other women to seek out

her husband. "Is it true," she demanded, "that you seek to replace my son with Prince Khurram?"

"At least Khurram is too young yet to rebel against me," he told her, meaning it as a jest.

Man Bai paled. Nur Jahan, bitch that she was, had obviously been speaking the truth. Salim had turned against their son, and why not? He had been appallingly disloyal. "Ahh, the shame of it," Man Bai whispered to herself hopelessly. Without another word, she fled the festivities. They found her in the morning. Dead. She had taken her own life by eating a lethal quantity of opium.

Salim was inconsolable over Man Bai's suicide. He fell back into his old habits of excess drink, now laced more heavily with opiates, and a general self-indulgence of the worst kind. His new companions were the absolute dregs of his father's court. They were greedy, ambitious sycophants who pandered to Salim's blackest moods, supplying him with whatever he desired, be it wine or young girls. A court news writer who was foolish enough to report the prince's behavior publicly was brought before Salim and murdered by being flayed alive.

Learning of his heir's latest atrocious behavior, Akbar decided to teach Salim a lesson once and for all. If his eldest son was to inherit his throne, his behavior had to radically change. If he was incapable of that change, then it was time for Akbar to settle the succession upon one of his grandsons. His other surviving son, Prince Daniyal, a charming, sweet-natured man, was an alcoholic incapable of little other than writing rather good poetry. Prince Murad had recently died from his overindulgence. Akbar shook his head in despair, and canceling his plans to visit his daughter in Kashmir, marched from Agra on August 21, 1604, toward Allahabad, where his eldest son held his own court.

The river between the two cities was low, and Akbar's boat stuck upon a sandbar. While he waited for it to be floated free, word came from Agra that Mariam Makani was ill and desired her son's presence.

"*Is she really ill?*" the emperor demanded sternly of the hapless messenger. He glowered at the man. "Or is this one of her ploys to wheedle around me so that I will not punish Prince Salim?"

"I will not deny, most high, that the dowager is upset by this new estrangement between you and the prince; but she is indeed quite ill," the messenger told Akbar. Then tears came into his eyes, for Mariam Makani was greatly loved. "My wife," the servant told the Mughal, "has served the dowager for forty years, most high. She fears that her mistress may be dying."

Akbar grew pale at the man's words. "*This is true?*" he half whispered fearfully.

The messenger nodded somberly. The emperor sighed deeply and sadly. Then he gave the order to return to Agra, and he hurried with all possible speed to his mother's side. Salim would keep.

Mariam Makani had shrunken into a mere wisp of a woman. She was so frail that she was unable to walk any longer. She had not left her bed in two months. Her skin was like delicate parchment. Her once fine black hair was now sparse and snow white. The pink of her scalp was quite visible to the naked eye. Only her dark eyes showed signs of vibrant life. As Akbar sat by her side, she clutched at him with a small, clawed hand.

"*Salim!*" she whispered.

"Safe from my wrath for now, Mother," he told her with a small attempt at humor.

"*He must come . . . after you,*" she said hoarsely.

Akbar shook his head. "I become more unsure each day as to whether he is fit to follow me, Mother. You know that I love him, but he seems to have inherited all the worst of the Mughals and the Rajputs. I may have to pass over him in favor of one of my grandsons if the empire is to survive."

Mariam Makani shook her head fiercely. *"No!"* she said. "Barbur. My Humayun. Akbar. *Salim!"*

He understood the importance of the Mughal succession to her, but Salim was half Hindu and most of his sons had even more Rajput blood in their veins than Mughal. It was a different world from the world of his grandfather and his father, who had spent most of their lives fighting for terri- tory on the subcontinent of India.

As if she sensed his thoughts, she rasped out to him with her last bit of strength, "Find a Mughal girl for Salim. Make their son your successor after Salim. These Rajput princesses weaken our blood." Then she closed her eyes and fell asleep, for the conversation had been much too much for her.

How simple it all seemed to her, he thought. *Find a Mughal girl for Salim. Make their child your heir after Salim.* Akbar sighed. If he were ten years younger himself, perhaps it would be possible, but not now. His mother, having lived to a great age, tended to forget that he was old too.

And then there was Salim. They had been at swords' points from the moment Salim realized that what Akbar had would one day belong to him. And Salim, impatient, had wanted his father's power and possessions from that time on. His mother's words, however, made Akbar realize that he would have to come to terms with his eldest son. Neither Khusrau nor any of his other grandsons were really old enough to rule India. His kingdom must have a grown man to come after him.

Mariam Makani never regained consciousness after her conversation with her son Akbar. She died on August 29, 1604, in her seventy-seventh year. Akbar shaved his head, his beard, and his moustache as a sign of filial respect; and led his nation in the brief, general mourning of his mother, whose death was much lamented by the general population.

Mariam Makani had been loved for her kindness and her charity to all.

A messenger was dispatched to Kashmir to inform Yasaman Kama Begum of her grandmother's passing. Yasaman wept at her loss. "You would have loved her," she told Jamal Khan. "Everyone did." Then she brightened. "But in the spring you will at least finally get to meet all of my family when we go to Agra for Papa's fiftieth-year celebration of his rule. Ohh, what a fine time we will have! And Mama Begum will come with us and be able to catch up on all the court gossip she so loves!"

"And I will finally get to meet your brother, Salim," Jamal Khan said to his wife.

"Yes," Yasaman replied. "It is important that you know Salim and that you like each other. Mama Begum says that Papa will confer the governorship of Kashmir upon you at the special Darbar that is to be held during the celebrations. We must choose a very special gift for my father, Jamal. It must outshine everyone else's. My brothers will give him elephants, as they always do." She laughed. "My father loves elephants, particularly good fighting elephants, and people who wish to please him are always gifting him with the beasts. The royal stables at all Papa's palaces are filled with elephants. Papa is always giving them away as gifts himself because he simply has too many of them. We will not give the emperor elephants."

"No," Jamal Khan agreed, thinking he liked the sound of her chuckle when she was happy and amused, as she was now. "A sapphire," Jamal Khan replied. "The finest sapphires in the world are mined here in Kashmir. Recently a particularly beautiful stone was brought to me. It weighs over three pounds and has been cut to show its perfection. I have named it the Wular Blue after this lake upon which we live."

He clapped his hands sharply and told the servant answering his summons, "Go to the high steward, Adali, and tell him to bring the Wular Blue to me."

"Very good, my lord," the servant replied.

Several minutes later Adali appeared and set a box before them upon the ebony table. The box was painted to a high gloss with black lacquer, and decorated with scenes of snow-covered mountains, lakes, and the natural flora and fauna of Kashmir. The corners of the lid were adorned with gold filigree which matched the lock. Adali undid the catch and slowly lifted the box's lid. Within, nestled upon a bed of white silk, was an enormous deep blue sapphire of such perfect beauty and clarity that Yasaman found herself at a loss for words.

"What do you think?" he asked her, smiling.

Yasaman finally managed to find her voice. "I have never seen anything so beautiful," she said. "It is rightly named, my lord. My father will treasure it."

"It is better than elephants?" he teased her.

She laughed. "Far better than elephants! My brothers will be green with envy at your cleverness. I, however, am not certain that I am not angry with you." She was unable to take her eyes from the magnificent sapphire.

"And why is that, my jasmine blossom?" he asked, his eyes twinkling at Adali, who was unable to restrain a quick grin.

"Why, my lord, you are to gift my father with this wonderful sapphire when you might have given it to me," she said, pretending an outrage she did not feel.

"The Wular Blue is a very special jewel," he told her in serious tones. "It is meant for an emperor." He nodded to Adali, who withdrew a flat ivory case from his robes. "This necklace, however, is meant to grace the pretty neck of a princess of Kashmir," Jamal Khan said, taking the box from Adali and handing it to his wife.

With a delighted little shriek, Yasaman snatched the box from him and opened it. Within was a marvelous necklace of perfectly matched deep blue stones set in pale white gold. "Ohhh, Jamal! They are wonderful!" she told him, lifting the necklace from the box to fasten it about her throat.

"The stones in the necklace are called the Stars of Kashmir," he said. "My father gave them to my mother when I was born. I thought you would enjoy wearing them to court in Agra. The wife of the governor of Kashmir should outshine all the other ladies."

"*Yes!*" Yasaman agreed, flinging herself into his arms and kissing him enthusiastically. "I will put all those gossipy old crows who are married to my brothers to shame. Even Nur Jahan will envy me the Stars of Kashmir. I know she has nothing half so fine," Yasaman gloated.

"Ahh, greedy one," Jamal said, taking her into his arms and cuddling her, "I am helpless before you. You have captured my heart. I shall never love another. Surely children born of such a love will be great in this land."

Children. Yasaman wanted children, but at first she had deferred to Mama Begum's wishes in the matter. Rugaiya Begum had worried that if a barely pubescent Yasaman became pregnant, it might injure, weaken, or even kill her. Consequently, Yasaman had taken a noxious brew that Toramalli made fresh every morning. It would, Rugaiya Begum told her daughter, prevent conception as long as she took it. Yasaman had dutifully followed her mother's instruction in the first year of her marriage, but shortly after her fourteenth birthday and the celebration of her first year as Jamal Khan's wife, she had ceased taking the medicine.

"I want his children!" she told Rugaiya Begum, and the older woman finally acquiesced, for Yasaman was obviously healthy.

In the company of her daughter and son-in-law, Rugaiya Begum traveled south to Agra during the early winter thaw. Akbar was to celebrate the beginning of his fiftieth year as India's ruler on the eleventh day of March. Both women knew that at this particular time Akbar would settle his affairs publicly a final time. Barring any further lapses in behavior, Salim would be declared once and for all his father's heir. That very open declaration should end any further attempts on Khusrau's behalf, hopefully putting a stop to the younger prince's thoughts of superseding his father to the throne.

Salim had been properly chastised for his horrendous behavior of the previous summer. In mid-autumn, using his grandmother's death as an excuse to see his father, he had come to Agra to pay Akbar a condolence call. He appeared publicly at the emperor's weekly Darbar bringing many gifts, including a fine diamond and two hundred elephants. Publicly, Akbar forgave his son; but he was not about to let him off as easily as Salim had anticipated. Elephants were not enough this time to placate the emperor.

The heir was arrested on his father's orders and brought to the zenana, where Akbar was awaiting him in Jodh Bai's apartments. The presence of his mother reassured Salim that he would not be harmed, but he was forced to listen to a catalogue of his sins as both his father and his mother chastised him.

His head ached from a night of debauchery and particularly strong wine. He was also aggravated because his father had ordered the arrest of his current best friend, Raja Basu of Mau. Fortunately, one of Salim's court spies had warned him in time, and Basu had been able to flee home. Knowing that sincere repentance was expected of him, Salim forced tears to his eyes. Weeping, he begged his parents' pardon for all the misery he had caused them. Tears and avowals of better behavior always seemed to work.

Jodh Bai, trusting and ready to forgive her son as ever, also wept. Then embracing Salim, she immediately forgave him.

Akbar was not so trusting this time. "You always say that you regret your bad behavior, Shaikho Baba, but I note you only regret it when you are caught and brought to account for that behavior."

"It is true, my father," Salim admitted, squeezing a few more tears from his eyes. "I seem slow to learn, but this time I swear I have done so. Never again will you have cause to chastise me."

"What kind of a ruler will you be," Akbar wondered aloud, "if you constantly give in to your own desires over the knowledge of what is good and right? Power is a gift, my son, but use that gift for ill rather than good, and eventually you will find your power taken from you. I have built this country province by province using all kinds of methods to gain my ends. Some pieces of land have cost me in the blood of my fighting men. Others I have won with the virgin blood of former enemies' daughters or sisters whom I have taken to wife.

"No ruler ever maintains total peace, Salim, and so he must be at peace with himself at least. The religious war constantly for men's souls and for the power it brings them. The Mughals and the Rajputs are never entirely comfortable with one another. The different castes struggle against each other. Now the Europeans have come, and I must balance them along with all the rest. It has never been easy, Shaikho Baba, but I have maintained control by virtue of my own self-discipline. This is a strength that you seem to have difficulty marshaling."

"I really will try harder, Father, I promise you," Salim said, his voice dripping with sincerity.

Akbar laughed, but there was little humor in the sound. Then he said, "And I will help you, Shaikho Baba, as I have always helped you." He signaled to the two guards who had brought Salim to him and had been discreetly awaiting his direction. "You have your orders," the emperor said. "Take the prince now."

Salim flung himself at his father's feet, his heart pounding. Had he finally gone too far? "Father!" he cried out, frightened. "Do you mean to murder me?"

Akbar looked pityingly at his eldest child. "No, Shaikho Baba. I will not harm you, but for your own salvation you will be locked away with my physician and two servants until such a time as I truly believe you have indeed repented your evil ways."

Salim looked to his mother, and when she smiled reassuringly, he let himself be led off, for of one thing he was certain. Jodh Bai had never in his life lied to him. So he was to be incarcerated for a brief time. It would not be difficult to endure, and then his father would be satisfied.

Salim quickly found, however, that his imprisonment was not to be one of luxurious restraint. He was brought to a marble bathroom which had been outfitted with several pallets for sleeping and nothing more. The food brought him was simple. Rice. Boiled chicken. Fresh fruit. Bread. *There was no wine.*

"I want wine," he demanded of his captors.

"The emperor has ordered that your system be purged of all evil humors, my lord," the physician, Sali-Vahan, told him. "He believes that wine and opiates cause a rotting of the brain. Your younger brother, Prince Murad, died of an excess of wine; and your youngest brother, Prince Daniyal, is so addicted to wine that he sees things that others do not see. Some of them are quite frightening, I am told. You may have either water or hot tea to drink."

"Wine!" shouted Salim. *"I demand you bring me wine!"*

The two servants restrained the prince, pinning him to his pallet as he first raved and demanded, then wept and tried to cajole, and finally threatened them with the most horrible of tortures if they did not instantly obey him. Dr. Sali-Vahan sat cross-legged next to his patient and began reading to him from the Koran.

For the next few days Salim alternated between anger and despair. Self-pity overwhelmed him for a time as, forced to face himself, he felt serious guilt over Man Bai's death. He wept for her, and he wept for himself. He thought of Khusrau, their son. He remembered the tears of joy she had cried upon his birth, proud to have given her husband a healthy son and heir. He recalled how loyal Man Bai had always been to him. He always came first with her. Once when he had been angry over some slight he imagined his father had given him, she had said, "Your father is India, Salim. One day you will be India and you will do things differently."

There was a lesson to be learned here. *India must come first.* Man Bai had said it, and his father had said it. *It had to be right.*

Jodh Bai came to visit her son and was shocked by his drawn appearance. "What has happened to him?" she demanded of the doctor.

"Do not worry yourself, gracious lady," Dr. Sali-Vahan told the prince's mother. "He had become dependent upon the delights of wine, and now that it has been taken from him, his body rebels. Soon both he and it will be in concert once again. When that happens, he will gain weight and be well."

"I will die from this treatment, Mother," Salim complained. "If I could just have but a tiny sip of wine to strengthen me."

Reassured by the physician, Jodh Bai was not taken in by her son's plea. "Wine is not good for you, Salim. We all know it." Then she said brightly, "Preparations have already begun for your father's fiftieth-year celebration. Yasaman and her husband are coming from Kashmir for the event."

"Yasaman is coming?" Salim's eyes visibly brightened.

"Yes," his mother told him. "You want to be well and healthy for your sister, don't you? She would be very distressed to see you in this condition. I know you will be pleased to learn that her marriage to Prince Jamal is a very happy one." Jodh Bai looked closely at her son, wondering if he still harbored a secret passion for his sister, as Rugaiya Begum had once claimed he did. Salim, however, showed only brotherly interest in the fact that Yasaman was coming.

"It will be good to see my little sister," he told his mother. "I look forward to meeting her husband. If my little monkey loves him, then he must be a good young man."

Jodh Bai was satisfied that whatever romantic notions Salim had once entertained for his half sister were now gone. "Tell me, Doctor," she asked the physician, "may the other ladies of the zenana visit with my son?"

"I think their visits would do him good, gracious lady," the doctor agreed.

Shortly thereafter, Akbar found himself assailed each time he visited the women's quarters by his wives, his daughters, his various female relatives, and his slave women. They pleaded with him to release Salim from his incarceration. The prince had at last learned his lesson, they argued. Too much more of the harsh treatment, and he would be a broken man. He must be released, the women chorused daily to the emperor.

Finally Akbar gave in, for he was weary of their constant pleas and growing short-tempered with their inability to comprehend that what he was doing to Salim, he was doing for his own good. The prince was paroled in the company of Dr. Sali-Vahan and rowed across the river Yamuna to his own palace, where he was, his father told him, to live in peace and sobriety or be disinherited. One more incident, the Mughal warned his heir, was all it would take. Salim swore he was a reformed man. Akbar, nonetheless, kept his eldest son under surveillance.

He need not have bothered, for having been forced to regain control of himself, Salim meant to remain in control, because his time was coming. The women in the zenana had been quite chatty. His father was not well at all, although he strove to hide it. Soon, Salim thought, I will be the Mughal. *And Yasaman was coming!* He did not want to be like his youngest brother, Daniyal, who was now so addicted to wine that despite his attempts to give it up, he could not do so. A man not in control of himself could not enjoy the power of the Mughal. *And Yasaman would be disgusted by a drunkard.*

The delegation from Kashmir arrived in Agra the first week in March. They were housed in a guest house within the palace grounds. Their quarters overlooked the Yamuna River and had terraced gardens that descended to the water. Jamal

Khan was astounded by Agra, for he had lived his entire life in Kashmir and had never seen a great city. Kashmir's own capital of Srinagar could not begin to compare to Agra.

It was a very ancient town, having been in existence in one form or another for over a thousand years. The major portion of the city was located on the east bank of the river and was made up of three- and four-story buildings. It was densely populated, and its streets were dirty. The warm climate encouraged whatever lay rotting in the streets to quickly become odoriferous. There were no city walls, but Agra was surrounded by a wide moat, and entry to it could only be gained by six gateways that had been erected by Akbar.

Every sort of business operated within the city. There were artisans of all kinds, iron workers, jewelers, miniaturists, goldsmiths and merchants who sold anything a person could desire. There were bazaars and shops of every description. The traffic, both two-footed and four-footed, was crowded and constantly on the move.

Yasaman hated it. Jamal Khan, however, was mightily impressed; and suddenly very aware of the total power his father-in-law wielded. He had never before realized Akbar's true strength. Now he was certain he should be a little afraid of this man who welcomed him so warmly, calling him "my son."

Jamal was particularly impressed by the great red sandstone fort that Akbar had caused to be built on the west bank of the river. It had been erected on the foundations of an older fort. The Mughal himself proudly showed his son-in-law the structure.

"The foundations go very deep, and the outer walls are nine feet in thickness," he told the Kashmiri prince.

"How high are the walls?" the younger man asked, craning his neck to look up.

"One hundred and eighty feet," Akbar said. "They are

utterly impossible to breach, and there are only two gates: a private gate on the south side for the family, and the public Delhi Gate on the west."

Jamal Khan admired the Delhi Gate, which was made up of two octagonal-shaped towers separated by an archway. The interior side of the gate had a beautiful facade with arcaded terraces above it, and soaring pinnacles, and kiosks atop the terraces. It was all highly decorated with patterns of white marble inlaid in the red sandstone. Above the gates the walls rose rife with battlements, breastworks, and loopholes for archers.

Red sandstone from Fatahpur-Sikri and gray stone from nearby Delhi had been used in the construction of the fort. It was surrounded by a moat sixty feet wide and thirty feet deep. Within the walls were five hundred separate buildings in the styles of Bengal and Gujarat. They housed the government and the court.

"I have never seen anything like this," Jamal Khan told his father-in-law. "It is magnificent!"

"Yasaman hates it," Akbar told him. "She has never really liked Agra, which is why she has spent most of her time in Lahore or Kashmir. She seems to have inherited her mother's constitution and dislikes the hot, sticky weather we have here in Agra."

"Yasaman does not like cities at all, I have discovered," Jamal Khan replied.

Akbar smiled at the young man and said, "Have you fallen in love with my daughter, Jamal Khan? When you speak of her, a soft look creeps onto your face and your voice is somehow different."

The prince flushed beneath his golden skin. "Yes," he said slowly, "I do love her, my lord." Then he smiled and a small chuckle escaped him. "I certainly must love her. Did you ever hear the tale of how Yasaman sold off my zenana women?"

Akbar burst out laughing. "No," he said, "I did not hear that story, but I cannot deny that it sounds just like the sort of thing she would do, my son."

"Yes, my lord. That sweet innocent you gave me as a wife can be a fierce, wild creature," Jamal Khan said. "You did not tell me that when you dangled her beauty before me. Oh, yes, I love her!"

"Tell me about the sale of your zenana women," Akbar said.

Jamal Khan proceeded to do so, first describing in detail each woman and her sexual prowess. When he finished, the emperor was laughing harder than ever.

"She used the profit to decorate her rooms!" he wheezed, delighted. "Her mother, Candra, had just as hot and spicy a temper," he told his son-in-law. "Ahh, I miss her!" Then he grew suddenly silent as sadness crept into his dark eyes.

For a moment Jamal Khan feared he had somehow offended the emperor. He did not know what to say.

The Grand Mughal broke the spell. "You will bring Yasaman to see me tonight? My son, Salim, will be with me. You have not yet met Salim. If you are to be the Imperial Mughal governor in Kashmir, you and Salim must like each other."

"I am certain we shall," Jamal Khan assured the emperor. "Yasaman loves him very much, and how can I fail to like someone whom my beloved so adores? With your permission, my gracious lord, I will pledge my fealty not only to you, but to Prince Salim as well."

"It is good," Akbar said, nodding.

In the evening, Yasaman, gowned in a rich, deep purple sari banded in gold, a necklace of large amethysts set in gold about her neck, went with her husband to visit her father. All of the Mughal's wives, surviving children, and grandchildren were also there. Yasaman was warmly welcomed, and her husband, particularly handsome and dressed all in white, was admired and fussed over. Rugaiya Begum beamed proudly as her daughter introduced Jamal Khan to her two elder sisters, Shahzad-Khanim Begum and Shukuran Nisa Begum, who had not been at her wedding nineteen months ago.

"He is beautiful, I will admit," Salima Begum said, coming to stand by Rugaiya Begum, "but you should have been a grandmother long since."

"Yasaman was just thirteen when they wed," Rugaiya Begum reminded her fellow wife. "They waited a time before consummating the marriage."

"Aiiiii!" Salima Begum sighed lustily. "The way he looks at her! Did Akbar ever look at any of us that way?"

"He looked at Jodh Bai and Candra that way," Rugaiya Begum said, her tone amused. "I remember it well."

"You remember the pain it caused in your heart," Salima Begum said low. "It is always that way when a first wife loves her husband too well. You do, old friend, but then our dear lord loves you back. He loves you enough to let you remain in Kashmir with Yasaman."

"I like it there," was the reply. "I am my own mistress now, Salima. I run my palace to suit me, and I answer to no one any longer. Yes, I quite like it!"

"I almost envy you," Salima Begum said, "but if I lived alone in my own palace, I would have no one to talk to, and there would be no gossip to brighten my life. No, I think I must remain as I am and where I am." She chuckled.

"The most gracious, the most honorable, the most high, Prince Salim Muhammad, enters the gathering! Make way! Make way!" intoned the servant at the door.

Salim stood for a moment, his dark eyes sweeping over the guests. He was dressed all in white, his jama coat brocaded and worked with both gold and silver threads. His patka sash was cloth-of-gold sewn all over with tiny diamonds. The small turban on his head was white silk with a decorative fillet of gold brocade sewn with pearls and diamonds, wound transversely about the turban. On his feet he wore slippers with pointed toes, which were decorated with gold and silver threads to match his coat. The slippers were called Salim Shahi in his honor.

Yasaman. Where was Yasaman? There! He spied her speaking with their sisters. A young man was with her. Salim strode into the room and went directly to his father, who sat upon a cushion beneath a gold canopy. He prostrated himself humbly before Akbar. The old man certainly did not look well at all. It would not be long now, Salim thought. Soon he would have everything he had ever wanted. He would have India. He would have incredible power. *He would have Yasaman!*

He felt himself being raised up, and lifted his head to look into his father's tear-filled eyes. "Father," he said, and kissed Akbar.

"Shaikho Baba, my most beloved son," the Mughal replied, and returned his kiss. "You are most welcome in my house. Now go and greet your mother and the rest of the family."

With a smile and a most correct bow, the prince obeyed his father. He saluted Jodh Bai quite affectionately. Having seen Yasaman, he was feeling very expansive now. He kissed each of the aunts and salaamed to his wife Nur Jahan and the Khandesh princess who was the mother of his second son, Khurram.

"Shahzad! Shukuran!" He hugged his two eldest sisters.

"Salim! Salim!" There was an impatient tugging of his sleeve.

"Aram-Banu, my dear, you grow lovelier each day!" he complimented the lady Waqi's daughter as he gently detached her clutching fingers.

Aram-Banu beamed with pleasure at his flattery.

"And who is your beautiful companion, my sisters?" he teased.

"Salim! Do you not recognize our little sister, Yasaman?" Aram-Banu giggled innocently.

"This cannot be my little monkey," the prince declared, pretending surprise, much to Shahzad and Shukuran's amusement and Aram-Banu's delight. "My Yasaman was an ugly little girl the last time I saw her."

"Villain! I have never in my life been ugly," Yasaman said. "Why, I am told I was even a most unusually beautiful baby!"

"Who grew into a vain young girl," he teased her.

"*Salim!*" Yasaman stamped her brocaded foot. "Is this how you greet me after almost two years, my brother?"

"No!" he told her, and swept her up into his arms. "This is how I greet you, my Yasaman!" He kissed her, his lips taking possession of hers, his tongue quickly darting in and out of her mouth with incredible sensuality. Then he released her. It had all been done so swiftly that Yasaman wasn't even certain she hadn't imagined the unseemly passion in his embrace.

She laughed nervously, pushing away the uncomfortable thoughts that had suddenly crowded into her head. "I am happy to see you, too, my brother," she said, forcing a smile onto her face.

Their sisters had melted back into the crowd of relations and close friends as the prince took Yasaman's hand in his. "You have grown more beautiful, if that is possible, my sister," he told her. His glance was warm. Nay! It was hot! "Marriage, I can see, agrees with you," he continued. "Your husband is a good lover, then?"

His words, and the attitude behind them, made her feel edgy. She was not imagining things, and for the first time in her life, Salim discomfited her. "I am very happy," she said stiffly.

"Do you love him?" Salim pried further.

"Yes, I love him, my brother." This was becoming most bothersome.

"Where is he, this little princeling of Kashmir? I would meet him, Yasaman, and decide for myself if he is the right man for you, *and* if he is the right man to govern one of my provinces for me."

Yasaman's turquoise eyes flashed angrily. "*Your provinces?*" she said softly. "Our father sits upon his throne yet, brother. He is no shade, or do you plan another of your little rebellions even as we come together to celebrate Father's fifty years upon his throne?" She yanked her hand from his grasp.

"A woman capable of great anger is also capable of great passion," he murmured.

"Your words are unseemly, my *brother*," Yasaman told him, and turned away from him.

His hand fell upon her bare shoulder, for she had chosen to wear no choli in the heat. His fingers pressed cruelly into the soft flesh. "I would meet your husband, my sister," he said.

She could not face him, but she still asked, "What is it you want of me, Salim?"

"That you sit by my side when I inherit the throne, Yasaman. You know that I have always wanted that," he told her.

"I am your sister, Salim. My place is by my husband's side," she answered quietly, unable to believe what she was hearing.

"*I want you!*" He spat the words urgently.

She could not keep from facing him, and so she turned about, only to be shocked to her core by the desire she saw in his eyes. "*Salim!*" she repeated. "*I am your sister!*"

"In ancient Egypt royal brothers and sisters wed," he said to her. "Have you forgotten all that I told you when you were a child, my beloved Yasaman?"

Yasaman suddenly softened, thinking that Salim's affection for her might make him understand the impropriety of his passion. "I am not a child any longer, Salim. We both know that what you are suggesting is a sin against nature and against all the religious faiths of the world. This thing you want cannot be. Put it from your heart and mind, I beg you, my brother. Look at our father. Though it pains me to admit it, he is dying. Soon you will be the Grand Mughal. My husband and I will rule our beautiful Kashmir most faithfully in your name." Reaching up, she stroked his cheek in a soothing gesture. "Come now and meet Jamal Khan, my brother. You will like him, I promise you. You can trust him, I can assure you. Come."

Taking his hand in hers again, she led him across the room to where her husband stood speaking with his own father and brothers, who had been invited to Akbar's celebration.

Seeing her, Yusef Khan salaamed, but Yasaman said, "No, father of my husband. It is not necessary that you salute me thusly. It is I who should honor you." Folding her hands together, she bowed to him. Then looking up, she smiled and greeted her two brothers-in-law, Yaqub and Haider. She had only met them briefly once before, but she had decided she did not like them. For Jamal's sake, however, she was pleasant.

Yusef Khan and his two elder sons now salaamed to Prince Salim, who nodded politely in return.

"Brother," Yasaman said, "this is my husband, Jamal Khan." She turned to the younger man. "My lord, this is my dearly loved brother, Salim, of whom I have so often spoken."

Jamal Khan salaamed politely to the brother-in-law who would one day be his overlord. "I am happy, gracious lord, to finally meet you. I pledge my fealty, as Allah is my witness."

Salim felt bitter jealousy pouring through him as he surveyed this handsome, polite, most correct young man who had stolen Yasaman's heart away from him. More than anything, he wanted to destroy Jamal Khan, but he had not survived this long by being stupid. His mouth turned itself up in a cordial smile. He held out his hand to the Kashmiri prince. "Younger brother," he said, "it is I who am pleased to finally meet the man who has made my little monkey so happy. I gladly accept your fealty and promise you that whatever my father ordains will remain in effect as long as you live, even after the Mughal passes from memory."

The two men shook hands, and Yusef Khan rejoiced in his heart of hearts. Kashmir was once again his family's, *and* without another drop of blood being shed. Jamal had pleased the very difficult Prince Salim, who had publicly promised that even after the Mughal's death, Jamal Khan would remain ruler of Kashmir. Yusef Khan beamed happily upon the prince, his three sons, and the adorable princess who had made it all possible. His kismet had taken many turns, but he was satisfied.

He did not see the bitter looks shared by his two elder sons. Salim Muhammad did, however, and smiled to himself, well pleased.

"Your brother Salim was most cordial to me," Jamal Khan said to his wife later that night when they had returned to their guest house. Yes, he thought, Salim had been pleasant. Yet some inner instinct warned him to beware. He could not shake it off.

"Salim can be very difficult, even with those of whom he is fond," Yasaman said slowly. "He is my brother and I love him, but you must never trust him entirely."

"But I must remain on his good side, my love," Jamal Khan answered. "Despite what he says, I think that what the lord Akbar gives, the lord Salim can take away."

"When he is Mughal," Yasaman told her husband, "my brother will no longer be called Salim. He decided a long time ago that he would change his name to Jahangir, which means World Seizer. It is not inappropriate. Salim has been

seizing everything he could get his hands on since childhood, my aunt Jodh Bai says."

Jamal Khan laughed. "You do not seem to dote upon him
like all the other women in your father's house. Why is that?"

"I love my brother, but I also know that he is nothing
more than a man like other men," Yasaman said carefully.

"Not quite like other men, my blossom," Jamal Khan replied. "Your brother will inherit a great kingdom and have
the power of life and death over us all. No, he is not like
other men."

The night was sultry, particularly for early spring. Yasaman wore a peshwaz with nothing beneath it. Jamal Khan
had divested himself of his court finery as well and wore a
dhoti.

"I do not want to continue speaking of my brother," she
told him, smoothing her hands over his chest. "It is hot
inside. Let us go out onto the terrace. Perhaps there is a
breeze off the river to cool us."

The sky was clear and silky black. A full white moon
made it almost as light as day and blocked their vision of all
but the brightest stars. The terrace off their bedchamber
hung over the river, although to the right and left there were
gardens that ran down to the water. A bird, tricked into
believing it was day by the moon, sang sweetly in a tree
somewhere nearby. There was the scent of roses in the warm
air. The river below flowed smoothly by with but the faintest
whispery sound. Across the river and around them the city
was almost silent. The occasional sound of music from some
tavern floated on the gentle wind.

The tiles of the terrace floor were still warm beneath Yasaman's feet. She threw off her gauze peshwaz, complaining,
"How I hate this heat so early in the season! It is a damp
heat unlike that of our Kashmir summers. On our lake it
does not even feel this hot in my birthday month, and it is
but spring here. Can you imagine what it will be like two
months from now? It will be totally unbearable."

"Your father told me that you have your mother's constitution," he answered. Allah! She was the most beautiful woman he had ever known. In the time that they had been here in Agra he had seen many lovely women, but there was no one like Yasaman Kama Begum. Already his loins were tightening in anticipation.

She flung her head back, rotating it to remove the stiffness from her neck and shoulders. Her breasts thrust themselves forward temptingly, and he succumbed, his hands fastening about her waist, his dark head lowering, his tongue snaking out to lick at her nipples.

Yasaman murmured and she lay her hands upon his shoulders, arching her body with pleasure.

"Temptress," he groaned, and she laughed softly.

"Would you rather I not tempt you, my dear lord?" she asked.

He nipped gently at her breasts, and she squealed even as he slid to his knees before her. "You are mine, woman!" he growled into the soft flesh of her belly.

Yasaman shivered, and wondered if all wives enjoyed their husbands as much as she enjoyed Jamal. Did passion always get better? How innocent she had been before her marriage. Other than her brief encounter with Salim, she had really known nothing. A Pillow Book told a woman nothing of reality. Every time she and Jamal made love, Yasaman realized that she still had so much more to learn.

He slid his hands down to fondle her buttocks, drawing her closer. His cheek rubbed against her belly as he nuzzled her. Instinctively she shifted in his embrace, parting her legs just slightly. His head moved lower and his thumbs gently parted her nether lips. She quivered again with anticipation even as the tip of his tongue touched the sentient little jewel of flesh her plump mont had concealed before being exposed to his view.

"Ahhhh," she breathed softly, her body arching slightly.

His tongue began to tantalize that tiny nub, tormenting

her deliciously and provoking a surprisingly quick burst of pleasure that left her feeling warm and content. He laughed happily and said, "You are such a greedy creature, wife. Can you never wait?".

She kneaded his shoulders, replying, "Can I not have more, my lord?"

"You may have as much pleasure and as much passion as your little heart desires, my jasmine blossom," he promised extravagantly.

"Get up, Jamal!" she ordered him impatiently. "It is now my turn to take the edge off of your appetite so we may enjoy the rest of the night at our leisure."

He arose and, wrapping her in his arms for a moment, they kissed deeply, their lips almost bruising in their intensity. Then Yasaman slipped to her knees before him. His lingham was totally engorged and thrust out to her.

"Ohhh," she said in a teasing tone, "this naughty fellow is every bit as eager as his female counterpart." She grasped her husband's male member in one hand, the other hand moving around to stroke his taut buttocks. Her tongue snaked out and encircled the deep ruby-red tip of his manhood. "Hmmmmmmm," she murmured, and then took him in her mouth.

Jamal Khan stiffened with almost painful pleasure as her mouth began to draw upon him. Her skill was such that had he not been absolutely positive of her virginity when they had first come together, he would have believed her the most skilled of courtesans. But she had been a virgin. A virgin with an incredible appetite and an equally incredible aptitude for sensual delights. There was little she did not enjoy or was not willing to do. He groaned as her tongue and lips worked him to a fever pitch. Being encased in her mouth was, he was certain, like being in the mouth of a volcano. Her tongue was like silken lava, swirling and flowing all around him. When he found himself in danger of imminent explosion, he grasped her dark head with his fingers and begged her through gritted teeth to cease her wonderful torture.

Reluctantly Yasaman obeyed him through the mists of her own desire. Bending, he raised her to her feet again and they looked deeply into each other's eyes. This silent communication between them had been there from the beginning. Jamal Khan lifted his wife into his arms and carried her over to the striped silk double couch where he lay her down. Yasaman held out her arms to him and he came into them.

Near their terrace was a small tower used by the Muslim clerics attached to Akbar's court to call the faithful to prayer five times daily. Within the tower Prince Salim stood viewing the terrace of the guest house. Hidden within the deep shadows of the structure, he watched his sister and her husband through the carved latticework, his face dark with lust. Jamal's buttocks contracted and relaxed as his lingham thrust back and forth within Yasaman's yoni. Salim half closed his eyes and imagined himself in his brother-in-law's place. Her love passage would be hot and tight, but she would gladly accept his mighty lingham even as she was now accepting that of her husband.

Jamal's seed overflowed his wife's womb, and, laughing together at the wonderfulness of their passion, they bathed each other's parts with the love cloths their servants had thoughtfully left earlier upon the terrace along with a basin of scented water. Once more they began to make love, kissing and caressing each other with growing fervor while the man in the tower above them continued to observe their deep and increasing desire for one another. Salim reached down and began to massage his own lingham, which was hard with his need.

Jamal Khan lay on his back upon the couch. Salim watched, fascinated, as his sister roused her husband once again, her dark hair spilling over his loins as she teased him with lips and tongue. When she deemed the time appropriate, Yasaman mounted him, lowering herself over his manhood, absorbing him slowly, inch by precious inch, her firm thighs grasping his narrow hips to hold them both steady. Leaning back upon her arms, she began to ride him, her beautiful face a mask of tempestuous, excited feeling. Her head thrown back, Salim could see her eyes were closed, her lips half parted. He could hear her small mewling cries in the stillness of the night. Jamal Khan reached up with both hands and, grasping her full breasts, began to fondle them as she moved upon him. Very shortly thereafter Yasaman collapsed upon him, once more spent.

Everything he had believed her possible of, Salim thought, she was indeed capable of doing. Yasaman was absolutely his match upon the field of love. He could scarcely wait to conquer her himself. Strangely, he found, he did not resent his young brother-in-law's possession of Yasaman. Virgins were generally boring. Now she would come to him somewhat experienced in the sensual arts, thanks to Jamal Khan. He looked back to the terrace to find that although Yasaman had been satisfied in her last bout with her husband, Jamal Khan was not.

Salim smiled and his lingham tingled with anticipation as he saw Yasaman turn onto her belly. Leaning forward and resting upon her arms, she arched her back, raising her bottom to her master for his pleasure. Jamal Khan knelt behind his wife, and then grasping her hips in his two hands, he thrust hard into her fiery yoni. Salim heard his sister cry out, but the sound she made was not one of pain. His own lingham was burning his hand and he groaned low, the erotic tableau before him arousing him in a way he had never been aroused before.

For a moment Salim thought that his brother-in-law was resting, but then peering closely through the moonlight he realized that Jamal Khan was thrusting with quick, tiny movements into his wife's yoni. The older prince nodded to himself with approval, silently admiring the younger prince's skill. The boy knew how to wield his lance well.

"Yes," Salim hissed softly to himself as Jamal Khan leaned forward over his wife's bent body and, reaching out, grasped her breasts.

Yasaman began to whimper in her inflamed need for release. Her graceful back curved more deeply and she pushed her bottom back at her husband with increasing rapidity as the intoxicating ecstasy engulfing them began to reach its climax.

"Please!"

Salim distinctly heard her even from his vantage point.

"Please!"

Jamal Khan's thrusts became faster and fiercer. His hands moved back again to her hips as he drove deeper and deeper into her burning body. Then suddenly they cried out in unison, their mutual heaven attained. And in his tower, still hidden by purple shadows, Salim Muhammad, heir to his father's throne, spilled his own seed. It spattered against the stone of the structure's wall, making a creamy puddle between the upturned toes of his slippers. He looked at it dispassionately, then he looked down onto the terrace where the two lovers, satisfied, had entwined themselves within each other's arms and had fallen asleep.

"Enjoy her while you can, my brother Jamal," he said to himself. "You will not have her much longer." Then he exited the tower as silently and as secretly as he had come, to return to his own palace.

Several days later the great celebrational Darbar honoring Akbar's fifty years of rule was held in the Hall of Audience at the Agra fort. A great procession preceded Akbar's formal entry. Every noble who could manage to come to Agra was there, and every one, whether he could afford it or not, had brought a gift for the emperor. Many were raised in rank, promoted to higher offices and given more land to have charge over. All had been warned beforehand of the honors to come, so no one honored was missing from the festivities.

The procession began with the clergy: Muslim muezzins, priests of the Hindu faiths, the Buddhists, the Jains, the Christians, and even rabbis from the two ancient Jewish communities of India. These were followed by those Akbar honored the most in his kingdom, the scholars. The one leading them, an ancient gentleman with a long white beard, recited Akbar's royal lineage that none doubt his right to his throne, or for that matter, Salim's right to follow his father.

The ladies of the royal household were seated in a balcony overlooking the Hall of Audience, where they had an excellent and unobstructed view of all that was going on below them. They had dressed themselves in their best finery, but in the heat of the new day, Yasaman thought, the commingling of the different and various scents was quite overpowering. She had had to arise early to be here and was uncharacteristically tired after another long night of lovemaking with her handsome husband. Nur Jahan was next to her, reeking of roses. Yasaman's head was beginning to ache terribly as the royal heralds entered the hall, preceded by drummers who beat upon their skin instruments, calling all to attention.

"Be aware! Be aware! There approaches the Protector of the People! The Provider of Grain! The Dispenser of Justice! The Pearl of Purity! The Diamond of Restraint! The Shadow of God on Earth!" the herald cried.

Behind the heralds came the standard bearers carrying the symbols of Akbar's monarchy. There was a large open hand carved realistically from ivory, the nails stained red, set upon a bejeweled golden pole that indicated the administration of the empire. Silver heads representing the elephant, the crocodile, and the tiger symbolized the Provider. There were standard bearers with glorious full sheaves of peacock feathers and beautiful white horse tails that fell gracefully from gold cones. These were the symbols of war and conquest. Finally came the fabulous royal sword of the kingdom, which stood for Justice.

At last Akbar was carried into the Hall of Audience, seated in his golden palanquin which blazed with diamonds and emeralds, the royal umbrella held high over his head. The pale blue silk parasol represented the sky, which was, of course, the emperor's direct access to God. His conveyance was set down. The Grand Mughal, garbed all in white and sparkling with diamonds, got out to seat himself cross-legged upon the simple red silk pillow set on the raised dais that was his throne.

Rugaiya Begum shook her head worriedly. "He does not look well," she whispered to Jodh Bai. "This is too much for him."

"I know," her friend agreed, "but you cannot tell our dear husband anything he does not want to hear."

Rugaiya Begum nodded, for Jodh Bai had spoken the truth.

The presentation of the gifts began. As Yasaman had mischievously predicted to her husband, there was a preponderance of elephants offered to Akbar. Salim presented his father with one quite magnificent fighting elephant, and his brother, Prince Daniyal, sent his father two female elephants and a fighting male. Daniyal was absent from the Darbar because he would not come to Agra while his brother was in residence.

Yasaman preened proudly before her female relations when her husband presented her father with the Wular Blue sapphire.

"What is it? What is it?" demanded Salima Begum. "I am unable to see clearly from here with these old eyes."

"Jamal Khan has given the emperor a sapphire as large as a cat's head," Rugaiya Begum answered.

"Aiiiii!" hissed Salima Begum. "He does well, Yasaman's

handsome young husband." She turned to the girl. "Does he love as well?" she teased, and then she cackled. "I can see he does from the purple circles beneath your eyes! Heh! Heh! Heh!"

Yasaman blushed, but she smiled. Salima Begum meant no harm.

The gift-giving continued. There were smaller jewels, and animals, and birds, and carved ebony and ivory boxes filled with pearls, and bolts of beautiful cloth, and rare books, and slaves of all races and both sexes, most young and beautiful, as well as chests of silver and gold coins.

Then came the honors Akbar was to bestow upon the loyal and upon those valuable civil servants without whom the Mughal could not have administered his vast empire. Prince Khusrau was honored. It was but the gesture of a loving grandfather. Akbar had already told those closest to him that in a few days the diwans of revenue, ministers, and officers would be placed under Salim's jurisdiction. Jamal Darya Khan was created governor of Kashmir for life, and publicly pledged his fealty to both Akbar and Prince Salim.

Yusef Khan could scarcely contain his pride, but his two elder sons were openly unhappy at Jamal's success. Salim noted this and several days later called Yaqub Khan and Haider Khan to him secretly. The two Kashmiri princes came, afraid, yet unable to refuse a royal summons.

Seeing them, Salim knew he had found the tools he needed to rid himself of his brother-in-law. "Sit down," he told the two men before him. "You will have wine, of course." He poured them goblets of a particularly good vintage he had imported from Europe, which had already been mixed with a very strong opiate.

"Wine is forbidden by the Prophet," Yaqub Khan said piously.

"Is not the forbidden usually the best of experiences?" Prince Salim rejoined. He raised his goblet. "To the new governor of Kashmir," he said and smiled toothily at the pair before him.

Reluctantly they raised their goblets to drink. What hypocrites, the prince thought to himself. He knew that both these Kashmiri lords drank regularly. He watched them over the rim of his goblet for a long moment, then lowering the vessel, he said, "You do not seem pleased that your younger brother has been appointed by my father to rule Kashmir."

Yaqub Khan and Haider Khan remained silent.

"Are you not relieved that one of your own is to again have charge over that land your ancestors have ruled for so many generations? Jamal Khan's mother was the daughter of one of your father's civil servants, wasn't she? Admittedly you are the eldest, Yaqub Khan, but still, even having the youngest rise above you to govern your homeland is better than having strangers sit in your father's palaces, is it not?" Salim smiled again at his two guests, wondering as he did so how long it would take for them to show their true colors. It was obvious that they were both terribly jealous of their youngest sibling. He did not have to wait long.

"I am my father's heir," burst out Yaqub Khan angrily. "It is I who should have been made governor of Kashmir by the Mughal!"

"You are a fool, Yaqub Khan," Salim replied coldly. "I remember you when you came to my father's court. You were cowardly and you were pompous. My father remembers it well too. You rebelled against the emperor even after he had conquered Kashmir. Your father had already sworn fealty to mine and taken a command in his army; but you rebelled, hiding out in the hills for months. Why would my father appoint you his governor? He cannot trust you."

"I have since proven my worth," Yaqub Khan said sullenly.

"How?" Salim answered him mockingly. "By lolling about your palace with your women and causing no further rebellions?"

"I am my father's firstborn," Yaqub Khan said angrily. "It should be I who received Kashmir back yesterday and not Jamal!"

Salim burst out laughing. "There is your greatest weakness, Yaqub Khan. Your overweening pride caused you to rebel in the face of defeat. Will it once again defeat you, I wonder, or can you be of use to me?"

"What do you want of us, gracious lord?" Haider Khan asked, perhaps a bit too eagerly. He had been silent until now.

Salim eyed him speculatively. Was this brother the wiser of the two? "You are ambitious, Haider Khan, are you not?"

"I must be ambitious for myself, gracious lord. I am a middle son. There is little for a middle son if he does not take it," came the honest reply.

Salim nodded. "And what do you want of me, Haider Khan?"

"A generalship in the future Mughal's army," Haider Khan told him frankly. "I enjoy war. There is still land to be taken in the Mughal's name. I like women, and I like good wine, gracious lord, but best of all I like to fight. I have no conscience at all where killing is concerned. Men, after all, are born to die."

"And what would you do for that generalship, Haider Khan?" Prince Salim demanded. He really didn't have to ask. He already knew.

"Whatever my gracious lord commands of me," came the predictable reply. Now Haider Khan smiled, showing strong white teeth.

Salim turned his dark gaze to Yaqub Khan. "And you, my poor disinherited friend, what would you do to regain Kashmir for yourself and for the sons and grandsons who will follow you?"

"Anything!" Yaqub Khan spat out. "Anything you want me to do!"

"Kill Jamal Khan?" Salim said softly. "Would you kill your

own flesh and blood, Yaqub Khan, to regain your rightful inheritance?"

"Yes! But why?"

Salim considered a moment, but then he decided it was best to answer. His real reasons must remain secret for now, but he would give Yaqub Khan an explanation to satisfy him. "My father and I do not agree on many things, and I have on several occasions struggled against him," Salim said. "It is an open secret that Akbar is dying. He has passed many of his responsibilities on to me already. Jamal Khan was not my choice to be governor of Kashmir."

"Who was?" Yaqub Khan asked.

"You were," replied Salim cleverly. "I, too, am an elder son, Yaqub Khan. Recently my own father has threatened to disinherit me because of our disagreements. I know how you feel. I told my father that your rebellions were a thing of the past; that I trusted your sworn word to us to keep the peace. Still, he would not listen to me. I do not want my brother-in-law as Kashmir's governor. *I want you!*"

"Then why not simply replace Jamal Khan with me after the Mughal's death?" Yaqub Khan demanded suspiciously.

"My father sealed Jamal Khan's fate when he appointed him Kashmir's governor for life. I cannot override that appointment even after Akbar's death. Therefore, the only thing I can do is have Jamal Khan killed," Salim explained reasonably.

"Why not hire an assassin?" Haider Khan asked.

"An assassin could later betray me," Salim said quietly, "but the new governor of Kashmir and one of my most powerful generals would not betray me, would they, Haider Khan?"

"I want the girl then too," Yaqub Khan told Salim.

"The girl?" Salim was puzzled.

"Your sister, Yasaman Kama Begum," Yaqub Khan answered.

"You would make her your wife?" Salim said, restraining his anger. Did this fool actually think he would give him Yasaman? Yaqub Khan's reply almost rendered Salim apoplectic, but because of what was involved, he managed by a supreme burst of will to remain calm.

"I have four wives. I see no advantage in divorcing any of them," Yaqub Khan said. "They have all given me sons. No, I want your sister as a hostage to ensure your kindness toward me. I will make her a concubine in my zenana. She will be well treated, I promise you. I am not unaffected by her beauty. I will probably give her several sons, which should bind us even closer once our blood has commingled. It is not that I do not trust you, gracious lord, but I am certain were you in my place, you would do all you could to protect yourself and your family."

"Of course! Of course," Salim said. "I suppose Yasaman would not object to remaining in Kashmir. She likes it there. Very well, Yaqub Khan, I will give you my sister for a concubine; but you must understand that I cannot let you have her until after my father is dead. I do not have that power. Besides, she will want a time to mourn her husband, as is only proper. She is young and fancies herself in love. Girls always feel that way about a man with a skillful lingham." He chuckled, and then as suddenly turned serious. "So it is agreed? You will kill Jamal Khan as quickly as possible?"

"Yes, gracious lord," the two brothers chorused.

"I have a suggestion," Salim told them. "It is best that it look like an accident. Find your brother and go with him to visit the emperor's elephants. The keepers are rarely in evidence at midday because of the heat. Render Jamal Khan unconscious and then throw him among the beasts. If they do not panic at the sight of his prone form, then stir them up so that they crush him beneath their mighty feet. When he is found, it will be assumed his death was a terrible happenstance."

Yaqub Khan nodded. "Yes," he agreed. "That is a fine suggestion, gracious lord. How soon afterward will I be appointed Kashmir's governor?"

"You must be patient, Yaqub Khan. There will be much distress over Jamal Khan's death. My sister, his wife, will grieve greatly at first, and my father's health may be affected by the tragedy. Trust me, my friend. I will be in your debt. I cannot betray you. When my father is ready to listen to reason, I will put forth your name again."

"And what if he again bypasses me in favor of another?" Yaqub Khan demanded. "I could do your bidding and once more find myself the loser. What guarantees do you give me, gracious lord?"

"You have my word, Yaqub Khan. I will not allow my father to appoint anyone else governor of Kashmir after Jamal Khan's death. Remember, Akbar is dying. We have time on our side. Trust me."

"I trust you, my lord!" Haider Khan told Salim.

"If you betray me, Salim Muhammad," Yaqub Khan said softly, "I will find some way to repay your treachery, even if I must come out of Hell to do it."

Salim smiled broadly. "You will have your due, Yaqub Khan, I swear it. Everything you deserve will shortly be yours, I promise."

The two brothers left him as secretly as they had come, and Salim sat contemplating his plans. Soon he would have everything he wanted. Soon he would be Grand Mughal and Yasaman would be at his side to share his life and his triumphs. He needed to be patient just a little longer.

※

7

※

The newly appointed governor of Kashmir, Prince Jamal Darya Khan, was dead. He had been found in an elephant stable, crushed beneath the feet of a frantic, newly delivered female. It was at first assumed that the young man had, in his curiosity, strayed too close to the baby elephant, and the mother had reacted in what she believed was a need to protect her infant.

The emperor was informed of this monumental tragedy by a nervous elephant keeper who was rushed into his presence. Akbar had been sitting enjoying a cup of mint tea with his wife, Rugaiya Begum, when the man was brought to him.

The keeper delivered his bad news, then seeing that they were alone, said suddenly, "It was not an accident, gracious lord. I saw it all!"

The Mughal stiffened. *"What?"* he asked, uncertain that he had heard correctly. "What did you say to me?"

"It was not an accident," the keeper repeated from his uncomfortable position, on his knees before his ruler.

"Explain yourself! If you do not tell me the exact truth, I

will have your tongue yanked from your head," Akbar said furiously.

"Prince Jamal came to the barns at midday with his two brothers, Prince Yaqub and Prince Haider, gracious lord. I warned them to beware of that female in particular, as she had only given birth this morning. Then I left to get some water. When I returned but a minute later, Yaqub Khan and Haider Khan were lifting the prone, unconscious body of Prince Jamal over the gate into the elephant mother's pen. She was wild with terror and had already begun to trumpet her fear." The keeper hung his head in shame. "I was frightened, gracious lord. I know I should have shouted to them, but when I saw what they were doing, I was afraid. I am a poor and humble man. They might have blamed me for the terrible deed, and because they are rich and powerful, they would have been believed. Besides, I was not in time to stop them. I feared that if they saw me, they would kill me too.

"As soon as they had deposited him in the female's pen, they began to cry for help as if it were an accident. I ran also to the pen to see if I could save Prince Jamal. But alas! His skull was already crushed beneath the feet of the terrified mother elephant. There was nothing else I could do but come to you, gracious lord, and throw myself upon your mercy," the keeper concluded. He prostrated himself fully before the emperor.

"You are absolutely certain of what you saw?" Akbar asked the elephant keeper numbly. "These are serious charges you make against Yaqub Khan and Haider Khan. How are you certain that it was them?"

The elephant keeper raised himself up slightly, saying, "Haider Khan keeps a magnificent fighting elephant in the royal barns. I have had the privilege of attending the beast, gracious lord. This prince has spoken to me on several occasions. Once he came with his brother, Yaqub Khan. Haider Khan introduced me to him and told him that I was the finest elephant keeper in all the royal stables. I would know him anywhere!" The keeper threw himself flat again.

Akbar could feel Rugaiya Begum shaking as she sat next to him. She was obviously suffering from shock. "Arise, good keeper, and go back to the stables," he told the man. "Say nothing of what you have seen or what you know to anyone, on peril of your life. I will administer justice fairly. Those involved will atone with their lives for this terrible crime before the hour is past. If Jamal Khan's brothers thought to replace him in Kashmir, they have committed this crime for naught."

The keeper scrambled quickly to his feet. He had known the emperor his entire life. He knew that his word was good. Bowing himself out of the room, he ran to do Akbar's bidding, thinking that the worst being over, he would gain a certain stature from being among the discoverers of Jamal Khan's body.

Rugaiya Begum began to weep softly, but Akbar ignored her, calling for his guard instead. "Find Yaqub Khan and Haider Khan, the sons of Yusef Khan," he told the captain of his guard. "Bring them here to me quickly with as much discretion as you can manage. And send someone to find my daughter, Yasaman Kama Begum. Bring her to me also."

The captain of the guard hurried off.

"What can we tell her?" Rugaiya Begum sobbed. "This will kill my child for certain. She loves Jamal Khan with all her heart and soul. There will never again be another man for her!"

"She must know the truth, my wife," Akbar replied, "even though it causes her great pain. She is my daughter. She is strong. I want her here when the murderers are brought before me so that she may hear their explanation for this horrific crime. There is more to this than meets the eye, Rugaiya. I feel it!"

"It is Salim!" Rugaiya Begum said bitterly. "He is behind this, and no one else! His desire for her must burn as strongly as it ever did. He knows his time to rule is coming. He but prepared the way for himself that he may have Yasaman as well. We must not let him, my husband!"

Akbar paled. "Do not say it, my wife. *Do not say it!* Salim knows that a sensual relationship with his sister is not only repellent, but forbidden by both man's law and God's law. Surely he would not try to defy nature."

"When did either man or God, or even Akbar, ever stop Prince Salim Muhammad in his quest for what he desired?" Rugaiya Begum replied harshly. "He has been out of control his entire life. You should have recognized he was unfit when he was a boy. Instead you made him the heir. Daniyal was more fit, but it is too late for poor Daniyal, lost in his grape and poppy haze."

They sat in silence for several long minutes. Then the door to the room opened to admit Yasaman. She was wearing a pale blue and gold sari, and her dark hair was braided with strands of small pearls. She looked so happy.

"You called me, my father?" she said, coming to him and kissing his cheek.

Akbar drew her down between Rugaiya Begum and himself. "I have terrible news, my daughter. I will not hold back because nothing will couch the blow I must deliver to you. Jamal Khan is dead." The emperor tightened his arm about his youngest daughter to comfort her.

"*How?*" Yasaman's voice was distant and without emotion.

"It appears he was murdered, my child," Akbar told her, and repeated the elephant keeper's tale.

"*Why, my father?*" She was suddenly cold. Terribly cold. Jamal dead? No! It could not be, but why would they lie to her?

"I have ordered Yaqub Khan and Haider Khan brought to me immediately, Yasaman, my child," she heard Akbar say. "They will tell us before they die why they have committed this deed."

Once more silence descended upon the room. Yasaman was struggling to digest what her father had told her, but she could still not quite believe his words. It seemed so unreal. Like some horrible dream from which she could not awaken, although she was sure when she did, Jamal would be beside her.

Rugaiya Begum had been rendered speechless. She did

not know how to comfort Yasaman for the loss of a husband. What did one say in such a situation? *There, there. Everything will be all right.* Everything was not going to be all right, particularly if, as she suspected, Salim was behind the matter. They had married Yasaman off to Jamal Khan to protect her from her brother's evil lust. How would they protect her now? The negotiations involved in arranging another marriage could not even begin until Yasaman had finished her period of mourning a year from now. Akbar was not going to live that long, Rugaiya Begum knew. Salim had planned well, damn his wicked soul, and now Yasaman, the beloved child of her heart, was in mortal danger.

The door to the room was once again flung open and several soldiers entered escorting Yaqub Khan and Haider Khan, who were protesting loudly at what they considered a great indignity.

"Send me two mutes, then dismiss all the men. You remain," Akbar ordered the captain. When the mutes had come and the others were gone, the door was closed. Akbar pierced Yusef Khan's two remaining sons with a hard look and said without preamble, "Why did you kill your brother Jamal?"

Neither of the Kashmiri princes answered him.

"The elephant keeper saw you. He came to me," Akbar told them quietly. "I repeat, why did you kill your brother?"

Yaqub Khan looked at his younger brother and shrugged. Both men were aware that the mutes were royal executioners. To deny the plot was now futile, but had they been betrayed by Salim? he wondered. Perhaps the truth would save their lives. Akbar was known for fairness. "Your son, Salim, promised me the governorship of Kashmir *and* his sister, Yasaman Kama Begum, for my concubine. To my brother, Haider, he promised a high military position," he said.

"Did you approach him in this matter, or did he approach you?" Akbar demanded, hoping against hope that it had been the two Kashmiri princes who had first gone to his son with the idea.

"He called us to him early in the morning, gracious lord," Yaqub Khan said. "We would not have done this deed had we not been assured great rewards by someone so powerful."

Akbar nodded. Yaqub Khan was speaking the truth, he knew. The man was a follower and not a leader. "You swear this on your miserable life?" he asked the two brothers.

They nodded, and Yaqub Khan said, "We swear it with our dying breaths, gracious lord." He suddenly understood the certainty of his fate, for he realized too late that the woman next to the emperor was his sister-in-law, Yasaman Kama Begum.

Akbar sighed deeply and looked to the captain of his guard. The captain silently nodded to the two mutes standing behind the Kashmiri princes. The mutes, with incredible swiftness, garroted Yaqub Khan and his brother Haider before they even realized what was happening. Then, under the direction of the captain, they removed the bodies for immediate burial, departing the room and leaving the emperor, his wife, and his daughter alone again. The captain did not need to be admonished to silence. His entire career had been at the Mughal court, and he knew that Salim would soon rule.

"They lied!" Yasaman burst out. *"They lied!"*

"No," Akbar said wearily, "they told the truth, my rosebud."

"Salim would not hurt me in this way," Yasaman whispered, her voice beginning to quiver with emotion. "He would not hurt me! He loves me."

"Yes," Akbar said, "he loves you, my daughter, but he does not love you as a brother loves his sister. He loves and desires you as a man desires a beautiful woman. I think perhaps that this is something you knew but dared not admit to yourself."

"He tried to seduce me the night of my thirteenth birthday," Yasaman half whispered to her father. "I thought it might be wrong, and yet . . ." Her voice trailed off.

"I know he tried to seduce you then," Akbar replied, "but you must not feel guilty about it, Yasaman. You were an innocent young girl filled with a new and burning passion you did not understand or know what to do with; but your brother, may God forgive him, knew, and he took shameful advantage of you."

"How did you know, Father?" Her cheeks were pink with the memory of the brief but torrid encounter with her brother.

"Adali was there. He had seen the looks your brother had lavished upon you over the past years. He was suspicious of him, and rightly so, it turns out," the emperor said. "Remember, Adali is loyal beyond question. He had long ago promised Candra to protect you from all evil. It was not a promise he made lightly, my daughter."

Yasaman nodded. "Is that why I was married in such haste to Jamal?" she asked her father.

"Yes. Your mother and I wanted to protect you, Yasaman. We believed such a marriage the answer to our problem."

"I had known Jamal's mother briefly," Rugaiya Begum spoke up. "I had even seen the prince on one or two occasions. He was handsome and seemed kind. His reputation was spotless. I knew you would not be unhappy to remain in Kashmir. In Kashmir you would have been far from Salim's eye and, we hoped, his thoughts. It would appear, however, that you are an obsession with your brother. He knows that your father is dying. He has acted to remove the final barrier to his possession of you."

Yasaman's world was unraveling about her even as they spoke. Jamal, her beloved husband, was dead by her beloved brother's command; and Salim was preparing to . . . to . . . what did he really want of her? To possess her body, she understood, but what place was she to have in his life? She had loved Salim her entire life, but now she hated him. She hated him with as deep a passion as he obviously loved her.

"I will kill him if I have to face him," she said finally. Her heart was gone and she was so cold.

"No," Akbar said quietly. "You cannot."

"How will you punish him, my father?" Yasaman demanded in a hard voice. "Will you replace him with Khusrau or Khurram? Will you have him garroted as you did his two hapless minions? No! He must bear a slow death. I want him to suffer!"

Rugaiya Begum looked at Akbar. How will you answer her? her mournful dark eyes asked of him. What comfort can you possibly bring to her?

"Khusrau is too volatile," Akbar finally said. "He has inherited the worst traits of both his parents. As for Khurram, he is too young, I fear, though he shows great promise. I cannot live long enough to assure his safe ascent to power if I destroy his father, Yasaman. Khurram is only fourteen."

"You were fourteen when my grandfather, Humayun, died," she reminded him. "You fought off uncles, cousins, and brothers to retain your throne."

"Times were different then," he protested. "I had not all of this land."

"Yes, they were harder times, my father! The Mughals had little left after their wars with the Afghan tribes and Sher Shah. You had an empire to conquer and half a dozen aspirants to your throne eager to bring you down so that they could rule in your place! Our world is nothing like that now!"

"No," he agreed, "it is a far more subtle and deadly world, my daughter. I have conquered almost all of this land by the sword and by the alliances I have so cleverly forged by virtue of the marriage bed. A boy of fourteen could not hold *this* empire together. India needs a man. Unfortunately there is but one son of my loins fit to rule. Your brother Salim."

"What of Daniyal?" she replied furiously.

"Daniyal is too often in his cups to function successfully,

I fear, my daughter. No, Salim is India's only hope. He may have tried me sorely over the years with his eagerness to fill my boots, but he is an able administrator and a fine warrior. The people fear him, and they respect him."

"How long would they respect him if they knew of his desire to commit incest with his sister?" Yasaman said bitterly. "How long would they respect him if they knew he had ordered his brother-in-law's murder in order to clear a path to my bed?" Her voice was beginning to rise as her grief began to overcome her. "You say you are dying, my father. How will you protect me then from Salim? I will kill myself before I will allow him to violate me! But if it comes to that, I will kill him too!"

"Be silent, my daughter!" Rugaiya Begum said sharply, and both Akbar and Yasaman turned to look at her, startled. "I will hear no talk of killing. We have but one course in this matter, but in order to take it, we must not let Salim know that we are aware of his perfidy. Your father is correct, Yasaman. There is no one who can follow him but Salim. That is unescapable fact. Nothing you say or do can alter it. Trust me when I tell you that no one would come to your aid if Salim forced you to an incestuous relationship. You are only a woman. Any cleric who protested would be killed to silence his chatter. We must, therefore, protect you from Salim and protect Salim from himself. There is only one way. You must leave India."

"*Leave India?*" Yasaman was horrified. "Where would I go, Mama Begum?"

"You must go to Candra's land; to your other grandmother. It is the only place where you will be safe. Your brother will not know where you are, and therefore cannot send after you. Obviously your fate is not here in India, my daughter. Before your marriage, your father's astrologer saw both happiness and tragedy in your stars, as well as several children. If you remain here, Salim will not permit you to have another husband to father those children."

"I cannot leave India," Yasaman said. "It is my home."

"Yes," Akbar said as if a sudden revelation had been presented to him. "Yes, Rugaiya, my wife, it is the only way! Why I did not think of it myself, I do not know. *England!* You will be safe in England, my beloved daughter. And Candra's family will surely protect you."

"You were not so certain of Candra's family when you permitted her to return to her own land without me," Yasaman said.

"I did not know them then, but over the years your other grandmother has corresponded with me. I believe her to be a woman of great morality and good sense. She will not refuse to shelter you," Akbar said.

"Yes, she has corresponded with you, my father, but never have you corresponded with her! What will she think when I suddenly appear upon her doorstep?"

"We will consult with Father Cullen," Akbar said. "He is one of them, a European. He will know; but I believe England is the safest place for you, Yasaman."

Before they might continue the conversation, however, Yasaman suddenly doubled over and cried out in pain.

"What is it, my daughter?" Rugaiya Begum said, frightened.

Yasaman looked up at her mutely, her eyes filled with anguish. "I think I may be with child," she managed to gasp.

Akbar scrambled to his feet. Hurrying over to the door of the chamber, he opened it and called to the guardsman outside, "Fetch the lady Juliana immediately! Quickly! Quickly!" When he turned back, Rugaiya Begum was cradling Yasaman in her arms.

Yasaman's eyes were closed and she was very pale. Tiny drops of perspiration beaded her forehead and upper lip.

They sat silently until finally the door to the room opened and Juliana Bourbon hurried in. "What has happened?" Seeing Yasaman, she knelt by her side and looked at Rugaiya Begum questioningly.

"She may be with child," Rugaiya Begum told the doctor.

"Not any longer," Juliana Bourbon replied, pointing to the ooze of blood staining Yasaman's clothing. "I am sorry, my princess," she told Yasaman, whose eyes fluttered open at the doctor's words. "How long since your last show of blood?"

"Eight, nine weeks," Yasaman murmured weakly.

"It will be all right, my child," Juliana Bourbon reassured the girl. "You are young and healthy. You will have other children."

Yasaman began to weep wildly.

"Jamal Khan has been murdered this day," Akbar told the doctor.

"Ahh," she replied, "then that is what has brought about this sad event. Sometimes a terrible shock will do that to a woman, and the princess is very young. Let me call for a litter. She will need immediate treatment."

"Take her to my quarters here in the fort," Rugaiya Begum told Juliana Bourbon, "and can you give her something to quiet her before you move her? I do not want this event to become a public scandal, under the circumstances."

"Of course," the doctor said. "Give me some water, my lady Begum," and she removed a gilded pill from a pouch that hung from her belt. Gently she inserted it between Yasaman's lips, the sobbing girl choking slightly as Rugaiya Begum forced some water from a goblet down her daughter's throat. Yasaman swallowed, and a few short minutes later her sobs died as she fell into a deep sleep.

The litter was brought and the young princess gently put upon it.

"Take my daughter directly to her mother's apartments," Akbar instructed the bearers. "Go with them," he told his wife, and Rugaiya Begum accompanied the doctor from the room. When she had departed, Akbar told the attending guardsman, "Find Father Cullen and send him to me."

• •

The priest came and Akbar told him of all the events that had transpired this day, concluding, "I know that you know the real reason we married Yasaman off so quickly, Father. Now, however, all our plans to keep her safe from Salim, and Salim safe from his own wicked desires, have gone astray."

"What are we to do then, gracious lord?" the priest asked.

"Rugaiya Begum and I have discussed it, Father. Yasaman must leave India. There is no other way. She must go to England to Candra's family. I will, of course, want you to escort her. Will the Church allow you to leave your post here, I wonder?"

"My post is with the princess, gracious lord," the priest answered. "My instructions, which came from my bishop, were to remain with her always. If she goes to England, then I must, of necessity, follow her."

"Is the Church so interested in the welfare of a single soul that it would assign a priest to its keeping?" Akbar mused aloud.

Cullen Butler laughed softly. "Has it never occurred to you, gracious lord, that perhaps the Church was not quite as involved with my coming as you assumed? That perhaps there were other factors involved in my being assigned to the princess's household?"

"I do not understand you," the Mughal said. "I myself requested that the Jesuits send me a priest for Yasaman's household."

"Indeed you did, gracious lord. In due time I was sent to you, a priest—*but not a member of the order of the Jesuits*. I was very surprised, although at the same time most grateful, that you never questioned the Church's decision. The Jesuits are a powerful order and very jealous of their foothold here in India. I have had to walk carefully and defer to them at every turn lest they grow too curious themselves as to why I, and not one of their own, was sent to your daughter's household. It was not an easy task that I was set when I was sent forth to India."

The Mughal stared hard at the pleasant-faced priest as the import of his words penetrated his brain. *"Who are you?"* he finally asked quietly. "And how did you come to be here?"

"I was sent at your request, which was forwarded by the Jesuits to Paris. There, Bearach O'Dowd, a priest high in the Jesuit order, came into the picture. He heard of your desire and communicated with his childhood friend, an Irish bishop, who communicated with his sister. The result was that I, and not a Jesuit, was sent to India. You have met this Irish bishop yourself, but once. He is Michael O'Malley. His sister is Yasaman Kama Begum's other grandmother, Lady de Marisco. I, gracious lord, am their nephew, the youngest son of Sine O'Malley Butler.

"When Father O'Dowd told my uncle Michael that a priest was required for the princess's household, Lady de Marisco insisted that I be sent. In that way my aunt was always able to have firsthand accounts of her grandchild. Although she understood your reasons for not allowing the princess to come to England with her mother, she grieved for the grandchild lost to her. My aunt is a woman of strong values, gracious lord, and for her, family is everything."

"If she knew of Yasaman's progress through communication with you, Father Cullen, then why was she always pestering me with her letters?" the Mughal asked curiously.

"It was my aunt's way of personally letting you know that she cared what happened to her granddaughter," the priest answered.

Akbar sighed. "I think I should be angry that Lady de Marisco's reach is so long. She must be a very powerful woman. Why did you not tell me until now, Father Cullen, that you are related by blood to my daughter? Perhaps you feared that I would send you away?"

"There was always that possibility, gracious lord. I was not sent here to spy, but rather to watch over my young relative. If you knew my aunt, you would understand, but I would not have you gain an incorrect picture of her. She is wealthy through her own efforts, proud, stubborn, and determined. She is the strongest woman I have ever known, and possibly the most noble."

"Will she really welcome my daughter into her family?" Akbar asked Father Cullen. "And what of Yasaman's mother, Candra? I cannot remember her other name. She has always been Candra in my heart and mind," the emperor told the priest.

"The princess's mother is called Velvet, and she is my cousin. I do not really know her except by reputation. I will take the princess to her grandmother, my aunt, in England. Velvet lives far to the north of her mother in another country called Scotland, although now that Scotland has inherited England's throne, the two lands will certainly be joined, I am certain."

"Has she other children, my daughter's mother?" He had never before wanted to know such a thing, for the memories had been too painful. Now, however, it was different. His life was coming to an end, and the one thing that had bound him to Candra, their daughter, must leave him to go to England.

"She has borne her husband five sons," Cullen Butler said.

"Five sons!" Akbar marveled. "What are their ages, Father?"

"The eldest is twelve, I believe, and the youngest five," the priest told the Mughal. "There is also a stepdaughter from another alliance Velvet's husband had. The girl is just a little older than the princess and will surely be a good sister to her.

"Lady de Marisco will, I think, want to keep the princess with her, however, gracious lord. As a beautiful and wealthy young widow, Yasaman will have a better opportunity to contract a fine marriage from her grandmother's house than she would have if she went to her mother in Scotland. There is no court in Scotland any longer."

Akbar nodded. "Yes," he said. "I want my Yasaman to

remarry and to be happy, Father. The love of a good man will help her to find contentment in her new life. Children too." He sighed deeply. "Ahh, I shall never see the grandchildren my daughter gives me! I shall never be able to dandle them upon my knee, or take them tiger hunting in my howdah as I did Yasaman when she was just a small baby. How Candra scolded me over it, Father Cullen. I wonder if she ever forgave me for refusing to allow Yasaman to go with her. Now I must send our daughter to her for protection. I can only pray that she will love and welcome her as I would were our positions reversed."

"The princess will be safe with her mother's family, gracious lord, I swear it!" Cullen Butler told the Mughal sincerely.

"My daughter will not arrive in England a pauper," Akbar said. "Your aunt's ships put into Cambay once yearly, in midsummer. Yasaman will travel to England on one and her fortune will accompany her. There will be gold, jewels, spices, and silks. She will live out her days like the queen she was born to be. Our preparations, however, must remain a secret. Only Yasaman, her mother, Adali, you, and I can know what we are planning. If Prince Salim learns of Yasaman's departure, he will stop her. I cannot prevent it. He is too strong for me now, and I am dying."

"Can you live long enough to see to your daughter's going, gracious lord?" the priest asked frankly. "It is a journey of several weeks to the coast. Such a large caravan will certainly attract attention."

"You have a factor in Cambay, do you not?" Akbar queried.

"Aye. He is one of our own people." A smile touched the corners of Cullen Butler's lips. "By coincidence, he is one of the princess's cousins, Alain O'Flaherty, the third son of Lady de Marisco's eldest child, Ewan O'Flaherty. He has been in charge of our establishment in Cambay for five years now, gracious lord."

Akbar could not help but chuckle. "Your aunt is a *very* wise woman, Father. This grandson, I assume, is a younger son, and she has given him a chance to make his own fortune by coming to India."

"Exactly, gracious lord! Family can usually be trusted, and in this case, young Alain was a good choice," the priest said. "He knows nothing, of course, about Yasaman, but I will explain everything to him when we reach Cambay. Our timing is most crucial. We must sail for England before the end of August, or we will lose the trade winds. The voyage, my lord, is some five to six months, but going overland would be far more dangerous, and take us close to two years."

"Send a messenger to him this very day, Father. I will provide you with one of my own people for the journey. Simply say that there will be shipments from Agra coming to him over the next few weeks that are to go to England. Tell him you will be coming to visit him midsummer and will then explain further. That should be soon enough. My daughter will need time to regain her strength, to try and recover from the shock of her husband's murder and the loss of their child."

"How will you keep her safe from your son, gracious lord?"

"Yasaman will remain in her mother's care. Salim cannot predict the term of a woman's grief. My daughter's grief will be very, very great. Jamal's body must be buried immediately according to his Muslim faith, but I will have his heart removed from his body to be buried in Kashmir. When it is time for Yasaman to journey to the coast, we will use a small ruse to cover her departure. Another caravan, this one carrying the heart of Jamal Khan, will depart for Kashmir. It will appear that the grieving young widow is with it. Salim dare not object to a wife accompanying her husband's heart to its burial ground. He will feel secure in knowing where she is and that he can get to her at any time."

The priest nodded. "You plan as skillfully as does my aunt," he said with a smile.

The emperor chuckled. "How I should like to know that woman!" he said. "Tell me, Father. Is she beautiful? Candra was beautiful."

"I only saw my cousin Velvet when she was a child, but my aunt Skye is probably the most beautiful woman I have ever known. None of her daughters had the same beauty. Strangely, it is your daughter who reminds me most of my aunt in her youth, although the princess does not really look like her. My aunt has fair white skin, and dark, dark hair, and the most beautiful eyes I have ever seen. They are blue-green in color. She will be sixty-five this year, gracious lord, but the last time I saw her, those wonderful eyes had not dimmed in color."

"Are her eyes then like my daughter's?" the emperor asked. "I have always wondered where Yasaman got her eye color. Her mother's were an emerald-green of incredible clarity."

"No, gracious lord. The princess's eyes are the blue of a Persian turquoise. My aunt's are more like the blue-green waters off the coast of Kerry, a province of my native Ireland," Cullen Butler replied. "My mother and her elder sisters were always jealous of my aunt's great beauty. My aunt is the youngest of the sisters. Yet it was she who defied all tradition and went out into the world to conquer it. She succeeded, too, much to their chagrin," the priest finished with a chuckle.

"Tell me of my daughter's grandfather. I remember that Candra adored her father," Akbar said.

"Adam de Marisco is my aunt's sixth husband. She outlived the other five. His mother was French, his father English. The de Mariscos are a very ancient family. Adam is brave, and clever and witty, gracious lord. He is a large, fierce-looking man with the heart of a lion and the soul of a lamb. He totally understands my aunt, allowing her to do exactly as she pleases, for he knows that she is not a foolish woman. He will be absolutely delighted to have Yasaman in

his house, and will undoubtedly spoil her every bit as much
as I am told he spoiled her mother."

The emperor smiled. "I send her to good people, do I not,
Father Cullen?"

"You do, gracious lord. Her English family will love and
cherish the princess. They defend their own. They will allow
no harm to come to her. Once she has gotten over losing
everything she has ever known, she will be happy with them.
It will not be easy, gracious lord, but the princess is a strong
woman, as her mother was strong; as Rugaiya Begum, the
mother who raised her, is strong; as both her grandmothers,
Mariam Makani of sainted memory, and my aunt Skye, are
strong. Your daughter springs from a race of fierce women,
gracious lord. Trust me. She will survive."

The priest's words sustained Akbar in the days that followed. They were turbulent days. Yasaman, after her first
outburst of grief, mourned her husband and child with hard,
cold eyes. She would allow no one to speak of the tragedy,
shutting herself away from her family to weep bitter tears in
the lonely hours of the night, when there were none to hear
or see her deep sorrow.

Yusef Khan had been devastated by Jamal Khan's death,
and even more so by the knowledge that his youngest son
had died at the hands of his elder brothers. Akbar kept
Salim's part in the murder to himself. Salim was his undis-
puted heir and needed no more enemies than he already
had. Yusef Khan resigned his position in the emperor's service in order to return to Kashmir to oversee his remaining
family, which included the wives and children that his older
sons had left.

"I applaud your swift justice, gracious lord," he told
Akbar, "even if it meant the loss of all my sons. I will see
my grandsons learn their loyalty to you and to your chosen
descendants."

Akbar nodded sadly, reluctantly allowing him to go, but

it was better this way. He knew that all of Yasaman's ties to Kashmir had to be severed.

Word reached the emperor in Agra that his youngest son, Daniyal, had died in Burhanpur on March 11, 1605, the very day that he had held his fiftieth-year celebration Darbar. Daniyal's father-in-law, under Akbar's orders, had attempted to wean the young man from his weakness for wine, but one of his servants had brought the forbidden beverage into the prince's chamber, hidden in the barrel of his favorite gun. The wine mixed with the gunpowder residue, and the rust of the iron interior of the weapon poisoned the prince as soon as he drank, killing him.

The family mourned Daniyal, who had been a charming man, and Salim became even more careful of his health than before. Both his brothers had died of an excess of wine. It was a warning he took most seriously, particularly as he saw that the news of Daniyal's death, coming as it did on top of Jamal Khan's death, took a great toll on Akbar. The Mughal seemed to shrink and grow more feeble before their very eyes. His mother and Rugaiya Begum, as well as the other wives, were visibly worried; but Salim, though filled with sorrow on one hand, secretly rejoiced. Soon his father would be dead. He would rule, and Yasaman would be his to possess forever without interference.

He had not seen her in several weeks now, for she had, it seemed, been with child when Jamal Khan had met his most unfortunate death. Yasaman had miscarried of her infant and was slow to recover her strength, or so Rugaiya Begum claimed. He had not considered the possibility that she might be pregnant when he had ordered her husband's death, but it was better the child was lost. He wanted no loving reminders of the Kashmiri prince who had captured his sister's heart. Eventually she would forget Jamal Khan, Salim thought, because there would not be room in her heart for anyone but himself.

• •

As spring moved toward summer, the prince learned that his sister would accompany her husband's heart home to Kashmir. Good! he thought. That will put an end to it once and for all. She will be where I can get to her when I want her.

His sister's departure was to be the morning after the Holi festival, and Salim intended to visit her the night of the festival. Though a Hindu fete, Holi was celebrated by everyone in India, for it was such a happy time. It fell on the day of the summer equinox, and the barriers between men and women, as well as between castes, magically disappeared. The legends concerning Holi were ancient. It seemed originally to have been a fertility rite.

The revels surrounding Holi were observed with wild abandon. Kama, the Hindu god of Pleasure, presided. He carried a bow made of sugarcane, its string a line of honey bees. His arrows were flowers which, in this season of floral abundance, was perfect symbolism. The flower arrows were said to be tipped with passion, and those touched by them were lost in love forever.

It was the custom at Holi for the celebrants to smear each other with colored powder which was made from crushed flowers. By evening the air was tinted with the reds and purples, pinks and yellows of the freely tossed powder. Some people mixed water and musk with the colors, filling hollow bamboos, which they then squirted at each other. People sang and danced and ate special sweetmeats, some of which were laced with opium and hashish, accounting for the most rowdy, abandoned behavior.

Yasaman could hear the celebration going on in the city all day. She was fully recovered physically from her miscarriage, and had been for several weeks now. Tomorrow she would begin the long journey that would take her from her home, from everyone and everything she had ever known. She was bitter and angry when word came to her that her brother Salim would pay her a visit.

"I do not want to see him, Mama Begum," she told Rugaiya. "How can I face him and not desire to kill him? He has taken everything I hold dear from me. My husband is dead! I have lost our child from the shock of Jamal's murder, and now I must go forth from India, from you and Papa. *I hate Salim!*"

"Listen to me, Yasaman," Rugaiya Begum told her daughter. "If you give in to your anger, you will allow Salim the very thing you seek to deny him. A victory over you. He would sooner see you dead than happy in another man's arms. Escape him! He will be forever forced to live his life without you, knowing that you have found happiness with others, knowing that given the choice, you left India. *Left him.* It will not kill him immediately, but it will rub him like an open canker for as long as he lives. This is a far better vengeance than any other that we could think of, my child."

"Come with me!" Yasaman begged Rugaiya Begum.

"I cannot, Yasaman. I am too old for adventure now. Besides, your father needs me as he has never needed me before. Akbar and I have lived our entire lives together. As a small boy, I am told, he was present at my birth. If the child my mother bore was a girl, she was to be his first wife. Your father saw me born into this world. I must be here to see him out of it. It is only right. I have been his wife longer than I have been anything else." Rugaiya Begum smoothed Yasaman's dark hair gently. "Your father has given me everything I hold dear—his love and his daughter to raise. I should be a poor wife if I left him now. The others will not care for him as I can."

Yasaman wept softly in her mother's arms. "I cannot bear the thought of my life without you, Mama Begum," she said. "This, too, I owe my brother, may God damn his black soul to eternal night! Do not make me receive him, I beg of you!"

"Yasaman! Yasaman! You cannot allow your own feelings to prevent you from doing your duty," Rugaiya Begum gently scolded. "Your father, Adali, Father Cullen, and I have worked diligently to make certain that your escape is assured. If you refuse to see your brother, he will become suspicious, my child. Do not destroy yourself, Yasaman, by foolish actions. Be strong! Always remember that you are the Mughal's daughter. Within you runs the blood of many mighty conquerors. Do not deny it!"

Yasaman sighed deeply. Then she drew away from her mother, saying, "I must see him alone lest he become apprehensive." When Rugaiya Begum looked worried, Yasaman reassured her, "I am not the child my brother tried to seduce almost two years ago, Mama Begum. No matter his lust, he will not press me right now, I am certain."

I must trust to her judgment, Rugaiya Begum thought. Tomorrow I will send her on a journey that will take her half a world away from me, and I will never see this child of my heart again. I can protect her no longer. "Very well, my daughter," she told Yasaman. "Do what you think is best in this matter. I will, however, be here to greet Salim when he comes, else he think my absence odd."

And when Salim arrived that evening, Rugaiya Begum salaamed politely. "Welcome, my nephew," she said.

"Aunt! It is good to see you again," he answered, and kissed her cheek affectionately. "How is Yasaman?"

"Ask her yourself, dear boy," Rugaiya Begum told him. "She is in the garden enjoying the roses and the pristine beauty of the summer moonlight. I will leave you together. As for me, I am an old woman now. I want nothing more of this night than my comfortable bed." She chuckled. "Do not keep your sister too long, Salim. She has a long journey to begin tomorrow morning, but once it is completed, a door is shut and another is opened to Yasaman. That is life, is it not?" She kissed his cheek and, with a smile, left him.

The garden of Rugaiya Begum's small palace within the fort was completely enclosed by red sandstone walls. It was not a large garden. The pebbled pathways were set out in the shape of a cross, and in the center was a beautiful white marble fountain filled with white lotus and goldfish. There were several tall orchid trees and a number of rosebushes which were currently in full, fragrant bloom. The flower beds had been planted with night-blooming blossoms that gave off their sweetness after the heat of the day. Beautiful, exquisite frangipani, exotic queen of the night, and creamy jasmine flourished in the silvery moonlight.

Salim found his sister sitting by the lotus pool. Her cotton sari was a pale purple in color and her dark hair was loose about her shoulders. He swallowed hard. It was far too soon for him to approach her, but she was the most desirable woman he had ever seen. In her simple garb and unadorned by any jewelry, she was more beautiful than any female he knew.

"Yasaman." He finally found his voice.

She looked up and, for the briefest moment, the look in her turquoise eyes was unfathomable, but then she smiled at him. "Salim, my brother. It is good to see you again. I have been ill, you know."

She was impossible to resist. Seating himself by her side, he put an arm about her. "I know, little monkey, and I wept with you," he told her, his voice thick with sincerity.

Liar, she thought, but she looked up meltingly into his face. "I have missed you, my brother. I have no one now, you know. My husband is dead, and I have miscarried our child. I am alone, Salim."

"You will never be alone as long as I am alive, Yasaman!" he vowed to her. "Must you return to Kashmir, my beloved sister?"

"Alas, yes, beloved brother. Jamal was good to me, and in my way, I cared for him. I will take his heart home to the land he so loved and bury it with honor. Afterward," she sighed sadly, "I do not know what will happen to me. Father is dying, you realize. Yet I would remain in Kashmir with its lakes and mountains, its many flowers and fields of saffron. Do you remember the saffron fields, Salim?"

His arm about her tightened, and with his other hand he caressed her face. He did indeed remember the fields of saffron with a fragrance so wonderful that if he had died at the very moment the scent overwhelmed him, it would have been enough. "Yasaman," he breathed, and his lips touched hers briefly. When she did not resist him, he pressed more firmly upon her mouth, thrilled when she parted her lips slightly for him. The hand that had brushed softly over her cheek now moved lower to fondle her full breasts. "Sweet little sister," he murmured against her ear, his fingers squeezing her nipples almost painfully as he struggled to restrain himself. "You will never be alone, Yasaman. Remember the princes of ancient Egypt, little monkey? When you have fulfilled your obligations to Jamal Khan, you will return to me and we will find our own destiny together. If you love Kashmir so, I will build a garden for you there that only you and I may enter. I will call it Shalimar, the garden of love. It will stand for all time as a testimony of Salim's desire and devotion to Yasaman. Will that please you?"

"Yes," she answered him with seeming shyness, casting her eyes down. "I believe that you have been correct all along, Salim, my brother. I believe our kismet is meant that we always be in each other's thoughts."

"And you will return to me next spring, sister?"

"I will return as soon as I have buried the heart of Jamal Khan in Kashmir, Salim. Father will need me first, dear brother," she murmured, struggling to remain calm within his hateful embrace. He must never suspect how she really felt. How at this very moment a cold anger burned within her belly, so painful in its intensity that it was all she could do not to scream. He could never know how she longed to claw his face to bloody ribbons, and then with her bare fists beat what remained into a bleeding pulp.

"I have never loved anyone like I love you, Yasaman," he told her passionately. "Our coming together will be like nothing that has ever happened in the history of man. I will even restrain my ardor for you until I have built you our Garden of Shalimar."

It is there we will consummate our union and our children will rule India for a thousand generations to come, he thought silently, triumphantly.

"Salim!" She drew gently away from him, her voice softly chiding him. "You go much too quickly for me. I love you, too, my brother, but I am not certain I can come to terms with what this love between us means."

The soft blush on her cheeks, her modest reticence, all combined to but arouse his unholy passions further. He caught her hand in his and held it against his swiftly beating heart. "I will convince you, my beloved Yasaman, that what we desire is good and right," he declared with fervor. "How could the love we feel for one another be wrong?"

She arose, pulling away from him. "You must go, dear brother. It is very late. I must leave for Kashmir before sunrise."

He caught her to him and, looking down at her, kissed her hard. *"Remember that,* and remember how deeply I love you until we meet again, beloved," he whispered to her. Then, releasing her, he hurried back through the garden into the house.

Yasaman stood in stony silence, listening closely. She could hear the low hum of voices as Salim bid the servants good-night. She heard the rumble of the doors to her mother's palace closing, the heavy bolt being lifted into place with a thud. Only then did she lean over and vomit the contents of her stomach onto the ground. She wanted a bath, although all the washing in the world could not cleanse her of this feeling of defilement. It amazed her that she had been able to remain so docile and acquiescent while her brother had kissed and caressed her.

Her only regret was that he would never know how much he disgusted her; but Salim was so wrapped up in what he desired, it never occurred to him that others might not want what he did. By remaining calm while his mouth and hands had ravished her, she had convinced him that she would shortly be his. Yasaman wiped her mouth with the back of her hand and, leaving the garden, found her way to her mother's private apartments.

Rugaiya Begum looked up anxiously as her daughter entered her bedchamber. "He is gone?"

Yasaman nodded. "Yes, he is gone. Gone believing that he has practically won me over, and that I shall return to him after I have closed the door on Jamal Khan. He has vowed to build a garden called Shalimar in Kashmir as a testimony of his love for me. How dare he!" She flung herself into Rugaiya Begum's arms. "I let him kiss me and fondle my breasts, Mama Begum. But at least now he believes me truly within his grasp. I vomited after he left me."

Rugaiya Begum held her daughter tightly, stroking her dark hair tenderly. In just a few short hours they would be separated forever, and she would never again hold her child in her arms. She would never again see Yasaman, or know the man who would one day capture her heart, or grow old with her grandchildren about her. She grappled with herself to hold back her tears. The situation was even harder for poor Yasaman. Yasaman must leave everyone and everything she had ever known. This was what Salim had brought them to. She would never forgive him for it. "I hate him, too, my child," she admitted softly.

The two women stayed together for a time. Then Yasaman arose to bathe and dress for her journey. A young mute girl with a vague but passable resemblance to Yasaman had been found among the several thousand women of the Mughal's household. From a distance it would be assumed she was the princess. The caravan was under the charge of a loyal young Kashmiri captain whose mission was to deliver the heart of Jamal Khan to Yusef Khan, his father, for burial. The mute slave girl would be given her freedom, a dowry large enough to overcome her disability, and be put into the care of Yusef Khan, who would be instructed to find her a good husband. These were the captain's instructions.

Knowing nothing of why she was really being sent to Kashmir, and unable to speak even if she did know, the girl would be safe. So would the young captain, for he was not aware he should be accompanying Yasaman Kama Begum. His instructions were simply to take Jamal Khan's heart and the young mute to Yusef Khan. As for Yusef Khan himself, he only knew his son's heart was being sent home.

Indeed, by the time Salim discovered his sister was among the missing, there would only be two people in India who could tell him of Yasaman's whereabouts: his father and Rugaiya Begum. Akbar might even be dead by that time, and nothing, even the threat of torture and death, would make Rugaiya Begum divulge her daughter's sanctuary. Salim would not dare to attack his aunt, they all knew. She was his mother's best friend and well loved within the household. Rugaiya Begum would live out her lonely old age in peace.

Yasaman's caravan was to leave from outside the city and not from the emperor's fort. It would depart several hours before the sunrise. Almost all of Yasaman's possessions, including Balna and her charge, Hiraman, had been sent to the coast weeks ago to be put into the care of the factor of the O'Malley-Small Trading Company. This caravan would be a heavily armed, swiftly moving unit. The soldiers accompanying it were unquestioningly loyal to Akbar. Their captains had only been told that a young person of importance was to be taken quickly and safely to Cambay. Eventually, of course, Salim might hear of this, but then again he might not if the trip was an uneventful one, for this group of soldiers frequently discharged duties of this exact nature.

There would be nothing, however, to indicate that this was the caravan of a royal Mughal princess. Yasaman was only close to Rohana and Toramalli, among her servants, and to her high steward, Adali. None of the trio would allow her to leave them behind despite the fact that she had offered them their freedom, along with dowries for the two sisters who were pretty and young enough yet to find husbands, and a monetary settlement for Adali so he might go into business for himself. All refused.

"Our life is with you, gracious lady," Adali had said, speaking for them all. "If you leave us behind, we will be in danger. Even if we were not privy to your plans, Prince Salim would not believe we did not know your destination. He would hunt us down and torture us for answers we could not give him. Besides, what would you do without us? We have served you your whole life."

"And served me well," she told them. "Very well, you may come with me, but you come not as slaves, rather as freed servants. If at any time you wish to leave me, you have but to ask. I will settle a sum of money upon you then for your term of faithful service. From this day, however, you will receive your wages yearly, as well as a clothing allowance, your room, and your board. Is it agreed?"

They fell to their knees before her, thanking her. Their princess had been more than generous. Then, to their horror, Yasaman had told them that they must learn to ride horses. That would be their means of transportation to the coast. Now, several weeks later, they prepared nervously for their upcoming journey over the dusty summer roads of India, heading for the sea which only Adali and Father Cullen had ever seen.

Adali escorted Rohana and Toramalli, dressed as young men, to the caravan site and returned for his mistress and the priest. Akbar had slipped away from his own palace and entered his wife's palace through an underground passage that connected them. Now father and daughter stood together with Rugaiya Begum.

"What can I say to you, Yasaman, that you do not already know?" Akbar asked his youngest child. "Will it help you to once again hear that you are my favorite child? That were I not dying, I should not be strong enough to send you from me and from this terrible danger you face at your brother Salim's hands? Ahhh, Yasaman, how I love you! Never forget that you were born of the great love that was once shared between Candra and me. I can only pray that she will welcome you into her heart as I once welcomed her into mine when she arrived in this land, frightened and alone. Tell her . . . tell her I have never forgotten what we once shared, and that I take the memory of her to my grave. I shall be dead before you reach this England that I am sending you to, my daughter, but you will know for certain that I have joined our ancestors by this sign that Rugaiya Begum shall send to you." He removed a strand of black pearls from about his neck and gave them to the older woman.

"I know I must go, and yet I do not want to leave you," Yasaman told him. "Still, my hatred of Salim is so great now that I dare not remain else I be driven to violence or worse to some plot against my brother's succession. I would not hurt you, Papa. I know that despite everything, you love your Shaikho Baba. If I remained, you would be forced to choose between your love for him and your love for me."

"The priest, your cousin, tells me that Candra's family will welcome you gladly and with love, Yasaman. Take courage in that knowledge, but never forget that no matter where you are, you are the Mughal Akbar's daughter. In your veins runs the blood of Genghis Khan, Kublai Khan, and the great Tamerlane; noble members all of a proud and ancient race. You are their descendant, and you must never bow your head before any man or woman, for none is your true equal!" Taking her by the shoulders, he kissed her forehead. "Go with the God who watches over us all, my child."

She struggled against them, but the tears sprang into her turquoise eyes, making them shine and glitter. "I will not forget, my father," she told him. "How could I ever forget that I am your daughter?"

He smiled weakly at her as he made a small attempt at

humor. "You are a handsome son for so dutiful a daughter," he told her, for she was dressed in man's garb, her dark hair tucked beneath a small white turban.

Yasaman bit her lip and quickly turned away lest her resolve not to weep openly weaken. "Mama Begum, you are my only mother and I shall love you forever! Do not forget me," Yasaman begged, hugging the older woman.

My heart is breaking, Rugaiya Begum thought sadly, but she answered bravely, "I am the mother fortunate enough to have raised you to womanhood. I love you with all my heart, my daughter, but Candra is the mother who bore you. We did not ever believe you should know her, but fate has dictated otherwise. There is much in her, I remember, that reminds me of you. She is intelligent, and kind, and her temper burned every bit as hot as yours does. Do not dislike her because your kismet has driven you from India. None of this is her fault, and I thank Allah that she is there, a safe haven for us to send you to, Yasaman." Rugaiya Begum kissed her daughter tenderly and then said, "Go now. Never look back, Yasaman. Always look forward as you travel through life. Memories are good things to have, but to live life is to obey Allah's wishes for us. Remember that too."

Adali took his mistress by the arm and quickly led her from the chamber where Akbar and Rugaiya Begum remained. She did not see the stricken look upon the Mughal's face, or hear the bitter sobs that came from Rugaiya Begum, who collapsed in her husband's arms, weeping.

Adali and Yasaman left the palace and, walking swiftly across the courtyards and walkways, through arches and over marble footbridges, exited the Red Fort through the small private south gate where the guardsman now slept a wine-induced sleep at his post. Cullen Butler was waiting for them with the horses. Mounting, they rode across the city of Agra to its outskirts, where their caravan awaited them.

The moon was bright as they traveled along, and Cullen

Butler could see the silent tears that rolled down Yasaman's face. "Are you all right?" he finally asked her.

Swallowing hard, she nodded. "If I don't weep a bit, I shall scream," she admitted. "It has been a terrible few hours."

"I want you to speak English from now on," he told her. "You need to practice, and besides, if you do, we won't have to worry about anyone overhearing and understanding us," he explained in that tongue.

"Very well, cousin," she agreed. "I had indeed best practice the use of Candra's native tongue. You and I must teach my maidens on the long voyage how to speak proper English."

He smiled back at her, and Yasaman wondered if the rest of her other family looked like Cullen Butler. They had explained his true relationship to her weeks ago when she had recovered from the miscarriage of her child. It had seemed a sign at the time. She had lost one family in Jamal and their baby, only to have gained another in Cullen Butler, whom she had actually known her entire life.

They arrived safely in the port city of Cambay, and Alain O'Flaherty, after his initial shock, greeted his newfound cousin warmly. As they had been several weeks upon the road, Yasaman welcomed the next few days of rest while they awaited the arrival of the O'Malley-Small fleet.

When, however, her companion saw the princess beginning to grow restless, an excursion to Cambay's marketplace was arranged. In the company of Alain, who was a younger version of Cullen Butler, and with Adali and her female servants, Yasaman walked through the market. Properly veiled and with such a prosperous-looking party, she was assailed on all sides by the shouting merchants hawking their wares. She bought several wonderful bolts of silk, and others of cotton. Blocks of foil-wrapped tea, both green and black, were added to her stash. A slipper merchant's stall caught her eye, but there was, to her disappointment, nothing to fit her slender foot.

"I should think not!" Toramalli huffed indignantly. "You are a princess and not some common creature who buys her footwear in an open market." She turned to Alain. "Why, good sir, all my mistress's slippers are made for her alone. Do you know how the foot of a princess is measured?" And before he could answer, she continued on. "Why, it is measured with a string of pearls, and the pearls not needed for the shoemaker, our lady has given to my sister and me." She held up a particularly beautiful strand from about her neck. "Those discarded gems over the years have gone to make me this fine necklace! No, indeed! A princess does not buy her footwear in a marketplace."

Alain was astounded. "Is this fact?" he asked Yasaman.

"Yes it is," she said with a small smile.

"Amazing! Here these last few days you have been questioning all of us about life in England, and yet your life is far more fascinating, cousin."

When they returned to the harbor, they found that eight ships of the O'Malley-Small trading fleet had arrived at Cambay. The fleet was under the command of Captain Michael Small, who told them that there were eight other vessels with which they would rendezvous off the African coast and were now in the Spice Islands picking up their cargos.

To Yasaman's surprise, Captain Small knew immediately who she was. He had been told of her by her uncle Murrough many years ago, he explained, for the secret of her existence had weighed heavily upon Murrough, who had captained the vessel that brought Velvet home from India. Michael Small's kindness reassured the princess, who was growing more nervous as the time of her departure approached.

Yasaman's fortune was loaded onto her family's fleet. She would travel upon *Cardiff Rose*. Captain Small had ceded his large quarters to his royal passenger and her companions. The simple, spare area was now lush with colorful silk cushions and seductive gauze hangings. Hiraman, the parrot, shrieked noisily from his perch. Fou-Fou and Jiinn had settled themselves regally upon the cushions. Only Baba, Yasaman's monkey, seemed truly unhappy.

"I have, on occasion, seen birds like this one in England," the captain told Yasaman, "and the cats will, of course, thrive quite nicely, but I fear for this little fellow." He cuddled the monkey in the crook of his arm. "He may not survive our cold weather."

"He is the first pet I ever had," Yasaman said. "My father gave him to me for my fourth birthday." She scratched the monkey's small round head and a tear slipped down her cheek. "I don't really pay a great deal of attention to him anymore, but I will miss him if I leave him behind. What will happen to him?"

"Give him to me," Alain said. "I'll give him a good home. He seems to enjoy playing in the courtyard trees by my office, cousin. He might even find himself a lady monkey to keep him company in his old age," the factor told Yasaman with a twinkle in his eye. "Every gentleman should have a lady to keep him happy when he has had his fill of adventuring. I think Baba has reached that stage of life. He seems to like me, don't you, old fellow?"

She sighed deeply, but then agreed. "Take him, Alain, but promise me you will be good to him. He doesn't like thunderstorms. He'll want to cuddle in your arms if there is one. And he loves fresh coconut and mango. You will see he gets those fruits, won't you?"

"I will treat him as my own."

Alain O'Flaherty departed the ship with Baba clinging to his shoulder, chattering excitedly with relief to be off the vessel. The factor remained upon the docks overseeing the raising of the gangway and the anchor. He watched as the sails on all of the ships were raised slowly, catching the gentle afternoon trade winds. He stood waving as the O'Malley-Small ships cleared the harbor.

. Captain Michael Small, having seen his ship safely out of the harbor and into the open sea, joined his passenger at the ship's rail. Yasaman stood silently watching the coastline as it quickly disappeared. *India.* The land of her birth. The blood of its people ran in her veins, but then so, too, did the blood of the English. She had always been so certain of who she was and where she belonged. Now she was not so certain.

The captain took her delicate hand in his big rough one and told her, "Do not be sad, my child. There is a saying among our people that when one door closes, another one is certain to open. You have so much to look forward to, Yasaman. Do not despair."

"As I have so much to anticipate, Captain," she told him, "I also have so many memories to recall. I can never forget India."

"You must not!" he said. "Ah, no, Yasaman, you must never forget any experience, good or bad. Learn from them, treasure them, but never, ever forget. That, dear girl, is life, and life, your grandmother Lady de Marisco has taught me, is good. It is to be lived to the fullest, even in the darkest of times. And now, Yasaman Begum, you have closed the door on one part of your life, only to find the next door wide open and ready for you to walk through." He squeezed her hand. "I will be with you, and Cullen Butler, and your Adali, and your women. Do not be afraid, Princess."

Remember you are the Mughal's daughter, she heard Rugaiya Begum saying in her heart. "I am not afraid, Michael Small," she told him. "If I am sad in leaving my home, so am I happy to have my . . . my mother's family to be going to in England."

"You're a brave lass, Yasaman, but then you come from a race of brave women," he told her.

"Not Yasaman, Captain," she replied, and she gazed a final time on the disappearing coast of India. "I have left Yasaman Kama Begum behind me. If I am to blend into this new world I must enter, it is best if I do not seem different. From this moment on you will call me Jasmine, which is the English translation of my name. And it is the custom, is it not, for the English to have surnames? Do you think my grandparents would mind if I took their surname as my own?"

"No," he said quietly, "I do not think they would mind. Rather, I think they will be most pleased."

"Then it is settled," she said with a smile. "I am Jasmine de Marisco from this day forth, *but*," she added, *"I will, nonetheless, always be the Mughal's daughter."*

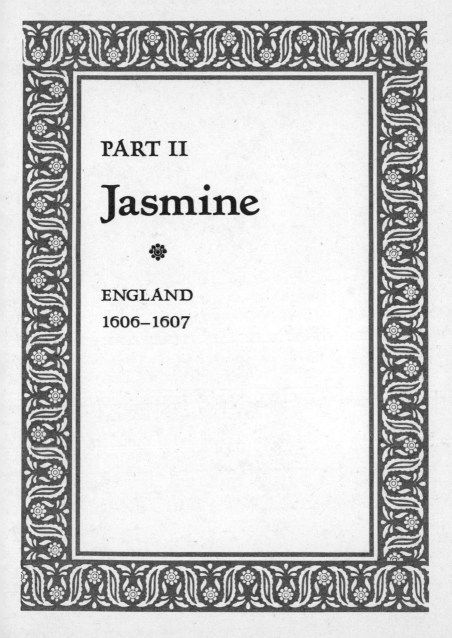

PART II

Jasmine

❋

ENGLAND

1606–1607

❀

8

❀

"*Thistlewood!*" Skye O'Malley de Marisco leaned precariously out of the window of her coach as it careened along
the London Road. Behind her, inside the vehicle, her husband,
Adam, sat calmly, a slight smile upon his handsome face.
"Damn it, Thistlewood! Can you go no faster?" Skye shouted
up to her coachman, who had his hands quite full with the
galloping horses and trying to remain securely upon his seat.

"The horses is full out, m'lady," the terse answer came back.

"God's foot! We're going to be late," Skye concluded as she
withdrew back into her coach, raising the window up to keep
the cold air out. Grumbling, she pulled the beaver lap robe
back over her knees. "Our little princess, the grandchild we've
never seen, has been at sea for almost six months. A wonderful welcome she'll receive when she gets to London and finds
no one to greet her. She'll think we don't want her, Adam!
Poor child!" Her Kerry-blue eyes grew misty.

"Sit back, little girl," her husband advised her quietly,
and he took her hand in his big one. "Adali left Queen's
Malvern before the storm blocked the roads between our

estate and London. He was safely in town two weeks ago. If our trading fleet arrives early, he will be there to greet his young mistress and to escort her to Greenwood House, where she will be safe until we can reach London. You sent word to the servants to open the house and prepare for our coming. Mrs. Winters will have an ample amount of lads trained for footmen, and Davis will have found his grooms for the stables. As for Mrs. Evans, she'll be in her glory planning menus." He patted the icy little hand in his. "We'll be there soon, Skye, but then when were you ever patient about getting something you wanted? No one knows better than I do how much you desire to get your hands on this particular grandchild of ours." He chuckled wickedly.

"Are you going to sit there, you maddening old man, and tell me that you aren't as anxious to meet Yasaman as I am? That you do not want her with us at long last?" she demanded of him. "That child is Velvet's firstborn!"

"I know," he said, "and I won't lie to you. I'm eager to meet the girl. I want to know what she is like. I'm not a man for mysteries."

"Ohh, Adam!" Skye continued. "Do you know what a shock it was to me when Adali arrived at Queen's Malvern on Christmas Day? And the servants! I thought their eyes would pop out of their heads when they saw him in that wonderful fur-lined robe with a turban upon his head. I am amazed they were able to keep him a secret from the family." She giggled, a sound he found charming in a woman of her years. "And the family still thinks us mad for our little outburst in the Great Hall after baby Adam's christening. Willow, in particular, thinks us quite dotty with all our teasing talk of a forty-sixth grandchild. And all our daughters and daughters-in-law were hotly denying that any of them was with child. We had the hall in quite an uproar." She laughed aloud with the memory.

"Particularly," he agreed, "as you would not explain yourself to Willow despite her persistence. How your eldest daughter dislikes being kept out of anything. Well, she'll know soon enough; and I, for one, want to personally be there to see her face when she meets Yasaman." He chuckled again. "Our dear prim and proper Willow is in for quite a shock."

"I hope their voyage was a good one," Skye said. "I remember how tedious the days seemed when we were going out and coming back from India on that expedition for Queen Bess."

"Adali told me that the voyage was quite pleasant up to the time he left them. Yasaman and Father Cullen spent their days teaching her female servants English. Adali, of course, learned it years ago from Velvet and Father Cullen. That is why the emperor entrusted him with that letter he sent us. I think it quite clever of Adali that he suggested to Captain Small he come ahead in a single ship rather than waiting for the entire fleet. It gave us a good month's warning so we might prepare for our grandchild's arrival.

"Aye," Skye agreed. "Adali is a very clever fellow. His purpose has always been to smooth our grandchild's way. He tells me that this is the first time in Yasaman's life that he has been separated from her for any period of time. He's terribly devoted to the girl. I hope he will be content in England. He says his father was a French sailor. He certainly has a Gallic look about him, but for his brown skin. I trust him, and I like him, Adam, don't you?"

"Aye, I do," Adam replied. "He fit right in, too, with all our good English servants. Your tiring woman Daisy confided in me that he was a 'real gentleman, m'lord.' He'll get no higher praise than that coming from our good Daisy," Adam de Marisco said with a smile.

The coach raced toward London. Outside it was a cold but quite clear day. It had snowed heavily several days before. Now the sunlight glinted off the crystalline whiteness with almost blinding intensity. The bare trees stood out black against the bright blue sky. Already, from his vantage spot atop the coachman's box, Thistlewood could see the spire of Westminster. He whistled to his horses, encouraging them onward.

• •

The O'Malley-Small trading fleet, fifteen vessels strong, slowly made its way up the Thames River toward the London Pool, where they would anchor. Jasmine de Marisco and her two women servants stood in the large bow window in the master's cabin watching the landscape pass by.

"There is no green," Rohana said nervously. "It is so stark a land and so cold."

"It is winter, but England, I have always been told, is a very green and beautiful land," Jasmine assured her. "Why are you so fretful? You have seen snow before in Kashmir, Rohana."

"That is true, my lady princess," the servant admitted, "but Kashmir was familiar to me. This place is not."

"It will be soon enough, sister," Toramalli said briskly. She had always been the braver of the twins. "I, for one, am simply happy to see land at long last! Desert isle or snowy hill, I will be glad to be off this ship after so many months at sea, and pleased to see our dear old Adali again. It has seemed so strange without him."

There was a knock upon the cabin door and Rohana ran to open it, admitting Cullen Butler. He was dressed as they had never seen him before, in black wool pantaloons and a black velvet doublet with the most modest amount of gold embroidery. There was a small ruff about his neck, and his leather boots came to his knees. Upon his head was a flat black cap of velvet with a small white plume.

Seeing their look of surprise, he explained, "Priests of the Holy Mother Church are not warmly welcomed in England anymore. It is best that I remain discreet with regard to my calling."

Jasmine nodded. "And shall I call you cousin Cullen?"

"Aye," he said. " 'Twould be best, and the lasses will call me Master Butler."

"Do you understand?" Jasmine asked her servants, and they nodded in the affirmative. "I think," she continued, "that you must go home to Ireland as soon as you can, cousin Cullen. If I am safe in my grandmother's care, then there is little need for you to chaperon me any longer, is there? Your duty to me is done, cousin. You long for your Ireland, I know, and for a little stone church somewhere in its hills. And your mother will want to see you, too, won't she? I do not imagine she ever expected to see you again."

"Nay, she surely did not," he agreed, "but I will wager she already knows that I am coming. Your grandmother will have written to her. It's true, Jasmine, you really do not need me any longer. You're educated, and you have grown into a beautiful woman. Your education I can take credit for, but as for your spiritual well-being, I have failed miserably."

"Is my grandmother a devout woman?" Jasmine asked him.

"In her own way, I suppose," he said glumly.

"In other words, just like me?" Jasmine teased him.

Cullen Butler thought a moment, and then he laughed. "Aye, I think you're probably correct, cousin. My aunt Skye has supreme faith in God and her own ability to handle anything that is presented to her. She once told me that God never gave us anything to do he did not truly believe we could handle. It was just before I came out to India. I was so fearful that the emperor would not like me, or that the Jesuits would attempt to interfere in my appointment, or that you would not want me to be your tutor and spiritual advisor."

"How foolish of you," Jasmine told him. "I loved you from the first. It will be hard for me to part with you, cousin Cullen, but you are a priest. Your first loyalty must be to God and service to Him. That is why I will send you home to Ireland. I do not need you, but there are many souls who will, I know."

Her astute words touched him. "Perhaps I have not failed with you after all, Jasmine de Marisco," he said quietly.

There was another knock upon the door, and Rohana

admitted Captain Small. "We'll be anchoring in another minute or two. The barge from Greenwood House is already awaiting you, my lady," he said. "I have brought you a fur-lined cape to wear. It is very chilly upon the river, and you have a bit of a row before you." He handed Toramalli the garment and, bowing, returned to his duties.

"I know that our clothing isn't warm enough, cousin," Jasmine worried. She and her serving women were dressed in salwar pajamas, baggy trousers gathered at the ankles that had been made of soft Kashmir wool. Over the trousers they wore jaguli dresses. Cullen Butler had given each girl several pairs of silk stockings to wear with their dainty slippers so that their feet would stay warm, but he wondered now, given the particularly cold weather, if it was enough.

"There will be a heater in the barge," he told her, "and hot bricks wrapped in flannel for your feet." He wrapped the cape about his charge and then escorted the three women out onto the deck. There was a light breeze blowing and it seemed, Jasmine quickly found, to go right through all her many layers of clothing. She looked to her servants and saw that they were already shivering. There was nothing she could do about it, Jasmine thought. She just hoped that they would reach Greenwood House quickly. She walked to the ship's rail and peered over. Beneath her a very elegant barge bobbed in the waves. It was large, and the cabin appeared to have glass windows.

A turbaned head popped from beneath the wooden canopy. A familiar grin split the face. "Gracious lady!" Adali called up to her. "Welcome to England! Your grandparents should be awaiting you at Greenwood House."

Jasmine nodded excitedly, suddenly eager once again. She turned and thanked Michael Small and his ship, *Cardiff Rose*, for bringing her in safely from India. She thanked his youngest son, who had been the cabin boy, giving the blushing lad a kiss on the cheek and a tiny ivory elephant for a souvenir. "Shall I take my grandmother any message, Captain Small?" she asked him.

"Just say it was a successful, profitable trip, my lady, and I will await her summons tomorrow. I thank you for asking. Do not fear for your possessions. They will be brought immediately upriver to Greenwood House."

Rohana and Toramalli had already been put into the Greenwood vessel. Cullen Butler now helped Jasmine into the bosun's chair, and as soon as she was settled, it was swung out over the ship's side and lowered to the barge where Adali helped his mistress out. The chair was hauled up to take the priest, who quickly joined them.

Jasmine and her two servants found themselves settled upon a well-upholstered velvet bench within the cabin. Heavy fur lap robes were tucked in about them. Hot bricks were placed at their feet. A small brazier of hot coals set upon the floor helped to assuage some of the icy, damp air. Adali was grinning delightedly. He and Cullen Butler settled themselves opposite the women.

"I cannot believe you are finally here, gracious lady," the eunuch said to her. "I arrived over a month ago. I reached your lady grandmother's house, a place called Queen's Malvern, on Christmas Day. Your newest cousin was being christened. You have a huge family, gracious lady. They are all most beautiful, but very noisy."

"Do they know about me?" Jasmine asked him.

"Not yet," Adali replied. "Your lady grandmother wishes to keep it a secret until your mother can be informed." He then said to Jasmine, "Lady de Marisco is most formidable, my princess. She hides a marble fist beneath a swath of silk, but her family all love and respect her. She is most happy to welcome you, and cried when I told her of your coming. Your grandfather is a wonderful old gentleman, gracious lady. He, too, looks forward to meeting you."

The Greenwood barge made its way up the river to

Chiswick-on-Strand, where Greenwood House was located, the very last house on Riversedge Street. From the water, Jasmine saw that, unlike its more magnificent neighbors, it was an elegant but small house of mellowed pink brick, one wall of which was covered in dark green ivy. The house, she would later discover, was set within a beautifully kept park with a small woodland.

The barge nosed its way gently into the small dock where a waiting footman made it fast and then helped the passengers from the vessel. For a moment Jasmine swayed, unable to regain her land legs, but then she stepped firmly forward onto the snowy lawn. Behind her came her women, the priest, and Adali.

"This way, my lady," the footman said politely, wondering to himself what manner of creatures they were. They surely looked like a pack of Gypsies with their odd, colorful garments and head shawls. He shook his head. He was paid to serve, and not to involve himself in the business of the gentry. Lady de Marisco was a good employer. The footman led the way up from the river's edge toward the house.

Suddenly, from the lovely brick building, a woman emerged. She was half running, and her dark green velvet skirts blew in the light breeze off the river. She was tall and more slender than not, yet she had the substantial look of a woman who had borne children. Her hair was very dark but for two silver wings that showed just above her ears, and she wore it in an elegant chignon dressed with silk flowers. There was a smile of welcome upon her face, and for a brief moment Jasmine wondered if this was Candra.

The priest jumped forward and hurried toward the lady. "Aunt Skye!" he said, catching her hand up as he reached her and kissing it. "Why is it you never age, madame? I shall return to Ireland to find my own mother, your sister, a white-haired little old lady."

A peal of rich laughter rang out at the loving flattery. "If I were going to age, Cullen Butler," Skye said, "I should have

done so years ago with all my adventures, but I have not."
She kissed him on the cheek, then gently pushing him aside,
moved past him, stopping before Jasmine.

For what seemed a very, very long moment, the two
women surveyed each other carefully, Skye's Kerry-blue eyes
hungrily scanning the slender girl for something familiar,
something of Velvet, but not really finding it; Jasmine absolutely astounded that this elegant, youthful lady was her
grandmother. Mariam Makani seemed ancient by comparison. Did Candra look like her?

"You are so beautiful," the girl finally said softly, breaking
the silence between them.

"So are you," Skye told her granddaughter, a half smile
touching her mouth, yet biting her lower lip to keep from
crying.

"Am I like Candra? My mother, I mean," Jasmine corrected herself, blushing. "I really am trying to think of her
as my mother."

"No. Yes. Perhaps a little," Skye replied, and she laughed
aloud. "Your face is heart-shaped like mine, but you have
your mother's mouth, and your nose is long and slender
like your mother's. Your eyes have the same shape as Velvet's, but there is a much different look to them, and the
color! They are like a Persian turquoise. As for that charming little mole between your upper lip and your left nostril,
I do not recognize it at all, but I do not doubt the gentlemen
will find it fascinating. You are yourself, I can see, my darling
girl. I am so happy to have you with me at long last! Welcome to England, Yasaman Kama Begum!"

"I have left Yasaman Kama Begum behind in India,
Grandmother," Jasmine told her. "With your permission, I
should prefer to be known as Jasmine de Marisco."

Tears threatened to totally overwhelm Lady de Marisco
for a moment, and then she said, "So you shall be, my darling girl! Welcome to England, Jasmine de Marisco!" Then,
unable to restrain herself any longer, Skye hugged the girl

hard, kissing her soft, perfumed cheek. Releasing her, she said briskly, "Let us go in! You and your ladies must be freezing in this river wind. Your grandfather is awaiting you in the house. I would not let him come out with me because I wanted to see you first. If we do not go in now, however, he will come stomping out and catch a chill from which it will take him weeks to recover." She linked her arm in the girl's and together they hurried into Greenwood.

Adam de Marisco had watched the women from the vantage point of his library windows. Even with less than perfect vision, he could see that the girl was extraordinarily lovely. This, then, was his firstborn grandchild. He wondered what his daughter Velvet was going to say about this development. He had wanted to write to her immediately after the arrival of Adali, but Skye had not let him.

"Let us see what the girl is like first," she said reasonably. "Perhaps she cannot speak English, or has no idea of English manners. If that be so, we will teach her that she show to her best advantage with her mother when they finally meet."

"What if she is presentable?" he had demanded of his wife.

"There is no great rush to write to Velvet," Skye had told him. "She and Alex and the children will be here as usual for their English summer. Time enough for Velvet and her daughter to meet one another. What a wonderful surprise it will be for Velvet to finally know the child she was forced to leave behind in India. I shall never forget how devastated she was over it, Adam."

"Nor will I," he had replied. "But do you think surprising her like this is really a good idea, little girl?"

"I cannot wait to see the look on her face!" Skye had answered gleefully. "Velvet has always loved surprises."

He was still not certain that his wife's idea was a particularly good one, but then the door to the library opened and Skye came in accompanied by his grandchild. Adam de Marisco opened his arms to the girl and, without a word, she went into them. He struggled not to cry, but the tears slipped down his weathered cheeks. He thought himself an old fool, but he could simply not help it. "Dear girl," he said. "I never thought to hold you in my arms, but now I can die happy."

"Stop talking of dying, Adam de Marisco," Skye scolded him. "You may be seventy-five years of age, but you're in better health and vigor than most men half your age! Now stop smothering Jasmine and let her go. You haven't had a proper look at her yet, and when you do, you will see what a magnificent beauty she is. Once the gentlemen get a look at her, we will have to hire men-at-arms to protect her. This new court is not as elegant, nor does it have the delicacy of manners that Bess's court had in its heyday."

Adam de Marisco released his granddaughter from the bear hug in which he had enveloped her and said to his wife, "*Court?* We have not been to court in years. What is this talk of court?"

"We never went to court because Bess banned me," Skye said airily, "but this Stuart king doesn't even know me. How are we to find a new husband for Jasmine if we don't go to court?"

"*Jasmine?*" He looked puzzled.

"Our granddaughter has Anglicized her name from Yasaman to Jasmine, and she has taken your surname for her own. She is Jasmine de Marisco now. Is it not perfect, Adam?"

"Indeed it is!" He beamed with approval, and then he looked at the girl, scanning her carefully with his smoky blue eyes. "She has your look about her, Skye," he said.

"Do you really think so?" the proud grandmother asked.

"Have you no granddaughters who look like you?" Jasmine asked.

Skye thought a moment and then she said, "Perhaps your cousin, Laura Southwood, or mayhap Thalia Blakeley, but they are so young yet, I cannot really be certain. Little Bessie Burke is certainly like me in temperament." She chuckled.

"Oh, darling girl, what a large and loving family you have here in England. They will love you on sight as I do!"

"How many grandchildren do you have, Grandmother?" Jasmine wondered aloud.

"Well, let me see," Skye considered. "My eldest son, Ewan O'Flaherty, has eight children, including Alain, whom you met in Cambay. Ewan's brother, Murrough, has six children; your aunt Willow has eight; your uncle Robin, the Earl of Lynmouth, has eight, three from his first marriage, five from his second; your aunt Deirdre has seven; and your uncle Padraic, Lord Burke, who was slow to marry, has but two so far. The baby, Adam Burke, was christened on Christmas Day when your Adali came to us with the news you were arriving in England within the month."

"And my mother? How many children has she now?" Jasmine inquired.

"You have five half brothers and a stepsister, my darling girl," Skye told her. "Your brothers are named James, although he is called Sandy; Adam Charles; Robert and Henry, who are twins; and last is Edward. They're fine boys, if a bit rough from growing up in Scotland. As for your stepsister, she is Lady Sybilla Alexandra Mary Gordon. She is just six months older than you. Perhaps you will be friends," Skye said. "Your mother and her family will be arriving at the end of April. Velvet's birthday is May first. We always try to be together on that day. You, darling girl, will be the best birthday present your mother ever had! You have no idea how she mourned leaving you behind."

"What does she look like now?" Jasmine asked her grandmother. "Our first night at sea after we had left India, Adali gave me this miniature of my mother." Jasmine drew it from the pocket of her jaguli dress and held it out to Skye. "Candra had given it to him before she departed India. Her instructions were that he give it to me someday when I was old enough, but over the years he forgot all about it. He found it when he was packing his possessions to come to England."

Skye looked at the little painting and smiled. "This was your mother at fifteen or sixteen," she said. "She will be celebrating her thirty-third birthday this year. The face in the picture is a girl's face, innocent and really quite unknowing of the world. If anything, she is lovelier now, but her features are more mature than the maiden's in this picture. Still, you will easily recognize her when you see her."

"In the spring?" Jasmine looked eager; and for the first time she seemed like the young girl she really was, Adam thought, watching her.

"Aye, in the spring," Skye promised her, "but until then we must keep your presence here a secret. I want no one spoiling my fine surprise. If one of your aunts or uncles know, soon the entire family will know. We will stay here in London until mid-April. If we go home to Queen's Malvern, Deirdre could easily discover you, for she and her family live nearby. She would tell her brother Padraic, who cannot keep a secret to save his soul. Soon Robin would know, and your aunt Willow, and both of your O'Flaherty uncles. Besides, you will need time to recover from your long voyage; and you will need a whole new wardrobe, my darling girl; and your servants will need new clothes more in keeping with their station here in England. Now, let me see," Skye said, "where shall we begin?"

Adam de Marisco grinned at his granddaughter, who was beginning to look somewhat overwhelmed by her grandmother. "Best to let her have her way, Jasmine," he counseled her. "She will anyway in the end."

"I have been told that my grandmother is *formidable*," Jasmine said mischievously. She already adored this great big man with his wonderful smoky blue eyes and his shock of silver-white hair.

"*Formidable? Me?*" Skye pretended to look offended, but

seeing the look in her companions' eyes, she could not help but burst out laughing.

The de Mariscos were astounded by the vast wealth that had accompanied Jasmine. If they had not been certain of it before, they were now quite sure of Akbar's deep love for his youngest child. The quantity and the quality of the rare, costly spices that had come to England with their grand-daughter, when sold, would make her a very rich woman for the rest of her life. There was yet another fortune in fine fabrics; the silks and cottons that the princess brought with her sent her grandmother into rapture. Skye, whose own collection of jewelry was one of the finest in Europe, was frankly amazed by the magnificent jewelry and uncut gemstones in Jasmine's possession. Indeed, her wealth was fabulous.

"My husband, Jamal, gave me this," Jasmine told her grandmother one day, showing her the Stars of Kashmir necklace.

Skye took the jewels and examined them carefully. "They are the finest sapphires I have ever seen, and each stone is flawless," she told her granddaughter honestly. "Do you see that tiny flame of green within each stone? Only the greatest sapphires have such a flame." She handed the necklace back to the girl. "Did you love him very much, my darling?" she asked. Jasmine had not spoken a great deal about her husband.

"It seems so long ago," Jasmine admitted. "He has been dead almost a year. I am not even certain that I can remember his face now. Is that awful of me, Grandmother? Did I love him? Yes, I did love him, and he loved me. He was charming and wise. He would have served my father and my brother well, but my brother arranged his murder. I will never forgive Salim for it, even if I live to be an old lady of one hundred!"

Jasmine had said little about her life in India, but she never failed to answer a direct question when asked. It was

just that she never volunteered any information about herself or her past.

"She is hurting," Adam said to Skye. "I think she finds it
easier to come to terms with herself and the life she must
now lead by putting her past behind her."

The winter was quickly over, for there was so much to do
and the long days sped swiftly by. A skilled dressmaker was
found to come and live in while she created an entire wardrobe for Jasmine. There were gowns of velvet, taffeta, brocade, silk and damask weaves. Jasmine's rich complexion with
its hint of gold favored rich shades of red, green, violet,
lavender, black, gold, peacock-blue, and cream. Skye insisted
that everything be in the latest styles. Farthingales were
smaller now, although the skirts were still bell-shaped, and
yet divided to show an undergown. Skirts were also slightly
shorter, coming to the ankle, but necklines were still square
and very low.

Jasmine was slightly shocked. "But my breasts can be
plainly seen," she wailed at her first fitting.

" 'Tis the fashion," her grandmother decreed. "You have
beautiful breasts, my darling girl. Besides, if one is to catch
a rich husband, one must bait the trap well, eh?"

Jasmine burst out laughing, and even the dressmaker
tittered.

"I'm not certain I want another husband, Grandmother."

"What do you want?" Skye asked quietly.

"I do not know yet," Jasmine said honestly. "This is a
new world for me. I would explore it and learn all I can
about it."

"But when you have finished exploring it," Skye said
wisely, "you will want a husband with whom you can settle
down and have children. What else is there for a woman if
not a family, Jasmine? Were things so different in your native
India? I do not think they were. Would not your Mama
Begum rejoice to learn you have found another true love

and happiness once again, darling girl? If she is the dear, wonderful lady you have told me that she is, I know she would."

"Aye," Jasmine admitted to Skye. "She would be very happy to know I had found happiness with a new love. Ohh, Grandmother! I miss her so very much! Here is another pain Salim has inflicted upon me. He is my brother and claims to love me, but he has caused me nothing but misery. He loved our father, too, but he was never happy being just his heir. He had to be the Mughal. Nothing else would do for Salim. He brought Father great unhappiness despite the love Father had for him. What matter of man is it that loves but constantly brings sorrow to those he loves?"

"I do not know," Skye told Jasmine, "but something good has come out of this all, my darling girl. You have come to England!"

The fittings continued. There were nightgowns, chemises, blouses, and petticoats to be made. Corsets, made of laths about two inches wide, banded together by silk ribbons, were the latest fashion from Spain. Jasmine would not wear one, despite the dressmaker's tsking disapproval.

"I cannot breathe in one of those things!" she said.

"Then you shall not have it," her grandmother agreed.

The dressmaker and her assistant sewed on, making high-waisted cloaks with full sleeves, jackets for riding and archery, and capes with hoods for rainy days. There were silk stockings bought, and shoes and boots made to order. Jasmine told her grandmother of how her foot had been measured in India, and the dressmakers listened, their eyes wide. There was clothing for the winter months, and clothing for the warmer months, and clothing for the in-between months. Jasmine's gowns were decorated with embroidery and beautiful buttons of ivory, bone, pearl, and precious gemstones. There were gloves sewn and handkerchiefs embroidered with the monogram *J de M.* The use of lace and silk ribbons was lavish.

"I shall be able to buy myself a shop with what I have earned sewing for you, my lady," the little dressmaker admitted on the day that she left them.

It was early April, and on that same day two messengers had arrived, one from the north and the other from a ship newly docked from the East Indies. The first messenger, wearing the livery of the Earl of BrocCairn, carried a letter for Skye. Opening it, she scanned its contents.

"We must go home," Skye said. "Your mother and her brood will be at Queen's Malvern in two weeks. I shall hold a family party!" Then she looked at her granddaughter, who had suddenly grown paler as she read the message that had been addressed to her. "What is it, darling child?"

"My father is dead," Jasmine said. She held up a strand of magnificent black pearls. "Alain has sent us the news via a late-departing merchant vessel." Silent tears began to slip down her beautiful face. "My father arranged this sign with me so I should be certain the messenger did not lie."

Skye enfolded the girl in a loving embrace. "Death," she said, "is always a shock. Even when it is expected, we don't quite expect it. I will always remember when my own father died. I came to his bedside, and he entrusted the well-being of the family into my hands, much to the shock of my sisters and brothers-in-law. Only my stepmother Anne supported me." She caressed Jasmine's hair. "Does Alain say when the emperor died, my darling?"

"He died on October fifteenth, 1605. In the evening. It was his sixty-third birthday. Mama Begum and Jodh Bai were with him," Jasmine said. "Alain is quoting the official statement." Then she sobbed her grief for Akbar upon the older woman's breast.

Being young, however, and being away from India, Jasmine began to recover from her sorrow within the next few days. She could never forget her dearly beloved father, but Skye kept the girl so busy that there was little time for her to mope about.

Cullen Butler came to say his good-byes, still wearing the dress of a moderately well-to-do gentleman. He had lingered long enough in England to be certain that Jasmine was adjusting to her new life, but then his aunt had certainly seen to that. He would ride down to Devon and sail from Bideford to Cobh.

"I do not know, Princess, if we will ever meet again," he said seriously, "but I would have you know that I am grateful for my years with you. Kneel, my child, and let me give you my blessing."

When she arose, Jasmine kissed her cousin on the cheek, saying, "Without your help, Cullen Butler, I should have had a much harder time coming to England than I have had. Thank you. I hope my great-uncle, Michael O'Malley, will give you that little stone church you have so longed for all those years you spent in India."

"Tell Michael there are harder times coming for Ireland than they ever had under old Bess," Skye told the priest. "Remind him that he's *the O'Malley* now, and not me. Tell him not to allow his duty to the Church to turn him from his duty to the family. In our father's time the O'Malley and his bishop were two people and not one. 'Tis hard for Michael, I know." She kissed her nephew. "My love to your mother, Cullen Butler. Tell her that her youngest son has done the family proud. I am grateful."

Cullen Butler departed, and an hour later the de Mariscos also departed for Queen's Malvern. Although accompanied by several coaches, Skye, Adam, and Jasmine preferred to ride. Her grandparents had given her a beautiful, fine-boned black mare whom Jasmine named Ebony. The girl loved racing the beast ahead of her party, letting the mare have her lead and feeling the warm spring wind in her face. The hillsides were awash with daffodils, narcissus, common red poppies, yellow rock rose, and purple gorse. Skye pointed out all these wild flowers new to her granddaughter. The neatly thatched, whitewashed cottages also fascinated Jasmine.

"Of course," she said, "there are more people in India than there are here in England, but our peasants do not have such fine houses as do yours. The land is all owned by the Mughal, and he parcels it out to his nobles in exchange for military units. The nobles, in turn, give over bits of the land to the farmers and lower peasant orders. In exchange, they must pay with part of their crop and with time given to the military. It is all very complicated. If the Mughal becomes angry with a noble and reclaims his land to give to another, very often chaos results. Do your peasants own their land or do they just farm it for the nobility? And look!" She pointed. "Do they own their sheep and cattle too? And their orchards as well? This is an interesting land!"

"Some farmers rent their lands from the nobility," Skye told Jasmine, "but others own their own land as well as their livestock and orchards. Men and women are all free here in England."

"So Cullen told me, Grandmother. I freed Adali and my maids before we left India."

They rode toward the Midlands, and on a bright, warm day in late April, Jasmine de Marisco saw Queen's Malvern for the first time. Built in the reign of Edward IV, it had been a love token given to that king's queen, Elizabeth Woodville. The building, set in a small valley within the Malvern Hills between the rivers Severn and Wye, had been constructed in the shape of an E. It had always been a royal property, and Elizabeth Tudor, the late queen, had loaned it to Skye and Adam in exchange for Adam's island of Lundy. Late in Elizabeth's reign, desperate for money, she had sold Queen's Malvern to the de Mariscos.

The house was built of warm, long-mellowed pinkish brick, and two of its walls were covered in shiny, dark green ivy. The windows were lead-paned, but tall and wide, allowing a good deal of light to enter into the house. As they rode up the graveled drive, the coaches rumbling behind them, Jasmine saw that the hedgerowed fields surrounding Queen's Malvern were filled with mares and colts.

"Your grandfather and I raise horses," Skye explained.

The front door to the house opened and the footmen came out to greet the travelers. They were accompanied by a gap-toothed woman who called, "Mistress Skye! And 'tis high time you got home! I was beginning to think it was the old days all over again and you had gone off without me."

"Ahh, Daisy, I'd never go off without you." Skye laughed, and drawing her horse to a stop, dismounted slowly. "I'm certainly not as agile as I once was," she complained ruefully.

"Well, m'lady, you just come along," the serving woman said, "and I'll have a nice hot tub prepared for you this minute." Then Daisy's sharp eyes saw Jasmine, who was next to her grandfather. "And who is this?" she demanded, peering closely at the girl, a puzzled look coming into her eyes. "She seems familiar. Do I know this lass, Mistress Skye?"

"Nay, Daisy," Skye told her tiring woman of many years. She slipped her arm through Daisy's and together they went into the house. "Come into the library, old friend, and we shall tell you who she is."

Once the door to the room closed, Skye motioned her servant to a chair and sat down opposite her. She drew Adam to her side while Jasmine settled herself onto a stool by her grandmother's knee. The girl looked particularly lovely in a midnight-blue velvet riding skirt with an elegantly tailored matching silk jacket with pearl buttons.

"This is Velvet's firstborn, Daisy. Though you have been discreet over the years, I know Pansy told you," Skye said simply, and then to Jasmine, "Daisy's daughter, Pansy, is your mother's tiring woman. She was with her in India, too, my darling."

"God Almighty!" Daisy gasped. "Then that's what that

heathen, Adali, was about with his arrival on Christmas Day, and all of us wondering and never knowing." She peered again at Jasmine. "No wonder you looked familiar to me, child. You've both your grandmother and your mother in you, but more of your grandmother, I'm thinking. I've been with her since before Mistress Willow was born, and 'tis going on fifty years, it is. I can remember when my lady was as fresh and as ripe as you are now, child. Now why did that daughter of mine not get word to me about this? Probably too busy with her life in the BrocCairn castle and all of Dugald Geddes's rambunctious sons—seven of them she has, but now that she's got her girl, there will be no more babies for my Pansy. Blossom is the last of 'em, you can be certain."

"Velvet does not know," Skye said quietly.

"What?" Daisy looked astounded. "You have had this child for over two months and her own mother doesn't know she is here? Shame on you, my lady!"

"Velvet will be here for her birthday on May first and remain for her English summer, Daisy. Jasmine is going to be my gift to her. She will be so surprised! I've sent invitations to Robin and Angel down in Devon; and to Murrough and Joan as well. They are to leave the children, however. 'Twould be too much for the children to absorb. Let my sons and daughters come to terms with all this first. Willow and James have been invited. Now that I'm home, Deirdre and John, as well as Padraic and Valentina, shall be sent for as well.

"And, Daisy, not a word to the other servants," Skye cautioned. "Ohh, I cannot wait to see the look of surprise on Velvet's face when she meets Jasmine for the first time! She never thought to see her child again, but fate, as I so often have warned Velvet, is a capricious but kind bitch when she chooses."

When Daisy had gone, taking Jasmine along to show her

her rooms and to carry out the other myriad instructions her mistress had given her, Adam poured his wife and himself goblets of rich red Archambault wine.

Handing Skye one of the goblets, he said, "Do you really still think it wise to surprise Velvet with her daughter's arrival? I have never heard her speak of the child since she came home to reconcile with Alex." He sipped thoughtfully as he looked at her.

"Because she has not spoken of her does not mean she has not thought of her, Adam," Skye answered. "No mother forgets a child she has borne and raised for even as short a time as she and Jasmine had each other. She is, I promise you, going to be thrilled."

"Will Alex? Does he even know?" Adam wondered.

"Of course he knows," Skye said with assurance. "He must. I am certain that Velvet promised me she would tell him. 'Tis true Jasmine will be a bit of a shock to him, but let us not forget that Velvet has raised the child Alex's mistress gave him while Velvet was in India. Indeed, Sybilla thinks of Velvet as her own mother and even calls her Mama. I think Velvet has poured all the love she could have lavished on Jasmine into raising Sybilla Gordon."

"I suppose," Adam mused, "that it will be all right, even if it does come as a bit of a shock to the family at first."

He smiled to himself, and Skye thought how handsome a man he was despite his age. Some men shrank with the passing of time, but not Adam. He stood as tall and straight as he ever had. The smoky blue eyes had never faded, and if his once midnight-black hair was now silvery white, she did not care a bit. They would be married thirty-four years in September. There had not been a year gone by that she had not been supremely happy with this great bear of a man.

Little had she realized all those long years ago when he so tenderly but firmly seduced her that one day he would be her dearest husband, not simply her lover and her best friend. Sometimes she would awaken in the night and listen for the sound of his breathing, afraid that he might have left her. But then he would resume his sonorous snoring and she would poke at him, admonishing him to roll over and cease his noise. Skye O'Malley frankly could not imagine life without her beloved Adam.

For the next few days the servants at Queen's Malvern worked diligently, readying the house for the coming guests. The night before the Gordons of BrocCairn were due to arrive, Skye and Adam called their granddaughter to them. "We had always planned to leave Queen's Malvern to your mother," Skye began. "We knew with Bess Tudor remaining unmarried that England's throne would eventually go to Mary of Scotland's son, King James. We married your mother into a well-connected Scots family believing that when that day came, she would come with Alex and their children to live in England.

"But when King James arrived in England three years ago, he brought with him a host of younger sons and assorted adventurers seeking whatever they could lay their hands upon. There has been much ill-feeling between the English and the Scots. The year after James inherited the throne, he made peace with Spain, England's traditional enemy. Last November there was a plot discovered to blow up the king and his parliament.

"Alexander Gordon, the Earl of BrocCairn, your mother's husband, is related to the king by blood, but he has chosen to remain in Scotland at Dun Broc, his own home. He was never much of a man for the court. The life he chooses to lead suits your mother well. In her youth she enjoyed court, but no more. She loves Scotland greatly, only wanting a milder English summer each year.

"It seems foolish, therefore, for your grandfather and I to leave our home to the Gordons of BrocCairn. We have rewritten our wills. You, Jasmine, will inherit this house one day, and Greenwood in London as well. Adam and I know you will offer your hospitality to the family whenever they need it, but we also feel you must have English roots of your own, my darling girl. That way you will always remain independent of others. Wealth, as you already know, gives you the power to run your own life."

"Will not my mother be disappointed if you leave me Queen's Malvern?" Jasmine asked. "Did she not grow up here? And what of my half brothers? Has one of them been expecting to inherit this house?"

"Your mother will never live in England as long as Alexander Gordon remains alive. It is likely, barring accident, that he will survive to be a grand old man," Skye answered. "We will be gone long before that, my darling. As for his boys, Sandy will inherit Dun Broc, and he will have no use for Queen's Malvern. The others, like all younger sons, will have to make their own way in the world. If I know Velvet, she will see them all wed to heiresses with lands of their own."

"And mother's daughter?"

"Sybilla?" Skye wrinkled her nose. "Velvet has raised the girl practically from infancy, but she is Alex's daughter and no blood kin of ours. I would never leave Queen's Malvern to her."

Jasmine sighed. "I am very grateful to both you and Grandfather, madame, but I would not offend my mother or any in her family."

Skye patted Jasmine's hand. "You will offend no one, will she, Adam? Your mother will understand and probably approve our decision. None of the boys, nor Sybilla, ever expected to inherit this estate from us. Oh, I feel so much better knowing that you are now landed, my darling girl. Just a few more hours and your mother will be here! I can hardly wait, can you?"

When the BrocCairn party was reported to be coming through the main gates of the estate, Jasmine and her servants hurried upstairs to her apartment, where they would remain until the appointed hour that evening. Jasmine was almost sick with excitement. If only her rooms faced the front of the house instead of the back, she thought, she might glimpse Velvet and her family, but her windows all looked out on the beautiful gardens, the fields and the woodlands beyond.

Meanwhile, the coaches rumbled up the driveway. They were accompanied by a party of horsemen, including the Earl of BrocCairn himself, and four of his five sons. Drawing his mount to a halt, Alexander Gordon swept off his broadbrimmed hat with its plumes and bowed to his in-laws from his saddle. His sons followed his polite example.

"Welcome back to Queen's Malvern, my lord!" Skye said.

The earl dismounted and kissed her. "Madame Skye, why do you never grow old? In Scotland there would be whispers of witchcraft, I vow." He turned. "Laddies, come and greet your grandmam!"

While Sandy and Adam Charles, along with Robert and Henry, the twins, crowded about their grandmother demanding her attention, the coach carrying Velvet, her youngest son Edward, and her stepdaughter Sybilla came to a stop. A footman rushed up to open the door and lower the coach steps.

"Grandsire!" Little Edward Gordon tumbled from the vehicle.

Adam de Marisco swept the boy up into a bear hug. "Neddie, my lad, 'tis good to see you again." He set the little boy down and said, "Go and give your grandmam a kiss."

"Sibby was sick all over the coach," Neddie volunteered happily. "She made a really awful stink! Did you ever see anyone turn green, grandsire? Sibby was quite green when she was sick."

Adam could not help but laugh. The idea of Velvet's stepdaughter turning green was an amusing one. Lady Sybilla Alexandra Mary Gordon was not his favorite grandchild.

He did not understand how it had happened, but Sybilla was a dreadful snob. She took great pride in her father's heritage, which linked her with not only one of the most powerful clans in Scotland, but with royalty itself.

That her natural mother was a London silversmith's daughter with the morals of a mink, and was now married to a semi-reformed bandit, she could not be persuaded to even acknowledge. As far as Lady Sybilla Alexandra Mary Gordon was concerned, Alanna Wythe Shaw had never existed. Velvet de Marisco Gordon, with her elegant and far preferable ancestors, was her only mother.

Adam often considered that his daughter's soft heart had gotten the better of her where Sybilla Gordon was concerned. His son-in-law had legitimatized the girl, a great kindness on his part. Velvet had raised her, spoiling her unconscionably. If Velvet had given Alexander Gordon another daughter, perhaps Sybilla would not have been so spoiled, but his daughter had borne only sons for Alex, allowing Sybilla to grow into a little madame. Her one saving grace, in Adam's eyes, was that she adored her stepmother above all people, even her father.

"Papa!"

Adam de Marisco snapped from his reverie and a smile split his face. "Velvet, my dear!" He held out his arms to her and she descended gracefully from the coach into them. They kissed, and then putting her back from him, he said, "You are lovelier than ever, Velvet."

Velvet de Marisco Gordon flushed with pleasure at her father's compliment. She was a beautiful woman with fair skin and rich auburn hair, whose voluptuous figure belied the fact that she had borne six children. Her face was oval-shaped with both the forehead and cheekbones high. Her long Norman nose she had inherited from her father's family. Her small, square chin bespoke a lady of firm opinions and determined nature. Her wide, sensual mouth suggested another, more passionate side to her nature. She was tall, but her bones were delicate.

"And you have certainly grown no older in the past year, Papa," she told him, her emerald-green eyes twinkling.

"Neddie says Sybilla was sick in the coach," he said.

Velvet laughed. "Only the first day," she replied. "Neddie will never get over seeing Sibby vomit all over her new traveling dress. They don't get on particularly well, you know. I suspect he adored seeing the idol pulled from her pedestal. He really is a most impossible little boy. I do not know what to do with him."

"He seems a perfectly normal lad to me," her father remarked blandly.

"Grandsire." Lady Sybilla Alexandra Mary Gordon stepped daintily from the coach, having waited until she was certain her entrance would be appreciated and admired. She was a petite girl, standing only about five feet, three inches tall. Her eyes, which she liked to make wide, were sky-blue in color, and not a golden curl upon her head was out of place. Her traveling gown was of pale blue velvet, and although the early afternoon had turned warm on this last day of April, young Lady Sybilla looked cool and comfortable.

"Welcome back to Queen's Malvern, Sibby," Adam said, placing a kiss upon the girl's forehead. "Is it possible you have grown fairer in the year since I last saw you? The gentlemen will be beating a path up that rocky hill to Dun Broc before long, my dear."

Sibby giggled. She loved nothing better than a compliment. "I have already picked out a gentleman, Grandsire," she confided to him. "He is James Leslie, the Earl of Glenkirk. He is related to the king, even as I am. His wife and children died five years ago. His wife was a Gordon cousin of mine. Everyone says he must finally remarry and cease his mourning. He is at court, and Mama says we may go to court! Papa is going to approach Lord Leslie about a match. Isn't it exciting? I shall be the Countess of Glenkirk!" Sybilla, unlike her half brothers, did not speak with a Scots accent. She had made a successful effort over the years to mimic her stepmother's speech.

"You shall be the Countess of Glenkirk only if Lord Leslie decides you are the right woman for him," Skye said as she joined them. "Velvet, my dear, you simply must train Sibby not to chatter so. A wrong word overheard and she could be ruined, as you well know."

Sybilla Gordon wrinkled her nose in disdain. Grandmam always put her off. She was a fussy old woman. What could she possibly know of life? She had spent most of it here in the country and had never gone to court. I shall be the Countess of Glenkirk, Sybilla thought to herself. *I shall!* Then she smiled sweetly up at Skye and curtsied prettily. "I am happy to be back in England again, Grandmam," she said.

Skye pressed a cool kiss to Sybilla's cheek and told her, "Run along inside, Sibby. You must take a nap if you are to stay up for your mother's birthday party tonight." Skye then turned to her youngest daughter. "I've invited your brothers and sisters this year. Padraic and Valentina have already joined Conn and Aidan at Pearroc Royale this morning. Willow, Murrough, and Robin are coming up from Devon and should be here by mid-afternoon."

"Good Lord, Mama," Velvet said. "The house will be as overflowing with relations and their offspring as it was last Christmas. Although I was not here, both Deirdre and Willow wrote to me that you swore you would never have such a gathering here again at Queen's Malvern."

"I have asked that my grandchildren remain at home, except, of course, for yours and for Adam Burke, who is nursing."

"Well," Velvet reasoned, "if it's only my siblings and their mates, I suppose we won't be too crowded."

"Particularly," her mother told her, "as I have arranged with your sister Deirdre to invite your youngest three over to Blackthorne Hall. Just until the others are gone, of course, Velvet."

"Gracious, Mama, you have thought of everything," Velvet told her, and she hugged Skye. "I'm so glad to be back at Queen's Malvern! 'Tis not my house, and I do not have to do anything. 'Tis not easy managing Dun Broc. Now that the king has left Scotland, it seems even harder than it was before, when he was there. I should tell you now that we have joined the new Kirk, mama. It is better for us now that James is gone. The old Kirk and its members are always in danger. I cannot do that to my children, nor can Alex. What was it old Queen Bess used to say about religion?"

" 'There is but one Lord Jesus Christ. The rest is all trifles,' " Skye answered her, and linking her arm in her daughter's, they strolled together into the house.

9

Skye's children had all arrived at Queen's Malvern but for Ewan O'Flaherty and his family, who lived in Ireland. Padraic and his Valentina had ridden over from nearby Pearroc Royale with Valentina's parents, Cónn and Aidan, Lord and Lady Bliss.

Deirdre Burke Blackthorne had come in her coach from Blackthorne Hall with her husband John. She was quick to reassure Velvet that Neddie, Robert, and Henry were safe, well-fed, and happily into naughtiness with their Blackthorne cousins. "Thalia and Penelope are delighted to have them and are worse than the boys," Deirdre said, smiling.

Murrough O'Flaherty and his Joan were up from Devon, as were Robin, the Earl of Southwood, and his wife Angel, and, of course, Willow, the Countess of Alcester, and her devoted husband, James Edwardes.

"I cannot imagine what is so special about Velvet's thirty-third birthday that we all had to be here," Willow said to her siblings. "After Adam Burke's christening last Christmas, I was certain that Mama would never have us all again, but she absolutely insisted we come." Then she smiled mischievously. "Of course, we were told to leave our numerous offspring at home. Did you know I am to be a grandmother? Cecily's first is due around All Saint's Day."

The hall had been decorated beautifully with flowering branches of hawthorn, fragrant pine, and early lilacs. There were places set for twenty at the U-shaped table. The best linen and the heavy silver were used along with silver goblets decorated with carnelians. The candles were of the purest beeswax and scented with rose oil. There were silver bowls filled with lilacs, apple blossoms, small, early roses, and lily of the valley. Applewood fires took the chill off the evening.

Skye was an excellent hostess and had always enjoyed entertaining. Tonight the festive meal consisted of fine salmon that had been brought by the Gordons of BrocCairn from Scotland. The creatures had been caught in nets and then transported in barrels of icy springwater to England, where they met their end in the kitchens of Queen's Malvern. They were served upon beds of fresh sharp cress that had traveled with them. The contrast between the thinly sliced pink flesh of the salmon and the bright green herb was a delight to the eye. Tubs of freshly caught North Sea oysters; large, meaty prawns that had been poached in wine; steamed mussels, their shiny black shells half-opened; and tiny little coquilles in a dilled cream sauce made up the rest of the fish course.

There was a side of roasted beef dripping its juices; a large, sweet pink ham; a platter of tiny lamb chops; two roasted turkeys; six ducks which were served with a fruit sauce; a fine pheasant; and a platter of tiny ortolans which had been browned to perfection. There were bowls of new peas, tiny beets, and lettuce braised in white wine. Several silver salvers were piled high with freshly baked breads. There was a wheel of sharp cheddar and one of French brie. Wines from Archambault and home-brewed ale were equally popular.

Velvet de Marisco Gordon had been born shortly after

midnight on the first day of May. It had been the custom of her family since her childhood to begin the celebration of her birth on the evening before, the festivities culminating with the gift-giving after the midnight hour. It somehow seemed a more festive occasion than usual this particular year, although none of the guests could say why.

The ladies were beautifully gowned. Skye wore a deep midnight-blue velvet. Willow was in an elegant rose-pink silk gown, while her sister Deirdre was garbed in a flattering shade of mauve and Velvet wore her favorite dark green velvet. Skye's daughters-in-law were equally lovely. Joan always looked her best in sky-blue. Angel was radiant in aquamarine-blue; Valentina magnificent in lilac silk. Young Lady Sybilla, quite excited to be included in her mother's party, was very pretty in apple-green.

The gentlemen were more sedate in black velvet suits with crisp white neck ruffs, including Alex Gordon's heir, Sandy, and his next eldest brother, Adam Charles. Both were feeling very grown-up and worked hard at aping their elders' manners lest they be sent from the table.

Skye looked about her and smiled, satisfied. The sweets had been brought, including a caramel creme brulée, which was Velvet's favorite desert. Her family was well-fed and happy, trading confidences and gossip. Soon it would be midnight and Velvet would sit in the place of honor at the high board and receive her gifts. Skye had already announced that the gift she and Adam planned to give their daughter would be the last gift she received.

" 'Tis midnight," Adam finally announced as the tall clock in the Great Hall began to strike. He stood up and, raising his goblet, said, "Happy Birthday, Velvet! May this birthday be the best one you have ever had, and may you remember it always!"

The other guests raised their goblets, calling out, "Happy Birthday, Velvet! Long life! Happiness!"

Velvet beamed appreciatively, and then her green eyes

grew as wide as a child's as her gifts were placed before her all at once, appearing magically from beneath the tables where her relatives had hidden them. There were perfumed leather gloves lined in sheer silk and embroidered with small gemstones, several small pieces of jewelry, a particularly beautiful set of paste buttons fashioned like flowers that rivaled real jewels, a charming loupe mask of black silk embroidered with floral sprigs in gold and silver threads, a handsome wide comb decorated with pearls around its arch, and finally a set of two silk handkerchiefs that had been monogrammed by Sibby in dainty stitches.

Velvet ohhed and ahhed appreciatively as each gift was opened and admired. When there was nothing left, she looked up and said to her mother, "Now Mama, what is this surprise that you and Papa have for me?"

Skye and Adam chuckled simultaneously, and then Lady de Marisco signaled to her servants, giving her husband a very arch look as she did so, her daughter Willow thought.

The doors to the Great Hall opened and several footmen guided in a square platform that had been set on wheels. Above the base of the contraption was a railing from which brass rings holding a blue velvet curtain hung. The curtain enclosed and hid from view the mysterious contents of the platform.

"Well, Mama, this is most curious!" Willow declared. What on earth was the curtain hiding? Her mother had certainly never given *her* anything like this as a gift, and why choose her youngest sibling's thirty-third birthday? What was so special about this birthday?

The platform was carefully wheeled into the center of the U-shaped table and brought to a halt directly before Velvet. With a great sense of drama, Skye and Adam came to stand on either side of it, even as everyone crowded about around Velvet so they might also see what was hidden. Slowly, slowly, the de Mariscos drew back the heavy curtain revealing to view what appeared to be a living tableau.

In the foreground of the platform stood a beautiful young woman dressed in the absolute height of fashion. Her gown was of scarlet silk with an undergown of cloth-of-gold embroidered with tiny pearls and sparkling diamante. The neckline of the dress was low and square. The sleeves were designed with small slashes through which showed little cloth-of-gold puffs of material. Cuffs of gold lace accented the wearer's delicate wrists. The lady's black hair was parted in the center and twisted into an elegant chignon. She wore red roses in her hair, and the ruby necklace about her neck was obviously worth a king's ransom, as were the rubies cascading from her ears.

She was accompanied by three companions. A gentleman of mid-height wore exotic garb that consisted of narrow white pants, a white coat embroidered lightly in gold thread and pearls that came to just below his knees, and a small white turban upon his head. The other two people upon the platform were obviously twin sisters, who wore even more exotic garb fashioned of green and gold silks, part of which covered their dark hair.

The audience ohhed.

Velvet stared hard. There was something familiar about these people. She had seen them before. She knew them. *Adali! Rohana! Toramalli!* The names came suddenly into her head. Her heart began to pound violently. She gripped the edge of the table, white-knuckled.

She looked again, this time directly at the beautiful girl. Incredible and very unusual turquoise-blue eyes stared calmly back at her. There was something in their expression that tugged at her memory, but she could not quite place it. She carefully searched the girl's face for something familiar, something she could recognize and identify. The room was deathly silent, the frank curiosity of the other guests hanging heavily in the air.

It was then that Velvet saw the small beauty mark on the girl's face. A tiny dark mole just below her left nostril and just above her upper lip. No. It could not be. *It simply could not be!* She gasped with shock as memories began to flood her very being. It was then the girl smiled tremulously and said, "Happy Birthday, Mama." With a shriek of dismay, Velvet de Marisco fainted.

Instantly the hall was in an uproar, but Skye and Adam quickly took charge. The Earl of BrocCairn was directed to carry his unconscious wife to a settle near the fireplace. Captain Murrough O'Flaherty was directed to escort the girl on the platform and her companions off their stage. The rest of the guests were told to be silent, and then Skye began to force wine between her youngest daughter's lips. Velvet moaned and opened her eyes.

"Ohhhh," she groaned. Seeing her mother's angry face, she closed her eyes again.

"Open your eyes, Velvet Gabrielle-Marie de Marisco," Skye snapped. "Open your eyes this instant! *You promised me!* You promised me that you would tell Alex, and you have not, have you? *You have not!*"

Velvet's green eyes fluttered open once more. Her mother was glaring furiously at her. She could not remember ever having seen Skye so angry. Alex, her darling Alex, was looking dismayed and confused. "I . . . I could not!" she finally managed to say to her mother.

"Sit up!" snapped Skye. "What do you mean, you could not?"

Velvet struggled into a seated position. She was very pale, and her face was already streaked with tears. For a brief moment she looked far younger than her thirty-three years. From beneath her wet lashes she glanced quickly at Jasmine and then as quickly away again. "Do you not remember, Mama?" she said softly. "Do you not remember that I said I should never tell Alex lest he reproach me with the knowledge?"

For a moment Skye looked confused. Was she getting old enough to have forgotten such a thing? "I thought that the pain being fresh and new was what made you declare such a thing," she told her daughter. "I thought that there would come a time when you could trust Alex and enlighten him fully."

"There was never such a time," Velvet said bleakly, her voice low. "He is a Scot and would not understand."

"In fifteen years there was never a time when you might have told your husband about your firstborn child?" Skye demanded, unbelieving.

"Ohhhh!" Willow and Deirdre gasped simultaneously, their eyes wide, their expressions unabashedly shocked.

"What?" the Earl of BrocCairn demanded, his face darkening with outrage. "What is this that your mother has said? *This girl is your child?* How, madame, can that be? And just when did you cuckold me, Velvet?" He looked angrier than any of his relations could ever remember having seen him.

"Tell him, Velvet," Skye said implacably. "Tell him this instant or I shall tell him. I am astounded by your behavior and cannot imagine what Jasmine must think of you. *Tell him!*"

"Aye, madame, tell me," the Earl of BrocCairn said menacingly.

Velvet looked nervously from her mother to her husband to Jasmine and then back to Alex. What was the use? The cat was certainly out of the bag now. There was no help for it. "Yasaman is my daughter," she told Alex Gordon. "Her father is the Grand Mughal, Akbar."

"How can this possibly be?" he demanded furiously.

Suddenly Velvet was angry herself. The memory of being forcibly separated from her daughter rose up, threatening to overwhelm her. All those years and so much between them lost. She had never seen this child take her first step or utter her first intelligent word. She had not kissed away bruises or helped her with her lessons. How dare he stand over her judging her, condemning her? She looked at Jasmine again. My God! she thought. By some miracle I do not even know yet, my daughter has been restored to me.

Standing up, Velvet said to her husband, "She was begat in the usual manner, my lord, but I was forced to leave her behind in India when I was sent home to you fifteen years ago. I never believed I would see my daughter again, Alex, but this is she. I have not a doubt. She carries her father's mark between her left nostril and her upper lip." Then she turned away from him and, opening her arms, said, "Come to me, Yasaman Kama Begum! You are the best birthday gift I have ever received! I long to embrace you as I have never before been able to do." Tears of happiness slipped down her face.

With a small cry of joy, Jasmine flew into her mother's arms. "Oh, Mama!" she said. "Ohh, Mama!" and she, too, wept.

Velvet hugged her daughter, covering her beautiful face with maternal kisses. "Oh, my darling," she told Jasmine, "you are more beautiful than I could have ever imagined! Why are you here? I believed you married and settled. What of your father?"

About them the family milled, stunned and questioning. It was obvious that they needed answers. "Wait," said Skye, and they all turned to her. "This story is too long to be told more than once. Gather around, my darlings, and together Velvet and my forty-sixth grandchild will tell you the story."

"So that is what you meant last Christmas when you said you and Papa had forty-six grandchildren," Willow said with a small laugh. "Have you known about her all along, Mama? Oh, of course you have! There is nothing in this family you do not concern yourself with, is there?"

"Sandy! Adam Charles! Sybilla!" the Earl of BrocCairn barked. "You will leave the hall immediately."

"Nay!" their grandmother sternly countermanded his order. "You will all please stay." She turned to her son-in-law. "This is a shock, Alex, I know. Jasmine, however, is a reality. Your children are her siblings. They should know her story from her own lips and from Velvet's, not from some vicious backstairs gossip." She put a gentle hand on his arm. "*Please.*"

"Very well," he agreed, unable to refute her reasoning. Although Sybilla looked clearly shocked by this turn of events and was obviously near to tears, Alexander Gordon had to admit that his sons looked absolutely fascinated by all that was transpiring. "You may stay," he told them tersely.

Chairs were brought from about the hall and drawn up around the fireplace. The ladies all sat, the gentlemen stood by their sides. The two Gordon boys settled themselves upon the floor, using their aunts' silk-covered legs as a back prop. All eyes were turned to Skye, Velvet, and the beautiful young woman.

"This," Skye began formally, "is Velvet's firstborn child. In her native India she is known as Yasaman Kama Begum. She is an Imperial Mughal princess. Here in England she prefers that she be known by the English translation of her name, which is Jasmine. She has taken her grandfather's surname for her own as well. Her companions are her high steward, Adali; and her maidservants, Rohana and Toramalli. They also served Velvet during her time in India. I believe, however, that Velvet will want to begin the tale."

"You all remember that shortly after Alex and I were wed, he fought a foolish duel over the long-lost honor of a strumpet," Velvet began, and she glared at her husband. Alex, not in the least intimidated, glared back. Jasmine, however, was fascinated to have this new piece of information to add to Mama Begum's tale of Candra. "Padraic, who was there, heard someone cry out that Lord Gordon was dead. Looking, he could see Alex sprawled upon the green. He rushed to tell me of this disaster before some stranger could." She turned to look at her brother, Padraic Burke, who flushed with the memory of his heedless youth.

"I was devastated by his news," Velvet continued. "Mama and Papa were in India, being held for ransom by the Portuguese governor. Murrough was to set sail that very day with the gold needed to obtain their release. I instantly begged him to take me with him. I could not bear to be left alone in my grief."

"You might have come to me or Deirdre," Willow said sharply.

Velvet laughed. "You would have tried to run my life, dear, bossy Willow. And sweet Deirdre would have sympathized so deeply with me, I would have slipped into the grave myself with my grief," she told her two elder sisters. "No, my decision to go to India was actually the best decision I could have made under the circumstances. I needed Mama's strength. But when we arrived in India, we discovered that Mama and Papa had escaped the Portuguese and were already on their way home.

"The Portuguese governor was furious. He removed me from Murrough's vessel and forced our brother to deliver the ransom anyway, in exchange for my freedom. What Murrough was not aware of was that Mama had so offended the governor, who had made lewd advances toward her that she quite harshly rebuffed, that he intended to be revenged upon her by sending me as a gift to Akbar, India's ruler, the Grand Mughal.

"By the time Murrough learned of the Portuguese deception, it was too late. The caravan was long gone, and me with it." Velvet sighed deeply and then took up the skein of her story once again. "I will not go into the harrowing details of either the journey or my arrival at the Mughal's then capital city, Fatahpur Sikri. You need only know that the Mughal, Akbar, fell in love with me and made me his fortieth wife under the laws of India. I fell in love with Akbar, and on August ninth in the year of our Lord 1590, our daughter Yasaman was born at my palace in Kashmir.

"Bearing a man's child binds a woman closer to that man than she has ever been before," Velvet said thoughtfully, and the women in the room, but for Sybilla, understood exactly what she meant. "I loved the man I believed to be my husband. I loved our baby girl. When Yasaman was several months old, however, our uncle, Michael O'Malley, arrived at Akbar's palace to tell us that Alex Gordon had not been killed in that infamous duel. He was alive and, despite everything that had happened, it was he and not Akbar who was my legal husband. I had no choice but to return to England.

"At the time I did not want to return. I had been married to Alex but a few months; to Akbar almost two years. We had a child! The Mughal, Akbar, however, is a man of deep honor. Despite what we had shared, he would not allow another man's wife to remain in his zenana. I was drugged and sent from him without my daughter. Akbar would not allow me to take her. She was all, he told me, that he had left of the great passion we had shared. He feared for her reception here in England. He is more than well acquainted with the European nature.

"I knew little of her after that, but that she was still alive. Each year on her birthday, Akbar would send a pearl to Mama, a small sign that my daughter thrived. Two years ago Mama said she had received a letter from Cullen Butler, Jasmine's tutor, saying that Jasmine was married and quite happy. Whatever small dream I might have harbored to meet Yasaman again, I certainly never expected to see my daughter after her marriage."

Robin Southwood looked at his new niece and, smiling, said, "It is Jasmine's turn now, I believe, to take up the story. Will you tell us, my dear, how you came to be here in England?"

All eyes turned to the girl. They admired her beauty and obvious good manners. The Earl of BrocCairn, however, could not help but feel anger toward this beautiful creature who had so changed his life. As for the earl's daughter, Sybilla, her anger burned even hotter than her father's. She was Velvet's daughter, not this exotic creature! She would not permit this *Jasmine* to have even the slightest share of Velvet. *Velvet was her mama!*

"I do not remember the mother who gave me birth," Jasmine began softly, "but never was I allowed, from earliest memory, to forget the woman who was called Candra, whom my father had so deeply loved. I am told that on the day she was taken from me, he ascended into a high tower on the palace grounds overlooking the road to the coast. He did not come out for three days, emerging only at the insistence of his mother, whom his frightened wives had sent for, as he would neither answer nor heed their pleadings. When my father finally came from his tower, his hair had gone white. He never really ceased to grieve for his Candra."

Velvet gasped. Tears sprang into her eyes. "He had such beautiful dark hair," she said, almost to herself. "It was so soft, yet strong, even as he was."

A spasm of pain crossed Alex Gordon's face.

"I was given to my father's first wife, Rugaiya Begum, to be raised," Jasmine continued. "I call her Mama Begum. My life was simple, surrounded by family. I had three half brothers and three half sisters. Then, on the night of my thirteenth birthday, my eldest brother, Salim, came to me. I will not go into lurid detail," Jasmine said, "but my brother began a seduction of me which he eventually hoped to carry to the fullest extent of the word. He was willing, however, to be patient and left my maidenhead intact that night."

Sybilla gasped, but her aunt Valentina pinched her sharply on the arm to silence any outburst which would arouse her father's ire. Sybilla, despite her virginal state, knew more, Valentina believed, than she pretended.

Jasmine continued her tale, telling them of her marriage, and finally Jamal Khan's murder. Then she stopped. The tears she had restrained before now slipped down her pale cheeks. *Remember, you are the Mughal's daughter.* She could hear Mama Begum's voice in her ear.

"Why was your father incapable of protecting you?" Murrough O'Flaherty asked gently.

Jasmine shook her head. "My father's health was precarious at best. For better or for worse, Salim was his eldest son and his heir. There was but one solution to our problem: that I leave India. My father and Mama Begum conceived a plan. I escaped incognito to the port of Cambay with Father Cullen and my servants. I learned after I reached England that my father, the Grand Mughal Akbar, had died two months after I set sail.

"Salim has now taken the name of Jahangir, which means 'World Seizer.' He is Grand Mughal of India today. Had I remained in India, I should have been forced into an incestuous relationship with my own brother. The very thought is horrifying to me. Mama Begum and my father believed I should be safe in England with my mother's family."

"Does your brother know that you are here?" Robin Southwood asked.

"No, my lord, to my knowledge he does not. No one but Mama Begum, my father, and my servants who have traveled with me knew of my destination."

There was a long silence as they digested what Jasmine and Velvet had told them. Then Padraic, Lord Burke, who was closest in age to Velvet, spoke.

"What will you do now, Jasmine?" he asked.

Jasmine laughed. "Grandmother says I must have another husband, but I do not think I am quite ready to settle down yet, Uncle."

"Jasmine will live with me," Skye told them firmly. "Adam and I have rewritten our wills. She will inherit both Greenwood House in London and Queen's Malvern one day. Although Velvet will inherit her father's title, it will eventually go to Jasmine as Velvet's firstborn daughter. None of you need Greenwood or Queen's Malvern. You cannot possibly object to our decision."

"But Mama was to have Greenwood and Queen's Malvern," Sybilla Gordon wailed. "And she said it would one day come to me!"

"She should not have said such a thing to you, Sybilla," Skye responded sharply. "Neither of those houses was hers to give. Although we had, for many years, thought to leave them to Velvet, the truth of the matter is that she does not need them. Your father has decided against making a permanent home in England, Sybilla. You, I am told, hope to become the Earl of Glenkirk's wife. You, too, will remain in Scotland then. Jasmine is my granddaughter of my blood, and she needs her own home."

"It will always be open to the family, as it always has been," Jasmine said in an attempt to soothe her stepsister's fears.

"*How kind of you,*" Sybilla said acidly, "but if you think I will ever come into this house or Greenwood once they are yours, you are sadly mistaken. I will not associate with some foreign-born bastard, even if she is my mother's child!"

Jasmine grew pale, but then before anyone else could speak, she said, "I was born in India, the legitimate issue of its ruler. You, however, were born in England, the illegitimate issue of a silversmith's daughter and my mother's husband. What does that make you, I wonder?"

"Ohhhh!" Sybilla wailed, and she stomped her foot angrily, her golden curls bouncing with her aggravation.

Jasmine burst out laughing. Although she found Sybilla annoying, she also thought her response silly.

"*Papa!* That bastard girl is laughing at me," Sybilla cried to Alex Gordon. "Make her stop this instant! I will not have it!"

Jasmine stepped forward and slapped her stepsister upon her cheek. "If you use that word to describe me ever again," she threatened, "I will claw your round blue eyes from your head!"

Sybilla shrieked and then her fury spilled over. She was Lady Sybilla Alexandra Mary Gordon, the daughter of the Earl of BrocCairn. The girl before her was nothing! *Nothing!* "My father legitimatized me, you bastard!" she screamed.

Jasmine slapped her again, this time harder. "I told you not to use that word," she warned her antagonist. "Being legitimatized has certainly not improved the low streak in your blood that you have obviously inherited from your mother."

"This is my mother!" Sybilla screamed, pointing to Velvet.

"No," Jasmine said. *"That is my mother."*

"Stop it you two!" Skye finally interceded. "Stop it this instant!" She grasped Velvet's stepdaughter by the arm. "Sybilla, you began this contretemps. Jasmine, however, has finished it. Velvet is mother to you both. She bore Jasmine, and she has raised Sybilla from her earliest memory. Now apologize to each other. I will not have my family torn apart by silly bickering."

"Apologize? To her? Never!" Sybilla spat.

"I can hardly apologize for speaking the truth," Jasmine told her grandmother angrily.

"Bastard girl!" Sybilla snarled.

Jasmine leapt forward and knocked her stepsister to the carpet, throwing herself atop her to pummel her with tightly clenched fists. She would teach this little bitch a lesson not to be forgotten. How dare she use such an epithet toward her? *Bastard?* She was no bastard. *She was the Mughal's daughter!* Sybilla shrieked and fought back. She was no mean opponent and defended herself with spirit.

"This is what your reckless behavior has brought us to!" shouted Alex Gordon to his wife.

"My reckless behavior?" his wife countered. "I was a helpless slave in the Mughal's zenana. Would you prefer that I had killed myself to preserve *your* honor? You hardly considered honor when you set about to swive Alanna Wythe with such vigor and openly made her your mistress. You even took her back to Scotland and set her up in your village in her own cottage, where she tormented me and almost got me killed! *My reckless behavior?"* Velvet rounded on her husband and hit him a blow that sent the Earl of BrocCairn reeling.

The Earl of Lynmouth burst out laughing. "Now here's a

sight I never thought to see again," Robin chortled. "The battling BrocCairns. Why, everything's been so lovey-dovey the last few years between Alex and Velvet, I thought for certain that contentment had finally turned them into dull beings. I love surprises, don't you?" He moved back as his nieces rolled screaming and clawing beneath his feet.

"Robin, how can you?" his wife, Angel, scolded, but Robin had already dissolved into even heartier guffaws, and was joined by the rest of the gentlemen, who wheezed with mirth, tears running down their cheeks.

"Men," Skye said grimly to her daughters and daughters-in-law, "are consummate fools. Aidan!" she called to her sister-in-law. "Give me a hand with these two wildcats. Willow, you can help as well!"

Not without difficulty were the two combatants separated and dragged apart by their female relations. Jasmine's three servants had been stunned and shocked by the melee. Now they looked helplessly to Skye for direction. She shook her head at them.

"This is a different world, and your mistress must learn to cope by herself." Then her Kerry-blue eyes twinkled. "I think she is doing quite nicely, do you not?" she whispered to them.

Unable to help himself, Adali grinned. "Yes, my lady," he said low, and then he chuckled as Rohana and Toramalli giggled helplessly behind their little hands.

Jasmine's beautiful black hair had been pulled from its elegant chignon, and there was a small purple bruise beginning to form high on her left cheekbone. Her gown had been ripped off one shoulder, but other than that she was little the worse for wear.

Her two half brothers, Sandy and Adam Charles, were wide-eyed with surprise. They had never imagined that girls could fight like boys. The younger of the two could not prevent the grin that split his face as he looked at Jasmine.

"Sibby hae almost blacked your eye," he said matter-of-factly.

Jasmine regarded him with equal interest. She had always been the youngest, but now suddenly she was the eldest of her new siblings. "I did black hers," she said.

"Are you really a bas—" He stopped, and then, "You know . . ."

Jasmine laughed. "It is difficult to explain," she told the boy. "We have the same mother, but different fathers. What is your name, boy? I think I should know your name as we are brother and sister."

"Adam Charles, but they call me Charlie," he answered.

"Well, Charlie," Jasmine said, "I know you've heard my story, but let me see if I can explain it in simpler terms. In my land I was born of a legitimate union. In your land, you and your brothers were born of a legitimate union, but there are some in your land who would think the marriage between our mother and my father illegal. In my land they do not. Does any of this make sense to you?" She looked down at the boy. He had dark hair and their grandmother's green-blue eyes. There was a sprinkle of golden freckles across the bridge of his nose.

"Aye, 'tis like the old Kirk and the new Kirk at home. Each says the other is wrong and wicked," Charlie answered.

Jasmine was surprised by his quick grasp of the situation. She knew about the religious squabbles going on throughout Europe from her studies and from her grandmother, who had explained the situation in England to her when she arrived. "Aye, Charlie, 'tis just like that," she told him. "You are a quick lad, I think."

"Can we be friends?" he asked. "I hae nae been friends wi a girl before, but I nae knew a girl who could fight so good. Aye, you've blackened Sibby's eye for her, I can see." He pointed to his other half sister.

Young Lady Sybilla had indeed gotten the worst of it. Her blond hair was pulled and, delicate of texture, it stood out in unattractive clumps. Her face was scratched, one eye was indeed blackened, and her skirt was in shreds. She was howling more, however, than was really warranted in the situation.

"She almost killed me! She did certainly try to kill me! Mama! Papa!" Sibby looked about for her parents, but they were still arguing with each other. She could not obtain their attention. She grew sullen and quiet, glaring at Jasmine, who glared back.

"Ohhhhh!" shrieked Sibby, suddenly drawing back. "She is going to come at me again, that wild woman! Keep her away from me! *Keep her away from me!*" Sibby threw herself at her aunt Willow.

Willow, however, was not one bit fooled by Sybilla Gordon's histrionics. She took her by the shoulders and shook her hard. "That is quite enough, miss!" she said. "Your half sister Jasmine has made no further move in your direction. Stop this nonsense or I shall myself slap you out of your hysterics, you silly chit!"

Sibby grew silent.

"Spoiled," Willow said to her sister-in-law, Joan O'Flaherty. "Velvet has spoiled her rotten. There has been no advantage in being the only girl in a family of boys. Now she has a rival for Velvet's affections and she is jealous."

Joan nodded. Whether you agreed or disagreed with Willow, it was best simply to nod. In this particular instance she did agree with her formidable sister-in-law.

The beautiful Countess of Lynmouth, however, was a bit more sympathetic toward her niece. "You cannot blame her, Willow," Angel Southwood said. "She has had Velvet to herself her whole life, and Velvet has perhaps worked harder at being a good mother to Sibby because Alanna was such a bad mother. Discovering that Velvet has another daughter must be a terrible shock for Sibby. Especially under the circumstances."

"If Alex would set his daughter a better example," Willow

noted, "Sibby would follow suit. But no. There he is, raging and ranting about something that happened almost sixteen years ago. Although I thought Velvet impetuous to run off with Murrough at the time, and I still do, the birth of her daughter by the Indian king is hardly her fault now, is it?"

Valentina St. Michael Burke burst out laughing. "I do not think Jasmine's father is totally responsible for her birth," she said. "Do you, dearest Willow? Velvet did play some part in the situation."

"I have heard enough!" Skye O'Malley de Marisco said. She turned to the gentlemen and said fiercely, "Sit down and stop braying like donkeys, the pack of you." When the room grew silent, she continued. "I will have no more quarreling about this. The facts are quite clear. Jasmine is Velvet's daughter by the Grand Mughal Akbar, now deceased. She was born of a legitimate union in her own land and is as legitimate as any of you, as far as I am concerned. She has come to us for refuge. She will have it, and anything else I choose to give her. Is that quite plain to everyone?

"Sybilla, you, too, are Velvet's daughter, for she has raised you from your infancy and loves you dearly. Whatever the circumstances of your birth, your father has legally legitimatized you. But I will not allow you or anyone else to unfairly blacken Jasmine's reputation or the de Marisco name. You are jealous that you must now share your mama. I understand that, but you must try not to be jealous. Velvet, I know, has more than enough love for both her daughters and all her sons too. Certainly you are not so stupid that you cannot understand that.

"Alex! Our daughter was a good and faithful wife to you before her adventures in India and certainly has been after them. Jasmine's arrival into our midst is, of course, a great surprise, but I would remind you that my daughter has raised with love the daughter born to your mistress. No one asked her. Velvet did it out of her love for you. You will not dare to mistreat her or my granddaughter Jasmine unless you wish to answer to me."

"It was different with me," the Earl of BrocCairn began, but his mother-in-law interrupted him angrily.

"If you tell me it was different because you were a man, Alexander Gordon, I shall kill you where you stand!" Skye threatened. "Now this has been more of a day than I expected ever to have. I am no longer a young woman. I am going to bed, and I suggest you all do the same. Adam!" She stamped from the Great Hall.

Adam de Marisco rose to his feet. "Good night, my dears," he said, and with a wink he was gone after his wife.

For a moment there was silence in the Great Hall of Queen's Malvern. Then Jasmine de Marisco curtsied to her relations and bid them good-night, leaving the hall with her three servants in her wake.

"Ohhh, Papa!" Sibby Gordon cried, flinging herself into her father's embrace, seeking sympathy.

Alex Gordon, however, was confused. He pushed his daughter away, saying, "Go to bed, Sibby. I've nae time for ye now, lass."

Velvet took Sybilla's face in her hands and kissed the girl. "Go along and obey your papa, dearest."

"Do you love me still, Mama?" Sibby said low. "Or do you love that bastard girl more?"

"I love all my children equally, Sybilla," Velvet said quietly, "and if you love me, dearest, you will not refer to my firstborn child as a bastard. She is not. It hurts me greatly when you say it. You will shame me and your father if you continue to do so."

Sybilla nodded. "I would not hurt you, Mama. I love you!"

"Come, Sibby," Aidan St. Michael said, taking her niece by the hand and leading her off. "Let Uncle Conn and me escort you upstairs."

When the doors to the Great Hall closed again, the children of Skye O'Malley settled themselves about the fire and began to talk with one another.

"Well," chuckled Murrough, "you say you like surprises, Robin. We have surely had one this evening. I thought we were past the time when Mother could surprise us, but obviously we are not."

"Mama," Willow said sharply, "will go on surprising us until she is gone. Frankly, I am not so certain that she will not reach from beyond the grave to surprise us all a final time or two!"

The others laughed appreciatively.

"What are we to do, then?" Padraic asked.

"About what?" Deirdre questioned her brother. "Surely we will all accept Velvet's child as one of our own?"

There were nods and murmurs of assent, but John Blackthorne, Deirdre's husband, said quietly, "What of your feelings, Alex? This affects you and your children more than any of us."

The Earl of BrocCairn looked up at them, and never had any of them seen Alex Gordon look so vulnerable. "Madame Skye is correct when she says that Velvet hae always been a faithful wife to me. She is correct when she says that Sibby is jealous. The lass is pea-green. There is nae doubt about it. She is correct when she says that Velvet hae raised Sibby wi love. She has.

"I want to be as generous to Velvet's daughter as my wife has been to my daughter. I want to love her child as she hae loved mine, but I cannot! Even though I knew that the Grand Mughal had made Velvet his wife, I could put it all from my mind because Velvet came home to me. Because she was a good wife to me and bore my sons. Because she was generous enough to take my daughter to her heart. As the years went by, I pushed that episode in our lives further away into some distant past that perhaps never really existed after all. There was nothing to substantiate it, was there?

"But now," he sighed, "Jasmine de Marisco stands as living proof of my wife's passion for another man. If Velvet would say that she was forced to his bed . . . but she will not. She loved him. The girl is proof of the love that existed between Velvet and the Grand Mughal Akbar.

"Perhaps if Jasmine were soft-spoken or plain I could find it in my heart to accept her; but she is neither, is she? She eclipses her mother in both beauty and in pride. She is the Mughal's daughter. She will always remember it. Her coming amongst us will, I fear, change everything."

"Aye," agreed his brother-in-law, the Earl of Lynmouth, "it will, Alex. It already has, but Jasmine is our own flesh and blood. I, for one, am glad that she has been restored to us."

"She is your blood, Robin," the Earl of BrocCairn said pointedly. "She is nae mine."

"Nonetheless, you will treat my daughter with kindness and with respect, my lord," Velvet told her husband.

"Your words have the unspoken ring of a threat to them, madame," he said. "I will do my best, but I will promise you nothing."

"At least when I went to the Mughal's bed, I believed myself widowed of you, and an imperial bride. You, however, knew that I lived, yet you could not keep your cock in your breeches long enough to await my return. Do not dare to judge me, or to judge the child of my union with Akbar. Was your lapse of fidelity any less than mine, Alex? And why should either of our daughters suffer for it?" Velvet said pointedly. Then, with a swish of her dark green skirts, the Countess of BrocCairn left the hall, her back quite straight, her head held high.

Without another word Alex Gordon arose and followed her.

"Well," said James Edwardes, the Earl of Alcester, to the remaining family members, " 'tis been a most interesting evening, has it not?"

❋

10

❋

"*Jasmine!*" The voice whispered into her ear with urgency. "Jasmine, wake up! Wake up!" Something tugged at her arm.

She swam up through the mist of a dream in which Jamal was alive again and they were boating together on Wular Lake at dusk. The voice hissed her name again. Jasmine, rolling over, opened her eyes to look into her half brother's young face. "Charlie," she groaned, "what is it? Is the house afire?" She turned her head, looking to her window, and saw that the sky was just growing light with the dawn.

He climbed up on her bed, snuggling against her companionably and said, "I want you to come a-Maying with me. 'Tis May morn!"

"What is May morn?" she asked sleepily, thinking that even if he had woken her up at this terribly early hour, it was nice to have a little brother who climbed into bed with you for a chat.

"You do not know what May morn is?" he asked unbelievingly. "Why it is the first day of May, Jasmine. Do you not have the first day of May in India? I thought everyone in the world had a first day of May."

"The calendar in India is based on the cycles of the moon," she told him. "May first falls somewhere between the months of Shawwai and Dulkaada, depending upon the moon's phases in a particular year. Now, tell me what is so important about today that I should get up out of my most comfortable bed, Charlie Gordon, and come with you?"

"On May morn," he patiently explained to her, "we arise early so that we can gather flowers, fresh hawthorn branches, and the first dew at dawn."

Jasmine yawned. "Why?" she demanded.

"The dew gathered on May morn has magical properties for the skin, and as for the rest," he answered impatiently, "I do not know why. We just do it! Now get up and get dressed, Jasmine!"

She laughed and pushed him from the bed. "Very well," she said, "but if you expect me to dress, you must leave, sir."

"Do not be long," he warned her, "and do not wear shoes. 'Tis not a formal occasion, Jasmine." Then he scampered from her bedchamber, a pleased grin upon his freckled face.

Jasmine climbed from her bed as the door closed behind him. How, she wondered, had he managed to find her? She had not told him last night where her rooms were. She smiled to herself. Her stepfather might not approve of her. Sybilla obviously did not like her. But her mother and this little brother were making her feel very welcome. If only, she thought, I could let Mama Begum know how happy I am.

Jasmine pulled a simple white blouse on over her chemise, and a red silk skirt on over her petticoats. Informal, her brother had said. No need for either a farthingale or a fancy bodice, and with bare feet there was no need for stockings either. Unbraiding her hair, she brushed it out and rebraided it neatly in a single plait, tying the end with a red ribbon.

Looking at herself in the mirror, she frowned at the little purple bruise on her cheekbone. Stepping back to view her whole figure, she was somewhat startled to find she resembled a young Englishwoman in her present garb far more than she resembled an Imperial Mughal princess. Had it always been so? She wondered if Salim would even recognize her without kohl about her eyes. Reaching for her flask of scent, she dabbed some on, thinking that if he did not recognize her, he would certainly recognize the jasmine fragrance she always wore. Salim, however, was as far away from her now as if he lived on the moon itself. She would never see him again.

Exiting her room, she found her little brother awaiting her in the hallway. "That was quick," he said approvingly. "Sybilla is never that quick, nor is Mama." He took her hand in his.

They hurried down the staircase of the house to find the front door opened wide. With a muttered oath the boy tugged Jasmine's hand and pulled her along.

"God's foot! There are some ahead of us!"

"Does it make a difference?" she asked.

"Probably not," he admitted, "but I like being the first out on May morn. Look! There are our uncles Robin and Padraic wi their wives! They are still in the same clothes they wore last night. I will vow they've nae been to bed. Did you ever stay up all night, Jasmine?"

"Not all night," she said, "but very late sometimes. How old are you?"

"I was eleven on St. Valentine's Day," he told her. "They say I am big for my age."

"I will be sixteen on the ninth day of August, by your calendar," she replied. "Tell me how old Sybilla and our brothers are."

"Sibby," he answered, "was sixteen on February the first. She's practically an old maid at this point. Most girls are married by sixteen, but Mama did nae want her forced to any prearranged match. She wants Sibby to find love. Sibby thinks she hae found it in Lord Leslie. I dinna know why she thinks such a thing. She hardly knows the fellow. She hae only seen him three times in her whole life. On two of those occasions his first wife was living."

"What about our brothers?" Jasmine pressed him. This business about Sybilla Gordon was interesting, but she wanted to know more about her mother's children. Her stepsister was quite unimportant.

"Sandy turned thirteen last month," Charlie said.

"Is Sandy his real name?" Jasmine asked.

"James Francis Henry Alexander is his full name," Charlie replied. "James for the king, but there are so many Jameses in Scotland that he was not called by his first name. Francis was for the king's cousin, the Earl of Bothwell, who was my parents' friend. The king doesna like his cousin, so my brother could not be called Francis. Henry was for the crown prince. One of the twins has that for a first name, so my brother is called Sandy, which is a shortened version of Alexander, his last given name. That way he is nae confused with Papa, who is called Alex. What is your full name?"

"In India I was called Yasaman Kama Begum. Yasaman is just the Indian way of saying Jasmine. Kama means love, and Begum was my rank. A Begum is a princess, Charlie. When I came to England I decided to Anglicize my Indian name. Father Cullen told me that when I was baptized as an infant, I was christened Jasmine Elizabeth Mary, for the priests insisted I have a good Christian name. So I am Jasmine Elizabeth Mary de Marisco now. Tell me of the other boys."

"The twins, Rob and Hal, will be nine at the end of June, and little Ned will be six in the autumn. The twins look exactly alike, and they dinna seem to need anyone but each other. Ned's a good little lad. 'Tis nae easy being the youngest, Mama says."

"I know," she told him. "Once I was the youngest."

"Good morning, Jasmine, Charlie," the Earl of Lynmouth greeted his niece and nephew. "Have you come to go a-Maying with us?"

"You nae went to bed last night, Uncle Robin," Charlie accused.

"No," laughed Angel, ruffling his dark hair, "we did not."

"What do grown-ups do when they stay up all night?" Charlie wondered aloud.

"We talk," Lord Southwood told his nephew, "and sometimes we sing songs, and sometimes—"

"*Robin!*" Angel warned her husband, and he laughed.

"You have never been a-Maying, my dear, I expect," Valentina, Lady Burke, said to Jasmine. "Has Charlie explained the custom to you?"

"He tells me we gather early dew for our complexions because it has magical properties," Jasmine said with a smile, "and flowers and flowering branches, but he has no idea why that is done."

Valentina laughed. "The custom extends back into the mists of time," she said. "Our Irish ancestors were called Celts. May first was one of the high holy days. It was called Beltaine. The Celts believed that the earth was their mother, and the sun their father. The mother renewed herself each spring with a new growing season. They celebrated that renewed fertility with dancing, flowers, and songs of praise. The coming of Christianity changed many of the old customs, but some, like May Day and All-Hallows Eve, which was the other great Celtic holy day called Samhein, survive."

"We have a festival in India called Holi, where the barriers of caste are dropped for a day. It, too, has to do with the growing season. People pelt each other with colored powder and flowers, eat special foods, and sing and dance," Jasmine told them. "It would seem that there are many things similar in our different cultures."

"Look," said Angel, "here come Sandy and Sibby to join us."

"God's foot," grumbled Charlie.

"Good May morning, my children," Angel called.

The two young Gordons replied, Sandy cheerfully, Sibby

in more subdued tones as she cast an unfriendly look at Jasmine. Her blackened eye was more obvious this morning.

They began to walk across the fields, and very shortly the sun slipped up over the horizon, gilding the world in its golden glow. The dew sparkled like tiny crystals on the grass, and they bent down to wash their faces in it. Jasmine followed the example set her. They plucked flowers from the field and the hedges: lilacs and buttercups, early roses, poppies, branches of flowering hawthorn and apple blossoms. A lark burst forth in song, and Jasmine almost cried. It was so very beautiful and peaceful. Suddenly she was filled with an overwhelming happiness. *England.* She loved it despite its vast difference from her native India. It was home. She could feel it in her heart and soul.

She walked on, taking in everything about her, sensing, rather than actually seeing, Charlie at her side. A small herd of deer had come from the woods to graze. There was a buck, three does, and four adorable fawns. Jasmine stopped to observe them until, finally aware of the human in their midst, they looked up startled, and with snorts of annoyance fled into the trees. She gazed down at arms filled with flowers.

"What are you mooning about?" Charlie asked.

"I was just thinking how lovely it all is and how happy I am," Jasmine told him. Looking about her, she saw that her aunts and uncles had already begun to make their way back to the house. Nearby, however, Sibby and Sandy were still gathering flowers.

"Let's go back," Charlie answered. "I hae found some pretty violets for Grandmother. She likes it when I bring her flowers."

"And you like it when she gives you sweetmeats, which she always does when you bring her something," Sybilla said meanly, overhearing him. "The old woman likes flattery."

"Perhaps she simply loves Charlie and is pleased by his sweet thoughtfulness," Jasmine said quietly.

"Hah! A lot you know," Sybilla sniffed. "Charlie is a second son. He will have to make his own way in the world. He is hoping that Grandmother will help him, and that's why he always fusses over her. The old woman has so many grandchildren, and he does not want to be forgotten."

"I swear," Charlie responded, "that your mother's teats ran vinegar, Sibby. You have the sourest tongue I hae ever known."

Sybilla Gordon lashed out and slapped her younger brother. A moment later she found herself upon her back in the grass. With a shriek she scrambled to her feet. "She pushed me! Sandy, you saw it!"

Jasmine was paying her no mind. She was far too busy examining Charlie's cheek. One of Sybilla's fingernails had scratched the boy's cheekbone and it was oozing blood. "When we get back to the house," she told him, "I have a special ointment that will heal this with no scarring," she promised him. "If it does scar, however," she teased, "you can say it was a dueling scar."

Charlie, who was still young enough to cry, manfully swallowed back his tears and gave a watery chuckle.

"Sandy!" Sybilla stridently demanded her brother's attention. "*She pushed me!* That creature attacked me! You must tell Father. She should be beaten for it. She is an uncivilized wild woman and does not deserve to be among gentle folk!"

"Wild Jasmine," Charlie said with another chuckle, and his elder brother, a serious boy, was forced to smile.

"You had no right to hit Charlie, Sibby," Sandy said quietly. "I believe Jasmine was just defending him."

"Ohhhhhh! I hate you all!" Sybilla wailed and, throwing down the flowers she had gathered, ran back toward the house.

"Thank you," Jasmine said to the eldest of her half brothers.

Sandy Gordon looked at her, and she saw that his eyes were amber in color. He was, in fact, his father in miniature, with his black hair and craggy features. "As my father's heir," he told her in the same quiet voice, "I will one day be head of this family. Although I am younger than you, I am your eldest brother, Jasmine. I would appreciate your respect. I dinna like to see you and Sybilla quarrel. If she is behaving childishly, it is because she is afraid that Mama will love you more, having found you after all these years. Though you are almost the same age, Sibby is still a girl wi girlish dreams. You are a woman, Jasmine. You have seen the world and lived a far more exciting life than Sibby can ever imagine."

"Who am I, Sandy?" Jasmine asked him.

For a moment he did not quite comprehend her, and then the light of understanding filled his eyes. "You are my half sister," he answered. "You are our mother's daughter by a previous and legitimate alliance to the Grand Mughal of India."

"You truly believe that?" Jasmine pressed him.

"If I didna believe it, Jasmine," he replied, "then I should shame our mother's good name. I will nae do that."

"Your father is outraged by the revelation of my birth," she said. "What of his good name, Sandy? Do you not owe him loyalty too?"

The boy smiled. "You are clever, like Grandmother," he told her. "Aye, my father is very outraged, but he loves Mother. It will take time, but he will eventually come to terms with all of this, if nae for his own sake, then for Mother's. Be warned, however, that he will protect Sibby at all costs. She is his only daughter and, as such, quite dear to him. Your father would have done no less."

Jasmine nodded. "In sending me here to England, my father was protecting me. I understand. I will try to be kinder to Sybilla, but she simply must stop provoking me. I will not be bullied. I am the Mughal's daughter."

As they spoke, Charlie had gathered up Sibby's flowers from the grass. Now, seeing that things were settled between his brother and sister he said, "Let's go back and bring Grandmother and Mother their bouquets."

Together the three young people made their way across the field. As they walked they heard hoofbeats behind them. Two horsemen soon came abreast of them. The animals upon

which they were mounted were beautiful, finely bred creatures, one a bay and the other black. The gentlemen were
dressed for the country in dark breeches, boots, and leather
jerkins worn over their doublets. They were both bare-
headed and wore no capes.

"Good morrow, children," said the first rider. "Would that
be Queen's Malvern?" He pointed to the house. "We seek
Lord de Marisco."

"Aye, my lord, that is Queen's Malvern," Sandy replied.
"We are three of Lord de Marisco's grandchildren."

"Bless me!" said the other gentleman. "How many does
he have?"

"Forty-six at present, sir," volunteered Charlie with a grin.

"And are all the girls as lovely as your sister, lad?" the
second gentleman asked. "She is your sister, isn't she?"

"My half sister, sir."

"Come along, Charlie, Sandy," Jasmine said briskly.
"Mama and Grandmother are waiting."

"Why, you are not a child at all, are you?" the second
horseman said, surprised.

Jasmine looked up at the gentleman, feeling distinctly at
a disadvantage in her bare feet. "No, my lord, I am not,"
she said coolly. "Now, please excuse us. Our family is waiting. While you idly chatter, our flowers are wilting and will
be dead ere we get to the house." Moving past their horses,
Jasmine shepherded her brothers off.

"By God, Rowan! I do believe you have been given a set-
down," chuckled the first man. " 'Tis to be expected. You
will find the ladies of this family strong, beautiful, and outspoken."

"Do you know who she is, Tom?" his companion asked.
"Did you see those eyes of hers? They were turquoise-blue! I
never saw eyes like that in my entire life. Nor did I ever see
so beautiful a woman. She is a woman too. No girl would
look so lush, so ripe for the plucking. *I will have her!*"

"If she is no girl, Rowan, then she is married. You had

best behave around the de Mariscos. They are very protective of each other, and their women are not wantons. If you
want to breed your mares with Lord de Marisco's stud,
Nightwind, then you had best mind your manners. The
Marquess of Westleigh does not need to chase after women."

"What about the Earl of Kempe?" mocked his friend. "You
chased halfway around the world after Valentina Barrows
and then lost her to her cousin, Lord Burke."

"Alas," Thomas Ashburne, the Earl of Kempe, replied,
"it was a cruel fate that I not wed with my divinity, but
Rowan, I always treated her with tenderness and respect. I
am happy to say that Val, Padraic, and I have remained
good friends. It is a friendship I treasure."

The Earl of Kempe was a most handsome young man.
He was tall and had an athlete's slender, well-built body.
His eyes were best described as misty gray in color, and his
thick hair and elegantly barbered Vandyke moustache were
a rich gold. He had set many a heart a-flutter in his day, but
the only lady who had ever captured his heart was Valentina, Lady Burke. There had been none to catch his fancy
since.

His companion was not quite as handsome. He was clean-
shaven and had a square jaw that was cleft in the center
with a dimple. Tall, he was heavier set, but his bulk came
from a larger bone structure. There was no excess fat on his
body. His skin was fair, which was to be expected, considering that his two most arresting features were a pair of deep-
set gold eyes and a shock of wavy, tawny gold hair. He
carried himself with an arrogance that might be expected of
a man who could trace his family back to the time of Alfred
the Great himself, and whose same family had possessed the
same lands since that very distant past.

Reaching the house, the two men dismounted and their
horses were taken away by a groom to be rested and fed. A
footman led the gentlemen into the house, taking them to a
small, bright receiving room.

"The Earl of Kempe and the Marquess of Westleigh to see Lord de Marisco," Tom Ashburne told the servant.

"Very good, my lord. If you will wait here. There are wine and biscuits on the table," the footman said, and then bowed himself from the room.

As it was early, and as they had not yet broken their fast, the two gentlemen helped themselves, settling into comfortable, tapestried-back chairs by a small, bright fire that took the chill out of the morning air.

Suddenly the door to the room burst open. A woman hurried in, smiling and saying, "Tom Ashburne, you scamp! Why did you not tell us you were coming? Padraic and Valentina are here. 'Tis Velvet's birthday." She embraced him, kissing him on both cheeks. "Have you found a wife yet, or are you still pining for my daughter-in-law?"

"Madame Skye!" He kissed her back, enjoying the damask-rose scent she always wore. She was undoubtedly one of the most feminine women he had ever known. "I am not even seeking a wife. Did you not promise to find one for me? I am going to rely on your good judgment."

"Still a rogue," she said with a smile, then turned her blue-green gaze on the other gentleman in the room. "But you must introduce me to your companion."

"Madame Skye, Countess of Lundy, my cousin, James Rowan Lindley, the Marquess of Westleigh. Rowan, this is Lady de Marisco."

The Marquess of Westleigh bowed low over Skye's hand and murmured a polite greeting.

Her eyes twinkled at him, amused, and then she said to Tom Ashburne, "Why are you here? It has been ages since we last saw you."

"Rowan has some particularly fine mares he brought from Spain. Travel is quite unrestricted since the peace. They have an Arab strain in them. He wants to put them to stud, and I told him that your husband's Nightwind is the finest stallion in all of England today. We came to speak with Lord de Marisco about it."

"Adam, I fear, is still abed. Our daughter's birthday fete always begins the evening before May Day, as Velvet was born just after midnight," Skye explained. "Adam is not as young as he once was, and our gift to Velvet caused a great deal of excitement amongst the family. Come into the Family Hall and join us for the morning meal."

"What did you give your daughter that caused such excitement?" the Marquess of Westleigh asked, curious.

"It is a very long story, my lord. Come and eat. If you are truly interested, I will tell it to you," Skye promised him.

In the hall, only the boys, Sybilla, and Jasmine were in evidence. The two girls were seated at the high board as far apart as they could get. Sandy had chosen to sit with Sibby, and Charlie was with Jasmine. Skye frowned, knowing there was certain to be a scene if she attempted to tell Jasmine's tale now. She saw, however, that her grandchildren were already well-fed, and so, smiling at them, she said, "Have you been to see your mother yet?"

"We were afraid she would still be abed, Grandmama," Sybilla answered primly. "We did not want to disturb her."

"Fete or no, it is past time your mother was up," Skye told the girl. "Go and tell her I said so, Sybilla."

"Yes, Grandmama," Sybilla said, arising, curtseying, and then gathering up a mass of flowers. "I shall take her these May morning blooms." She hurried from the hall, her blond curls bouncing.

"Is she also your granddaughter, Madame Skye?" Tom Ashburne asked.

"She is my son-in-law the Earl of BrocCairn's daughter, and has been raised by my daughter, Velvet, his wife. I have always considered her my grandchild, although we are not related by any blood."

"Do you remember you once promised to find me a wife from amongst your granddaughters?" he said seriously.

"Sibby has her heart set upon the Earl of Glenkirk," young Sandy volunteered.

"But there is no betrothal yet," Charlie chimed in.

Tom Ashburne chuckled. "And who are these two fine young fellows?" he asked Skye as they settled themselves at the high board.

"My grandsons, Sandy and Charlie Gordon," she told them, "and a pair of scamps they are, I can promise you. They are Sybilla's half brothers."

"And this lady?" the Marquess of Westleigh said, looking at Jasmine, his gaze perhaps a trifle more intimate than it should have been. Indeed, it was quite obvious she had piqued his interest.

"This is my granddaughter, Yasaman Kama Begum, an Imperial Mughal princess. She will be known here in England as Jasmine de Marisco. Her father was the late Grand Mughal, Akbar; her mother, my daughter Velvet. She was the birthday surprise that caused such a stir amongst my family last night. Shall I tell you her tale as you eat?"

They were both, of course, absolutely fascinated.

"The women in your family seem to have a penchant for adventure," Tom Ashburne noted with a smile. "You, Lady St. Michael, Val, and now, I learn, the Countess of BrocCairn. Say on, dear Madame Skye!"

She spoke, and while she did the servants brought them a breakfast the like of which neither had had in a long time. There was oat porridge mixed with cream and bits of dried apple and pear; eggs poached in cream and marsala wine; sweet, pink country ham; tiny baby lamb chops; fresh bread, warm from the ovens; honey; a crock of newly churned butter; a small wheel of sharp cheese; flagons of nut-brown ale and red wine.

The two gentlemen ate appreciatively and with gusto as Skye unfolded Jasmine's tale before them. When she had finished, Tom Ashburne shook his head wonderingly.

" 'Tis the most amazing story, Madame Skye. Did I not

know you and your family as well as I do, I should be dubious of such a tale. Having accompanied your son and darling Val to Turkey, however, I am not. Perhaps I should seek a wife from among a quieter family."

"Hah!" she told him. "I do not believe you seek a wife at all, my lord, else you would have found one by now. You have turned your broken heart into a fine art, I think," she teased him. "Besides, most of the women in my family are a dull lot at best. If you are serious, Tom Ashburne, in your intent to marry, I can find you a pretty and biddable girl who will breed you up a houseful of children. What say you?"

He laughed. "What of Mistress Jasmine?"

"Oh no, my lord," Jasmine told him. "I have been widowed a year now and think to remain unmarried for a time longer. Besides, I am not in the least biddable. The Mughal's daughters seldom are."

They all laughed, and then Skye said, "Jasmine, my darling, take our guests out into the gardens for a stroll while I awaken your grandfather. You will stay, my lords? As most of my grandchildren have remained home, there is plenty of room for guests."

They accepted her gracious invitation. Sandy and Charlie Gordon, after a whispered conversation, announced that they were riding over to Blackthorne Hall to tell their brothers of their newfound sister. Tom Ashburne, a contented look upon his face, said that he would remain by the fire in hopes of seeing Valentina shortly.

"Are you really interested in visiting my grandmother's gardens, my lord?" Jasmine asked the Marquess of Westleigh. "She does have some particularly fine roses, I will admit."

"I am a lover of roses," he said, taking her arm in his. "Lead on, Mistress de Marisco." As they walked through the house and back out into the fresh spring morning, he remarked, "You have the most elegant little feet I have ever seen. They are not only beautiful, but there is something incredibly sensual about them."

"God's nightshirt!" Jasmine swore, using her grandfather's favorite oath. "I had forgotten I was without shoes, my lord. I hope you will excuse me. In India I wore slippers only on state occasions, but here in England I must have footwear on at all times except in my own chambers. When my little brother awoke me to come a-Maying with him, he told me not to wear shoes. He said it was the custom." She laughed. "I wonder if he was teasing me? I suspect him to be a young rogue, although I already adore him. I have never had a little brother before."

"When I was a child," Rowan Lindley said, "my cousins and I always went barefooted on May Day morn."

They entered Skye's rose garden and walked slowly along the grassy paths where the bushes were just beginning to come into bloom.

"Did you grow up near the Earl of Kempe?" Jasmine inquired politely. She bent and inhaled the spicy fragrance of a newly opened pink damask rose, finding it headily delicious.

"My father, God rest him, and Tom's mother were sister and brother. My own mother died when I was four. My father, when I was six. My father had appointed his brother-in-law, Henry Ashburne, who was then the Earl of Kempe, as my guardian. I was brought to Swan Court to be raised with his children. I had no brothers or sisters of my own.

"My uncle and aunt, however, had four children at that time. Tom was eleven, and five years my senior. He had three younger sisters. My aunt Anne was again with child. Robert was born in the spring of the following year. He was far too young for either Tom or me to be bothered with. For want of another male sibling, Tom took me under his wing. We have been friends ever since. As we both grew older, the five years between us seemed to dissipate until it no longer existed."

"You speak of your cousin with such fondness in your voice, my lord," Jasmine told him, "that I suspect that yours was a happy childhood. Where, pray, is your home? I find England so fair a land."

"Nearby to Tom's own Swan Court. My estate is called Cadby. It is set upon the bank of the river Avon. It is but two days' ride from Queen's Malvern and quite near your uncle, the Earl of Alcester's, home. You are absolutely the most beautiful woman I have ever seen!"

Jasmine stopped. Turning, she looked up at him, startled. She was shocked to see the barely masked passionate look in his unusual gold eyes. "Are all Englishmen so direct, my lord?" she asked him, keeping her voice cool. "Other than my family, I have had little contact with the English so far." His look was so intense that she finally had to lower her eyes.

In answer he said, "There is a necklace and earrings that I bought in Spain from the same gentleman who sold me my horses. His family had come upon hard times. The necklace, he told me, was part of the booty his ancestors claimed when they drove the Moors from Spain. It is made of Persian turquoise and diamonds. Your eyes are the exact color of that turquoise, Mistress de Marisco."

"In India a gentleman does not speak with such familiarity to a lady he has just met," Jasmine told him primly, her heart beating nervously. "Are all Englishmen as bold as you are, my lord?"

"Some are," he said. "If I am bold, it is because it is not often that I see something I truly want."

Jasmine found herself confused. Although she had spoken English her entire life, she was finding that there were certain nuances of the language that she was not familiar with, or did not quite understand. "What is it exactly that you do desire, my lord?" she asked him politely.

"*You*," he answered calmly.

Astounded, she felt her cheeks growing warm. "Ohh!" was all she could manage to say, wondering if she looked as big a fool as she surely felt. She stood very still, unable to move. She had thought herself so sophisticated. She was a widow and had known a man. In India her life had been set, like a jewel, into a prescribed setting. There was nothing in either her experience or her base of knowledge that told her how to handle a situation like this, *or* a man like the Marquess of Westleigh. She was as helpless as any innocent maid.

Looking down on her, Rowan Lindley smiled softly. He easily read the confusion in her face, and reaching up, he cupped her face with his hand. Her eyes widened slightly at his touch. His fingers splayed outward, caressing her cheek, running a thumb over her lips. "Your skin is softer than anything I have ever felt," he told her. "I mean to have you, you know."

"Have me for what?" she managed to gasp, shocked by the effect his warm, strong touch was having upon her.

He laughed briefly, showing even, white teeth. "For my wife, Jasmine de Marisco. I mean to have you for my wife."

"I have no wish to remarry at this time," she said.

"I will wait," he replied, his golden eyes making her feel as if her blood was boiling over.

"I am certain I hear my mother calling me," she said suddenly, pulling away from him and picking up her skirts to hurry off. Thank God she could move. She had believed her legs would never function again.

"I would not have thought that the Mughal's daughter was a coward," he called after her, and then he laughed as she stopped and whirled about.

"*I am not afraid of you!*" she declared vehemently. "And what could you possibly know of my father?"

"I have several shares in the East India Company," he said, staying where he was, not moving. "I went to India several years ago. I find it a land of incredible variety. There was no one I met, native to the land, who did not love, admire, and revere Akbar. I even saw him once in Agra. You have his look about the eyes, and the beauty mark you bear approximates the mole upon his face."

"So I have been told," Jasmine replied dryly and, turning, hurried back into the house.

Rowan Lindley laughed softly to himself. He wanted Jasmine de Marisco with every fiber of his being. From the very first moment he had seen her this morning, he had known that she must be his. She was young, and her life, he realized, had been very sheltered until now. Let her taste this new freedom she had just found. He could wait. He suspected that Jasmine would be very much worth the wait. Bending, he sniffed the damask rose she had smelled earlier. Its fragrance reminded him of her. Elusive, yet heady.

Jasmine had fled to her rooms. She stood in the shadow of the draperies, looking out over the gardens at Rowan Lindley. He excited her, making her feel as she had never felt, even with her dearest Jamal. Yet he did frighten her as well, despite her denials to the contrary. There was a deep, passionate intensity about him that seemed almost dangerous. His tawny, wavy hair fascinated her. She wanted to touch it, to let her fingers slide through it. She had been astounded when he had touched her. The intimacy that his touch had engendered was equally surprising.

She was so lost in thought that she did not hear the door to her bedchamber open. She started at the sound of her grandmother's voice, turning about to face Skye, her cheeks pink with a guilty blush.

"Adali tells me you rushed into your rooms as if you were pursued by the seven evil jinns," Skye said, noting the blush but not remarking upon it. Walking to the window, she looked down into her gardens where the Marquess of Westleigh strolled alone now.

"Adali worries too much," Jasmine replied shortly. "He is worse than half a dozen old women." Her eyes strayed back out the window.

"Did you show Tom Ashburne and his cousin the gardens, my darling?" she asked her granddaughter.

"The earl preferred to remain by the fire," Jasmine said.

"And Lord Lindley?" Skye gently probed.

Jasmine turned suddenly and looked directly at her grandmother. "He is an incredibly bold man," she said. "He says he wants me for his wife! He touched my face with his hand! In India a man would have been executed for taking such a liberty with any woman of good breeding."

"Ahhhh," Skye said, her eyes a-twinkle. "I see."

"What do you see?" Jasmine demanded nervously, unconsciously worrying the lace edging of her fine lawn handkerchief.

"That you are attracted to this man," Skye answered. "He is quite handsome, my darling. Tell me exactly what he said."

"He said that he would have me," Jasmine began, "and when I asked *what* he would have of me, he laughed and replied, 'I mean to have you for my wife.' I told him I had no wish to remarry at this time, and he said that he would wait! Grandmama! What am I to do?"

Skye laughed merrily. Then she said, "Why, my darling, you are to go on living your life exactly as you wish to live it. You do not have to marry anyone until you choose to remarry."

"I am not ready yet," Jasmine told her.

Skye patted the young woman's hand. "I will ask Tom Ashburne about his cousin. I find it odd he has no wife. I wonder what his age is? He and Tom are obviously close," she mused.

"He is five years the earl's junior and was raised with him from age six," Jasmine told her grandmother. "His father and the earl's mother were brother and sister. His parents had died."

"Hmmmmmm," Skye said. "Tom is a year older than Padraic. That would make him thirty-eight now. The Marquess of Westleigh is therefore thirty-three years of age. It is a good age for a man." Skye gave her granddaughter a hug. "Go and bid your mama a happy May morn. Sybilla has been with her long enough, and 'tis time she got used to the idea that she has a sister."

Lady de Marisco left Jasmine's rooms and descended to the hall, where she found her husband already deep in conversation with the Marquess of Westleigh. Tom Ashburne dozed by the fire, obviously quite content. Skye gave him a sharp poke with a finger. "Wake up, you rogue!" she said. "I want to talk with you."

His misty gray eyes opened, regarded her lazily. Then he stretched his large frame. "Here?"

"No, outdoors in the gardens where we cannot be overheard," she told him, and took the arm he offered as he stood.

When they were well away from the house, Skye said, "Tell me about Westleigh. He has made advances toward my granddaughter. What are his circumstances? Is he a fortune hunter?"

"God's foot, no, dear madame!" the Earl of Kempe said vehemently.

"Your mother and his father were siblings, I am told."

"Aye. Rowan was orphaned young. My father was his guardian until he was twenty-one."

"You have no wife, Tom, and your cousin has no wife. I understand your circumstances. Tell me of Rowan Lindley's," she asked.

"My parents treated Rowan no differently than they treated the rest of us," the earl began. "By the time Rowan reached his majority, he was like all young men. Eager to throw off the parental shackles he thought were binding him. My father had made no match for him. He, like you, dear madame, was a great romantic. He had fallen in love with my mother and he wanted that privilege for all his children.

"At twenty-one my cousin returned to his own home, which is called Cadby. Within several months' time he had made a match with the heiress of an adjoining property. He had seen the girl out riding and found her attractive. Like him, she had been orphaned from an early age. Her guardian, however, was a bachelor uncle. The girl seemed neither enthusiastic nor unenthusiastic about Rowan. My parents were worried, but nothing could dissuade Rowan from the path he had chosen. He is a very stubborn man, Madame Skye.

"The wedding was celebrated, but when my cousin entered his bride's bedchamber on their wedding night, he found it empty. Seeing the windows wide open, he went to close them, only to discover that his new wife had thrown herself out those windows. He could see her lying in a crumpled heap below. Sadly, she was still alive, but she was totally incapable of moving her lower limbs and never did so again. She lived on for eleven years, but in all that time she never spoke a word to anyone.

"A little over a year ago Rowan's wife contracted a lung fever. It was obvious that she was dying. As he sat by her bedside giving her what comfort he could, she spoke to him, to his great amazement. She had not wanted to marry anyone, for she was afraid and ashamed of what a husband would think when he found her not a virgin. Her guardian, you see, had robbed her of her maidenhead when she was but eleven, and not satisfied with that, had continued to force her. In another time she might have entered a convent to escape her fate."

"Poor girl," Skye said with genuine feeling. Then she asked him, "How did her guardian dare to believe that a husband would not realize the girl was not a virgin?"

"The man was obviously a terrible blackguard. He told his niece that, once married, her husband would not dare to admit to her imperfection for fear of embarrassment. And if she told Rowan of her uncle's behavior toward her, the uncle said he would disclaim the girl's accusations and shame her publicly. He told his niece that there were no witnesses to his lust, for indeed he had been very careful. The girl knew it to be the truth, but she was an extremely ethical little thing. She had fallen in love with Rowan and would not cheat him. So she chose to kill herself instead."

"What happened to the uncle?" Skye asked.

"When he heard of his niece's attempted suicide, he decided to flee England, realizing that Rowan would believe whatever his wife told him under those tragic circumstances. He fueled his flight with the girl's fortune, leaving only her land for Rowan. Rowan never told her this, even as she lay dying. He did not feel that she should believe herself under any obligation to him. The uncle never knew that the girl spoke not a word against him until her dying day."

"And your cousin loved and supported her despite everything," Skye said. "I am pleased to hear he is that sort of a man, Tom Ashburne."

"I do not know if Rowan really loved his wife, Madame Skye. If he did, it was not a deep love; but aye, he is a kind man."

"What else is he, my lord?" She fixed him with a sharp look.

The Earl of Kempe laughed. "You love this newly found granddaughter of yours very much, I can see, madame."

"Why Tom," she told him frankly, "I love them all! My children, and grandchildren, my whole family! Now tell me more of your cousin, the Marquess of Westleigh. He has greatly disturbed Jasmine."

"He is stubborn, as I have said, but a good man."

"Has he wealth of his own?"

"Aye, and strives to increase that wealth. He went out to India several years ago and returned to invest in the East India Company," the earl said.

"Which Church?" she demanded.

"The Anglican Church," came the answer.

"Good!" Skye said. "He is no fanatic, thank God! Does he follow the court? And what of women? Do not tell me he led a monastic life all those years of his unfortunate mar-

riage. I will not believe you, Tom Ashburne, if you do. Tell
me of his women."

"He goes to court to amuse himself, as we all do," the earl
told her. "As for women, yes, he has them, but he is discreet.
No lady has ever captured his heart to my knowledge, or
even become important in his life. When he first saw your
granddaughter this morning, however, he was immediately
taken with her." He chuckled. "I find it most annoying that
my cousin can find a lady to woo amongst your female relations, Madame Skye, while I am once more left languishing
by the wayside." He sighed dramatically. "Unless, of course,
you would like to put in a good word for me with Mistress
Sybilla."

"You are too old for Sybilla," Skye said.

"Nonsense," he told her. "A spirited girl needs an older
husband to keep her in check. I think her absolutely adorable with her golden curls and pouting mouth."

"She has set her heart upon the Earl of Glenkirk, although I know not the man," Skye warned him. "Why is it,
Tom Ashburne, that you always seek the impossible when
dealing with women? I think you do it deliberately. Disappointment gains you far more attention and keeps you a
wicked bachelor, you naughty rogue!" She teasingly tweaked
his elegantly barbered moustache.

The Earl of Kempe caught her hand and kissed it. His
eyes looked deep into hers. "A lady of your years, dear Madame Skye, should really not be so damned attractive," he
told her.

Skye laughed aloud. It was a joyous sound. "It is rare that I
long for my youth, Tom Ashburne, but with you I almost do!"

"Only almost?" he said, sounding quite disappointed.

"Almost," she repeated. "If I were young again, you see,
I should have to give up my darling Adam. I simply could
not do that."

"He is the most fortunate man alive, I think," the Earl of
Kempe said gallantly.

"Indeed he is," Skye agreed, and she laughed again.

He laughed with her, and when the humor had finally drained away, the earl said, "Are you satisfied that my cousin is an honorable man, madame? Your granddaughter could do no better, I vow."

"As much as I should like to see Jasmine married, happy and settled once more, she is simply not ready for it, I fear. I should like to take her to court, but first I will need to quell my son-in-law's outrage over her existence," Skye told Tom Ashburne. "Without BrocCairn's cooperation, it could be quite difficult for Jasmine."

"And Mistress Sybilla presents a problem also, I would imagine," the earl said wisely. "The lack of warmth between those two this morning at the high board, each separated by a brother, did not escape me."

"Sybilla has been spoiled by both her parents. She is not simply jealous of Jasmine. She is afraid as well. You do not know her, Tom. Sybilla is not a girl to turn the other cheek. She strikes back when she feels she is being attacked."

"A girl with spirit, as I have previously said," the Earl of Kempe remarked. " 'Tis just the sort of girl I like."

"Very well, my lord. Go and get your fingers burned once again," Skye told him. "Perhaps if the little witch has such a beautiful gentleman as yourself fawning over her, she will feel less hostile to her stepsister Jasmine. Do not say I did not warn you, Tom."

He laughed, but then quickly grew serious. "And do not say I did not warn you, dear madame. The court is not what it once was."

"I know," Skye told him. "Can it ever really be what it once was under Bess? Even I must admit to the truth. When Valentina was at court, it was a sad place. I do not imagine Scots James had enlivened it greatly. I am told he is a man with a dislike of ceremony."

"He is, madame, but his queen is not. She adores masques, and games, and beautiful clothing. If James will not partake in her frivolity, the rest of the court does. The king loves to hunt. That is his great passion. The queen loves to play, and she plays hard. The court has become a most licentious place. Our good queen Bess would be shocked and disapproving.

"I think both you and the Earl of BrocCairn will not be pleased. Mistess Sybilla is a virgin of gentle breeding. I do not believe the court is a good place for her to take up residence. You would be wise to beware. Mistress Jasmine, however, by virtue of her widowed state, has less to lose as long as her behavior is discreet."

"We are so isolated here in the country," Skye said. "My interest in the court died years ago, but now, with a new granddaughter to see to, I know not what else to do, Tom. As for Sybilla, her interest lies in one direction. She will adhere to a straight path and not deviate from her goal, I promise you.

"Gossip is slow to come to Queen's Malvern these days," she continued. "Eventually it does arrive, however, but how much distortion there is in it, I know not. I am told that the king was accompanied by a large group of his countrymen, many of whom are improvident."

"Aye," the Earl of Kempe told her. "And the king is quite a sentimental fellow. Do him the smallest kindness, and he wants to reward you with a munificence he can ill afford. Elizabeth's courtiers are very scornful of him, for poor King James is a fearful fellow. He is afraid of his own shadow, and hence not good with the people.

"To make matters worse, he dislikes the grandeur and magnificence that is necessary to the pageantry of court life. He can barely stay still while indoors, and is only happiest when out hunting. The Scots courtiers, of course, understand him far better than the English courtiers. They are kinder to him in their eagerness to advance themselves, while the English are aloof, believing themselves better than their northern counterparts. The king is not stupid. He knows the English for what they really are."

"Poor man," Skye said. "I do not envy him following in Bess's footsteps. Still, there he is, and so must we be, if but for a little while."

11

The Countess of BrocCairn sat beneath a willow tree in her mother's garden working upon a tapestry. Beside her sat her two daughters: Sybilla, embroidering her monogram upon some fine linen pillow slips, Jasmine reading. The late afternoon was unusually warm. There was no breeze, and the air was somewhat heavy. The Earl of Kempe lounged lazily in the green grass by Sybilla's side, gazing up at her admiringly while handing her fresh threads from her work-basket as she required them. He had made it quite clear to everyone in the de Marisco household that he was paying serious court to the young Lady Sybilla.

Sybilla pricked her finger and cried out. "Ohhh! How I dislike sewing, Mama! I shall be glad to go to court come the autumn." She snatched her hand away from Tom Ashburne, who was ardently kissing the injured digit.

"Sewing is a skill that every gentlewoman should possess, my dear," her mother told her. "What if some clumsy fellow should step on your gown and tear the hem from it? Your skill with a needle would enable you to quickly repair it, and you would not be thought a slattern."

"I have never learned to sew," Jasmine said, putting her book aside. "In India I had women to do such tasks for me."

"Do you never stop your ridiculous boasting?" Sybilla asked nastily. "You may have been a princess in India, but here you are nothing more than a common ba—" She stopped short, seeing the dangerous look in Jasmine's eyes, and smiled sweetly. "Well, we all know what you really are," she finished.

"I cannot understand how so sweet a mother could have raised so spiteful a shrew," Jasmine replied in equally sugary tones. "You must really be more careful, Sybilla dear. We all know what you *really* are. Your true colors are showing. You will surely frighten away my lord earl."

"I should adore my darling beauty if she were naught but a beggar maid," Tom Ashburne said gallantly.

"Well!" Sybilla huffed, rising to her feet and throwing down the cloth upon which she had been working. "I am not a beggar maid, my lord. I am related to the king. I am the only daughter of the Earl and Countess of BrocCairn. Do not ever forget it!" Then she dashed off into the depths of the gardens, the earl in pursuit, eager to make his apologies and regain a place in Sybilla's good graces.

"You should not bait her," Velvet admonished Jasmine.

"She should not take every opportunity to attack me," Jasmine replied. "I was not boasting about my life in India." Her face grew hard. "I will not allow her *any* latitude, Mama. Even Lord Gordon was good enough to speak with her, but she will not obey him either. If I continue to defend myself, perhaps she will eventually cease. She is my elder by six months, although I am certainly far more grown-up than Sybilla. I would like to try and be friends with her, but she will not let me. Her jealousy eats away at her, and you know it."

Velvet sighed deeply. "It is hard for her," she began, but Jasmine interrupted her.

"It is hard for me also!" she declared fiercely. "Why should it be so unusually difficult for Sybilla? She is in her native land, surrounded by a family who loves her. She has a noble suitor and aspires to go to court, where I doubt not she will find more hopeful swains.

"I am half a world away from my homeland. I have been torn from the mother who raised me and whom I love. I am bereft of both my husband and my father. I have lost my unborn child. It is, I think, far harder for me than for Sybilla, but I do not use my situation to try to hurt her.

"Why should she strike out at me because I am your child too? She is spoiled, and she is unpleasant, Mama. I will not allow her to slander me or my good name in her petulance! If she continues to do so, I will find a way to punish her, I promise you." Jasmine then arose and, with an angry swish of her skirts, returned to the house.

Velvet sighed again. She could not ever remember having been this uncomfortable in her entire life. Caught between her stepdaughter and Akbar's daughter, she was trying, though unsuccessfully, to keep the peace between the two girls. It was, however, a waste of her time. Jasmine, to Velvet's intense mortification, was correct in her assessment of Sybilla. She was behaving in a spoiled, unpleasant manner toward her stepsister. There was really no reason for her to do so. As each day passed, Sybilla grew more and more out of hand. No one, not Velvet herself, nor Alex, could reason with her, for her jealousy was, as Jasmine had so wisely observed, all-consuming.

Jasmine. Velvet smiled to herself. It was really very hard to think of that beautiful young woman as her daughter. There was so much of Akbar in her. I have missed so much, she thought sadly. Rugaiya Begum had done a wonderful job bringing up their shared child. Far better, Velvet considered guiltily, than I have done with Alanna Wythe's daughter. Although the two girls were the same age, Jasmine had far more poise, and certainly more elegance than Sybilla. Jasmine also had a highly eligible suitor in the person of the Marquess of Westleigh, although she pretended not to realize Rowan Lindley's intentions and did her best to ignore the handsome gentlemen.

Alex, of course, was pleased to see the marquess's interest. "Good!" he had said to his wife. "We'll marry her off before the truth of her birth can cause us any embarrassment. Jasmine will be far more respectable as his marchioness than as Lady Gordon's bastard get."

It was then that Velvet had struck her surprised husband. "My daughter," she said in a low, tight voice, "is no bastard. Why, my lord, do you persist in this? This is why I cannot bring Sybilla to heel, and she continues her assault upon her stepsister."

He rubbed his cheek ruefully. "I dinna mean to offend you, sweetheart. I am trying to accept the girl, but she will nae give an inch, and I fear for Sibby. She hae her heart set upon Glenkirk, and the Leslies of Glenkirk are a proud clan. If James Leslie sniffs any hint of scandal around Sibby, he will nae even consider my proposal. 'Twould break my lass's heart."

Velvet sighed. If only she could get Sybilla and Jasmine to cooperate. If Jasmine said black, then Sybilla said white. Her stepdaughter was constantly baiting her daughter, who would not ignore the girl, but like a cobra, struck back with all her own venom. Sybilla did not seem to have the good sense to cease her vindictive behavior, but it had to stop before the autumn, when they went to court. If the girls did not stop their backbiting, a scandal was certain to ensue. Alex would be furious if his Sybilla lost her chance to marry Glenkirk.

"Why are you frowning so?" Skye asked her daughter as she came to join her. "Have Sybilla and Jasmine been quarreling again? My granddaughter returned to the house with an expression as dark as a thundercloud."

"I cannot seem to exercise any control over them," Velvet

admitted wearily. "How can I take them to court if they continue to behave like two squabbling wildcats?"

"It is Sybilla's fault," Skye said bluntly.

"Jasmine gives back as good as she gets," Velvet replied, defending her stepdaughter.

"Sybilla begins the contretemps every time," Skye answered firmly.

"Where is she now?"

"Somewhere in the gardens with Tom Ashburne. He truly seems to adore her, but she will give him no quarter. She claims to want only Glenkirk, and yet I think she would be happier with Tom," Velvet told her mother. "He is warm, and amusing, and so devoted to her."

"What of Glenkirk? Tell me about him," Skye said, and she took the small low-backed chair previously occupied by Jasmine.

"I knew his mother briefly," Velvet began. "Next to you, Mama, she was the most beautiful woman I have ever seen. Dark, honey-colored hair and leaf-green eyes. She was my senior by some eleven years. Like me, she had been betrothed in the cradle and pushed to the altar, for like me, she resisted her first husband Patrick Leslie."

"Did she love him?" Skye wondered aloud.

"Aye, Mama, she did. Unfortunately, the king interfered in their marriage, and it led to terrible unhappiness for them all. It was then that she fell in love with Alex's and the king's cousin, Francis Stewart-Hepburn, the Earl of Bothwell. She is his wife now. They live in Italy with their children, as Bothwell was banished by the king from Scotland.

"Her son, James Leslie, is the current Earl of Glenkirk. He married another of Alex's cousins, Isabelle Gordon. They had two sons. Five years ago Bella was enceinte with her third child when she paid a social call to a nearby convent where a cousin was a nun. While she was there, it was attacked by a large group of religious fanatics. These zealots had been terrorizing the countryside for weeks, targeting the old Kirk and its institutions. They were utterly merciless and set the convent aflame.

"Both of Bella's sons had accompanied her. They died in the fire. Bella herself was found within the smoking ruins of the convent's courtyard, violated and hacked to bits. About her were the bodies of all of the nuns. The youngest of them had been first raped, Mama, and then crucified. It was the most horrendous atrocity ever perpetrated in our region. Even the preachers of the new Kirk were outraged. What was worse was that afterward these fiends disappeared and were not heard from again.

"Jemmie Leslie was, as you can imagine, totally devastated by his tremendous loss. He and his clansmen rode the high-lands for weeks afterward, but they could not find the crim-inals who had murdered his family and done those other dastardly deeds. If was as if the earth had opened up and swallowed them. Perhaps if he had been able to take his revenge, it would have helped purge the blackness from his soul. I have known him since I first came to Dun Broc. He and Bella were our nearest neighbors. After his family died, however, the gentle man with the delicious sense of humor that I knew turned into a cold, harsh creature. I hardly rec-ognize him. Yet I cannot blame him."

"And he has never remarried," Skye said thoughtfully.

"Nay. His family has begged him to take another wife, but he will not. He has two Leslie brothers, both with chil-dren, who could succeed him. When Jamie became King of England, Glenkirk accompanied him south. It was some-thing he would have never done if his family were alive. He serves as the king's unofficial minister of foreign trade for the New World and the East. 'Tis all he does these days, I am told. Work, work, and more work. 'Tis his life."

"Then why on earth does that silly chit Sybilla want him?" Skye demanded irritably. "He hardly sounds like a good catch to me."

"Sibby visited Glenkirk Castle with us when she was just

a little girl," Velvet explained. "Jemmie was always particularly kind to her as he had no daughters and very much desired one. I think she fell in love with him when she was four. She believes that if he can just see her grown, he will fall in love with her. She thinks she can ease his grief and make him happy again. She is so very hopeful, Mama. She has prevailed on her father to pursue the matter, and frankly, Alex likes the idea of marrying his only daughter to Glenkirk. He loves her very much and it would mean he would not really lose her. He thinks if Jemmie had a new wife, he would return home to Glenkirk."

"And what do you think, Velvet?" Skye looked sharply at her youngest daughter. "Are Alex and Sibby wasting their time?"

Velvet's brow wrinkled as she considered the question. She nibbled upon her lower lip with little white teeth. Finally she said, "I am not certain, Mama. Have not you and I known love to conquer the worst of troubles? Yet Jemmie has lived five years with his grief and bitterness. He seems to grow harder with time rather than softer." She shrugged. "Perhaps Sibby can win him over. I do not know."

Skye nodded her understanding. "I hope the chit will not break her heart over the man. Though she be difficult and wickedly rude to my darling Jasmine, I cannot wish her ill."

"Mama," Velvet teased her mother gently with a smile, "I have never seen you so taken with a grandchild as you are with Jasmine."

"Aye," Skye admitted grudgingly. "I love the girl greatly, and I'll not deny it to please any! I thank God your father and I lived to see her." Skye chuckled. "Adam dotes on her almost as much as he doted upon you, Velvet. Jasmine delights him with tales of her childhood escapades. Did you know that she first went tiger hunting with her father when she was only three? And she learned to shoot at five? Musket *and* bow! And how that big blue and gold parrot of hers can make Adam laugh! Why, he's almost human with his talking.

He has learned to imitate my voice, which drives Daisy wild. She is never certain if it is me calling or that wicked bird!"

"Jasmine will not remember it," Velvet said with a sad smile, "but Akbar took her tiger hunting when she was just an infant. I roasted him for it, as did Rugaiya Begum and Jodh Bai. Imagine taking a baby up upon his great fighting elephant! Ohh, Mama! I have lost so much!"

"Aye, you lost much with Jasmine, but 'twas not your fault," Skye sympathized. "And you have much with Alex in return. My poor Velvet, you were placed in a position I cannot envy any woman. Caught between two men you loved. Fate made the decision for you, and it has now all worked out for the best. You have *all* your children with you at last, and a husband who loves and adores you. You are certainly to be envied, Velvet!"

At that moment the Earl of BrocCairn exited the house and, walking across the lawns, called to his wife and mother-in-law. Velvet arose from her seat. She ran to him, holding her face up for a kiss, which he most willingly offered. Skye smiled. All her children had found love, and it made her happy to know that they were happy. Together the Broc-Cairns came to join her.

"You are going to hae company, madame," Alex Gordon informed his mother-in-law, and he bent to kiss her cheek.

Skye arose from her seat. *"Who?"* she demanded of him.

"The king."

"The king?" Skye was truly astounded. "Why on earth would James Stuart want to come to Queen's Malvern? Did you invite him? I most certainly do not want to entertain a king! God's nightshirt! It is the terror of every good family that the king should want to come and visit. It will cost us a fortune to entertain him! The lawns will be ruined! His retainers will eat us out of house and home! And nine months from the day, the housemaids will start giving birth to a flock of bastards, you mark my words, Alex Gordon!"

"The king comes incognito, madame. He brings with him

but a body servant and one companion, *the Earl of Glen-kirk!*" This last was said triumphantly.

"What does he want of us?" Skye asked suspiciously. "Why does he travel like a beggar instead of the king he is?"

"He wanted to come fishing," Alex said with a laugh. "So I invited him. He is nae like your old Queen Bess wi all her love of pomp and show. Jamie is on his summer progress, visiting a great house nearby. There are half a dozen masques planned for him and several banquets. The king is nae exceedingly fond of such things. The queen and Prince Henry will preside in his place. His hosts will be told he is abed with a summer flux of some sort or another. This will allow Jamie the opportunity to escape for a day or two of fishing. I have warned him Queen's Malvern cannot offer him the salmon that our icy, swift-flowing Scots rivers can, but he will be satisfied to fish for perch, rudd, and pike.

"He will also enjoy the peace of simple family life and plain meals. He doesna like food that is oversauced. The life you lead here at Queen's Malvern is more to his taste. He will be no trouble at all, belle-mere, *and* it will give me an opportunity to display our wee Sybilla to her best advantage before Glenkirk! 'Tis an excellent plan for him to get to know her again before she goes to court to serve the queen." He grinned, looking very pleased with himself.

"Perhaps," Velvet said, "it is a good idea that Jemmie Leslie renew his acquaintance with Sybilla under less formal circumstances."

"Humph!" her mother snorted. "She'll have no choice unless you intend to send her over to Blackthorne Hall or Pearroc Royale. Well, if she's to impress this Glenkirk, she had best sweeten her sour temper where Jasmine is concerned, Alex. They have fought again this day, and over nothing, as usual," Skye told her son-in-law.

"Perhaps, then, madame," he replied, "it would be better if you sent *your* granddaughter to Blackthorne Hall or Pearroc Royale. I will nae hae her spoiling my Sibby's chances wi Jemmie Leslie."

"Only Sybilla can do that," Skye told him sharply. Why was Alex so blind to Sybilla's faults? she wondered. " 'Tis she who starts these altercations, and well you know it. This is Jasmine's home. I do not intend to send her away from it to please any of you. Let Sybilla mind her manners for a change. 'Tis time she was forced to practice a little self-control. If she really wants to be the Countess of Glenkirk, she will have to. If battling with Jasmine means more to her, then so be it! Now, since you've invited the king, Alex Gordon, I'll take my leave of you. The entire house will need to be turned out to receive such a guest. When are we to expect him?"

"The day after tomorrow, madame," the Earl of Broc-Cairn replied.

"You have certainly given me a great deal of time to make my preparations, haven't you?" Skye answered him sarcastically, and turning, hurried back across the lawns into her house.

"I thought she would soften wi age," Alex Gordon said, bemused.

Velvet burst out laughing. "*Whatever* made you think that?"

After informing Adam of the impending royal visit, Skye gathered her servants together in the Family Hall and told them they would be receiving a very important guest in another day. "*He* comes to us in private," she said meaningfully, and only the densest of her retainers did not understand what she was telling them. Skye smiled, amused by the gasps of surprise. "*He* comes to fish for a day. None of you may leave the house until *he* departs. I want the entire house turned out and ready to receive him. Mrs. Bramwell," Skye addressed her housekeeper. "The four housemaids will do nicely. You need bring no others in from the village. Our guest comes with only one body servant and is accompanied by the Earl of Glenkirk and his servant. His visit is not official. I am happy to say we will not be burdened with half the court. *He* is to be accorded every respect, but prefers an informal way of life such as ours."

"Yes, m'lady," the housekeeper replied, relieved, but at the same time disapproving. What kind of a king was it who traveled without a great retinue and liked a simple country life? The old queen would have had none of such behavior if she had ever visited Queen's Malvern. Mrs. Bramwell was still entertained by the tales told by Lady de Marisco's tiring woman Daisy and her daughter Pansy, both of whom had been to court in the days of the great Elizabeth Tudor. Now there was a real monarch!

"Mrs. Garman."

The cook stepped forward. "Yes, m'lady?"

"Our guest likes good country food. Nothing is to be oversauced. I know that you should like to show off your great culinary skills, but please keep your menus simple and hearty."

The cook curtsied. "If that's what *he* wants, that's what *he'll* get, m'lady, but more's the pity, for I've several new recipes from France I've been wanting to try." Mrs. Garman looked very aggrieved.

"You may try them on us," Skye answered her, "once our guest has left. Our palates are not quite so finicky as the royal one is."

The house was in a frenzied state as the servants cleaned, swept, dusted, and polished everything they might lay their hands to. Even Violet, Velvet's old nurse, was called upon to arrange the flowers, for she had a great talent for such work, and because Velvet's sons, but for little Ned, were quite able to fend for themselves.

On the appointed day, the king's body servant rode ahead of his royal master to warn the de Mariscos of his lord's impending arrival.

"Shall I have the servants line up in the drive to meet his majesty, m'lady?" Bramwell, the majordomo, asked.

"Nay," Skye answered him. "The king would be incognito, and so we shall let him be."

Bramwell bowed himself from his mistress's presence.

"Well," said Daisy, "he sounds to me like a queer fellow, this Scots King of England. Old Queen Bess would have really had us jumping, and she did when she came to Lynmouth House, didn't she, m'lady?" Daisy tucked an errant lock of her lady's hair into place. "There, that's done!" She stood back and admired her handiwork.

Skye smiled into the mirror at her faithful tiring woman. "Aye, Bess always had us on our mettle, Daisy, but 'tis a new century, and with it, a new king. We're past our time, you and I."

"Yet yer going off to court come winter, aren't you?" Daisy said. "Well, you'll not go without me, m'lady!"

Skye arose and smoothed down the dark blue silk of her gown. "I go for Jasmine. She is the Mughal's daughter and must have every chance at happiness here in England."

"Seems to me," Daisy noted sagely, "that Mistress Jasmine is very happy right where she is. According to Toramalli and Rohana, yer granddaughter lived a country life in India. And that Marquess of Westleigh seems an eager enough suitor for all Mistress Jasmine pretends not to notice. She can see he's hot for her, and one day soon, I expect, she'll return his ardor. She's been widowed long enough. The women in this family don't like to be too long without a man."

"Daisy!" Skye laughed. "You are a shameless old biddy."

"I only tell the truth as I sees it," Daisy said with a chuckle.

There was a knock on the bedchamber door and Molly, an apple-cheeked maidservant, popped her head in. "The king is coming up the drive, m'lady. M'lord says ye'd best hurry."

"Indeed I had," Skye said, and hurried from the room, Daisy in her wake.

In the main hallway of the house, Skye found her daughter Velvet and son-in-law, their five sons, Sybilla, Jasmine, and Adam, all awaiting James Stuart. The gentlemen were garbed formally in black silk suits with starched white linen ruffs. Six-year-old Neddie looked as if he was strangling, his small fingers wedged between his neck and his collar. Velvet wore a silk gown the color of violets. Jasmine was in crimson.

It was obvious, however, that a great deal of care had been taken with Sybilla. Her gown of pale blue silk with its delicate lace embroidery made her look extraordinarily virginal. There was not a curl out of place, and she seemed to be enveloped in a cloud of lavender. Skye caught Adam's gaze, looked toward Sybilla and rolled her eyes. Lord de Marisco's cough sounded very much like laughter to those about him, but he maintained a dignified demeanor.

They watched through the open door of the house as their guests rode up. Seabert, the head groom, was waiting with Will and John, the two stablemen. Bowing politely to the king, the three men hurried the horses off as soon as the riders had dismounted. Skye and Adam then stepped through the door of the house to greet James Stewart. The king and his companions were garbed simply. Only their son-in-law's description of his kingly cousin allowed them to know him. Lady de Marisco curtsied low, even as her husband bowed gallantly.

As Skye arose, pleased that her left knee, which had gained a stiffness lately, had not failed her, she said, "Welcome to Queen's Malvern, Your Majesty. We are honored by your presence."

"Welcome, sire!" Adam echoed his wife's greeting.

The Earl of BrocCairn quickly stepped forward and bowed. "May I present my in-laws, sire? Your host and hostess, Lord and Lady de Marisco, the Earl and Countess of Lundy."

James Stuart smiled. The king had not inherited either his parents' great height or their unusual good looks. He was well-built, and of medium height. Although his legs were slightly bent from a childhood illness, he was not deformed, though when he walked, his steps were slightly uneven. His hair, the Stuart family red in his youth, was now turning reddish-brown in his fortieth year. He had a long face with a long nose and a small mouth, but his most compelling feature was his heavy-lidded amber eyes, which, whatever James's mood, seemed filled with an unfathomable sadness.

"I thank ye, Lord and Lady de Marisco, that ye would hae me, and on such short notice," the king said. "I am weary of all the folderol of the court, and a wee bit of fishing will soothe my soul. I'm told ye hae some wickedly large pike on yon river."

"Aye, sire," Adam returned. "You will not be disappointed, I am certain. May we offer you a bit of fresh baked bread, some of our ham and October ale? A man should not sport on an empty belly."

"Aye," the king agreed, and it was obvious he was pleased with the old Earl of Lundy's friendly, but respectful courtesy. Although he preferred a simpler lifestyle than he was ordinarily permitted, he never forgot his high position and insisted upon being treated with the courtesy and respect he believed a king deserved. James was glad he had come.

They reentered the house, and the Earl of BrocCairn presented his sons and daughter. The boys were in open awe of the monarch, while Sybilla blushed and simpered prettily, to James's pleasure.

"And who is this lovely lassie, Alex?" the king asked, coming abreast of Jasmine.

"My stepdaughter, Mistress Jasmine de Marisco, my liege," Alex said in even tones.

"My daughter from a previous marriage, sire," Velvet put in.

"You will undoubtedly be interested to know that my granddaughter is the youngest daughter of the late emperor of India, Akbar," Skye said briskly. "She has only just arrived in England this past winter. Her father, as you know, died almost a year ago. She has been widowed almost two years. In India she was known as Yasaman Kama Begum. She chose to Anglicize her name, which means Jasmine, and take our surname for her own. It is less confusing. Perhaps at dinner we may entertain you with her miraculous tale."

"Ahh, aye," the king said, a trifle confused, but willing to accept this rather formidable lady's word. Still, his mind stretched back over the years. He seemed to remember that the beautiful Countess of BrocCairn came a maiden to her husband. Was his memory failing him? The king thought not. He would indeed be interested in Lady de Marisco's story.

"Run along, children," Adam said. Then he turned to the king. "Will Your Majesty introduce us to your traveling companion?" he inquired politely.

"Och," the king replied. "I hae almost forgot ye were wi me, Jemmie. This is the Earl of Glenkirk. He's a quiet fellow, aren't ye, Jemmie? I like to hae him wi me because he doesna talk me to death as so many others do."

The Earl of Glenkirk nodded with a brief, amused smile. Then he bowed to Adam and kissed Skye's hand. "Thank ye for having me," he said.

Velvet pushed forward and kissed James Leslie's cheek. "It has been a long time, Jemmie," she said quietly. "We miss you at home."

"There is naught for me at Glenkirk now, Velvet. I live my life best serving my king," was the quiet reply.

Velvet drew Sybilla forth. The girl's blue eyes were wide with admiration and adoration. "I will wager you do not remember our daughter Sybilla, Jemmie. She has become quite a fine young lady and will go to court this winter to serve the queen. Your friendship would mean much to her, I know. Court is a frightening place when you are new to it, and young, and inexperienced," Velvet said, her voice brimming with maternal concern. "I remember my own days there."

James Leslie's eyes flickered dispassionately over Sybilla. He gave her a small, wintery smile, even as he kissed her hand. "You, of course, have my friendship, Lady Sybilla," he told the blushing girl politely. Then he turned away from her before Sybilla even had a chance to speak, looking directly at Jasmine. "Will you introduce me to your other daughter, Velvet?"

"This is Jasmine de Marisco, Jemmie," Velvet said nervously. It was not going at all as they had imagined it would.

Glenkirk kissed the elegant little hand offered to him. His green-gold eyes stared directly into Jasmine's turquoise eyes. "Madame," was all he said, but his look said far more. Even Sybilla noticed it.

"How could you?" she demanded of Jasmine shortly afterward, when the gentlemen had gone off to the river to fish. She was near to tears, and she stamped her little foot, as she often did when she was angry.

"What can I possibly have done to displease you now?" Jasmine said irritably. "Please, Sybilla, let us not quarrel while the king is here. We promised Grandmother we would not."

Sybilla stamped her foot again. "I saw how you looked at the Earl of Glenkirk, you low-bred hussy! *He is mine!* I will not have you with your exotic, whorish ways flirting with the man I am to marry. If you so much as speak to him again, I shall tear your heart out! Do you understand me? *Do you understand me?*" Her voice rose in dramatic intensity, and her pretty face grew red with anger.

"Ohh, Sybilla, what a little fool you are," Jasmine replied impatiently, her own anger giving an edge to her voice. "I could hardly look away from the earl when he was introduced to me. There was nothing in my look but dispassionate curiosity. I would be more careful of how I spoke, *stepsister*. Your father has not yet broached the subject of a match between you and the earl. What if you were overheard by the earl's servant and he spoke with his master? You yourself could ruin everything you hope for, and then what would you do, Sybilla?" Jasmine wisely ignored the girl's remarks about her background. She knew who she was.

"Jasmine is correct, dearest," Velvet said, agreeing with

her daughter. "You simply must learn to master both your temper and your tongue."

"And high time too," Skye put in.

Sybilla's lower lip began to tremble. Her beautiful blue eyes filled with tears of self-pity. "You are *all* against me," she declared. "Only Papa understands me!" Sybilla sobbed dramatically.

"God's nightshirt!" Skye exploded. "The wench should be smacked!"

"No one is against you, Sybilla," her mama said in rather sharp tones. "You are anxious about Lord Leslie, to be sure, but you must not take out your apprehensions on those who love you. I wonder if indeed you are old enough to marry. Your behavior is most childish."

As evening approached, Skye sat with her granddaughter Jasmine in her own day room and again considered Lady Sybilla Gordon.

"I hope Alex will approach the Earl of Glenkirk quickly," Skye said. "If Sybilla wants him, 'twould be just as well to see her married off to the fellow as soon as possible. Why go to the expense and the trouble of sending her to court?"

"And if she were married and back in Scotland," Jasmine teased her grandmother, "you would not have to be bothered with her at Queen's Malvern ever again, eh, Grandmother?"

" 'Tis truth, my darling girl, that you utter," Skye admitted. "I have never been able to warm to the wench. As a little one she was always demanding of Velvet's entire attention, even when Velvet's elder lads were small and Velvet enceinte with another of them. Sybilla could hardly bear to be out of her sight. She has ever been her mama's girl, a whining, troublesome chit of a creature. Velvet has overcoddled her out of a sense of both pity and guilt."

"She does not look like Lord Gordon," Jasmine noted.

"She looked more like him as a child," Skye said. "I expect

she resembles the creature who bore her, the silversmith's bold wench."

"Do you think I looked at Lord Leslie in a flirtatious manner, Grandmama? Since I would just as soon be rid of Sybilla also, I do not want to ruin her chances with the gentleman," Jasmine said with a mischievous smile.

"I think it was Lord Leslie who looked at you with interest in those fathomless green eyes of his," Skye replied. "You are most extravagantly beautiful, my darling girl. Sybilla is a pretty thing, but she cannot hold a candle to you. Alas, I think she knows it."

"Oh dear," Jasmine fretted.

Skye laughed. "As long as you do not encourage him, my darling girl, you cannot be blamed for whatever happens."

"I do not wish anything to happen," Jasmine declared vehemently. "It is bad enough that the Marquess of Westleigh has been a constant visitor every few weeks since spring. Why will no one understand that I simply want to be left alone to myself? I have been quite happy since I came to England last winter, Grandmama. I have a family, and I am safe."

"And that is enough?" Skye asked.

"For now it is, Grandmama. When I left India almost a year ago, I was heartbroken and quite devastated by the events surrounding my departure. The husband I loved was dead at my beloved brother's behest. My father was close to death. But now that time and distance have had their effect upon me, Grandmama," Jasmine said, "I find that I both want and need time to enjoy life before I must settle down to being a wife and mother again. Can you understand that? I know I must eventually remarry, *but not now*."

Skye nodded. "I understand," she reassured Jasmine.

"Sybilla, on the other hand," Jasmine continued, "very much desires to be married to the Earl of Glenkirk. Perhaps I can help her in a roundabout way. I think I shall have my dinner in my room tonight. I find that after the strain of today, my head is aching fiercely."

Skye chuckled. "You are indeed anxious to be relieved of your stepsister's company, my darling girl, but I will not have her driving you from your own board."

"She is not, Grandmama," Jasmine replied, "but I do fret her. She cannot seem to help herself. She will be at her best if I am not there. Perhaps she will even impress the Earl of Glenkirk enough that he will consider Lord Gordon's proposal. Everyone is correct when they say that Sybilla must make a good impression on Lord Leslie before she goes to court. It will be far harder there for her to attract his attention if the English court is anything like my father's court was. It was a noisy, gossipy, busy place."

"Royal courts are royal courts the world over," Skye said. "Very well, darling girl, you may absent yourself from the board tonight that Sybilla have an opportunity to shine before the object of her desire. It is unfortunate that she will neither understand nor appreciate your motives. You are far more generous to her than she to you."

Jasmine's absence was duly noted that evening, but Skye's explanation was so easily given that no one thought any more on it. Mrs. Garman, the cook, had done her very best to follow her mistress's instructions. The meal was a simple, hearty one which began with some excellent perch that had been caught that very afternoon by the visitors to Queen's Malvern. The fish had been delicately broiled and were served with dill and lemon. There was also a large dish of mussels that had been steamed in white wine until their shiny black shells had opened. There was a single side of beef that had been packed in rock salt and roasted over a slow fire; a large game bird pie with rich wine-flavored gravy oozing from its crisp golden crust; and a platter of lamb chops. There were turnips and fresh peas, fresh bread, crocks of sweet butter, and a wheel of sharp, hard cheese. October ale and a rich red wine were served to drink.

"Madame," the king said as he wiped his mouth prior to digging into a second serving of plum tartlet, "ye keep a verra fine table, to be sure. I canna remember when I hae enjoyed a meal last as much as I hae enjoyed this meal. My compliments to your cook."

"Would it be too much trouble, Your Majesty," Skye said, "if I ask Mrs. Garman to come out of her kitchens that Your Majesty might tell her yourself. She is a simple country woman who would never, in her wildest dreams, have expected to serve Your Majesty. 'Twould be a rare moment she would treasure for the rest of her life."

"Aye," the king said expansively. "Bring the lady before me that I may praise her most excellent skills."

Mrs. Garman was called for and, accompanied by Bramwell, the majordomo, came from her kitchens, flushed, beaming, and quite nervous. She curtsied so low before James that Skye feared the poor woman would be unable to arise without tumbling back upon her well-padded posterior, but Bramwell, one hand beneath the lady's elbow, guided her successfully to her feet again.

"A verra fine meal, good lady," James Stuart said. "I canna remember ever having eaten a better one."

" 'Tis a pleasure to cook for Yer Majesty," Mrs. Garman replied. She was then escorted out and returned to her kitchens to tell Priss and Mary, the kitchen maids, and little Wat, the knife boy, that though she could barely understand the king, for he spoke with a very thick tongue, he was a most fine gentleman indeed.

When the meal had been cleared away, Skye cleared her throat, saying, "I will now tell Your Majesty of how my granddaughter Jasmine came into this family."

"Twill nae be necessary," the king replied. "Lady Sybilla herself told both Jemmie and me before dinner the whole sad tale. Velvet, my dear, yer a brave lass, but then I always knew that ye were," the king said with a warm smile at the Countess of BrocCairn.

"*Just what did Lady Sybilla tell you, sire?*" Skye asked pointedly of the king, and she sent both her daughter and son-in-law a fierce look.

Alex Gordon was visibly white about the lips, while his daughter Sybilla wore the pleased expression of a cat that had just cornered a plump mouse. The girl's look was, in fact, such a look of pure triumph that Skye wanted to slap her.

The king looked quite confused. He could not understand what was wrong.

The Earl of Glenkirk came to his monarch's aid, saying, "Lady Sybilla has explained to us how her mother was kidnapped years ago and forced into a shameful, carnal bondage, during which captivity she was forced to bear a child which she gladly left behind upon her rescue. Indeed, we have been told that Lady Gordon was so ashamed of this tawdry incident in her life that she did not even tell Alex. Lady Sybilla has elaborated on how this child, now grown, came to England and forced herself upon the good natures and good hearts of Lord and Lady de Marisco. Is that not so?"

"No, my lord, it is not so. What Sybilla has told you is an outrageous fabrication," Skye said quietly, although those about her who knew her realized that those well-controlled tones represented just the merest tip of her outrage.

Sybilla, however, unwisely arose and cried out, "*It is true! I have not lied!*"

"Leave this table and go to your room," Skye told the girl. "*At once!*"

"Jasmine seeks only to ruin my life!" Sybilla wept uncontrollably, obviously overwrought.

Skye turned to her horrified majordomo. "Bramwell, escort Lady Sybilla from the hall," she ordered. Her gaze swung to her son-in-law, the Earl of BrocCairn. "I hold you entirely responsible for *your* daughter's behavior, my lord. You will send her home to Dun Broc tomorrow. I will no longer have her in my house."

Velvet cast a beseeching look toward her father. "Papa," she pleaded weakly.

"I am in entire accord with your mother, Velvet," Adam said.

"What is wrong?" the king asked, finally finding his voice.

"Lady Sybilla has lied to Your Majesty," Skye replied.

"Lied? To me? To her king?" James Stuart looked astounded, as if such a thing were not possible.

"Jamie, I apologize for my lass," Alex Gordon said, shamefaced. "Please forgive Sibby and allow my belle-mere to explain."

"Madame, enlighten us, if ye will," the king said, now fully recovered from his surprise and quite curious to know what was really going on. "This situation is strange, most strange indeed."

"Once, Elizabeth Tudor and I were friends," Skye began, "and then I was a thorn in her side, but that is another tale altogether."

"Do ye nae then believe in the divine right of kings, madame?" the king demanded, interrupting. His divine royal rights were a very sore point with James Stuart, who strongly believed in them and in himself.

"Aye, Your Majesty, I do," Skye said with a small twinkle in her Kerry-blue eyes, "but Elizabeth Tudor was a queen, *not a king.*"

James Stuart stared at Lady de Marisco, and then understanding dawned in his amber eyes. "Hch! A *queen, and not a king!*" he chortled. "Heh! Heh! Heh! 'Tis a fine jest, madame. A verra fine jest indeed. Heh! Heh!"

The atmosphere about the table was more visibly relaxed now as Skye took up the thread of her tale. She spoke movingly of that time so many years ago when all their destinies had been changed by Elizabeth Tudor's seemingly innocent demand that she and Adam mount a trading expedition to India. Skye chose her words carefully in order to protect both her beloved daughter and granddaughter, that James might understand not just their plight, but also the difficulty presented to the Indian emperor when Velvet's uncle had come to take her home.

"Velvet tells me Akbar was a most moral man who had studied all the world's religions. There were even Jesuits at this court, and their daughter was baptized a Christian," Skye told them.

"When the Mughal learned that Alex was alive, there was no question that Velvet must be returned. Alex, however, had only been her husband for a few months. Akbar had been her husband for almost two years, and they shared a child.

"The Mughal would not compromise his principles. Since she would not go willingly, she was drugged and removed forcibly. She was not allowed to take her child, for the Mughal knew of the prejudice practiced in Western lands. He knew there were those who would call his daughter base-born, yet under the laws of the land in which she was born, the land to which she was native, she was not only true-born, but a royal Mughal princess as well."

"Aye," James Stuart agreed, "of course she would be. I can find no fault wi this reasoning, though I know some would."

"Thank you, Your Majesty," Velvet said, her eyes bright with unshed tears. The king might be called "the wisest fool in Christendom," but he was really quite intelligent and had a kind heart. He had fully understood her plight.

"Unfortunately, Sybilla Gordon, whom Alex fathered and legitimatized, and whom my daughter has raised with love, is wildly jealous of her stepsister. We have remonstrated with her, but to no avail, sire."

"The lass needs to be beaten," the king said. "A good beating and a diet of bread and water will bring any recalcitrant child to its senses, Lady de Marisco. Now, I think, I will seek my bed. The fish are up early, as ye must know."

When the king had left the hall in the company of Lord

Leslie, Skye and her family sat back down at the high board, the wine cups were refilled, and they discussed the evening past.

"I meant it when I said Sybilla is to return to Dun Broc on the morrow," Skye told her son-in-law.

"I'll nae argue wi you over that," Alex Gordon said. "She behaved shamefully and is obviously nae fit for civilized company. Let her cool her heels at Dun Broc until late autumn. Then she must return to England to go to court. She hae been promised a place amongst Queen Anne's maids, and we canna renege now."

"She will be heartbroken to be sent home," Velvet ventured, her soft heart going out to the daughter she had raised.

"She hae brought it all upon herself," Alex said harshly. "Perhaps Jamie is right. Perhaps I should gie her a good beating as well. She surely deserves it."

"Mama!" the Countess of BrocCairn cried softly to her mother.

"No, Velvet, she cannot stay," Skye said in answer to the unspoken question, "though I realize what Sybilla did was out of her fear that her stepsister was proving more attractive to Lord Leslie than she. Had I not been so angry, I should have laughed at the Earl of Glenkirk's recital of Sybilla's tale. He was obviously quoting her very words. 'Carnal bondage'? 'Tawdry incident'?" Skye laughed.

"The lass must learn to live wi the consequences of her actions," the Earl of BrocCairn said angrily. "Ye hae spoiled her, Velvet."

"I have spoiled her?" Velvet looked positively outraged. "I was not the only one who spoiled her, Alex Gordon! You have ever doted on the child. 'Tis not I who have filled her head full of Gordon history and how she is related to the king. I am responsible in part for what she has become, but you must accept your responsibility in this matter as well."

"Cease your bickering," Skye sharply ordered them both.

"Nothing will come of it. You are Sybilla's parents. It is up to you to make her see the error of her ways. You had best warn her that this sort of behavior will not be tolerated by her majesty Queen Anne. If she does not wish to lose her place at court and disgrace her family, she will behave herself."

The Gordons of BrocCairn left the Great Hall of Queen's Malvern and found their way to their apartment. There upon their bed lay Sybilla, sleeping, her pretty face tearstained.

"Oh, Alex!" Velvet whispered, her soft heart touched.

"I'll nae be moved," he whispered back, "and I'll nae allow you to be." He gave her hand an encouraging squeeze and then said in a hard voice, "Sybilla! Wake up! Yer mother and I would hae words wi ye."

The girl slowly sat up, her blue eyes wide. "Did you speak to Glenkirk about a match between us?" Sybilla asked. "What did he say? Will he have me to wife? Ohhh, Papa! Is he not the most handsome man in the whole world?"

Alex Gordon felt a shiver go down his spine. How was it possible, he wondered, that Sybilla was suddenly so like Alanna Wythe, the woman who had birthed her? Sibby certainly was exhibiting the same selfishness that Alanna had always shown. The Earl of BrocCairn shook his head wearily and said to his daughter, "I most certainly didna speak wi Glenkirk, Sibby. Can ye nae understand? Ye hae behaved quite badly and brought shame upon both yer mother's family and my own. No man would want a wife who did that. Perhaps if ye shine in Queen Anne's service when yer at court, however, ye will make a favorable impression upon him. Then I may finally suggest a match between ye."

" 'Tis not fair," Sybilla Gordon whined. " 'Tis not fair that I suffer because of that Jasmine. This is all her fault!"

"Nay, lass, 'tis yer fault," her father said harshly. "Ye cannot blame Jasmine for this. Now ye hae best find yer own bed and get some sleep. Ye leave at dawn for Dun Broc."

"Mama!" Sybilla clutched Velvet. "Please don't send me away! Oh, please do not!"

"You must accept your just punishment with better grace than this, Sybilla," Velvet said, smoothing the girl's hair.

"The matter is settled, lass," Alex told his daughter. "Now gie us a kiss and go to bed."

"I will not!" Sybilla said, and stamping her foot, she turned and ran from the room.

"Oh, Alex! What are we to do with her?" Velvet groaned.

"Stand firm, sweetheart," he told her. "Sybilla is out of hand, and I am ashamed I dinna see it before now—before she hurt Skye and Adam."

"And Jasmine too," Velvet said.

"Jasmine," the Earl of BrocCairn said slowly. "Now there's another problem to solve."

"Perhaps with Sybilla returned home to Dun Broc," Velvet suggested, "you will be able to get to know her better."

"Aye," the earl said absently. "Perhaps." And he gave his wife a kiss.

❋

12

❋

The court was back at Whitehall for the winter season, and a group of young English nobles clustered about, observing everyone at the evening's entertainment with a sharp eye.

"The queen has two new maids of honor, I'm told," remarked a young man with dark, saturnine good looks.

"One is a horse-faced heiress from Lincoln," replied another of the group, a large fellow with sandy hair. "Best leave her to our Scots compatriots. They'll marry *anything* English with a plump purse."

His friends chortled at this witticism.

"You seem to be the best informed of all of us, Henley," the dark gentleman, Lord North, said. "Tell us, who is the other new maid of honor?"

"The daughter of a Scots earl," came the reply.

"God's nightshirt!" exploded Lord North. "Is it not bad enough we are overrun by young, impoverished second sons out of Scotland seeking to marry our ladies? Eager, uncouth fellows pushing us from our own court! Now they are sending us their bold, freckle-faced women."

"Do not despair," Baron Henley told him. "This girl has an English mother, and frankly, my dear North, she is divine. Petite, skin like cream. Golden curls, and eyes so blue a man could drown in them. She is absolutely adorable. The Earl of Kempe is already making a fool of himself over her. She is the Earl of BrocCairn's only daughter, and the man absolutely dotes upon her. She'll have a fat dowry, you can be certain of it. Not only that," Baron Henley lowered his voice. "I am told she is the granddaughter of the Countess of Lundy."

"*Who is the Countess of Lundy?*" Lord North inquired, puzzled.

"God's foot, North! You really know nothing. The Countess of Lundy is the magnificent Skye O'Malley herself. She was old Bess's great rival, and was banned from court after her marriage to Lord de Marisco, the Earl of Lundy. They say she was the most beautiful woman in all the kingdom. Few, except her family, have seen her in years, if indeed she is even still alive. She is rich beyond all knowing, I am told. Why, you've met several of her children here at court. The Earl of Southwood is her son, and so is Lord Burke of Clearfields. The Countess of Alcester is her daughter. They say the mere mention of her name could infuriate old Bess."

"Why?"

Baron Henley looked confused. "*Why?*" he repeated. "I have absolutely no idea, North. It just could, I am told."

Lord North laughed. "Point out the little Scots girl to me, Henley," he said.

"There," his friend said, his finger delicately thrusting forth, "next to the queen herself upon a stool. The pretty girl in sky-blue velvet."

Lord North peered. "Very nice," he finally said. "Indeed, she is quite acceptable, Henley. Perhaps we should go over and encourage Anglo-Saxon relations. 'Twould surely please Old King Fool. While he is so generously handing out tokens of his friendship to all and sundry, why should we not be included amongst the fortunate?"

Just then the majordomo stationed at the entry of the hall banged his staff of office upon the floor and announced, "The Earl and Countess of Lundy. Mistress Jasmine de Marisco."

The large Baron Henley almost tangled himself in his storklike legs turning about to gape with surprise. "God's foot!" he said. "It cannot be, and yet . . . and yet it must be! Lord, how old Bess must hate it that her greatest rival has outlived her! And who is that spectacular creature with them! I have never seen such a beautiful woman in all my life. Look at the sapphires about her neck, North! They are surely worth a king's ransom! Ahhh, perhaps the winter will not be dull after all."

"How you spend your winter, my lord, is, of course, up to you," a voice murmured softly in his ear, "provided that you do not attempt to accost Mistress de Marisco. *She is mine.*"

Startled, Baron Henley turned about to find himself face to face with the Marquess of Westleigh and his cousin, the Earl of Kempe.

"I believe," Tom Ashburne said, "that my cousin is warning you off, Henley. He staked his claim to Mistress de Marisco some six months ago when they first met. You would not, of course, want to hinder his courtship of the lady. And North, my dear fellow, the dainty Sybilla Gordon—for that is her name—is mine. You will do well to remember it lest I be forced to remind you."

"A cat may look at a king or a queen as the case may be," Baron Henley said with a weak smile.

"There are easier pickings to be had here," Lord North remarked, shrugging. "Usually an orphan or a girl without powerful connections is best, I have found. No need to distress yourselves, my lords." And arm in arm with Baron Henley, Lord North lost himself in the crowd of courtiers within the hall.

"As fine a pair of blackguards as I've ever seen," Rowan Lindley said, annoyed.

"But cowardly and easily dismissed," Tom Ashburne replied. His eyes turned to where the queen sat, Sybilla at her side. "Is not my darling the most precious creature you have ever seen, Cousin?"

The marquess laughed. "Tom, you are impossible. In all the time you've known that unbearable little chit, she has scarcely given you the time of day. She is determined to be the Countess of Glenkirk, but Glenkirk's eyes, I fear, stray in another direction. But now that Mistress Jasmine de Marisco has come to court, Cousin, I will redouble my efforts to make her my wife. I am not a man to give my heart easily, as you know."

The two gentlemen made their way through the crowds to the dais where the royal couple sat. They were just near enough to hear the conversation that ensued.

The de Mariscos made their obeisance to the king and the queen.

James Stuart smiled broadly. " 'Tis verra good to see ye, my lord and my lady. I am pleased that ye took my invitation to heart." He turned to the queen. "Annie, 'tis BrocCairn's in-laws and his stepdaughter, the Indian princess I hae told ye about."

The queen was staring hard at Jasmine's necklace. "I've never seen such beautiful sapphires in all my life," she said by way of greeting.

"They were a gift from my late husband, madame," Jasmine replied. "The stones in the necklace are called the 'Stars of Kashmir.' " Then she proffered a small ivory box to the queen. "I am told that Your Majesty is fond of pearls. Will you accept this small token of my pleasure at being here in England?"

Sybilla Gordon, being nearest the queen, took the delicately carved box from her stepsister and handed it to her royal mistress.

The queen, with a childlike delight, opened the box and gasped, her large jaw falling slack with her surprise. There, nestled upon a pillow of black velvet, was a baroque pearl the size of a Seville orange. "Gracious!" she finally managed to say. Then she looked directly at Jasmine. "Mistress de Marisco, yours is truly a most magnificent gift. I've never received its like before."

"If I have pleased Your Majesty, then I am content," Jasmine answered with a smile and, knowing she was dismissed, she curtsied, backing away along with her grandparents.

"Nicely done, lass," the Earl of BrocCairn told her with a smile of approval as he joined his in-laws. In the months that Sybilla had been exiled to Dun Broc, he had come to know his stepdaughter Jasmine better. Although it was still hard for him to reconcile himself to the fact that his beloved wife had borne another man's child, *her first child*, he found he could not hold that fact against Jasmine. It was impossible not to like the girl. He fully approved the strong streak of good common sense she possessed and that he only wished his daughter would emulate. Although Sybilla no longer struck out at her stepsister, she was still not one bit won over by Jasmine; particularly as she was barred from staying at Greenwood when she was in London with the court. Greenwood would belong to Jasmine one day, as would Queen's Malvern. Had it not been for the kindness of Velvet's elder brother Robin, the Earl of Southwood, who allowed Sybilla to stay at Lynwood House when she was off duty with the queen, the girl would have had no place to live.

"Hae ye come to enjoy Robin's Twelfth Night fete?" Alex Gordon asked his in-laws.

"Aye," Skye told him. "With all these Scots newcomers, it is important that old English families like Robins' remain noticed. The queen loves masques and fetes. The more elaborate the better, I am told. When the king inherited the throne, Robin began at once again to celebrate Twelfth Night as lavishly as his father did in Elizabeth Tudor's time.

The queen just loves it. She spends half a year, Robin says, preparing for it." Skye smiled wistfully. "Bess always loved Twelfth Night too," she said, allowing her memories to engulf her for a moment. Then she asked, "Will you go, Alex?"

"Aye, Velvet insists. Besides," he lowered his voice, " 'tis an excellent opportunity for us to prevent Sybilla to Glenkirk. She's behaved herself quite well, Madame Skye, and the queen is very fond of my lass."

At that moment Sybilla joined them. She ignored her grandparents and her stepsister, saying, "Did you see that vulgar pearl Jasmine gave the queen, Papa? I have never seen an uglier jewel."

Skye arched an elegant eyebrow. "Your father has been telling us, Sybilla, of how well you have been behaving. Yet you have no greeting for your grandfather, your stepsister, or me?"

Grudgingly, the girl curtsied first to Skye and then to Adam.

"What, Sybilla?" her father pressed her. "No greeting for Jasmine?" He glowered threateningly at his daughter.

"I will not curtsey to *her*," Sybilla snapped angrily.

"She is your stepsister, Sybilla," Skye said quietly. "You have had more than enough time to resolve your feelings in this matter."

"I will not like her," Sybilla said pettishly.

"Are you this rude to all those you dislike, Sybilla?" Skye queried. "Perhaps you are not as mature as we believed you. Perhaps you are not ready for marriage after all. If you continue to allow your emotions to overrule your good judgment, you shall remain an old maid forever, I fear. What a pity!"

Sybilla sighed with irritation, but she finally curtsied to Jasmine, who quickly curtsied back with great annoyance.

"There," Alex said. " 'Tis how I like to see my girls."

Sybilla gasped. "She is not your girl, Papa. *I am!* Ohhh, have I lost you to her as well as Mama?" Her eyes welled with tears.

"Your father is being kind to me, Sybilla," Jasmine quickly spoke. "You and only you are his daughter, although I do have the honor of being Lord Gordon's stepdaughter."

Before Sybilla might think on her stepsister's words, however, the Earl of Kempe arrived, sweeping his hat off in greeting to them all and then declaring, "Beauteous one, I have waited all evening to speak with you. But say a kind word to me, and I shall be satisfied."

"Go away!" Sybilla demanded of him. "Is there no place I may be safe from your silliness? Why will you not believe me when I tell you I will marry the Earl of Glenkirk or no one?"

"He is a cold, harsh fellow, my beauty," Tom Ashburne insisted. "He will freeze the blood in your veins, but I shall set you aflame with my passion and my love, I swear it! Just give me a chance, beauty!"

"God's foot!" Skye declared. "I am inclined to side with Sibby against you, my lord. You babble like an idiot!"

"Madame, you devastate me," the Earl of Kempe said, a twinkle in his eye. "I but seek to convince your granddaughter that I am the proper husband for her. Glenkirk cannot love her as I will love her, and my home, Swan Court, will be a fine setting for this beauteous jewel of a girl. My lord!" He turned to Alex. "Will you not reason with your daughter?"

Alex Gordon controlled his amusement. "My lord," he finally said, "I think you a most fitting suitor for my daughter, but it is the custom of this family to allow their daughters to choose their own husbands, provided they are acceptable to us. Both you and Lord Leslie are eminently proper candidates, but I must listen to Sibby first."

"Go away, Kempe!" Sybilla Gordon repeated.

"Nay, Sibby," he told her. "You are young, and you have no experience in matters of the heart. Glenkirk will disappoint you, but I will not. I will be here for you when you want me." Taking her dainty hand in his, he kissed it.

Sybilla snatched her hand away, glaring at Tom Ashburne as if he had done a terrible thing. "*My lord!* Cease, I beg you!"

Then suddenly into their midst came the Earl of Glenkirk. James Leslie was dressed in the height of fashion in very short, black velvet breeches, his dark stockings cross-gartered at the knee with cloth-of-silver bows. His tight, long-waisted doublet, embroidered with silver and small pearls, accentuated his elegant torso. The cuffs on the doublet were of the finest lace and matched the fraise that edged his standing collar. A short Spanish cape trimmed with marten completed his attire. About his neck he wore a heavy gold chain, but his long supple fingers were bereft of jewelry except for a single gold band. "My lord, my ladies," he said.

Sybilla almost swooned at his dark-haired good looks. His green-gold eyes fascinated her, but she was also distressed to find that he made her uncomfortable. There was something forbidding about James Leslie, unlike Thomas Ashburne, who never made her nervous. Surprised by her own thoughts, Sybilla quickly pushed them away. She meant to be James Leslie's wife. It was what she had always wanted.

"Mistress de Marisco," the Earl of Glenkirk said quietly, "there is to be dancing. Will you allow me to partner you?"

Sybilla grew pale with her frustration at his words.

"Thank you, my lord, but I have not yet learned your English dances," Jasmine responded politely. "It is not the custom of my native land for men and women to dance together as the English do. Please excuse me." She curtsied, keeping her eyes modestly lowered.

The Earl of Glenkirk bowed in return. Then with a nod to the others he moved away.

"Oh, bitch!" Sybilla hissed furiously, and, despite her best efforts to control them, tears slipped down her pink cheeks.

"Apologize to your stepsister, Sibby," her grandmother said furiously. "Jasmine dances our *English* dances quite well, as you would know had you not been sent home to Dun

Broc last summer. She has done you a great kindness in refusing the earl so cleverly."

"Why did he not ask me?" Sybilla wailed softly. *"Why her?"*

"Who is to know why a man does anything?" Skye responded with a small laugh. She was most resplendent tonight in a midnight-blue velvet gown, the underskirt of which was fashioned from gold brocade designed in a pattern of swirls and decorated with tiny diamante that sparked with her every step. The neckline of the gown was square and low. Skye was quite proud of the fact that her bosom was still attractive despite her sixty-six years. The sleeves of her gown were leg-of-mutton, held by many narrow deep blue- and gold-striped ribbons. About her neck she wore a fine necklace of diamonds, while diamonds and rubies sparkled in her ears. Her hair was done in its usual chignon and dressed with hairpins studded with the same stones.

"Do not fret, Sybilla," Skye continued. "If it is meant that Lord Leslie marry you, he will."

"He does not even know I exist," Sybilla said with a trace of self-pity in her young voice. "Why does he see *her*, and not me?" she demanded, pointing an accusatory finger at Jasmine. "I see the way he looks at her. He hardly looks at me at all."

"You must know I am not encouraging him, Sybilla," Jasmine protested. "I am not in the least interested in Lord Leslie, or any other man for that matter. I wish to be left alone to mourn my husband, Jamal."

"You can hardly be said to look like a woman in mourning," Sybilla said dryly, looking with a jaundiced eye upon her stepsister's beautiful, rich burgundy velvet gown with its rose-colored ribbons and rose brocade underskirt.

"Jasmine's husband is dead almost two years," Skye quickly put in. "She is out of deep mourning and can certainly wear whatever she chooses, particularly here at court."

"I mourn Jamal in my heart, Sybilla," Jasmine said quietly. "The heart never really forgets."

For the briefest moment Sybilla Gordon allowed her own basically good heart to sympathize, but just as quickly she put the feelings aside. *Jasmine was her enemy.* She had taken her mother from her, and even her father was now supportive of the bitch. As for James Leslie's obvious interest, she would soon put a stop to it. Jasmine would regret coming to court!

With Christmas past, the entire court looked forward to the famous Revels and Fete to be held at the Earl of Lynmouth's magnificent house on the Strand. Twelfth Night at Lynmouth House was legend from the time of the current earl's father, and an invitation to the fete was eagerly looked forward to by all the courtiers. Even those who were not certain they would be invited had costumes at the ready. London's dressmakers were booked for months in advance, designing and executing their creations.

Skye and her family always kept a dressmaker on staff. Bonnie had traveled with the family down to the city from Queen's Malvern in late autumn, her materials and half-finished costumes, along with her young apprentice, Mary, snug in their own comfortable coach.

The gentlemen, of course, had complained bitterly, as they did each year, but they stood patiently for their fittings. Sandy and Charlie Gordon had been allowed to come to London for their first visit and would be allowed to go to their uncle Robin's party. Like their father and their grandfather, they would be garbed in scarlet and orange silks, representing flames of fire. Skye, Velvet, and Jasmine would be costumed as colorful moths. Sybilla had been invited to join them, but she preferred to be dressed as a perfect English rose.

"There will be at least two dozen English roses," Skye

said, disgusted. "She will be disappointed, I guarantee it. Why could she not have chosen a more original idea? With her lovely coloring, she would make a perfect Dawn."

Sybilla, however, could not be moved in her intent, until two days before her uncle's fete when she learned from court gossip just how many perfect English roses would be represented at the party. "I am ruined!" she sobbed. "Glenkirk will not notice me at all, and I did so hope he would! What am I to do, Mama?"

They had been gathered at Lynmouth House for a family dinner.

"Wear my costume," Jasmine said generously. "You are smaller than I am in stature and have not as much bosom as I do, but there is time for Bonnie to alter the garment to suit you. I was to be the silver and gold moth. The colors will suit you as well in this instance."

"What will you wear?" Sibby demanded suspiciously. "Or do you intend drawing attention to yourself by your marked absence?"

Jasmine laughed. "I most certainly would not miss Uncle Robin's fete for you or anyone else, Sybilla. I, however, can wear my native garb. It will seem like a costume to the other guests."

"Well," Sybilla considered, and her family held its collective breath, not daring to encourage her lest she turn petulant. "Very well, I will take your costume, Jasmine," she finally decided.

"The wretched girl might have thanked you," Skye fussed at Jasmine afterward.

Jasmine laughed. "Now, Grandmama, 'twas very hard for Sibby to accept my offer of help. Under normal circumstances she would have sooner died, but her desire to attract Lord Leslie is paramount. She will do anything to capture his heart."

"The man is as cold as ice," Skye said, "although when he looks at you, my darling girl, I see fire in those eyes of his. Poor little Sibby does not have a chance, but you, I believe, do, if you would show just the slightest bit of interest. If you will not have Westleigh, then why not Glenkirk?"

Jasmine laughed, but it was a forced sound, and Skye noticed it immediately. "He is attractive," she said, "Glenkirk, I mean. But I am not ready to marry again quite yet. Besides, Sybilla Gordon would be driven to murder me if I stole the one man she desires."

Jasmine did not tell her grandmother that she had been walking in the gardens belonging to Greenwood one afternoon recently when the Earl of Glenkirk had arrived on his first of several impromptu visits, coming through the park that surrounded the house, mounted upon a large dappled gray stallion. He greeted her, and she curtsied politely.

"Have you come to see my stepfather?" she asked him politely.

He dismounted, and putting his arm through the reins, walked with her. "Nay. I have come to see you, Mistress de Marisco."

"We are barely acquainted, sir, and I mourn my husband," she answered him, her heart beating just a bit faster.

"We could be better acquainted, madame, if you would not work so hard to avoid me," came the amused answer. "As for mourning your husband, I respect you for it. I mourn my Isabelle and the children we lost. The sadness, I think, will remain wi me my whole life."

"Aye," she said softly. "Your wife and sons, I am told, died needlessly. I understand your sadness. My husband was murdered also, but worse, my lord, he was murdered by my own brother."

"Ahhh, so that is a part of the mystery surrounding you, Mistress de Marisco," James Leslie said.

"There is no mystery, my lord. If you ask, I will tell you. But you should not, I think, be here," Jasmine told him. "It is an open secret my stepfather seeks to make a match between you and his daughter. Sybilla and I are not friends.

She would be very distressed to learn that you were here with me."

"Then we will not tell her, Mistress de Marisco, will we?" he teased her.

She had sent him away, of course, but he had come again. Believing her widowed state a neutral ground, Jasmine had shared her memories of Jamal Khan with him, and he had proved sympathetic. James Leslie, in turn, had told her of his sweet and merry Bella, and their two little boys.

This common bond between them, at first comforting, was beginning to prove difficult. Now, as she dressed for her uncle's fete, Jasmine wondered if she would see James Leslie tonight. She was, to her deep distress, beginning to be attracted to him. She must put those feelings aside, she scolded herself. Alex Gordon had chosen this very night to speak with James Leslie. By morning a betrothal would be set between the Earl of Glenkirk and Lady Sybilla Gordon. It was how it should be, Jasmine thought reluctantly.

Toramalli poured jasmine oil in her mistress's bath the evening of the gala. Rohana had already washed her lady's hair, toweling it dry and brushing it with a boar's-bristle brush by the fire until it was free of dampness. The serving woman then polished the raven tresses with a silk cloth until they shone. During the summer past, the ladies had made good hard-milled soap, scenting it with jasmine for their princess, and damask rose for Skye. Jasmine's hair was carefully pinned atop her head so none of it would get wet. Settling herself in her tub, she sighed.

" 'Tis colder than Kashmir, these English winters," she said with a small smile at her servants.

"The summers are not too warm either," Rohana remarked dryly, taking up a cloth, soaping it, and then bathing her lady.

"You are both free now," Jasmine reminded them. "If at any time you desire to return to India, I will dower you and

have you transported upon one of grandmother's ships. Her
fleet will be leaving for the east next month. You must go
then or wait another year."

"The cold will not kill either of us," Toramalli said, speaking for them both. "What would we do if we returned to
India? There would be no one to arrange marriages for us.
Even free, we have no caste. What if the emperor learned of
our whereabouts? He has eyes and ears everywhere. Besides,
our life is with you, my lady." She helped her mistress from
her tub. "Come, Rohana, do not be so slow with the towel!
The princess will catch a chill!"

Jasmine's costume lay upon her bed. It was a traditional
Mughal jaguli. The beautiful high-waisted dress was made of
turquoise-blue silk, which was shot through with threads of
beaten gold. The long, tight-fitting sleeves had two-inch gold
bands at the wrists which were sewn with tiny diamonds,
pearls, and turquoise Persian lapis. The graceful, long-flowing
skirt was edged with a band of gold, and the banding on the
high, round neckline matched that upon the sleeves. The
dress, although fastened with a large diamond button at both
the neckline and the waist, had a narrow opening between
that allowed a tantalizing glimpse of Jasmine's full breasts.
Upon her feet she slipped dainty heelless slippers of kid that
had been covered in thin sheets of beaten gold and sewn all
over with little diamonds so that with every step she took,
her feet appeared to twinkle with a thousand lights.

Rohana fastened the Stars of Kashmir necklace about her
lady's neck. She attached ear bobs of sapphires and pearls
to Jasmine's ears. Toramalli plaited the princess's hair into a
single, thick, long braid which she interwove with strands
of pearls and Persian lapis strung upon thin gold wires. Rohana knelt and clasped anklets of dainty gold bells about
Jasmine's ankles while her sister pushed delicate bracelets of
gold, silver, and costly jewels upon her mistress's arms. The
princess herself touched the deliciously elusive jasmine per-

fume to her pulse points and watched in the mirror as Rohana carefully placed over her head a gossamer sheer turquoise-blue silk orhni embroidered with small gold stars.

"So this is what an Imperial Mughal princess looks like," Skye said, coming up behind her granddaughter.

"Wait until my eyes have been painted with kohl, Grandmama," Jasmine said, and sat to allow Toramalli to do it.

The serving woman worked skillfully and quickly, and when she had finished, Jasmine stood and faced Skye.

The older woman shook her head. "You are even more beautiful than I was at your age, my darling child," she said quietly. "Come, let us show your mother. Rohana, bring the fur-lined cloak for your lady. Even though we do nothing more than travel next door, the night is cold, and it has started to snow. I hope Robin's guests will be able to get here. The roads, I am told, are icy already."

Jasmine laughed. "Grandmama, there is no one in London in possession of an invitation to Uncle Robin's fete who would not freeze to death in the snow rather than miss the occasion."

Her grandmother chuckled. "You are probably correct, darling child."

Velvet gasped softly as they came down the main staircase of the house. "Oh my," she murmured. "You are every inch your father's daughter, Yasaman Kama Begum. In your Mughal garments you are so exotic and foreign-looking; yet this morning you appeared so English."

"Indeed, Jasmine, your transformation is quite amazing," agreed Lord Gordon. "Indian garb is very beautiful, I see, and far more graceful than our English clothing." He sighed. "Is it not possible for you to look less magnificent? Sibby will be quite put out, I fear. Pray God she will not cause a scene before I have had time to approach the Earl of Glenkirk, or after for that matter. It is not easy to maintain one's dignity and paternal authority while dressed as a flame of fire."

"Perhaps the flame should threaten to burn the moth if she does not behave." Jasmine giggled mischievously.

Alex Gordon chuckled. Yes, he thought, I like this girl, no matter her paternity. I could wish she were mine, but would she be the same girl if she were? Or would she be like my little Sibby?

Jasmine allowed her gaze to take in her relations in their costumes. Her mother and grandmother were garbed as moths, Velvet in blue-green silks with painted wings edged with gold paint. Skye, a mauve and purple moth, had wings edged with silver. Sandy and Charlie capered about in scarlet velvet breeches and doublets that were decorated in gold beads and small garnets. Their stockings were cross-gartered with cloth-of-gold bows, and they trailed orange, red, and yellow silks in imitation of flame. Their grandfather and father wore identical costumes.

"I feel like a bloody fool," grumbled Adam. "At my age I should be allowed to wear my good black velvet suit and white lace ruff."

"Why, my darling," Skye said, kissing his mouth softly, "I rather like being a moth to your flame. Have I not always been so?"

"Wanton," he murmured back, a twinkle in his deep blue eyes. "And at your age, too, madame, but do not change on me. I am too old now to sustain such a shock."

Jasmine watched her grandparents. She thought that one day she would like to find such a love as they obviously shared. For a moment she remembered Jamal and, in remembering, realized that theirs had not been such a passion, nor would it ever have been, she suspected. They had been a royal match. It was a marriage of convenience, and fortunately they had liked one another enough to make it work. Whether that friendship would have withstood the test of time she did not know. Nor would she ever know.

The guests were beginning to arrive at Lynmouth House

despite the falling snow. Sybilla Gordon, greeting them, took one look at her stepsister and frowned, but wisely held her tongue. She was rewarded by lavish praise from her family for her own appearance. Indeed, Sibby was a most charming, petite moth in her silver and gold silks, her dainty cloth-of-gold wings fluttering with her every movement. Her younger half brothers, dancing about her, did most certainly give the flattering illusion of flames to her moth.

Lord Southwood and his beautiful wife Angel were costumed all in white velvet, their garb sparkling with crystals and pearls.

"We are the Winter King and his Queen," Robin announced. "What think you, Mama? Would my father have approved?"

"Most certainly he would have," Skye told her son, remembering Geoffrey Southwood, Robin's father. The "Angel Earl," they had called him, and he had been Elizabeth Tudor's favorite courtier. He was an elegant, golden creature of wit and style, with whom she had shared a great passion. Forty-five years ago this very Twelfth Night she had come to Lynmouth House for that first of many Twelfth Night fetes. She had been carrying the very son who now hosted this gala. She had been too proud to tell his father, but Geoffrey had learned of it and finally convinced her of his love that they might marry. *Twelfth Night.* It had always been such a magic night for her family ever since. She felt Adam squeeze her hand, and Skye smiled into his face. "I cannot help but remember," she said quietly.

"I don't want you ever to forget," her husband answered. "You loved him once, and Robin is proof of it, even as Velvet is proof of the love we share, little girl. I am far more fortunate than Geoffrey Southwood, or any of your other lovers for that matter. 'Tis I who have been the man lucky enough to be your husband all these years, Skye."

The king and queen arrived. James, who disliked costumes, had not worn one. The queen, however, was garbed in a grass-green velvet gown, sewn all over with multicolored silk flowers. Atop her grizzled blond head was a golden sunburst. She beamed coquettishly at her host, and Robin smiled back, bowing over Anne of Denmark's plump hand.

Straightening himself, the Earl of Lynmouth said, "Why certainly Your Majesty is the fairest springtime I have ever seen."

"You see, James," the queen crowed triumphantly. "I knew that Robin would understand my costume at once, even if you did not."

James Stuart snorted irritably. He hated parties, and this one was known to go on until dawn. If he left much before, he would spoil everyone's fun, and they would complain about it behind their hands for the next two months. He was their king, and he shouldn't care, but he did. "And what do I represent, my lord of Lynmouth," he groused at Robin, peering at him sharply for the answer.

"England, my lord, and may God bless and save Your Majesty," Robin Southwood said quickly.

"Hah!" The king barked a single laugh. "You are a silver-tongued serpent, my lord earl. I thank God you prefer to spend your time in the country and out of politics."

"Politics, Your Majesty, is for kings and fools, I think," Lord Southwood replied, his lime green eyes twinkling. "Kings are born to it and cannot help themselves. Fools involved themselves because they think that they can change the world. There is, however, one exception to my rule, sire."

"And what is that?" the king demanded, very amused by the Earl of Lynmouth's swift repartee.

"Cecils, Your Majesty. They, too, seem to be born to politics, and England is the richer for it, I think," was the clever reply.

James Stuart chortled with laughter. "You are right, my lord of Lynmouth, absolutely right!" He turned and poked

Robert Cecil, Lord Burghley, the Secretary of State, with a sharp finger. "What think you, little beagle? Lord Southwood is quite correct! Hah! Ah-hah! Hah! Hah!"

"He is as clever as his father when he chooses to be," Skye murmured softly to her husband. There was a hint of pride in her tone.

The musicians in the minstrel's gallery played throughout the evening and well into the night. There were tableaus done by the various costumed guests. Skye and her family received much applause for their "Moths to the Flames." Charlie and Sandy were ecstatic with their success at their first adult party.

Jasmine was presented in simple tableau, a turbaned Adali on one knee by her side, the magnificent blue and gold macaw, Hiraman, perched upon his raised white-coated arm. The guests gasped with amazement as the bird, looking directly at the king, said in a clear, if raspy, voice, "God save the king! God save the king!" There was much enthusiastic clapping, and James, fascinated, was shown how to offer Hiraman a piece of cake.

The bird took the cake from him, bobbing his head in a bow and telling James, "Thank you, sire."

The king stepped back nervously. " 'Tis witchcraft?" he said softly, obviously quite uncomfortable.

"Nay, my good lord," Jasmine swiftly assured him, for she knew the king was most superstitious. "In my land there are many birds who speak as does Hiraman. Among God's creatures, parrots have the reputation of being very intelligent, my lord."

"Oh," the king said, feeling less threatened. Nonetheless, he did not offer the bird any more treats.

Jasmine scratched Hiraman's neck affectionately and then said quietly to Adali, "Return him home quickly, lest someone try to steal him. Take several of my uncle's footmen with you across the garden."

"Yes, my princess," Adali replied.

"How clever of you to amuse the king so well," the Marquess of Westleigh murmured, coming up next to Jasmine.

She turned her turquoise eyes upon him. "I was born knowing how to entertain kings," she teased him. "It is in my blood."

"Dance with me," he begged her, smiling.

"I do not know if I should encourage you so, my lord. You insist upon calling upon me, and my grandmother, even though you know I do not wish it."

"You cannot mourn forever, my love," Rowan Lindley said wisely, and he held out his hand to Jasmine.

She laughed, for his charm was almost impossible to resist. Taking the proferred hand, she allowed him to lead her to the floor.

While the guests had been distracted by Jasmine and her parrot, Alex Gordon had taken the opportunity to gain James Leslie's attention. Together the two men adjourned to Robin Southwood's library, where they might speak in private. Seated comfortably before the blazing fire, large goblets of rich Burgundy wine by their sides, they remained silent for a long moment, and then Alex Gordon spoke.

"I am nae a man to dissemble, Jemmie. I prefer to come straight to the point. I would like to propose a match between you and my daughter Sybilla. Isabelle is dead almost five years. You hae no legitimate heirs of your own body. I realize that your brothers have sons, but do you really want Glenkirk given to one of them and not to your own son? I know your brothers would nae be unhappy should you remarry. Surely you dinna intend to spend your life alone and bereft of a wife and children?

"Sybilla is my only daughter. Legitimatized to be certain, for Velvet is nae her natural mother. Sibby's ma is an English silversmith's wench, Alanna Wythe. Alanna is now married to Ranald Torc. Velvet hae raised my daughter, and she is a fine young lady now, Jemmie. She'll come to ye wia verra generous dowry, I promise you. Property as well as gold and plate. I'll nae stint wi her, and 'tis nae secret I want ye for her husband."

James Leslie, the Earl of Glenkirk, sighed deeply. He had known for months that BrocCairn would eventually approach him. If he had not heard it from others, the girl herself would have given it away. She had mooned after him quite openly since the day she had come to court as a maid of honor to Queen Anne. There were few secrets at Whitehall. Indeed, a lady of his acquaintance who was also in the queen's service told him one evening as they spent a relaxed hour together that Sybilla Gordon had bragged so openly in the queen's chambers of how she would be the next Countess of Glenkirk that the queen had finally bidden her hold her foolish tongue.

James Leslie did not know if he would ever be of a mind to marry again, but if and when he did remarry, it would not be Lady Sybilla Gordon he took to wife. Oh, she was pretty enough, if that had been all he was seeking in a wife; and he had no doubt Alex Gordon would dower the girl magnificently; and the fact that she was Scots-born could not be discounted, despite her English mother. The circumstances of the girl's birth were of no bother to him either. But the girl herself did not attract him one whit. She was obviously spoiled, quite spiteful, and had all the charm of a lump of suet pudding, as far as he was concerned.

"Do you love your wife, Alex?" he asked the Earl of BrocCairn.

"Aye!"

"From the beginning?"

"Aye!"

"I do not love Sybilla, Alex. I fear I am nae in the least attracted to her. I never will be." Then, to end any future discussion of the matter, he told Alex Gordon a small lie. "I dinna like blondes."

Alex Gordon drank down his wine in three gulps and

nodded. "I canna change the color of the lass's hair," he answered. "A man could learn to like blondes if he so chose, but if ye dinna love my Sibby or believe ye can love her, 'tis better we end this discussion now. I dinna want my little lass unhappy. Ye'll understand if ye ever hae a lass of yer own."

"Aye, perhaps I will," James Leslie agreed, relieved to have escaped the matter so easily. "There are nae hard feelings, Alex Gordon, are there? I would keep your friendship."

The Earl of BrocCairn offered the Earl of Glenkirk his hand. "Of course there are nae hard feelings, Jemmie. I am a doting father, I fear, and Sibby fancies herself in love wi ye. I wanted to make her happy, but now I shall consider an offer I hae had for the lass and try to convince her to accept the gentleman."

The two men shook hands and, after a few more minutes of conversation, returned to the party.

"You will keep this to yourself, won't you?" Alex Gordon said, thinking that he would not tell his daughter until the morrow. Let her enjoy the fete tonight. Tomorrow was time enough for a broken heart.

"Aye," the Earl of Glenkirk agreed, his eyes already sweeping the room for Jasmine de Marisco. Now that this business with Sybilla Gordon was settled, he was free to pursue other delights. Then he saw Jasmine dancing a graceful lavolta with her grandfather, and his green-gold eyes lit with pleasure. She was certainly the most beautiful woman he had ever seen, although he knew that the standard of beauty was very different for each man. When the dance was over, he approached her and bowed.

"Will you take supper with me, Mistress de Marisco?" he asked.

The elderly Earl of Lundy grinned, pleased, and said, "Aye, she will, my lord." Then he kissed Jasmine upon the forehead. "Run along now, my girl, and enjoy yourself. I thank you for the dance."

Jasmine laughed. "I can scarce refuse you now, can I? My grandfather has made it quite impossible, and I expect he knew just what he was doing. Grandmama says he was quite a wicked rogue in his youth. He possessed an island called Lundy, and being the last of his line, and with few funds, he pirated, she says."

The Earl of Glenkirk tucked her hand in his arm and they walked slowly toward the buffet.

"Your heritage fascinates me, madame. The daughter of a king, the granddaughter of a pirate. And how quickly you have become proficient in our English dances. You grow more intriguing by the minute."

"You should not be with me, I suspect," Jasmine said, ignoring his teasing. "I saw my stepfather spirit you off before while the rest of the guests were overwhelmed by my parrot. Fortunately, Sybilla was not aware that you had gone, for Lord Ashburne was doing his best to amuse her."

"I can trust you, I know," James Leslie told her, and his voice was low. "There will be no marriage between Sybilla Gordon and myself, madame. Her father, however, will nae speak of it until tomorrow."

"Poor Sybilla," Jasmine said honestly. "She did have her heart set on you. She will certainly find a way to blame me for this turn of events, and particularly if she sees us together having supper."

"I want to be with you, Jasmine de Marisco," he said.

"My lord," she answered him, "what is it that you want of me? You seek me out constantly, even knowing the distress it causes my stepsister, who, as you know, is not very fond of me."

"I do not know what I want of you. I only know," James Leslie said, "that I would be with you. I would know you better. There must be someplace that we might escape prying eyes. Let us find our cloaks and walk together in the gardens. You do not mind the snow, do you?"

She half laughed. "You are mad, my lord. Besides, I have not the footwear for such a stroll. Diamonds are not particularly warm."

I am mad, he thought. He could feel a rashness sweeping over him, and though unfamiliar, the sensation was not unpleasant. "There must be somewhere we may be alone, Jasmine de Marisco," he told her. "Think quickly, or I may be forced to cause a scene."

"We cannot leave before the king and queen," she protested. "My grandmother told me that just this very evening."

"Jamie and Anne will nae miss us. There must be over three hundred people here. Did you know that you have a mouth that I suspect was just made for kissing? I would like to kiss it very much."

She stared at him, surprised, but at the same time she thought that she might like to kiss him too. How long had it been since she had been kissed? she wondered. When was the last time Jamal had kissed her? She could not remember, and felt a burst of sadness with the realization. Jasmine turned away from Glenkirk that he might not see the tears that sprang into her eyes.

James Leslie, however, had seen the change as it appeared upon her beautiful face. "Were you thinking of your husband?" he asked her with unfailing intuition. "You have not kissed a man since his death, have you, Jasmine de Marisco? I did not mean to make you sad."

Wordlessly she shook her head at him.

The Earl of Glenkirk steered her away from the rooms where the Twelfth Night fete was in progress and led her up the staircase of Lynmouth House.

Halfway up the second flight of steps, Jasmine regained her senses and asked, "Where are you taking me, my Lord?"

"To my apartments," he said bluntly. "I am staying here as your uncle's guest."

Jasmine stopped. "I do not believe it is wise that I continue to accompany you, my lord," she told him. "In fact, I think it most unwise for me to accompany you."

James Leslie said nothing. Instead he tipped her face to his with a strangely gentle hand and kissed her mouth with a deep, passionate kiss. Her lips yielded beneath his instinctively, and their breaths mingled sweetly. He lifted his mouth from hers just slightly, his green-gold eyes looking deeply into her magnificent turquoise ones.

"We are both very lonely, Jasmine de Marisco, yet neither of us is ready yet to remarry. Let us share our loneliness tonight. I want to make love to you, madame. Nothing more. Nothing less. I believe that you want to make love with me. If I am wrong, then you have but to turn about and go down the stairs. I will nae follow you, nor force you to my desire."

She stared at him, speechless. How dare he presume. How dare he even suggest such a thing. . . . Then he touched her face with the back of his hand, gently stroking it from the jawbone up, and with his touch Jasmine realized, to her shock, that she did indeed want to make love with him. She was no stranger to passion, and her young body was at this very moment crying out to her for surcease.

"We are both free to indulge our desires," James Leslie said quietly. "You are so beautiful, I cannot help myself. I know that you are no wanton and have been sheltered, but you are a woman, no maid, else I should not even suggest such a liaison, madame."

She nodded, unable to find the right words. Then he took her hand again and began to lead her up the staircase once more. She followed mutely, knowing that there was now no turning back. Nor did she want to turn back. She did not believe herself in love with James Leslie, but she longed for the intimacy that could be shared by two lovers.

They entered his apartments, and a small man hurried forward. James Leslie said, "Go discreetly, Fergus More, and fetch us some supper. Leave it upon the board in the day room and then go to bed." Drawing her along, he entered the bedchamber. It was a square room of medium size with paneled walls. A fire burned brightly in the fireplace. A great oak bedstead hung with crimson velvet took up almost an entire wall. He closed the door behind them firmly and, turning, took her in his arms.

"I think I must be mad," Jasmine said, finally finding her voice. "This cannot be right, my lord."

"Are you afraid?" he asked her, and he undid the diamond button on her jaguli, bending and leaning forward to kiss the erratic pulse at the base of her slender throat.

"Nay," she whispered, enjoying the sensation of his warm mouth on her skin. "I have never been afraid of what men and women do together."

In answer he slipped the second diamond button open, and her gown was opened from neck to waist. James Leslie pushed the fabric off her shoulders, his hands sliding slowly down her torso until the jaguli slithered into a silken puddle about her ankles. "Do not move!" he ordered her harshly, and literally tore his own garments off until he was as naked as she.

Jasmine struggled for breath. She was simply burning with sudden and overwhelming desire. Her eyes took him in as he pulled his clothing away. He was so fair in comparison to Jamal. His body was tall and hard-looking, his shoulders broad, and a tangled mat of dark hair lay upon his chest. Indeed, his long, sturdy legs were covered in dark hair, as was the triangle between his legs where his manhood lay, already half rampant. She had never seen a man with so much hair! The men of her country had only hair upon their heads. At least the men she had known. James Leslie pulled her roughly against him, and the first impression she had had of hardness was at once borne out. He was hard. There seemed to be no fat upon him at all. The look in his eyes, however, was both admiring and tender.

She needed to touch him. Reaching up, she caressed his

face, feeling the faint stubble of whiskers beneath her finger-tips. His dark eyebrows were an unruly mass, and she smoothed them, but they immediately sprang back to their original disorder. Jasmine laughed softly, and he smiled down at her. Then, picking her up, he carried her across the room to where the large bed awaited them. He placed her gently upon it and followed, his own body sinking into the feather bed next to hers.

He cradled her in the curve of an arm, a hand reaching out to touch her breasts. Fingers lightly caressed her nipples, setting them aquiver with arousal. Bending his head, he took first one nipple and then the other within the warmth of his mouth, suckling upon them and tonguing them while she murmured with pleasure. She caressed the graceful back of his neck, feeling the hairs erecting themselves beneath her touch.

His lips found their way into the cleft between her breasts. Pressing kisses upon the soft flesh, he murmured, "What is that intoxicating scent you wear, my love? It is so deliciously elusive, but most wonderfully seductive. I have never smelled its fragrance before."

"I am named for that fragrance, my lord," she told him. "It is the perfume of the night-blooming jasmine flower."

"Then you are well named, for you are exactly as you have described it, Jasmine, although surely your mama could not have known that when she named you." He placed an-other warm kiss upon her skin and then looked into her eyes. "My friends call me Jemmie. You and I would not be here in this bed, Jasmine, were we not friends, would we?"

She smiled back at him. "Nay, Jemmie, we would not."

He bent his head once more to kiss her, the pressure of his mouth parting her lips, his tongue slipping between her lips to meet with her tongue. She shivered with delight at the intimacy of the embrace. When he had sated himself with the nectar of her tongue, he began a slow, leisurely exploration of her body with his kisses. Fascinated, she

watched his deliberate progress as his skilled lips warmed
her, moving over her breasts, her torso, her belly, her right
thigh, knee, and from her shin to her foot. With a chuckle,
he removed her right slipper, then transferring his attention
to her left side, he removed that slipper also before continu-
ing his progress back up her body to her mouth again.

Placing a playful kiss upon her lips, he said, "Delicious!"
And then to her surprise he turned her over. Warm kisses
played across her shoulders and down her spine, while ahead
of them raced a series of very pleasurable shivers preceding
his lips, right to the soles of her feet. Relaxed and embold-
ened by his love play, she rolled away from him with a laugh.

"You shall not have all the fun, Jemmie Leslie," she said,
and pushed him, surprised, upon his back.

The Earl of Glenkirk had enjoyed a loving marriage, but
neither Isabelle nor the few women he had taken to his bed
after her death had ever really made love to him as this
beautiful girl was now doing. She covered his body with
kisses and nibbles, and then taking his lance within her
mouth, she drove him to near madness before mounting him
and sheathing him within her wonderful young body. With
a groan of pleasure greater than he had ever known, he
rolled her onto her back, pumping himself into her over,
and over, and over again. He could not seem to get enough
of her, and for a moment he believed himself incapable of
release until he realized that he had been waiting for her to
find her own pleasure.

Beneath him Jasmine writhed frantically. Dear God! It
had been so long since she had felt a man's passion. It had
been so long since she had allowed her own passions to run
wild as they were now doing. She had honestly forgotten
how sweet the conjunction of two hungry bodies could be.
She had forgotten until now. She could feel his hard thighs
pressing against her, could feel the urgency in his manhood's
desire communicating itself to her by its insistent throbbing,
throbbing, throbbing. With a cry of pleasure, she found her

heaven, and in the misty satisfaction that followed and suffused her entire being, she heard him cry out his delight as well.

Afterward they lay together, holding hands, and he finally said, "I do not think I have ever known a woman like you, Jasmine de Marisco. No woman has ever been so free with me."

She laughed softly. "I told you I was not afraid of what transpired between a man and a woman. In my land we are taught that such things are God-given and good. There is no wantonness, you understand, but passion is not thought of as wrong or wicked."

"Stay with me tonight," he begged her, and Jasmine agreed, feeling less on edge than she had felt in months, and realizing, to her amusement, what had been missing from her life. She knew now that once a girl becomes a woman, there could be no going back. Fearful and in mourning, she had come to England a year ago. She had reveled in the love of her grandparents and her mother. She had allowed herself to be a child again, but the truth of the matter was that she was not a child. She was a woman, and she had a woman's needs. There was only one person who would understand that. *Her grandmother*. She would speak with Skye tomorrow about this turn of events.

They slept and awoke to make love again. They ate the food that had been placed upon the sideboard in the day room by the discreet Fergus More and made love again. They fell back asleep, only to be awakened by the sound of a woman's outraged screams pealing over and over again in their brains until Jemmie Leslie and Jasmine de Marisco sat up in bed to find themselves facing a furious Lady Sybilla Gordon.

"*Bitch! Bitch! Bitch!*" Sybilla shrieked, tears pouring down her face. "You had to steal him from me, didn't you? First my mother, then Papa, and now the only man I have ever loved, or will love! I will never forgive you! *I will kill you!*" and so saying, Sybilla Gordon threw herself at Jasmine.

James Leslie leapt from the bed in an attempt to protect his lover, and, seeing a man stark naked for the first time in her entire life, Sybilla's eyes grew wide with shock. She gasped and backed away. A hand flew to her throat and then, with another great cry, she fainted, even as her family, drawn by her screams, poured into the bedchamber. Jasmine, a coverlet clutched to her bosom in an attempt at modesty, did not know whether to laugh or to cry. Her eyes met those of her grandmother's, and she would have sworn that Skye found herself in a similar predicament.

For a moment all was silence, and then Alex Gordon, the Earl of BrocCairn, demanded furiously, "What the hell is going on here?"

There were several snickers from among the people crowding into the room, and then Skye said dryly, "God's nightshirt, Alex, is it not obvious? Sybilla has caught Lord Leslie and Jasmine in what can most certainly be called a very compromising situation. Velvet, see to Sybilla! James Leslie, either get back into bed, or put on your breeches. We've seen quite enough!"

The Earl of Glenkirk had the good grace to flush, and reaching for his breeches, drew them quickly on.

Skye turned about. "The rest of you go to bed! I can but thank God the guests are all gone and a serious scandal has been averted. Not one word of this is to be spoken of by any of you. Do you understand?" They nodded and departed.

Sybilla was regaining consciousness. *"Mama!"* she whimpered piteously. *"Ohhhhh, Mama!"*

"There, my darling, 'tis all right," Velvet soothed the girl, stroking her blond head.

"It will never be all right again," Sybilla sobbed. "She has stolen my betrothed husband from me! Ohhhhh, I shall die!"

Velvet patted her stepdaughter's hand sympathetically and helped her up and into a chair. "Do not weep, Sibby. No man is worth that many tears. Jasmine has not stolen Lord

Leslie from you. He was never really yours, dear heart." She hugged the girl comfortingly.

"We were to be married! Papa promised!" Sybilla wailed, pulling away from Velvet.

"Alex!" Velvet looked to her husband. "Tell her the truth!"

Alex Gordon knelt beside his daughter's chair. "He'll nae hae ye, Sibby," he began. "We spoke last night, but I didna want to tell ye until this morning. Ye were having such a good time at your uncle's fete."

"He'll not have me?" Sybilla Gordon's tone implied that such a thing could absolutely not be possible. "Why not? It is the bitch! He would have her instead of me! Is that it?"

"Nay," her father answered.

"Then why?" Sybilla demanded. "Why will he not have me?"

"He doesna fancy blondes," Alex replied helplessly. He would not hurt his daughter with the rest of Glenkirk's answer.

"He does not fancy blondes?" Sybilla echoed her father's words. She jumped to her feet, fully recovered, and stalked across the room to where James Leslie stood. "What, my lord," she shouted at him, poking a sharp finger into his bare chest, "what do you mean you do not like blondes? What a ridiculous excuse! I am the only daughter of the Earl of BrocCairn. I am related to the king himself! How dare you refuse me!" She stamped her small foot, and her visage was crimson with her fury. No one in her family could ever remember seeing Sybilla so enraged.

"Very well then, Lady Gordon," the Earl of Glenkirk said coldly. He, too, was angry. He had been publicly embarrassed by this irritating girl, as had Jasmine. He no longer felt the need for tact. "If it is the truth you want, 'tis the truth you'll get. *I do not like you.* I find you spoiled and mean-spirited. I could not possibly ever love you, and I would not marry you if you were the last female on the face of the earth! *Do you understand now?"*

"I suppose you would prefer to wed with your whore?" Sybilla said acidly, casting a scathing glance at Jasmine and struggling to hold back her tears. She would not let him see her cry. She would never cry over a man again. Her mother was right. Men were not worth a woman's tears. But God, her heart ached so from the blow he had delivered with his hard, unfeeling words! How had she ever believed herself to be in love with James Leslie? He was a terrible man!

"My daughter brings up an interesting point, my lord," Alex Gordon said quietly. "You have most certainly compromised my stepdaughter. I think perhaps you must marry her now if the wrong is to be righted. We want no scandal."

"But I do not want to marry him," Jasmine spoke up quickly.

"This is not your decision!" Alex Gordon snapped at her. He was angry at the girl, and yet he had no right to be. James Leslie had been quite honest in his refusal of Sybilla last evening. He should be angry with Sybilla for causing all this furor. What the hell was she doing creeping about the Earl of Glenkirk's bedchamber in the first place?

"It most certainly is my decision," Jasmine told him. *"I am not your daughter."*

"Nay, you are not," the Earl of BrocCairn said. "But you are my wife's daughter, and as such, you are legally in my charge. This man has seduced you. He can only restore your honor by marrying you."

"You are wrong, my lord," Jasmine told him with a little laugh. "Jemmie did not seduce me. *We seduced each other.* I am a widow, no virgin. We were lonely last night and but sought to comfort each other. I will not be forced into a marriage for such a trifle. I do not choose to marry Lord Leslie, and he, I am quite certain, does not wish to marry me."

If Jasmine had fascinated James Leslie before, she fascinated him even more now. Any other woman of his acquaintance would have jumped at the chance to marry him.

For his part, he said nothing, but his silence was far more eloquent than anything he might have said.

"Velvet, Alex," Skye said, "take Sybilla to her room and put her to bed. Jasmine, get dressed and come home."

"Yes, Grandmama," was the obedient reply, but Jasmine's eyes twinkled mischievously, even as did her grandmother's.

The room emptied, but for the Earl of Glenkirk and Jasmine de Marisco. She stepped naked from the bed and began to quickly dress herself, for the room was cold and the fire had burned itself to embers.

"Why do you not wish to marry me?" he asked her, curious.

"There are several very good reasons, Jemmie," she replied, buttoning her jaguli. "First, I am not yet ready to marry. Nor, I believe, are you. My family tells me there is no other life for a woman but marriage. I will accept their wisdom in the matter, but not quite yet. I am sure your family wants you to remarry and sire sons, do they not?"

"Aye," he nodded. "They do. Isabelle and our lads will be dead five years this spring." His handsome face was suddenly sad.

"Neither of us should be forced into another union for the sake of others, Jemmie," Jasmine said wisely. "When we wed again, it should be because we *want* it. For me, I must be in love! Perhaps I am a fool, but I do not believe I can be happy without love. I did, in my own way, love Jamal, but 'twas not, I think, a deep and abiding love. That is what I want next time. Every woman, I think, deserves that kind of love!"

"If you have not had it, how can you know of such love?" he asked her. He picked up the strings of Persian lapis and pearls that had been entwined in her hair and handed them to her. Her long, dark tresses had come undone during one of their love bouts, and the thin gold strands with their beads had become entangled with the sheets.

"My grandparents have such a love. Can you not see it? I can! I will have that kind of love when I wed again, and so should you, dear Jemmie! Do not settle for any less!" Jasmine slipped her slender feet into her diamond-studded slippers and smiled at him. "I have enjoyed our time together very much," she said quietly, and then, blowing him a kiss, she left the room.

He felt strangely bereft at her departure. She was a most intriguing woman. He had been drawn to her from the first moment he had laid eyes upon her. He thought, perhaps, that he should get to knew her better, and then he smiled at himself. After last night he knew her quite well. It was time, as his relations were forever reminding him, that he remarry. Jasmine de Marisco would certainly make a very elegant Countess of Glenkirk, but he would need, he realized from her words, time in which to court her, time to convince her that her place was by his side.

My God! he thought. *Am I falling in love with her?* It would certainly not be hard to fall in love with her. Yet she was so very different from Isabelle. His marriage to Isabelle had been a carefully arranged one, and although they had liked one another, there had been no great passion between them. Bella had been more like one of his sisters, but for the children they shared. Still, he would have remained faithful to her had she not died.

Unlike his father, who had a roving eye, James Patrick Charles Adam Leslie was a one-woman man. Jasmine de Marisco would like that, he realized. Her involvement with him last night had not really been a casual one. She would not have given herself to him lightly. She would be, he instinctively knew, a one-man woman when she found the right man. He knew now it was up to him to convince her that he might be that one man who could make her happy. She would not have him otherwise.

13

The falling snow made the January mid-morning seem darker than it actually was. Skye and Adam de Marisco, forced by circumstance to relent their decision in the matter of Sybilla Gordon, had allowed the girl to return to Greenwood House temporarily.

"It is simply not proper that she remain at Lynmouth while Lord Leslie is there," Skye told her husband.

Sybilla Gordon now stood before her father in the library of Greenwood. Her grandparents and her mother were also present, as was her hated rival. If they had expected her to be chastened by all that had transpired earlier, they were mistaken.

"I want the truth, Sybilla," Alex Gordon said in a hard voice that Sybilla had never heard him use toward her before.

"What truth, Papa?" she answered sweetly.

"Why did ye go to Lord Leslie's room early this morning?" the Earl of BrocCairn demanded. "You certainly hae no business there."

Sybilla bit her lip in vexation. Her father was correct. No

virgin of good family and breeding would go to a man's bedchamber, yet she had.

"Well, Sybilla? Hae ye no answer for me?" Alex pressed. "Am I to believe that ye went to play the wanton, the better to further yer cause wi Jemmie Leslie?"

Sybilla flushed. "I did not go to play the wanton," she lied. "I simply wanted to say good-night to Lord Leslie. You said you would speak with him, and I believed a match had been made between us." The truth was that she had indeed gone to compromise James Leslie in hopes that he would have no choice but to marry her. Sybilla was no fool, and she realized that all her maidenly wiles had neither impressed nor intrigued the Earl of Glenkirk. Then she noticed late in the evening that she had not seen either James Leslie nor Jasmine de Marisco for some time. She was desperate and she was afraid. But most of all, she had been enraged to think Jasmine might be with the man she loved.

Alex Gordon did not believe his daughter, but he loved her. Sibby was obviously hurt, and she was certainly angry. Whatever the truth of the matter was, it no longer mattered. He had come to a decision about Sybilla, and now he told her of it.

"I spoke wi the Earl of Kempe this morning. Ye will be married to him on St. Agnes Day, Sybilla," he said. "Tom Ashburne is a good and decent man. He loves ye and will make ye an excellent husband."

Sybilla grew pale. *"No!"* was the single word she uttered.

"This is nae your decision to make, Sybilla," her father said firmly. "Ye hae made a fool of yerself over James Leslie, but now 'tis over, lassie. Ye'll wed and settle down like a proper maid."

"I'd sooner enter a convent!" Sybilla declared dramatically, tears filling her blue eyes.

" 'Tis nae an option open to ye, Sibby," her father replied, amused, his tone softening a bit. "Think about it, lass. Ye'll be a countess, *and* an English countess to boot. Ye'll be welcome at court, and Ashburne will dote on ye, I fear. He'll gie ye the world."

"He is very handsome," Velvet volunteered. "You will make a most stunning couple, dear heart. Ohh, we have so much to do and such a short time in which to do it, but you will have a fine wedding!"

"Why should I be forced to the altar?" Sybilla Gordon wailed. "I have not shamed the family behaving like a strumpet. *She has!* And then, bold baggage that she is, she will not even marry the man with whom she has so wantonly sported the night away! Why do you not punish her?" She turned to her stepsister. "I will destroy you when I return to court tomorrow! I will tell all who will listen of your lewd behavior with Lord Leslie! No decent man will every marry you after that!" Sybilla declared triumphantly, shaking a finger in Jasmine's face.

"You will say *nothing* of what transpired at your uncle's house last night," Skye told the girl sharply. "If you do, Sybilla, I will see that you suffer in ways you cannot even imagine. We are not simply talking of Jasmine's reputation, but yours and this family's as well. If, in your childish desire for revenge, you gossip freely, your father and mother, whom you claim to love, will suffer as well. Kempe will certainly withdraw his suit, and no one, Sybilla, *no one* will want you. A scandal such as the one you could cause would not die easily. Therefore, in an effort to protect our family, I should have to declare that you were mad and have you locked away where your behavior could harm no one ever again. Is that what you truly wish?" Skye looked implacably at Sybilla Gordon, who knew her grandmother was not a woman to make idle threats.

"Well," Sybilla grumbled, not quite willing to give in yet, "I do not see, Grandmam, why I should have to suffer for Jasmine's sins."

Jasmine laughed. "Making love with a man is no sin, as you will learn."

"Be silent, Jasmine!" Skye said sharply. *"We will deal with you shortly."* She returned her attention to Sybilla. "Marriage to a man who adores you and can afford to indulge your every silly whim is hardly a punishment, you foolish chit. What is it that you object to in the Earl of Kempe's character? Is there something about his personal habits that disturbs you? Speak up, girl!" Children today, she thought, were so contrary.

Sybilla thought a moment, but there was nothing about Tom Ashburne that she could actually dislike. He really did love her, and he was wonderfully wealthy, thanks to his skill at picking the most successful trading ventures to finance. He was handsome, and clever, and witty. If she couldn't have James Leslie, and she certainly did not want him now, Tom Ashburne was certainly an excellent candidate for a husband.

"Well?" Skye demanded an answer, and then gave it herself. "You can find nothing wrong with the man, can you?"

"Nay, I cannot," Sybilla agreed, shaking her head.

"Then you'll marry him without a fuss?"

"Aye, Grandmam, I will," Sybilla said, unable to find a reason to continue her protest.

"Good! Now that's settled, sit down. Jasmine, come here, my darling girl. We have your future to see to as well this day."

Jasmine arose and came to stand obediently before her grandmother and her stepfather. "I can see to my own future, Grandmama," she said.

"Nay, my girl, you cannot," Skye told her firmly. "This is England and not the Mughal's realm. You may have been born a princess, but here in England you are plain Mistress Jasmine de Marisco, wealthy widow. I have told you over and over since your arrival a year ago that your future lies in a good marriage. Your beauty and your extraordinary fortune make you prey to some very dangerous types. Last night's episode tells me that you are certainly ready to wed again, and so you shall, my darling girl. So you shall!"

"Jemmie Leslie is no fortune hunter," Jasmine defended

the Earl of Glenkirk. "What is so terribly wrong about what we did, Grandmama? We were lonely. Did you *never*, during any of your widowhoods, comfort yourself with a kind and loving man?"

The remark struck very close to home, Skye thought, uncomfortable. Too close. She and Jasmine's grandfather had first become lovers when her third husband, Geoffrey Southwood, had died. They had been lovers on and off between two other husbands until finally she had married Adam. Skye straightened her back and glanced at him. His mouth had a faint twitch of amusement to it, but he said nothing.

"We are not speaking about my life, Jasmine," Skye said sternly. "Granted Lord Leslie is no fortune hunter, but what if you had decided to console yourself with a man who was? You have been protected your entire life, and have no real knowledge, despite your marriage and the contretemps with your brother, of how difficult the world really is. Marriage with Lord Leslie is apparently not a consideration. So, you will marry the Marquess of Westleigh at the end of April, and that is an end to it."

"Why does she get to have a spring wedding, and I must marry in January?" Sybilla demanded pettishly.

"Because, you silly chit," her grandmother said, "we must first make certain that your stepsister's foolishness will not lead to a child."

"Ohhhh," Sybilla murmured, her eyes wide, and she cast a quick glance at Jasmine as if seeking to ascertain if she were already enceinte.

"Besides, Sybilla, your betrothed is eager to marry you," Skye continued. "Winter is a beautiful time for a wedding. I am certain that at least one or two of my weddings was celebrated in winter."

"I will not marry the Marquess of Westleigh," Jasmine said.

"Why not?" demanded her grandmother.

"I do not love him. Ohhh, Grandmama, I want what you

and Grandfather have! I want a deep and abiding love!" Jasmine cried.

The older woman gave a deep sigh. "I detested my first husband, Dom O'Flaherty, and yet two fine sons came of the marriage. I loved Willow's father and mourned him deeply, but it was not until I met Geoffrey Southwood, your uncle Robin's father, that I found my first deep and abiding love. My fourth husband was Niall Burke. I fell in love with him when I was fifteen and promised to another man. Niall was the son of my father's overlord and came to my wedding as his representative. He claimed *droit de seigneur* of me. Do you know what that is, my darling girl?"

Jasmine shook her head, fascinated. "No, Grandmama, I do not."

"The overlord may claim a bride's virginity of her bride-groom, and he must give it. There is no choice. Ahhh, Niall! He was handsome and reckless, and heedless of the conse-quences of his actions. I loved him well, but he would not have changed; he would have grown old being reckless and heedless. I do not think I could have borne it, but I did not have to, for he died young." A look of deep sadness passed over Skye's face as she remembered, but then she brought herself back to the present and said, "My fifth husband was Fabron de Beaumont, the Duc de Beaumont de Jaspre. It was a political alliance I made at Elizabeth Tudor's behest. Then at last I married your grandfather. He is my second deep and abiding love, and I thank God for the many good years we have had together. Alas, my darling girl, we cannot always have what we want. Not even a princess can have what she desires all the time.

"You learned to love your Jamal Khan. You have told me what a kind and good young man he was. Now you will learn to love Rowan Lindley. You have been so determined to maintain your status as a widow, you have not given the Marquess of Westleigh a fair chance, Jasmine. He offered for you months ago, but your grandfather and I would not even consider it because we knew you needed time to adjust to your new life here in England. After last night I believe you to be quite settled in, my darling girl," Skye said with a twinkle in her eye, "but there can be no more instances like that one. Rowan Lindley will call on us later today, Jasmine, and you will agree to marry him when he asks."

"If I promise *never* again to allow my emotions to get the better of me, will you reconsider, Grandmama?" Jasmine begged Skye.

Skye laughed. "Ahh, darling girl! The women in this family cannot promise to restrain their passions. It is beyond them. Now stop looking as if you have been condemned to Tower Green, my darling girl. Like Sybilla, you have a betrothed husband who adores you. Use such knowledge to your advantage and you will be very happy, I promise."

"You must fetter his soul before you bind your body to his in lovemaking," Jasmine said softly, but Skye heard her.

"Who said that?" she asked.

"They are lines from the *Kama Sutra*, a book of love," Jasmine answered.

"They are wise words, my darling girl. You would not be foolish if you lived by them. Now run along and get some rest. You look simply exhausted, and you must be at your best this afternoon. You, too, Sybilla."

When the two young women had left the library, Adam de Marisco poured four goblets of red wine and, handing them about to his wife, his daughter, and his son-in-law, said, "To Jasmine and Sybilla!"

The goblets were raised and their healths drunk.

Velvet set her wine down. "I know Sybilla will be quite happy with Tom Ashburne no matter her irritation over James Leslie. Tom will get 'round her quickly enough, and she will immediately decide herself in love with him. She is like that, and once she gives him her loyalty, he will have it always, provided he does not play her false. I think it a good thing he is so many years her senior."

"He is more than twice her age," Alex fretted.

"Sybilla will be seventeen next month," Velvet said. "It is late for a first marriage. Besides, Tom Ashburne is only ten years older than Lord Leslie."

"She needs the stability of an older husband," Skye agreed. "Some girls are like that. An older husband will be more indulgent and more patient. Sybilla is not easy, Alex."

" 'Tis Jasmine I worry over," Velvet continued. "I know that Rowan Lindley is Tom Ashburne's cousin, but what do we really know about him, Mama? What kind of a match will this be, and what if she is unhappy?"

Skye smiled. "She will not be unhappy. I know all I need to know about Rowan Lindley. His family is good. He is no fortune hunter. Although he will receive a generous dowry, that dowry comes from us. Jasmine's wealth remains hers to oversee as she chooses, and he has agreed to that. He's made for her, Velvet, and what is more, he is man enough to manage a Mughal princess without breaking her spirit."

"Then we are fortunate, Mama, are we not?" Velvet sipped at her wine. "Will he be kind to her? I wonder. She can be so imperious."

"He will be kind," Skye assured her daughter, and then she told them of how Rowan Lindley had cared so devotedly for his first wife for all the long, tedious years of their tragic marriage.

"There, ye see," Alex Gordon told his wife. "Do ye really think yer mother would allow Jasmine to marry the man if he were nae a gentleman? Yer mother dotes upon the wench far more than upon any of her other grandchildren. Now, in the matter of Sybilla's wedding, I'll nae be beggared by the two of ye wi a lot of shopping. I trust ye understand, madame, and will at least try to obey me in this matter."

"Are we back to *horses and dogs* after all these years, my lord?" Velvet said. "They may be taught to obey, but a de

Marisco cannot. Sibby is your only daughter, and I will not allow her to go to the Earl of Kempe like some cowherd's offspring! Your purse had best be opened wide to me, my lord, and it had better be full!"

That afternoon both swains came calling at Greenwood House. Sybilla, looking adorable in a rose-pink velvet gown, was at first coy and then haughty by turns. Tom Ashburne quickly had her giggling, and they disappeared into the library together, closing the door behind them.

"Take Lord Lindley and show him the picture gallery," Skye ordered Jasmine, who had chosen to garb herself in black velvet and was outrageously stunning despite her attempts to look otherwise.

The gallery was a small one with long windows upon one side which faced the river. The walls were hung with the portraits of all of Skye's husbands and her offspring in various stages of childhood, as well as a painting that had been done of Skye herself when she was the Countess of Lynmouth.

"You certainly do favor your grandmother," Rowan Lindley remarked when he saw the portrait.

Jasmine smiled, flattered. Next to her father and Rugaiya Begum, she had come to love and admire her grandmother more than any other person she knew. Her mother was sweet, of course, but she seemed much too young to be *her* mother, Jasmine thought. They had become friends, and they would undoubtedly remain friends, but no more than that. Too many years had been lost. But in Skye, Jasmine had come to sense a kindred soul, even if they occasionally disagreed. There was no doubt to anyone in the family that she was her grandmother's child first and foremost.

Jasmine led the Marquess of Westleigh down the short length of the picture gallery, identifying her relations as her grandmother had identified them to her well over a year ago. When she had finished, she began the return journey along the window wall, stopping suddenly to gaze out upon the snowy lawns and the dark gray river. It was almost dark now, and the wind had begun to whip the trees about.

"It has stopped snowing," she noted.

"Aye," he said, and then, "Do you remember I said I would wed you, Jasmine de Marisco?" He stood directly behind her, hemming her in.

"I slept with Lord Leslie last night," Jasmine told him bluntly.

"I suspected something of the sort when you disappeared from Lord Southwood's fete," he replied calmly. "You will not, of course, do anything as naughty again, will you, Jasmine? You will remember that you are to be my wife?" He kissed the top of her head softly.

Jasmine turned about. She was both angry at him and shocked by his attitude, which bordered upon amusement. *"Do you not care that I lay with the Earl of Glenkirk?"* she demanded furiously, looking up into his handsome face. Did she mean nothing to him that he cared so little about her behavior? And why was that thought so irritating? She did not love him. It was unlikely she would ever love him!

Rowan Lindley looked down at her. His golden eyes grew hard and his voice was harsh when he spoke. *"Care?* Aye, madame, *I care!* It infuriates me to know that James Leslie has had you naked and weeping with pleasure beneath him. The picture I can so well imagine burns into my soul like a blazing brand." His hand reached up, catching her throat, encircling it gently, yet she could feel the power in it. "How many times before did you lie with him, madame?"

"Only last night," she half whispered, suddenly afraid, but struggling not to show it, "and never again if I am to be your wife. I am the Mughal's daughter, and I have my honor as well as yours to protect. Last night I was a free woman. *Free to do as I chose.* Today that is no longer so. I will not dishonor you, my lord. Or will you cry off because of what I have just told you?"

His hand dropped from her neck and he laughed weakly.

"Would it please you if I say yes? Well, I will not, Jasmine de Marisco. Can you not see that you drive me to madness? Never before have I put my hands upon a woman in violence or anger. This is what you do to me, and I suspect even when you are mine, I shall still feel this way if another man should dare to look at you with anything less than respect in his eye, may God help him!"

Then he pulled her roughly to him, and his mouth crushed down upon hers, bruising it, yet sending a thrill of anticipation through her slender frame. "You are a fever in my blood, Jasmine de Marisco," he murmured against her lips. "A burning, hot fever." He nibbled at her mouth, his golden eyes suddenly soft and tender. "I want more than just a night with you. *I want eternity.* I want sons and daughters of our making, my beautiful Jasmine."

"Aye," she told him, swept up in the moment, "I would have children too! When Jamal was murdered, I lost our child. I love children!"

"Then marry me and I will give you those children. I will give you whatever you want, Jasmine. *Anything!*"

What if she said no? What could they do to her? she wondered. Then she realized that if her grandmother had chosen the Marquess of Westleigh for her husband, he could be naught but a good man. Again, there was no real choice, but she did trust her grandmother.

"Aye," she told Rowan Lindley. "I'll marry you, my lord."

He took her face in his two hands and gently kissed her. "I will make you happy," he promised her gravely.

Jasmine felt tears welling behind her eyelids, but she opened them, gazing up at him through the veil of moisture, and said, "I think I must make you happy also, my lord."

This man makes me feel safe. I have not had this feeling since I was a child, she thought. I have not had this feeling since Salim robbed me of it. *Now*, the notion slipped into her consciousness, *now* my brother can never find me. Even if his agents eventually trace me to England, he does not know my mother's real name, or my grandmother's, *or my husband's.*

"One thing I must know," Rowan Lindley was saying, and Jasmine forced herself to pay attention to him.

"What is it, my lord?" she asked.

"What does the Earl of Glenkirk really mean to you, madame?"

"Jemmie Leslie?" Jasmine smiled. "Why, he is my friend, sir."

"But last night . . . ?"

"There is much in common that we share," Jasmine began. "We have both lost mates in a violent manner. We have lost children. We were lonely and sought only to comfort each other. I do not love him, nor he, me. My stepfather thought that he should wed with me, but I said no. I should not like to think I forced a man to the altar," she finished with a smile.

"I needed to know, Jasmine," he told her.

She put her hand upon his cheek in a comforting gesture. "I know that you did. I will never betray your honor, my lord, nor my own. Are you certain, however, that you still really wish to marry me? Certainly you realize my grandmother has decided I must be wed lest my *baser* instincts publicly embarrass the family. There will be no scandal about last night, for the discovery that Jemmie and I were together was not made until after my uncle's guests had gone. Still, should you decide that a marriage between us was not wise, I would understand."

"You are mine," Rowan Lindley said simply. "You have been since I first set eyes on you last May Day." Then, taking her hand in his, he led her from the picture gallery. He said nothing about the wedding date nor the reason behind the delay. He was touched by her honesty and knew that she would be a good wife to him. *I can trust her,* he thought, satisfied, and he squeezed the slim hand in his lovingly.

It is settled then, Jasmine realized as she signed the contract of marriage between herself and James Rowan Lindley, Marquess of Westleigh, that evening. The contracts for Sybilla's marriage were also signed. A small dinner party was held in the betrothed couples' honor.

"Thomas is taking me to France in May," Sybilla announced grandly. " 'Twill be a belated honeymoon as there is nowhere we may go in January. We shall visit Paris and Grandfather de Marisco's relations at Archambault. Mama says there is a special château there, Belle Fleurs it is called, where she spent her early childhood." Sybilla turned eagerly to Skye. "May we stay at Belle Fleurs, Grandmam? Mama says that you and Grandfather spent a part of your honeymoon there and 'tis a very romantic place. Oh, please, Grandmam!"

"The place has not been lived in for years," Skye said, "but oh, very well, you silly chit. I will send word that the château be made ready for another generation of honeymooners." Though she grumbled, Skye smiled with her words. *Belle Fleurs!* It has been so long ago. She had been so much younger, she thought ruefully, and her back had not ached so much in the mornings. "No place to go in January indeed. You can go to court and lord it over all those other silly chits who serve Danish Annie with you," she told Sybilla.

"I am offended, beauty," the Earl of Kempe said mournfully. "No place to go? Why, I shall take you to heaven and back, my adorable Sybilla. You may trust my word on it." He kissed her little hand, his gray eyes twinkling mischievously.

Sybilla was not so dense that she did not comprehend his meaning. She blushed to the roots of her golden-blond head.

The first of the family weddings being less than three weeks away, Bonnie, the seamstress, and her assistant found themselves immersed in work eighteen hours a day. The London seamstress who had sewn Jasmine's new wardrobe the previous winter was called from her shop to lend a hand. Remembering the generosity of the old Countess of Lundy,

she came gladly. Lady Sybilla Alexandra Mary Gor
would not go to her new husband with less than a full trous
seau. The Earl of BrocCairn had begged the queen's indu
gence, and Sybilla had been relieved of her duties as maid
of honor. Her place in the queen's household was quickly
filled.

"So she is indeed to be married to the Earl of Glenkirk,"
Queen Anne said, smiling, when Sybilla's father requested
her release. " 'Tis time Jemmie wed again."

"Nay, madame," Alex Gordon corrected the queen. "Sybilla
is to be married to Thomas Ashburne, the Earl of Kempe.
Glenkirk was but a childish fantasy she hae carried wi her for
years. Kempe offered for her last summer, but we hae promised
her she could come to court to serve ye. Nay, madame, Glenkirk never entered the picture except in Sibby's girlish dreams.
She is quite besotted by Tom Ashburne now, and he in love
wi her."

"Then," the queen said, " 'twill be a good match, my lord.
You and your wife are to be congratulated on your daughter's good fortune."

"We hae been twice blessed, madame," the earl told her.
"My widowed stepdaughter, Jasmine de Marisco, will remarry in the spring. Her betrothed husband is the Marquess
of Westleigh, Kempe's cousin. Both gentlemen came to visit
my father-in-law, Lord de Marisco, last May at Queen's Malvern and fell in love wi the lasses then." Alex Gordon felt
safe in telling the queen this additional bit of news. Jasmine's
monthly flow had come upon her two days after her liaison
with Lord Leslie. There would, thank God, be no scandal!

The day before Sybilla's wedding to Tom Ashburne, Jasmine
sought out her stepsister. She found Sybilla in her bcham-
ber alone.

"What do you want?" Sybilla demanded. She had not
been quite as obnoxious to Jasmine of late as previously been.

1 want you to have this," Jasmine said, proffering a large, ...t, red leather case to Sybilla. "It is my wedding gift to you."

Sybilla looked at Jasmine with surprise. "Why are you giving me a wedding present? You hate me. You must."

"I do not hate you," Jasmine said. "Remember, Sibby, that we share something very special. *Our mother.* I cannot hate my mother's daughter, and I do not believe that you really hate me."

"Perhaps if Mama had had a daughter and not four boys," Sybilla began, and she sighed, "but she did not. I was her little girl, and then you came. I realized then that all the love she had lavished on me was really the love she had wanted to lavish on you. Her love did not belong to me. It belonged to you. I was hurt and angry, Jasmine. Would you not have been if you were me? I love Mama more than anyone in my life!" Here Sybilla's voice broke and large tears slipped down her pink cheeks.

Jasmine put a comforting arm about her stepsister and, strangely, Sybilla did not pull away. "Oh Sibby," Jasmine told her, "had it not been for you, I do not believe our mother would have survived leaving India, nor would her marriage have been a very happy one. When my husband Jamal was murdered, I lost the child I was carrying. I did not know that child except in my imagination. Yet its loss hurt me dreadfully.

"Try to imagine what it must have been like for Mama, knowing her child and then being forcefully separated from that child. Then she came to Dun Broc and you were there! are only six months apart in age, Sibby, but that would no have mattered. *You were there.* A little girl who needed mo ing, and a mother who desperately needed her little girl. ma must have thought it a miracle.

ve and care she gave you was always yours, never mine, y. Did she think of me? I do not know. Perhaps sometir ut perhaps not, for I would have thought it far too painful for her. All she could remember was a baby. She never expected to see me again, and she had you. You became her darling little girl. Not me. Her joy at our reunion was no more than that. She gave me life, and yet, try as I may, I cannot *really* think of her as my mother."

"You cannot?" Sibby was astounded. She looked up at her beautiful stepsister in surprise. *"She is your mother, Jasmine!"*

Jasmine laughed. "I know she is, but because I never really knew her, it is Rugaiya Begum, the woman who raised me, that I think of as my mother. Do you ever think of Alanna Wythe as your mother?"

"Never!" Sybilla said. "I loathe and detest her, if the truth be known. Mama always grew upset with me when I said things like that, but it is true. Alanna Wythe but used me to blackmail my father. She was no mother to me.

"When I was small she would come to Dun Broc to see me, but every time 'twas really to wheedle something out of my father. Cattle, or horses, or grain to get her and that outlaw she wed through the winter. When I was six she came, big-bellied with a runny-nosed brat hanging upon her skirts. She coyly introduced him as my baby brother. The little horror was every bit as tall as I was, yet he was but two. His father, whom I've seen but once, is a huge giant of a man.

"I told my father after she left to simply send the creature her tribute, for I never wanted to see her again. I haven't, either, since that day."

"Yet she is your mother. She gave you life," Jasmine said.

Understanding dawned in Sybilla's blue eyes. Then she replied, "At least the mother who gave birth to you truly loves you."

"But the love she has for me takes nothing away from the love she has for you, Sibby," Jasmine responded. "We are two totally different girls, are we not? Cannot our mother love all her children without taking love away from one to give love to another of them? I never had a sister close to

. in age, Sibby. I was the youngest, the last of the Mughal's
nildren. My father's daughters were nearly all grown when
I was born. I lived mostly apart from the court with my
mother. I had no friends my own age. When I learned of
your existence, I was so happy. It never occurred to me that
we would not be friends. We should be. We are sisters."

Not stepsisters. She had said sisters, Sybilla thought. "Do
you like me?" she asked Jasmine.

"Not always," came the honest answer. "You are very
spoiled."

"And you can be imperious," Sibby retorted quickly.

"I am the Mughal's daughter," Jasmine replied regally.

Then the two girls' eyes met and they burst out laughing.

"Ohh my," Sybilla gasped, finally catching her breath, "I
think we can be friends, Jasmine. I know we can, dear sister!"

Then she began to sob again, and Jasmine wept too. It
was thus that Velvet found them. "What is the matter?" she
cried out.

"We are sisters," Sibby said, her tears making her little
nose quite rosy.

"Isn't it wonderful?" Jasmine hiccuped.

"Have you two been imbibing the wedding wine?" Velvet
demanded suspiciously. What on earth had happened to
bring these two together?

"Jasmine brought me a wedding gift," Sybilla finally said,
"and then we talked and we decided we don't want to be
enemies any longer. We are sisters, Mama, and we are marrying cousins who are like brothers to one another."

Velvet shook her head. "I have been a mother all these
years, and I still do not understand children," she said. Then,
"Let us see what Jasmine has given you, Sibby. Open the
box. Ohhhh, gracious! It is magnificent!" she exclaimed, as
Sybilla revealed a necklace of diamonds and pearls nestled
along with ear bobs upon a satin background.

"The diamonds come from my father's mines in Golconda, and the pearls are from the waters of the Persian

Gulf. The finest pearls in all the world come from the gu.
my father used to say. I did not know if Sibby had any
grown-up jewelry, but I thought she should have some to
wear on her wedding day. It will go perfectly with your gown,
Sibby."

"Ohh, do you really think so?"

Velvet was astounded. Quickly forgotten, she tiptoed from
the room while her two daughters, their ebony and golden
heads together, discussed the merits of Sybilla's wedding
gown.

Skye laughed heartily as her daughter told her of how the
two girls had made peace between themselves. " 'Twas only
a matter of time," she said. "Sybilla was jealous of Jasmine
because she unexpectedly had to share you. Now she has
Tom Ashburne's love, and yours does not seem to matter as
much to her anymore. As for Jasmine, she is feeling secure
in her new life. Rowan Lindley will be good for her as well.
Adam and I will have two more great-grandchildren before
the year is out, and you, my sweet Velvet, will find yourself
twice a grandmother!" Then Skye laughed.

Lady Sybilla Alexandra Mary Gordon was married to Lord
Thomas Henry Kempe on the very sunny morning of January 26, 1607. The bride wore a gown of white velvet with a
cloth-of-silver underskirt and a bodice sewn all over with
pearls and crystals that sparkled in the morning sunlight.
The groom was garbed in black velvet. The sun, which had
not shone in almost two weeks, was considered a very go
omen for a happy marriage; and all the guests admired
bride's necklace.

The marriage was celebrated in the chapel at Ly
House, and the feast held afterward was attend
king and the queen, as well as all the more imp
bers of the court. The king's own Anglican ch
over the nuptials, a great honor. The Earl o
at the first news of his niece's betrothal

ent word to his brother, Lord Burke. Padraic and Valentina
nad been on the road within two days and struggled through
the winter weather to reach London in time.

Now, as he and Sybilla stood receiving the congratulations of the guests, the Earl of Kempe's smile widened at the
sight of the Burkes. "How did you know?" he exclaimed.

"Robin sent a message," Padraic said. "I wouldn't have
missed seeing you wed for the world! Now you can no longer
flirt with my wife, you rogue! My dear niece, Sybilla, will
certainly destroy you if you do, I have not a doubt. Mama
says you're besotted by the wench."

"Stop teasing Tom," Valentina interjected, and she kissed
the earl's cheek. "I always told you that you would one day
find the perfect woman for you, my dear friend. How glad I
am I might be here today to see you married." Then she
lowered her voice. "But *Sybilla?*"

Tom Ashburne laughed merrily. "She is the perfect mate
for me, divinity. I swear it! I should be lost without her." He
caught his bride's hand in his and, raising it to his lips,
kissed it as Sybilla beamed with pleasure, love shining from
her blue eyes.

"I wonder how long until you're a grandmother, Velvet,"
Padraic asked the bride's mother mischievously, and then
ducked the blow she aimed at him. "Do I see a wrinkle,
madame?" he teased, and turned away with his wife before
his youngest sister could do him serious harm.

The Marquess of Westleigh promenaded through the ball-
rom of Lynmouth House with his betrothed wife displayed
on his arm. Jasmine looked most magnificent in an orange
vet gown with a gold brocade underskirt. Tiny brocade
each with a miniature topaz center, decorated her
Her About her neck was a necklace of yellow diamonds.
chign-dark hair was parted in the center and worn in a
decont hugged the nape of her neck. The chignon was
th cloth-of-gold roses.

B E R T R I C E   S M A L L 413

"Look at how proudly she holds herself," Skye said to Adam. "She should be a queen!"

"She is you all over again, but for the turquoise eyes and that damnably fetching mole," Adam de Marisco said.

"She is far more beautiful than I ever was," Skye replied.

"Nay," he told her. "You are the most beautiful woman who ever lived. Do not argue with me, little girl. *You are!*"

"I never argue with you," Skye told him, and Adam laughed.

Jasmine saw little of court after her betrothal to the Marquess of Westleigh. It was not proper for an unmarried woman of good family to be seen there without an express purpose, unless in the company of her relations or her husband-to-be. Rowan Lindley did not like the court.

" 'Tis full of hangers-on and low types," he said. "I will show you London instead. As soon as the danger of severe storms is over, we must all return home. You will need time to prepare for our marriage."

"Will we ever visit London after we are wed?" Jasmine asked him. "Greenwood is to be mine one day and we are always welcome to stay here."

"If you wish to visit London, of course we can come," he told her, "but are you not more of a country girl? I seem to remember the first time I saw you, you were barefooted and had an armful of fresh flowers with the dew still on them. That is the woman I fell in love with, Jasmine de Marisco."

"I cannot always promise to remain the same," she told him honestly.

"Good, then I shall not promise that either," he replied, and they laughed.

He took her across the London Bridge to Southwark, where the Globe Theatre was located. One of the owners of the Globe was Master William Shakespeare, the famous playwright. There they saw several of his plays. *Macbeth. Henry V.*

King Lear. Although these plays gave her a stronger sense of English and Scots history, Jasmine preferred Master Shakespeare's comedies, of which she saw two: *Much Ado About Nothing* and *A Midsummer's Night Dream.*

The Globe itself was a bawdy, noisy place located directly next to the Bear Gardens. Rowan always bought them seats upon the stage itself. The pit below was a roiling mass of humanity. Of the playgoers, some were respectable, some not. Orange girls were selling their fruits from Spain, and ofttimes themselves for a greater coin. In the boxes about the theatre, where no respectable woman would dare to be seen, there were expensive whores openly plying their trade, calling boldly to the gallants below; and gentlemen with their mistresses, some well-known ladies of the court who hid behind the boxes' curtains.

"Would you like to see the bear-baiting?" Rowan asked her one day.

"What is a bear-baiting?" Jasmine wondered aloud.

He told her and was rather relieved by the look of revulsion upon her face. Rowan Lindley did not enjoy bear-baiting himself.

"That is dreadful!" Jasmine exclaimed. "It is cruel! To hunt an animal is one thing, but to set beasts against each other for mere amusement is horrible! No thank you, my lord!"

"You have hunted, then?" he inquired, turning the subject.

"Aye, with my father and brothers. Tiger, antelope, and gazelle mostly. Sometimes we rode horseback and other times we pursued our quarry from the backs of our elephants. I am a reasonably good shot with both gun and bow, and I can use a spear accurately if I must. Do you hunt, my lord? And what?"

"Deer, rabbit, game birds for the table mostly," he said. "I do not believe in killing for sport alone. It is wasteful."

They were sitting together in the library of Greenwood House, trying to decide what to do.

"I learn more about you each day," Jasmine told him. "I am beginning to think perhaps my grandmother is right about you."

"And what does that magnificent woman say about me?" he asked her with a smile.

"That you are a good man and the perfect husband for me," she said frankly.

"Aye, I am," he agreed, "but, madame, there is more I need to know about you, yet you give me no opportunity to learn it. Come here to me, Jasmine."

Curious, she arose and stood before him, crying out in surprise when he pulled her down into his lap, her skirts ballooning about her. *"My lord!"*

"Rowan," he said to her. "I am called Rowan. I want to hear my name from your lips, Jasmine."

"Rowan! What are you about?" She struggled to arise, but he would not let her, pinioning her firmly within his embrace, half laughing at her spirited outrage.

"The night we agreed to wed, I kissed you," he said. "Since then you have given me no chance at all to kiss you or to caress you. Should we not be lovers as well as husband and wife, Jasmine?"

"We are not married yet," she said primly, but her cheeks were pink with her blushes. She felt suddenly shy.

"We are certainly not lovers, either, madame. Why are you so coy with me? You were not so coy with Glenkirk," he said suddenly.

She gasped as if stung, struggling once again to escape him, and then, unsuccessful, she replied furiously, "Is that all you want of me, Rowan? What Jemmie Leslie had? I am no wanton, my lord, whatever you may think!"

"I will have more of you than *he* ever had, Jasmine," Rowan Lindley answered jealously, and he kissed her.

It was an angry kiss, and she met it with equal anger. He bruised her mouth, forcing her lips apart, plunging his tongue into her mouth to do battle with her tongue. But their anger gave rise to passion, and suddenly he groaned. The kiss grew soft as he felt her rage draining away as well. Nibbling his way across her lips, his hot mouth found her cheekbones, her eyes, and finally the edge of her jawbone just beneath her left ear.

Jasmine quivered. He made her head spin, and she was very surprised to find the stirrings of desire beginning to infuse her body. He bit down gently upon the lobe of her ear. His tongue slowly explored the shell of it, his soft breath sending shivers down her spine. He passed a hand lightly over her breasts, then plunged it into her bodice. Jasmine was amazed the gown did not burst asunder with his invasion, for her breasts felt tight and swollen. Taking a nipple between his thumb and forefinger, he worried it back and forth until she whimpered.

His mouth found hers again. They kissed until she believed they could kiss no more, their lips mashing against one another warmly, wetly. She pulled away, gasping for air, only to feel a hand slipping beneath her voluminous skirts. The hand slid smoothly up her slim thigh, finding her most sensitive spot with unerring aim.

"*Rowan!*" she softly cried his name.

"I need to touch you there," he murmured desperately against her cheek, and a single finger began to move sensuously against her tiny jewel.

She could feel herself getting moist with her desire. He was wicked! *Wicked!* She struggled feebly to sit up, but could not. "*Rowan!*" she gasped, unable now even to breathe quite properly.

He said nothing. The finger rubbed, and rubbed and rubbed, until finally he felt her stiffen, shudder, and then collapse, sobbing as she turned her face against his chest.

"*I hate you for that!*" she wept.

" 'Twas not enough, was it?" he said low.

"*No!*"

"It was not meant to be, Jasmine."

"Then why? Why did you do that to me?" she demanded, pulling herself into a sitting position and looking into his golden eyes.

"Because I want you to want me as much as I desire you, my love. You are no virgin to be satisfied easily. You are a woman. I want you to be my woman; to hold back nothing from me—*ever*."

"You are cruel," she said weakly, aching with her need for him.

"I can give both pleasure and pain, even as you can, my love," he replied. Then he kissed her lips softly.

"Never bring Jemmie Leslie between us again," Jasmine told him. "There is naught for you to be jealous of, Rowan. I swear it! Is there no way in which I can convince you of this?"

"Perhaps when I have loved you as you were meant to be loved," he said. "Perhaps then I can wipe out the pictures my mind insists upon fabricating to torture me with, Jasmine. Perhaps I can replace the nightmares with dreams of my own, my love. Until then, jealousy burns a hole in my gut that aches unbearably."

"Then have me now, Rowan," she said softly, caressing his tawny hair. "I cannot bear that you suffer over something so trifling. Those few hours I spent with the Earl of Glenkirk were not important to me, nor to him either. We only sought a moment of comfort with each other. Make love to me now, my lord, and ease your pain."

"No," he told her. "I cannot take advantage of you. I would never want you to believe I did so, Jasmine. I must learn to control myself, but dear heaven, I want you!"

"Passion is the sweeter for the waiting," she teased him gently.

"Glenkirk is a fool," Rowan Lindley replied.

"Why do you say that?" she asked.

"Because he could have had you, Jasmine, and he was not wise enough to take you," her betrothed husband answered.

• •

James Leslie, however, was even now bemoaning his lack of foresight. Several days after he and Jasmine had been found abed, he had called upon the Earl and Countess of Lundy, asking their permission to court their granddaughter. They had refused.

"Jasmine is now betrothed to the Marquess of Westleigh," Skye had told Lord Leslie.

"But what if she carries my child?" he demanded.

"She does not," was the stiff answer.

"Is she in love with Westleigh, or do you force her to this match because of me?" James Leslie queried.

"Listen to me, my lord," Skye said quietly. "Rowan Lindley met our granddaughter last May. He fell in love with her and sought our permission to marry her. We refused him because we felt Jasmine needed more time to acclimate herself to her new life in England. We were also thinking of ourselves, and of how much we enjoyed having this grandchild we never expected to know with us. There is, however, no other path in life for a respectable woman, as you yourself know, but marriage. Jasmine's petite adventure with you made us realize that it was time she be settled."

"And she agreed to the match?" the Earl of Glenkirk asked.

"Of course she did, my lord. We have never forced any of our children or grandchildren to the altar," Skye told him. "This disappointment is all your own doing. You had the opportunity to wed her, but when asked, you said nothing, which was every bit as good as saying no."

"But she said she did not want to marry me," he protested.

"And you believed her?" Skye felt genuinely sorry for James Leslie. He had realized too late his mistake.

"I thought she was being sporting, madame. We were caught, you will admit, in a most compromising situation. Jasmine is obviously not a woman to take advantage of a

BERTRICE SMALL 419

gentleman, and then, too, there were her stepsister's feelings to consider. I know her well enough to see she is a kind woman."

"You learned all of that in just a few short hours with her?" Skye teased him, trying to lighten the moment.

"Mistress de Marisco and I had spoken at length on several occasions in your park when I came calling upon her. For young Lady Sybilla's sake, she would not encourage me further," he said stiffly.

"Until the night of my son's Twelfth Night fete," Skye murmured. "She says you were both lonely and but comforting each other, my lord."

"Aye," he replied, and she could read pain upon his handsome face. James Leslie straightened his shoulders and said formally, "I thank you for seeing me, my lord. My lady. Under the circumstances, I will trouble you no further. Will you tell Jasmine that I was here?"

"No, my lord, I will not," Skye answered honestly. "There would be no point to it now, would there? She is formally betrothed to marry Rowan Lindley and the marriage will be celebrated April thirtieth."

"Should you not give her the choice?" Adam asked his wife when the Earl of Glenkirk had departed.

"Her future is in England, not Scotland," Skye said fiercely. "I have lost Velvet to that wild and wet land. I will not lose my darling Jasmine to it, Adam. Besides, if Glenkirk really loved her, he would have said it immediately. This is an afterthought. Perhaps he learned of her fortune. Wealthy men are never satisfied with their own fortunes. They are always desirous of adding to them."

And so the matter had been closed, and the servants had been warned not to tell Mistress de Marisco that the Earl of Glenkirk had called upon her grandparents that day. Rowan Lindley had won Jasmine. When the mid-February air was mild with the promise of spring, the Gordons, the de Mariscos, and the Ashburnes left London to travel home.

"You will come to Swan Court soon, won't you, Jasmine?" Sybilla begged her sister. "I will be so lonely without you!"

"As soon as Grandmother lets me," Jasmine promised. "She says I must be fitted for my trousseau first."

"Send word as soon as you can," Sybilla said, smiling. Then the coach carrying the bride, her parents—who were going with her to see her home—and her bridegroom turned off the main highway and onto the road that would take them to Swan Court.

❈

14

❈

"**P**oor Bonnie," Jasmine said with a sympathetic smile. "You shall have no fingers left with which to sew by the time my wedding day comes. First Sybilla and now me."

The seamstress smiled back at the young woman. She *was* tired, and her poor little assistant was equally so; but neither of the women minded. They knew that their work would be appreciated, and unlike so many in service to great households, they were well-fed and warm at night in their attic bedchamber with its pretty casement windows which looked down across the fields. " 'Tis a pleasure to sew for you, m'lady," Bonnie said. "We've had far more time to complete your trousseau than we did Lady Sybilla's. Now you just hold still a moment more and I'll have that hem basted. 'Tis a beautiful wedding gown, m'lady, and needs just a tiny bit of remodeling. Styles have not changed so much over the years. You're taller than your grandmother, but a wee bit shorter than your mother, so the hem must come up again."

"My grandmother *and* my mother's wedding gown," Jasmine said softly. "Oh Bonnie! I am so happy at last!"

"He's a fine man, the marquess," Bonnie said with a smile, and then she bit off the thread holding the basting stitches. "There, m'lady. Now let's get you out of this and then you can run off to your handsome lover. Just a few more weeks and you'll be his wife!"

"A moment," Skye said as she entered the room with Velvet, who had come from Swan Court. "Let me see you, darling girl. I never saw your mother in this gown, for I was in India when she wed Alex. Ahh, how beautiful you are!"

"Wearing your wedding gown, Mama," Velvet told them, "made me feel as if you and Papa were almost with me. My daughter, however, far outshines me with her radiance. The gown could have been tailored specifically for you, Jasmine. The color is perfect! Look at yourself!"

Jasmine, who had not dared to espy herself before, now turned and stared into the tall glass in the sewing room. The gown she wore was the very one that Skye had worn when she had been married to Adam; the same one her mother had worn when her marriage to Alex Gordon was celebrated at Queen's Malvern. It did indeed fit her as if it had been fashioned for her and her alone. The gown had been made in France, for that is where her grandparents had wed.

It was pure, shimmering silk, apple-green in color. The low, square bodice was embroidered with gold butterflies, daisies, and tiny seed pearls. There was a slightly darker green velvet underskirt embroidered to match the bodice. The sleeves were of the style called leg-of-mutton. They were decorated with tiny gold ribbons, and the wristbands were turned back to form a cuff, each one of which had a gold lace ruff. The long wasp waist and the bell-shaped skirt were still very much in style.

Skye had managed to have duplicated the silk undergarments as well as the pale green silk stockings embroidered with grapevines and the delicate silk slippers that had also been a part of her wedding outfit. Bonnie had, on her mistress's instructions, made cloth-of-gold silk roses to decorate the bride's dark hair. "You will wear my pearls," Skye told her granddaughter, and there were tears in her eyes.

Jasmine hugged each of the women in turn. "You are both so good to me," she told them.

"Tell me what you wore on your wedding day to Prince Jamal," Skye asked as Jasmine finally removed the wedding gown.

"I was garbed like an idol to show both my father's wealth and to honor my husband's family," Jasmine told them, and she described her red silk and diamond-studded outfit. "I am quite certain I prefer my lovely silk gown. India and the life I lived there is fast fading from my consciousness. I am an Englishwoman, and I am proud to be one."

Bonnie helped Jasmine out of the gown and its bodice. She had been listening avidly to the young woman's description of her previous wedding finery and now asked, fascinated, "What did you wear under all them silks, gold, and jewels, m'lady? I can't help being curious as a magpie."

"Why nothing, Bonnie," Jasmine told her, her turquoise-blue eyes twinkling mischievously.

"*Nothing?* Go on with you, m'lady!" the seamstress said.

"The climate is hot, Bonnie. Hotter than you can imagine, and, except on formal occasions, we wore few garments in India. There are no chemises and other undergarments as you have here in England," Jasmine said.

"Ohhh," Bonnie replied, shocked.

Her wardrobe just about completed, Jasmine went to visit Sybilla at Swan Court. Her stepsister had been pleading that she come that she might show off her new home. Jasmine was quite impressed with Swan Court, for although it was not a large house, it was a most charming one, with a lovely lake which was home to both black and white swans. Tom Ashburne's widowed mother had died three years previously, and so the house had been without a mistress to guide it. Sybilla, well-trained by her mother, quickly set everything in order, and now with spring upon them was directing the gardener in her efforts to restore the gardens. Jasmine stayed with the Ashburnes until a week before her wedding, when Rowan Lindley arrived to escort her home to Queen's Malvern.

"We'll be just two days behind you," Sybilla told Jasmine. "We must come slowly." She smiled archly at her stepsister.

"You are not riding? I far prefer to ride. The coach is so slow and too stuffy," Jasmine said.

"Tom will not let me ride . . . *now*," Sybilla replied, and she was unable to keep the smile from her face.

For a moment Jasmine stared at her as if she had gone mad, and then she shrieked, "You are going to have a baby! That's it, Sibby, isn't it? You are going to have a baby! Does Mama know?"

"Not yet," Sybilla said as the two hugged each other. "You must not tell her either. Your wedding is April thirtieth, and on Mama's birthday the following day, Tom and I intend gifting her with the news of her first grandchild. 'Twill be born in mid-autumn. I think I may have conceived on our wedding night. Ohh, I wish the same for you, dear Jasmine! I am so happy! Please be happy too!"

Riding across the English countryside with Rowan Lindley by her side, Jasmine considered that she was happy. The feeling had slipped up on her and, casting a look from beneath her eyelashes at the tawny-haired man riding by her side, she also considered the possibility that she might be falling in love with him. She wondered exactly how he felt about her. That he desired her was something he had not hidden even from the very beginning, but Jasmine was wise enough to know that desire would not be enough for her, nor for him either.

"You are thinking," he said, "and serious thoughts too."

"How can you know that?" she responded, smiling at him.

"Your forehead wrinkles when you are pondering, and the wrinkles deepen in relation to the seriousness of your thoughts," he told her.

Jasmine laughed. "How can you know me so well and in such a short time, Rowan?"

"I watch you," he said, "and we have known each other almost a full year now, Jasmine."

He made her feel almost ashamed, for she was not certain that she knew him as well as he seemed to know her. Daringly she asked him, "Do you love me, Rowan Lindley?"

"Aye, Jasmine, I do," he replied in all seriousness. "I have loved you from the beginning, my dear. Tom can tell you that I am like that. So it was with my first wife. I saw her. I fell in love."

"No, no, you cannot possibly love me," she insisted. "That you desire me, I know, but love me?" Her mare shied nervously at the tone in her voice, and Jasmine calmed the beast with a soothing pat.

"I love you," he said firmly, and then, "Are you beginning to love me, Jasmine? I would like it very much if you did."

She drew her animal to a halt and he followed her lead. "*Love you?* Aye, I think I am beginning to love you, Rowan."

They moved forward again in silence. The road stretched on ahead of them over the green hills which were dotted with colorful spring blossoms and frolicking lambs who resembled small, fluffy white clouds. Behind them, somewhere in the distance, the de Mariscos' coach rumbled forward, heading toward Queen's Malvern, Toramalli within, watching over her mistress's possessions. Jasmine kicked Ebony into a gallop. She needed to run almost as much as the mare herself did. Rowan Lindley's chestnut stallion kept pace with them.

The day, which had been gray to start with, began to look even more ominous. The wind picked up and dark clouds blew helter-skelter across the horizon and above them. There was a rumble of thunder and then the skies suddenly opened up, the rain pelting down on them in large, flat droplets. The coach had been far behind them to begin with, and their gallop had taken them even farther away from it. There seemed to be no shelter in sight. Jasmine pulled up the hood of her cloak and hunched down. They rode doggedly on until Rowan Lindley's sharp eye spotted a small building ahead of them set back slightly from the road. It was obviously inhabited, for from its chimney came a thin stream of smoke. He pointed to it, and Jasmine nodded, directing her horse to follow his.

As they drew near he shouted to her over the rain, " 'Tis an inn!" He pointed to a small sign hanging over the gate which read, THE ROSE AND CROWN. "We're in luck!"

They rode into the inn yard and dismounted, leading their beasts quickly into the small stable that was attached to the main building. There was one rather elderly horse housed within and several empty stalls.

"Can you unsaddle Ebony yourself, Jasmine, or will you need help?" he asked her.

"No, I can care for her, thank you," she replied, working to unfasten the girths from around the mare's belly. Setting the saddle aside, she found the feed and poured some grain into the stall's feed box. "There, my girl, you are settled for the time being," Jasmine told the creature, and she patted her lovingly, looking about. " 'Tis a clean place and the roof does not leak," she noted.

"Aye, the horses will be safe here," he agreed. "Now we must brave the rain again to get into the inn." Taking her hand, they stepped out into the wet weather again and hurried to the inn's front door.

The innkeeper was a pleasant-faced lady who jumped, startled as they came through the door. "Why bless my soul," she exclaimed. "I did not hear your coach, m'lord, m'lady. I am Mistress Greene."

"The coach is behind us some miles," Rowan Lindley said. "We rode and have stabled our horses ourselves. We will need rooms, good madame."

The innkeeper shook her head. "I am sorry, my lord, but I only have one chamber. 'Tis not often I see overnight guests, for the Red Bull is just down the road five miles or so. 'Tis quite large and comfortable, and most travelers stop there. Perhaps if the rain lets up you can go on. In the meantime I will be happy to serve you a good supper if you do not mind that the service is slow. My husband has gone off to market and will not be home tonight. 'Tis just my daughter Lizzie and me."

Jasmine looked around her. The inn was small but immaculately clean. There was a lovely fire burning in the big fireplace that took up almost an entire wall, and the tables were well-scrubbed. A large old black and white dog lay sprawled by the fire snoring. Jasmine smiled and look up at the marquess. "Let us remain here the night, my lord," she said. "I am not of a mind to brave the elements any longer, and 'tis so private and peaceful here."

"I could sleep down here by the fire," he mused.

"Or you could share the bed with me," she said softly and put her hand upon his arm, looking up at him with a melting glance. "We are to be married next week, my lord. What is the harm of it?"

The innkeeper could not hear their conversation, but she was not surprised when the gentleman said, "We will take your guest chamber, Mistress Greene, and have our supper here by the fire when you are ready to serve it."

"Very good, my lord!" she replied, and then moved to help them with their wet cloaks. "I'll take them into the kitchen, m'lord, and dry them by the fire. They'll be just fine come morning."

"I'm afraid," Jasmine said, "that you will have to take my skirts as well. I am soaked practically through. Would you or your daughter have a skirt I might borrow while I eat supper?"

"Ah, poor lamb," the innkeeper sympathized. "You come into the kitchen with me right now, m'lady, and I'll take care of you. Lizzie," she called, and a fresh-faced girl of about sixteen appeared from the direction of the kitchen. "Run, child," her mother commanded her, "and fetch your Sunday best. The lady is wet clear through to her petticoats." She turned to the marquess. "I'll bring you a tankard of good ale and some cheese, my lord, if you'll wait but just a moment."

"See to my lady first, goodwife," Rowan Lindley said as the woman hurried off out of his sight. His feet were dry in his boots, and his breeches just barely spattered with rain. A woman's skirts were far more vulnerable to a blowing storm. Settling himself in the large single chair by the fire, he reached down and scratched the half-sleeping dog's silky head. Dark eyes viewed him a moment and then closed. The marquess laughed softly. "So you've correctly ascertained that I'm no threat, have you," he said to the dog, and stretched out his legs toward the fire.

Shortly, Mistress Greene returned with a large pewter mug filled with foamy brown ale which she gave him along with a plate of bread and cheese. "This will ease your lordship's appetite until supper," she said. "'Twill be a wee time, for your lady's chilled and I've had my daughter bring the oak bathtub so your lady can bathe by the kitchen fire and get some warmth back into her little bones. Why, the lass is as slender as a reed and there's no meat on her at all." So saying, the innkeeper bustled off, leaving the Marquess of Westleigh chuckling.

In the kitchen, Jasmine found herself quickly divested of all her clothing and settled into a hot tub before the enormous fire where several iron pots bubbled and a joint of beef was being turned on a spit by Lizzie. Their wet clothing was spread on wooden racks at one end of the fireplace so it could dry. She was handed a clean cloth and a cake of soap by the innkeeper. The soap smelled of lavender, clean and brisk. Then left to herself, Jasmine washed the stink of the horses from her body and watched, soaking in the hot water, as Mistress Greene vigorously kneaded dough for the cottage loaves she would be serving in the morning.

With the dough left to rise within the bowl, her hostess helped her from the tub, and Jasmine toweled herself off with a rough, clean cloth. Her petticoats and chemise had been dried, for they were but fine lawn cotton, and she was offered Lizzie's Sunday best skirt of red linen along with a low-necked white blouse.

"I've nothing for your feet, and your stockings are still very damp, m'lady," Mistress Greene told her.

"Even fine ladies are known to go barefooted on occasion," Jasmine said with a smile. "The inn is warm, and my feet will not freeze."

"Then go and keep your fine gentleman company while I see to the supper," the innkeeper said. "I'll have Lizzie light the fire in the bedchamber so 'twill be warm for you later."

That she was dying of curiosity, Jasmine could see, and because she had been refrained from asking, Jasmine said, "I am Mistress Jasmine de Marisco, the granddaughter of the Earl and Countess of Lundy. The gentleman accompanying me is my betrothed husband, Lord Lindley, the Marquess of Westleigh. I am on my way home to Queen's Malvern to be married. My coach and servants will arrive later. They will be quite comfortable in your stable, but they will need to be fed."

Mistress Greene nodded. "I'll be happy to serve you, m'lady. More than likely, however, your coach will pass us by for the Red Bull, believing you to be there. If they do, you can catch them in the morning." The innkeeper curtsied as Jasmine turned and went into the tap room to join the marquess.

"Ohh, Ma, do you think she is telling the truth?" Lizzie wondered, very impressed by it all.

"Aye, she's a de Marisco girl. I saw her grandma once and never forgot it. She was on her way to visit a daughter and they stopped here at midday to water the horses and have a meal. You was just a wee thing and wouldn't remember, but I never forgot her ladyship. She was the most beautiful woman I ever seen. Mistress de Marisco favors her grandma. I wondered why she seemed so familiar when she came in earlier, and now I know. And a marquess for a husband!"

"He's really good-looking, too, Ma, with those gold eyes of his," Lizzie noted, and then she jumped as her mother slapped her. "Maaa!"

"You keep your eyes to yourself, Lizzie Greene! More than one girl's found herself in trouble flirtin' with the gentry!"

"I wasn't flirtin', Ma. I just looked at the gentleman," Lizzie sniffed.

"Well, don't go lookin' at gentlemen, my girl, or so much the worse for you," Mistress Greene warned her daughter. "Now get yourself upstairs and see a nice fire's lit in the guest chamber so's the lord and his lady don't freeze later. Then get back down here and we'll be serving the supper to them. That lass needs food, I can see."

Rowan and Jasmine sat at a small table pulled next to the fire and enjoyed the meal that Mistress Greene offered them. It was simple country food, but well-seasoned and hot. There was a rabbit stew with chunks of tender meat, onions, and carrots; thick slices of the beef Jasmine had seen roasting in the kitchen; a dish of mashed turnip with a knob of butter melting in it; fresh brown bread; and small, hard cheese. When they had managed to consume a goodly portion of this, washed down with brown ale, Mistress Greene presented them with a sweet pudding made with eggs, cream, bread, sugar, and currants.

The Marquess of Westleigh loosened his belt and said to the innkeeper, "If more people knew of your culinary skills, madame, your inn would be overrun with travelers, I vow it!"

"We do quite well, thank you, m'lord, with the day traffic and the occasional overnight guest," she told him with a pleased smile as she cleared the table of the last dishes. "When you're ready for your bed, you'll find the guest chamber at the top of the stairs."

"Will someone wait up for the coach, Mistress Greene?" Jasmine asked her, worried about Thistlewood and Toramalli.

"No need, m'lady. My daughter and I sleep here on the ground floor. If they come, we'll hear them for certain, but I think they have already passed us by for the Red Bull. I thought I heard a vehicle go by earlier on, but with the wind and rain, I could have been mistaken." She curtsied and returned to her kitchen.

Rowan Lindley and Jasmine sat silently for a few minutes before the fire, and then he asked, "Do you wish to retire, madame?"

She stood up and stretched languidly. "I am tired, my lord," she admitted, "and the rain upon the roof does have a soothing effect."

"Go up," he said. "I will join you shortly."

Opening the door at the top of the stairs, Jasmine found herself in a tiny room that was overwhelmed by a bed hung with homespun linen hangings decorated with colored threads. Stepping in, she closed the door behind her. The chamber was as immaculate as the rest of the inn. A well-laid fire burned in the small fireplace, warming the area quite well despite the blowing storm outside. The only other piece of furniture in the little space was a small wooden chair. Jasmine removed her skirt, petticoats, blouse, and chemise, laying them neatly over the rungs of the chair back. She loosened her hair from its chignon, combing it with her fingers. Then she hurried to climb into the bed. Though the lavender-scented sheets were cool, the feather bed beneath them would quickly warm her, she knew. Pulling the quilt over her, she snuggled down, her eyes closing.

Jasmine did not know what it was that woke her, but Rowan was in the chamber and about to enter the bed. "Do you always wear your shirt to bed, my lord?" she asked sleepily.

"Nay," he told her. "I generally sleep without any covering at all. 'Tis more comfortable, I find."

"So do I," she answered him.

Rowan Lindley removed his shirt and laid it with his other

clothing upon the seat of the chair. After adding a few more twigs to the fire, he climbed into bed with her. For several long, deeply silent minutes they lay side by side, and then Jasmine began to giggle.

Surprised, he raised himself up upon an elbow and looked down into her beautiful face. "What, may I ask, is so amusing, madame?" he demanded of her.

"We are!" she managed to gasp before being overcome by a fresh fit of laughter that brought tears to her eyes. Finally, however, Jasmine managed to control her mirth, and said, "Oh, Rowan, my love! For months you have lusted after me, and I most boldly have offered to share my bed with you tonight. Here we lie, side by side, naked as the day we were born, and neither of us dares to make a move toward the other. Do you not find that amusing? I do!" And she began to laugh softly again.

Unable to restrain a grin, he chuckled with her, but then he grew serious and said, "Are you certain that you want this, Jasmine?" His heart was beating so fiercely within the cavity of his chest that he wondered that she could not hear it. If he were to restrain himself much longer, he thought, he would burst into a thousand pieces.

Reaching up, she caressed his face with her hand. "We are to be married in seven days, Rowan Lindley. My grandmother, God bless her, is so enthusiastic about this wedding that you would think it was my first marriage and not the second. She has planned a huge celebration. The house will be filled to overflowing with all of my relations and their offspring, some of whom I have not even met. The king and queen, thank God, cannot come. Amid all of this, you and I will be put to bed with great ceremony upon our wedding night. I'm told any sound heard issuing forth from our nuptial chamber will be snickered at and fully interpreted as to its meaning by those up and avidly listening as they swill their wine in the Great Hall of Queen's Malvern."

"Good God!" he said, looking appalled. "Is there no escape?"

"We cannot offend my grandparents by fleeing the scene immediately following our wedding ceremony," she said, and there was genuine regret in her voice. "We are forced to remain and take part in *all* of the festivities. I therefore propose we make tonight our wedding night, Rowan Lindley. Here at this little inn we are safe and secluded, our privacy protected from prying eyes. Here, tonight, we may make love to each other with all the passion of which we are both capable so that on our official wedding night we may sleep peacefully and foil the gossips."

"You are a devious woman," he said softly.

"I am my father's daughter," she replied. "Now what say you?"

In answer he threw back the quilt that covered them. "Stand up, Jasmine," he said. "I would see you as God has fashioned you."

She arose, and in the flickering firelight she saw a little stool upon the tiled hearth. Stepping up upon it, she looked directly at him. Slowly she raised her arms up, placing them behind her head, revealing the firm, full cones of her breasts to him. Her nipples were large and a deep brownish-rose in color. "Well, my lord?" she purred at him, her turquoise eyes glittering darkly at him.

He devoured her beauty slowly. The magnificent breasts, the long shapely legs, the full hips. She was incredibly voluptuous for such a delicately boned girl. The flames from the fire played over her creamy skin, bringing out a faint hint of gold that darkened just slightly upon her smooth Venus mont. *"Turn,"* he softly commanded her, and with the hint of a smile upon her lips, she obeyed him, revealing to him her long shapely back and a bottom that was surprisingly fuller than he would have suspected, given the way her skirts fell. Her raven-black hair hung just to the small of her back. She faced him again.

Rowan Lindley arose from the bed. Offering her his hand, he gallantly helped her from the stool and stepped up upon it himself. "Now madame, I offer myself to you for your inspection," he said.

Jasmine stepped back slightly and boldly surveyed him. He was tall and sturdily built, with very long legs. His chest was broad and smooth, his shoulders wide. He had big feet, with toes that seemed quite long to her.

"Turn," she told him, and he did, revealing a hard buttocks and a long, broad back. He faced her once again and Jasmine asked him, "Why is the hair between your legs darker than the hair upon your head, my lord? Other men have the same color in both places."

"The hair upon my head is lightened by the sunlight," he explained with a grin. *What a question to ask a man!*

Her eyes lingered between his legs where his manhood lay at rest. It was larger than any she had ever seen. Both Jamal Khan, her brother, and Glenkirk had been more than well-endowed, but Rowan Lindley seem to her to be larger than other men. Her questioning look met his eyes. "Your manhood is very big, I think," she said slowly.

He nodded and agreed, "I've seen none bigger, Jasmine. Boys like to compare their attributes, and mine was always the largest by far."

"Will it fit me?" she wondered aloud.

"Quite nicely, I think," he said with a small chuckle. "I have never met a woman it did not fit." He stepped down from the stool and took her in his arms, his lips brushing the top of her head.

Her cheek lay against the smoothness of his chest. Her fingers made little circles upon his skin. She could feel the rhythmic, steady beat of his heart beneath her ear. Lifting her head just slightly, she licked at his nipple, then kissed it with soft lips, moving to the other nipple, which she saluted in the same fashion. Rowan Lindley stood very still, allowing her to set the pace of their lovemaking. She rubbed her head

against him, then sliding her palms slowly up his torso, she
lifted her face to him.

Taking her head between his two hands, he bent, brushing his mouth softly over hers. Her tongue licked at his upper lip and then the lower lip as she pressed herself against
him. The pliant mounds of her breasts aroused him, particularly as she slipped her arms about him, murmuring against
his ear seductively. He could feel her firm thighs and her soft
belly molding themselves against his thighs and belly. Then,
as one of her hands caressed the back of his neck, she lowered her other hand to fondle his manhood. Her touch was
like being scorched by flame. He had been touched there
before, but never like this. Her slender, skilled fingers
brought him as close to losing his control as he had ever
been without actually being sheathed within his lover.

"God's nightshirt," he groaned, catching her hand and
pulling it away from him. He was as near to spilling his seed
as any green lad.

"Does it shock you that I touch you?" she asked him curiously.

He shook his head. "Your touch has magic in it, my love,
but I am aroused almost beyond all bearing."

" 'Tis anticipation," she replied wisely.

He laughed weakly. "Aye. I do not think I have ever desired a woman as much as I desire you, Jasmine, but I want
to enjoy this wedding night of ours. More important, I want
you to enjoy it with me. I think, perhaps, that I should make
love to you rather than you make love to me. Afterward I
will be pleased to have you caress me as you have just now
caressed me. Will you let me lead the way, my darling?"

"Men are quick to pleasure, my lord. Far quicker than a
woman," she told him. "Since I but sought to please you,
then you must, if it pleases you, gain your pleasure as you
will. If in doing so you give me pleasure, so much the better!"

He laughed again. "I do not believe that any woman has
ever spoken so freely with me, Jasmine de Marisco. You are

honest and, it would seem, totally without guile. I fell in love with a beautiful girl, but the woman I wed is, I think, far better than I deserve."

"All women possess some guile, Rowan. Never believe it otherwise," she told him. "I am frank with you because it is my nature to speak thusly."

"Let us be done with talk," he said softly, and one arm about her supple waist, he reached up with his other hand to cup a breast within his warm palm. Gently he crushed the soft flesh, and his thumb stroked at the tender nipple. "Such perfection," he murmured softly into her perfumed hair. Then he bent, taking the nipple into his mouth and suckling hard upon it.

Jasmine's eyes closed, and she sighed deeply. Each tug of his mouth upon the sensitive nub sent a shiver of sensation deep into the secret places of her body. When he straightened himself, lifting her into his arms and walking with her to the bed, it was almost a relief of sorts. Gently he lay her upon the feather bed, joining her immediately, his mouth closing over her other nipple. Fiercely he drew upon it, causing her to cry out softly.

His tongue licked at the nipple and then began a leisurely exploration of her person. "I need to taste you," he said low as he moved from her chest to her belly to her thighs. Then turning her over on her belly, he licked her flesh from ankle to shoulder, nipping occasionally at her, causing her to squeal and squirm nervously. Rolling her over onto her back again, he slid down the bed to kiss her feet, saluting each toe in its turn and making her giggle. Moving slowly back up to where he was level with her, he slid a hand along the inside of her legs, rubbing, stroking, caressing. His gentle fingers insinuated themselves between the folds of flesh protecting that most sensitive of places a woman possesses.

Jasmine could feel that she was already moist with her rising passion. She bridled anxiously at his touch, remembering the last time he had touched her there; touched her and made her wild with a desire he had left unsatisfied. *"Please,"* she said, flushing at her own word.

He continued to softly caress her, and she shivered with the sensation. "Open yourself to me," he said low, pushing gently at her closed thighs, and when she answered his request, his tawny head dipped between her legs and he drew them over his shoulders, his tongue finding her with an unerring aim. "Ahh," he groaned, "you are sweet, my love! So very, very sweet!"

"Ahhhhh," she half sobbed, his teasing tongue taunting her with long-awaited pleasure. "Ohh, yes Rowan! Please, yes!" She was aching with a need so great that it threatened to overwhelm her in its intensity as his tongue played havoc with her. She shuddered with her first release, but despite it the edge of her passion was greater than it had been before. "I need you inside me, Rowan," she pleaded with him. *"Please!* I will die if you do not put yourself within me!"

He rose up above her. "Look at what you have done to me, my love!" his voice grated harshly at her. "Open your eyes and see what I will pleasure you with, Jasmine, *and I will pleasure you, my love,* more than any other man has ever pleasured you! *Look at me!"*

She was fast being overcome with her own desire, but Jasmine forced her eyes open and almost cried aloud with joy, for his manhood, aroused, was huge. Rather than being afraid, she welcomed it, reaching out to caress it, guiding him eagerly into the depths of her very being. With a groan he sank into her flesh, feeling her young body encasing him tightly, yet at the same time opening to allow him passage deeper and deeper until finally he could go no farther. Slowly he withdrew himself almost to the tip of his spear, and then he began to pump her vigorously over and over and over again until their soft cries of pleasure, mingling with their kisses, drew them over the brink of sanity and down into the depths of unbridled passion.

Jasmine bit her lip until she could taste blood. Her nails raked savagely down his back. He filled her as no man had ever filled her, stretching the walls of her sheath until she thought they could stretch no more. His manhood throbbed its message of desire within her fevered body. She could barely breathe, and gasped desperately as the intensity built and built inside her until finally she gained release.

He could feel her tensing within, and then her quivering little flutters of satisfaction as she crowned the head of his manhood with her own sweet honeyed libation of pleasure. The warmth of it sent him out of control, and his own love juices burst forth in greater measure, searing her hidden garden with an intensity of ecstasy that left Jasmine weeping wildly with relief and happiness. Gathering her in his arms, he held her against him. There was nothing left for either of them to say. Together they had experienced the kind of passion known to few lovers, and they were both sophisticated enough to realize it.

After a time Jasmine said low, "I do not know if I can live through another such bout, Rowan Lindley. Never have I known such a lover as you, my lord. *Never!*"

"Not even Glenkirk?" He hated himself even as he said the words. What the hell was the matter with him? He could not allow his jealousy to eat away at him like this. He would drive her away.

"Not even Glenkirk," she answered him, understanding and wanting to reassure him. "He has neither your skill nor your other far more superior attributes," she teased, gently patting his manhood. "In fact, I find my appetite for you has increased rather than decreased, Rowan Lindley, my dear lord, my betrothed husband."

"You are worldly-wise enough to know that even the best lover must have rest, my darling," he said with a smile.

In answer she arose from the tangle of sheets and, walking across the room, found a basin and pitcher of water by the fire. Pouring some of the water into the basin, she took her chemise, dampened it, and wringing it out, returned to the bed to gently bathe his sex. He was fascinated by her actions, especially as she told him, "In India we always keep a basin of perfumed water and half a dozen love cloths by the bedside. It aids lovers in their renewal." Finished with her task, she bent over him and took his flaccid manhood in her mouth.

Rowan Lindley gasped with surprise, but as her mouth began to suckle upon him, he found himself unable, not unwilling, to make her cease. "God's foot, Jasmine!" he groaned. My God, he was being aroused by her teasing little tongue and mouth so quickly that he was scarce able to believe it himself. He felt himself growing hard, and hot, and aching with a renewed need to possess this incredible woman who was to shortly be his wife. Roughly he pulled her head from him, yanking her into their bed, driving himself back into her and reveling in her cry of pleasure. This time neither of them gave quarter; driving each other beyond desire, beyond passion, to a white-hot intensity that scorched their very souls.

When the spring dawn came, they arose from their bed and tenderly bathed each other with the remaining water. They should have been exhausted, but rather, each felt renewed and alive. Rowan left the bedchamber and returned with Jasmine's clothing, which was warm and dry after its night before the kitchen fire. She folded the damp chemise and stuffed it in the pocket of her skirt. Together they devoured a huge country breakfast of barley cereal, ham, boiled eggs, bread, cheese, and apple cider.

"Your coach never came," Mistress Greene told them. "It surely went on to the Red Bull. You'll catch up with them quick enough and be home by noon, m'lady, m'lord." She beamed at them as she bid them a farewell, her usual good nature made even more good-natured by the single gold coin the Marquess of Westleigh had pressed into her hand. It was more money than she and her family would see in five years,

and she realized that Rowan Lindley's generosity was due to
his obvious happiness. Curtseying, she stuffed the gold piece
in her pocket and waved the lovers off with a cheery, "God
go with you and bless you with many children! Sons!" she
amended.

"Ohh, Ma! Is that a real gold coin?" Lizzie's eyes were
wide with amazement. "Wait till Pa gets home and sees it!"

"You'll not be telling your pa about this coin," her mother
said warningly. "Think, girl! Since the Red Bull opened up
we just get by, thanks to my cooking, but if I was to die,
where would you and your pa be? This gold coin will buy
you a farmer's eldest son, my girl! You can be the wife of a
propertied man, Lizzie. Your father would waste this coin
on some fool scheme or another, and who would have you
to wife then? Some itinerant tinker? Oh no! This coin can
be your dowry and our little secret, eh?"

Lizzie grinned at her mother. "I hope I can be as happy
as them two," she said, gazing after Jasmine and Rowan
Lindley.

"Happiness is for the gentry," her mother said. "A God-
fearing man with a good farm is all you'll ever need," Mistress Greene said, but she smiled as she watched her guests
departing.

"You gave her far too much money for an evening's lodg-
ing," Jasmine scolded Rowan Lindley as they rode. "You
should not be so generous, my lord."

"Not even to you, my love?" he teased her.

Jasmine laughed. "Now do not go twisting my words, my
lord. My grandfather loves to do that to Grandmama."

"And does she fluster as easily as you do, my love?" His
gold eyes were twinkling with merriment. "I adore you, Jasmine. I do not think I can wait a week to marry you."

"But you must," she said primly. "Besides, who is to know
if you steal into my chamber at night? I cannot bear to be
without you, my darling!" Her glance was meltingly torrid

as it caressed the region between his legs, and she licked her lips suggestively.

"Witch!" he groaned, feeling a familiar tightness in the area of his groin. "You will simply have to behave yourself, Jasmine. I do not want your grandparents, or your mother and stepfather for that matter, privy to our affairs, er, personal matters."

But Skye took one look at Jasmine as the betrothed couple returned to Queen's Malvern and chuckled wisely. Jasmine was radiant, and Rowan Lindley had the look of a cat who had swallowed a particularly delicious canary, despite his great effort at dignity. She was pleased to see that her judgment had not failed her. Jasmine was more than ready to begin a new life with a new husband.

As the wedding day drew nearer and Queen's Malvern filled with all the children and grandchildren of Skye O'Malley de Marisco, Jasmine grew quiet and a trifle withdrawn. How different this all was from her first marriage to Jamal Khan, and yet there was a sameness to it. She remembered all the *aunts*, and the pleasure they gained from her wedding. How were they now? Did they all still live? Salim, of course, would be kind to them. His mother would see to that. She thought of her little palace on Wular Lake in Kashmir; of Ali the fisherman. Did he ever think of her? *And she thought about Ruqaiya Begum.*

"What is it, my darling girl?" Skye asked Jasmine the night before her wedding, when the young woman's thoughts were particularly troubling. "What disturbs you? You have begun to love Rowan Lindley, that I can see, but something else distresses you greatly. Tell me and perhaps I can help to ease your mind of whatever worries you have."

"I cannot bear that my mother not know how happy I am, or that I am remarrying. It pains me that she will never see her grandchildren, Grandmama. She did not deserve to be alone in her old age," Jasmine said. "She was a good and loving mother."

Skye nodded. Loyalty was something that she well understood. "There is always a way," she said thoughtfully to her granddaughter. "We need to find a means by which we can communicate with Rugaiya Begum so that your brother does not learn of it. You know these people best of any of us. Think, Jasmine! Is there such a way for us to speak to Rugaiya Begum so that only she can hear and understand? Your cousin in Cambay can deliver the message, but how? Only tell me how and I will see it done!"

"My mother enjoys her garden," Jasmine said thoughtfully, "and she would know that my father often called Candra his English Rose. What if Alain O'Flaherty, himself, brought two rosebushes to Mama Begum. *English rosebushes!* He could speak to her using the roses to explain my situation. She would understand. *I know that she would!*"

"Perhaps," Skye said. "Perhaps you are right, my darling girl, but it will be at least ten months before our ships leave again for India. In that time you may have other news for your Mama Begum. That, too, would please her every bit as much as I know it will please me and Velvet."

"Now I can be happy," Jasmine said softly. "Thank you, Grandmama! I do not know what I should do without you. May I never have to know it!" She hugged Skye hard.

"Nonsense, my darling girl," Skye O'Malley de Marisco said. "I shall be with you for many a year yet. I am just now skirting the edges of old age, but there is a great deal of living left in me! A great deal of living indeed!"

At dawn the next morning the family and their guests crowded themselves into the chapel at Queen's Malvern. As there were but four carved oak benches within, most were forced to stand about the room, in the rear, and out into the hallway. The rising sun lit the stained-glass windows, casting shadows of red, blue, gold, rose, and green that gave the place a magical glow. Upon the marble altar with its Irish lace cloth sat a gold crucifix which was flanked by tall gold candlesticks burning pure beeswax tapers.

The bride, radiant in her apple-green silk gown with its charming gold adornments, was escorted by her proud grandfather. Adam looked extremely handsome in his elegant suit of dark green velvet. He beamed with pride, and tears shone in his blue eyes as they traversed the narrow aisle. He and Skye had been in India when Velvet had married Alex. He had not had the privilege of giving his daughter away, and had always felt the loss of that singular, special moment. When Jasmine had asked him to do the honors for her, he had been overwhelmed with delight, and readily accepted.

Now as they reached the altar rail, which was carved around with grapevines, he bent down to place a kiss upon his beloved granddaughter's cheek, even as he put her hand into the hand of a besotted Rowan Lindley.

Jasmine smiled at him, and reaching up touched his cheek tenderly with her other hand. "I love you, Grandpapa," she told him softly.

Adam stepped back to join Skye, the tears now slipping quite unashamedly down his cheeks. Wordlessly, his wife handed him a handkerchief, squeezing his hand in hers as the Church of England priest began to speak the beautiful words of the marriage ceremony.

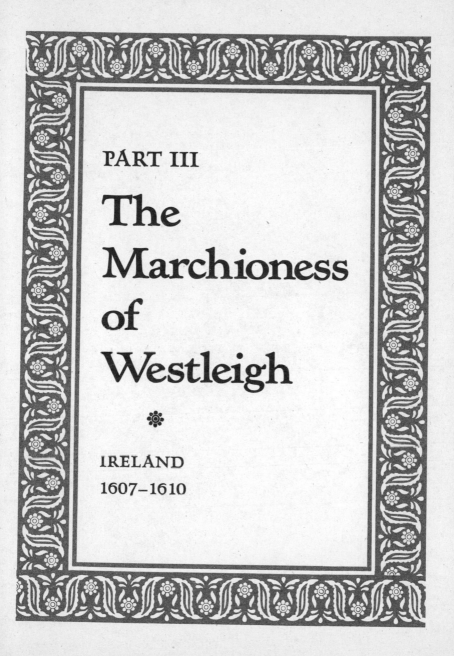

PART III

The Marchioness of Westleigh

❊

IRELAND
1607–1610

❀

15

❀

In the summer of 1608, in the garden of Rugaiya Begum, a young European gentleman came to speak with the late Mughal's eldest widow. She greeted him politely. He was a diversion in the otherwise drab existence of her days. He was a factor of an English trading house, she had learned.

"Why do you come to me?" she asked him. "I have no influence with the Mughal. He is not my son," she explained. Too often Europeans did not realize that Akbar had had many wives. Because she had been his first wife, they assumed she was Salim's mother.

"I have been told that you are very fond of your gardens, gracious lady," the young gentleman said. "My name is Alain O'Flaherty. I seek no favors of you, but recently there came into my possession some particularly fine rosebushes." He paused. "*English roses*. They flourish more freely than do the roses of India," Alain O'Flaherty said. "Knowing of your love for roses, I thought to perhaps bring these two bushes to you, gracious lady. I had to make a trip to Lahore on business matters, and though you modestly claim no influence with the Mughal, your friendship is important to me."

"What are these bushes called?" she asked him. "One is white, I see, the other red. Do they have names, good sir?" Am I growing mad, Rugaiya Begum wondered, or is this gentleman trying to tell me something?

"The white bush is called the Jasmine rose, gracious lady. Note that it bares a faintly elusive scent similar to the night-blooming jasmine flower. The red is named for the Marquess of Westleigh, a most worthy gentleman," he told her.

"Ahh," she said, and arose to examine the bushes in their porcelain tubs. Her head lowered, her fingers playing with the deep green leaves, she said in a voice so low he barely heard her, *"Is my daughter happy?"*

Alain nodded and replied in equally low tones, "We are cousins, gracious lady. She is married to the Marquess of Westleigh, and was, when our grandmother's fleet set sail from England last February, already great with child."

Rugaiya Begum straightened herself and said to Alain O'Flaherty, "Your bushes are of an excellent quality, good sir. You may bring me more of these English roses when they are available. I should like to see a garden full of them, Allah willing!"

He bowed. "I shall do my best, gracious lady," he promised. *"God willing."*

She watched him as he departed her presence. He could not know how his visit had cheered her. It was August ninth, and Yasaman, her beloved daughter, was eighteen this day. A tear slipped down the old begum's face. In all the years she had lived in India, Yasaman had never allowed a birthday to go by that she had not gifted her Mama Begum. Yasaman would never know that today she had given Rugaiya Begum her best gift of all. The knowledge that she was safe and happy once more.

• •

The young Marchioness of Westleigh awoke early at Cadby on the morning of her eighteenth birthday to find her bedchamber filled with flowers. "Rowan, have you gone mad?" She laughed happily as her husband entered the room carrying their daughter in one arm and a squirming red and white spaniel puppy in the other. "Give me India. She will want her breakfast at once or her little Mughal temper will burst forth," Jasmine said, and bared her breast, causing her daughter to grunt eagerly in anticipation.

Rowan Lindley dumped the puppy upon the bed and handed Lady India Lindley to her doting mother. "I have been mad with happiness ever since we married, my love," he said. "I wish you would find a wet nurse for India. She takes far too much of your time, and I wish to do that."

Jasmine put her daughter to her breast and the baby suckled noisily, now content. "Soon," she promised him. "What did you get me for my birthday, Rowan?"

"You will have to wait until your birthday dinner, madame," he told her with a smile. " 'Tis a most special gift, I promise you."

"Did your going to London have anything to do with my gift?" she wheedled him. "Is this why you left me for almost three weeks?"

He chuckled. "In time, Jasmine. In good time you will know everything you desire to know, but not until tonight! For now, be satisfied with this charming puppy I have bought you. Her name is 'Feathers,' and eventually, I am certain, she will learn not to pee on the bed." He scooped the puppy up with a rueful grin. "Rohana! A cloth!"

Jasmine shook her head at him, but she was laughing too. Rowan was always bringing her gifts of one kind or another, be it an occasion or no occasion. The one thing he would not give her, however, was jewelry, the only exception being her wedding ring.

"I could not possibly give you anything as magnificent as what you already possess," he told her honestly. "Between the separate pieces and the caskets of gemstones you hold, there is nothing left for me to give." She had to agree, but of all the jewelry she owned, the wedding band he had given her was her most treasured possession.

India's nursemaid arrived to take her little mistress. After Jasmine kissed her daughter's dark, downy head, she waved her off. "I'm starved!" she announced. "I think I may be breeding again, Rowan. 'Twill be a son this time, I promise you! We cannot allow Tom and Sybilla all the glory with their lads. My mother simply dotes upon them."

"Your grandmother dotes upon India," he replied. "Should you have another child so quickly, my love?"

"Why not?" she demanded of him. "I am healthy. Besides, my lord, you cannot seem to keep your cock in your breeches for very long when we are together," she teased him. "A puppy is but a little birthday gift. Have you nothing bigger for me?" She had not fully replaced her chamber robe, and flaunted her bared breasts at him.

"Madame, you are a shameless creature," he told her, pretending an outrage he was far from feeling. Indeed, if he was feeling anything, it was pure and unadulterated lust for his wife. His delicious, naughty, and totally uninhibited wife. The randy beast between his legs stirred.

Jasmine saw the movement beneath his nightshirt and she giggled. Though they both continued to sleep together in the nude, they dressed in the morning for the sake of their servants' modesty.

Although it would not have disturbed Rohana and Toramalli to see their master and mistress as God had fashioned them, Cadby's English servants would have been shocked. They were just now becoming used to the idea of having Adali as their majordomo. Many of the servants at Cadby had been elderly when Jasmine arrived sixteen months ago as her husband's bride. She had retired most of them to cottages and replaced them with those of her own choosing who had known no other mistress. Only the cook, a plump, middle-aged woman, remained, and she, poor creature, was completely in Adali's thrall.

Jasmine threw back the bed covers and smiled invitingly. "Come back to bed, my lord. Why the sun is even now just barely up."

"I am bound to take the gentlemen hunting," he said.

"This early?" She slipped a hand beneath his nightshirt, fondling his stiffened rod and pouch.

"Jasmine!"

"Yes, my lord?" Her fingers tangled themselves within his bush, tickling him.

"You will make me late," he protested weakly.

"You will be later if you do not come into this bed and give me a little gift," she teased mischievously. "Do I no longer attract you, Rowan, my love, that you will not dally with me of a morning?"

He glanced toward the windows. "It does look like rain," he reasoned. Her hand was driving him wild. "Perhaps a few minutes will not matter, you incorrigible little witch!" He pulled away from her and yanked his nightshirt off, then threw himself upon the bed.

Giggling, Jasmine scooted away from him, pulling her own garment fully off and sticking her tongue out at him. "I am not incorrigible," she said. "I am the very model of a good English wife!"

"Your aunt Willow is the model of a good English wife," he answered, laughing. "You are deliciously, naughtily, delightfully incorrigible." Tackling her, he flung himself atop her and kissed her soundly, sheathing himself within her even as he did so.

"Oohh, you are a terrible beast," she murmured, running her tongue across his lips.

" 'Tis a beast you like well," he teased her back, moving on her slowly at first and then more quickly as their mutual crisis drew nearer. "Ahhh, sweetheart!" he groaned as he filled her with pleasure.

"Rowan, my love!" she answered, sighing gustily with a shudder. "I adore you, husband, and I should even if you were not the most wonderful lover any woman could have!"

He lay pillowed upon her breasts for a few moments and then reluctantly arose. "I would rather remain here abed with you, Jasmine, and you know it, but we do have guests. You invited them. *All of them!* Even now your grandfather, your stepfather, your brothers, your uncle, and Tom are making their way downstairs that I may take them hunting this morning. As their host, I cannot fail to appear and do my duty, having done it here with you now!"

"Oh, villain!" She threw a pillow at him as he left the room, laughing, to quickly bathe and dress. Jasmine lay back amid her pillows. She loved him. Aye, she did. When she had married him, she had not been certain that she was going to truly love Rowan Lindley, but after two years of marriage she knew she did indeed love him. Was it a deep and abiding love? She was not certain, but she had to admit that she was happy. Her mind turned to more frivolous things. *What had he gotten her for her birthday?*

The weather was lovely and warm and Jasmine had arranged for her birthday celebration to be held that evening upon the green lawns of Cadby overlooking the river Avon. Paper lanterns had been strung through the trees, and a high board and tables had been set up with a view of the river. The day being a long one, archery butts had been placed about for sport. Jasmine's brothers were playing a game with a ball, dashing around and shouting noisily.

"Have you no control over those wild creatures?" Skye demanded of Velvet. "Sandy is fifteen and certainly past games. Why is he not at court? How do you expect him to get ahead if he does not make the proper friends? He will not find them at Dun Broc."

"Sandy will be the Earl of BrocCairn one day," Velvet

told her mother irritably. "He's a Scot, and not an Anglicized Scot like those who hang about the court currying
favor with the king. Court has changed, Mama. 'Tis not like
it was in the queen's day. I want no children of mine there.
It has become a cesspit of immorality."

"My lads went to court and lived to be gentlemen," Skye
said sharply. "The court has always been a dangerous place,
Velvet."

" 'Tis different today, Mama, than it was in your day,"
was the reply.

"My *day?*" Sky looked mortally offended, and seeing it,
Jasmine hurried to defuse the situation.

"The king, they say, Grandmama, is partial to handsome
young men these days. 'Twas not always so, my stepfather
tells me, but 'tis now." She sighed dramatically. "I think
perhaps Mama is correct in keeping Sandy and the others
from court. I would not want one of my sons—if I had sons—
involved in such goings-on. Don't you agree?"

Skye looked at her granddaughter and chuckled. "You
know better than any of them how to get around me, Jasmine de Marisco Lindley. Aye, I agree with you. You make
it impossible not to agree with you. Ah, you would have
driven old Bess Tudor mad, even as I did in 'my day.' "

Jasmine kissed her grandmother's cheek. "I may be breeding again," she said. "I wanted you to be the first to know
after Rowan. I told him this morning before he took the
gentlemen hunting."

"I am not surprised," Skye replied. "You can scarce keep
your hands off each other, my fine young marchioness, but
should you have another babe so soon after India? 'Tis not
easy, I know."

"Perhaps if India had been a son instead of a daughter,"
Jasmine said thoughtfully, "but Tom and Sybilla have two
lads already."

"Nonsense!" Skye told her. "India is a wonderful child,
and if you had none but her you would be fortunate."

"This will be a son," Jasmine said, "and then I shall rest upon my laurels for a time. I love children, Grandmama! I want a houseful of them. Besides, did you not produce Uncle Ewan and Uncle Murrough within fifteen months of each other? And Uncle Robin's little brother who died was born the year after he was, wasn't he?"

"Murrough and Ewan could not be helped. I knew no better. As for Robin and my wee John, God rest him, I was young, and I was a foolish woman in love with a fascinating man," Skye said, defending herself.

"So am I, Grandmama," Jasmine said softly. "So am I!"

Skye O'Malley de Marisco put a loving hand upon her favorite grandchild's cheek and said, "May your happiness come sooner and stay forever, my darling girl. You are so like I was at eighteen."

The gentlemen had an archery contest while the servants brought the food from the kitchens. It was more of a picnic meal than a formal dinner. There was fish caught that morning in the river, a roe deer roasting over an open pit as well as a suckling pig. There were capon and rabbit pies; beef and pheasant; beets, carrots, and turnip from the gardens; loaves of fine white bread; tubs of butter; and a variety of cheeses. Fresh fruit in large silver bowls decorated the tables: peaches, pears, apples, and grapes. There were cakes soaked in marsala wine; puddings of eggs, dried fruits, and bread with clotted cream. The best wine from Archambault filled the goblets, although some among the guests preferred Cadby's fine ale instead.

They ate in a leisurely fashion, and when at last the tables had been cleared, a moon was rising over the river, dappling the placid waters with a pearly iridescence. Jasmine's family had gifted her throughout the day. Velvet had given her daughter all the exquisite jewelry Akbar had once given her.

"I have never been able to wear it since my return, as you must understand," she said. "It is a part of my life that is so far from me I can barely remember it, but I do remember some things that might make an interesting tale for your children one day. When you were four and half months of age—India's age, in fact—your father learned that gifts were appropriate on each of the twelve days of Christmas. These emeralds were my first day's gift. On the third day he gave me this carved ivory box filled with these strands of pink pearls. The sixth morning he presented me with diamonds; on the tenth a necklace of rubies with matching bracelets," Velvet told her daughter, sliding the jewels through her fingers. "On the twelfth day of Christmas I was weighed three times. I received my weight in gold, silver, and precious gems. They are now all yours, Jasmine. They have not seen the light of day in many years. Wear them and be reminded not just of Akbar, but of me as well and the love we once shared. A love, my dearest, that gave us you."

"Mama!" Jasmine kissed Velvet sweetly. "When India is older I shall enjoy telling her that story of her grandmother and grandfather. She will be a most proper little English girl, but I do not want her to forget that other part of her heritage. That is why I called her India. It is unlikely she will ever see that land."

"Do you miss it?" Velvet asked her daughter.

"Aye, but not greatly, and less as time goes by. Perhaps if I had not had a family to come to here it would have been different for me, but even Toramalli and Rohana have grown used to England, and as for Adali, he would never go back even if he could," Jasmine said.

Wearing the rubies her father had once given her mother, Jasmine smiled. Gazing about the lawns at the small part of her family gathered tonight, she felt a deep sense of contentment.

Sybilla and Tom looked every bit as happy as she and Rowan were. Petite, elegant Sybilla was plumper than she had been just two years ago, but she did not seem to mind, and certainly neither did Tom. Her Gordon brothers were growing up so quickly, Jasmine thought, looking at them. Sandy was fifteen now, almost a man, and Charlie at thirteen was not far behind him. Neddie, chubby with baby fat at six, was as thin and wiry at eight as his ten-year-old twin siblings were.

Uncle Padraic and Aunt Valentina had left their children at home, but Bessie and Adam Burke had a third sibling, young James, a russet-haired toddler just a year old. Her stepfather Alex was showing silvery strands in his hair, but her mother seemed to grow lovelier with the passing years, even as did her grandmama. The patriarch of the family, however, seemed ageless, Jasmine thought. Her grandfather, but for his white hair, was young as ever despite his seventy-eight years.

"You are happy," Rowan said, kissing her shoulder as he came up next to her. "I am happy, too, my love, and 'tis because of you. Would you like your birthday gift now," he asked her, "or shall I put it aside for another time, mayhap?"

"No! No!" Jasmine cried, and then she said to her assembled guests, "Rowan has a special gift for me. He would not present it to me until tonight." She stood and grabbed at his pockets. "Where is it?"

He laughed. "Such insatiable greed, madame." He signaled to a waiting footman, who came forward with a silver tray upon which rested a sealed parchment. "This is yours, Jasmine, my love. A most happy birthday and may we celebrate many more together."

Jasmine reached for the parchment. "What is it?" she asked, breaking the seals. Her eyes scanned the document.

"Well?" demanded her grandmother. *"What is it?"*

"It is a deed to three thousand acres, a village called Maguire's Ford, a small castle in a place called Ulster. Where is Ulster?"

Skye grew pale. "It is in Ireland," she said.

There was a deathly silence among the guests, and then Jasmine said, "What is wrong? Why are you all so quiet?"

Finally Padraic Burke spoke up. "King James is giving away land that does not belong to him, Jasmine. 'Tis stealing."

"That is not so!" Alex Gordon replied angrily. "James Stuart is an honorable man."

"What else would you call it?" Padraic Burke said quietly. *"Maguire's Ford, Alex.* 'Tis Maguire land and not James Stuart's land to parcel out as he desires. The Irish are being driven off their property and it is being repopulated by foreigners—Scots and English."

Alex Gordon looked at his brother-in-law as if Padraic had just lost his mind. "What the hell has Ireland to do with you?" he demanded. "You were raised in England. You possess an English estate given you by an English queen, Padraic."

"Both my mother and father were Irish," Padraic Burke said. "My maternal grandfather was Dubhdara O'Malley of Innisfana; my paternal grandfather, the McWilliam of Mid-Connaught. I was raised in England because Elizabeth Tudor willed it so. I possess English lands because she gave them to me to replace my hereditary lands, which she stole from me and turned over to English settlers. It pains me to see the same thing happening to others who, God help them, are not even compensated for their loss, and if I were not an English-raised Irishman, Alex, I should still object to what is happening in Ireland because it is wrong!"

"Rory O'Donnell, Hugh O'Neill, and Conor Maguire left Ireland almost a year ago," Alex Gordon replied. "Barely ahead of the king's men coming to arrest them for treasonous activities, so 'tis said. Papers were found in Dublin Castle implicating them all in some new plot. Sir Cahir O'Doherty testified against them himself."

"My God, you cannot believe that dirty traitor!" Padraic Burke said. "The charges were fraudulent, as any intelligent man could see. O'Doherty lied and then revolted against the king this April past, when, having served his vile purpose, he decided his reward wasn't great enough."

"Well, he is dead now," the Earl of BrocCairn said matter-of-factly, "and the assizes just held have declared that the bulk of the land in Fermanagh, Tyrone, Coleraine, Donegal,

Cavan, and Armagh be forfeited to the king because of the former owners' treasons."

"Guilty or innocent, the Irish must suffer," Padraic said.

"Jasmine's grant is one of the very first given," Rowan Lindley told them. "I was able to gain it through the kindness of the queen. A friend at court wrote me that these lands would be parceled out by the end of the year. The competition for the acreage is quite hot. The northern bishoprics of the Church of Ireland will get some. Trinity College in Dublin will have a share. The more deserving of the Irish who fought on the king's side, some former landowners, and the lord deputy must all be compensated first."

"But why did you want this land for Jasmine?" Skye finally spoke up. "The king will give much of it to the hangers-on and the adventurers who have besieged him ever since he came to the throne. I can only imagine the sort of people they will send to Ireland. It is a disgraceful project, and no decent person should want to be connected with it in any way! I was born Irish. It is true I have lived most of my life in England. Fate made it so, but my heart is Irish, and my soul is Irish and will ever be, no matter where I reside!"

"I never meant to offend you, madame," Rowan Lindley said quietly, "but I wanted a very special gift for my wife's eighteenth birthday. Jasmine has all the jewelry a hundred women could want due to her heritage. There was nothing I could think of until my friends at court told me of these lands. They are in Jasmine's name alone, not mine. I went to Queen Anne and explained my plight. It was she who gained the king's permission and his signature on the documents making Jasmine Lindley, Marchioness of Westleigh, the new owner of Maguire's Ford, and all that goes with it."

"What is the land like?" Jasmine asked, surprising them all.

"Very fertile," was her husband's reply. "A small village with a church surrounded by meadows, gentle hills, well-watered and green. 'Tis on the shores of Lough Erne. The castle, I am told, is several hundred years old, but livable."

"I shall raise horses there," Jasmine said. "We will take Nighthawk, the young stallion Grandpapa gave us as a wedding gift, and the best of the Cadby mares to be bred to him."

Skye looked distressed but said nothing. What could she say that would have made any difference in the matter? The deed was done.

Padraic Burke, however, said angrily, "How can you speak so dispassionately about raising horses on stolen lands, Jasmine?"

Jasmine looked at her uncle, puzzled, and then she replied, "Uncle Padraic, it is the way of the world that one people conquer another, and when that happens, the land exchanges hands. It has always been so in India. Has it not been so here? I seem to remember from the history lessons that Father Cullen taught me that your Irish ancestors came to Ireland from another place. The English who inhabit this land today are descendants of both Norman and Anglo-Saxon invaders who came to these shores, not of the original tribes who once populated it. Nothing is graven so deeply in stone that it cannot be changed.

"Your Irish lands were taken from you, and Clearfields, the lands you now possess, once belonged to someone else. What happened to them? Did you ever consider them or their feelings?" Jasmine turned to her husband. "Thank you, Rowan. I am thrilled with my gift! I have never had one better in all my life." She then kissed her husband, and turning about, looked at her family defiantly. "I shall keep my new lands."

Skye shook her head. "Her damned logic is flawless," she said, "and I find I cannot argue with it." She gave a sharp bark of a laugh.

"*Mother!*"

"Do not glower at me, Padraic Burke. God, how like your father you look at this very moment! Jasmine is correct. As long as O'Donnell and O'Neill and Maguire remained, their lands were theirs. By fleeing, they forfeited everything. 'Twas winner take all, and Scottish James did."

"They made it impossible for the chieftains to remain," Padraic answered his mother. "When O'Neill submitted to James Stuart in 1604, the English, though allowing him to retain the lands, took control by installing all the adjuncts of English government. They appointed sheriffs for each county; coroners; justices of the peace. They weakened the authority of O'Neill and the other earls. My God! What could they do but leave? There was no other choice!"

"How typically Irish of you, my son, but Irish pride offers little comfort to the widows, the orphans, the dispossessed. There are always choices, Padraic," Skye told him. "When Elizabeth Tudor stole your lands, and broke her promise to me, I made her give you English lands, that you not be dispossessed, and vulnerable.

"O'Neill and his cohorts could have stayed, but they departed because times were changing and they did not want to change with the times. They left their people alone, helpless, to struggle on while they reestablished themselves in comfort in Rome. The Irish, God help them, cannot survive on tales of their former greatness, Padraic. If they continue to live in the past, allowing the bards with their songs of Celtic heroism, and the Church with its narrow view of life, and the English in their arrogance to rule them, Ireland will never know peace again, nor will her people be truly free."

"Your mother speaks wisely, Padraic," Valentina Burke told her husband. "Remember that the survival and prosperity of this family has always been first and foremost in her mind and heart." She turned to her niece. "When will you go and see your new acquisition, Jasmine?"

"Not until after the baby is born," Jasmine told her. "This one will be a son, I am certain of it!"

"I felt the same certainty when I was carrying little Adam after Bessie was born," Valentina told her, and suddenly the tension surrounding Rowan Lindley's gift was dissipated.

Several musicians came from the house and, settling themselves, began to play the spritely tunes that were the accompaniment to the country dances so favored by the family. Partners were chosen and the evening progressed upon a more pleasant note.

On Rowan and Jasmine's second wedding anniversary, Lord Henry Thomas Lindley made his first appearance. He was a healthy, ruddy baby with a large appetite and sweet disposition. Although, like his elder sister, he possessed a headful of dark curls, his eyes were blue like his mother's. India Lindley had their father's golden eyes.

"You see," Jasmine said smugly. "I told you I would give you a son this time! Is he not the most beautiful baby you have ever seen?" She touched her son's cheek, and he turned his perfect little round head toward her breast, nuzzling at her. "Just like his papa," she teased Rowan with a smile.

Rowan Lindley gazed down at his son. The boy was big, they said, and yet he looked so small. Bending, he kissed his wife first and then the baby's soft head. There were tears in his eyes as he said to Jasmine, "Thank you, my love." He could scarce believe his good fortune. After all those years with his tragic first wife, he had finally found happiness with Jasmine and their children.

The Marchioness of Westleigh nursed her son for a month before turning him over to a wet nurse, a young farm wife carefully chosen by both herself and Adali. The majordomo knew all the local gossip down to the smallest detail and was able to tell his lady that Mistress Brent had lost her new baby to a spring flux but was healthy herself and produced excellent milk that had already nourished three other children. The wet nurse was required to live at Cadby, but as her husband had both a mother and a younger sister in the house, he did not mind.

"I hate giving little Hal to someone else," Jasmine fussed.

"You have no choice if we are to visit your estates in Ireland," Rowan told her. "I can go alone if you desire, my

love, and you come next year. Henry is too young right now
to travel with us."

"I know," she sighed. "Hal will be safe with Mistress Brent.
Adali and Rohana are here to oversee his and India's safety.
I want to go to Ireland with you, Rowan. 'Twill be the first
time since the children came that we have had time alone
to ourselves," she told him with a mischievous smile. "Do
you not want to be alone with me?"

Rowan Lindley smiled and shook his head. "Incorrigible,"
he lamented. "You are simply incorrigible, madame, and I
hope that you will never change. To think of you turning
into the very model of your aunt Willow terrifies me." Pulling her into his arms, he kissed her dark head. "I love you,
Jasmine, but then you have always known that I did, from
the moment I first laid eyes upon you that May morn."

Jasmine closed her eyes and reveled in his warm strength.
He loved her and she loved him, more than any man she
had known. Her grandmother had never explained to her
that a deep and abiding love is one that grows with each
passing day with a sharing of joined lives, with the birth of
wanted children. How could Skye have explained that to
her? She had to learn it herself by living it.

The Marquess and Marchioness of Westleigh departed
Cadby in late June, traveling north and west to Holyhead,
where they embarked upon the *Cardiff Rose* for Dun Deal-
gan, which the English called Dundalk. The vessel had been
refurbished that it might carry the Marquess of Westleigh's
great traveling coach; his carriage horses; the stallion Nighthawk, son of Adam de Marisco's great stud Nightwind; and
six young mares of the best breeding stock.

" 'Tis a short voyage," Michael Small assured them, "and
the weather is better than I've seen it in years here in the
Irish Sea. We'll be there in two days' time, m'lady. So you're
to live in Ireland are ye?"

"Not all year, Captain Small," Jasmine told him. "Cadby

is the Westleighs' seat, but 'tis said Ireland is a fine place for
raising horses. The Irish are said to be good with them."

"Aye, so I've heard," the ship's captain replied. Good with
horses and good at fighting, he thought silently.

"This is the very boat that brought me from India," Jasmine told her husband nostalgically. "Toramalli, Rohana,
and I shared this cabin for all those months. It was our little
home."

"And it got littler with every mile of sea we traversed,"
Toramalli said dryly. "The day we reached London, it was
snowing and as damp a cold as I had ever felt piercing my
bones, m'lord, but I was delighted to leave the *Cardiff Rose*,
for all she'd brought us to England in safety. I certainly never
thought to set foot upon her again!"

He chuckled. " 'Twill be but a little while, Toramalli, or
so Captain Small assures me. You're becoming a most traveled woman."

"Humph," came the reply, but Toramalli was smiling. She
and Rowan Lindley had become fast friends.

As they sailed into Dundalk Bay, there was a light rain
falling. The *Cardiff Rose*, which normally would have an-
chored in the bay, was made fast to the dock so that the
coach and horses could be off-loaded. The agent appointed
by the crown to oversee the estate until its new owners arrived was awaiting them.

As Jasmine and Rowan disembarked, he came forward, a
small, thin wisp of a man with sharp features and colorless
hair, with eyes to match. He bowed, perhaps a bit too obse-
quiously, and identified himself. "My name is Eamon Feeny,
m'lord. Welcome to Ulster. I stand ready to serve yer lordship in any way that I can." He bowed again and smiled,
showing a mouthful of rather bad teeth, and as an afterthought, snatched the cap from his thinning hair. "I've
brought a coachman for ye."

"Very good, Feeny," Rowan Lindley said, "but before we
proceed further, you must understand that the Maguire's

Ford plantation belongs not to me, but to my wife, Lady Lindley. Unless otherwise instructed, you will accept her authority in all matters pertaining to the plantation. Do you understand?" The marquess regarded the agent carefully. He did not like the look of the man at all, but what the hell did James's government in London know about the agents it appointed in Ulster? Very little, the Marquess of Westleigh suspected. Unless this Feeny proved himself a decent sort, he would have to go.

Feeny looked aghast at the Englishman's words. *A woman in charge of Maguire's Ford?* It had to be a joke. Women were good for several things—cooking, sewing, fucking—but a woman capable of overseeing an estate? It simply wasn't possible. He cocked his head questioningly at his new master and said nervously, *"Lady Lindley in charge?"* Of course it was jest. The Englishman had to be testing him in some way.

The marquess, however, nodded his head slowly at the horrified royal agent. "Aye," he drawled.

"Is the coachman familiar with the roads, Master Feeny?" Jasmine asked. "How long will it take us to reach Maguire's Ford? I am told the castle is habitable. Is that so? And you have, of course, engaged servants for me, haven't you?"

Feeny gaped at her like a fish out of water, and it was then that Jasmine noticed a very tall young man with a shock of red-gold hair standing nearby. As their eyes met, he stepped forward and bowed to her with an elegance that would have befitted a courtier at Whitehall.

"Rory Maguire, m'lady. I've been engaged to drive yer coach. There's not a road between here and Lough Erne that I'm not familiar with, I assure ye. 'Twill take two days of hard driving if we start now, and three if we don't." He bowed again to her, his blue eyes twinkling.

"Then we had best get started now, hadn't we?" Jasmine said. "But I prefer to ride one of my horses rather than sit in that stuffy coach. Can you ride, Rory Maguire?"

"Aye . . . m'lady."

"And you, Master Feeny. Can you handle the coach by yourself? Of course you can!" she answered for him. *"Handle the coach?"* Feeny sputtered, outraged. "Madame, I am the royal land agent, not some stableyard servant!" The woman was obviously featherbrained, and shouldn't be allowed to make any decisions outside of her house and garden. He pulled himself up straight and looked disapprovingly at Jasmine. To his shock, however, she did not wither beneath his stern condemnation; rather, those strange blue eyes of hers grew hard for a moment as she looked at him.

Then she turned to her husband. "Rowan, you take Nighthawk and I'll ride my Ebony. Toramalli, you will ride in the coach. Master Feeny, take care—Toramalli has been with me since my birth and is very dear to me; you must treat her as you would your own child." Jasmine smiled brightly at the royal agent. "Choose yourself one of the mares, Rory Maguire," she told him, "and use her gently. With luck, her children will soon be gamboling in Irish meadows and growing fat on green grass."

Rory Maguire was unable to suppress a grin. The English lord must really have his hands full with this spirited filly. He cast a surreptitious glance at Rowan Lindley from under his outrageously thick eyelashes as he was choosing his mount. The man looked hard. She was obviously no English rose, but the Irishman could see that Lord Lindley had a soft spot in his heart for his beautiful wife. *And who was she?* She had the look of Ireland about her, and yet there was something else there as well.

Jasmine thanked Captain Small for a safe voyage.

"I can get you back to England anytime you want to go, but the seas get nastier between England and Ireland as the year grows older. Not all voyages are as smooth as this one," he said.

"I may want my children once I see what kind of conditions we face at Maguire's Ford," Jasmine told him. "I do not like leaving them for a long period of time, and we must really remain a year or two if we are to begin a successful breeding farm."

"Before September if you can, m'lady, else it will be too hard on the little ones," Captain Small told her, and then he bowed respectfully.

The coach horses were being affixed into the carriage traces by two young grooms who had come with them from Cadby.

"The mares can be attached behind," Jasmine told them. "Do not drive too quickly, Master Feeny. I do not want my little beauties winded." She patted each of the mares affectionately.

Mounting Ebony, Jasmine smiled at her husband and then looked to Rory Maguire to lead the way. They were but a few miles from the bay when the sun began to shine, but several miles farther on the day clouded over and it once again began to rain. It was not really a heavy English rain. Rather, it was a fine mist of a rain.

" 'Tis what we call a *soft* day," Rory Maguire told them.

"Is it always like this, Maguire?" the marquess asked.

"Aye, most days, m'lord. Ireland is both a magical and a most confounding place, or so the English have found," was the bland answer from the young man.

"Are you the Maguire of Maguire's Ford?" Jasmine asked, coming directly to the point. It was one thing to talk about invaders and lands changing hands, she thought, but it was another to come face-to-face with your property's former owner.

"There are many Maguires in Ulster, m'lady," he told her. "The former owner of your lands was Conor Maguire himself. He departed Ireland almost a year ago. You'll not be embarrassed in any way, I assure you." His blue eyes remained fixed on some distant horizon.

They rode for several hours before Rory Maguire led them into a farmyard. A tall young girl, her eyes lowered, ran out with tankards of ale while a smaller child followed, carrying a tray upon which were slabs of freshly sliced bread covered with cheese.

"There's no inn such as you are used to," the Irishman told them. "I arranged with this farmer's family to feed you at midday."

"I must get off my horse," Jasmine said, and Rowan quickly dismounted to help his wife. "Is there no place we may sit ourselves, Master Maguire, while we eat? It is beginning to rain again, and while I do not mind riding in the rain, I do object to picnicking in it." Jasmine shook her damp green velvet riding skirts irritably. She hated riding sidesaddle, and wet skirts were the most damnable inconvenience.

"We can eat inside," Rory Maguire said, "but 'tis a poor place, like many in Ireland. It may shock yer ladyship."

"Your solicitude is commendable, Master Maguire," she told him, annoyed. This coachman was behaving in a manner far above his station, but then she had been warned that the Irish were an overproud race.

The farmer's house was stone with a thatched roof. Inside they found a dirt floor and a single fireplace around which were gathered a very pregnant woman and several children. The inhabitants looked wide-eyed at the visitors, and the woman drew her children closer as if afraid. There was but a single table in the room and several benches.

"I should like to sit by the fire and warm myself, please," Jasmine said to the woman, who looked at her terrified when she spoke.

"She does not understand you," Rory Maguire said. "She speaks only the Irish tongue." He then turned to the woman and from his mouth came what sounded like a stream of gibberish to the English lord and his wife. The woman answered back, and then the Irishman said to them, "Mistress Tully bids you welcome to her home and asks that you sit by her fire. She apologizes for the meal, but 'tis all she has."

Jasmine smiled at the woman and her children and, settling herself on a bench by the fire, replied, "Tell her, Master

Maguire, that I appreciate her hospitality. Her bread is the best I have ever tasted."

He repeated her words to their hostess in the Irish tongue, and the woman asked him, "What manner of Englishwoman is this, Rory Maguire, who *asks* to come into my house instead of just barging in and then thanks me?"

"Her ladyship is the new *owner* of Maguire's Ford, Sosanna Tully," he told her. "I've just met her myself, but I'd say she's not quite what we expected to have at Maguire's Ford." Then he grinned at Mistress Tully and set about demolishing the food.

When they had finished and were ready to leave, Rowan Lindley asked, "Has the woman been paid for her kindness, Master Maguire?"

"Usually English travelers just take, m'lord, no offense, but 'tis truth," Rory Maguire responded. "If, however, you were of a mind to give her a little something, 'twould help. Her husband is no longer with her, and she's been struggling along alone. Her bairn is due any minute now, as you can surely see."

"Where is her husband?" Jasmine asked.

"Sean left Ireland with his chieftain last autumn, m'lady."

"Leaving his wife and children behind?" Jasmine was outraged.

"She would not leave the land," was the answer. "There are many like her now. Women alone with their children, tending their farms as best as they can. As long as their men are alive, they cannot take new husbands, and so they struggle on alone. As long as she can pay her rent to her English landlord, m'lady, she'll survive. Mistress Tully is luckier than most. Her farm is on the road to Erne, and she feeds the travelers passing by. Sometimes she takes them in overnight. It helps her to manage while her children work the land."

Rowan Lindley pressed a coin into Mistress Tully's hand. Jasmine saw the glitter of gold and smiled, remembering Mistress Greene at the Rose and Crown.

But Rory Maguire spoke up. "Do not give her gold, m'lord. She will not be able to pass the coin for fear of being called a thief. If you would be generous, let her have whatever coins of silver or copper you have in your pockets. Those she can exchange with ease."

"Tell her to keep the gold for an emergency," Rowan Lindley told the Irishman, and then he gave the woman several additional coins, those of copper and silver as Rory Maguire had suggested.

The Irishman explained to their hostess, adding, "The man's a damned fool, I'm thinking, Sosanna Tully."

"Nay, he's a real gentleman, Rory Maguire, and his wife a woman with a heart. Thank them for me." Then she bobbed a curtsey at the Marquess and Marchioness of Westleigh, favoring them with a slight smile as well. "If more English were like them, life might not be so hard."

"And if wishes were horses, beggars would ride in grand style, Sosanna Tully," he answered her with a grin. " 'Tis not likely to happen."

They spent several more long hours upon the road, until Jasmine was frankly quite tired. "Does it never get dark in Ireland?" she demanded irritably of their guide. As much as she disliked riding inside the coach, she would have welcomed it right now, but to her great annoyance, it was nowhere in sight.

" 'Tis summer, m'lady, and we have long days, marvelous twilights, but very short nights," he told her with a small smile. She had a temper, did she? The woman had to have Irish blood in her.

"Where are we to stop the night, Maguire?" Rowan Lindley asked.

"I've arranged for you to stay with Sir John Appleton and his wife, m'lord. 'Tis just over the next hill," was the reply.

Jasmine felt slightly more cheered by that revelation and looked about her with more interest. The on again, off again rain had disappeared, and the day was really quite beautiful now. About them the green hills rolled gently away toward the horizon. There were vast meadows of grass that boded well, she thought, for their enterprise. Here and there a single gray stone tower rose up, but none seemed inhabited. Occasionally they rode through a cluster of cottages, and wherever those cottages appeared there was always a small square with a cross in its center and a church. The land, however, seemed sparsely populated.

Sir John Appleton was a portly gentleman with a fat red face. His wife was equally plump but pasty-faced. They welcomed their guests effusively, ordering their servants about harshly, fretting over the fact that the coach had not arrived as of yet.

"They'll be here in good time," Rory Maguire assured them.

"Who is this person?" Sir John demanded.

"Our guide," Rowan Lindley replied.

"He is Irish," Sir John said suspiciously.

"This is Ireland," the Marquess of Westleigh answered, amused.

"Young, able-bodied Irishmen in Ulster who did not flee with their traitorous masters are usually troublemakers," Sir John said ominously. "What is your name, fellow?"

"Rory Maguire, if it please yer lordship," and the younger man bowed in a servile manner, bobbing up and down several times.

"*Maguire?* 'Tis a common enough name in this country," Sir John said, mollified somewhat by the seemingly humble manner of the man before him. "Well, Maguire, you may sleep in the stables and cook will give you your supper in the kitchens."

"Aye, m'lord, thank ye, m'lord, very good, m'lord," Rory Maguire responded and backed himself out of Sir John's presence.

"A sly fellow, I can see, and not to be trusted, but then none of these Irish are," Sir John told his guests. "Won't have 'em in the house, even as servants. No! No! Not even as servants!"

"They make terrible servants," Lady Appleton confided to Jasmine. "Lazy, dirty people, and they'll steal anything that isn't nailed down, they will. Are you bringing your servants from England, Lady Lindley?"

"Only a few," Jasmine said. "I had intended employing local people for the most part. I felt that it would be best."

"Oh no, my dear!" Lady Appleton said in a concerned and motherly tone. "If you do not bring your own people, then you must hire only English, or Scots at the worst, but frankly I think them not much better than the Irish, for all our dear King James is a Scot."

They sat down to supper and, as the meal was served, Rowan Lindley asked his host, "Where is your home in England, sir?"

"Oh," Sir John replied, "I had only a little house in London. I was recently knighted by the king himself for my services to the crown."

"And what were those services?" the marquess asked.

"I was secretary first to the old Lord Burghley himself and then to his son, Sir Robert Cecil, the Earl of Salisbury. When I was knighted, I was given this plantation of five hundred acres here in Ireland," Sir John explained. "Our daughter and her husband will be joining us next year, as will our son, who is a merchant in London."

He made himself sound quite important, the marquess thought, and the less knowledgeable might have been impressed. Rowan Lindley was not, for he knew that old Lord Burghley and his son had at least half a dozen secretaries to serve them.

"I shall be so glad to see our children," Lady Appleton twittered. "There is no social life here at all, and we have been so lonely since we arrived. One can hardly be friends with the Irish. Why, most of them don't even speak English, and when they do, one can barely understand what they are saying. A most ignorant people, but what can one do? We have served England our whole lives and now we have come to Ireland to help civilize it for the king."

Jasmine choked on a mouthful of soup and cast her husband a despairing glance. Later, when they had finally escaped their host and hostess and lay abed, she said, "I have never heard such arrogance! If all the English coming to Ireland are like them, no wonder the Irish don't like us. It is not easy to be a conquered people, but to have to take such abuse from one's conquerors in addition is untenable, Rowan. I do not want to treat the people on our land like that."

"You will not, Jasmine. I know you well and your heart is kind. You will try your best, but be warned, my lady, that there are those who will not respond even to your kindness and will be your enemies. Do not be surprised by them. Be hard. For those people will only understand you if you are. 'Twill not be easy, and most like Feeny do not think a woman capable of managing a large estate. I, however, know you can."

The coach arrived shortly after they had gone to bed, and they heard Toramalli creep into the dressing room off their bedchamber where she was to sleep.

"Toramalli." Jasmine called her in. "Have you eaten?"

"Aye, though that dough-faced creature who is the lady of the house was not of a mind to feed us so late, until I told her my mistress would be very angry to learn we were mistreated."

"I had begun to fear for you," Jasmine said.

"We are lucky to be here and alive," Toramalli answered, her dark eyes showing her annoyance. "That Feeny fellow is the most incompetent man who ever lived, m'lady. The grooms finally had to take the reins, and I, God help me, was forced to ride with the fool while he puffed himself up like a frog and croaked of his importance in the scheme of the world. Please, m'lady, let the coachman sit upon the box tomorrow even if you ride, else I kill that Feeny fellow!"

Rowan chuckled from beneath his coverlet. He had rarely heard Toramalli discourse so passionately about anyone other than her mistress. Rolling over, he grinned at the servant. "We'll make him run behind the coach with the mares tomorrow, Toramalli, I promise you," he said.

Toramalli giggled and, curtseying to her master, went to her bed. " 'Twould be a good thing if he did," she was heard to say as she closed the door behind her.

"She adores you," Jasmine said with a smile.

"As much as her mistress?" he teased her.

"No one," Jasmine said firmly, "could love you as much as I love you, James Rowan Lindley, my dearest, darling lord and husband."

"Then show me," he replied wickedly. "I will wager these bedsprings have not been well sprung in ten years or more, madame, if ever."

"Have you not had enough of riding for today, my lord?" she said mischievously, already purring beneath his caressing hands.

"With you for a mount, I could ride forever," he declared.

"Well, perhaps a short trot about the park," she considered, "but remember, my lord, that the dawn comes very early in Ireland, or so Master Maguire would have us believe. Ummmmm, Rowan! Ahh, yes!"

He had unlaced her chemise and fastened his mouth about a nipple. Slowly his tongue encircled the nub, flicking at it teasingly. She murmured softly beneath his delicious ministrations, her fingers kneading at his tawny head, feeling the prickle of the hair upon his neck rising with his arousal. She arched against him, murmuring with pleasure as his hands began to caress her body.

"Flawless," he groaned, lifting his head and meeting her gaze. "You are absolutely flawless, my love." He nuzzled against her slightly rounded belly, alternately kissing and tasting the flesh while his hand fondled a plump breast.

"Did you not have enough supper, my lord?" she teased him.

"There was no sweet," he replied mischievously, "and I cannot sleep without a sweet. Any sweet will do, of course!"

"Oh, villain!" She smacked at him playfully. "Ohhh, Rowan!" she then cried as he entered her in a single stroke. She was surprised by the suddenness of his action. "Ohhh, my love!"

He moved smoothly upon her, his mouth finding hers and kissing her passionately. Jasmine sighed happily, letting herself relax, drifting with the delightful sensations that each stroke of his mighty manhood evoked within her. Mindful of her admonition that the dawn came early, he brought her to complete fulfillment, taking his own pleasure at the same time; and then together they fell asleep, limbs entwined.

They departed Lord Appleton's house shortly after first light. Rory Maguire sat upon the coachman's box, to Tora-malli's great satisfaction. Master Feeny had his own mount, for which Jasmine thanked providence.

"Look at the way he saws at that poor beast's mouth with his reins," she said to her husband. "He is surely no horse-man."

Hearing her, Rory Maguire grinned to himself. Feeny was a pitiful specimen to begin with, but seeing him upon a horse was a comical sight at the least. Rory whipped up the carriage horses, knowing that the English milord and his beautiful wife would have no trouble following.

"We'll be home by suppertime, my beauties, and there will be a fine dry stable for you and a full measure of oats."

It rained all day. It was a chilly, steady downpour that turned the road to mud, but Rory Maguire was a skilled driver and brought the horses along at a steady pace. Finally, he drew the great traveling coach to a halt and waited for the mounted party to draw abreast. "Just over the next hill is Maguire's Ford, m'lady. There isn't much to it. Just a wee village and a small bit of a castle, but the land has good grass. 'Twill be a grand place for your horses, I promise you."

"Maguire! Do not get above yer station," Master Feeny said sharply. "Ye were hired to drive the coach. 'Tis not yer place to tell his lordship about Maguire's Ford. I shall do that."

"Do you come from Maguire's Ford, Master Feeny?" Jasmine inquired. The little man annoyed her with his airs.

"Me? Gracious no, yer ladyship! And if I did, I'd not admit it, for 'tis a poor place to come from, I'm thinking. No, no! I was born and raised in Belfast. 'Tis a fine civilized town, Belfast!"

"If you were born in Belfast, Master Feeny, then pray, how can you tell me anything about Maguire's Ford, which you indeed seem to hold in great contempt? A closed mind, I have found, is seldom a good judge of anything, but perhaps I mistake your words," Jasmine said.

Rory Maguire swallowed back his laughter. The little crown estate agent was clearly almost apoplectic with his outrage, but he dared not voice it. Ye'll not be with us long, I'm thinking, the tall Irishman predicted.

"M'lady, I have carefully inspected the plantation and its premises thoroughly. I can tell you whatever you need to know, I assure you," Master Feeny insisted. "Indeed, I know my duties better than most. There has never been a complaint about Eamon Feeny."

"Let us move on," the Marquess of Westleigh said quietly. "I am most anxious to see Maguire's Ford, and I know my wife is as well."

At the top of the next hill they stopped once more. Below, a beautiful body of water stretched out before them, blue and inviting in the sudden late afternoon sunshine.

" 'Tis upper Lough Erne," Rory Maguire told them. "The lough bisects Fermanagh and runs the length of it, turning into a river of the same name that pours out into Donegal Bay at Ballyshannon."

"It's lovely," Jasmine told him. "In India my home was also on a lake, and beyond it were great snow-covered mountains. Your green hills are softer and somehow more friendly."

"*India?* What and where is that place?" he asked.

"It is a land across the eastern seas, six months in traveling time from London," she told him. "I was born there."

"Are ye not English, then, m'lady?" Rory Maguire was puzzled.

Jasmine thought a moment. "My father was Indian. My mother is half English, half Irish. I suppose that makes me Anglo-Irish and Indian."

"I knew that there was Irish in ye," he said, chuckling. "Would ye happen to know where yer grandmother came from, m'lady?"

"My grandmother is an O'Malley from Innisfana in Connaught," Jasmine said. "I do not even know how far from here that is, do you?"

"*An O'Malley!?* O'Malley is a famous name in Connaught," he told her. "Your grandmother's home is several days' ride, on the sea." Then Rory Maguire caught himself. They should not be speaking like friends. He pointed down the hill. "There is the village of Maguire's Ford, m'lady, and the castle just beyond it on the lough. Can you see it?" He gently urged the horses on again, leading them down the hill.

They entered the village and it was oddly silent.

"Where are all the people?" Jasmine called to Master Feeny. The stone cottages were obviously deserted, and weeds were growing in the little kitchen gardens. There were no barking dogs, nor cattle, nor sheep to be seen.

·"I have had them driven off, m'lady. You'll not be wanting Irish in your village. It can be repopulated as soon as you desire with God-fearing English or Scots settlers. There are plenty waiting to come."

"*You drove my villagers off?*" Her voice was high with her

outrage. "Where are they expected to go, Master Feeny? Certainly there were whole families—women, children, oldsters—and you drove them off? How long ago? Get them back at once!"

"They were Irish, m'lady," he said, in a tone that implied she was a silly woman and could not possibly understand.

"*This is Ireland*, you pompous fool!" Jasmine shouted furiously. "Now answer me! *Where are my villagers?*"

"In the bogs, in the woods, I suppose, m'lady. 'Tis not my business to keep track of a bunch of peasants," he protested rudely.

"Go back to Belfast, Master Feeny," Jasmine said coldly.

"*What?*" The estate agent looked startled.

"Go back to Belfast," she replied. "Your services are no longer required by me. You are dismissed. There is no law that says I must keep you on, and if there were, I should defy it!"

"My lord, I must protest," Master Feeny said, red-faced.

Rowan Lindley shrugged his shoulders. "I told you, Master Feeny, that Maguire's Ford belongs to my wife. Her wishes will be law on this plantation, and there is nothing I can or will do about it. In any event, I believe her right in this matter. It was very foolish of you to drive the villagers away."

"They are Irish malcontents," Feeny attempted once again to explain. "They will cause trouble with their ungovernable attitude and their wicked popery rebels."

"You are a fool, Master Feeny," Jasmine said angrily. "I condemn no one before I have given them a chance, and as for their wicked popery, I agree with our late queen. 'There is but one Lord Jesus Christ. The rest is all trifles.' I do not believe there is but one correct road that leads to God's front door. I think there are many roads!"

" 'Tis mightily tolerant of you, your ladyship," Master Feeny said nastily, "but the priests will be no more tolerant of your silly attitude than a preacher from the Church of

Ireland would be. As for the villagers of Maguire's Ford, if you allow them back here, they will defy you at every turn and cause you nothing but trouble. Do not say I did not warn you. You'll see!"

"You may stay the night, Master Feeny," Jasmine said coldly. "In the morning be on your way." She turned away from him and said, "Rory Maguire, I have no doubt you know exactly where the people of Maguire's Ford have gone. Find them as quickly as possible and tell them to come home. I have need of them, and I will be fair to all who give me their honest loyalty. Those who cannot had best be on their way, for I will deal harshly with insurrection of *any* kind."

"They'll want a priest," he warned her.

"They can have one. I even have one in mind for them," she said with a small smile, and then she lowered her voice so only he might hear her words. "My great-uncle, Michael O'Malley, is the bishop of Mid-Connaught. He will supply me with a cleric."

"Michael O'Malley is one of the few important churchmen who has remained here in Ireland despite the English," Rory Maguire said admiringly. "Most have fled to Paris or Rome." Then he caught himself. Jesu. The woman had a way of putting a man at his ease. He had to be more careful. "Let me bring you to the castle, m'lady, m'lord. Then I shall go out and see if I can find your villagers. They'll not have gone far despite Master Feeny. They've all lived here for generations and would not know where else to go."

"Does the castle have a name, Master Maguire?" Jasmine asked him as she rode beside the coach through the village.

" 'Tis called Erne Rock, m'lady. You see it sits upon a wee promontory and is surrounded by the waters on three sides. From the lough 'tis said to resemble a rock, and hence its name, Erne Rock Castle," he told them. "You will soon see how one might gain such an impression."

"How old is the castle, Master Maguire?" Jasmine queried him.

"Oh, I couldn't be certain, m'lady, but 'tis said to have been here for over two hundred years or more. It began as a tower house, the customary type of home for the Irish gentry, and was added on to over the years until it became what you see before you."

The coach drew up before Erne Rock Castle. It was a small building, but obviously it had been well-maintained over the years. Its entry was across a drawbridge that lay over what appeared to be a moat. Upon closer inspection, however, Rowan Lindley could see that the narrow land side of the castle had been dug open, allowing the lough to surround it. When the drawbridge was raised, the castle was fairly impregnable. He smiled admiringly. "Clever," he said softly. "Very clever indeed."

The Marquess of Westleigh encouraged his horse onto the drawbridge and over it into the courtyard of the castle. The others followed. Like the village, the castle was also deserted. "Did you drive the house servants off as well, Feeny?" he said wryly to the estate agent. "You'll get no supper, I fear, if you did. Though my wife is expert in many things, the culinary arts are not among them."

"The servants were ordered to remain, my lord, I swear it!" the beleaguered Feeny protested. "Their disobedience just proves my point. These Irish peasants are not to be trusted."

"Master Feeny," Jasmine said, aggravated by his attitude. "Are you not Irish yourself?"

"I am a Belfast man, m'lady," Feeny replied proudly, as if that should explain everything.

"Belfast is in Ireland," Jasmine answered solemnly, "or it was the last time I inquired. Is that not so, my lord?"

"Aye," Rowan drawled. "You are correct, my love."

Maguire climbed down off the coachman's box and, opening the carriage door, helped Toramalli out. "If I might have the loan of a horse, my lord," he said to Rowan, "I'll go and track down the poor souls who belong to Maguire's Ford for ye and tell them to come back."

"The castle will be open, I assume," Rowan Lindley said.

"Aye, my lord, it will be," was the reply.

"Then go along, Maguire," the marquess instructed him.

Rory Maguire untied one of the mares from behind the coach and, without even bothering to saddle the creature, swung himself upon its back and rode out of the castle courtyard, guiding the animal with his knees, a hand gripping the mare's mane.

"Yer mad to trust that one!" Feeny said. "He'll murder you in yer beds before 'tis all done, I'm certain."

"Where did you find him, Feeny?" the marquess asked, curious. Rory Maguire was no servant, or farmer for that matter, Rowan Lindley knew. He was too well-spoken, and his hands, although hard, were not a workman's hands. Feeny, of course, would not have realized any of that. He had not the wit.

"He was just here, m'lord, when I arrived to take possession of Maguire's Ford in the king's name," Feeny told the marquess. "He seemed more intelligent than the others. When I offered him employment, he was happy to take it. Still, he's Irish and you must be careful."

"Hmmmmm," Rowan Lindley replied, and then he said, "Come, Master Feeny, we must get the horses into the stable and the coach unhitched. You may help me. Jasmine, my love, you and Toramalli go into the castle and see just what it is you have been given by Jamie Stuart. Having never been to Ireland, I just took what I was offered. It does not seem to be a bad bargain, though I feared it might be. Come along, Feeny! The horses."

Eamon Feeny seethed with his outrage as his stubby fingers struggled to undo the buckles and straps that fastened the horses to the coach. What kind of people were these English lords? Certainly unlike any he had met before. No real gentleman would unfasten his own coach animals and lead them whistling into the stables as this Marquess of Westleigh was now doing. And what kind of man allowed his wife to give orders to others, except, of course, female servants?

The woman was obviously a witch. An evil, ungodly creature who would tolerate popery. A foul creature who had lured her husband into his besotted state with her beauty, and probably ensorceled other men as well. That Rory Maguire looked as if he'd like to get his hands under her fine silk skirts. Ohhh, yes! He saw this Marchioness of Westleigh for what she really was. She could not fool Eamon Feeny. If it were not for Lady Lindley, he would still be retained as land agent of Maguire's Ford. Ahh, the shame of it! That he, Eamon Feeny, should be dismissed from a position—*and by a woman!* He would be a laughingstock in all Belfast if he returned now. The damned woman had ruined him! What was he to do? He glared fiercely after Lady Lindley and her serving wench.

The two women entered the dwelling to find a warm home with well-polished floors on the upper level and well-swept stone floors on the main level. There were two fireplaces in the Great Hall, which was not much bigger than the Family Hall at Queen's Malvern. There were fireplaces in all the bedchambers. The furniture was golden oak, well-rubbed with beeswax over the years. It had a comfortable look and feel to it.

"Well," said Toramalli, "I'm surprised. From all I had been told, Ireland is a barbaric place, and yet it seems not so, m'lady."

They were standing in the largest of the bedchambers. Jasmine was looking out over the fields through the lead-paned windows, watching Rory Maguire as he rode away. "Hmmm, what, Toramalli?" she said.

Toramalli followed her mistress's gaze and then said, "This Ireland is not so awful after all, is it? I think you should send for the children. Adali and Rohana would like it here too." Then she giggled. "That Master Maguire is a handsome fellow, m'lady, isn't he? I never saw hair so red-gold, and those blue eyes of his are just like the sapphires in the Stars of Kashmir necklace, aren't they?"

"I did not notice his eyes as you did, Toramalli," Jasmine teased her serving woman. "His hair, however, is something else. I think you could probably see him coming on a dark night with that hair."

The object of their discussion had now disappeared from view. Rory Maguire rode like a man who knew just where he was going, and in fact he did. Entering a wood, he stopped the mare and whistled several times. He was answered by another whistle, and a young boy came forth from the thick trees.

"M'lord! Yer back, then. That's a fine mare yer riding!" The boy reached out and ran an appreciative hand over the mare's neck.

"Indeed, and I'm back, Brian lad. Is everyone just where I told them to go? I've brought the new English landlord with me." He gave an amused chuckle. " 'Tis a fine lady, my lad. What do ye think of that?"

"*A lady?*" The boy's mouth fell open and then he said, "Naaah! Yer jesting with me, m'lord! 'Tis no lady!"

"Aye, Brian, it is. Lady Jasmine Lindley, the Marchioness of Westleigh. She's a rare one, I can tell ye, even on our short acquaintance. She's sent that Belfast man packing already. He's to go at first light, she says."

They moved deeper into the woods until finally they came to a clearing within which was the half-camouflaged mouth of a large cave. All about them, suddenly, people appeared, calling out to Rory Maguire, nodding and smiling. He dismounted the mare and tied it to a tree. Then he gathered the people together within the mouth of the cave and spoke to them.

"I want ye to all go home now," he said. " 'Tis safe, I promise ye. I should not tell ye otherwise."

"Have the English gone then, m'lord?" a voice in the crowd asked him. "Are we safe from the English, and are the earls back, then?"

"Nay, Fergus, the English are not gone. I've brought the new landlord of Maguire's Ford to Erne Rock myself this day."

" 'Tis a lady, he says," Brian burst out, unable to contain such important news.

There were murmurs of discontent among the Irish gathered before Rory Maguire, but he held up his hand and said to them, "It is indeed a lady who has been given these lands. A beautiful young woman whose grandmother was an O'Malley. She says she will be fair to all who give her their loyalty, and I believe her. She will return a priest to the church, and she has sent that Belfast man on his way."

"Maguire's Ford belongs to the Maguires," the man called Fergus protested. "How can ye, the lord of Erne Rock, give it over so easily? When the earls return—"

"They will not return," Rory Maguire said bleakly.

A low keening began among the women.

"Do not say it, my lord," Fergus begged, tears in his eyes.

"O'Neill is in Rome and the others are with him," Rory Maguire said quietly. "O'Donnell has died of a broken heart, they say. I heard it at Dundalk from a ship's captain just in from Spain. They will not return. I knew it the day I rode to Lough Swilly with my kinsman and overlord, Conor Maguire, to bid him farewell. I could see it in his eyes that he knew it too. O'Neill and his wife Catherine, their sons; O'Donnell, his brothers, and his sister Nuala; my cousin Conor. They knew as they set foot on that French ship and gazed out over the waters at our blessed hills that they would never see Ireland again. They will not return, my lads. *Not ever*."

Many in the crowd surrounding Rory Maguire wept openly and unashamedly at his words, and then Fergus said, "We can still fight the English, my lord. We can still fight them!"

"To what purpose?" Rory Maguire asked him.

Fergus and many of the other men looked astounded at

their lord's words. This was Rory Maguire, as fierce a fighter
as any man would want for a son. What was the matter with
him? What was he saying?

He saw their puzzlement and told them, "We have been
fighting the English for over four hundred years or more,
my lads. O'Neill, O'Donnell, Conor Maguire, and their ilk
have left us in a grand gesture of defiance, but we must
remain. Do we remain to live or to die? If we attempt to fight
the English as we have always fought them, then we die. If
ye would die, Fergus, then drown yerself in the lough and
save yer family further misery. If ye would live, however,
then listen to me.

"My branch of the Maguire family have held this land
and Erne Rock for the Maguire chieftains since the beginning. I will not leave ye, nor will I leave my lands. The
English landlord says she will not mistreat ye. I truly believe
her. If ye do not return to the village, she will be forced to
repopulate it with Scots or English. She has brought a stallion and several mares as fine as this one I rode. She means
to raise horses on my lands, and she means to stay. I mean
to stay as well."

"Does she know who you are, my lord?" a voice inquired.

"Nay, but she probably suspects. I know her husband
does," he told them with a small smile. "The man is no
foppish courtier, but I believe he will let me be as long as I
do not challenge his authority and I continue to be useful
to him. I could almost like him, lads, if he were not so
damned English."

There was a great deal of murmuring among the crowd,
and then one of the women spoke up. "I'm going home
now," she said loudly in firm tones. "I've lived at Maguire's
Ford my entire life, and my family before me for so many
generations we cannot count. I'll not be kept from my home
any longer, and that's an end to it. Children!"

"I'll not have it," Fergus answered his wife angrily. "I'll
not have my children raised in a heretical faith, woman!"

"Did I not mention that there will be a priest in the church?" Rory Maguire said slyly. "I know I did, but ye were not listening."

"*A priest?*" Fergus was disbelieving.

"I told ye that our new landlord has an O'Malley for a grandmother. She says her great-uncle is Michael O'Malley himself, the Bishop of Mid-Connaught, and that she'll request a priest of him for our church. If she does this for us, then she proves her good faith, doesn't she?"

"Wellll," Fergus considered.

"And when have I ever lied to ye, lads?" Rory Maguire demanded.

"*He never has!*" Fergus's wife, who was called Bride, spoke up and, hands on ample hips, looked around her. "Can any of you deny it?"

"Nay!" came the collective reply from the crowd.

Bride gathered her children about her and, with a toss of her head, walked from the clearing. "I'm going home," she repeated, and to no one's surprise the other women, with their children, began to follow after her. Bride had always been a leader in the village.

"Put out the fires in the cave, lads," Rory Maguire said quietly, "and let's all go home. Fergus? Ye'll come?"

"Ye, my lord, I'll come, but if there's any trouble from this new English landlord, I'll be cutting a few English throats and not have a moment's guilt over it, I tell ye."

Watching from the windows of the master's bedchamber, Jasmine de Marisco Lindley was not in the least surprised to see the villagers begin streaming forth from the woods.

❀

16

❀

Rory Maguire returned to Erne Rock in the twilight.
Behind him lights were already twinkling in the cottages and
smoke rose from their stone chimneys. Beside him walked
an enormous gray dog who was obviously as familiar with
the territory he trod as was his tall, flame-haired master.

"Good evening, m'lord," the newly restored guard at the
gate said pleasantly as man and beast passed him, crossing
the drawbridge into the courtyard.

Rory Maguire nodded affably, and climbing the flight of
steps that led into the castle itself, he headed for the Great
Hall. There he found the Marquess and Marchioness of
Westleigh, seated at the high board eating their supper. The
servants stood attentively, watchful of the new owners' every
need. The dog, moving away from his master, stretched its
great length before one of the two fireplaces, and, with a
sigh, closed his eyes in utter and rapt contentment.

"Come and join us," Rowan Lindley said, "though
it seems strange to ask a man to sit at his own table,
Maguire."

"This place belongs to Conor Maguire, my lord," was the reply.

"But held by your family for him for how many generations?" Rowan Lindley replied. "Do not fence with me, man. I am not stupid."

"Why did you not go with your kinsman?" Jasmine asked him as he seated himself at her right side.

"If it were your holding, m'lady, would you have deserted it, and its people?" he responded. "I can fight with the best of them, but I'm tired of fighting. I have done little else my whole life. When my cousin decided to leave Ireland it was because he, too, was sick and weary of the battles. His action will be seen by history as noble and magnificent. Mine will not be remembered at all. That will suit me well. I am no high and mighty nobleman, m'lord. I am a simple Maguire chieftain. If I must humble myself before you, then I will, if you will but let me remain with my land, and treat my people with kindness."

"But can you live with the unassailable fact that you no longer *possess* this land, Maguire?" Rowan Lindley asked him, leaning across Jasmine to make eye contact with the other man. "Can you accept my wife's rule, for that is what you must do if you would remain? I do not know if I could, were I in your place, Maguire." His gold eyes carefully scanned the Irishman's face for answers.

"Let me manage the estate for you, m'lord, m'lady," Rory Maguire asked them. "The people will listen to me and give no difficulty, I promise you. They are good folk, but change will come hard for them. Everything they knew is gone, and they must begin afresh."

"And if we say no, Maguire? What will you do then? I do not know if it is wise to allow the former lord of Erne Rock to remain. You could undermine my wife's and my authority here," the marquess said.

"If you would have me go, m'lord, then I will go," Rory Maguire told them quietly, "and I will instruct the people to give you their loyalty and their respect. They will obey me as long as you treat them fairly. 'Tis little to ask. We are not enemies, you and I. We are simply three people caught up in something not of our own making."

"I want him to stay," Jasmine said suddenly, and she put a beseeching hand on her husband's arm, looking into his face. "I know far better than you, Rowan, my love, the pain of exile. I will not send this man from here. But be warned, Rory Maguire," Jasmine told him, her gaze now moving from Rowan Lindley's to meet the Irishman's, "if you betray me in any manner, I, and not my husband, will seek you out and destroy you. I am a king's daughter, Rory Maguire. I have been taught when and how to be hard. Do not be misled into believing because I am a beautiful woman that I am not capable of being fierce. It would certainly be the biggest and the last mistake you ever made." Then her tone softened. "What is the dog's name? I've never seen one so big."

"Finn, m'lady. He is a wolfhound. I swear before God that I will never betray you," Rory Maguire answered her solemnly, thinking as he gave her his fealty that he did indeed believe her. Her magnificent turquoise-blue eyes had grown hard as flint as she spoke to him. *A king's daughter, was she?* What king? And what land? It would be interesting to learn more about this king's daughter with the O'Malley grandmother. "Ye'll not forget the priest, m'lady, will ye?" he asked.

"Nay, I'll not. Is the gatehouse habitable, Rory Maguire?" she demanded of him, and when he nodded, she said, "Then make it your own. That is where I want you to live. If there is anything within Erne Rock of particular sentimental value to you, you may take it. I had to leave so much behind," she mused softly.

It was settled, and so quickly, he thought, amazed. "What would ye have me do as my first duty to ye, m'lady?" he asked her.

"In the morning," she said gravely, "you will escort Master Feeny from my lands, Rory Maguire. I somehow think you will enjoy it," and her eyes twinkled.

"Yes, m'lady," he told her with equal seriousness, but his lips were twitching with suppressed amusement. 'Twould be a fine start to a new day to hustle the irritating little Belfast man from the place.

The encounter, however, proved to be far more unpleasant than he had anticipated. Feeny, after a night in the stables contemplating the abuse he believed himself subject to, was filled to the brim with vitriol. He did not hesitate to vent his anger at Rory Maguire.

"Think yer clever, Maguire, don't ye?" he snarled. "Think ye've got yer new English masters wrapped around yer finger with yer oily charm. Ye'd best toe the mark, or they'll turn on ye as quickly as they did on me. Then where will you be?"

"I find Lord and Lady Lindley pleasant and reasonable people," Rory Maguire responded stiffly. "Come on, Feeny, and get on yer pony."

Feeny clambered onto his mount and grinned nastily at the younger man. "Especially the woman, eh, Maguire? Well, ye'd best watch yer step there! She's trouble, I can tell ye. If it weren't for her, I'd still have my position. I know her kind. Uses a man, and takes all he has, then discards him. Look at her poor husband, enchanted with her he is, and doesn't see her evil, but I do."

"Begone!" Rory Maguire said impatiently, and smacked the rump of Eamon Feeny's pony. Feeny grabbed his reins tightly as the beast bolted off. "And don't let me catch ye on this plantation again, Feeny. Yer not welcome here!" Maguire watched with relief as the Belfast man disappeared down the road.

The summer passed while the mares that the Lindleys had brought to Ireland grew fat on the lush grass growing on the plantation and four of the six swelled with new life. Nighthawk was proving a good stud. Little India and her baby brother were sent for, and came with Adali, Rohana, and their wet nurses in attendance. India was soon toddling on fat little legs among the children of Maguire's Ford, while her brother rolled over in his cot for the first time and grinned, drooling, every time he spied his mother. Fergus Duffy was dispatched to the Bishop of Mid-Connaught, and returned several weeks later with Cullen Butler in tow.

Jasmine hugged her cousin warmly. "Grandmother said that Great-Uncle Michael would not let you leave him, but I did return you to Ireland so you might have your little stone church, cousin Cullen. Now you do! The people of Maguire's Ford have been eagerly awaiting you. There are over a dozen babies to be baptized, and at least two unions to be properly blessed. Isn't that so, Rory Maguire?"

"Aye, m'lady, it is."

"Cousin Cullen, this is Rory Maguire, the estate manager. My cousin, Cullen Butler, is the priest I told you I had in mind for Maguire's Ford. Father Cullen was my tutor in India."

The priest shook hands with Rory Maguire. "Lady Lindley," he said, "has told you of her childhood, I assume."

"Aye, Father, she has. I would have never imagined such a place as she describes existed. It sounds like a fairyland."

"India is certainly exotic, and exciting, but it is no fairyland, my son," the priest told him.

Afterward he asked Jasmine, "Just who is this Rory Maguire, my child? Where did you come upon him?"

"Actually the royal estate agent, Feeny, brought him to us. Feeny was such a fool, cousin Cullen. He did not realize that Rory Maguire was the lord of Erne Rock. Rowan and I quickly perceived it, for he is better spoken than most, and can speak the English. He asked to remain on this land, and we agreed. He is a good manager. His father, the former lord of Erne Rock, his mother, and a younger brother, along with his three sisters, their husbands, and families, left Ireland last year with Conor Maguire. Only Rory remained. Is that not sad, cousin Cullen? Why can the Irish not learn to get along with the English? One nation conquering another is nothing new."

Cullen Butler smiled at Jasmine's reasoning. He had almost forgotten what it was like to be Irish during all those years he had spent in India, but these last months at home had brought it all back to him. He despaired for the people of this green island. Religion now divided them, but even when it had not, there had been an antipathy between English and Irish seemingly too great to overcome. The Irish race was simply not one to easily, if ever, accept a conqueror. The Anglo-Norman peoples seemed to antagonize the Celts more than anyone else could. Although he had lived with it most of his life, even Cullen Butler did not understand why that was so. It simply was.

The priest settled comfortably in Maguire's Ford. He was finally doing what he loved best, ministering to the souls of his fellow man. The babies, some as old as four years, were quickly baptized, the two unions formally sealed, and just in time, he thought, for both of the brides were visibly great with child. He celebrated mass daily each morning and vespers each evening. Rowan and Jasmine rarely came, for the marquess was Church of England, and Jasmine—Cullen Butler smiled to himself—like her grandmother, trod an individual path toward God's door. He knew he should admonish her, but he did not.

Jasmine desired to remain in Ireland until her mares had been safely delivered of their colts. "At least until next year," she told her husband. "There is a magic to Ireland, and I like it."

"But the children are English," he said. "I want them raised in England. Ireland is never safe for very long."

"Do you think the hereditary earls will return, my love?"

He shook his head. "Nay. Not this time. The heart is gone out of them, as it would have gone out of me had I been in their position. The Irish population, however, will chafe beneath our rule; and sooner or later the matter of religion will rear its ugly head, Jasmine. Then there will be fighting again. I do not want you or the children here when that happens. The past history of this land is one of incredible cruelty on both sides when they war. It would be difficult to get to the sea and make an escape should fighting break out. For now I believe there will be peace, but in a few years . . ."

"India loves it here so," Jasmine noted.

Her husband laughed. "Aye, she does. She races about the village just like all the other little children, but she is not like them, Jasmine. She is Lady India Anne Lindley, the eldest child of the Marquess and Marchioness of Westleigh. She must learn her place."

"Rowan!" Jasmine didn't know whether to laugh or to scold him. "India is not even two yet. Surely there is time for her to 'learn' her position."

"You were taught from birth to never forget that you were a king's daughter, Jasmine," he said quietly, reminding her.

Now she did laugh. "So I was," she agreed, "but this is such a different place, Rowan, that I thought perhaps I might raise our daughter more gently. Look how happy and healthy she is."

He smiled, but said, "She looks like a little urchin. No shoes, no napkin on her, and when she wants to pee, she lifts her skirts and squats with all the other little girls. 'Tis hardly dignified."

Jasmine giggled. "But it is far more healthy and practical than running about with a soggy napkin, Rowan."

"You are going to defend her, I can see," he said.

"Oh, my love, if she plays with the village children an-other year it matters not. Little ones are very adaptable, and she will readjust to life in England again just as easily as an apple falling from a tree."

Autumn came, and with it several mild and surprisingly sunny days. The Marquess and Marchioness of Westleigh rode out each afternoon with Rory Maguire to inspect their mares as they grazed contently in the meadows. The scene was bucolic: the villagers working in the nearby fields, the children playing, while in the background Lough Erne shimmered deep blue. The sight never failed to fill Jasmine with a sense of overwhelming contentment.

"Will there be enough grain for winter this year, Maguire," the marquess asked one afternoon as they walked their horses down the road, "or shall I send to market for more? I want no hunger among either the animals or the villagers."

" 'Tis been a very substantial harvest, m'lord. We can more than make do with our own grain," Rory assured him.

"Mama! Mama!" Little India came from the fields, her skirts flying, trailed by Bride Duffy's eldest girl, Sine, who was ten and had taken to watching over the child.

"Barefooted as usual," Rowan said, half laughing.

" 'Tis the custom in India to be barefooted except on formal occasions," Jasmine defended her daughter.

"Well, I cannot argue with that since I like the other Indian customs you've so kindly shown me, my love," he teased her, and Jasmine blushed becomingly, remembering the passionate night they had just spent.

India had finally reached them, and holding out her arms, she demanded, "Up! Up! Mama, up!"

Sine Duffy grasped the little girl about her waist and lifted her as high as she could as Jasmine bent in her saddle, reaching out for her daughter. At that moment a shot rang out, and looking into Sine Duffy's face, Jasmine saw the young girl's eyes widen with horror even as her mouth made an almost silent O. Straightening, Jasmine turned. Her husband's mount was sidestepping nervously, its saddle empty. Rory Maguire was already dismounting, and Jasmine, her heart pounding, let her eyes slide to the ground where her husband lay, a bright crimson blossom of blood staining his doublet.

"Mama! Dia wants up!"

Jamal. His name slid unbidden into her consciousness even as she stared down at Rowan Lindley. *This was not happening.* It could not be happening. Why was her husband lying so still? Why did he not get up? "Rowan, my love!" Her voice sounded like it was coming from a great distance away. *"Rowan!"* Why was she screaming?

Rory Maguire knelt by the marquess's body. He leaned forward, as if listening for something. He felt for a pulse, but there was none. Jesu, he thought! *Jesu!*

"Rowan!"

Rory Maguire looked up into her beautiful face. "He's dead, m'lady," was all he could say to her, watching helplessly as she slid from her saddle.

"There!" Fergus Duffy came running, pointing to a man running through the brush on the slope. "Up on the hillside, Rory lad!"

Bride Duffy was immediately behind her husband. "I'll take care of her ladyship, Rory Maguire! Find the devil who did this!" She knelt by Jasmine's side, then looking up, said to her daughter, "Sine, take her little ladyship back to the castle and fetch Father Cullen. Quickly, lass, or I'll whip the flesh right off yer bottom!"

Rory Maguire quickly remounted his horse and with Fergus Duffy running ahead of him, he directed the beast up the hillside. It did not take either of the men long to spot the culprit, a small man running for all he was worth, ahead of them. Rory Maguire urged his horse ahead of Fergus Duffy, easily riding down his prey. Leaning from his horse, he grasped the man by the back of the collar and hauled him across his saddle. As he turned about, smacking the man none too gently on the head when he attempted to struggle, he heard Fergus Duffy call out to him, "I've his musket!"

When they reached the spot where Rowan Lindley had been murdered, Jasmine was regaining consciousness. For a moment confusion reigned in her eyes, but then a look of intense pain filled them. With Bride Duffy's aid she struggled to her feet, her gaze avoiding her husband's prone body.

"Here's yer murderer, m'lady," Rory Maguire said, yanking the man from his uncomfortable perch and flinging him at her feet.

"Stand up," Jasmine said to the man. *"Stand up!"* Her voice was stronger now.

The fellow struggled to his feet, glaring at her. "Ye must surely be a witch, woman, to have escaped my bullet."

"Feeny!" Jasmine and Rory Maguire said the name in unison.

"Aye, 'tis me," the little man answered them.

"Why did you kill my husband?" Jasmine asked him. She could feel her legs shaking beneath her skirts, and prayed that they would not give way beneath her. She needed her strength to deal with this.

"I did not intend to kill his lordship," Feeny replied. " 'Twas ye I sought to kill. Ye had no right dismissing me as yer agent. I've not had a day's good luck since ye did it. Yer a witch! Ye must be to have so enchanted a king into giving you a plantation this size; and yer husband who told me I must obey ye. *Obey a woman?* What nonsense!"

"Hang him," Jasmine said tonelessly.

"With pleasure, m'lady," Rory Maguire answered her.

Feeny stared at them, open-mouthed. "Ye've enchanted him, too, have ye? I must go to the authorities about this!"

"Now!" Jasmine spat the word.

"We have no rope, yer ladyship," Fergus Duffy ventured.

"Take my husband's belt, then," Jasmine said coldly, "but I want this creature dead. That he has lived any time beyond my Rowan's departure is a sin. Hang him from that tree over there."

Feeny, realizing that the village men who had gathered from the fields would obey their mistress, began to babble. "Ye can't hang me! I am a representative of the king's government! This is king's business! No! No! I am Eamon Feeny of Belfast town. No! No!"

A strong young man scrambled up the designated tree, the marquess's leather belt in his hand. Feeny was boosted into the saddle of Rowan Lindley's horse, his hands bound behind him with a strip of Bride Duffy's petticoat, and was then led beneath the tree. The belt was carefully fastened about the condemned man's neck, the long end returned to the man in the tree, who carefully drew it around a strong, thick limb, still holding it. Without a word Jasmine slapped her husband's horse upon its shining rump. The beast cantered off while the man in the tree, his arm straining, bore the burden of Eamon Feeny's swinging body.

Jasmine watched dispassionately as the Belfast man struggled, his face slowly turning from rose to red to blue. His tongue shot out of his mouth, and an unpleasant odor filled the air as his bowels emptied. Still she stood and watched, as if the murderer's own pain could ease hers, but it did not. The man in the tree looked nervously to Rory Maguire, who nodded. With a deft crack of his wrist upon the leather belt, the executioner snapped Feeny's neck, breaking it, and dropped the body into a heap upon the ground.

"It was too soon," said Jasmine bleakly, and then she collapsed, unconscious, onto the ground beneath the tree.

Rory Maguire and the villagers crossed themselves even as Fergus Duffy asked, "What do we do with the body, m'lord?"

"Bury it in the woods in an unmarked grave, Fergus. Let the grave be deep and impossible to find by either man or beast. I don't want her to ever see it, lest she remember."

"She'll remember," Bride Duffy said wisely. " 'Tis her husband, Rory lad, that's been murdered this day. She'll never forget, but yer wise to try to make her forget, poor lady." Bride Duffy's blue eyes filled with tears. "Poor, good lady to suffer so, and what's to become of the wee ones? Why, the lad will not even remember his father, and the lassie is so young too. She'll remember only because her mother teaches her to remember. Ahhhh! This is such a great tragedy!"

Cullen Butler came running up. His horrified gaze moved

from Rowan Lindley's dead body, to his cousin, still unconscious, to Feeny, at the base of the tree, the belt wrapped
tightly about his neck. "God almighty, and His blessed
Mother have mercy on us all," he said, crossing himself.
"What has happened, Rory Maguire?"

"Feeny, the former estate agent, shot the marquess, but it
was actually her ladyship he meant to kill. Her ladyship ordered his execution. We, her loyal servants, obeyed her, and
with great pleasure, I might add, Father. If ever a man deserved hanging, it was Feeny."

There was nothing Cullen Butler could say in response
that would have suited the moment. Kneeling, he gave his
cousin's husband absolution, for although Rowan had been
born into the Anglican communion, Cullen could not allow
Jasmine's husband to lie unshriven. He would have to bury
him, too, for the nearest Church of Ireland cleric was in
Enniskillen, too many miles away to be called. The priest
next moved to Feeny, and made the sign of the cross over
him, his lips moving in silent prayer.

"Don't waste yer prayers on that one, Father," Fergus
Duffy growled.

Cullen Butler then looked to his cousin. She was still pale
and unconscious. "Master Maguire," he said quietly, "could
you please carry her ladyship to the castle? Her servants can
attend to her better there. She has sustained a most severe
shock this day, more than you can possibly know." Aye,
Cullen Butler thought sadly. One husband murdered was
bad enough, but two? He did not know if Jasmine would
recover from such a tragedy. "Fergus Duffy. Are you brave
enough to carry a message to England for me? To her ladyship's grandmother?"

"I am!" came the swift answer. Though he would have
denied it with his dying breath, Fergus Duffy liked his English mistress well.

"Then come back with me to Erne Rock, and I will arrange it, but first see to his lordship's body. We cannot leave

him lying out here in the fields. The crows are already gathering for carrion."

They did the priest's bidding. Jasmine was carried to her chambers, where Rohana and Toramalli, already apprised of the events that had transpired this afternoon, were waiting to attend her. Rowan Lindley's murdered body was brought to the church and lain upon the altar to await its coffin. Adali, ever his lady's right arm, kept everyone in perfect order, including the two English wet nurses, whose first instincts were toward hysteria.

"Calm yourselves," he told them. "There is no danger, and the children need you. If you become frightened, your milk will dry up and the babies starve. All will be well, I assure you."

Rohana and Toramalli undressed their mistress and bathed her now feverish body with cool, perfumed water. Tenderly, they laid her in her bed, and took turns watching over her. A day passed. And another. Jasmine remained unconscious, barely breathing, barely moving. Then, in the night between the second and third days, she began to cry softly in her delirium. The two serving women half listened at first, but when Jasmine repeated the same words over and over again, Toramalli sought out Adali.

"You must come," she told him. "She is speaking, and yet she remains unconscious to everything about her. We are afraid, Adali."

He followed her to Jasmine's bedchamber and stood over his mistress, looking down upon her, his heart aching. She was so pale, and for all her nineteen years, she looked so young and helpless.

"We have kept her clean, and comfortable, Adali," Rohana said. Both sisters had dark circles beneath their eyes, he noted. "Now she has begun to rave, and her words frighten us. Watch with us awhile. You will see, and you will hear also. We do not know what to do."

He sat by Jasmine's bedside with them, and just as he was about to nod off with his own exhaustion, Jasmine spoke.

"Rowan. Rowan! Love me! I cannot bear it that you leave me without loving me a final time." Her eyes were tightly shut.

Adali sat straight up. Had he heard her correctly? It could not possibly be. He must be more attentive to his mistress.

"Rowan. Rowan! Love me! I cannot bear it that you leave me without loving me a final time."

Adali stiffened with shock, his brown eyes meeting those of Rohana and Toramalli.

"There is more," Toramalli said softly. "But wait."

"I will follow you, my love," Jasmine said. *"I will follow you into death rather than be without you. Oh Rowan, love me but a final time! I do not think I can live without you!"*

And Adali watched horrified as tears slipped from between Jasmine's closed eyes and ran slowly down her pale cheeks. "How long has she been crying thusly?" he asked them.

"For several hours, Adali, and with each passing hour her life force grows weaker. What are we to do? She is willing herself into death. We speak to her, but she hears us not. We have reminded her of her children, but there is nothing for her but her husband," Toramalli said, her voice edged with deep concern.

"I must think," Adali said, his brow furrowing. When the thought first came to him, he pushed it away, shocked by his own notion; but Jasmine began to cry out again, and her desperation burned into his very soul. He arose, telling the two women, "I must find Father Cullen. Remain with our mistress. I will be back as quickly as possible."

On the previous day, when it was clear that Jasmine would not quickly recover from her shock, the priest had said the mass of burial over Lord Lindley, entombing his body in the stone vault beneath the church where were buried generations of the lords of Erne Rock Castle. Now, in the hours before the dawn, he knelt before the altar in the church praying for Rowan's soul. Hearing someone enter behind him, he arose and turned to face Adali.

"We must talk," the eunuch said to him.

"Come into my cottage," the priest directed. The two men entered the small house, settling themselves before the fire, which just barely glowed with still-alive embers. Cullen Butler placed some peat bricks upon the coals, and fanned them into a flame. The room began to warm. "Is it Jasmine?" he asked, knowing that of course it was.

"My mistress is dying, Father Cullen," Adali said quietly.

"You are certain?" the priest responded.

Adali nodded. "I am, but I think I can save her. Before I do, however, you must know what is involved. I cannot bear this burden by myself. It is far too great a responsibility for me to carry alone."

"I will shoulder my part of your load willingly," Cullen Butler replied. "Jasmine is my cousin, and I love her too. Tell me what it is you must do to save her from a premature death."

Adali began slowly to explain, repeating his mistress's words to the priest, then saying, "Her body must be physically satisfied so that her mind can release its hold upon Lord Lindley. If that happens, I believe she will regain consciousness again and we can prevent her demise. Her own sense of duty to her children, to the marquess's memory, to Maguire's Ford, and to Cadby will eventually overwhelm her grief."

"Are you proposing that a man be sent into her bed, Adali?" Cullen Butler asked him, shocked by the very thought.

"I am," the eunuch replied.

"It is unthinkable!" the priest cried.

"She will die unless we do it, and she may die anyway, but I will not give her to death willingly, without a battle,

Father! I was nothing until my French father's blood gave me the opportunity to serve as her mother's eunuch. When Lady Gordon departed India, she placed Yasaman Kama Begum into my keeping, and I have never failed to do my duty toward my mistress. It was I who ferreted out Prince Salim's wicked intent toward the princess! It was I who kept her safe from him! She is the daughter I could never have! *I will not let her die!*" Adali declared with more passion than Cullen Butler had ever seen him exhibit in all the years that the two men had known each other. Adali had always gone about his duty with a calm, deliberate air. He had always been the voice of reason in an otherwise turbulent world. His great distress now was evidence of his fear.

"Why do you think such a thing would save her?" the priest asked, realizing that he was weakening in the matter.

"You lived in India long enough, Father, to learn the truth of how the mind can overcome the body. Remember the yogis on their bed of nails? The firewalkers whose feet were never burned? The holy men who could go for weeks without food or drink? And the snake charmers who could put away their fears for their own bodily safety while handling the deadly cobra snake? I think the same principle may apply here. If the princess's mind can be made to believe that her husband has come to her and made love to her a final time, I think she can recover. We cannot just stand by, Father, and allow her to die."

"I will pray by her bedside," Cullen Butler said.

"Your prayers will be certainly welcome, but whether by her bedside or in your church, what matter? And you have been praying for her already, haven't you? It has done no good, Father. God helps those who help themselves, and we may have the solution if we are but bold enough to execute it," Adali said. "Time grows short."

"Who?" the priest asked, realizing that he was giving in

to the eunuch's persuasion, and wondering if God would forgive him this apparent denial of everything he had ever been taught and was trying to pass on to others. Still, he reasoned, if Adali were right . . .

"Rory Maguire," Adali told him. "He's already in love with the princess, although I doubt he has ever dared to admit it to himself. He is a young man of great honor and good sense. We may trust him."

"Will he do it, Adali?"

"I will persuade him," Adali replied.

"Let us go, then, and find him," the priest said. "This deed had best be done as quickly as possible, and before the dawn of another day. If Jasmine is growing weaker by the hour, she may not have much time left, in which case neither do we."

The two men hurried from the priest's cottage to the gate house where Rory Maguire had taken up residence. They knocked upon the door until they were finally admitted by the sleepy Irishman. Closing the door behind them they pushed their host into his day room, and when they were certain he was awake, they laid their plan before him.

Rory Maguire flushed, startled, by their explanation of the situation and their unorthodox method for resolving it. "*I cannot!*" he cried. "My God, Father, how can you even be party to such a suggestion?"

"If you do not do as we bid you," Adali said stonily, "and my mistress dies, you will have killed her. Her death will be upon your head, lord of Erne Rock Castle. Can you live with that? Can you live with the sight of her orphaned children each day?"

Rory Maguire groaned with despair.

"You love her, lord of Erne Rock," the eunuch relentlessly continued. "Only your honor has kept you from admitting it to yourself, but I am a man who sees into the heart. I see your love for her because I love her also. I will do what I must to save her, and you must too."

"What if she awakens and finds me with her, and not her husband?" Rory Maguire demanded. "She will cry rape, and I will have brought shame upon my family's good name. I did not remain in Ireland to do that, Adali. What will you do if that happens?"

"I will give her a mild sleeping potion before I let you enter her chamber. You will then make love to her and depart. If God is with us, then she will awaken tomorrow unknowing of what has transpired, but alive. We three will carry the burden of what we have done, but it will be an easy burden if my lady recovers her health, will it not?"

"And what of her serving women?" Rory Maguire asked.

"I will send them to their beds even before you come," was the answer. "The fewer people who know of the deed done, the better."

"Ye've said nothing, Father," Rory Maguire said. "Have ye no words for me in this matter?"

"You have my blessing," Cullen Butler told him softly.

The young man shook his head wonderingly. "Two more unlikely conspirators I've never seen," he told them. "Very well, I will do yer bidding, though I am ashamed of it. Still, I cannot live with the thought that my actions might have saved her should I refuse you."

"In half an hour's time," Adali told him, "Rohana and Toramalli will be in their own beds, and all will be in readiness for you. Do what you have to, and then return here."

The priest and the eunuch left the younger man.

"Your scheme is worthy of a cardinal," Cullen Butler told Adali as they parted company. Then he returned to his place before the altar of the little stone church that Jasmine had given him.

Adali hurried into the castle and up the stairs to his mistress's apartment. Within her bedchamber Rohana and Toramalli continued their watch. "How is she?" he asked them.

"Weaker," Toramalli replied, and Rohana wept.

"Go to your beds, and do not return until the morning is fully two hours old," he told them firmly. "I will keep watch over her."

Putting a comforting arm about her twin sister, Toramalli led her from their mistress's apartment and to their own chamber at the top of the house. She wondered what plan Adali had concocted to save their princess. There was no doubt in her mind that he would save her. That she and Rohana had not been invited to share in that plan could only mean that Adali did not want them to know of it. *What would he do?*

Rory Maguire left the gate house and walked slowly down to the lakeshore. Gritting his teeth, he plunged into the dark waters, ducking his red-gold head beneath to cleanse it. A man never entered a lady's bed without bathing. His mother had always told him that, and although there had been many times he had not obeyed her admonition, this time he would. Hurrying back to his quarters, he put on clean breeches and a clean shirt. He decided against wearing his boots, and then changed his mind. If he was seen by anyone barefooted within the castle in the early morning, gossip would ensue for certain.

His heart was beating more quickly than usual. He could hear it faintly within his ears. He hadn't allowed himself to think about what he was about to do. Yet now, walking up the staircase of the castle to her chambers, he must. The eunuch had said that he loved her, but that his honor had prevented him from admitting to himself. Had Adali been right? He sighed wearily. Aye. Adali had been.

From the first moment he had seen her, he had been lost. It wasn't just her beauty, which was certainly formidable. It had been her bold, nay, regal manner that had enchanted him. Irish women were hardly shy and retiring creatures, but this simple woman, he thought, would have taken a sword up to defend what was hers if she had had to do so. Her

swift actions regarding her husband's murderer were worthy
of a Celtic warrior. Then he remembered that it was women
warriors who had once taught the men of Ireland how to
fight. He knew nothing of this India from whence she had
sprung; but she certainly exhibited her Irish ancestry.

The castle, to his relief, seemed deserted as he turned the
handle on the door and stepped into the master chamber.
Walking through the day room, he hesitated at the bedchamber door; finally, with a soft sigh, he entered. The place
was gently lit with beeswax candles, and a good fire burned
within the fireplace. Walking to the bed, he gazed down at
Jasmine. God, she was so pale! She seemed hardly to breathe,
and her closed eyelids were purple with her agony. This isn't
right, he thought unhappily. Then Jasmine began to cry out
as Adali had said she would.

*"Rowan! Rowan! Love me but a final time! Ohh, how shall I
live without you, my love? Please, love me!"*

Rory Maguire felt his heart contract painfully within his
chest. How could he let her die? Reaching out, he gently
touched one of the crystal tears as it ran down her cheek.
Wearily, he drew off his boots, his breeches, his shirt. He
had never felt less like making love to a woman in his entire
life. Then, to his shock, her eyes opened, and as he stood
frozen with fear, she held out her arms to him.

"Rowan! You came back to me!"

Looking down at her, Rory Maguire realized that her
wonderful turquoise eyes, though open, were totally unfo-
cused. Jasmine could only see what she wanted to see, and
he had become Rowan Lindley for her. He wasn't certain if
he felt anger or shame at the revelation. Drawing back the
coverlet, he stared at her exquisite nudity. The candles and
the fire cast a golden glow over her body. Her breasts were
probably the most beautiful he had ever seen on a woman.

The sightless eyes looked up at him, and she smiled seductively.

Unable to help himself, he reached out and fondled one

of the cone-shaped orbs. She murmured with pleasure at his touch, her eyes closing once again. Kneeling by the bedside, he leaned over her and, finding her mouth, kissed her softly at first, then more passionately. Her lips parted beneath his, her tongue sought his out, teasing at him with little flickering jabs that sent fire into his loins, to his great mortification. It was wrong to want her under these circumstances. He wanted her to be aware that he loved her, that he desired her, that he wanted her to desire him. Not Rowan Lindley. *Him. Rory Maguire!*

"Come into bed, Rowan. I want to feel you against me," Jasmine whispered against his ear, her tongue poking teasingly into it.

He was overcome momentarily with a deep feeling of self-loathing, for his male member was suddenly as hard as iron and tingling with lust to possess her. Climbing into the bed, he gathered her into his arms, kissing her eyes, her mouth, her cheeks; his desire rising with every passing moment, for her response to his passion was incredible. He had never known a woman to react with such unfettered sensuality. He could feel her breasts beneath his chest swelling with her arousal, the nipples taut. Unable to restrain himself, he lowered his head and suckled hard upon one of the sentient little tips.

"Oh, Rowan!" she half sobbed, her fingers threading themselves through his unruly hair, arching herself against him as he transferred his attentions to the other nipple.

He was half sprawled across her, and gasped, startled as she reached down with her hands to capture his manhood and caress it fervently. She cupped and fondled his pouch, tickling it gently with the fingers of one hand while the other stroked his rod to the bursting point.

"I can wait no longer," she moaned. *"Put yourself inside me, my love!"*

He needed little encouragement, and mounted her. She squirmed seductively beneath him as he pinioned her be-

tween his thighs, reaching out to guide him into paradise.
A groan escaped his lips as he sank into her passage. She
was as hot as fire and as sweet as honey. Matching her
rhythm to his, she met each thrust with enthusiasm. She
surrounded him, enclosing and squeezing him with a magic
he had never believed possible. He couldn't stop. He was
never going to stop. He would ride her forever. He had never
felt so strong or so sure of anything.

"*Ohhh, Rowan!*" she cried, piercing his heart with the re-
minder that he but played a part. "*Ohhhh, my love! Yesss!*"

He didn't want it to end! It couldn't end! *Not yet! Dear
God, not yet!* But he could feel her spasms, strong and hard,
demanding the final tribute of him, and unable to stop himself, he poured his love juices in fierce bursts of passion into
her, pressing a burning kiss upon her lips as he did so. For
what seemed a long few minutes he lay atop her, and then
with reluctance he withdrew from her, slipping from the bed
to look down at her. To his surprise, she was asleep, but
there was faint color in her cheeks that had not been there
before. Her despair and restlessness seemed to have left her.
Rory Maguire drew the coverlet back over Jasmine.

He was drained. Not simply physically, but emotionally.
If she survived, she could never know the part he had played
in her recovery. As for his future, it was bleak. He was a
simple Irish chieftain of virtually no importance, and no fit
mate for a king's daughter. He lived on her goodwill, dis-
enfranchised within his own native land. What future could
there be for them? He knew the answer. *There was none.* Yet
he would not leave her as long as she needed him, and he
would not leave this land that had been in his family's trust
for so many generations.

Rory Maguire drew his shirt, his breeches, and his boots
back on. Through the windows, he could see the faint beginnings of the new day. Quietly he slipped from her chambers, and to his great surprise he found Finn awaiting him
in the passageway outside her apartments. The big dog arose

from the floor where he had been sleeping, and pushed a cold, wet nose into Rory's hand, as if comforting him. Together master and dog left the castle, unseen, and returned to the gate house.

Adali watched him go from the windows of Jasmine's bedchamber. Although the Irishman had been unaware of his presence, the eunuch had been in his mistress's chambers the entire time. It had been necessary in order to be certain that Rory Maguire performed as he had been requested to perform. Adali realized even better than his co-conspirator, Father Cullen, the deep sense of morality ingrained in Rory Maguire. While he admired and appreciated the young man's ethics, his first concern was for Jasmine. She would survive if he could make her survive.

Turning away from the window, Adali walked to the bed and looked down at his mistress. She seemed to be sleeping quite peacefully and deeply now. Her cheeks were faintly pink. He drew back the coverlet and lifted her tenderly from the bed, propping her on the settle by the fireplace. Quickly he remade the bed with fresh lavender-scented sheets, for the Irishman's love juices had been so profuse that her womb had overflowed with them. Adali then bathed Jasmine's female parts with a basin of perfumed water, erasing all traces of the lovemaking. If she remembered, she would think it but a dream. Dressing her in a clean nightgown, he placed her back in her bed, drawing the coverlet over her. Finally he burned the used sheets in her fireplace. Now there was no evidence at all of what had transpired in the room over the past hour. Adali smiled, satisfied. Both Akbar and Rugaiya Begum would have approved his actions. Their daughter would live. He drew up a chair and settled himself by her bedside to watch over her. Aye! *She would live!*

❁

17

❁

Skye O'Malley de Marisco had not set her eyes on her native land in almost forty years. When Elizabeth Tudor had taken away Padraic's heriditary Burke lands, she had also forbidden Skye's return, although she had rescinded that order once so that Lady de Marisco might gain her O'Malley brothers' aid for England. Now, looking out over the beauty of Lough Erne, Skye sighed gustily.

" 'Tis the most beautiful place on earth, Adam? Is it not?"

"When it is not raining," her husband agreed. "I am too old for such damp, madame. It rains here more than in England, and I never thought I should say such a thing of any other place. How long must we stay?"

"The seas are already winter-wicked," Skye told her husband. "Go, if you will, my darling, but I must stay with Jasmine, and she cannot travel until her baby is born. It is a blessing, and yet at the same time a tragedy that Rowan has left her with this parting gift. The child is due at the end of June, the beginning of July. If it is healthy, we will return to England in August. 'Twill not be a pleasant trip, I fear, for we will be returning poor Rowan's body to Cadby on the same ship." Her eyes filled with tears. " 'Tis so unfair, Adam!"

He put a comforting arm about her. "There now, little girl, how many husbands did you bury before we found happiness? I do not, of course, wish the same fate for our granddaughter, but I know she will marry again, and find happiness even as we did."

"I hope so," Skye said, sighing. She had grown used to a peaceful life, but the last few months had been dreadful. First Fergus Duffy had arrived from Ireland with a written message from Adali and Cullen Butler. She and Adam had been astounded and heartbroken by the news he had brought. They had hurried to Ireland, even though the seas between the two lands were not particularly safe at this time of year. There they had found their granddaughter, weak and grieving for her husband. That she was alive, Cullen Butler told his aunt, was nothing short of a miracle. When, several weeks after her grandmother's arrival, Jasmine had discovered she was enceinte, her joy had known no bounds. This child would be Rowan's final gift to her. It was a sign, she told them, that she must live on, not just for his memory, but for their children.

"But you will come home to England, won't you?" her grandmother had queried her. "You will return to Queen's Malvern with your grandfather and with me, come late summer of next year, Jasmine?"

"I must go to Cadby, Grandmama," Jasmine said. " 'Twas Rowan's home. He wanted Henry and India raised there. We had spoken on it just before . . . before he died. We were going to return after the first of the mares foaled. We both knew that we could leave Maguire's Ford safe in Rory Maguire's hands. He will look after the plantation diligently and carefully because he loves it and it was once his family's lands."

Rory Maguire. Now there was a puzzle, thought Skye.

As soon as Jasmine had regained consciousness, Cullen had told her, they had sent to Sir George Harding, the sheriff for Fermanagh, telling him of the Marquess of Westleigh's murder and the subsequent execution of his murderer. Sir George had taken it upon himself to come to Maguire's Ford to hold an inquiry.

"I cannot believe," he had declared pompously, "that an agent of the crown acted so despicably." He had pierced Cullen Butler with a sharp look that said he distrusted a priest of the old faith.

"My lord," Cullen Butler said quietly, "I realize that you are as shocked as we were upon hearing of Lord Lindley's demise, but I assure you, the agent Feeny did commit the crime. Lady Lindley had dismissed him upon her arrival at Maguire's Ford. Before he was hung, he admitted that it was actually her ladyship that he was attempting to assassinate, not his lordship. As both the marquess and the marchioness are very beloved of their tenants, I regret we were unable to hold Master Feeny over for judgment. Having admitted his guilt, he was immediately hung, may God have mercy on his soul," Cullen Butler said solemnly, crossing himself.

"Hmmmm," replied Sir George, and then, "I should like to see her ladyship, sir. I am still not content with this matter."

"Of course, my lord, but you cannot stay for too long. Her ladyship has been devastated by her grief, and has almost died of it, poor lady."

Sir George Harding was admitted into Jasmine's bedchamber. She sat, propped by several pillows, in her bed. She was garbed modestly but richly in a dark, fur-trimmed velvet gown, a lace-edged lawn cap upon her head. Her eyes seemed very big in her small heart-shaped face, and her dark hair made her skin seem even paler than it was. Her eyelids were purple, and there were matching smudges of purple beneath her eyes.

His brief talk with her convinced Sir George that however the Marquess of Westleigh had died, his wife was innocent in the matter. Her grief was simply too overwhelming. "I shall send an estate agent to you," he said magnanimously, but she had shaken her head.

"No, my lord. Maguire's Ford belongs to me, and did not belong to my husband. The patent is certainly filed in Enniskillen to prove the truth of my words. Master Maguire is our estate agent."

"The former owner of these lands?" Sir George was horrified.

"A relative of the former owner," Jasmine said weakly. "My husband appointed him. He has been doing an excellent job, my lord."

"I cannot allow it!" Sir George huffed.

"It is not your decision, sir!" Jasmine had said angrily, two spots of bright color appearing upon her cheeks. "The king himself gifted me with Maguire's Ford. It is mine to do with as I please! Now, get out! I am sick, and weary with my grief! I can abide no more!"

Which, Skye thought, brought her back to Rory Maguire. *Polite. Deferential. Concerned.* And whose bright blue eyes always strayed to Jasmine when he thought himself unobserved; but Skye had noticed.

"He is in love with her," she said to Adali one day when they were alone in the Great Hall. Jasmine and Maguire had just passed through, discussing the mares in foal.

"Yes, madame," Adali replied. "He is, but he knows better than to climb so high. Besides, she will never love him. The timing is not correct for them. So it is written in the stars."

"Still, he pines for her," Skye said. "It is sad. I will be glad when my granddaughter has delivered of her child so we may return to England." She laughed, almost bitterly. "This is my native land, and I have been denied it for so long, yet here I am longing for England. Do you ever long for India, Adali?"

"Only rarely, my lady. You see, I believe that wherever one is at a particular moment is exactly where they are supposed to be at that moment. So, if I am in Ireland now, or in England tomorrow, it would be a great waste of my emotion to long for India, would it not?"

Skye laughed. "You remind me of an old friend, Osman, the astrologer, but he is long dead. He would have said something similar to me if I had asked him such a question, Adali. Your wisdom gives me comfort in a tragic time."

The winter passed, and with the coming of spring the mares in the pastures of Maguire's Ford dropped their foals. The sight of the mothers running with their babies in the meadows brought a smile to Jasmine's face for the first time in months. Of the four foals, three were fillies and one a fine black colt with but one white stocking.

"Mine!" Lady India Lindley said, pointing at the little colt from the vantage point of her great-grandfather's arms. "Mine, Anpa!"

"Hah!" chuckled Skye, who was holding the young Lord Lindley, who had just celebrated his first birthday. "What think you, my little marquess, shall we let your sister have the colt?"

Henry put his thumb in his mouth and stared at her with large blue eyes. He appeared to be actually considering the matter.

"They are all so healthy, thank God," Jasmine said. "I wish Rowan had lived to see the success of our experiment. This is a good land for raising horses, Grandmama. Maguire should do well for us after we've gone. I shall, of course, come back at some point, but Cadby must be our home from now on. Perhaps when Henry is older he will want to spend some time here, or mayhap I shall give the land to India one day. What do you think?" It was now June, and Jasmine was large with child. Still, she had recovered both her health and her strength, and seemed to bloom with an inner beauty.

"I think India will grasp anything she can lay her hands on, darling girl. There is a great deal of the Mughal in her temperament, I suspect," and Skye laughed. "There is plenty of time to decide who is to receive what, Jasmine. For now Henry has his father's holdings, and India will one day have yours. Perhaps you should give Maguire's Ford to this new baby. Lad or lassie, it will need something of its own for either an inheritance or a dowry. Then, too, one day you will remarry and there will be other children to provide for as well."

That Jasmine did not deny a possible third marriage, Skye found interesting, but then, perhaps, her granddaughter simply did not wish to argue with her.

Jasmine went into labor with her third child on the eighth day of July.

"Exactly nine months to the day of his lordship's death," Adali said fatalistically.

But unlike her first two children, this child was difficult to deliver. Skye had wisely sent to the convent of St. Bride's of the Cliffs for her elder sister, Eibhlin, who was a doctor. Eibhlin was well past seventy, but still practicing her beloved medicine. She had arrived on the first day of July and declared, " 'Tis not right, Skye. I am a bent old lady, and you still look like a woman half your age!"

Skye had laughed and embraced Eibhlin. "I will be seventy before Christmas, Eibhlin. If you do not remember how old I am, I do." The two sisters had not seen each other in many years.

Now, with Jasmine in apparent difficulty, Skye was relieved that she had had the foresight to fetch Eibhlin.

" 'Tis like it was with your Deirdre," Eibhlin declared. "The child is turned about. I can feel its little toes."

Jasmine winced as another sharp pain tore into her. "Damn!" she gasped. "It was not so terrible with India and Henry. They were born so quickly, Grandmama, and with little hurt."

"There, my darling girl," Skye soothed her granddaughter. "The little one is not in correct position, and your great-aunt must turn it about. Your aunt Deirdre gave me the same difficulty." Skye took up a cloth and wrung it out in a basin of cool, perfumed water. Then she smoothed it across

Jasmine's hot brow. "Each child is different. I should know, having had eight myself."

Carefully, Eibhlin turned the infant about, but Skye saw her sister's brow furrow in concentration as she worked, and when their eyes met, Skye knew that something else was wrong.

"What is it?" she asked low.

"The cord may be about the baby's neck," Eibhlin replied softly.

Another pain washed over Jasmine, and she shrieked aloud. Tiny beads of perspiration dappled her forehead, and she gasped as if seeking breath. "I cannot bear it," she sobbed.

"I can see the baby's head quite clearly," Eibhlin said calmly. "If you will just push a bit harder, niece, this business of birthing will be over for you quite quickly." She almost sounded cheerful.

Jasmine sent her a fierce look, but she stopped feeling sorry for herself almost immediately. "This baby is a boy," she declared. "Only a lad would be so insensitive of his mother."

Skye laughed. "More than likely 'tis a girl. Girls are always quarreling with their mothers, are they not, my darling?" She chuckled once more. "I will wager a gold piece with you, Jasmine, that I shall shortly have another great-granddaughter."

Jasmine's turquoise-blue eyes twinkled. "Done, Grandmama!" she said, and then she paled and gasped once more.

"Push, child!" Eibhlin demanded. *"Push!"*

Jasmine glared at her, but screwing up her face, she did as she was bid, pushing with every bit of strength that she possessed. To her great relief, she could feel the baby begin to slip from her body as the spasm subsided.

"Good lass!" Eibhlin said. "We'll have it with the next push, my dear." She carefully turned the child, who was now born to its shoulders, gently untangling the umbilical cord from the little neck about which it had been loosely wrapped. "Nothing serious," she said low to her sister. " 'Twas not tight, but I knew it was there. I felt it."

"Ahhhhhhhhhh!" Jasmine cried out, and pushed again.

The infant slid from her body, and almost immediately began to wail. Eibhlin worked with an efficiency and swiftness that amazed Skye; wiping the child free of birthing blood, clearing its little mouth of mucus, handing the infant over to its great-grandmother, then snipping and tying off the cord neatly.

"You owe me a gold piece, darling girl," Skye informed her granddaughter as she wrapped the baby in its swaddling clothes.

"Let me see her," Jasmine demanded. "Does she look like Rowan? Both India and Henry do."

"I think she looks like you," Skye said, handing the baby to her. "What do you intend to call her?"

"Fortune," Jasmine replied. "I lost her father through a turn of bad luck, but by good fortune we had made love the night before, and 'twas then I must have conceived her. So she shall be Fortune Lindley, I think. Since I know that cousin Cullen will want to baptize her himself, even though I shall raise her in England's church, I will add Mary to her name, which should please him. Lady Fortune Mary Lindley. What think you Grandmama? Aunt Eibhlin?"

" 'Tis a good name," Skye said, and turning away, wiped her eyes. "I am becoming a sentimental old woman," she grumbled, "but seeing a child born never fails to fill me with amazement and awe."

"I have brought more children into this world than I can even remember, and I, too, feel the same way, sister," Eibhlin admitted.

Jasmine gazed down at her daughter. She had to agree with her grandmother. There seemed to be nothing of Rowan in the baby, but then Fortune was so newborn that it was difficult to tell. The child had stopped howling now and was sleepily observing its mother. Jasmine smiled at her. "Welcome, Lady Fortune Mary Lindley," she said softly. "I'm sorry you won't know your papa, for he was a wonderful man, but I shall love you with all my heart, as will the rest of your family."

"Give her to me," Skye said, reaching out for the baby. "Rohana and Toramalli are desperate to see this child, as is the rest of the household. You've been in labor all of yesterday and the whole night past with Fortune, but 'tis morning now. I can hear already India outside the door to these rooms. She will want to see her new sister."

Rohana and Toramalli, who although they had been in their mistress's bedchamber during the birth, had had little to do with it, crowded in to see Fortune.

"She has the Mughal's mole, as you do," Toramalli remarked to Jasmine.

"And your blue eyes, my lady," Rohana said. "Your lady grandmother is correct. She looks like you, but for her tawny hair, which I think is a small inheritance from her father."

"Her hair is more red than tawny," Toramalli remarked.

"Her grandmother, Velvet, has auburn hair," Skye said. "Aye, she's more de Marisco, I think, than anything else." She gathered the infant up and hurried from the room to display it to its great-grandfather, its siblings, and Adali, all of whom were waiting eagerly for news of the newest member of the family.

"I think Jasmine must have looked like this as an infant," Adam said, cradling the baby in his arms. He gently touched the tiny beauty mark Fortune carried between her nostril and her upper lip.

"See! See!" Lady India Lindley demanded, and her nursemaid lifted the little girl up to inspect her new sister. "Baby," India said, sounding a bit disappointed. "Dia wanted a pony, Anpa."

"And so you shall have one when we return home to England, Mistress India," Adam promised. "What color pony do you want?"

"Black!" India said without hesitation.

"A fine, fat black pony, my pet!" he promised her, and

then turned to his wife. "Fortune seems a healthy lass. Can we travel within the month, Skye? Ireland is a fair land, but I long for Queen's Malvern."

"Jasmine must gather her strength before we can travel, Adam," Skye told her husband. "I think six weeks, if she and Fortune remain healthy, and then we may begin the journey back to England."

Eibhlin visited with her sister for a few days following Fortune's birth, and then she prepared to return to St. Bride's.

"Be careful," her younger sister cautioned her just before her departure. "The English have an iron grip on Ireland now, and 'tis not likely they will let go. I thank God St. Bride's is off the beaten path, but what happened in England to the monasteries and the convents all those years ago could just as easily happen in Ireland. Religious houses have been burned before. King James is a nice enough fellow, and given the choice, he would allow full freedom of religion. Those around him, though, for whatever their reasons—greed, fanaticism, or ignorance—prefer the chaos that religious dissent brings. Be watchful, and I will send you whatever news I can."

"I will be dead long before there is any change, and I praise God for an easy deliverance," Eibhlin said. "There is a canker growing in my breast, Skye. I will live a year or two at the most."

"*Eibhlin!*" Skye was horrified by her sister's blunt words.

Eibhlin, however, smiled serenely. "You and I, of all our sisters, have lived our lives as we chose to live them, Skye. We let no man tell us what we might do or not do. I am one of only three women physicians in Ireland today. My life has been filled full aiding the ill, bringing new souls into this world, easing the burden for the dying, seeing my skills heal the sick. Life has been a joy for me, and I praise God with every bit of my being that he allowed me such total happiness and complete fulfillment. Now I am dying. Have

I the right to complain over it? I am seventy-four years old, sister. It is a venerable age. Why, neither our sisters Moire, Peigi, or Bride lived to such an age!"

Eibhlin patted her sister's hand comfortingly. "Do not grieve hard for me, Skye. When God wills my time at an end, I go gladly, serving Him with my obedience, as I have ever tried to serve Him. Mourn me a little in your heart, Skye, for I know you will do it even if I forbid you, but do not mourn me too long, little sister. There is nothing to weep over. I have had it all my way, and how many of us can say that? Not even you, Skye O'Malley. Not even you!"

Watching her sister ride off down the road upon her small brown mare, Skye knew that she would never again see Eibhlin O'Malley in this life.

"Where the hell have all the years gone?" Skye muttered irritably to herself. "How can Eibhlin be dying? How can I be facing my seventieth birthday? And God's nightshirt! Adam will be eighty next month! I am beginning to have an aversion to mirrors, as did old Bess Tudor. Admittedly I look better for my age than I should, but already I am beginning to feel the hot breath of old age in my aches and pains. Yet inside my head I am yet young, and filled with the juices of life and living! I am not, damnit, ready to be old!" She grimaced. "I will *never* be old," she decided firmly. Looking back to the road where Eibhlin and her horse were even now disappearing out of sight, Skye whispered softly, "Godspeed, Eibhlin O'Malley, until we meet again." Then she stamped back into the castle, her step firm, her skirts swinging about her.

Fortune Lindley was baptized in the village church of Maguire's Ford by Cullen Butler. The baby's godparents were a particularly clever choice on the part of her mother, Skye thought. Bride Duffy, in her absolute best, and only, gown, was Fortune's godmother. Rory Maguire was her godfather. They stood proudly by the ancient stone baptismal font as the child was welcomed into the Christian community. A shaft of sunlight came through the narrow little stained-glass windows that were the church's pride and touched the infant's head.

Skye looked hard. Fortune's hair, which was generous for a girl, was a rich red-gold. Velvet had never had hair like *that*, Skye thought. Velvet had been dark-haired, in fact, when she had been born. It was only when she was about six months of age that her black hair had fallen out and regrown a rich auburn. Fortune Lindley's hair was not auburn, nor anything like it. I must be getting old, Skye thought. Why did I not notice before that my great-granddaughter's hair is red-gold? Why, 'tis the same color as Rory Maguire's.

Skye stiffened. What was she thinking? There was nothing between Jasmine and Rory Maguire. *Absolutely nothing!* Aye, the young fool loved Jasmine, but she was totally, completely, unaware of it. She was still in love with Rowan Lindley, and would be for a time. Skye knew the pattern of grief that followed the loss of a beloved husband. *Yet where had that red-gold hair come from?*

In the days that followed Fortune's baptism, while they prepared to depart Ireland and return to England, Skye could not help but wonder about the new member of her family. Her eyes would stray to the young Irishman and then back to the baby. With each passing day, the more convinced she became that Fortune Lindley was not Rowan Lindley's daughter. What she could not decide was how such a thing could have happened. Jasmine did not seem like a woman with a guilty secret. She was always speaking to her children about their father, and even to the baby. There was apparently no deceit in her.

"Am I growing dotty?" Skye wondered aloud to herself. This was not a secret she would burden Adam with, but she needed to speak with someone about it. *Adali.* Jasmine had no secrets from him. He knew everything, but would he tell her? "I will tear his fingernails out one by one if he does not," Skye muttered darkly.

The night before they were to leave, she waited until they were alone in the Great Hall. Everyone else had gone to bed.

"Adali, I would speak with you," Skye told him.

He came immediately, deferential and polite as always. "Yes, my lady? How may I serve you?"

"You can tell me the truth, damnit!" Skye said.

"What is it you would know, madame?" he asked her warily.

"Why does my great-granddaughter, Fortune, remind me so of Rory Maguire, Adali?" Skye demanded bluntly.

"Because he is her father," Adali replied as candidly. There was no use lying to this glorious woman, Adali knew. She would accept nothing but the truth.

Skye let her breath out in a long hiss. *So there it was.* No deceptions. No evasions. She accepted the rather large goblet of wine Adali now poured her, and sat down heavily in a chair by the fire. Motioning him to sit opposite her she said, "Explain this phenomenon to me."

Choosing his words carefully, Adali told Skye how he and Cullen Butler had engineered their plot to save Jasmine's life. He concluded by saying, "I tell you honestly that I felt sorry for the young Maguire. He truly loves her, yet realizes that there can never be a marriage between them. He would always be torn between this land and her. If war comes to Ireland again, and I suspect from what I have seen here that it will, they would be on different sides of the issue. She is loyal to England's king, but he cannot ever really be."

"No," Skye said. "He cannot."

"The princess never suspected our plot, nor does she now, my lady. When she announced she was with child again, it did not occur to me that the one brief encounter with the Irishman would bear fruit. She had made love with her husband the night before he was murdered, and regularly prior to that last night. It was not until I saw the child that I realized the truth of what had happened. There is much of her mother in little Fortune, but more of her sire, I fear. It is good that we are returning to England. There will come a time when, if Rory Maguire and Lady Fortune Lindley are in the same room together, there will be no denying their relationship. Still, I saved my mistress's life, and that is to the greater good, I believe, my lady."

"Aye," Skye agreed, "it is, Adali, and as long as we can keep Fortune from Ireland, who is to know? India and Henry are too small to clearly remember Maguire. Jasmine, although pleasant to him, pays him very little heed, poor fellow. As long as I harp upon Velvet's auburn hair, if the question of Fortune's hair comes up, we will be safe. Rowan Lindley's tawny-blond hair had a bit of red in it, I think. Perhaps her hair will grow darker with age," Skye considered. "But if not, I shall tell all who listen that Fortune resembles my late mother."

"Will you tell the good father of your knowledge, my lady?" Adali asked Skye.

"Aye," Skye responded, "I will. Perhaps I can ease his sore conscience in the matter, Adali, for his religion will yet be warring with his more practical side in this matter. Does he know that Fortune is Maguire's child? Oh, poor Cullen!"

"Aye, he knows," Adali said. "He noticed the hair almost immediately. It has troubled him greatly, but he will say nothing, for he feels the baby is an innocent and must not be harmed. Besides, as everyone, including my lady, assumes that Lord Lindley was Fortune's father, he will not stir up a hornet's nest."

"I will go and speak with him now," Skye said, placing her goblet on the stone floor and arising. "Thank you, Adali, for your candor. I feared I was growing old, and foolish."

"Your eye will ever be sharp, my lady," Adali told her. "You love my mistress even as much as I love her. You will never hurt her."

Skye found her nephew in his cottage and faced him with the truth. Her words at first brought a flush to his cheeks, and then he grew pale with his distress. "Do not wallow in your supposed guilt," she scolded him sharply. "You and Adali did exactly what needed to be done in this matter. To have allowed Jasmine to die would have been criminal. Thank you for having the courage to act as you did, my dear Cullen." Then she kissed his cheek.

"Why is it that you make what I know to be a moral wrong, right, Aunt Skye?" he asked her with a small smile.

"Standing by and allowing someone to die without doing your utmost to save them is a far greater crime than anything that is legislated by our society's supposed morality," Skye told him.

"Are you saying that the Church can be wrong, Aunt?"

"I certainly am," she replied spiritedly, "and many before me have said it, and many after me will too. The Church and its laws have been made by men, Cullen Butler. Men are fallible. God is not, mind you, but men are. 'Tis far better to use one's common sense!"

The priest laughed aloud. "You will never change, Aunt Skye, will you? Independent in mind and spirit always."

"And do you think God will condemn me for it, Cullen?"

"Nay, Aunt. He knows your heart is good. As he made you, and has let you go your merry way for so long a time, I must assume he is satisfied with his handiwork. Try to keep Fortune out of Ireland, Aunt. If she grows up favoring her father, and they are ever seen together, 'twould, I fear, be a great embarrassment to us all."

"Do you think he suspects?" Skye asked her nephew.

"Nay." Cullen Butler shook his head. "He was, of course, happy that his actions produced Jasmine's recovery, but he still carries a burden of shame at having done what he did. You see, he truly loves Jasmine, though I'm sure he realizes a union between them would be impossible."

"He should marry," Skye said. "A good woman would ease him."

"Nay, Aunt. The political situation is too unstable in Ireland. Rory has lived his whole life with it. He has seen his family and his overlord forced to leave here. He no longer has the possession of these lands, but husbands them for an English landlord. In another short generation or two that could lead to difficulties between his descendants and Jasmine's. Nay, 'tis better he remains single, devoting his life to Maguire's Ford, its people, and the horses. They will all survive under the protection Jasmine's ownership affords them."

"And what will you do, Cullen, and what will you advise the people here to do when the bigots finally rear their heads again? They will, you know, my lad," she told him.

"I will tell each one of my parishioners to follow their conscience," he said quietly.

Skye snorted at him impatiently. "By that you mean adhere to the teachings of the Holy Mother Church and be slaughtered, Cullen. For shame! I expect better of you, my lad. You will have to advise these people how to survive. If there are two branches of a family, brothers perhaps, or a sister and a brother, one branch must follow the teachings of the Church of Ireland, and the other branch will remain as they have always been. In this way no family may be wiped out entirely. If the two faiths live side by side, there can be no mystery about either. Ignorance, my lad! Ignorance is what turns people against one another!"

In the morning, Skye sought out Rory Maguire.

"Do not be a patriot, Maguire, but if you must, disassociate yourself from Maguire's Ford first," she warned him quietly.

The Irishman shook his red-gold head. "I am weary of fighting," he said, "yet I could not run as the others did. I love this place too much to ever leave it. Your granddaughter has been more than kind to me in allowing me to remain. I promise you that I will not fail her."

"You have more courage than the others," Skye told him. "Running away was the easy way out. Remaining, and finding a way to make peace, even if the peace was not to your liking, was far harder, Rory Maguire."

"You learned the same lesson, I think," he said with a smile.

"Many years ago, and 'twas not a lesson easily learned for me," she replied, returning his smile and giving a small chuckle. " 'Twas Adam who became my rock and my salvation, I tell you honestly."

Jasmine came to them. She was dressed in her traveling garments, a burgundy silk skirt, and a jacket for riding. She wore a small starched ruff at her throat, and the long sleeves of the jacket were edged in ecru-colored Irish lace. Her hair was parted in the center and affixed in its usual chignon. She was today, as she had been that first day Rory Maguire had seen her, the most beautiful woman in the world.

Jasmine smiled at him. "Grandmama has, I have no doubt, given you instructions to follow, Maguire. I will not overrule her for her advice is always good. I will add, however, my own small admonition to take good care of the horses. Nighthawk, his wee brood of mares, and the babies must be carefully watched over. Put Nighthawk to those two mares who did not conceive last year, and see what happens. There will be a vessel arriving at Dundalk shortly with several other mares. You will be sent word. Bring them home yourself, and breed them to our stallion as soon as they are rested and over their journey."

"What of the little colt, my lady?" he asked. "Shall we geld him in the spring? And what shall we name him?"

"He's useless to us gelded," Jasmine replied. "I know that once he matures a bit more his father will be jealous, but you must keep them apart. When he reaches maturity, put him to stud as well, but not just with our mares. Nightbird will grow into a handsome and swift fellow. We'll race him in two years, and then those wishing his offspring will come to us, Maguire." She laughed. "Am I not clever?"

"If he proves a winner," her grandmother chortled, "you are clever. If he does not, it is another matter, eh, Maguire?"

The Irishman grinned. "Aye, m'lady, it is." Then he turned back to Jasmine. "Nightbird, is it, then?"

She nodded. "His mother is Swallow, his father Night-hawk. I think Nightbird is a good name, Maguire."

"May we please get going," Adam de Marisco grumbled, sticking his silvery head from the coach. "I'd like to get home before winter!"

They all laughed at his impatience, but Skye nodded to Rory Maguire, and with a footman's help clambered up into the coach to join her husband.

"Godspeed, my lord, and my lady," Maguire said.

The priest came up to them. "Good-bye, Aunt, Uncle Adam. Go with God," Cullen Butler said.

"Yes! Yes!" Adam could be heard agreeing with him from inside the carriage. "God's nightshirt, let us be on our way!"

Thistlewood, who had come to Ireland with his master and his mistress, grinned down at them. "We cannot sail until we're all in Dundalk," he noted, "but I'd best go before his old lordship has a fit." Gathering up his reins with an expert hand, he cracked his whip over the horses' heads and they were off.

Jasmine ran to the second coach, and, satisfied that her children and their nurses were comfortable, told India's nurse, "Now, when Fortune becomes hungry, you have but to call to me and we will stop, Martha."

"Aye, my lady," was the crisp reply.

Adali, Rohana, and Toramalli took up a third coach, and there were three baggage carts as well behind them. Satisfied that all was in order, Jasmine mounted Ebony and looked down at Maguire.

"You are a true and faithful friend, Rory Maguire. I shall not forget you, and your good heart. I need not ask you to watch over Maguire's Ford and her people. They are more yours than mine, if the truth be known, but I know you will not break your trust with me, or the memory of my beloved husband. I thank you for the loan of your family's vault in which his body has lain until two days ago. Now I shall take him back to Cadby to lie in his native soil."

"I will never forget you, my lady," Rory Maguire told her. "I will indeed watch over this land for you, and your children." He took her hand in his, his lake-blue eyes devouring her face for a swift moment, and then he kissed her gloved hand reverently. "God grant you a safe passage to England, my lady. I hope you will return to Ireland soon. If all the English were like you, madame, we should be friends with them instead of bitter and deadly enemies." He released her hand.

"Farewell, Cousin," Cullen Butler said, making the sign of the cross over them all. "I hope we will meet again, but if we do not, I thank you for my little stone church."

"Watch over them all, Cullen," Jasmine told him, and then turning her mare, she led the caravan of carriages and carts off down the road after her grandparents' coach.

They watched her go, each man wrapped in his own thoughts. Cullen Butler wondered if Ireland would remain at peace now that the English were settling Ulster in such great numbers. Or would there be bitterness that continued through the next hundred generations? Antipathy between Celt and Anglo-Saxon seemed to be a way of life, ingrained into their very souls. Yet there was no real difference between them. The priest shook his head. He did not understand it at all.

Rory Maguire thought the eyes would fall from his head. He stared intently after the departing people and horses, silently desperate to keep her in his sight. *Farewell, my only love*, he thought sadly. *Farewell, my heart*. He felt the tears pricking at the back of his eyes. *I will not cry! Men do not weep like disappointed maids.* Then, as they reached the bend in the road, he saw Jasmine turn in her saddle a moment and wave at them a final time before disappearing around the curve in the path. Waving after her energetically, Rory Maguire, the lord of Erne Rock Castle, scrubbed vigorously at the tears slipping down his handsome face with his other hand.

Men did not cry.

PART IV

Jasmine

❀

ENGLAND
1611–1613

❀

18

❀

"**Y**ou have been in mourning for Rowan for over a year now. I really do believe it is time enough," the Countess of BrocCairn said to her daughter, Jasmine Lindley. "Quite frankly, my dear, any further display of sorrow on your part is quite excessive."

"How easy it is for you, Mama," Jasmine replied bitterly. "You have never lost a husband to death, have you? I, however, have lost two." She stared with deep concentration at the pastoral view outside of her day room windows. The late summer hills were lush with greenery, and the river flowed as serenely as it always did.

Velvet drew a deep breath to keep from losing her temper. Rowan's death had been an unexpected tragedy that could not be changed. He was gone, and would not come back. It was time for Jasmine to begin thinking about another marriage. She could not spend the rest of her life alone. She was simply too young.

"Alex and I want you to come to court with us in the

autumn," Velvet said. "Sibby and Tom are going as well. The court is really a very exciting place these days."

"The court," Jasmine said primly, "is a sewer, I have heard. I am amazed that my stepfather would consent to go there. I believed him to have better sense, Mama, but perhaps he finds it easier to humor you than to have to argue with you. I cannot go. I have the children to consider. They are far too young to accompany me."

"God's foot, Jasmine!" her mother said, irritated. "The children most certainly should not accompany you. One goes to court for pleasure. My grandchildren are perfectly safe here at Cadby. All are sturdy, thank God!"

"They are too young for me to leave," Jasmine insisted.

"Nonsense!" Velvet said firmly. "India is practically three and a half; Henry is two and a half; and Fortune is past her first birthday. They all have their nurses, and if you think for one moment that Adali would let any harm come to them . . . Why, he is devoted to them all."

"Your mother is right," Skye said. She had remained seated and silent until now.

"*Grandmama!*" Jasmine had counted on Skye to back her.

"Well, she is," Skye said. "Rowan would dislike it intensely that you have shut yourself away here at Cadby. He was so full of life, the rogue! As long as you remain here, my darling girl, you become more ingrown. You are making a saint out of a man who was very much a man, and what is worse, you are spoiling your children terribly."

"They have no father!" Jasmine cried, tears welling in her eyes.

"That is no excuse for giving in to their every whim and wish," her grandmother said sharply. "I have raised enough children myself to know certain danger signals. India is an absolute little terror these days. Henry follows her every lead. As for Fortune, for all her wee size, she is a tiny tyrant, screaming herself red in the face if she is not immediately gratified. Do not delude yourself into believing that they will outgrow these bad habits, that it is only because they are small. They will grow worse with each day, each week, each month, each year, unless you begin to discipline them, Jasmine. If you cannot, then you must allow others to do so. Let me have my great-grandchildren at Queen's Malvern for a little time. Go to court with your mother and the rest of the family. You must think of marriage eventually, Jasmine, even if you do not think of it now."

"The queen gives the most delightful masques," Velvet enthused.

"Which the king never attends," Jasmine replied.

"Oh, Jamie is such an old sobersides." Velvet laughed. "He always was."

"Except when it comes to his *laddies*," Jasmine said. "I hear that young Kerr is still his majesty's favorite. They say he has taught the fellow Latin, but I hear he should have taught him English, for his Scots English is almost unintelligible."

" 'Tis true," Velvet admitted, and then she added, "He has Anglicized his name, my dear, and calls himself Carr these days."

"How does the queen bear it?" Jasmine demanded.

"Bear what?" Velvet replied. "The king is devoted to her, and to their children. She has had nine, even if they did not all live. Although the princes are her favorites, Henry most of all, Princess Elizabeth is her father's pride and joy. The king and the queen have different interests, and were they not so much the center of our universe, we should notice nothing amiss with their relationship. The king is given to being demonstrative with those of whom he is fond. Lady or gentleman, there would be gossip, Jasmine. Now we must think about your wardrobe. Styles are changing, and you will need a new one."

"If I go, will you come with us, Grandmama?" Jasmine asked.

Skye laughed. "Nay, darling girl, I am past that, I am

happy to say. I shall remain quite contentedly at Queen's
Malvern, and attempt to instill some respect and some manners into your children. Henry will benefit from having a
man around the house. Your grandfather may be an old
man, but he is still a vital one. Why, he hunts several times
a week even now. It is time that both Henry and India learn
to ride."

A small spasm passed briefly over Jasmine's face. "My father taught me to ride," she said. "I remember him saying
that it was not the custom for Indian ladies of high birth to
ride horses, but that as Candra had been a most excellent
rider, he thought perhaps that I should enjoy learning. I did,
and was so glad he taught me. It meant that I could go hunting with him, and with my brothers, unlike my elder sisters."

"How old were you when he taught you?" Velvet asked.

"I was just three," Jasmine replied.

"Well," Skye said briskly, "it is settled then! You will go
to court with your mother. As for your clothing, Velvet is
correct. You will need a new wardrobe. Fashions are finally
changing. Though the necklines are still square and low in
front, they have become high in the back. Necklines are
wider, too, on the shoulders, and large collars of linen or
lace are now quite de trop. Skirts are shorter as well, and
not quite as full. I shall send Bonnie to you. She is such a
clever seamstress."

"Well," Jasmine considered, "perhaps I could go to court
for a little while, Grandmama. I know the children are safe
with you, but you must promise me that you will not be too
harsh with them. They do miss their papa so very much. I
know I spoil them, but I cannot help it."

"They would not even remember their papa if you were
not constantly reminding them of Rowan," Skye replied
tartly. "Your idealized picture of him gives him the burnish
of saintliness that he most certainly did not possess. It is
good that you do not allow your children to forget their
father, my darling girl, but do not make him so perfect that

your son will be unable to live up to his memory, and your daughters forever comparing him to their suitors, who will also be unable to measure up. That would be a great tragedy." Skye patted her favorite grandchild's hand lovingly. "You have not forgotten how sweet love can be, my darling girl. Do not deny your daughters the experience when the time is right for them."

Bonnie was sent for, and arrived from Queen's Malvern with her assistant Mary. Together the two women set about in the waning days of summer to sew Jasmine's new wardrobe. A traveling jeweler and his apprentice arrived at Cadby and fashioned a number of beautiful buttons for the new clothing, using the gemstones that Jasmine supplied. While the jeweler set the stones within their frames of silver and gold, his apprentice dexterously carved additional buttons from ivory, bone, and polished wood.

"I am positively green with envy," Sybilla declared as she examined her stepsister's new clothes before Rohana and Toramalli packed them carefully for the journey to London. Sybilla had grown plumper with the birth of each of her four children, the youngest of whom had been born in late winter of that year.

"I have much too much," Jasmine declared. "Take whatever you fancy, Sibby. I haven't had time to grow attached to anything yet."

Sybilla sighed, and then she laughed. "I couldn't possibly fit into anything of yours, Jasmine. You remain impossibly willow-slim, while I am as plump as a partridge ready for the table. Tom, however, doesn't seem to mind. He says he likes having more of me to love, and swears I keep him quite toasty on cold winter nights."

"Tom has put on a bit of weight too," Jasmine noted. " 'Tis all your love, and the good food you see he has. He is disgracefully content for a man who was such an old bachelor."

Sybilla laughed again. There was a new softness about

her. All the sharp edges seemed to have gone. "I fear that I am content too," she admitted. "Tom is the best husband in the world."

"I am glad you are happy," Jasmine replied softly.

"Ohh!" Sibby cried. "I did not mean to sadden you, Jasmine."

"You did not," Jasmine hastened to assure her stepsister, and then she cleverly changed the subject. "Are you looking forward to the court, Sibby? I am not certain it is the place for a respectable woman without a husband in attendance. What do you think?"

"I think you fret too much," Sibby said. "Court is really quite exciting. We went last autumn before I was too uncomfortable with Elizabeth. Oh, Jasmine, 'tis so nice to have a little daughter. She is so much easier than the boys. Girls are, aren't they?"

Jasmine chuckled. "I had not noticed. Neither India nor Fortune strike me as easy. In my family 'tis Henry who is the easiest."

In early October Jasmine, in the company of the Gordons of BrocCairn and the Earl and Countess of Kempe, traveled up to London to join the court. After settling themselves into Greenwood, they went to Whitehall to pay their respects to their majesties.

The king, Jasmine thought, seemed to show his age more now. His skin had become coarse-looking, and he was a trifle jowly, but he greeted the young dowager Marchioness of Westleigh in kindly fashion.

Jasmine was looking particularly lovely this evening. Her gown was of heavy burgundy-colored silk with a large collar of ecru lace that extended low on her shoulders. The simple underskirt was of deep rose brocade. The same brocade showed through the small slashes upon her sleeves. The ankle-length, bell-shaped skirt of her gown revealed elaborate silk-covered shoes decorated with pearls, and when she turned suddenly, a glimpse of rose-colored silk stockings dec-orated with delicate gold-thread vines could be seen sheath-ing her slender legs. She wore a long necklace of large pearls held in front by a brooch of diamonds and rubies. From her ears hung long, pear-shaped pearls, and upon her arms were several bejeweled gold bangles.

The young widow curtsied low to the king, allowing both him and his handsome young favorite, Robert Carr, an un-restricted view of her beautiful bosom. "Your Majesty is most kind to receive me once again," Jasmine said softly as her skirts blossomed about her.

"We are pleased to see ye returned safely from Ireland," James Stuart replied, motioning her to arise, which she did. "We hope ye will bide wi us a wee while, Lady Lindley. Yer beauty can but enhance our court, is that nae so, Robbie luv?" The king looked up at the young man lounging against his throne. His eyes were misty with his affection.

Barely interested blue eyes swept over Jasmine and dis-missed her as unimportant. "Aye, my dear lord," came the expected reply.

"Ye hae nae met our Robbie before, hae ye, Lady Lindley?" the king said, sending the young man another loving look.

"Nay, my lord, I have not," Jasmine replied, feeling as if she were intruding upon a lovers' rendezvous, and not stand-ing in the middle of a crowded receiving room.

"Robbie luv, Lady Lindley is a most wealthy widow. She will need a new husband ere long, will ye nae, my lady?" The king smiled.

"Eventually, my lord, I hope to remarry," Jasmine said in cool, measured tones, "but for now I still mourn my beloved Rowan." Reaching into her bosom, she withdrew a scrap of linen edged in delicate lace and wiped away a tear. "This is my first venture into the world since his untimely death. Do you like children, Viscount?" she queried Robert Carr, whom the king had made Viscount Rochester earlier in the year. "I have three little ones at home, and although my dear grandmama says they are badly spoiled, I adore them. When I finally remarry, I shall want more children."

The king, who was sentimental over his own offspring, smiled at her. "Aye, bairns are a true blessing, Lady Lindley, but ye canna spare the rod if ye dinna wish them to grow up unruly. Is that nae right, Robbie? The bairns must be whipped well to instill respect and Christian behavior into their wee souls. 'Tis a parent's duty."

"Oh, aye, my lord," Robert Carr agreed, looking as if children were the furthest thing from his mind right now. Indeed, his glance kept straying in the direction of the beautiful and voluptuous Lady Essex.

"Ohh," Jasmine said, "I could never allow my darlings to be whipped. It is too cruel, sire."

"Mothers are generally as soft as custard," the king said, in a tone implying that women, bless them, were weak. "Well, I am yet glad to see yer return. Now go and pay yer respects to the queen, madame."

Jasmine curtsied to James Stuart once again and backed from his presence.

A hand was placed firmly beneath her elbow, and a voice said in her ear, "A most masterful performance, Lady Lindley."

Jasmine whirled about to see who would dare be so bold, and with a tiny gasp, curtsied in mid-stride. "Your Highness!"

Prince Henry grinned at her mischievously. He was a very handsome young man who favored his mother and his grandfather, the unfortunate Lord Darnley. Blue-eyed, with red-blond hair and an inordinate amount of charm, he was beloved by all who knew him, and was considered England's great hope. "Did you see the look on Rochester's face when you said you had three children, madame, and desired more? He must have been absolutely terrified that my father was going to propose a match between you." The prince chuckled. "Did I not fear the formidable reputation of your grandmama more than I dislike Robert Carr, I should have encouraged my father to the deed. His Robbie is secretly courting Lord Essex's wife."

Jasmine laughed. "You would do better to fear me, my lord, rather than my grandmama," she teased the prince, "should you encourage your father to match me with *anyone*! I will choose my own husband."

"Do you have anyone particular in mind, madame?" he queried her, fascinated.

"I am really not of a mind to marry at all, if you would know the truth," Jasmine replied. "I think, perhaps, that I am a jinx to any man who loves me and makes me his wife. Both of my husbands have been murdered. I am intelligent enough to manage my own life, and I already have children to comfort me in my old age."

"But what of someone to comfort you now?" he said softly, dropping a quick kiss on her bare shoulder. "Did you know that you have the most incredible blue eyes, madame?"

"So I have been told, sir," Jasmine said dryly. "I am four years your senior, and you, my lord, are very bold."

"So I have been told, madame," he mocked her, his eyes twinkling.

Jasmine laughed helplessly before his charm. "I really must go and pay my respects to your mama," she said. "My family has already done so, and they will wonder why I have been such a laggard, sir."

"Allow me to escort you, madame," the prince said politely.

He led her across the room, not just a few heads turning to see who the prince was with, for most at court did not remember Jasmine's previously brief visit. The word was quickly passed. *'Tis the dowager Marchioness of Westleigh. A most wealthy woman. She has the king's favor.*

Jasmine curtsied to the queen.

"Ahh," said Anne of Denmark, "I am happy to see you, my dear, but so sad at your loss. Still, you will be a definite asset to the court. Can you learn lines easily? We have the most divine masques, and a lady of your beauty cannot help but want to be a part of our revels."

The queen's reputation for frivolity was more than well-deserved. Still, she had done her duty to the crown, producing nine children, though only three, Prince Henry, Prince Charles, and Princess Elizabeth, had lived to maturity. The king loved his Annie, and as long as she did not involve him in what he referred to as her "silliness," he was happy to allow her whatever she wanted. Aiding her in her many lighthearted endeavors was Master Inigo Jones, who planned her masques and designed both the jewelry and the costumes.

"I am just now coming out of mourning," Jasmine told the queen, attempting to escape her royal clutches.

"You would make a magnificent Autumn, would she not, Master Jones? We are to do a masque next week celebrating the harvest, Lady Lindley. You must be our Autumn!" the queen insisted.

"I am going to portray the Lord of the Harvest," Prince Henry said, wickedly encouraging his mother onward.

"Yes! Yes!" the queen replied, beaming at her eldest and most favorite offspring. "Henry does not often indulge me in my little entertainments, but he did promise me this time, did you not, my love?"

"Indeed, madame, I did," the prince answered, kissing his doting parent's plump white hand. "And if Lady Lindley will take the part of Autumn, I believe your masque will be a great success, Mama."

"Then it is settled!" the queen said, smiling brightly at Jasmine.

The dowager Marchioness of Westleigh curtsied again to the queen, and escorted still by the prince, eased from her presence.

"Traitor!" she hissed at the prince once they were away from the queen's hearing. "You did nothing to help me at all. Instead you encouraged your mother on in her charming folly."

"I will help you with your lines," Henry Stuart said. "Indeed, we will have to spend a great deal of time together rehearsing."

"You are impossible!" Jasmine said, unable to refrain from laughing. Henry Stuart was a very delightful young man.

"Now there is a word I have never heard describe my most royal and august self," the prince told her. "I am considered quite the opposite of my dear parents, you know. Mama is a delightful silly creature who would harm no one, and my kingly father, though wiser than most would believe him, is unorganized and overly sentimental. I, on the other hand, am considered orderly in my mind and habits, sensible to a fault, and possessing a great wit; not to mention, madame, a strong healthy body, and a disgracefully handsome face."

"And Your Highness is modest to a fault as well," Jasmine said wryly.

Henry Stuart burst out laughing, and those around them turned to stare, wondering at the prince's amusement, and also at the beautiful woman he was escorting. "Ahh," the prince said with a knowing smile, "now they will all begin to talk. Are you prepared to be gossiped about, my dear Marchioness of Westleigh, for you will be gossiped about, you realize."

"I am the *dowager* Marchioness of Westleigh," Jasmine corrected him, "and why will I be gossiped about? Why, none of these people know me. Why would they gossip about me?"

The prince led her to a windowed alcove with a cushioned seat, and invited Jasmine to seat herself. Settling himself next to her, he said, "There are many reasons to gossip about you, madame. You are outrageously beautiful, for one thing. You are an unknown factor here at my father's court, which in itself arouses curiosity. You are in my company, and obviously have the facility to amuse me, which, of course, leads shallower minds to wonder what else you might do for me. You see, I have no mistress at the moment. In fact I have never had a formally recognized mistress.

"People cannot help but wonder what kind of a Stuart I am. Am I like my father, who, although he has loved the ladies in his time, now seems to have a tendre for young men? Or am I like my great-great-grandfather, and my great-grandfather, both of whom had large capacities for loving women?" The prince took her hand in his and, raising it to his lips, kissed first the back of it, then, turning her hand over, kissed her palm and the sensitive skin of her wrist. His blue eyes met hers in an unspoken question.

Jasmine found herself flushing with surprise. She knew immediately what kind of a Stuart Henry was. A passionate Stuart. This young man had caught her with her guard quite down. "I am a king's daughter, my lord," she said quietly. She must put him off without offending him. One did not anger a prince, particularly one who would one day be a king of England. "You have taken me by surprise, I fear."

Henry Stuart laughed, obviously pleased with himself and with her answer. "I have not *yet* taken you, my love, but I shall. When you arrived tonight, I could not believe how beautiful you were. We did not meet when you were last at court, for I was at Richmond, keeping at my studies. My mother, of course, wrote to me about you. She was fascinated by your heritage, your wealth, your beauty, particularly your unusual, magnificent eyes.

"When I returned to court, eager to meet you, I learned that you had returned to your grandmother's home in the Midlands to be married. I was truly disappointed. Then tonight you came to Whitehall. I recognized you immediately, although we had not met. 'Twas your wonderful turquoise-blue eyes that gave you away. I immediately sought out Lord Salisbury, and he told me that you were now widowed. God bless little Cecil! He knows everything."

Jasmine was astounded. "I do not know what to say, sir,"

she told him. His interest was certainly obvious, his intent quite crystal clear. Jasmine was not certain what she should do.

"Lean forward," he said to her.

"What?" she responded.

"Lean forward, madame. I wish to kiss you," the prince replied.

"Sir!" She feigned outrage. She must put a stop to his boldness as quickly as possible. It was a most difficult situation, which seemed to be growing more difficult with each passing minute.

"Lean forward," he said a third time. "Surely you do not want to cause a scene, madame, and you will if you refuse me. But one kiss, my love. What is the harm in it? You are widowed, I, a bachelor."

He was right, Jasmine thought, silently chiding herself for being foolish. There was really no harm in a simple kiss in a practically public place. The prince was not yet betrothed, and she was a widow. It was quite flattering, actually, that he wanted to kiss her. With a little laugh, and a shake of her head to indicate that she thought him quite naughty, Jasmine leaned forward, closing her turquoise-blue eyes and pursing her lips as she did so.

Henry Stuart grinned to himself, well-pleased. With one hand he cradled her head, his sensuous mouth slowly meeting hers in a series of small kisses that finally became a very deep, passionate one as his lips worked seductively against hers. She stiffened, obviously thought better of it, and relaxed, only to tear her head away from his, gasping with shock as his other hand plunged into her bodice to cup a breast.

"My lord!"

He forced her head back to his and said softly against her lips, "Open your mouth for me, my love." His roaming hand caressed her fervently. "God's boots, your skin is like silk!"

She felt his tongue pushing against the shield of her teeth;

her nipples growing taut with the gentle strokings of his skill-ful fingers. How had a simple kiss become so damned in-volved? Jasmine wondered muzzily. His tongue plunged into the hollow of her mouth, finding her tongue, which he brushed against with growing ardor. Desperately she mar-shaled her strength, and placing her hands against his velvet-clad chest, shoved him away. "Stop, my lord, I beg you!" she managed to whisper. *"Stop it this instant!"*

"You intoxicate me, madame," he groaned, his head dip-ping to her cleavage, his lips kissing the bared flesh of her bosom, while his marauding hand continued to fondle her with growing urgency.

The bodice of her gown felt tight. She could hardly breathe. What on earth was she to do? His passion was such that he would have her on her back shortly, futtering her for all the court to see! The thought was overwhelming, and her stomach suddenly roiling, Jasmine said with total can-dor, "Stop, my lord! I am going to be sick! Would you have me vomit all over your fine, bejeweled doublet?"

Henry Stuart lifted his head from the perfumed softness of her breasts and met her gaze. What he saw brought him sharply back to reality. Jasmine was very pale. Tiny beads of perspiration had broken out upon her smooth, high fore-head. "My love!" he cried. "What is it? Dear heaven, I have been a complete fool! I have taken you unawares in my ea-gerness. Forgive me, Jasmine, but I cannot seem to control my desire to possess you. I see now that I must." The prince arose and signaled a passing servant. "Wine!" he com-manded.

The request was quickly met. Henry Stuart pressed a gob-let into Jasmine's hand even as he gulped down several mouthfuls from his own goblet. The wine seemed to calm her upset stomach, and Jasmine drew a clear, deep breath. "Thank you," she said, but nothing more. What was she going to do about this situation? She had never imagined that such a thing could happen to her. She was totally confused. *Oh, Rowan!* she thought. *What am I to do?* God, if only her grandmother were here!

Her legs were shaking slightly as she forced herself to her feet, leaving the goblet on the seat behind her. "I must find my family," she said. "They will wonder where I have gotten to, my lord."

"I will escort you, madame," he told her, his hand slipping beneath her arm once more.

Jasmine realigned the bodice of her gown with as much dignity as she could muster. "I am ready," she said.

"Are you?" he murmured, bending to kiss the lobe of her ear.

"Stop it!" Strength flowed back into her limbs with her anger, and Jasmine stamped her foot. Two bright spots of pink colored her cheeks.

"Excellent, madame!" he said with a chuckle. "You have fully recovered. Did you know that I quite adore your little mole? I shall kiss it the next time that we meet, which will, I hope, be soon."

"I do not know how long I will remain with the court," she quickly replied. "I have my children at home. I have never yet been separated from them until now. I miss them. I think I shall return to Cadby within the week."

"I shall forbid it," he answered her with a laugh. "I want you here at court where I may enjoy your company, my sweet marchioness."

"I am the *dowager* marchioness," she responded sharply.

"You are far too young to be a dowager," he chuckled. "Ahh, BrocCairn, I return your lovely stepdaughter to you, Cousin. She is to take part in my mother's masque next week. I shall be calling upon her so we may rehearse our lines together. You will see that she is available to me when I call? You are staying at your mother-in-law's house on the Strand as usual? Greenwood, I believe?"

"Yes, Your Highness," the Earl of BrocCairn replied, bowing politely to the prince. "We are at Greenwood."

"Madame." The prince bowed over her head, and then left them.

Alexander Gordon raised a quizzical eyebrow. "Indeed, my dear Jasmine, it would seem you have made a conquest, and a very, *very* important conquest at that. Henry Stuart has certainly never before shown such a public interest in a woman. You may consider yourself honored."

"Honored?" Jasmine looked slightly appalled. "He has made it quite clear, my lord, that he wishes to make love to me. I cannot countenance such a thing! I am not some light-skirted creature with low morals. I did not come to court for this!" Her cheeks were pink with her outrage, and the Earl of BrocCairn thought that his stepdaughter looked particularly beautiful at this moment.

"If Prince Henry wishes to make love to you, Jasmine," the earl said slowly, his deep voice so low that only she could hear him, "you do not have any choice but to gracefully acquiesce, my dear. You have no maidenhead, nor a husband's honor to protect; and Henry Stuart will be England's next king. It would not be politic, I fear, to refuse him."

"Are you telling me, my lord, that I have no choice in the matter? What of my honor? I am an emperor's daughter, and every bit as royal as this prince!" Jasmine declared vehemently.

The Earl of BrocCairn took his stepdaughter's hand and patted it comfortingly. "You know that I am related to the king, my dear, but do you know how the relationship came about?"

Jasmine shook her head.

"The king and I share the same grandfather, King James the Fifth. My grandmother, Alexandra Gordon, was his mistress for a time. My father, Angus Gordon, may God assoil his good soul, was the result of their passionate union. Stuart kings, and Stuart princes, are notorious for their loving natures. Why, it is said that they are related to half of Scotland or more." The earl chuckled. "There is no shame in being beloved by a Stuart, I assure you. If indeed this is what Prince Henry desires, you must accept his suit graciously without protest. It would not be very wise, Jasmine, to cause a scandal, or to embarrass the prince."

"If I remove myself immediately from the court," Jasmine told her stepfather, "then the matter is ended, and no one the wiser. I shall leave tomorrow for Cadby, my lord."

"You will not," he replied, and when she gasped with surprise, Alexander Gordon said, "The prince has made it quite plain that he wishes you to remain here with the court, Jasmine. Neither of us misunderstood him. He has made me a direct party to this matter. If I allow you to go, I will be guilty of disobeying the king's son. I cannot be. Now that the prince has noticed you, the very well-being of our family depends on his royal goodwill. You cannot simply think of yourself, Jasmine. You have *all* of us to consider."

"That is not fair!" she cried. "I did not ask for this *honor*, and I do not want it, my lord!"

"What is the matter?" Velvet joined them, looking worriedly at her daughter. "Jasmine, my love, you look pale. Are you all right?"

"No, Mama, I am not all right," Jasmine replied, distraught.

"Prince Henry seems to have become enamored of your daughter, madam," the earl told his wife. "She is not pleased about it."

"Oh, dear," Velvet said nervously. "How enamored, Alex?"

"Totally enamored, my darling," he answered her.

"Ohhh dear!" Velvet exclaimed. "What are we to do, then?"

"We can do nothing," he said. "Jasmine, no matter her strong objections, will have to accept the inevitable. What is so terrible? She is not being asked to give up her life, or her wealth. A handsome, charming young man wishes to make love to her. I do not understand all the fuss being made over it," the earl concluded testily.

"I shall leave for Cadby tonight!" Jasmine declared desperately.

The Earl of BrocCairn said nothing in response to his stepdaughter's dramatic proposal. Instead, when they returned to Greenwood, Alexander Gordon gave orders to the household staff that Lady Lindley, who was suddenly unwell, was to not leave the house. He then personally locked Jasmine in her apartments with Toramalli and pocketed the key, to his wife's deep distress.

"Jasmine will never forgive you for this, Alex," Velvet fretted. "She is a princess born and raised. How can she tolerate being asked to be the prince's whore? It really is quite untenable, my lord."

"Being a royal Stuart's mistress is hardly considered a deep dishonor," the earl insisted to his wife. "Give her a few days and she will think better of it, I am certain. This is not India, after all."

"Would you want this for Sybilla?" Jasmine shouted at her stepfather the following day, when he came to reason with her.

"Placed in your situation, Sybilla would know her duty, and do it, damnit," Alexander Gordon said heatedly.

Jasmine threw a vase of roses at his head, which the earl ducked as he swiftly retreated.

"She is certainly your daughter, madame, with her hot temper," he told his wife in the hallway. "I was reminded of our youth as I fled that vase. It seems I remember similar incidents between us."

"And despite all the years I have been your wife," Velvet teased him mercilessly, "you have learned nothing about dealing with the women in my family, Alex. I shall remonstrate with my daughter. I would not have missed my target."

Henry Stuart ended the contretemps by coming to call at that moment. When Jasmine refused to come down to receive him, he was directed to her apartments by the earl, who accompanied him.

"How dare you!" Jasmine said furiously at their appearance. "Leave my apartments this instant, my lords! I am not receiving today!"

"Toramalli, come with me," the earl ordered the tiring woman.

"I am sorry, my lord," Toramalli replied, "but I take orders from no one but my mistress."

Alexander Gordon advanced upon the small woman, and picking her up about the waist, hauled her kicking and shrieking from her lady's presence. Henry Stuart closed the doors to Jasmine's apartments behind them, and turning the key in its lock, slipped it into his pocket.

Jasmine watched him wide-eyed. "If you come one step near me, I shall scream!" she told him.

"Why?" he asked her, moving past her to seat himself by the fire. "May I have a goblet of wine, madame?"

If his intent was to make me feel foolish, Jasmine thought, he has certainly succeeded. "What are you doing here, my lord?" she demanded.

"We have our lines to practice for the masque next week," he said blandly. "Mama says to tell you that Master Jones and his seamstress will come to Greenwood tomorrow to fit you for your costume." He smiled at her, and then said, "My wine, madame. I am fair parched."

Jasmine moved cautiously around him and poured a deep red wine from a crystal decanter into a small chased-silver goblet. Handing it to him, she stepped quickly back, standing silent as he drank.

"Ahhh," Henry Stuart said, swallowing his wine. "This is

a most excellent vintage, madame. Who is your wine merchant?"

"The wine comes from my great-gandparents' estate in France," she answered him. "I will arrange to have several barrels sent to Your Highness. The estate is called Archambault."

"Come and sit by me, Jasmine," he said, motioning to an upholstered stool by his chair.

She shook her head, remaining where she was. "What do you want of me, my lord?"

"Many things," he said quietly.

"You must be specific with me, my lord. I do not wish to misunderstand you. My family and I have been quite at odds over our meeting at Whitehall last night. I do not think I am the sort of person to enjoy court, and I would go home to Cadby, but my stepfather will not allow me to go. He says I cannot offend Your Highness. He says that you obviously desire me, and 'tis an honor."

"I do desire you," Henry Stuart responded with a small smile. She was so charmingly serious, he thought. He had never before met a woman like Jasmine. "You, however, my love, do not consider my interest in you an honor, do you? Why is that?"

"I am an Imperial Mughal princess, my lord," she replied, knowing that he, a prince born, would certainly understand.

He did, but said, "I have never taken a mistress before. Oh, I have had my share of women, the first when I was eleven, but I have never fallen in love with a woman enough to want her for myself. Not until I saw you, Jasmine. A royal Stuart would not settle for anything less than an Imperial Mughal princess," he concluded with a small smile.

"I have been told that your ancestors were not quite as discerning as Your Highness. Indeed, it has been reliably reported to me that your family is related to more than half of Scotland," Jasmine answered pertly, a trifle more relaxed, and with a twinkle in her eye.

Henry Stuart laughed. "Now, there is another thing," he said. "You can make me laugh. You have a wickedly sharp wit, madame." Then he grew serious. "Jasmine, I admit to wanting to make love to you, and eventually we will, but when we do, it will be because you desire me as well. I apologize for accosting you at Whitehall, and frightening you. I am ashamed to say I could not help myself. I hope you will forgive me, my love. Now may there please be a pax between us?"

"Will you unlock the door to my chambers?" she said.

Reaching into his doublet, he withdrew the key and held it toward her. "Do you trust me now, madame?" he asked.

Jasmine stared a moment at the key he proffered. Her stepfather was correct when he said she could not refuse Henry Stuart's overtures. This was England, not India. She was no princess here, but he was the heir to England's throne. She could not afford to incur the king's ill will. She had her children to consider. If she were forced to flee the royal wrath in England, where could she go this time?

"Keep the key, my lord," she told him. "I have your word that you will behave yourself, and the word of a royal Stuart can be trusted, I am certain." Jasmine approached and sat down upon the little stool by his side. "What are the lines I must learn for this masque of your mama's?" She tipped her face up to his, looking deep into his light blue eyes.

Henry Stuart gently caressed her dark head, and then he said, "Look away from me, madame, else I be overcome with my desire for you," and when she blushingly complied, he said, "I shall tell you the story we are to perform for the masque. It is quite simple, as are all of Mama's little entertainments. The emphasis is upon the music, the dance, the costumes, and the beauty of the players.

"Summertime, who shall be portrayed by my cousin, Arabella Stuart, does not wish to yield her hold upon the earth to her sister, Autumn. She has drawn the flowers to her side. They fear Autumn's frosty fingers upon their dainty petals.

The trees, however, are overcome by their own vanity, for they wish to exchange their plain robes of summer-green for Autumn's colors: scarlet, gold, and purple. The two sisters and their allies war back and forth, but Autumn, cleverer than Summertime, enlists her lover, the Lord of the Harvest, in the battle. Once he has decreed that the growing season must end, Summertime has no choice but to yield to her sister, Autumn. She departs sadly while Autumn and the Lord of the Harvest dance together in triumph."

The prince chuckled. "As I have said, 'tis quite simple. Mama, however, adores such follies. You, my love, will be a beautiful Autumn. You shall quite put to shame poor Arabella, who is, in my opinion, a bit long in the tooth, and overripe for her role as young Summertime. Arabella ought to be married and with a houseful of children, but alas, she is my father's first cousin, and the only direct heir to his throne who is of his generation. Their fathers were brothers.

"When old Queen Bess died, there were some who talked of putting Arabella on the throne of England instead of my father. She is fortunate to be living in this time, for in another time she would have been imprisoned, and perhaps even murdered for her unfortunate bloodlines. Instead my father keeps her in an unmarried state at court. Poor creature. She has hot Stuart blood running through her veins, even as I have."

"These three roles, then—Summertime, Autumn, and the Lord of the Harvest," said Jasmine, "are the only speaking roles?"

"I believe so," Prince Henry replied. "The trees and flowers may have a line here or there. Young ladies of the court will play the flowers, and young gentlemen the trees. Roles in my mother's masques are quite coveted."

Henry Stuart then explained the dialogue to Jasmine, and together they rehearsed their parts. When they both realized that the day was waning, the prince arose and took his leave of her. He did not attempt to kiss her, which Jasmine found reassuring, yet strangely disquieting.

"May I come tomorrow?" he asked her.

She nodded. "We will need more practice, I fear, if we are to do this well. Perhaps you should bring your cousin Arabella, so we may practice together, my lord. I do not wish to be taken unawares by another player, and disappoint her majesty with an awkward performance."

"That is an excellent idea," the prince agreed, and departed.

When he had gone, Toramalli flew back into Jasmine's rooms, inquiring anxiously, "Are you all right, my lady? The door was locked, and I could not get back in after the earl had removed me. Your mother gave him merry hell for it, I can tell you." Toramalli chuckled. "She accused him of behaving like a whoremaster, and the earl grew red in the face and shouted that he would not allow *her daughter* to destroy them all just because the prince sought to bed you! Does he really seek to bed you, my princess? He is certainly a merry, handsome young man."

"Indeed he does desire me, Toramalli," Jasmine replied slowly. "Eventually I shall have to yield myself to him, as he is to be England's king one day. I really cannot offend him."

"It does not seem too terrible a task, my lady—I mean, to fall in love with Prince Henry. He appears most amiable," Toramalli observed. "You are not, after all, in love with another, or betrothed. You are your own mistress in all matters regarding yourself and your children."

"You are absolutely right, Toramalli. I thank you for your common sense, which for my part I seem to have lost," Jasmine said, then she smiled a soft smile. "He is very handsome, isn't he? And he is certainly kind and amusing."

"It is time that you took a lover, my lady," Toramalli told her. "You have mourned your good lord and husband well over a year, and that is quite enough. You are young, and you are beautiful. Your juices of life flow generously, and should be mingled with those of a strong, young lover."

It seemed to Jasmine as if the whole world was conspiring against her to place her in Henry Stuart's bed. Her stepfather insisted that such a role was acceptable within the polite society in which they moved. Royal bastards were also, if recognized and doted upon, acceptable. Jasmine found that very perplexing in light of the attitude that would be taken had the full truth of her birth been known by the court. It appeared that the king had kept her secret to himself. It was obvious that the English court had one set of standards for themselves and another for the rest of the world.

Prince Henry, in the company of his cousin Arabella, arrived the following afternoon. Jasmine had to agree with the prince. The "Fair Arabella," as popularly known, was, in her late thirties, far too old for youthful Summertime. She was, nonetheless, a pretty woman with fine eyes, and graceful hands which fluttered constantly with her nervousness. Still, she spoke her lines well, and generously complimented Jasmine on the way in which she played her part.

When Inigo Jones and his seamstress arrived to fit Jasmine's costume, Arabella Stuart departed, but the prince remained.

"If you will disrobe to your chemise, Lady Lindley," the royal designer said.

"*Sir?*" Jasmine was most startled by his request.

"I cannot fit your costume over your own garments, madame," was the reply.

The prince sat smiling. He was obviously not about to leave.

Toramalli bit her lip to keep from giggling, and moved to help her mistress. Jasmine sent her a dark look.

"You will be barefooted for the masque, my lady," Inigo Jones informed her politely, "but I must measure your ankle, for it shall be bedecked with a small wreathlet of grapes.

Your natural coloring is really quite marvelous, you know. I shall gown you in shades of crimson and gold! You must wear your hair loose, my dear. I shall personally show your tiring woman how to dress it."

Master Jones and his assistant tossed lengths of colored silk about, twining certain colors together, wrapping her this way and that. It seemed to Jasmine that their efforts were quite useless, particularly when, after a period of time, she was set free from their ministrations. As they gathered up their materials to depart, Master Jones told her, "You will have your costume in three days, madame. It shall be delivered to Greenwood. Make certain you take good care of it."

"I cannot believe that my costume will resemble much of anything, my lord," Jasmine told the prince afterward. "I do not know what he did."

"He is an extremely clever fellow," Henry Stuart reassured her. "Wait and see, my love, you will be quite surprised by his efforts. May I take supper with you, Jasmine?"

"I do not know if supper will be available at Greenwood tonight, my lord," she told him. "My mother and stepfather had planned to dine at Whitehall with Sybilla and Tom. Toramalli, go to Mrs. Evans and see if she can prepare something sufficient to satisfy a royal appetite."

After wrapping a scarlet velvet chamber robe trimmed in thick, soft marten about her mistress, Toramalli curtsied and hurried off.

"We will eat here before the fire," he said, as if it had already been settled. Henry Stuart knew it unlikely that the cook would refuse to feed him. She would consider it an honor. He stretched his long legs out, warming the soles of his boots before the dancing flames.

Jasmine said nothing. Instead she moved to pour him some wine. She had hoped to have more time, but it was obvious he would not give her any more time. He was clever, she had to admit. He had chosen an evening he knew her family to be gone from the house, and he would seduce her in her own bed, where she was most likely to feel more comfortable. Jasmine smiled to herself admiringly. Henry Stuart would be a marvelous king one day. He was an excellent tactician.

"My lord." She handed him his goblet.

Placing it upon the little table next to his chair, he reached out and drew her down into his lap. "I want you in my arms where you belong, madame, not seated primly across from me with your marvelous eyes watching my every move with trepidation. When I kiss you, I want you to open your mouth," he commanded her, taking a drink from his goblet. Then he did kiss her, and slowly transferred the wine from his mouth to hers, his eyes never leaving hers.

Jasmine swallowed the liquid, shocked by the sensuousness of the act. Henry Stuart might be young, but he was obviously no stranger to passion. "You have never had a mistress?" she queried him.

His blue eyes sparkled with amusement. "Are you jealous already, madame?" His hand slid beneath her robe and stole slowly up between her legs. "I came to England's court when I was nine. I have told you that I became a man at eleven. When I was thirteen, I dallied a bit with Frances Howard, who is now Lady Essex. Being a very spoiled and proud lady, Frances likes to believe she was my mistress. She was not. I have never considered keeping a mistress until now." His slender fingers caressed the soft flesh of her Venus mont. Then, a single digit sought for, and found, the tiny jewel of her womanhood.

Jasmine could feel the tip of his finger, motionless on her flesh, simply touching her. Her cheeks grew warm and her heart jumped within her chest nervously. She pressed her cheek against his shoulder, her breath catching in her throat as she struggled to breathe normally. She could feel his lips brushing the top of her head, and all the while, she was more and more intensely aware of his finger touching her. Just when she thought she could bear it no longer, the single finger began to stroke her little jewel with a tender, light touch.

"Look at me," he whispered to her.

"I cannot," she murmured back, feeling inexplicably shy.

"Aye, you can, my love," he told her. "I adore it that you are so demure with me, but you must not be reticent, Jasmine. Now, my darling, look up at me. There is nothing so terrible about what we do. I am simply touching you, my love. Look at me," he crooned low.

Slowly she raised her head, and when finally their eyes met, he bent to kiss her. His mouth was warm and incredibly sensuous on hers. He kissed her tenderly at first, his kiss deepening until she was so overwhelmed with its sweetness that she silently prayed it would never end. She arched herself, twisting her body to meet his lips, aching suddenly with her need to be possessed by him. *"Please!"* she half sobbed as the seductive workings of both his mouth, and the marauding finger, began to arouse her more than she thought she could bear.

It had been so very long since she had known passion, and Jasmine was very aware now that she needed passion in her life. She was more than just the mother of Rowan Lindley's three children. *"Please!"* she repeated, and cried out softly as she felt two of his fingers penetrating her, moving quickly to ease her need until finally she collapsed against him, weeping bitterly, half relieved, half shamed by her own conduct.

He cradled her tenderly within the security of his arms until her little sobs had dissipated. Then he arose, setting her on her feet. "You can stand," he told her as he walked across the room to the door and, turning the key, locked it. "Where is your bedchamber?" he demanded.

Wordlessly Jasmine pointed, and Henry Stuart nodded, removing her velvet robe first. Then, hooking his hand into the neckline of her chemise, he ripped it open in a single stroke and pulled it off of her. He stood silently for a long moment, his blue eyes sweeping over her. With impatient fingers he yanked his own clothing off. When he was as naked as she, he stood for a brief time allowing her to see him. He was tall, with long, graceful limbs, a smooth, broad chest, and a manhood already engorged with his desire for her.

Silently he lifted her up in his arms and carried her into the bedchamber. Near the fire, which burned brightly, giving the room its only light, was a tall mirror in a carved silver casing. Henry Stuart stood Jasmine before the mirror, standing behind her so they might both gaze on their naked images, erotically reflected in the dim, smoky glass. His hands moved from her shoulders down her torso to cup her breasts in his palms. Tenderly he fondled the proud, high cones of flesh, teasing the dark, rosy nipples into sharp little points. His red-blond head dipped low to kiss her neck and shoulder with deep sensuous kisses, his mouth hot and moist upon her flesh.

Jasmine's dark head fell back against him. She had never in her life, she realized, felt so helpless before a man's passion. He was in full and total control. She was not afraid, however. For some reason, what was happening between them was right. His teeth sank into her shoulder, and she moaned with her rising, overwhelming desire. He turned her about to face him, their lips met fiercely and they kissed each other until their mouths were bruised and aching.

Slowly he forced her to her knees before him, his hand cupping his throbbing member, offering it to her, and she took him in her mouth. Henry Stuart's eyes closed and he groaned with the pleasure she so quickly gave him. Her mouth drew strongly and rhythmically upon him. Her tongue swept over and around him, teasing lightly but insistently. He struggled against his own lust, and won. He wanted far more than just the little they had shared so far.

"Enough!" he growled harshly. He pulled her to her feet as she released her hold on him, pushing her back so that

she fell upon her bed, her legs hanging over awkwardly. Kneeling quickly, he drew her slender limbs over his shoulders, his head pressing forward between her shapely thighs, his tongue seeking her out.

Jasmine cried out sharply at his touch, which was almost painful to her in her aroused state. She felt as if she were close to bursting into flames, and gasped desperately for air. Her limbs felt leaden and weak. She was helpless before his sweetly marauding mouth, and yet the pleasure filling her was almost too much to endure. She didn't want him to cease his divine ministrations even if she died from it.

"Sweet! Sweet!" he groaned low against her moist flesh.

She arched to meet him, encouraging him in his lust, needing it, craving it, pleasured beyond her wildest dreams by it. She had loved Jamal Khan with a girl's first love. She had loved Rowan Lindley with a woman's love. She did not love Henry Stuart, but she did need him. She needed this passion. She wanted it. She would have it! *Or she would die!*

The prince released his hold upon her and, standing, pulled her completely onto the bed. His strong young body covered hers. She felt him penetrating her, and Jasmine wrapped herself around her lover, encouraging him in his efforts. He thrust furiously into her passage, rousing her further and further until she cried out with fulfillment, but even then he was not satisfied. Once again he drove her up passion's peak, this time, however, tumbling over into the sweet abyss with her.

Returning slowly to his senses within the comfort of her embrace, he said, "Madame, you are a fit mistress for a king."

He laughed when she replied, "And you, my lord prince, are certainly more than a fit lover for an Imperial Mughal princess!"

"Then it is settled between us, is it?" Henry Stuart asked.

"Aye, my lord. I will be yours, but you must be faithful to me, my Hal," Jasmine told him.

"And if I am not?" he teased her.

"Then I shall not be faithful to you either," she said with utmost seriousness. "I shall never forget that you are to be England's king one day, Hal. But you must not forget that I am a princess born. Who could you bed who would be my better? There is no one, and therefore you would bring shame upon me. I will not countenance it, my lord."

"Someday I will have to take a wife," he said.

"A wife is a wife," she answered. "I will forgive you a wife."

Henry Stuart laughed again, genuinely amused. "My darling Jasmine, I absolutely adore you! There has never been anyone in my life who could satisfy my passions as you do, or make me laugh as you do. Swear to me that you will never leave me, my love."

She looked into his eyes and thought that he was a very sweet man. If she was the prince's official mistress, she would always be safe from marriage. She would be her own mistress by being the prince's.

"I will never leave you, my Hal," she told him. "Unless, of course, you no longer desire me."

"I cannot," he said with utmost seriousness, "ever imagine not desiring you, Jasmine, my love."

"Then it is truly settled," she replied.

❋

19

❋

The Earl of Glenkirk had returned to court after an absence of some months. He had been in Scotland overseeing his vast holdings. It was becoming increasingly difficult, he found, to serve both James Stuart and his own interests. Glenkirk was his home, and he loved it, but without Isabelle and the children, it was a place overrun with lonely memories—not just of his late wife and children, but of his mother, his father, his grandparents, and that magnificent matriarch he had never known but who was still spoken of by the Leslies of Glenkirk, his great-great-grandmother, Janet Leslie. But they were all gone, and he was alone. He did not like being alone.

He knew that he should remarry. His brothers and sisters constantly importuned him to remarry. His mother wrote him long, serious letters from Italy, where she now lived with her second husband, begging him to remarry. His father wrote him once yearly from the Americas, where he lived with his new wife and family. He, too, preached remarriage and duty to Glenkirk.

James Leslie found his father's letters particularly irritating. Patrick Leslie had gone off, leaving his family in order that he might explore the new world. When his ship was reported sunk, they had believed him dead. He had survived, however, but neglected to inform them. A charming but spoiled man, Patrick Leslie had continued on with his explorations, returning home in secret almost ten years ago to confront his eldest son and heir with the fact of his existence.

He had not been at all interested in picking up his old life. He was, in fact, openly relieved not to have to do so. His son had agreed to keep the secret of his survival between themselves, and the former Earl of Glenkirk never lost touch with his son again, writing him yearly.

His father had been very sympathetic over the death of Isabelle and the children, but then he began to nag his son regarding remarriage and his obligations to the family. But it was the pleas of his brothers, Colin and Robert, that concerned James Leslie most. They did not wish the responsibility of Glenkirk thrust upon them.

"There must be some woman you would be content to marry, and father children upon," Colin Leslie had said to his brother the night before James began his return trip to England. "It is not as if Isabelle was the great love of your life, Jemmie. And how long have she and the bairns been gone now?"

"Aye," Robert Leslie had chimed in seriously. " 'Tis past time you remarried, and had new heirs. If there is no one in Scotland who takes your fancy, then look about the English court, man. We will settle for any strong, healthy lass, Jemmie. Even a Sassenach!"

James Leslie sighed to himself at his brother's words. There had been a woman he might have married, but he had not been quick enough. She had wed another. *Jasmine de Marisco.* He had never known a woman like her. His brothers could not know that it was not the memory of his dear Isabelle that prevented him from remarriage now. It was the memory of Jasmine de Marisco, and one incredible night that sometimes he was not even certain had really happened. Isabelle had been his wife by an arranged marriage, but this time he would follow his mother's lead. He would marry only for love. Without love there was nothing.

And now, newly returned to court, who should he happen upon first but Lady Frances Howard Devereaux, the Countess of Essex. Frances Howard was considered one of the most beautiful women at James's court. A voluptuous woman with large, dark eyes and rich chestnut-brown hair, she was one of the Earl of Suffolk's daughters. At thirteen she had been forced into marriage with young Robert Devereaux, the Earl of Essex, and her dislike for him was no secret. But despite her arrogant and willful personality, she had great charm when she chose to exhibit it. Even one of her great enemies described her as "a beauty of the greatest magnitude in the horizon of the court . . . every tongue grew an orator at that shrine."

"Glenkirk, you rogue! I did not know you were returned to court," Frances Howard effusively greeted James Leslie. "Little has changed, I fear. The same old faces; the same old scandals. Oh, yes! Prince Henry has taken a mistress, and not on the sly. It is quite in the open, my dear." Frances kissed his cheek familiarly, and for a moment he was enveloped in the fragrance of violets. "How is your Scotland?" she asked him, tucking her hand through his arm to walk with him.

"Same old faces, but alas, the scandals have moved south with the king," he told her mischievously. "The weather, I might add, was abysmal, as it frequently is in Scotland. Tell me of the prince. Who is the lady who has found favor with him? I thought that you were his favorite, Frances, but I hear, even in Scotland, that you have turned your sights upon Viscount Rochester. Oh, yes, how is your husband?"

Frances Howard, dressed in a gown of tawny orange and gold brocade with a wickedly low neckline that revealed her plump breasts, chuckled, and rapped the Earl of Glenkirk upon the arm with her gold and lace fan. "I but toyed with Henry Stuart, my dear. A lovely boy, but a boy nonetheless. My husband is as always. *Boring.* As for the prince, he has taken the dowager Marchioness of Westleigh to his bed. I must say that she is every bit as beautiful as I am," Frances concluded generously. "She is half foreign, I am told. Born a princess in her native land. Her mother is the Countess of BrocCairn. She and the prince are mad for one another, my dear. One cannot help but wonder how long it will last, but still it is encouraging to know that Henry Stuart does not have his father's proclivities."

"The *dowager* Marchioness of Westleigh, Frances? I did not know that there was one. Surely she must be a bit old for the prince. I have met the young Marchioness of West-leigh, but not her mother-in-law," the Earl of Glenkirk re-plied. "It is young Lady Lindley who is foreign-born."

"My goodness, you have been gone a long time," Frances Howard told him. "The Marquess of Westleigh was killed in Ireland, Glenkirk. It is his young widow who is Prince Hen-ry's mistress. Lady Jasmine Lindley is her name. Is that the same lady of your acquaintance?"

He nodded, stunned. "Aye, it is. I did not know she had been widowed. How long?"

"Well over a year, I understand. She has three children, but they are in the country," Frances Howard said.

"They cannot be very old," the Earl of Glenkirk said. "She ought to be with her children, and not at court whor-ing for the prince!"

Frances Howard laughed. "Oh, Glenkirk," she replied, "do not be so old-fashioned! One has servants to look after one's children. Lady Lindley does her children a better service here at court pleasing England's next king than she would remaining at home with them. Why, I think her a most excellent mother, for she is ambitious, and her position in Prince Henry's life cannot fail but help her children."

James Leslie was outraged, but he could not understand

why. Jasmine Lindley was not his responsibility, and yet the thought of her as Prince Henry's mistress was galling. He voiced his concern to Lady Lindley's stepfather, and was further outraged by Alex Gordon's attitude.

The Earl of BrocCairn looked at the Earl of Glenkirk as if he were a half-wit. "God's nightshirt, Jemmie, what business is it of yers? My own father was a royal bastard. Yer own mother was this king's mistress in his youth. Where is the harm in it? Jasmine was no virgin, but twice widowed. She was willing."

"Willing?" he ground out. "Willing to whore for a prince?"

"Aye, willing," BrocCairn replied. "She likes Henry Stuart. She has told her mother so. Besides, it canna hurt the future of her bairns that she is the prince's mistress. Little Henry Lindley will benefit by the association, as will our two granddaughters."

James Leslie felt himself overcome with rage at the Earl of BrocCairn's reasoning. Excusing himself, he hurried off before he hit the man. What was it about the Stuarts that drew women to them? And what was it about the royal Stuarts that led them to believe that they had a perfect right to appropriate any woman that took their fancy? But he knew the answer. James Stuart and his family believed most seriously in the divine right of kings to do what they pleased, when they pleased. Henry Stuart, if he had learned nothing else, had absorbed this lesson at his father's knobby knee.

The Earl of Glenkirk stopped in his flight and looked about. He was in a stone corridor, and completely lost. A sound caught his ear, and instinctively he stepped back into the shadows. A door at the end of the corridor opened, and in the shaft of light that spilled forth momentarily, he saw two people hurry through, one a man, the other a woman. He could not yet make out their features for they were too far away from him. The woman ran ahead of the man, who chased after her and finally caught up almost directly in front of the Earl of Glenkirk's hiding place. Shocked, he recognized the two. He was unable, however, to reveal himself.

Jasmine Lindley laughed low, seductively. "You really are very naughty, my lord," she told Henry Stuart.

"*I won!*" he said.

"*You cheated!*" she responded. "I have been playing chess since earliest childhood, and I could even beat my father, who was one of the finest players in India. You, sir, are not his equal. I saw you palm that bishop! You did not win, my lord!"

"Nonetheless you will pay the forfeit, madame, else I expire right here in this darkened corridor," he told her. "Surely you would not want to be responsible for my death? Then brother Charles would become king one day, and the poor little fellow is much too serious to be a King of England, madame. I shall make him Archbishop of Canterbury instead," Henry Stuart finished with a laugh, and he reached out for her.

In the dim torchlight that lighted the interior hallway, the Earl of Glenkirk saw Jasmine Lindley step quickly aside to evade the prince. Now, he thought, now I must make my presence known to them, but somehow he could not bring himself to step forward, to speak up. Instead he watched as the two lovers played a game of dodge and catch which the prince eventually won, drawing Jasmine into his arms to kiss her.

Pressing her against a stone pillar, he murmured against her mouth, and Glenkirk, in the shadows, not even daring to draw a deep breath, heard and saw everything.

"Witch! You have surely bewitched me, Jasmine, my love," Henry Stuart said. The tone in his voice was that of a young man in love but trying to keep control of the situation.

Lowering his head, the prince kissed the exposed flesh of her bosom. Then, with skillful fingers, he managed to undo her laces just enough that her breasts spilled from the gown. Bending, he suckled on each of her breasts while Jasmine sighed softly.

"Someone could see us," she protested faintly.

"We are quite alone, my love," he assured her.

I should turn away since I dare not reveal my presence, the Earl of Glenkirk thought, but he did not.

"I want you, my love," the prince told her. "Now!" He pushed the skirts of her gown up, eagerly seeking her.

"Oh, Hal! *Not here!*" she begged him, but it seemed to Glenkirk that she was not truly distressed by her situation. "What if someone comes, my darling? 'Twould be a terrible scandal."

"Who would dare admit to seeing such a thing?" He laughed, pressing against her sensuously, his tongue licking at her ear. "Why, Jasmine, my love, there could be someone hidden in the corridor at this very moment, and they would not dare reveal what they saw to a living soul. Does it excite you to think of fucking me before an audience? God's boots! I would not care if the entire court were present now, I desire you so very much!" He fumbled with his own clothing, releasing his greatly swollen manhood. "I want you, my darling! *I want you now!*" Henry Stuart said, his hands cupping her bottom and lifting her up to impale her upon his fleshy rod.

"Ahhhhhh," she cried softly, and wrapped both her arms and her legs about him, her naked breasts pressing hard against him.

James Leslie almost groaned aloud at the sight. As the prince thrust rhythmically into his most willing partner, her beautiful face became an erotic mask of pure pleasure. The earl closed his eyes for a moment, listening to the sensual sounds of their lovemaking, imagining himself in Henry Stuart's place. It had been almost five years since he had lain within her embrace, and he had been half in love with her then, a fact brought home to him when he learned of her impending marriage to Rowan Lindley. Now she was widowed, and he might have been free to court her had she not been Prince Henry's mistress. He struggled to prevent the overwhelming jealousy he felt from boiling over.

"Ohhh, Hal, my darling!" Jasmine cried.

"My love!" the prince replied, his voice harsh, and he shuddered with his release even as she half fainted within his arms.

All was silent for a few moments, except for the sounds of their rough breathing, gnawing at the quiet of the corridor. Then Jasmine laughed softly and said, "You *really* are naughty, my darling, but do not, I beg you, ever change your most wicked ways, Hal. I fear I enjoy them much too much."

Listening to her, James Leslie's jealousy grew even stronger. He watched from his hiding place as they carefully straightened their clothing so that no one they met might know of their dalliance. The earl studied his rival with a close eye. Henry Stuart was barely out of his boyhood, but then, Jasmine was not much older than her lover. The young man had an oval face that narrowed toward his chin, which had a small cleft in it. His eyebrows were bushy over fine gray-blue eyes. His cheekbones were high, his forehead broad. His nose was probably his weakest feature, being long and like his father's, but broader toward the tip. His upper lip was narrow, but his lower lip was full and sensuous.

"Would you be angry, Jasmine, if I said that I loved you?" Henry Stuart asked her, his eyes lowered, his fingers redoing her laces.

"You must not love me, Hal," she told him quietly. "We are friends, and that is more than enough for me. I would take nothing from the girl you will one day marry. I want you to love your wife. Without love, life is very lonely, my sweet lord. The wife chosen for you will be a princess from some foreign land. She will leave her family and all she has known to come to you, Hal. You must not just welcome her publicly. You must learn to love her so she will be content with you. Then you also will be happy. It is not easy to leave one's native land, one's family, and everything familiar that one has known. Had I not had my most wonderful grandparents awaiting me when I came here from India, I do not know what I should have done."

Her gentle, wise words surprised the earl in light of her most licentious and very abandoned behavior of the past few minutes. "You are a princess," Henry Stuart said. "I would marry you!"

"Oh, Hal! I do not know when I have been so flattered," Jasmine told him, and she kissed his cheek. "In India neither my father, God rest him, nor my brother would consider a royal Stuart worthy of an Imperial Mughal princess. Here in England the reverse would be true. The situation surrounding my birth has been delicately explained away because of my family connections, and my wealth. If you ever seriously contemplated a match with me, you would be horrified by the ensuing uproar. In England an Imperial Mughal princess is fit to be the Prince of Wales's mistress, but certainly not his wife. Besides, my darling, I have no wish to ever remarry," Jasmine concluded.

"Why?" he asked her, looking into her face tenderly.

"I believe I may be cursed, as I told you, Hal," Jasmine replied with utmost seriousness. "Both of my husbands have died violently, and both their deaths have been because of me. My brother Salim had Jamal Khan murdered because he sought an incestuous relationship with me. Rowan Lindley was killed by an assassin who meant for me to die. Only fate, unpredictable creature that she is, saved me both times. Because my grandmother had insisted on remaining in contact with my father, I was able to escape my brother. Had I not bent down from my mare to pick up India, the bullet meant for me would have buried itself in my heart and not Rowan's. To lose a husband to death is not unusual, but to lose two husbands to murder is most unusual. I have my children, Hal, and I would not send another man to an untimely end; particularly the man who is to be England's next king."

"I would not have believed you capable of such superstitious nonsense," Henry Stuart said, half angrily. "You sound like my father, with all his fears and crotchets over the supernatural, or the occult."

"I will not argue with you, my lord," Jasmine answered him quietly. "Whatever I may or may not believe, a marriage between us would never be countenanced. Why should we quarrel over it, my darling?" She kissed the tip of one finger and touched it to the cleft in his chin, smiling. "Come, my lord. We shall be late for vespers, and you know what people will think if we are. I do not wish to displease the king, else he think me a bad influence upon you."

"You are the best thing that has ever happened to me," Henry Stuart declared vehemently, but nonetheless he took her arm, and the young couple hurried off down the torch-lit corridor.

James Leslie stood silently in the dim light, listening to their footsteps as they faded. So Henry Stuart would marry Jasmine, but she would not have him. She was right, of course, in one sense. He did not believe for a moment that she was, as she stated, "cursed." But she was correct when she said that she would not be considered an eligible wife for England's next king. The tragedy was that she would probably make Henry Stuart a good wife. She was loving, and sensible, and knew what was expected of a queen. She obviously cared for the prince, although she had not admitted that she loved him when he had declared his passion.

Did she love him? James Leslie wondered about it. It was unlikely that she would admit to it if she did. Being sensitive to the prince's situation, and no adventuress, she would not want to encourage Henry Stuart in his folly. And when the prince one day was suitably matched and married, what would become of Jasmine? the Earl of Glenkirk thought curiously. Whoever became England's future queen would be unable to hold a candle to Jasmine for beauty. How would she feel about her husband's beauteous mistress? Would Jasmine even be welcomed at court then? And if she was not welcome, where would she go? Would she consider remarriage then? *To him?*

Christmas was celebrated at Whitehall that year. With the arrival of the holidays, Jasmine realized, as she had realized many times in the last months, how very much she missed her children. Court, her grandmother wrote her, was no place for children. They were happier and safer at Queen's Malvern. The dowager Marchioness of Westleigh was reluctantly forced to agree with Skye.

Although Jasmine had a home at Greenwood House, she had also been given rooms at St. James's Palace, Henry Stuart's London residence. It was an unspoken acknowledgment of her position at court. Everyone, even James Leslie, had to admit that Jasmine had great style. Whatever happened between the dowager Marchioness of Westleigh and the Prince of Wales, she did not allow any member of the court to forget she was a princess born.

When Henry Stuart insisted that Jasmine be installed in her own rooms in the palace, Jasmine sent for her other servants. Now the turbaned, white-coated Adali oversaw his mistress's apartments. Rohana and Toramalli, used to English clothing, reverted to their colorful and exotic silks. The younger members of the court vied for invitations to Lady Lindley's suite, for her intimate entertainments were considered a mark of having arrived within the inner circle, which Jasmine found quite amusing. She only invited clever, intelligent people who could amuse the prince with their wit and their conversation.

Robert Cecil, the Earl of Salisbury, became disturbed by Jasmine's position in the prince's life, and spoke to the king. "Is it wise for the prince to flaunt his mistress, sire, when we are actively seeking a wife for him? A young and gently reared princess would surely be distressed."

"Dinna fret, my little beagle," the king replied. "Lady Lindley is the perfect light o' love for Henry. She is charming and modest."

"She is intelligent," Robert Cecil condemned Jasmine dourly.

"I dinna hold wi intelligence in a woman either," James Stuart answered. "Still, if she is, she dinna flaunt it, and she makes my laddie laugh. 'Tis a rare quality in a woman, Cecil."

"But what if she becomes enceinte, sire?" Robert Cecil persisted.

"We'll pray for a grandson," the king said with a smile. "If Lady Lindley proves fertile, so much the better for my son's reputation. The Stuarts are known throughout Europe as good breeding stock."

The Earl of Salisbury sighed deeply. In his father's day there was no such worry. Elizabeth was a maiden queen. There were no royal offspring to cause scandal. He knew the amorous reputation attributed to the royal Stuarts, but he had somehow hoped that Prince Henry, being more sensible than his parents, could overcome it. Obviously he could not. If only Lady Lindley were not the granddaughter of the Countess of Lundy. Lady de Marisco had given Elizabeth Tudor great difficulties, and now here was her incredibly beautiful granddaughter futtering the Prince of Wales, and enchanting him totally. What if a match for Henry Stuart was agreed upon and she caused difficulties? His father's son, Robert Cecil could not allow such a thing to happen. He requested that Lady Lindley meet with him. To his deep annoyance, she sent back a message that she would be delighted to speak with him . . . in her apartments.

"In other words," Robert Cecil muttered irritably to himself, "on her terms! Just like her grandmother, I vow!" Still, he went.

Jasmine greeted him politely, inviting him to be seated. Her servants brought them wine, and then when they had been dismissed, Lady Lindley, taking hold of the situation, said, "What is it you want of me, my lord Cecil? I cannot imagine there is some way in which I may aid you."

"Your relationship with the prince disturbs me, madame," Robert Cecil said, equally direct and open.

"My relationship with the prince is not your concern, my lord," Jasmine told him bluntly, "but I understand your fears. I do not expect to wed Prince Henry. When he is finally married, I will leave the court, although I have promised the prince that I will always be there for him should he need me. It is a promise I will keep. Nonetheless, I believe it important that he learn to love his wife, and she him. I will cause no scandal."

"What if you should have his child, madame?"

"I should consider myself blessed, my lord. I like children. I have three now. A son, and two daughters," Jasmine said.

"*Madame!* You are as exasperating as your grandmother has always been. On one hand you soothe my fears with your sensible words, but then you terrify me with the possibility of a royal bastard. There has not been an acknowledged royal bastard since the days of the late queen's father. Royal bastards make for unnecessary difficulties," the Earl of Salisbury grumbled, glowering at her.

Jasmine smothered a giggle. "Please, my lord, you must not fret yourself," she counseled him. "I cannot stop the course of nature should she get it into her capricious head to give me a baby."

With a despairing shake of his head, Robert Cecil departed Lady Lindley's apartments. What would be would be, unless, of course, he could convince the king to marry Lady Lindley off to some worthy gentleman who would remove her from court. *Aye!* That was the answer. The prince might play in peace with his mistress until they had found him a suitable bride, but once the papers were signed, Lady Lindley must be married off to a strong man who would not take kindly to being a cuckold. It was such a simple solution that

Robert Cecil was ashamed that he hadn't thought of it before. The lady herself had promised him that she would leave court when Prince Henry married.

Relieved, the Earl of Salisbury did not distress himself further even when the prince and his mistress were the center of the holiday revels. Ben Jonson had written a new masque, *Oberon, Prince of Faery*, and Inigo Jones would be designing the costumes and the sets. Prince Henry would, of course, play the title role in the masque. Jasmine Lindley would be Titania, Oberon's queen.

"Bare feet again, Master Jones?" Jasmine teased, as she stood patiently at her costume fitting.

Inigo Jones looked up at her with a grin. He was kneeling before her, measuring the distance from the floor to Jasmine's ankle. "And a costume so diaphanous that no other lady at court could dare to wear it, madame," he told her, and chuckled. "You must appear to be clothed in cobwebs and moonbeams."

"And who shall play the other roles in this masque?" Jasmine asked him, wondering if her lover would approve of the costume.

"Lady Essex has been chosen to be Aurora, the Goddess of Dawn, madame," Inigo Jones said. "Now that poor Lady Arabella is confined to the tower because her secret marriage to William Seymour has been revealed, we may expect Lady Essex's star to shine more brightly, especially given her close friend, Viscount Rochester."

"Poor Lord Essex," Jasmine said sympathetically. "He seems a very pleasant young man. The prince says he is quite loyal as well."

"That may be, my lady," Inigo Jones replied, "but young Carr is quite his majesty's pet. As long as he keeps on the king's good side, he'll go far. Wait and see. There will be a bigger peerage in it for him before it's all over." Inigo Jones lowered his voice now. "Lady Frances has charm, my lady, but she is spoiled, and determined to be the brightest star in the firmament of the court. How better to attain her goal than to become wife to his majesty's favorite?"

"But she already has a husband," Jasmine said low.

"With her connections, my lady, he's easily divorced when she so chooses to rid herself of him. I hear things. Her majesty would be delighted, I can tell you, to have young Carr removed from the king's sphere. That young man is most greedy, and never satisfied with all he gets. King James is a good man, but too generous with those he loves."

Inigo Jones, who had also served the queen's brother, King Christian of Denmark, was intimately acquainted with the royal family. Jasmine listened to him, fascinated. Anyone else might have dismissed him as a simple gossip, but she did not. She was also careful of what she said before him lest it be repeated. She only told Master Jones what she desired the king and queen to know. It was no secret that she was the Prince of Wales's mistress, but discretion was a very important part of her position in the court.

"You can wear nothing beneath this costume," Inigo Jones said as he stood up, satisfied with the length now. "You must remember that you are a faery queen clothed in gossamer garments."

"I am not certain that the prince will approve," Jasmine replied.

"I have shown him the costume, my lady. He has given his permission that you may wear it. Speak with him yourself," Inigo Jones said. "I will admit it is daring, but authenticity is so important."

That evening as she lay abed naked with her lover, Jasmine asked him, "Are you aware of how diaphanous my costume is, Hal? Master Jones says I am not to wear anything beneath it. My nudity shall be quite visible to all. He says he has your permission."

"Aye," Henry Stuart answered her. He was seated, equally naked, in her bed. Jasmine, her back to him, was settled between his legs. With one hand he cupped and fondled a breast, while with the other he pushed aside her long black hair that he might kiss her neck. His lips brushed the smooth, soft column. "I want every man at court to be jealous of me, my love. I want them to see your perfection, and ache with the knowledge that you are mine, and mine alone." His tongue swept up her neck wetly.

"I am yours because it pleases me to be so," she said softly, and her fingers trailed up and down his thigh thoughtfully. The light golden down on his legs bristled slightly, and she smiled to herself.

He sharply pinched the nipple with which he was toying, causing her to gasp. *"I will never let you go, Jasmine,"* he said fiercely. Then bending his head again, he bit her shoulder. *"You belong to me!"*

Pulling away from him, Jasmine scrambled about and knelt before him. "I am not a possession, Hal. Yours, or any man's. I left India because I would not allow myself to be owned. I belong to no one but myself. I am not some simple little English milady honored and overwhelmed by your attentions. I am an Imperial Mughal princess, though I be far from my homeland." Behind her the flames in the fireplace crackled noisily, as if adding emphasis to her words. "You are in my bed because I wish it, my lord, not just because you wish it."

For a moment his face darkened with his own anger, but then he laughed. "What a proud creature you are, Jasmine, my love," he told her blandly, but then he pushed her upon her back and flung himself atop her, pinioning her beneath him. *"You are mine, princess or no, madame!"*

Furiously, Jasmine squirmed beneath him, but he was heavier than she, and used his weight to his advantage. He had forced her arms behind her so that she could not use them against him. Now, straddling her, he laughed down into her face. "The gentlemen of the court shall admire you through a sensuously taunting curtain of fluttering silks, my love. They shall observe the exquisite high cones of your creamy breasts. When you dance before them, you shall think of me, of us, of how we are now. The nipples of your breasts will pucker with your remembrance." His free hand brushed possessively over her bosom, his fingers teasing at the nipples which had indeed grown taut and tight.

Jasmine said nothing, but her turquoise-blue eyes glowed angrily.

"Any gentleman with whom you make eye contact will believe you aroused by him, and will ache with his own desire to possess you," Henry Stuart continued wickedly. Then sliding himself down her body a ways, he leaned forward to take a nipple within his mouth.

The tug of his lips upon her flesh was delicious, but Jasmine remained silent. Their dispute was one of perspective, not passion. His behavior no doubt stemmed from his growing frustration over her place in his life. He wanted her for a wife, but being intelligent, he knew that Jasmine was correct when she said a marriage between them would not be allowed. The thought that he might lose her one day drove him to recklessness. His mother had only recently mentioned that they were considering the possibility of a match between him and the Spanish Infanta, Maria Anna, daughter of King Philip III and his queen, Margaret of Austria.

"You must do what is best for England," Jasmine had told him sternly when he mentioned it. He knew that she was right.

His anger had come to the boiling point. Wife or no wife, he would not lose her to another man! He suckled hard upon her breast, and Jasmine was no longer able to keep from crying out. *"You are mine!"* he repeated, and he pulled himself up level with her face that he might cover it with his hot kisses.

Her eyes closed now, Jasmine didn't know whether to be angry with him or not. He was so wise for a man of his tender years, and yet he was so young. She would wager she knew more about being a king than did Henry Stuart, for all his proud boasting. He had only recently said to his father, annoyed with the king's reprimand for some minor fault, "I know what becomes a prince. It is not necessary for me to be a professor, but a soldier, and a man of the world."

But the man within him yet warred with the boy. Jasmine struggled to free a hand, and successful, caressed the back of his neck tenderly.

"I cannot lose you, my lamb love," he groaned within the fragrant cloud of her dark hair. "I will not let them separate us! Whomever they shackle me to, I shall love only you, Jasmine. *Only you.*"

She felt the tears pricking at the back of her eyelids. Damn! Why was life so terribly complicated? *I love you, Henry Stuart,* she thought silently, but I will never tell you. It would not be fair to the lady who will one day be your wife. I have been a wife, and I know how much a woman needs to know that her husband loves her. But I will stay with you, my dear lord, as long as you desire me.

She felt him slide within her, and she arched herself to meet him. Fiercely he rode her, and freeing her other hand, she put her arms about him, holding him close to her, returning his kisses with fiery kisses of her own. He thrust into her over and over and over again until Jasmine was aflame and shuddering with her own passion. Still, he could not seem to satisfy himself.

"It is not enough!" he half sobbed. "It is not enough! I cannot have enough of you, my lamb love!" He ground deeply into her.

"Ahhhhh, my Hal! Ahhhhhh, my dearest!" Jasmine cried out to him as her voluptuous body reached its crisis for a third time. "No more, I beg you! It is too much!"

"No! 'Tis not enough!" Henry Stuart insisted, and he pressed his aching loins harder against her, forcing her legs up and back that he might propel himself deeper into her hot passage. His manhood was a weapon that thrust, parried, and withdrew as he plunged himself into her again and again.

Never, Jasmine thought dreamily through the haze of sensation enveloping her—nay, overwhelming her!—never had a man plowed her furrow so deeply. His rod was like iron, driving into her with a painful sweetness, until she thought that she could surely bear no more, that he could give no more; yet he pushed onward. Thrice she had gained pleasure from him in this one encounter, but now she could feel a wildness building up within the very core of her deepest being. He lay atop her, his loins pistoning against her, his hands clutching at her breasts for balance. She had long since ceased to hold him. Her arms lay helplessly over her head as he drove her onward into madness.

Their bodies were wet with their striving. Henry Stuart suddenly tensed. *At last*, he thought. At last he would gain victory over her sweetly yielding body. The walls of her passage tightened like a nutcracker about his throbbing member in a manner he had never before experienced. He groaned. It was as if she were struggling to extract every drop of his life force from him. He felt as if he would explode as she gripped and released, gripped and released him. It was almost enough, he realized with relief.

Sobbing with her passion, Jasmine gasped, but half aware, beneath her lover. He had never loved her like this before. It was wild, and it was wonderful. She was going to die, and she did not care. She could hear someone crying out with a sound of intense pleasure even as the waves of joy washed over her, drowing her in such happiness that it didn't matter if she ever saw the light of day again. Then she was swept down into a whirlpool of dark warmth, and with a cry, she yielded herself to it, unafraid.

When she finally came to herself again, it was to find

Henry Stuart sprawled across her body, shuddering with his own pleasure, still buried deep within her. "Ohh, Hal! You are still so hard!" she whispered.

"You fainted, my love," he whispered back. "I flooded your sweet womb but did not withdraw. You must give a little more, Jasmine, before I am content this night." Raising himself slightly, he kissed the corners of her mouth.

"You almost killed me, and you want more?" She ran her little pointed tongue swiftly over his sensuous lower lip.

"Aye, I do," he murmured against her mouth.

"Then love me sweetly and gently this time, my lord," she told him, and he did, finally withdrawing from her utterly satisfied.

As they lay quietly now, Henry Stuart said, "I want you to have my bairn, Jasmine. I have never before had a bairn."

"That must be as God wills it, my lord," she returned, "but I should not be unhappy if I could please you in this matter." The thought of Robert Cecil arose in her mind, and she giggled.

"What is it?" he asked her, and she told him. "Damn Cecil for an impertinent dog!" Henry Stuart grumbled.

"He tries to think of what would be best for you, my darling," Jasmine told him, surprised to find herself defending the king's chancellor.

"What they want is for me to marry some pious, ugly virgin of impeccable royal lineage. Have you seen the miniature of the Infanta Maria Anna? She has an overbite, and looks like a rodent, I vow!" he groused. "This is what they would have me get my sons on."

"I have indeed seen the Infanta's miniature, and you do her a great injustice, my lord," Jasmine scolded him. "She is a lovely young girl with fine large eyes, a most dainty nose, and a luscious-looking mouth. Her hair is fairer than yours too."

"And short! I do not like short hair, but her aunt, the French queen, has made it fashionable. A woman should have hair that is at least shoulder length," the prince announced. "Besides, there is the matter of religion. The Spanish are as obdurate about it as are the English. At least a French princess, though holding to her faith, would not interfere with the bairns. I think a French lass would be more acceptable to the English."

"You are so old-fashioned, my lord," she teased him. "Why, you are beginning to sound just like your royal father."

"God's boots," he groaned, "not that!"

The Christmas season arrived. Viscount Rochester was appointed the Lord of Misrule over the entire court. Jasmine, in concert with Sybilla and their mother, oversaw the decorations at St. James. The palace was decorated with a variety of greens. There was yew, reputed to be a good defense against sorcerers and witches, of which King James was sore afraid. Since the king would certainly visit his son at some point during the season, the yew was hung in deference to him. Bay was an ancient sign of power, and as Henry Stuart would one day be England's king, Jasmine thought it appropriate. The bright red berries on the deep green holly leaves stood for the drops of blood that fell from Christ's crown of thorns. The ivy garlands—ivy being sacred to the ancient god Bacchus—were believed to protect against drunkenness, of which there seemed to be much at court. Mistletoe was held to protect against evil spirits and to promote peace among men.

Her own apartments Jasmine decorated with laurel garlands. Laurel was thought to be a protector, and symbolized honor. Woven in with the laurel was bay, and rosemary for remembrance and friendship.

Although Jasmine knew many people at court now, she had no real friends except among her family. Her position as Prince Henry's mistress made her an easy target for gossip, but her family and her servants would not gossip about her

and the prince. They could not be bought, nor even importuned to intercede for some petitioner eager for royal favor.
Most amazing of all to those who peopled the court was that
neither Lady Lindley nor her family sought any gain for
themselves from her most advantageous position.

"They must be very stupid, provincial people," a courtier
said in the hearing of Lady Essex and the Earl of Glenkirk.

"Nay," Frances Howard replied, a small, amused smile
upon her face. "They are simply very rich."

"But they could be richer!" the courtier said in disbelief.

"There are some people in this world who put honor
above personal gain," the Earl of Glenkirk explained to the
surprised courtier. "Lady Lindley and her family are such
people."

"I still think them foolish not to benefit when they could
benefit most handsomely, my lord," the courtier said.

"Are you going to Robin Southwood's Twelfth Night
fete?" Frances Howard asked the earl, dismissing the courtier, who was not particularly important. "Ben Jonson and
Inigo Jones have devised a most magnificent masque for the
occasion. The prince will play the role of Oberon, the faery
king, and Lady Lindley, Titania, his queen. I am told that
her costume is most scandalous. One of my maids knows
one of the women who sews for Master Jones. They say you
can see right through it, and that she will wear it with nothing beneath! Do you think she would dare?"

"I have absolutely no idea," the Earl of Glenkirk replied,
sounding bored. "Tell me, madame, what costume will you
wear?" he asked, diverting her attention to herself.

Frances Howard looked about her, and then said in a half
whisper, "Will you swear to me, my lord, that you will tell
no one if I tell you? There is so little imagination among the
court, and a good idea is pounced upon to be duplicated a
dozen times over. I do not wish to see myself coming and
going at the Earl of Lynmouth's gala."

"I swear, madame," he whispered back, and then said, "I

shall even share my own secret with you first. I intend to come as myself."

"*Yourself?*" Frances Howard made a little moue with her mouth. "That is really not particularly interesting, Glenkirk. Have you, like the king, no fondness for a fete? Is this a Scottish trait perhaps?"

He laughed. "Actually I do enjoy a fete, madame, and when I tell you that I am coming as myself, I mean that I shall be garbed in my full Highland dress. Have you ever seen a Scot in a kilt?"

Her eyes grew round. "Nay, I have not," she admitted. "Is it true that your knees will be bare, my lord?"

"*Very bare,*" he teased her with a smile. "Does it excite you, madame, the thought of my bare knees?"

"Are your knees attractive, my lord, or are they knobby?" she teased him back. "I like a man with shapely knees."

"You shall judge for yourself, madame," he told her with a laugh. "Now you must tell me what your costume will be, for I have confided mine."

Frances Howard stood on tiptoes, but even so the Earl of Glenkirk had to bend down so she might whisper in his ear. "I shall be coming as Venus, the ancient Roman goddess of love. My lord Rochester is to be Adonis. What think you of that?"

"Will your husband come as Vulcan, then?" Glenkirk asked her, deadpan. "And perhaps the king will be Jupiter himself."

Lady Essex burst out laughing. "Lord bless me, my lord, you are most droll. I have no idea what Essex intends to wear, but I will wager that I could get him to come as Vulcan. I know I can! What a deliciously amusing idea! Shall I do it?"

"Would it be kind?" James Leslie asked her, now regretting that he had even suggested such a thing. This was a cruel court, and he found he sometimes fell into its unkind spirit without meaning to do so. Young Lord Essex had enough of a cross to bear with Frances Howard for his wife. She was neither dedicated to her task nor even particularly domesticated. She made a poor spouse, Glenkirk thought, though she was amusing. The rumor was that poor Essex had not even consummated the union, for his wife resisted all efforts on his part, disliking him so.

"I do not care if it is kind or not, Glenkirk, it is most clever, and I shall be admired greatly if I can pull it off. Essex will certainly look the fool, and so much the better," Frances concluded.

"Why do you hate your husband so?" he asked her, curious.

"I did not want to marry him, but my father thought the match an advantageous one for the Howards. I told Robert Devereaux quite plainly how I felt, but he agreed with my father because he thought the marriage a good one for his family too. They said that I was a silly chit of a girl and must do as I was bid. I was literally forced to the altar. Why, my father beat me twice before the wedding day for my refusals, but I've had my way despite them both."

"You are a formidable opponent, Frances Howard," Lord Leslie said.

"I am," she agreed calmly. "Now tell me, what think you of my costume? Is it original? Will I be admired?"

"Aye, it is, and you will be, madame," the Earl of Glenkirk told her.

Jasmine returned to Greenwood the day before her uncle Robin's annual fete. "I cannot, my lord, keep my costume secret," she told Henry Stuart, "unless I am in my own house."

Reluctantly, he allowed her to go.

Secretly, Jasmine was delighted to be back at Greenwood again. St. James Palace and Whitehall were overrun with courtiers and petitioners, and rife with intrigue, deception, and all other ills afflicting a royal court. Her every move was watched. Her every word was analyzed for deeper meaning. It was a constant strain that she did not enjoy, but bore for the sake of the young prince who loved her so passionately.

But even Jasmine's family could not help but discuss her status as they sat together at dinner that evening.

"Well, my dear, you have certainly surprised us all," her aunt Willow said sharply. "I would not have thought you capable of such a thing, and yet you have conducted yourself with dignity. I cannot, however, help but wonder what Mama must think of you now."

"My grandmother worries about my future," Jasmine replied.

"Do you mean she approves of your conduct, my child?" Willow demanded, looking slightly scandalized, yet at the same time thoughtful.

"Grandmother has known great love in her time. She well understands my position in this matter, Aunt," Jasmine responded softly.

"Hummmph," the Countess of Alcester snorted, retiring defeated. "Well, my child, I hope you will get *something* out of it. A manor, or a town house perhaps," she said. "Something. You've gems enough, I vow!"

"Jasmine is to play a major role in tomorrow evening's masque," Velvet said proudly. "Sybilla also has a part. She will be the nymph of the river Wye; and Robin's youngest daughter, along with my little Neddie, will join Prince Charles as mischievous wood sprites, Willow. 'Twill be a most beautiful and exciting masque, I believe."

"I miss the old days," Willow admitted. "We had such a fine time dancing at Queen Elizabeth's court. 'Twas better than these silly and most expensive masques. Why, the king is constantly in debt, with all the queen's expenditures. The treasury is not bottomless, you know, Velvet. Next they'll be taxing our trading houses even more than they do now to pay for all this nonsense."

"The king is generous," Jasmine said.

"With other people's money!" snapped her aunt. "Where will it end? I ask you. I must say I am grateful that all my daughters are married to country gentlemen. 'Tis better to stay clear of a court where rampant spending is the order of the day, and a woman's virtue may be so easily compromised," Willow concluded emphatically.

"My daughter's virtue was hardly *easily* compromised," Velvet told her sister testily. "To have refused Prince Henry would have caused a far greater scandal than to accept his suit. But then, dear Willow, as you have spent most of your life down in the country, you could hardly be expected to comprehend the etiquette of the Stuart court, could you?"

Sybilla kicked her stepsister beneath the table, her eyes twinkling with merriment as their mother and their aunt battled back and forth. Their aunt Willow very much disliked being considered ignorant on any subject.

"I would be mortified if *any* daughter of mine comported herself in the fashion that Jasmine has," Willow declared.

"And, indeed, Aunt, you would have every right to your distress," Jasmine agreed, "for your daughters are all married to living husbands. I have not that good fortune, however, and as the prince is unmarried as well, we harm no one with our love affair, do we?"

"What happens when Prince Henry marries?" demanded Willow, ever sensible. "What will become of you then?"

"Of course the prince will marry eventually. He must for the good of the realm. I will leave court when that time comes. I have told Hal that. His wife must not be embarrassed by my presence. 'Twill be no hardship, I assure you. I have no great love for court life. Indeed, I miss my children and the country."

"God's foot!" Willow swore. "You are Mama all over again. I can remember how maddening it was to try and deal with her when I was a girl. You think as she thought, God help us all!"

Those gathered about the high board laughed heartily,

and Willow's brother, Robin, sympathized mockingly with her. "Aye, poor Willow! She has forever been unable to force Mama to behave like a dull goodwife. It has been your cross, big sister, has it not? And now to have a niece who is equally difficult. Ahhhh!"

"Laugh if you will, Robert Southwood," Willow said, "but no good will come of Jasmine's behavior with Prince Henry. She but draws attention to the family. Our security has always been in being unknown."

"I am the king's blood relation," the Earl of BrocCairn said. "It is impossible for us to be unknown in this court, Willow. I am sorry if it discommodes you, but there it is. I seem to spend at least half my year in England now, though I would have it otherwise."

The talk now moved on to costumes for the Earl of Lynmouth's fete on the following evening.

"I hear the costume you are to wear in the masque is quite scandalous, Jasmine," her aunt said. "Is it so?"

"I fear you will be quite shocked, Aunt," Jasmine admitted. "But of course in India we wore fewer garments, and the body was not considered shameful. It should comfort you, however, to know that I shall change into another costume following my participation in the masque. The prince shall dress as the Sun itself, and I shall be the Moon."

"Ohh," Lady Southwood cried. "Our minds have been attuned, I think, dear Jasmine. Your uncle Robin is to come as the Evening Star, and I, the Morning Star. Our costumes will be mostly blue."

"The prince will be in cloth-of-gold," Jasmine said, "and I will be gowned in cloth-of-silver, Aunt Angel." She turned to Willow. "And you, Aunt, how will you be garbed for Uncle Robin's gala?"

"I will come as the ancient goddess of home and hearth," Willow replied tartly.

"How perfectly appropriate," murmured Lord Southwood, and he looked to his brother-in-law, James Edwardes.

"And you, James? What clever idea has struck you, and does Willow approve?"

"I approve of everything James does," Willow snapped at Robin. "He is, and always has been, the most sensible of men." She beamed quite lovingly at her patient spouse, for Willow loved her husband dearly.

"I have found some old robes in our estate church," the Earl of Alcester replied. "How long they had been there, I have no idea. Probably since the time of old King Henry. Willow most kindly restored them, and I shall come as a monk."

The other gentlemen at the table, unable to help themselves, burst into fits of uncontrollable laughter. James Edwardes's mild blue eyes twinkled, and even the ladies tittered.

Willow, feeling sore-pressed by her relations tonight, glared at them all and said, "If any of you says one word!"

Her family, however, was too overcome by amusement to utter a single syllable.

❀

20

❀

The Earl of Lynmouth's Twelfth Night gala was to be the largest he had ever held. The weather being unusually mild for January, lanterns were strung among the trees in the gardens of Lynmouth House, which bordered the river Thames. Bonfires were to be set in select areas of the gardens and kept burning all the night long. At midnight the guests would stream out from the house to view a magnificent display of fireworks that were set off from a large barge in mid-river. No one had ever done such a thing before, and many who must entertain the king in future were certain to be overcome with envy at the handsome Earl of Lynmouth's cleverness.

The great ballroom had a stage constructed at one end. Inigo Jones had come himself to oversee the placement and building of the temporary structure. The Earl of Lynmouth, however, had borne the expense of it all. Although he would have never admitted it to his sister Willow, he was beginning himself to consider the great expense of this court and whether it was worth it. The brief magnificence of a masque was wonderful to look upon, but the values it instilled were not those values that Robert Southwood wished to pass on to his children, or grandchildren. His three eldest daughters from his first marriage were safely married; but the children his beautiful second wife, Angel, had borne him ranged in age from his heir, Geoffrey, who was twenty-one, to his youngest daughter, Laura, who was just eleven.

Laura Southwood, who was her father's pet, had been rehearsing her role for days with her cousin, Neddie Gordon, and little Prince Charles, both of whom were ten. He had never seen her more excited over anything than she was over this masque. Lady Laura Southwood, for all her father's worries, loved the Stuart court.

The family gathered at Lynmouth House in mid-afternoon in advance of the guests. A single room had been set aside for the costumes. There were tables set up by the various tiring women, and valets for their mistresses and masters; and beautiful decorative screens behind which they would don their costumes. There were several large mirrors set in carved, gilded frames, so that the masque's participants could view themselves prior to their performance. They would not appear before then.

A light meal was served, and then the family scattered, each to bedchambers assigned to them. Jasmine had eaten lightly. She had not felt particularly well these past few days. Her mother asked the obvious question as they sat together before a cozy fire.

"Are you with child, Jasmine?" The Countess of Broc-Cairn looked genuinely concerned, for no matter what her husband said, it was disturbing to her that Jasmine should give birth to a royal bastard.

"I am not certain yet, Mama," Jasmine replied serenely.

"How long since your last moon cycle?" her mother asked.

"Five weeks," Jasmine answered. "It is not enough yet for me to be sure. Please say nothing, Mama. I should feel quite the fool if it were not so, and Hal would be disappointed."

"But you are sure, aren't you?" Velvet probed.

Jasmine's turquoise-blue eyes met her mother's distressed green ones. How sweet she is, Jasmine thought, feeling almost protective of Velvet de Marisco Gordon. She is more of a sister to me than a mother, Jasmine considered, and then she nodded. "Aye, I am sure, Mama. I am sorry that it distresses you, for I am happy with the knowledge. It is what the prince desires most of all."

"But the baby will be a bastard!" Velvet fretted.

"A *royal bastard*, Mama. 'Tis quite a different thing. Was not Lord Gordon's father a royal bastard? The Gordons of BrocCairn do not seem to have suffered from the stigma of bastardy."

"That was Scotland, Jasmine," Velvet said. "This is England."

"King Henry the Eighth had a well-loved bastard son, Mama, upon whom he heaped honors and love. 'Twill be the same for my child, I know. I realize the idea is difficult for you to digest, and poor Aunt Willow will rant and rave over the news when I choose to tell her; but Grandmama would understand."

The two women sat in silence before the fire for a time, and then Velvet said, "When will you withdraw from court, Jasmine? You will certainly have no great desire to parade a big belly before the court, I know. Discretion has always been your finest quality."

"Why, thank you, Mama," Jasmine said with a small smile. "I shall wait until May, I think. The roads will be good then, and I shall go to Queen's Malvern, not Cadby. I always feel safest with Grandmama."

"What will the prince say? I wonder."

"He will be pleased with the idea he is to be a father, but unhappy that I would leave him. It must be, however. I will not remain at court while I grow as fat as a shoat and wagers are made as to when I shall deliver my child, or whether it will be a boy or a girl," Jasmine said to her mother. "I shall stay with Grandmama until after the baby is born. Perhaps

I shall rejoin the court next winter, and perhaps not. The king and the queen argue over a choice of a bride for Hal, but they will make their decision quickly once they learn I am with child by their heir. It is past time Henry Stuart had a wife. You must say nothing of this, Mama. Not even to Lord Gordon. *Promise me!*"

Velvet nodded. "I promise," she told her daughter wearily.

The Earl of Lynmouth's guests began arriving with the early evening. A long parade of carriages lined the drive leading from the high road, through the park, and to the earl's front door. Ladies and gentlemen, masked and in utterly magnificent costumes of every possible color and hue, stepped from the vehicles and tripped lightly into Lynmouth House. There were all sorts of amusements for them. They danced. They drank. They gossiped, played cards, and watched cockfights in a special cockpit that had been set up in one of the beautiful salons. There was much wagering back and forth amongst both the men and the women.

A buffet was served. There were barrels of oysters just up from the coast that same day. The oysters were devoured mostly by the men, who were unable to refrain from lewd remarks on how the shellfish would increase their sexual prowess that night. Next to the oyster barrels was an entire table devoted to fish. There was Scotch salmon in calf's-foot jelly, trout baked whole in pastry, smoked sturgeon, smoked eels, creamed cod with dill, salted herring, and prawns that had been steamed delicately in fine white wine and set a-swimming upon their platters with wedges of carved lemons.

A second table was devoted to game birds and poultry. It had a centerpiece fashioned from a magnificent peacock with its colorful tail spread full. Upon the table was roast goose, and ducks stuffed with saffroned rice and herbs in plum sauce. There were capons filled with dried fruit in a lemon-ginger sauce, large roast turkeys, platters of partridge, quail, and ortolons, and large pies of lark and sparrow, oozing rich brown gravy.

A third table was groaning with six sides of beef that had been packed in rock salt and roasted over the great, open kitchen fires. A servant in livery stood by to carve for the guests. There were legs of lamb, two roast pigs, country hams, and several dozen large rabbit pies, not to mention a new dish from France consisting of chunks of beef, red wine, and carrots and onions, which seemed to please everyone who tasted it, and there were many who did.

Another table held braised lettuce in white wine, bowls of peas, beets, carrots, turnips, and marrows. There were loaves of bread, plenty of sweet country butter, and great wheels of cheese for the guests to sample, which came not just from England, but France as well.

A final table held sweets of all kinds: cakes, jellies, sugar wafers, custards, tarts of dried fruits, candied angelica, violets, and rose leaves. There were bowls of pears and apples as well as oranges from Spain for the guests. Ale and wine flowed without ceasing.

The queen would not allow any of the players to either eat or drink before the masque. Several years prior, before she had sternly instituted this rule, Ben Jonson had written a masque to be performed during her eldest brother's visit from Denmark. Unfortunately, the fete during which this masque was to take place had gotten quite out of hand. Most of the ladies that evening were swept up in the spirit of the moment and became intoxicated.

The masque, which dealt with the seven virtues, turned into a riotous scandal as Faith vomited upon the King of Denmark's boots. Hope, too drunk to utter a syllable, stammered unintelligibly, and Charity was found behind a curtain futtering Lord Oliver, which one wag declared at least gave evidence that she understood the meaning of the virtue she was portraying, for Lord Oliver was neither handsome, rich, nor particularly likable.

Inigo Jones had designed wonderful scenery for the masque this particular Twelfth Night. The story was set in the faery kingdom. Its inhabitants lived the vital part of their lives during the warmer months of the year. They did not like the few winter months when the Frost King and his minions, the brownies and elves, were dominant. The faeries slept that time away in secure little nooks and crannies.

The court settled itself, and as the music began, the curtains of dark blue velvet were drawn back by two young pages garbed in pale blue velvet and lace ruffs, their soft velvet caps dripping white plumes, the toes of their shoes upturned in medieval fashion. The little lads drew the curtains open but halfway, revealing the oak tree bedchamber of the faery king and queen. Oberon lay sleeping alone, the coverlet next to him thrown aside.

Suddenly Oberon awoke, rubbed his eyes, stretched, and then saw that Titania was gone. He leapt up. The audience applauded as Henry Stuart stood before them, and the ladies of the court nudged each other over the prince's costume. His gilded leather boots were studded with gems and had wings upon the heels. Far more of interest to the ladies was the fact that the prince's legs were quite bare above his boots all the way to mid-thigh. He wore short, close-fitting pants striped in silver and gold, and trimmed with gold lace. The upper part of his costume was fashioned to resemble a sleeved breastplate such as might have been worn in Roman times. A royal-purple silk capelet was artfully draped from front to back.

Angrily the faery king aroused his court. He ordered them to find the queen. The faeries dashed to and fro, diligently seeking the missing Titania. Finally the three adorable wood sprites—played by Prince Charles, Edward Gordon, and Lady Laura Southwood, garbed in forest-green tights, green and brown blouses with ragged edges, and with small wings of a pearly hue edged in gold attached to their backs—hurried to tell the king that they had overheard some young brownies gossiping in the forest. The wood sprites danced quite charmingly as they told their tale, their tiny wings appearing to flutter realistically.

The Frost King had stolen Titania! He intended by means of enchantment to make her his own queen, for he had long envied Oberon the beauteous faery woman. Titania had been put beneath a spell which had caused her to forget Oberon. The wedding was set for dawn of the following morning.

Oberon was devastated. Then, as he placed a plumed gold helmet encircled with a gilded victory wreath of laurel upon his head, he had an idea. If he could convince Springtime to come early, the Frost King and his court would be banished until next winter. Under the influence of the birds and the flowers, Titania was certain to regain her memory.

As the masque progressed, Inigo Jones's genius was evident to all who watched. The scenery, beautifully painted and affixed to tiny wheels, was moved effortlessly by liveried servants with each change of scene. The costumes tonight were thought to be the absolute best that the designer had ever created.

Aurora, the glorious goddess of the Dawn, arrived, bringing with her the new day. Party to Oberon's plot, she moved slowly, drawing her colors lazily across the sky. The Frost King, played by Viscount Rochester in silver and white, prepared to take his bride. The court waited avidly for Jasmine's entrance. The gossip surrounding her costume was scandalous. A large snowflake, which had been made from wood and painted silver, was lowered from the ceiling. Seated upon it was Lady Lindley in her role as Titania.

At first the audience was disappointed, for it seemed that her costume was nothing out of the ordinary. The Frost King moved forward to help her from her precarious perch, and when she stepped forward into the lights, a collective gasp arose from the spectators. Never had anyone seen a costume of such gossamer quality. It could have very well been fashioned from moonbeams and spiderwebs, for it was both alive and pearlescent at the same time. The hem of the garment was deliberately ragged, and consequently allowed for glimpses of long, slender legs. A silver ribbon had been tied beneath her bosom, thereby underlining her full breasts, and her nipples had obviously been painted carmine-red. Jasmine's long, dark hair was loose, and dusted with both gold and silver dust. Atop her head was a delicate crown of crystals and pearls, set in a gold frame. When she danced with the Frost King, her buttocks and belly glowed pale and tantalizing beneath the sheer silk.

"I shall swoon," Willow, the Countess of Alcester declared dramatically, a hand going to her heart.

"Do not bother, my dear," her husband James told her. " 'Twill not divert attention from our niece, I assure you."

Willow glared at him. " 'Tis outrageous and shocking, James!"

"Aye, my dear," he agreed, his mild blue eyes upon the stage.

"God's nightshirt," murmured Tom Ashburne softly. "What a pity my cousin Rowan died. To leave such a woman is more than just a tragedy."

"Do you think her more beautiful than me?" Sybilla demanded, a tiny worm of jealousy gnawing at her heart. What was it about Jasmine, she thought irritably, that made her so fascinating to all men?

The Earl of Kempe heard the annoyance in his young wife's voice, and turning to her, he looked deep into her eyes. "No one, my Sybilla, is more beautiful to me than you are," he said sincerely.

"Oh, Tom, you are such a rogue," she replied, pleased, soft color flooding her cheeks.

"Jasmine's costume is certainly daring," Angel Southwood whispered to her husband. "I am surprised that the prince allowed it."

"He would show his prize to all the court," Robin Southwood said quietly. "They'll marry him off soon enough. 'Tis time, I think."

"Have you no feeling for my daughter, Robin, and her position?" Velvet hissed angrily. "What of Jasmine!?"

"Jasmine, like our mother, dear Velvet, will survive quite magnificently, I assure you," the Earl of Lynmouth told his sister, patting her hand comfortingly.

Onstage, the Frost King's hall was suddenly overrun with warm southern zephyrs. They danced gaily about. Birds were heard chirping spring songs. Mistress Springtime and her maidens, attired in flowing silken robes of varied pastel hues, flowers entwined in their long, loose hair, entered the hall of the Frost King dancing and singing. Springtime was being played by the delightful Princess Elizabeth, younger sister of Prince Henry. Betrothed to Prince Frederick V, the young Elector of the Palatine, she was to be married in the coming year.

With Springtime's arrival, the Frost King was thwarted. The warm zephyrs dancing about Titania, the fragrance of the flowers, all worked to restore the faery queen's lost memory. The spell was broken. Rejecting the Frost King's overtures, she flew to the arms of her lover, Oberon. Vowing revenge, the Frost King was banished for another year while Oberon, Titania, their court, and their allies all danced joyfully, celebrating their victory.

The Earl of Glenkirk watched the masque, his green eyes fixed upon Jasmine. It was ridiculous, he knew, but it seemed that she flaunted herself expressly for him. *He wanted her!* Why had he not said that he would marry her that morning several years back when they had been caught abed? Their combined pride had cost him so much. He watched as the masque came to a triumphant end. Jasmine and Henry pirouetted together with joyous abandon, surrounded by all the members of the faery court.

The curtain closed briefly, only to be drawn halfway back once again. The royal bedchamber in the oak tree was revealed. In the pale golden light of the candles on stage, Oberon, king of the faeries, walked across the stage, his beautiful queen, Titania, in his arms. Gently he laid her upon their marital bed, joining her, their lips meeting in a tender kiss even as the candles on stage were extinguished by the three wood sprites, and the two young pages drew the curtains discreetly closed.

For a moment there was complete silence in the ballroom of Lynmouth House, and then the audience commenced a thunderous clapping. The curtains were drawn back to reveal the players who took their bows, and then the curtains were closed a final time. Those members of the court who might have wished to get closer to Jasmine in her revealing costume were disappointed, for she and the prince quickly disappeared from the room.

"Ohh, you have outdone yourself, Master Jonson, Master Jones!" Queen Anne enthused. "What a charming and romantic masque you have given us this Twelfth Night. I do feel that Lady Lindley's costume was perhaps a bit daring, however." The queen was garbed this evening as Bel-Ana, Queen of the Ocean, a role she had played in a previous masque two years prior entitled *The Masques of Queenes*. She had always loved the costume with its magnificent crown and floating plumes.

"Thank you, Your Majesty," Ben Jonson replied. He wisely left the matter of the costuming to his compatriot.

"Lady Lindley's costume was indeed daring, my gracious queen," the designer said, "but 'twas necessary for authenticity. Had she not agreed to play the role, I could not have had such a costume. Her figure is quite perfect, and her skin tone marvelous. Did you see how it glowed beneath her silks? She is a charming woman as well, madame. There is no artifice or deceit in her. A most pleasant change."

"Indeed," the queen said thoughtfully. She was more than aware, for how could she not be, that Jasmine Lindley was her son's mistress. Royal mistresses could be difficult, and yet Inigo Jones was perfectly correct in his estimation of Jasmine. The queen wanted to dislike her son's mistress, but she could not. Jasmine cared for Henry Stuart, and was respectful to the other members of the royal family. Recently, Princess Elizabeth had wanted a particular silk for her trousseau, and no London merchant had been able to supply it.

"I would be honored if Your Highness would accept this small token of my genuine affection," Lady Lindley had said, presenting the silk to the young princess. "I brought it with me from India, but it has been lying in my grandmother's warehouse. I know Your Highness will make good use of it, and it suits you so well."

Jasmine Lindley had also strived to bring Henry and his little brother, Charles, closer together. Charles had been born prematurely, and had been physically ill fit his entire life. He could not walk until he was past four, and then his little legs had been spindly and weak. Henry enjoyed teasing his younger sibling, saying that he would make him the Archbishop of Canterbury one day since his legs would not show beneath his long clerical robes. The younger boy used to get furious when his brother said that. Of course, the angrier Charles got, the more Henry teased.

Jasmine had taught Prince Charles to fight back in a most clever way. "You must tell Hal when he becomes king, and you the archbishop, you will oversee his morals closely," she said. "He only teases you because you react so angrily. If you do not get angry with him, he will not tease you. He loves you dearly, my lord."

"He does?" Charles Stuart was quite surprised to hear this. He was amazingly advanced intellectually for his age, and his elder brother's behavior did not seem particularly loving to him.

When the younger lad, however, teased the older back, Henry Stuart laughed, surprised but pleased. "So you'll watch my morals closely, will you, runt? And what will you do if you don't like them?"

"Why, I'll excommunicate you, Hal!" Charles shot back.

"But I will be head of the Church of England, laddie." His brother chuckled smugly, certain he had the boy.

"Not if I excommunicate you, you won't," Charles Stuart told Henry Stuart. "Remember, I shall be the archbishop, and you just a king. God always takes precedence over man, brother. Even Father admits to that."

Henry Stuart had appeared astounded for a moment, and then he had laughed heartily.

Aye, the queen thought, Jasmine Lindley was certainly not a bad influence on her son, but she could also see that Henry was in love with her. There was, of course, no future in it. It is time that he married, the queen mused. His deep and obvious devotion to Lady Lindley proved that he was more than ready for it.

She had been party to a conversation between her husband and eldest son just a week ago. Henry had told his father that he wanted to marry Lady Lindley. James, to give him credit, had not lost his temper, but he had said to Henry, "She is nae worthy of ye."

"Jasmine told me that you would say that if I should ever ask you," the Prince of Wales told his father.

"Did she, laddie?" The king was surprised.

"Aye, she did," the prince replied. "She says that I must marry into France, or Spain, or the Germanies."

"*Did she?*" King James said, pleased. "Well, Henry, the lass is far wiser than ye are, and she obviously knows her duty."

"*I want her!*" Henry Stuart said fiercely.

"Ye hae her," his father replied blandly. " 'Tis nae secret that she is yer mistress, laddie. 'Tis all she can ever be to ye."

"What if she has my child?" the prince asked his father.

"I would certainly expect ye to recognize the bairn," the king said, "and we will provide for it. This family hae never been negligent toward the bairns it's spawned, no matter the side of the blanket they're born on, Henry. Blood is blood, laddie."

The prince had left his father afterward, and the queen

had come to sit by James Stuart, taking his hand in hers. "We must settle this matter of Henry's marriage," she had said. "Old King Philip's daughter would be perfect for him. She is well-schooled, and the family are proven breeders."

"Yer mad, Annie," the king responded. "The Spanish lass is a devout member of the old Kirk. She'll nae change, nor will Spain allow his grandchildren to be brought up in England's Kirk. The French, however, are not so stubborn. I say we look to France. Old Queen Marie has a little daughter, Henrietta-Marie, who would serve us well."

"Spain is stronger!" the queen insisted. "Besides, how could King Philip interfere in the raising of *our* grandchildren so far away?"

"I hae nae love for the Spanish," James Stuart said stubbornly.

"If you had chosen the Spanish Infanta, we could have had the young Spanish king for Bessie's husband instead of that German prince!" the queen said, losing her temper. "But no! You must pander to your Protestant subjects, and Henry sides with you in all of it. Well, Jamie, you may forget your French princess for Henry, for he tells me he will not marry *any* Roman Catholic for fear of dividing the country once again. For love of him have I accepted Prince Frederick for our daughter, and for no other reason. Now, I defy you to find a Protestant princess worthy of our son and heir!"

So they were stalemated, and while they sought a wife for Henry Stuart, he fell more and more in love with his mistress.

The holidays over, the court descended into winter and the Lenten season. Jasmine's scandalous costume was quickly forgotten by most in the wake of the many new scandals associated with the Stuart court, notably the growing and most public affaire de coeur between Frances Howard, the Countess of Essex, and Viscount Rochester.

By the end of February, Jasmine was absolutely certain

that she was with child again, and told her lover of the impending birth. Henry Stuart was, as she had predicted, ecstatic. He was less ecstatic to learn that Jasmine desired to leave the court in early spring.

"No!" he said. "You will have the child here at St. James."

"Our baby is not due until autumn," Jasmine told him. "Would you have me remain in London in the plague season, Hal? Despite the fact this palace is on the edge of the city with a park about it, and green fields to the north, it is still London. I am going to Queen's Malvern. I would be with my grandmother and grandfather when our child is born. You cannot deny me this, Hal. I must be happy now."

"You can go to my palace of Nonsuch, in Surry," he said.

"Nonsuch is too close to London," Jasmine complained.

"I shall send you to Richmond, then," he suggested.

"*Richmond?*" Jasmine looked horrified. " 'Tis in the north, in Yorkshire. I do not want to go to Yorkshire."

"Have you ever been to Yorkshire?" he asked her slyly. " 'Tis certainly far enough away from London, my love."

"I have heard of the Yorkshire moors, my lord. 'Tis a wild and desolate place. How can you even consider sending me to such a place?" She began to weep. "You claim to love me, Henry Stuart, and yet you would send me to some terrible, dank castle in the north of England."

"But you said you wanted to leave London before the plague season, Jasmine," he said, confused. "Nonsuch and Richmond belong to me."

"I want to go home to Queen's Malvern," she told him. "I need to see my children, Hal. I have not seen them in over six months. They are very little, my babies. My grandmother's house is a wonderful and peaceful place, Hal. Worcester is green and inviting. I love it there. 'Tis there I would have our child. You have been neglecting your position of late because of me, and you are not well, I know, though you try to hide it from me. You are overburdened with your duties, my lord. You need more rest. If I return home, you will get it. I want to leave the last week in April. The roads will be passable then, my darling, and 'twill still be safe for me to travel a long distance. I want to go home, Hal. *Let me go!*"

He sighed deeply. "I want to be with you, Jasmine, particularly now when you are ripening with our son, but I know that breeding women are subject to certain vagaries. If you would truly go home to your grandmother's house in Worcester, then I will allow it. The royal progress is to be made in the Midlands this summer. I shall join you then to be with you for the birth of our son. May I, my love?"

"Aye," she promised him, feeling better now. Then, her eyes twinkling, she asked him, "What makes you so certain that I shall deliver a son? I have two little girls, but only one little lad, my lord."

"Stuarts generally spawn lads," he said, his own eyes twinkling. "A daughter, however, would suit me as well if she looked like her mam." He bent and kissed Jasmine's forehead, his hand running lightly over her belly, which had only just begun to round slightly.

"A lad will be better," Jasmine said. " 'Twould be harder for a girl to bear the stigma of her birth."

"*What stigma?*" He looked genuinely perplexed.

"My child will be bastard-born, Hal. Is that not a stigma? Oh, I have bravely told my family it will not be, but won't it?"

He knew what she needed to hear now. "I will recognize my child, madame, and it will bear my name, I promise you. I would call a son Charles Frederick; the Charles for my brother, and the Frederick for me. Will that please you, madame?"

"The Charles for *my* brother," she told him happily. "The Frederick for you, my lord. *Charles Frederick Stuart.* It has a nice ring to it."

"May I tell my parents of our child?" he asked her.

Jasmine laughed. "I think you had best tell them soon,

before my belly begins to show," she said. "As for the rest of the court, let them speculate. It will not be hard for them to decipher once I have left court, but until then let us keep them guessing."

"You have a wicked sense of humor, madame," he approved.

"I hate the gossip," Jasmine told him. "Sometimes I could but wish we were just a simple man and woman, Hal, that we might wed and live our lives together in peace."

"Then you do love me," he said quietly.

She looked up at him, startled. What had ever made her say such a telling thing? Jasmine forced herself to laugh lightly. "I did not say that, my lord. I simply desire a less complicated life than I seem to have. 'Twould be easier. Do you always relish your position and impending fate, my love? Ahh, well, perhaps you do. I know my brother Salim could not even wait for our father to die, so anxious was he to rule."

"I want both you as my wife *and* England to rule," Henry Stuart told her honestly. "I will make a fine king, Jasmine. I know it!"

Again she laughed, but this time her amusement was more genuine. "There is an old saying about the acorn not falling far from the oak tree, and you are certainly proof of it, my lord. You will make a good king, my darling. You want it all! Sadly, however, even kings do not always get everything that they desire. It is God's way of keeping them humble."

"You were meant to be a queen," he said with sincerity.

"Perhaps I was," Jasmine admitted, "but I shall not be Queen of England, Hal. That honor will go to another woman, and 'tis best we realize it, else we bring great unhappiness to each other. I do not want that."

He tipped her face to his and kissed her softly. "I do not want that, either, my love," he told her. "I know what you tell me is true and what must be, but I cannot help but dream, Jasmine. I weep secretly in my heart not just for my personal loss, but for England's loss. You would be a great queen-consort."

But she was not his queen-consort, nor would she ever be. Jasmine had accepted her fate, though not perhaps as easily as she had previously believed she might. As her child grew within her, she thought of how if she were Henry Stuart's wife this child would be England's king after his father. But of course he would not be. He would be Lord Charles Frederick Stuart, for Jasmine was convinced the baby she carried was indeed a boy.

The winter was a relatively quiet one at court, for even Queen Anne dared not hold her beloved masques or dances during the penintential season of Lent. The only exception was the English New Year, which fell officially in March, although every other civilized nation celebrated this occasion on January first, and actually so did many of the English. Parliament, however, could not be convinced to make the calendar change that all of Europe, even Scotland, had made long ago. It would be another hundred years before it did.

The spring was early and wet. In the fields to the north of St. James Palace, the daffodils bloomed copiously, and in the common pasturage, lambs nursed upon their grazing mothers. As April drew to a close, Jasmine's servants packed up all her possessions both at St. James and at Greenwood. There were at least six baggage carts sent on their way as soon as they had been loaded. They were attended by a group of men-at-arms the de Mariscos had sent from Queen's Malvern. The roads were not always safe, and Jasmine did not want to lose her belongings.

Prince Henry had had London's finest coach maker at work all winter long building a traveling coach for Jasmine. "Your grandmother's vehicle is old," he said. "I want you to return home in safety and the utmost comfort, my love. With your new carriage I can be assured of it. We must do nothing that would endanger our child."

The coach was indeed a magnificent one. Its springs were firm and tight, yet possessed just the right amount of give so that the ride was a smooth one. Inside, the entire vehicle was padded thickly; the walls in beautifully tanned soft, white leather, and the seats in matching tufted velvet. The seat facing the front was extra wide on the chance that Jasmine would want to lie down. The back of the seat sloped just slightly in order to give her back better support.

Inside each door of the coach, a panel six inches wide, four inches deep, and six inches high had been hollowed out, and lined in iron. There was a tiny grate over each door, and another within the iron box upon which small pieces of coal and kindling might be placed for the purpose of heating the interior of the vehicle. When these miniature stoves were not in use, a decorative panel fit over them, hiding them from view.

The day of Lady Lindley's departure, the head cook at St. James's Palace personally oversaw the provisions that she would carry in the coach with her. The journey, usually just a few days in duration, would take far longer, for Prince Henry did not want his mistress wearied in her delicate state. A full dozen bottles of wine from Greenwood's cellars were put into the coach. There were two fully cooked capons, three loaves of fresh bread, a dozen hard-cooked eggs, half a small ham, a large wedge of hard, sharp cheese, some pears and oranges, which would take Lady Lindley through her first day.

"I have sent one of my undersecretaries ahead, my love, to see to your accommodations. You will be provided with a fresh basket of food for your journey each day, and should your wine give out, you will also be supplied with the best wines available," the prince told her.

"There is more than enough wine," Jasmine told him,

thinking that wine did not agree with her particularly now as it was. She far preferred springwater, and her Assam tea.

"I do not like to let you go," Henry Stuart said tenderly at their parting. He put his arms about her.

"I do not like being parted from you, my lord, but I would see my children, and I am told that plague has already broken out in the poorer sections of London. I am safer with my grandmother, and our bairn is too," Jasmine told him.

He smiled at her use of the Scots for baby, and placed his hand upon her belly, which was beginning to swell visibly now. "God keep you, my love. I will come to you in September. I cannot come before, for the press of my duties is great."

Their lips met in a tender kiss, and Jasmine felt tears prickling behind her closed eyelids. She did love this handsome prince, and she was unhappy to be leaving him, but the safety of their child depended upon her behaving in a sensible and responsible manner.

She sighed deeply, and breaking off their embrace, he looked deep into her beautiful turquoise-blue eyes. He wanted to beg her to stay, but Henry Stuart realized all too well that he could not be selfish. A future king made decisions based on what was best, not on what he personally desired. Only sometimes were the two the same.

"I love you, Jasmine," he told her softly, and he helped her into the carriage, where Toramalli was already seated. "Watch over your lady well for me, Mistress Toramalli," Henry Stuart said, and then he closed the door of the coach. With a last silent farewell to her, he signaled the coachman, and the vehicle began to move slowly off.

Jasmine lowered the windows of the vehicle and looked out at him. "Farewell, my lord! Farewell, my love!" she called to him. He could not see the tears shining brightly in her eyes now, and he waved back to her, but there was no smile upon his face.

• • •

It took nine days to reach Queen's Malvern, but as she stepped from the coach into Skye's open arms, Jasmine knew she had been right to come home. *Home!* Aye, Queen's Malvern was home, and so she told her grandmother, who beamed with pleasure at both Jasmine's return and her words. The two women hugged once again, and then Skye released Jasmine.

"Thank God you are home safe!" she said fervently, and putting her arm through her granddaughter's, led her into the house to the Family Hall, where the fires were blazing merrily, for the spring day was damp.

Jasmine laughed. "I but went to court, Grandmama," she said.

"And came back with something you did not leave with," Skye replied, reaching out to touch her granddaughter's belly.

"I love him, Grandmama," Jasmine said softly, "though I shall never tell him. He is young, and would in one moment cast aside his obligations, while telling me in the next what a fine king he will be someday. But he is a good man, and he will be good to his child."

"I will not scold you, Jasmine, my darling girl," Skye told her. "In my youth I would have done the same thing you have."

"In your youth you did worse!" Adam de Marisco teased as he came into the hall. "Welcome home, Jasmine, my love!" He enfolded his granddaughter into his large embrace.

She kissed him heartily, and then stepping back, said, "Grandpapa, you are limping. What is the matter?"

"What is the matter?" Skye interjected. "I will tell you what the matter is! Your grandfather is an old fool, Jasmine, who will hunt all day in a driving rain and then drink wine and eat foods that are too rich for his stomach. That is what the matter with him is!"

"I have the gout in one knee," the Earl of Lundy said with as much dignity as he could muster, allowing his granddaughter to seat him by the fire. "Now what is this I hear about another baby, madame?"

"Mama has written to you?" Jasmine sat next to him as Skye took the place opposite them.

"She has," Adam said. "Are you happy, my love?"

"Aye, and nay," Jasmine admitted. "I am happy to be having this child. Even though I know its father and I cannot ever wed, and I always knew it, I am yet disturbed by it."

"Of course you are," Skye told her, "but you knew when you began this affaire de coeur with Prince Henry what your life would be if you bore him a child. Put all distress from your mind, my darling girl. It is wasted effort. The prince loves you, your mother tells me, and he will be good to both you and his child even when he finally takes a wife."

"When is my new grandchild due to enter this world?" Adam asked her. He reached for a goblet of wine the servant offered, ignoring the glowering look his wife shot at him.

"In mid-September, Grandpapa," Jasmine said. "Hal has said he will come when the baby is near to being born. It is his first child, you know. The royal progress will be made through the Midlands this summer, and 'twill not be hard for him to slip away."

The de Mariscos nodded. Skye was pleased that Henry Stuart wanted to be present at the birth of his child. It spoke well of the young prince.

"Where are my children?" Jasmine asked her grandparents. "I have missed them greatly, and long to see them."

Skye nodded to a servant, who hurried out. A few minutes later the three little Lindleys entered the Family Hall in the company of their nurses. "Here is your mama, back from court," Skye told them. "Come and make your curtsies, lasses, and Henry, make your bow."

Jasmine was astounded by the change in her offspring. She had only left them nine months ago! Now here was

India, her silky dark hair coaxed into ringlets, her golden eyes—so like Rowan's—wide with curiosity. She wore a gown of rose-colored velvet that was most becoming to her. She was both neat and subdued. *And Henry!* "You have breeked him," she said surprised. Her three-year-old son was wearing dark blue velvet breeches, and a doublet with ivory lace.

"I do not hold with the custom of keeping children swaddled so that their limbs develop crookedly and they cannot walk until they are four or five," Skye said emphatically. "I also do not believe in leaving little boys in skirts until their fifth birthday. It is ridiculous!"

"I did not swaddle the children past their first month," Jasmine said weakly. The children were so quiet. Even Fortune. *Fortune!* Her baby was close to two years of age. "Her hair has not darkened," she noted, and fingered one of Fortune's curls. It was silky soft. Large blue-green eyes stared back at her. "Why, Grandmama, she has your eyes!" Jasmine said excitedly. "What a beauty she will be one day!" Fortune was also clad in deep blue.

" 'Tis a fine litter," Adam observed. "Even this little fox vixen," he chuckled, tweaking one of Fortune's curls.

"Welcome home, Mama." Lady India Lindley curtsied prettily. Her brother bowed neatly, and her little sister spread her tiny skirts in imitation of India, glancing from beneath golden lashes to be certain she was doing it correctly.

Jasmine bit her lip to keep from giggling. It was just the sort of thing she would have done as a little one. She would wager that Lady Fortune Lindley's fires were merely banked, but not extinguished. "Grandmama, you have tamed them very well, I must admit," she said.

"Boundaries!" Skye said. "Children must have boundaries, my darling girl! They need to know what is correct and what is not, what they may do and what they may not do. You were far too lax with them, and I hope when you return home to Cadby, you will not undo all our hard work. *Man-*

ners! Above all, manners. Good manners will cover a multitude of sins and other deficiencies, Jasmine."

Jasmine bent as much as she could and enfolded each of her children in a warm, loving embrace. Then straightening up, she said, "I am happy to see you all, my loves. India, you have become quite the young lady, I vow. I have seen none finer at court."

India beamed with pleasure. "Thank you, Mama," she said, and Skye gave her granddaughter an "I told you so" look.

"You have grown muchly, my lord," Jasmine told her son. "Perhaps when you are older you may serve the king at court as a page. Would you like that?"

"Thank you, Mama," Lord Henry Lindley said, but nothing more.

Jasmine looked to her grandmother, and Skye told her, "Henry is very deep, darling girl. He has many thoughts, it would seem, which he keeps to himself, but he is a good lad."

"He seems so serious for three," Jasmine said, and bending again, she asked her son, "Would you like to serve the king, Henry?"

Henry nodded, but there was fear in his eyes. "Must I go to court soon, Mama?" he asked.

Jasmine hugged him and gave him a kiss. " 'Tis many years away, my son. You must not fret yourself," and she was relieved to see Henry smile at her revelation. God's boots, he was just a baby, for all his fine clothes!

"Mama! Mama!" Fortune tugged at Jasmine's skirts. "Kiss me! *Kiss me!*"

Jasmine laughed, and turned her attention to her littlest daughter. She kissed her on each cheek, and Fortune giggled. "Like kissing!" she announced enthusiastically.

"We had best teach her discretion," Jasmine said merrily.

In the weeks that followed, Jasmine experienced some of

the happiest times of her life. Surrounded by her family, cosseted and fussed over, she grew more content with each passing day as the child within her grew. She took walks with her children in her grandmother's gardens, and in the fields and orchards belonging to Queen's Malvern. The days grew longer and the weather warmer as spring moved into summer and the summer progressed toward autumn.

She had explained to her children that there would be a new baby in the family by the end of September. They were fascinated by her growing belly, and pressed ears against it to *hear* the infant.

"Why is the baby in your tummy, Mama?" India asked one day.

"That is where it must grow until it may live safely in the world," Jasmine told her little daughter.

"How did it get there?" India persisted.

Skye looked at her granddaughter, amused. "Indeed, my darling girl, how did it get there?" she teased Jasmine.

"The papa put it there, India," Jasmine replied serenely.

"*My papa?*" India demanded.

For a moment a look of sadness flitted across Jasmine's face, but then she smiled down at her eldest child and said, "No, India, not your papa. Another papa."

"Will the other papa be my papa, Mama? Will he come and live with us one day?" India inquired curiously.

"Nay, India, he cannot come and live with us, but soon you will meet him. He will come to be here when the baby is born. You will like him, and he will like you, I promise," Jasmine told her daughter.

On the third day of September a messenger arrived from Henry Stuart. He was ill. Having spent an afternoon at his palace at Richmond in the tilt yard overexerting himself, he had gone swimming in the river afterward and come down with an appalling chill. He would, he assured Jasmine, be with her by the fifteenth of the month at the latest. She was not to give birth before then. Jasmine laughed at that although she was worried. There was still plague about the countryside, and in his weakened condition, the prince was vulnerable.

"How is he, really?" she demanded of the messenger.

"Feverish, and he has a cough," the royal messenger told her. "He'll not die, madame, if that is what frets you. I've seen him like this before, and he has always recovered."

Jasmine heard no more. On the fifteenth of September she watched the road nervously the entire day long, but Henry Stuart did not come. Finally, when they had sat down to the evening meal in the Family Hall, he arrived. Jasmine, who had been pale with worry all the day long, regained the color in her cheeks as she ran awkwardly toward him across the hall.

"My love! You have come at last!" Dear heaven, he looks so wan, she thought. He was not fully recovered, and yet he had come to her. Her arms went about his neck, and she kissed him passionately, realizing as she did so how very much she had missed him.

He kissed her in return, and then setting her back, smiled as his hand reached out to caress her large belly. "My love," he said, "you bloom beautifully, and the sight of you does my heart good. Ahhh, my darling one, I have missed you so these past few months!"

A look passed between Lord and Lady de Marisco, and they smiled at one another, pleased. Jasmine had not exaggerated. Henry Stuart was deeply in love with her. They were content now that even if their beloved granddaughter could not be his wife, he would care for her and their child, no matter a royal marriage.

Jasmine now brought her lover to the high board to introduce him to her family.

Adam de Marisco arose slowly and bowed low. "My lord,"

he said, "with your permission I will see to your men. Their horses will need stabling, and they will need hot food as well as shelter. I can see you have ridden hard."

"There is no need, my lord," the prince told him. "I have but come with my valet. This is no time for pomp and show, but a private time between us. I thank you for your gracious hospitality." Then he broke off and began to cough.

"Cherry bark syrup," Skye said. "I will see that your valet has a goodly supply. 'Tis a wicked cough you possess, my lord, and it needs tending. Have you no physician at Richmond?"

"I do not like doctors," the prince replied.

"How so like a man," Skye said sweetly, and Prince Henry looked startled. "You could be one of my grandsons," Lady de Marisco continued, "and so I intend to treat you as I would treat one of them, my lord. We will get you to bed right away! You need some competent nursing, not the quackery and mumbo-jumbo that always surrounds a royal court and its physicians."

"You have been to court?" he asked her, amused. He liked this determined old woman. Seeing her with Jasmine, he noted the very obvious resemblance of not just face and form, but of manner. Lady de Marisco was very beautiful for one of her years.

"Bess's court, and a nest of vipers it was!" Skye responded, leading the prince from her hall. "I suppose you have your vipers too."

She saw him tucked into bed, with bricks wrapped in flannel set at his feet. She fed him delicate, nourishing foods, and her own cough syrup made from the bark of the cherry trees in her orchards. To his great surprise, Henry Stuart found himself feeling better within a few days' time, so that when Jasmine went into labor with their child on the morning of September eighteenth, he felt well enough to attend her.

"I have never seen a bairn born, madame," he told Skye.

"Pray, what is it like? I want to comfort my love in her travail."

"Well, my lord, if I may speak plainly," Skye began, "birthing is painful, noisy, and bloody. If such things disturb you, I would ask that you remain in the hall. We have no time for anyone right now but my darling girl, and the little one she is working so hard to bear."

"Lead on, madame," the prince said, and he followed her into Jasmine's bedchamber.

There he found his beautiful mistress pale and dripping with perspiration. Her loose hair was lank and swung about her as she paced the room nervously. " 'Twill be quick this time, Grandmama," Jasmine said, ignoring Henry Stuart. "I can sense it. This child is anxious to be born."

"All the better!" Skye said, her glance sweeping about the chamber to be certain that all was in readiness. The birthing table was in its place. There were plenty of clean cloths, and water. The cradle and swaddling were in evidence.

"Ohhhhhh!" gasped Jasmine, and she doubled over.

"Help me get her on the table, my lord," Skye said to him.

"Is she all right?" he asked low.

"As all right as any woman in the throes of childbirth can be, my lord," Skye answered him, amused. But she fully approved of how the young man took charge of Jasmine, lifting her up to lay her gently upon the birthing table. "Get behind her, my lord," Skye instructed him, "and brace her back. She will need your strength."

Henry Stuart did as he was instructed, bracing Jasmine, bending low to murmur encouragingly to her, reaching forward to massage her distended belly with gentle hands. He seemed to have an instinctive knowledge of what was needed in this situation, and encouraged by his presence, Jasmine relaxed, pushing her child into the world.

"Ahhh!" Skye said. "The head!"

"Adali!" Henry Stuart barked. "Take my place!"

Adali leapt forward to obey the prince, and Henry Stuart moved around the birthing table to join Skye.

"God's bones," she muttered beneath her breath. This was all she needed. He would grow faint with all the blood, especially in his weakened condition. But to her surprise, the prince did not falter. Instead he watched the birth with great curiosity, encouraging Jasmine in her efforts, and when it became apparent that the baby would be born, he gently pushed Skye aside and birthed his child with his own hands, even as Skye cut the cord.

The infant began to howl immediately. Henry Stuart grinned as he noticed the tiny genitals. "A son!" he crowed to Jasmine, and he held the screaming boy up to show her. "We have a son, madame!" Then he thrust the baby at Skye and came around to kiss his mistress. "Thank you, my love," he said softly. "Thank you!"

"I would not have believed it," Skye told Adam afterward in the privacy of their own apartment. "What a king he will make, young Henry Stuart! A king even I can respect and admire. He did not falter once, Adam, and he thrust me aside to birth the lad himself! What a man! No wonder Jasmine loves him, and what a pity that they cannot wed. How unfair life can be sometimes. She would be a fine queen. Do you realize that if they were wed, this child should be England's next king after his father? God's bones! 'Tis not fair! He will wed some overbred royal virgin who will give him weaklings and stillbirths while our magnificent great-grandson is so strong and filled with life!"

"The babe is better off a simple Englishman," Adam said to his wife. "If he were Henry Stuart's heir, he would be taken from us to be raised by strangers. They would instill their values in him, and not ours. We would never see him, Skye. I thank God he is not England's heir, because he will be ours to love and know, ours to watch grow from infancy to boyhood. I shall never see him a man, but I will live long enough to see our little Charles Frederick Stuart a boy to be reckoned with, sweetheart. 'Tis good enough for me!"

Skye looked at her husband, stricken. She had never before heard Adam de Marisco speak of his own mortality.

He patted her hand, instantly understanding her fears. "I am eighty-two, little girl. I know my time is short, but not too short," he finished with a deep chuckle, and leaning forward, gave her a kiss.

Lord Charles Frederick Stuart had been born at twelve noon on the eighteenth day of September in the year 1612. Prince Henry, fascinated with his blue-eyed, auburn-haired son, could but stay with mother and child another three days. He left them on the twenty-second of September to join his royal parents as they made their progress from the Midlands back south. Before he left, he spoke privately with Skye, Adam, and Jasmine.

"I have taken the liberty, my lord," he told Adam, "of making a change in the line of descent for the Earldom of Lundy." Then he looked to Skye. "Robert Cecil told me last spring before he died, madame, that you arranged with the late Queen Elizabeth for the line of descent to come down through the female line. Your daughter, the Countess of BrocCairn, will have no need for this title; nor will Jasmine, who is Marchioness of Westleigh."

"*Dowager Marchioness,*" Jasmine corrected, and he laughed.

"Dowager Marchioness then, my love."

Skye was ahead of him. "You have arranged for your son to inherit the title from my husband, my lord. Is that it?"

The prince nodded. " 'Twas bold of me, and if you are truly distressed, I will see that the matter is reversed, but I did not think you would mind. I can ask my father for a title for my wee Charles, but I think this is a more discreet way of handling the matter."

Skye nodded. "It is," she agreed, and looked to Adam.

"I concur," he said.

Jasmine was yet too weak to leave her bed, and so Henry Stuart bid her farewell in her bedchamber, where she was nursing Charles. Fascinated, he watched as his son suckled strongly on her nipple. "I am jealous of the wee laddie," he told her with a smile. "When will you rejoin me at court?"

"Charles must come first, my lord, and he is much too young to travel. It is my desire to nurse him myself. It is better for him," Jasmine said. "I nursed India and Henry both."

"I want you back at court for Elizabeth's wedding in February," the prince told her. "Either you must hire a wet nurse, or Charles must travel with you, which I do not think advisable in the winter weather."

"We will discuss it further when Charles is older," Jasmine evaded him, not wanting to refuse him, but her maternal instincts overrode her passion for this man.

"In time for Bessie's nuptials, madame," he warned her. "I will brook no disobedience from you in this matter."

"Yes, my lord," she told him with false sweetness.

"Toramalli, take the bairn," the prince said, and the tiring woman hurried to obey him.

"Now, madame, you must bid me a proper farewell," he told her.

Their lips met, and Jasmine was quite startled to find her dormant passions being aroused by her lover.

He chuckled as she pulled away. "You see, my love, your desire for me is already warring with your desire to mother our child." Giving her a final quick kiss, he said, "I will try to visit you before you must return to court, my darling." Then he arose from her bed and, with a wink, departed.

"Adali," she called. "Carry me to the window that I may see my lord's departure."

He rushed to obey her, cradling her in his grasp as she

leaned forward to watch the prince below, bidding her grandparents farewell.

"Now keep taking the syrup for your cough," Skye said. "I have given your valet the recipe for it. The ingredients are easy enough to obtain, so don't let him tell you he cannot. That cough is still deep in your chest, my lord. My syrup just keeps it at bay."

Henry Stuart bent and kissed Skye's cheek. "I never knew my grandparents," he said. "I consider you both their surrogates." Then he mounted his horse and rode off down the drive with his valet in his wake. Turning to wave to them, he smiled to see Jasmine in the window above saluting him. He blew her a kiss.

"A fine young man," Adam said.

"Aye," Skye agreed. "A fine young man."

Above them Jasmine watched from the security of Adali's arms as her lover departed Queen's Malvern. Why, she wondered, do I feel so sad? Tears slid down her cheeks. Farewell, my love, she thought silently. God go with you always. Now why did I say that? she wondered. It was the sort of thing one said when one did not expect to see a person again. Jasmine shivered, and Adali fussed at her.

"Back to bed with you, my lady, else your grandmother blames me should you catch a cold," and he placed her in her bed again as she brushed away the tears on her face that he discreetly ignored.

21

Henry Stuart rode most of the day, to meet his parents, who were staying at Sudley Castle, the home of Lord and Lady Chandos. From early afternoon on he and his valet, Duncan, traveled in a driving rain, but the prince was anxious to reach his family that he might tell them of his son's birth. They stopped once to allow the horses a small respite and to eat something. The inn was small, and the innkeeper had absolutely no idea of who he was serving. Duncan told him, and the man's mouth dropped open with surprise. The innkeeper had heard the royal family was hereabouts, but he had certainly never expected to see one of them, let alone bring him an ale.

"Have ye any hot food?" Duncan demanded.

"There's no time," Henry Stuart told his servant.

Duncan had been with the prince his entire life, and now he invoked the privilege of a beloved servant—forthright speech. "I'll nae go another step, my lord, wi'out something hot in my belly. I'm nae as young as ye are, and while I'm about it, a wee bit of something warm would nae hurt ye either. Yer cough is still wi ye, and this weather will do ye nae good."

" 'Tis easier to agree with you than to argue with you, Duncan," the prince said with a chuckle, and then he began to cough.

"Ah-hah!" the valet said. "Ye see, my lord? Ye need food, rest, and Lady de Marisco's elixir before we can go another step." He turned to the still open-mouthed innkeeper. "Food, man!"

"Right away, sir, my lord," the innkeeper babbled, and fled into his kitchen, almost knocking over his wife, who had been listening wide-eyed behind the half-open door.

In short order a hot soup appeared along with a rabbit stew, several thick slices of ham, and a capon. There were bread, cheese, and a small tartlet of dried apples. The prince, who had not thought himself hungry, found that despite his cough, he was famished. When they had finished eating, Duncan paid the innkeeper generously, and the two men went out to the stables where they had left their horses.

"I've fed 'em and given 'em a bit of water, my lord, but only after I cooled 'em off," the young stable boy said.

"Good for you, lad," Henry Stuart said, and flipped the youngster a coin. "They've a bit of a ways yet to go. I know they're as refreshed by your good care as we are by the meal we just had." He led his horse from the stall and mounted it.

"Tell yer grandchildren one day, laddie, that ye cared for the horse of England's next king," Duncan told the amazed boy. "This is Prince Henry Stuart himself." Then he mounted his own horse, and the two men were off again into the downpour, leaving the astounded youngster looking after them with wide eyes and an open mouth.

When they finally reached Sudley Castle, the king and the court were already at supper in the Great Hall. Still booted, Henry Stuart joined them, kissing his mother, who frowned when she heard the wheeze coming from his chest.

The prince ignored her and took up a goblet of wine, saying, "Your Majesties, my lords, and my ladies, I ask you to raise your goblets to the good health and long life of Charles Frederick Stuart, *my son*, born at Queen's Malvern on the eighteenth day of September!"

There was a deep, stunned silence. It was not that the court was ignorant of Lady Lindley's condition, but until now everything had been so discreet. This was hardly a circumspect moment, and they did not know what to do.

Then the king clambered clumsily to his feet, his goblet raised, and said, "To the health and long life of Lord Charles Frederick Stuart, *my firstborn grandchild!*"

The court rose as one. "Here! Here!" they said.

Henry Stuart was grinning ear to ear now, and graciously accepted the congratulations of those around him.

Then his mother hissed up at him, "Sit down, Henry! You are making a spectacle of yourself. You are certainly not the first man in the history of the world to sire a son, nor the first Stuart to sire a royal bastard. Sit down! God bless me, you are soaked clear through. Get up from the table and find dry clothes. Your father and I will see you in our privy chamber when the meal is finished."

The prince was relieved to be released, and with a quick grin at his mother, he left the Great Hall.

Lord Chandos's majordomo hurried forward. "Your Highness, allow me to escort you to the apartments that have been prepared for your arrival. Your valet is already waiting, and I have given orders to have a tub and hot water brought, for he says you have ridden all day in this downpour."

Once within the safety of the rooms that had been set aside for him, Henry Stuart found that his teeth were chattering. Muttering balefully, Duncan stripped the wet clothes from his master and settled him in the hot water.

"Ye've no more sense than an unbreeked laddie, my lord," he said. "We'd have done better to stay at that wee inn instead of riding in the rain all these miles. My old bones are aching, and yer coughing again. Get yourself warm, and then I'll tuck ye into bed."

"My parents wish to see me in their privy chamber," the young prince answered his valet. "We drank a health to my wee Charles in the hall, Duncan. The entire court drank, and my father led them!"

"Yer getting into bed, my lord, and I'll hae no nonsense about it. I'll tell yer parents myself. They can come to ye. Yer royal mam would agree wi me, and 'tis nae lie."

Henry Stuart did not argue any further with Duncan. The truth of the matter was that as his euphoria faded, he was beginning to feel simply dreadful again. He remained in his bath long enough to let the hot water take the ache and the cold from his bones, and then he let Duncan dry him. Wrapped in a warm nightshirt, the prince climbed into his bed and accepted a small portion of Lady de Marisco's cough mixture. He wasn't even aware that he had dozed off until he realized that his mother was gently shaking him awake.

"Your cold is worse for your journey to Queen's Malvern," she said quietly, "although Duncan tells me old Lady de Marisco cared for you like one of her own, and you were better for a time."

"I'll be all right after a few days of rest, madame," he assured her. "I helped birth my son, Mama. I took him myself from his mother's womb even as he gave his first cry. It was magnificent!"

Anne of Denmark was astounded, and not just a little appalled. James had always fled the palace when she was giving birth. She was not even certain she would have wanted him there, let alone in the same room with her, helping her to bear her child. "Is the boy strong?" she asked her son.

"Strong, beautiful, and well-formed," Henry told her. "He has the Stuart auburn hair, and though his eyes are now blue, Jasmine says that they could change as he grows older."

"That is true," the queen agreed, and then she said, "How is Lady Lindley? She came through her travail easily?"

"Aye! She's nursing the laddie already, but I have told her I want her at Bessie's wedding in the winter, so she must wean our son to a wet nurse by Twelfth Night. How long are we to stay at Sudley?"

"Five days," his mother said. "You need your rest, Henry. I am not at all pleased by your condition, and I will brook no defiance from you in this matter. You will remain abed until I say you may arise."

"As you will, madame," he said meekly, but his eyes were twinkling at her, and the queen knew that as soon as her son felt better, there would be no keeping him in one place.

In the morning, Henry Stuart awoke to find that his parents had left Sudley quite early.

"They've gone to Queen's Malvern," Duncan told him.

"Why did they not tell me?" the prince complained, and he gave a cough. "I would have gone with them."

"They dinna tell ye because they dinna want ye running about the countryside sick as ye are, my lord. 'Tis twenty-five miles or more. They'll nae be back for two days, and no one else must know. 'Tis being said the king is sick wi the headache, and the queen is nursing ye. Lord Chandos is part of the plot. He'll keep the court busy wi hunting, and dancing into the night. They'll nae miss the king."

A rider had been sent ahead to Queen's Malvern at first light to warn the de Mariscos of the impending royal visit. The king and the queen, incognito, traveled with just half a dozen retainers. Both were used to being in the saddle all day, and were hardly fatigued by the time they reached Queen's Malvern in the late afternoon.

Skye and Adam de Marisco made an elegant obeisance to the royal couple as they entered the house.

"Welcome to Queen's Malvern, sire," Adam said. "I apologize that my granddaughter is unable to greet you, but she is not yet recovered from Charles Frederick's birth but a few days ago."

"We hae come to see the laddie," the king said, stripping his gloves and his long cloak off.

"Will you have some wine and biscuits after your long journey, sire, madame?" Skye asked politely.

"May we see the bairn first?" the king asked, almost shyly.

"Aye, my lord," Skye said, smiling. She remembered her first grandchild. "If Your Majesties will come with me," she told them, and led them up two flights of stairs to Jasmine's apartments. "The baby is with his mother now, nursing."

Jasmine had known that the king and queen were coming, and so she was not surprised when her grandmother escorted the royal couple into her bedchamber. Her new son was cradled in her arms, sucking lustily upon her breast. She was looking extraordinarily beautiful, her long black hair full and loose about her. Soft color had returned to her creamy cheeks. She wore a white chamber robe whose sleeves were trimmed lavishly in fine French lace as she sat propped by her grandmother's best pillows.

"Sire, madame," she greeted them, and gave a small nod.

The queen hurried to the bedside and gazed down upon her grandson. "Ahh, he's beautiful!" she said, and she smiled warmly at Jasmine, thinking that it really was a pity Henry could not have her to wife. She was not simply beautiful and fertile, she had dignity. She knew how to be royal. The situation was really very sad.

"Gie me the laddie," the king said, joining them, and when Jasmine had detached Charles from her nipple, he picked the baby up.

Charles Frederick Stuart began to wail. He had been quite comfortable within his mother's arms, suckling his supper.

"Nah, nah, laddie," his royal grandfather crooned, and the baby, intrigued by the sound of an unfamiliar voice, ceased his howling to stare at the king. "Aye now, and he's a beautiful laddie, as my Annie says, Jasmine Lindley. Ye hae done my son proud. I understand that Henry hae arranged wi Salisbury, before he died in May, that if he sired

a son on ye, 'twould inherit yer grandfather's title and estates one day. When that day comes, I will create the lad
Duke of Lundy, and nae just Earl. For now, lassie, he will
be known as Viscount Lundy. He's a royal Stuart for all his
birth. We Stuarts watch over our own, as yer stepfather
BrocCairn can tell ye, madame."

"Thank you, Your Majesty," Jasmine said softly.

"Let me have him, Jamie," the queen demanded. "Now
just look at that! You are holding him all wrong. You
would think you had never held a bairn before. Support
his wee neck!" She took her grandson from her beaming
husband. "Your mother and stepfather have come with us,
my dear," she said to Jasmine. "I thought you would want
to see them, and your mother, of course, is eager to see
her grandchild."

The royal couple stayed for a few minutes longer, promising to return on the morrow before they departed back to
Sudley Castle.

"Please, madame, how is the prince?" Jasmine asked the
queen as Anne prepared to leave the chamber.

A sharp retort was about to spring to the queen's lips
when she looked at Jasmine and saw the genuine love and
concern in the girl's face. "His cold lingers, my dear," Anne
of Denmark reported gently.

When they had left her, Toramalli took the baby and set
him back in his cradle by Jasmine's side. "He's sleeping, my
lady. No need to wake him up and continue feeding him.
He's full, right enough, else he'd howl to wake the dead.
He's a true Mughal."

"And a not-quite-royal Stuart," Jasmine said with a small
smile.

Velvet now rushed into her daughter's bedchamber, Alex
behind her. "Let me see him!" she demanded. "Let me see
my Stuart grandson!"

"Why, Mama," Jasmine said with humor, "I did not know
you were such a snob. He is in his cradle, having fallen

asleep in his royal grandmama's arms. The king will make him a duke one day, he says."

Velvet looked down at the baby who lay upon his stomach, his small head turned to one side. "He's lovely," she said, "and I do not begrudge the queen her few moments with him. 'Tis I little Charles Frederick Stuart will call 'Grandmama'; and 'tis I who will see him grow. I am glad I am not a queen. There are too many disadvantages to it, I fear." She looked at her daughter. "You are content?"

"Aye," Jasmine told her. "Why should I not be? Henry Stuart loves me, and I have his son. There is nothing more for me but Hal, and all my children. My life is complete."

Velvet nodded, pleased with her daughter's answer.

"Henry Stuart will make a good king one day," Alex Gordon noted. "He considers everything. I understand he arranged through poor old Cecil before he died last May to gie the bairn yer grandfather's titles one day. 'Tis just what my grandfather did for my father."

"And 'tis as canny of him as it was of his grandfather," Jasmine teased her stepfather. "By passing on a title that is already in the family, he does not have to create a new one, nor offer an allowance to support a new peerage. I am certain that Robert Cecil highly approved of that. He did so disapprove of my affair with Hal."

The Earl of BrocCairn chuckled. "Aye," he agreed. " 'Twas a consideration that would hae pleased Cecil mightily, God rest him. He was always so careful of the king's purse. Poor little royal beagle. He worked himself into the grave. The king hae replaced him with Robert Carr, and created that idiot Earl of Somerset to boot. A poor choice, I fear."

"I hear that Frances Howard has divorced Essex and plans to wed Carr," Jasmine said to her stepfather. "Is it so?"

"Aye, the bitch," BrocCairn told her. "But 'twas nae a divorce. She had her marriage to Essex annulled, and not satisfied to seek the annulment on the grounds of *propter maleficium versus hanc*—that he was impotent only toward her—she embarrassed the man by declaring *propter frigidita-tem*. She claims he is impotent to all women, and the whole damned court knows that isn't so, but the archbishop looked the other way. The annulment is a fact, although it has not been declared so yet. She and Carr will wed next spring."

"Jasmine needs her rest, Alex," Velvet declared. "Let us go. We will see you in the morning, my dear."

"Are you returning to court with the king and queen, Mama?"

"Nay, 'tis time we returned to Scotland," Velvet told her daughter. "The boys have been running wild since spring without us, I can be certain. It is time to bring order to their lives. Sandy and Charlie must go to university. God knows what mischief they have gotten into in our absence. Or," she said archly, "what girls they have impregnated at Dun Broc. Your stepfather does not see my concern."

Alex grinned over his wife's head, and winked at his step-daughter.

"I am sure the boys have done fine, Mama," Jasmine said.

"Aye, and I hope so," the Earl of BrocCairn said.

"*Alex!*" his outraged wife declared. "This is why I have no control over our sons any longer. You encourage them to bad behavior."

"There is nae wrong wi a lad chasing after a perty lassie," the earl said staunchly. "I did it myself before I wed ye, sweetheart."

"You have two sons, Jasmine," her mother said. "Do not let loose of the reins for one moment, or you will have chaos. I warn you."

When they had left her, Jasmine considered that her mother was beginning to sound more and more like her aunt Willow.

In the very early morning, the king and queen came a final time to see their grandson before returning to Sudley Castle. The king gave Jasmine a purse, which she accepted although she felt uncomfortable doing so. The royal purse was always empty, or near it, she knew, and she was a very wealthy woman. She did not refuse, however, for she would not offend their majesties.

"There is the matter of the bairn's baptism," the king said.

"The prince and I had hoped that Prince Charles and Princess Elizabeth would be permitted to stand as our son's godparents," Jasmine said.

"And what Church will he be baptised in?" the king asked.

"Why, the Church of England, Your Majesty," Jasmine answered.

"Is nae this family of the old Kirk, Madame?"

"We were all born into it, my lord," Skye interposed, "but the politics of the times being what they are, sir, we worship with the Church of England now. Elizabeth Tudor was fond of saying that 'there is but one lord Jesus Christ, and the rest is all trifles.' 'Tis possibly the only matter on which she and I ever agreed. My family and I are peace-loving peoples. We wish to remain at peace."

The king was forced to chuckle, and he nodded at Skye. "How well I understand, Lady de Marisco," he said. "How well I understand. When will the baptism take place?"

"In a few days' time, my lord," Jasmine said. "We will, of course, have proxies stand in for Prince Charles and his sister."

"They will be told, Lady Lindley," the king said, and then he and the queen took their leave.

The Earl and Countess of BrocCairn stood in for the royal godparents at the baptism of their grandson, but Prince Charles and his sister each sent fine gifts to their godchild. From the princess came six silver goblets with the Stuart crest engraved upon them, and a length of fine lawn to make infant dresses. Prince Charles sent his namesake a dozen silver spoons, and a fine gold ring with a sapphire for a seal. The king and queen sent a beautifully bound copy of the new Book of Common Prayer.

• •

The queen, who had accepted her husband's choice for Princess Elizabeth's husband only at the behest of her eldest son, now greeted Frederick V, the Elector Palatine, with less than her usual enthusiasm. Although the marriage was scheduled to be celebrated on St. Valentine's Day, Prince Frederick arrived in England in mid-autumn. Henry Stuart, his illness now visibly draining his strength, greeted his brother-in-law-to-be at Gravesend when he landed, and personally escorted him up to London.

On October 24, 1612, there was to be a magnificent dinner given by the lord mayor, but Henry was so ill now that he could not attend, and the affair was called off. The superstitious English now began to murmur nervously about the prince's health. That same autumn, the remains of Mary, Queen of Scots, had been disinterred from Fotheringay Castle and brought with much pomp to London, where they were reburied in a beautiful sepulchre commissioned by King James for his mother in Westminster Abbey. There was an ancient English saying that when the grave of a family member was disturbed, another family member would die. Then a lunar rainbow occurred, lasting several hours. Another omen, the superstitious declared, and indeed by October twenty-ninth Henry Stuart's condition had grown much worse.

The Londoners came in great numbers to stand outside of St. James's Palace awaiting the latest news. They watched as the queen and Princess Elizabeth arrived to visit the sick man. Then the physicians declared that the prince's fever was infectious, and the royal family were barred from further visits, much to the queen's sorrow. She had always been fearful of contagious diseases, and now her fears were borne out. She had not, to her shame, the courage to defy the doctors and stay with her firstborn child. Instead Anne fled to Somerset House in great sorrow. The king stubbornly remained with the prince.

The crowds grew bigger, until they lined every street between St. James's Palace and the queen's residence. They wept as the news grew more dire, and a thousand rumors of various natures swept through the press of people. Finally, just before midnight on November fifth, Henry Frederick Stuart breathed his last, to the great shock of all. He had been so young, and so vital.

James, despite all advice, had stayed by his eldest son's bedside until Henry had lapsed into an irreversible coma. Then, weeping bitterly, he had departed for Theobalds, only to return to London to the house of Sir Walter Cope. But he could not rest. Finally, word was brought to the king of his son's death, and James Stuart, before he retired to mourn in private, gave orders that his son should lie in state at his palace of St. James, his coffin to be set upon a bier in the chapel royal, with its beautiful painted ceiling.

When the pomp and circumstance of the funeral was finally over, James Stuart remembered Jasmine Lindley and her infant son. He called for his private secretary and dictated a message that was to be carried by royal messenger to her with all speed at Queen's Malvern. He had no idea if she knew of the prince's death, for her grandmother's home was isolated.

She did not, and consequently Jasmine collapsed in shock upon reading the royal missive. As Skye knelt to see to her granddaughter, Adam de Marisco snatched up the parchment as it fluttered to the floor.

He scanned it quickly and then swore beneath his breath. "Jesu! What a damned tragedy for us all, and for England."

"*What is it?*" Skye demanded, looking up at him as she attempted to revive Jasmine back to consciousness.

"Henry Stuart is dead," Adam said bluntly, and then he read,

"Madame, it is with deep regret we report to you the untimely death of our beloved son, and heir, Henry Frederick. His last thoughts were of you, and of our grandson, Lord Charles Frederick Stuart. We will communicate with you again in the future regarding your welfare, and that of our grandson.

Signed, James R."

Jasmine, half revived, was beginning to weep piteously.

"How did he die?" Adam demanded of the royal messenger.

"Well, my lord," the messenger said, "he wasn't well at all the whole autumn long. The prince took to his bed almost two weeks before the end. Some said he had smallpox, but 'twas not. I've heard that typhus or typhoid killed him, but many say the king should not have removed his mother's bones from Fotheringay Castle and reburied them in the abbey. 'Tis a great loss."

"Aye," Adam agreed. "A great loss for everyone."

The messenger stayed the night, and went his way back to London the following morning. Jasmine was so brokenhearted that her milk dried up, much to her great distress, but a healthy young wet nurse was found for Charles Frederick and quickly moved into the house.

"Why is it," Jasmine bemoaned sorrowfully to Skye, "that every man I love dies? Ohh, Grandmama, I should have told Hal that I loved him, but I did not want to complicate matters any more than they were complicated!"

"You did exactly the right thing," Skye assured her grandchild. "As for losing men to death, that, my darling girl, is a part of a woman's life. I lost five husbands to death before I married your grandfather, not to mention a son, my wee Johnnie. I know that you loved Henry Stuart, and I am so sorry, Jasmine, but all your weeping will not bring the prince back. You have lost your lover, but England has lost a great future king. A lover can be replaced. Perhaps not easily, but 'tis possible.

"Will poor little Prince Charles, however, be able to fill

his brother's boots, I wonder? Henry Stuart was strong and vital until the end, but Prince Charles has been a sickly child. What will happen if we lose him, too, and the queen past her prime for childbearing? 'Tis been five years since she lost that last little princess. I think we had best pray for the little prince that God will spare him and keep him safe for England."

Christmas came, but Jasmine could not celebrate, although she tried to confine her mourning to the privacy of her own apartments for the sake of her children. India would be five in March, and was a wise little girl for her age.

"Are you sad," she asked her mother one day, "because Prince Henry has died, Mama?"

"Aye," Jasmine said, turning away so India would not see her tears.

"Has he gone to Heaven? Will he see my father?"

Jasmine nodded.

"We have no papa," India said. "None of us."

"Nay," Jasmine told her eldest child. "None of you have a papa anymore."

In the middle of January another royal messenger arrived at Queen's Malvern with a missive for the dowager Marchioness of Westleigh. Jasmine was commanded to come to London for Princess Elizabeth's wedding on February fourteenth. Under normal circumstances the marriage would have been postponed because of Prince Henry's death, but the young bridegroom had come so far, and he was unable to remain away from his domain much longer. It was deemed wiser to celebrate the royal match and send the newlyweds on their way, than to send Prince Frederick V home to return another time.

Skye concurred, as did Jasmine, who said, "Hal would not want Bessie to wait. The princess has been so excited about her impending marriage."

"What will you wear?" her grandmother asked. "It cannot

be mourning, for this is a wedding, despite all the tragedy that has preceded it. What about that magnificent ruby-red velvet you possess?"

Jasmine shook her head. "I shall wear black," she said.

"You have a midnight-blue gown that is just perfect," Skye said, ignoring her granddaughter. "The Stars of Kashmir go just beautifully with it, as I remember, my darling girl."

"I shall wear black," Jasmine insisted.

"The black velvet with the silver lace?" Skye inquired hopefully.

"The black velvet with the high neck, and the white lace ruff," Jasmine replied stubbornly. "I will not flaunt myself."

"The black with the silver lace is more appropriate to a wedding, my darling girl," Skye wheedled. "Even if the prince is dead, you are his chosen representative. Will you have people wonder what it was he ever saw in you in the first place, Jasmine? Where is your damned pride? He was proud of you."

"The neckline on the gown you suggest is too low, Grand-mama. I do not intend to exhibit myself for the amusement of the court. It will look as if I am peddling my wares seeking another protector, when the truth of the matter is I do not care if I ever make love to another man again, even if I live to be one hundred!" Jasmine declared vehemently.

When Jasmine reached London, however, she found that the gown whose packing she had so carefully supervised was no longer in her trunk. In its place was the magnificent black velvet and silver lace gown her grandmother had wanted her to wear, along with a wonderful necklace, and ear bobs of rubies.

"Damn her for a meddling old woman," Jasmine muttered, and then she laughed. "God's boots, we are so alike! I would have done the same thing had our positions been reversed," she told Toramalli.

"I know," giggled her faithful servant, "and 'twas exactly what your lady grandmother said when she pulled that plain black gown from the luggage. She is right, though, my lady. The prince would want you to be the most beautiful woman at the wedding, next to his sister."

Jasmine had sent word of her arrival to the king, but she had insisted upon staying at Greenwood. James, still deeply distraught over his eldest son's death, bridled at this, but the queen soothed him, saying, " 'Tis most proper and discreet of Lady Lindley, my dear. I fully approve of her behavior in this most delicate matter. She is not our son's widow, after all. Only his mistress. When will ye speak with her about little Charles Frederick?"

"After the wedding," the king replied absently.

Although the king had complained that he could scarce afford such a grand affair, the wedding of Princess Elizabeth to the young, handsome Elector Palatine was a magnificent one attended by every member of the court from the highest to the lowest. The crown jewels were put on display, including a large pearl pendant, the Brctherin, the Portugal Diamond, and an even larger diamond set in a gold setting, called the Mirror of France. Jasmine had never seen these jewels, and although she found them beautiful, she thought she had better in her possession.

It was a strange celebration. In Westminster Abbey, where Frederick V was created a Knight of the Garter, the effigy of Henry Stuart was yet on display. Jasmine bravely fought back her tears. Then the king forgot to dub the new knight, but no one dared to tell him.

The wedding itself was celebrated on February fourteenth in the royal chapel at Whitehall. It was the first royal marriage using the new form of common prayer in England. The little princess glowed with happiness, for she and her bridegroom had fallen madly in love in the four short months in which they had known each other. The marriage had become a love match, to the surprise of everyone.

Elizabeth Stuart wore a magnificent gown of silver tissue. Her long, blond hair was unbound, signifying her innocence. Atop her head was a crown of diamonds and pearls. Her young bridegroom was garbed in scarlet and silver, the garter about his neck. The bridal attendants all wore pure white satin. The queen was gowned in cloth-of-gold and diamonds. The king, however, had given little care to his garb. He was dressed all in black, and his stockings quite obviously did not match. A rather bedraggled pheasant's feather hung from his cap, and he had a short black Spanish cape with its half-erect collar and hanging cowl about him.

At the party that followed the religious ceremony, James Stuart fidgeted, and complained about the expense of it all and about the overwhelming boredom he felt at the masque presented. "My brave laddie's dead, and yet they dance," he said sadly at one point. Jasmine felt deeply sorry for James Stuart, and she knew exactly how he felt. She could see the queen struggling to keep up a good front for the sake of her daughter, whom she truly loved. It was like being in a bad dream.

Jasmine had attempted to keep herself very much in the background. A royal page had come to Greenwood the afternoon before the wedding, and brought her a message from the king. She was not to leave London. He would see her in a week's time. She wondered what it was all about. Perhaps the king wanted to make some sort of provision for her infant son. She would, of course, tactfully refuse. She did not need a royal pension to support her children.

"Good evening, madame," a voice said at her ear.

Jasmine looked up to see James Leslie, the Earl of Glenkirk, towering above her. "My lord," she answered politely.

"Will you allow me to escort you through this crush, madame?" he asked her politely.

Jasmine opened her mouth to refuse him, and then thought better of it. It was unlikely that she would be pestered by the bold young men about the court if she was being escorted by the Earl of Glenkirk. She wanted no scenes or misunderstandings. "Thank you, my lord," she said.

"Your children are well?" he inquired solicitiously, having found them a quiet corner in which to sit.

She nodded politely.

"How old are they now?" Glenkirk persisted in the conversation.

"India will be five next month, Henry four in April, Fortune three in July, and my wee Charles will be five months old in four days," Jasmine said. "And you, my lord. Have you satisfied your family's pleas yet to remarry, and have more children?"

"I am yet a bachelor, madame. There has been but one woman to attract me over the years, but I did not speak up, and she married another gentleman. Now, however, she is a widow." His green-gold eyes looked directly at her.

Jasmine looked at him with shock. "Surely I misunderstand you, my lord," she said coldly.

"I do not think so, madame," he responded calmly, taking her hand in his.

She grew pale. Then she arose, snatching her hand back. "How dare you, my lord? How do you dare to presume to solicit me under the circumstances!"

"I lost you once, Jasmine, because I was too proud to say I wanted you, and you were too proud to admit to wanting me," James Leslie told her bluntly. "When Rowan Lindley died, I dared to hope I might begin anew with you, but Henry Stuart came between us."

"There is no *us*, my lord," Jasmine said furiously.

"*I will not lose you again,*" the Earl of Glenkirk said, and reaching out, he took her into his arms, and kissed her with all the pent-up passion in his soul.

Jasmine pulled from his embrace and slapped him as hard as she was able to do. "Do not ever approach me again, Lord Leslie," she told him icily, tears of outrage prickling her eyes. "Your presumption goes beyond the bounds of decency and certainly beyond those of good taste! I will mourn Henry

Stuart until the day I die, my lord!" Then turning, she walked angrily away from him.

James Leslie cursed softly under his breath. A less determined man might have lost heart, but he was only annoyed that he had perhaps misjudged the depth of her feelings for the prince. Of course she had loved Henry Stuart. She was not the sort of woman who gave herself to a man for gain. She was an honorable woman, and for her, love was paramount. He remembered their brief encounter of almost six years prior. She had been relatively newly widowed, and he was still hurting from his wife and children's untimely deaths. Together they had comforted each other, but it had been more for him. He had always believed that it had been more for her as well.

Jasmine pushed her way through the crowds of courtiers who made up the wedding guests. Her cheeks felt hot, and her Mughal temper was as close to out of hand as it had ever been since her arrival in England seven years ago. *What was she doing here?* She knew virtually no one, and frankly, there was no one she cared to know. Who was to know if she left? It was a breach of etiquette to be certain, but in this mob, who would even miss her? She would go back to Greenwood, and she would stay there until her appointment with the king next week.

Then a page was at her elbow. "Are you the dowager Marchioness of Westleigh, madame?" he asked her.

"I am," she said. "What is it you want of me?"

"Her majesty requests your presence, my lady," the young boy said. "If you would be so kind as to follow me."

God's boots, Jasmine thought irritably, and just when I was about to make my escape from this madhouse. But she followed the page to the queen, curtseying low before Anne of Denmark.

"A stool for Lady Lindley," the queen said, and then, "Come and sit next to me, my dear. Are you enjoying the wedding?"

Jasmine seated herself, spreading her black velvet skirts prettily around her. "The princess is a most beautiful bride, Your Majesty," she said.

"But court is not quite the same without him, is it?" the queen answered, nodding her head. "Like me, Lady Lindley, you hide what is in your heart, and put on a good face. What a pity you could not have been his wife, but tell me, how is Charles Frederick Stuart?"

"He thrives, madame. I became unable to nurse him when—" Her voice shook a moment, and the queen put a comforting hand on her hand.

"I understand," she said low, her gaze sympathetic.

"I have an excellent wet nurse for my son," Jasmine continued bravely. "He grows more beautiful every day, and he has two tiny teeth already. His brother is very protective of him, and his sisters adore him. He has the best nature, madame, even when he first awakens."

"I can see how much you love your children, my dear," Queen Anne said. "That is good. I, too, came from a large and loving family. There were five of us. I have two sisters and two brothers. We were a very happy family, perhaps even spoiled. Do you know that I was carried everywhere until I was nine? I never walked until then. I think I may have even learned to dance before I learned to walk," she said with a small chuckle. "Henry, of course, told you how different life for him was in Scotland."

Jasmine almost winced at the sound of his name.

"Ahh, how little I knew of the Scots when I married my Jamie," the queen continued on. "They took my son from me right after he was born. I was not allowed to nurse him, and I was not allowed to care for him. That pleasure and privilege went to the Earl and dowager Countess of Marr. They are the hereditary guardians of Scotland's heir, but I did not know that before I gave birth to my son. I was not allowed to even see him except by making an application in advance to Marr and his old mother.

" 'Twas they who felt my Henry's little gums for his first teeth. 'Twas they he greeted with his first smile. They who saw his first steps. I have never forgiven them for it, and now I never will! They took time from me that should have been mine, and they had no sympathy for my feelings in the matter. They were arrogant and stiff-necked about their position as the heir's guardians," the queen said.

Then she leaned even nearer to Jasmine. "Do not let *anyone* take Charles Frederick Stuart from you, my dear. He will be safer with his mother, and 'tis far better for him to grow up in a warm, loving family with his sisters and brother. Then, too, your family is a very large one, isn't it? Are your grandparents still alive?"

"Yes, Your Majesty, they are. My grandmother and I are best friends. I do not like being parted from her."

"You are very fortunate," the queen said.

Shortly afterward Jasmine was obliged to join the women of the court in preparing the bride for her marital bed. Elizabeth Stuart was all rosy with anticipation, for she loved her handsome young husband. The only sour note to these final wedding day festivities came from the king who told the young couple he would expect proof come the morrow that they had done their duty, and done it well.

Jasmine returned to Greenwood. She did not take part in any further celebrations, but rather waited the time until she was to see the king.

Her appointment was set for the early morning a few days later.

"With luck," she told Toramalli, "we can be on the road back to Queen's Malvern by noon. I cannot wait to get home. It seems as if we have been parted from the children for months instead of just weeks."

Toramalli dressed her mistress carefully for her meeting with the king, choosing an elegant gown of deep violet velvet with a large collar of fine lace which extended low on her shoulders. The sleeves, which were long, had small slashes through which puffs of deeper violet silk showed. Jasmine wore a heavy gold chain about her neck, to which was attached an oval brooch edged in pearls. In the center of the brooch was a small clear crystal through which could be seen a small lock of hair. It was Henry Stuart's hair. She wore no head covering, her hair affixed in its usual chignon, but the hood of her violet velvet cloak, which was trimmed in ermine, could be pulled up in inclement or cold weather.

To her great surprise, Jasmine was brought into the king's privy chamber. Both the queen and the Earl of Glenkirk were in the room, but no one else. Jasmine curtsied to their majesties, and ignored James Leslie.

"Come and sit by the fire, lassie," the king said. " 'Tis a raw day, though I think springtime will eventually come."

Jasmine loosened her cloak and laid it over the arm of the chair. Then she sat, her hands resting nervously in her lap. It was not her place to speak until the king had spoken his piece to her, but although she understood the presence of Queen Anne, she was confused by that of the Earl of Glenkirk. He had but nodded politely when she entered. The queen smiled at her encouragingly.

James Stuart sat himself opposite his guest. "How is my wee grandson, madame?" he asked her.

"He is well, Your Majesty. He has two teeth, and is of a most sunny disposition," Jasmine told the king.

The king nodded. "But for an accident of fate," he said, "that child might be England's next king." Then catching himself, he looked directly at Jasmine. "You are remaining at Queen's Malvern, madame? Not Cadby?"

"Aye, Your Majesty. I prefer being with my grandparents, and although I promised Rowan that his children would be raised at Cadby, our circumstances have changed since I made that promise. I believe it best we remain at Queen's Malvern. We will visit Cadby each year, and starting when Henry is six he must live there three months of the year for his tenants' sake."

"Is Queen's Malvern a safe house, madame?"

"Safe, sire? I do not think I understand you," Jasmine said.

"Safe from attack, madame?" the king replied.

"*Attack?*" She looked astounded. "Who would attack Queen's Malvern, and why, my lord?"

"Madame, you are the mother of a royal Stuart," the king told her with utmost seriousness.

"Sire, this is England. Queen's Malvern is in a quiet little valley which encompasses the whole estate. I do not believe there has been an attack of *any* kind there since before the days of William Norman, when the Welsh used to raid, or so my grandfather says."

"It is the custom of the royal Stuarts, madame, to assign a guardian to each of its children," the king told her.

"Sire, my son is not an heir to your throne," Jasmine said. "There is no need for him to have a guardian. I, as his mother, am more vigilant than any guardian could be. Besides, Charles Frederick Stuart is quite safe in the bosom of his family. My family is a large one."

The king ignored her as if she had not even spoken, and he continued on. "My grandson must be educated, madame."

"I agree, sire," Jasmine said.

"But what can you know of the education of a prince?" the king demanded.

Jasmine bit back the sharp retort that came to mind, and drawing a long, slow breath, said patiently, "I am a princess born, sire, and my father was a man who believed strongly in education for women, as well as for men. I am fluent in several languages including Portuguese, Latin, and French, and some languages you have never even heard of, my lord. I have been taught mathematics, and can keep my own estate and household accounts. I have learned philosophy, and history, and can tell you about the creeds of many religions, each of which thinks it is the best and only faith. I read, and I can write in a legible, fine hand in all the languages that I am capable of speaking. Are these not the things my son, indeed all of my children, should learn?"

"I dinna hold wi so much learning for a woman," the king replied infuriatingly. "The raising of a boy is a man's province, madame. Can you teach him to ride, or use a weapon?"

"Aye, my lord, I can," Jasmine replied with a smile. "I learned to ride at the age of three, when I began accompanying my father to the hunt. I can fire a gun accurately, and my aim with a spear was always deadly. As for the sword, sire, I can hire a good swordmaster for my sons, can I not?"

Behind the king's chair the Earl of Glenkirk hid an amused smile. He had known James Stuart his entire life, and he knew that the king was about to lose his royal temper.

"Damn me, madame, if you are nae the most irritating woman I hae ever known," James Stuart said. "A lad needs a man about him to learn things that a woman could nae possibly imagine."

"*What?*" Jasmine demanded. "Besides, my lord, my sons have my grandfather, and for all his age, he is an active gentleman. Then there is my uncle Conn; and my Aunt Deirdre's husband, Lord Blackthorne; and a whole host of young male cousins living nearby. Neither of my sons will lack for male company, I assure you."

"*Enough!*" the king roared. "I will nae be argued wi any further, madame. I hae made my decision. It is true that my grandson, Charles Frederick Stuart, will nae ever inherit England's throne. That great responsibility will go to my son Charles, the bairn's godfather. Nonetheless, no royal Stuart hae ever shirked his duty toward his own. I will nae be the first, and besides, I promised my Henry before he died that I would look after you and the bairn. I have this day affixed my royal seal to a document making James Leslie, the Earl of Glenkirk, guardian over my grandson, Charles Frederick Stuart, Viscount Lundy."

"No!" Jasmine shouted, her own royal temper exhibiting itself. "You have no right! I will not allow you to snatch my child away from me, my lord! What can a man, particularly a man without a wife in his house, know about raising a tiny baby?"

"It is not as dreadful as you think, my dear." The queen finally spoke up. " 'Tis not at all as it was with me. My Jamie has had the most wonderful idea. But listen."

Jasmine looked at the king, but her turquoise-blue eyes were angry.

"Nah, nah, madame, dinna fret yerself," James Stuart said. "I am a man who learns from his errors, and times are changing. My Annie hae reminded me of all the fuss we had over Henry in his infancy and childhood when I gave him to Marr. I realize now that a woman should nae be separated from her bairn until the bairn is grown. A man wi'out a wife is indeed a poor choice to raise a bairn, but is nae a woman wi'out a husband his equal?

"I hae known Jemmie Leslie since he was a bairn. His father was my friend, God assoil his bonnie soul. Jemmie hae been a loyal and true friend to me my entire life. His sweet Isabelle, and their bairns, died an untimely death, but he hae been a widower for eleven years now. Your husband died an equally untimely death, madame, four years ago. 'Tis time ye were both remarried. The Leslies of Glenkirk hae petitioned me regularly to make their earl do so. Well, now I will. Pick the date, madame, for I am commanding you to marry the Earl of Glenkirk as quickly as possible. Together you will raise my grandson. How is it I am told you put it, madame? The 'not-so-royal Stuart'?" The king chuckled, pleased with himself and with his decision.

Across from him Jasmine sat in stunned silence. *Marry James Leslie?* It was absolute madness. It was ridiculous. *It was impossible!*

"Is that not the most perfect solution to all of our problems, my dear?" the queen burbled, well pleased by her husband's cleverness.

Jasmine could still find no words to express herself.

"I believe," the Earl of Glenkirk said with great understatement, "that Lady Lindley has been taken by surprise by Your Majesties' decision in this matter. When she recovers herself, I am certain she will desire to speak with you to voice her thanks, even as I give mine now to you both." The earl came around the king's chair. "With Your Majesties' kind permission, I will escort Lady Lindley to her home at Queen's Malvern. I believe that she had intended to leave London almost immediately following her audience with Your Majesties." He clamped his hand hard beneath Jasmine's elbow and gently forced her to her feet. "Allow me, madame," the earl said softly.

James Leslie bowed to the king and the queen. Jasmine somehow managed to curtsey, and then he was leading her from the king's privy chamber.

"Say not one word, madame, until we are in the privacy of your coach," James Leslie warned her. "You will shortly recover your wits, but we will cause no scandal here at Whitehall, Jasmine, for all the court sycophants to gossip about."

She nodded silently.

"Where to, m'lady?" her coachman inquired as they exited Whitehall. "Back to Greenwood, or home? The baggage coach has already left." The coachman peered down at her.

"Queen's Malvern," the Earl of Glenkirk said to him, and then, "That is correct, madame, is it not?"

Jasmine nodded again.

The carriage moved off from Whitehall. James Leslie took the fur rug that was upon the seat and wrapped it about Jasmine's knees. Then he seated himself facing her. He was very impressed by the luxury of the coach, and soon realized that there was heat coming from the grates in the doors.

Ingenious, he thought, and sat back, stretching his long legs out before him. Very soon the city was left behind them. The countryside lay couched in bleak midwinter on either side of the road. There was no snow, but it was cold, and there was frost in the brown fields. Smoke wafted from the farmhouse and cottage chimneys as they passed by them. Now and then a dog would dash madly from a farmyard to pursue the carriage, barking wildly as it raced along, snapping at the wheels until it finally tired of the game.

After some time James Leslie said quietly, "Do you intend not to speak to me at all, madame, or is it that you have truly lost your tongue?"

"I will not marry you," Jasmine said. "Do you think yourself clever, my lord, to have convinced the king to give you guardianship over my Stuart son? And what foresight you have, Jemmie Leslie! Did you actually believe that by having custody of Charles Frederick, I should have no other choice but to wed you?"

"I did not ask the king for guardianship of your son, madame," he answered her, "and as for marrying you, 'tis true I desired to court you, and to eventually convince you to take me as your husband, but 'twas my damned brothers, importuning first Jamie and then his Annie, that resulted in a royal command to wed. I will admit, however, to feeling no regret at that command, which I will obey gladly."

"*I will not marry you,*" Jasmine repeated.

"I love you," he said.

"You lie!" she retorted.

"Nay, Jasmine, I do not lie. When we were caught abed, and BrocCairn said I must wed you, I refused to speak because I was angry at myself for having been so stupid as to expose you to such embarrassment. Surely you know I was already in love with you then, but the situation with Sybilla was a difficult one. And you, sweetheart, were so coolly gallant in your refusal to force me to the altar. Afterward, I came to Greenwood and told your grandmother that I wished to court you."

"I did not know that," Jasmine said softly.

"Ask her," the earl told her. "She said that you were betrothed to Rowan Lindley and that it would be best if you did not know of my visit, or the reason for it. She sent me away. I left court shortly after that, staying only long enough to meet my obligations to the king. When I returned to Glenkirk, I seriously sought out a new wife, for my brothers have been most adamant that I remarry. There was no woman, however, who pleased me. I finally returned to court to learn that you were widowed, but by then you had involved yourself with the prince. I could hardly reveal my feelings to you under those circumstances, could I?"

"I am not a child, my lord. I am twenty-two, and I will not be forced to the altar by this Scots King of England," Jasmine said firmly, ignoring his explanations.

"Madame, we do not have any other choice but to obey," James Leslie told her. "I will make you a bargain, however. Allow me to pay you court at Queen's Malvern. In a month or so we will set a wedding date, and so inform the king. 'Twill give us time to renew our acquaintance with each other."

"What of my Stuart son?" she asked him.

"Why, he will remain with you, Jasmine," James Leslie told her. "As you so scathingly pointed out to the king, a man without a wife is a poor choice to be guardian for a bairn." The Earl of Glenkirk smiled across the coach at her, and Jasmine, in spite of herself, felt the corners of her mouth turning up slightly.

"I will make you a bargain, my lord," she said finally in return. "The king's ultimatum came as a shock to me, as you know. I need time to accustom myself to it. You see, I never told Henry Stuart how much I loved him. I never told him at all that I loved him. He wanted to marry me, and of course such a marriage was not possible between us. If I had admitted my love for him, he would have been all the more obdurate regarding the choice of a wife. You know he would have, my lord. Then he died, and I could not tell him of my love. I have lived with that these past months, and the pain it has given me is beyond knowing.

"Now, the king, my Hal's father, has ordered me to marry you. That he has done it for reasons that make no sense to me, in his grief, and in the mistaken belief he is protecting his grandson, does not help me to come to terms with that royal decision. You say you love me, James Leslie. I am not certain that I believe you, although I think you believe it. Very well then, if you love me, take me home to Queen's Malvern, and then leave me be for a short period of time. With my children about me, and my grandmother's wisdom, I will be able to accept what must be. Can you do that?"

"When may I return to begin our courtship?" he asked her.

"Come on the first day of April, my lord. 'Tis less than six weeks from now," she said. "I will set our wedding date when I see you again. I promise you that, and a royal Mughal princess would never break her word, Jemmie Leslie."

She said his name softly, and the tip of her tongue flicked out to moisten her lips. He almost grew dizzy with the sensuality of the action, and thought ruefully that he had best gain a firmer hold upon himself lest she rule their household. Then he thought of his mother and smiled. It was the sort of bargain Cat Leslie would have struck in the same situation. She would play for time, and God only knew 'twas little enough she asked him. If it would ease the path that they must travel together, then how could he refuse?

"Very well, madame," he told Jasmine. "I will bring you in safety to your grandmother's home, but you must give me a few days with you before I depart. Then I shall return on the first day of April, to plan our wedding."

"I agree, my lord," Jasmine said quietly.

"I will be a good stepfather to your children," he promised her. "Even now I yet miss my own lads, but you will give me beautiful sons and daughters, Jasmine, I know. You like children, don't you?"

"Aye," she said, "I do. I was the youngest of my father's children, and my siblings were grown but for one sister, and she lived with her mother at court. In my little palace on the lake in Kashmir, it was as if I was an only child. Perhaps that is why I enjoy having a household full of children." She smiled at him. "Grandmama says I spoil my little ones, but I do not believe loving a child as I do can spoil it."

"My mother loved her bairns like that," he told her.

"Where is your mother?" she asked him.

"In Italy," he said. "Someday I will tell you the whole story of Cat Leslie and her love, which in Scotland was called 'wild and fair.' "

"I shall look forward to your tale, my lord. Does the story have a happy ending?" Jasmine said.

"Aye, a very happy ending, even as our story will have a happy ending," the Earl of Glenkirk promised her.

Jasmine looked directly at him, her turquoise-blue eyes bright. "Are you then so certain of our fates, my lord?"

"Aye!" he replied with a wide grin. "I am!"

"I am not," Jasmine told him solemnly. Then she turned away from James Leslie to watch the gray and brown countryside as it passed by their carriage. Above them the sky had grown dark, and it began to snow.

Epilogue

❀

QUEEN'S MALVERN
APRIL 1, 1613

"*Gone?* I do not understand you, madame. What do you mean gone?"

Skye O'Malley de Marisco looked at the Earl of Glenkirk and thought he was an extraordinarily handsome man, with his midnight-black hair and his green-gold eyes. It was obvious that he had stopped somewhere nearby to change from his traveling clothes into this more elegant black velvet suit with its gorgeous lace collar. The earl had come dressed for courting. He carried a bunch of colorful spring blooms in his hand, and she reached for them now, fearful that he was going to squeeze the life from their stems. Skye took the flowers and handed them to her tiring woman, Daisy Kelly.

"Put these in water, Daisy, and make certain that we are not disturbed by anyone."

"Yes, m'lady," Daisy said, and bobbed a creaky curtsey. Then, unable to resist, she whispered to her mistress, " 'Tis just like the old days, m'lady, isn't it? Except now 'tis Mistress Jasmine causing all the difficulty, and not you."

Skye swallowed her laughter and shooed her old servant

off. She then sought to compose herself before turning to face the earl.

"Where is Jasmine?" James Leslie demanded once again.

"She has gone, my lord, as I have previously told you," Skye said calmly.

"Gone where?" he pressed her.

"I do not know," Skye replied blandly.

"God's boots!" Anger darkened the earl's handsome face, and he struggled to maintain his composure.

Seated in a large comfortable chair, Lord de Marisco felt a pang of sympathy for James Leslie. Adam certainly knew how aggravating the women in his family could be when they chose to be, and at this moment Jasmine had chosen to be particularly difficult. Slowly sipping Archambault wine, Adam remained silent for the moment, allowing his wife to handle the situation. One of the nice things about being old, he thought, was the fact that one did not have to get involved if one chose not to be involved.

"Where is Lord Stuart?" the Earl of Glenkirk finally managed to say. "The child is legally in my charge, madame."

"Viscount Lundy is with his mother," Skye answered quietly. "You would hardly expect my granddaughter to go traveling without her children, my lord, would you?"

"She has deliberately disobeyed the king!" James Leslie shouted. "This is treason, madame! You are obviously a party to it!"

"Nonesense!" Skye retorted briskly. "You are distraught, my lord, and overreacting to the situation, I fear."

"Your granddaughter, promised in marriage to me by the king, has gone *traveling*, but you do not know where?" James Leslie said through gritted teeth. "She has removed the king's grandson from this place, and taken the lad, *my legal charge*, with her, and you believe that my outrage is an overreaction, madame? I think not, Lady de Marisco. I think not! It is indeed treason to disobey the king's direct command."

"I disobeyed a greater queen than this king," Skye said

with emphasis. "I am here to tell the tale, my lord. Do not raise your voice to me in my house again! Now sit down, James Leslie. I am no longer as young as I once was, though it aggravates me to admit it. I prefer to sit. I will not have you towering over me, glowering darkly. Take some wine to calm your irritation, and bring me some as well. My nerves are frayed with all this shouting."

Skye sat down next to her husband, giving him a mischievous wink which caused him to chuckle. As angry as James Leslie was, Adam thought, Skye would not long be able to play the frail old woman with him. He was no fool, this young Scots earl; and Skye was too used to being in charge of her world. Whether James Leslie knew it or not, he was now very much a part of Skye O'Malley de Marisco's world.

The earl poured the wine as she had bid him. His hands were shaking with his anger. He swore softly beneath his breath as he spilled some of the wine upon the silver tray where the goblets and the decanter were set. He swallowed down a mouthful of the liquid to calm himself, and then, turning, he walked across the room to give Lady de Marisco a goblet before sitting down opposite her.

"Why has Jasmine gone 'traveling'?" he asked.

"She yet mourns Henry Stuart," Skye said truthfully. "She does not wish to remarry at this time, my lord. You were wrong to encourage the king to arrange it so. Jasmine is a king's daughter, raised in a royal court. She prefers to make her own decisions. You took that right away from her when you, and the king, settled her future and that of her children between you, without even asking her opinion in the matter. She took back her rights when she decided to depart Queen's Malvern. I do not thank you for that, my lord. This is my granddaughter's home. My husband and I are no longer young, and having Jasmine with us has been the joy of our old age. Your actions have taken that from us also."

"I love her," the earl said. "I have for years. I simply did not want to lose her again, madame. I did not encourage the king to any match, I swear it! He asked me to oversee his grandson's raising, as is the custom in Scotland for royal Stuarts. It was the queen, romantic fool she is, who decided that Jasmine and I should marry.

"I have been widowed for eleven years now, madame, and my brothers, even though they might take my earldom if I died, do not want it. Neither do their sons. They would have to leave Scotland, you see, and they love it too much to do so. They have been petitioning the queen to find me a wife. When King James decided to appoint me Lord Charles Frederick Stuart's governor, the queen determined that they could kill two birds with one stone by not just putting their grandson in my charge, but by marrying me to Jasmine as well. They have no idea at all that I love her. I had resolved to court her when she had composed her life once more."

"Then why did you press her with this April first date?" Skye asked him gently, feeling a bit more disposed toward the earl now. Impatience was such a charming, yet irritating, trait in a lover, she thought to herself.

" 'Twas not my idea, madame," the earl replied. " 'Twas Jasmine's. If she had but spoken honestly with me, I would have been willing to wait until she had mourned the prince a full year. Then we might have planned our wedding for the following spring, or summer. I would have given her a reasonable amount of time, madame. Truly I would have!"

A small smile touched Skye's lips. "There was one thing that Henry Stuart loved in particular about Jasmine," Skye told him. "She could always make him laugh. My granddaughter has, I fear, a rather wicked sense of humor, my lord. She has certainly played a very fine jest upon you."

Understanding suddenly awoke in James Leslie's green-gold eyes. "I have been made quite the *April fool*, madame, haven't I?" he said, a little smile erasing the grim line of his mouth.

"I am afraid so, my lord," she answered him, and a giggle escaped Skye. She simply could not help it.

James Leslie, however, was also a man with a sense of

humor. He chuckled for a moment at himself. Then he said, "Where is she, madame? I beg you tell me where she has gone."

"I cannot, my lord," Skye told him. "I have given my word, and I have never knowingly or willingly broken that word once given."

Before the earl might protest, Adam de Marisco finally spoke up. "Have you been to France lately, my lord?" he asked. " 'Tis a most magnificent land. My mother was French. The wine you drink comes from the family vineyards at Archambault in the Loire Valley. Beautiful place!"

The Earl of Glenkirk arose. He bowed solemnly to Adam and said quietly, "Thank you, my lord." Taking Skye's hand up, he kissed it. "I admire your ethics, madame. They are to be commended." Then he looked again to Adam and asked, "Why, my lord?"

"I did not give my word," Adam de Marisco said, his deep blue eyes twinkling.

The Earl of Glenkirk smiled broadly, appreciating the subtlety, and then he said, "I will find her. I swear it!"

"Finding her is the easy part," Adam told him wisely. "Remember, James Leslie, that I once courted her grandmother, and a fine chase my Skye gave me before she was willing to settle down and behave herself."

"I have never behaved myself," Skye O'Malley declared vehemently. "You would have been bored silly, Adam, if I had."

The Earl of Lundy laughed, his deep laughter filling the room. "Aye, little girl, I probably would have," he admitted. Then he looked to James Leslie again. "Godspeed, my lord, but be warned, take nothing for granted where the women of this family are concerned. They are devious, but well worth the battle if you can but gain the victory."

The earl nodded, and then, bowing, departed Queen's Malvern.

"Do you think he'll find her?" Adam wondered. "After

all, I did not tell him she is at Belle Fleurs. I only mentioned Archambault."

"He will find her eventually," Skye answered with certainty. "He is a most determined young man, my darling, and he loves her."

"But will she marry him, I wonder?" Adam replied.

"One day, I think," Skye said, "but not right away," and then she began to laugh. "God's nightshirt, Adam! I regret not one single moment of my life, not even the hard parts, but by God 'tis good now to sit by the fire, a goblet in my hand, watching the antics of our descendants! These are the best compensations of age, I think."

"Nay, little girl, not the best. The best of it all is being here with you," Adam de Marisco declared, and reaching out, he took his wife's hand in his, kissing it as their eyes locked and their hearts soared as one, even as they always had. This was everything good, the Earl of Lundy decided happily. He could but pray God that their darling wild Jasmine one day find the same contentment and happiness in her life as he and Skye had found in theirs.

A NOTE FROM THE AUTHOR

Wild Jasmine concludes the O'Malley Saga. I hope that you have enjoyed it, and if you have not read the other five books in the series, that you will do so. Although they are threaded together, each book is an exciting story in itself.

Next year Ballantine and I will bring you *Dark Destiny*, a novel that will sweep the reader from fifth-century Britain to the decadence of Byzantium. Its heroine, Cailin Drusus, is an unforgettable and gallant young woman.

As always I look forward to your input. If you are so-minded, I hope you will write to me at P.O. Box 1575, Tryon, NC 28782.

ABOUT THE AUTHOR

Bertrice Small lives with her husband, George; Deuteronomy, the long-haired Maine Coon Cat; Checquers, the fat black and white cat with the pink ears; Nicky the Cockatiel; and Gilberto, the cranky Half-Moon Conure in the foothills of North Carolina's Blue Ridge mountains. The family heir, Tom, is now a college man. Bertrice Small is the author of: *The Kadin, Love Wild and Fair, Adora, Skye O'Malley, Unconquered, Beloved, All the Sweet Tomorrows, This Heart of Mine, Enchantress Mine, Blaze Wyndham, Lost Love Found, The Spitfire, A Moment in Time,* and *A Love for All Time.*